The
SHADOWMAGE
TRILOGY

An Abaddon Books™ Publication
www.abaddonbooks.com
abaddon@rebellion.co.uk

This omnibus published in 2012 by Abaddon Books™,
Rebellion Intellectual Property Limited,
Riverside House, Osney Mead, Oxford, OX2 0ES, UK.

10 9 8 7 6 5 4 3 2 1

Editor-in Chief: Jonathan Oliver
Desk Editor: David Moore
Cover Art & Maps: Pye Parr
Original Series Cover Art: Mark Harrison & Greg Staples
Design: Parr & Preece
Marketing and PR: Michael Molcher
Creative Director and CEO: Jason Kingsley
Chief Technical Officer: Chris Kingsley

ISBN (UK): 978-1-907992-92-6
ISBN (US): 978-1-907992-93-3

Printed in the US

TWILIGHT *of* KERBEROS

The
SHADOWMAGE
TRILOGY

MATTHEW SPRANGE

The Twilight of Kerberos Series

**The Lucius Kane Adventures
by Matthew Sprange**

Shadowmage
Night's Haunting
Legacy's Price

**The Kali Hooper Adventures
by Mike Wild**

The Clockwork King of Orl
Crucible of the Dragon God
Engines of the Apocalypse
The Trials of Trass Kathra

**The Silus Morlader Adventures
by Jonathan Oliver**

The Call of Kerberos
The Wrath of Kerberos

**The Gabriella DeZantez Adventures
by David A. McIntee**

The Light of Heaven

**Twilight of Kerberos – The Final Adventure
by Mike Wild**

Children of the Pantheon (coming soon)

INTRODUCTION

Welcome to the world of Twilight, overshadowed by the god planet Kerberos and packed with heroes and monsters, villains and magic. When Matthew Sprange and I sat down to plan out this shared-world series, right from the off I wanted to celebrate the pulp fantasy written by the likes of Fritz Leiber, Robert Howard and Clark Ashton Smith. I wanted us to look away from the epic doorstep tomes produced by writers such as George R.R. Martin and Steven Erikson (brilliant though they are) and instead create a collection of punchy fantasy adventures, each of which would stand alone but also continue to add to the world we were creating. This is more Swords and Sorcery than Tolkeinesque high fantasy; the emphasis is on fast-paced tales of sword wielders and spell slingers. Sprange's world is very Lieber-esque but there's also something of the tales of Conan here, while the stories remain very much Matthew's own.

This is the first of several Twilight of Kerberos omnibus editions and is a great place to start if you are unfamiliar with the series. Subsequent editions will follow different heroes as the series moves towards an apocalyptic climax. So pour yourself a tankard of mead and turn the page of this mighty tome. There is high adventure here and magic, just beware the wrath of the Lord of All and the warrior priests of the Final Faith!

Jonathan Oliver (Editor)
January 2012

Sarcre Islands

Nurn

Drakengrat Mount

Vosb

Oweilau

Malmkrug

Scholt

Turnitia

Allantia

Allantian Channel

Volonne

Freiport

Miramas

Gargas

as Territories

Pontaine

Sardenne Forest

Andon

yence

World's Ridge Mountains

SHADOWMAGE

Original cover art by Mark Harrison

PROLOGUE

SHOUTS FOR HIS blood echoed off the walls of the narrow alley, the worn buildings bouncing the sound so it seemed as though he were surrounded. Casting an anxious glance over his shoulder, he saw nothing through the shadowy gloom and guessed they were still on the street behind.

Not wanting to push his luck, he ran faster, legs straining under the effort and ankles aching from the unfamiliar exertion. A shape shuffled from the darkness of a doorway to his left. He nearly screamed in panic, thinking the murderers behind had caught up with him. The grey-haired beggar gave him a curious look, perhaps wondering why a wild-eyed man was in this region of the city at so late an hour, then shuffled back into his temporary home.

The alley jinked crookedly and, rounding the last corner, he saw the expanse of Meridian Street opening up before him. He slowed down, trying to control his breathing and appear normal, lest he draw attention from revellers or some of the less desirable types he knew frequented the thoroughfare. Drawing his hood up, he wrapped his cloak about him and continued north at a measured pace. The shouts were gradually receding and he began to give a silent prayer of relief. While the events of the evening had been painful, there was still a chance that something could be salvaged from the disaster.

Meridian Street was lit only by the torches and lanterns of the taverns, clubs and brothels that choked its wide midway stretch as it reached, arrow-straight, to Turnitia's northern gate. Even those lights were slowly being doused as all but the most stubborn establishments, or those most patronised, depending on how you looked at it, began to call an end to the evening's trade. Only the pale blue giant overhead continued to provide an eerie grey illumination, its cloud-strewn surface leering down on the city as the sphere dominated three quarters of the night sky.

He hoped his ancestors, soaring high in the clouds of Kerberos above, were watching over him now, providing whatever aid and protection the true God permitted. Discretley, he made the sign of the Brotherhood under his cloak, and then hurried north, hoping to appear like a young party-goer finding his way home, but fearing he appeared more like an old man on the run.

Few others were on the street, and even fewer paid him more than a scant glance, having the delights of heavy drink and loose women on their minds. For this, at least, he was grateful, for he could not afford any sort of confrontation, not tonight. The Faith had eyes everywhere, it seemed, and it might not take them long to arrive here if some sort of altercation broke out.

Crossing the cobbled road to avoid two young men obviously, and loudly, looking for a tavern that was still serving new arrivals, he strode purposefully onwards, eventually reaching the point where Meridian Street narrowed. A few closed shop fronts marked the undeclared barrier between entertainment and residential district, and he stopped for a few seconds, watching the road behind to see if any furtive shapes broke from the shadows to continue pursuit. Seeing nothing, he released the breath he had unconsciously been holding, though he knew he would not feel completely safe until he reached home. Perhaps not even then – that, however, was something to deal with in the morning. If he could just survive this night...

He continued his frightened trek and, a few hundred yards further along the road, he turned into a side street he had come to know well. Another turn and he was in the alleys that ran behind the row of close knit dwellings, the simple two storey townhouses of a type that sheltered the majority of the inhabitants of the city. Such humble accommodations were perhaps surprising for the man he was to call on, but he had learned they were entirely fitting for the Preacher's outlook on life. In Pontaine, the man would have been revered as a bishop, at the very least, but here, in subjugated Turnitia, the Faith and its lackeys in the Empire of Vos had ensured even this great man remained hidden.

Pausing once again to make sure he was not being followed, ears straining to hear soft footfalls in the twilight, he quietly entered the shadows cast by the house, and tapped on its back door, flecks of paint breaking loose from its ragged surface. Three taps followed by a pause, then two more.

A middle-aged woman opened the door, peering anxiously past him into the alley before focussing on his face. He could sense the fear emanating from her as she hustled him in quickly but that did little to stifle his own relief at, finally, reaching safe territory.

Inside, the kitchen was small and the same as in every other house in the street. A small cast-iron stove sitting under the chimney flooded the room with warmth, the fires behind its latticed grate combining with the lantern on the central dark wood table to provide a homely atmosphere, something he was glad of. The man seated at the table grabbed a bottle and poured a generous amount of wine into a clay cup.

"Tabius." The man nodded in welcome. "You look as if you could use this."

"Preacher," Tabius acknowledged. "We should get you to safety. The Faith could have discovered your location by now. They have taken enough of us tonight."

The Preacher waved his concern aside. "I did not run when the Empire descended on our city, even though we all knew they would bring the Final Faith with them. I am not going to start now. Have a drink man, steady your nerves. We don't believe it breaks the divine connection between man and God."

"I heard the Anointed Lord had passed that law," Tabius said, finally accepting the cup and relishing the first sip as it warmed his throat and stomach. "Think her followers will accept it?"

"They had better, if they know what is good for them," the Preacher said, then with a wry smile added, "Whether the Anointed Lord and her closest cronies follow it too, ah, that would be the question. Still, what can you expect when women are allowed into religion? Now, sit, and tell me how we fare this evening."

Tabius sat across from the Preacher and smiled in thanks as his wife laid out a plate of bread and ham, though he did not touch the supper, instead cradling the cup of wine in his hands to warm it.

"They knew where we were and what we were doing," he began, wincing slightly as the screams of dying friends echoed in his ears once again. "Someone gave us up. Tanner, maybe. He was a little too ready to offer us his cellar, knowing the risks it carried."

The Preacher shook his head. "I find that difficult to believe. I have known Tanner a long time, and would declare him righteous. He accepted the risks because he knew they were necessary. However, we have taken in new believers recently, and who knows whether they are all truly genuine? Even with recommendations, it is within some men to only deceive."

"Truly. The Rites of Protection and Good Health had barely finished when the Faith arrived. They were among us before we knew it, striking with swords at anyone within reach. Not just the men – they were after everyone."

He stopped to take another sip of wine, hoping the motion would conceal the shaking he felt enter his hands. The compassion in the Preacher's eyes told him he had failed, and he took a deep breath before continuing.

"It was complete chaos. People were running in all directions, trying to get out. And the screaming. It filled the cellar. We were slipping on the blood running across the floor, men were struck down as they tried to help their wounded sons. Gregor rallied first and began to fight back – I remember a hammer in his hand. We followed him as he headed for the stairs. I saw him cut down, but some of us, I don't know, maybe a dozen, managed to get out. Once we were on the street, we just ran."

"And you were chased?"

"Yes. We split up. I don't know if the others escaped. I was hoping I would find some of them here, as I went all the way round the Five Markets before coming back towards Meridian Street. I know Sanser, Mikels and Dornire got out with me, and I think I saw Kurn as well."

"Did the guard not come?"

"I saw a couple but..." Tabius paused. "The thing is I could have sworn they were in on it. Or, at least, some of them were. Since the city fell, the guard step in if you so much as knock a barrel over in the market. They must have seen what was happening, they just had to – but I did not see any of them act."

The Preacher nodded. "We have no friends in the Empire of Vos, and the Faith is fast taking root in the highest levels of their leadership. This Katherine may be a woman but as Anointed Lord, she has garnered a great deal of support among the Lord Dukes. I shudder to think what favours she has granted them, but her power is undeniable. Even here, in Turnitia, we feel the weight of her growing authority. We will find no justice from the city guard."

He reached across the table to top up Tabius' cup, though it had barely been touched. Tabius took this as a sign to drink, and he dutifully raised the cup to his lips.

"Gregor gone, you say? He will be missed in this hour of need." The Preacher sighed as he watched his wife fussing over the stove. "Aldene wants us to pack up and head for Pontaine. Perhaps even Allantia, she says. The Brotherhood is welcome there, she believes, or is at least not persecuted."

This caused his wife to glance over her shoulder with a reproachful look at her husband, and he smiled fondly back at her. Tabius shifted uneasily as he witnessed the love between them speak silent volumes.

"Perhaps that would be for the best," he ventured.

The Preacher hooted at that. "Would you?" he asked. "Really? Leave behind everything you have built up here for a new life? The grass is always greener, as they say but, in truth, you have sweated and worked too hard to leave behind your little empire here. I have worked just as hard, my boy. While you have amassed a small fortune in gold with your warehouses, I have become just as rich in spirit, bringing new blood into the Brotherhood and guiding those who believe to the best of my ability."

He fell silent for a moment, and Tabius stared into his cup. "No," the Preacher finally said. "I will stay and do what must be done. Our people will be scared after tonight, and will need reminding that the trials God puts before us are necessary for the salvation of all of us. Yes, even those poor misguided fools of the Faith. They have their part to play in his grand design too."

"So, what do we do now?" Tabius asked. Though he knew, come morning, a thousand problems would be waiting for him in his growing business, the Preacher had a knack of inspiring him to always work that little bit harder for the Brotherhood. His money and connections among the merchants of Turnitia had already benefited their congregation. All the Preacher had to do was ask, and he would serve as best he could.

"We start again," the Preacher said confidently. "Our beliefs are strong enough to survive the cruelty of the Final Faith. No matter how many of us they threaten, bully or kill, you cannot stamp out the truth, my boy. And truth is on our side. They have twisted the word of God beyond all recognition, turning it into a dream of conquest. But that is all it can be – a dream. We carry the burden of God's will, Tabius, and so we cannot fail. Whatever the tests put before us, we are God's chosen. Take comfort in that."

"As you say, Preacher."

"Now, come morning we will have a clearer idea of what our losses are. We will need a new meeting place – you can help with that, I trust?"

Tabius thought hard. Though one of his many warehouses by the docks would be a perfect venue for their gatherings, they had avoided it up to now, as it had seemed too dangerous with agents of the Final Faith constantly looking for signs of the Brotherhood growing in the city. Still, he had several that were away from the main trading areas, and his own name was nowhere near their legal documents of possession.

"It may be possible, yes," he said slowly, still thinking. "I'll start making arrangements tomorrow. I might be able to have something ready by evening."

"Please make sure you do. I must address our people by then at the latest. They will be terrified and in need of guidance. Perhaps just in need of assurance that everything will turn out the way it should." He smiled. "One thing is for sure, though. If we can–"

A loud crash of splintering wood resounded in the tiny kitchen. Tabius jerked in shock, looking past the Preacher to where the sound had come from.

"They're here!" cried the Preacher's wife, and she raced across to her husband to put a hand on his shoulder.

The Preacher looked at Tabius. "Go," he said simply.

Tabius stood immediately, as much out of habit of doing whatever the Preacher told him to do. Only then did he hesitate, looking into the man's eyes. He opened his mouth to speak, but the Preacher cut him off.

"Go! Quickly, while you still have time!"

Another crash, this time followed by a triumphant cry, and there were heavy footsteps in the hall outside the kitchen. Panic took over, and Tabius bolted through the back door, leaving the warm kitchen, the Preacher, and his wife behind. He heard shouts and a scream cut short.

Outside, a cry went up from a shadow in the alley to his right, and he dashed blindly left. Stumbling past houses on either side, he heard heavy footsteps with the chink of mail following, and fear gave him extra speed.

Behind, someone called out. "By the law of Vos – halt!"

That only served to drive Tabius on. A gap between houses to his left beckoned, and he dove into the darkness, crashing into a barrow that had been left casually propped up against one of the walls. The noise of man and barrow clattering onto the cobbles seemed deafening to him, and he scrabbled to his feet, ignoring the sting of grazed palms and shins as he burst out into another small street. Looking to each side, he ploughed forward into another alley that ran behind the next row of houses, changing direction to head back to Meridian Street.

Breathless after several minutes of fear-filled flight, he stopped, leaning against an abandoned cart outside a provisions store. His pursuers had been outpaced for now, no doubt weighed down by their armour and weaponry. Behind, he saw an orange glow silhouetting the city's skyline, and he strained his ears to hear massed cries in the distance. Smoke rose in columns from fires near the centre of Turnitia to lazily float in a growing cloud across the face of Kerberos, the massive sphere uncaring and unchanging in the face of human misery, even on this scale. The city, he saw, was descending into riotous chaos, and fellow members of the Brotherhood, people he knew, were the target of the mob, whipped into a frenzy by the Faith.

Slowly, his mind tried to come to terms with what was happening, but the implications of the city guard openly helping the Faith to track down their rivals – or dangerous heretics, as the Brotherhood was no doubt being described – filled him with a sick, creeping dread.

Had he been recognised at the Preacher's house? Tabius thought not, his escape had been too quick, and there had been no time to see his face clearly. Then he thought of the Preacher, and what he might be forced to tell his captors. If, indeed, the man was still alive.

Though weary, he pulled himself up straight and, doing his best to ignore the riots claiming the roads, markets and homes of the city, he carried on up Meridian Street until the north gate came into view. Taking the road that ran behind the city's fortified ramparts, he turned east until the tightly packed houses gave way to much larger dwellings, with their own gardens and protective walls hiding their grounds. This district was known intimately to Tabius. It was home.

Even through his fear, despair and fatigue, he possessed enough awareness to circle his own property twice, staring into the shadows for any sign of movement or presence of the guard. There was nothing, and he guessed the guard would not permit the riots to extend to this part of Turnitia, as there were too many men of power and money living here. Such men rarely entangled themselves in religious conflicts and, living here high on the hill on which Turnitia's foundations were built, they demanded nothing less than a total separation from the common rabble.

Gingerly opening a small wooden gate in the side wall of his home's compound, he silently slipped in and, closing it behind him, he breathed a heartfelt sigh of release. For the first time that night, he was truly safe. He opened his eyes and looked at his home, a large and finely built townhouse that took enough space to accommodate perhaps six or seven dwellings of the type the Preacher lived in. Light radiated from several of the downstairs rooms, and Tabius suddenly yearned to see his family, to make sure they were still safe, even though he knew no harm would reach them here.

His wife whirled round as he entered. Standing in front of the roaring fireplace in the drawing room, he guessed she had been pacing fretfully until he returned. With a cry of relief, she ran into his arms and, for a moment, they just held one another.

"Arthur came by earlier," she said once tears had been choked back. "He said the whole city has turned against you."

Tabius hushed her. "We will be safe. The mob won't climb the hill. There are too many interests to protect here. For once Vos might actually help us, however unintentionally."

"I hope you are right. Arthur said–"

Tabius held his wife at arm's length and smiled reassuringly. "While I appreciate Arthur looking after my family while I am away, he is an old man, and I really must have a word to him about scaring you unnecessarily."

"He said people were being killed in the streets. And the fires, I saw them from the landing. Half the city is aflame..."

"It is not as bad as all that. Where are the children?"

"Maggy is asleep. Lucius is pretending to be. He wanted to go down into the city to find his father."

Tabius grinned at that. "Thank God you convinced him otherwise. Now, I have a great deal of work tomorrow. Let's have supper and get some rest. Everything will seem better in the morning, I promise."

She wiped away a tear and nodded. "I'll rouse the kitchen."

Leaving Tabius' side, she walked proudly away, causing him to admire her fortitude, not for the first time. She paused at the door, then turned round. "Tabius... do you hear that?"

Straining his ears, he listened hard, not sure what his wife was getting at. Then it suddenly hit him – the mob was ascending the hill. He could hear their cries, muffled and distant now but slowly growing stronger.

"Impossible," he muttered. "The guard would not dare let them loose. Not up here."

His wife rested against the door for support. "Tabius," she said, worry and strain evident in her voice. "Are you sure about that? Really sure?"

One glance at his wife, standing by the door, strong in her faith but unsure of what to do, convinced him.

"Get the children. Do it now!"

As his wife fled upstairs, Tabius crossed the hall to his study, striding to the unlit fireplace to unbuckle the sword that hung there. Though it had belonged to his father and the blade had not been drawn in anger in decades, the lessons hammered into him during adolescence began to flood back as he grasped the hilt and drew the weapon. He fervently hoped he would not have to use it, especially in front of his children, but he would not permit anyone to hurt his family.

Striding back into the hall, he saw his wife leading little Magallia down the stairs, still in her night clothes and rubbing sleep from her eyes. Behind them was Lucius, his pride, about to enter adulthood and take on the responsibilities of the family business. Spying the sword, Lucius had just one question.

"Are we fighting them, Father?"

"I sincerely hope not," Tabius said, though he could not fully suppress a smile at his son's spirit.

A rap at the main door of the house caused them to freeze before it was followed by several more. Three raps, then a pause, followed by two more.

Tabius looked at his wife as he went for the door. "Arthur."

Unbolting the door, he opened it a crack at first, then threw it open when his suspicion was confirmed. Arthur, a stooped man in his seventies but with all the energy of someone far younger, shuffled in.

"You are preparing to leave?" he asked.

"Right now," Tabius said. "I'm not taking any chances. Have you seen anything?"

Turning to gather his family, Tabius stopped when he realised Arthur had not answered. He looked at the old man, and saw tears in the familiar face.

"The guard are already outside," Arthur said. "They are funnelling the mob straight here, avoiding everyone else. When they let me through their line, they said they were happy to let me burn with the rest of you."

Tabius sagged against the door, furiously trying to think what to do. His first thought was for the children. He walked slowly to his wife and took her hand.

"Get the children into the cellar. They will be after the three of us, not the children. They may be... missed in the confusion."

She put a hand to his cheek, and his heart broke at the look of anguish on her face.

"Tabius..." she said, searching for the words. He had nothing of comfort to tell her.

"It is too late."

CHAPTER ONE

ONCE AGAIN, HE found himself waiting for his opponent's decision. Leaning back on two legs of his chair, Lucius propped his feet up on the table and closed his eyes, knowing this could take a while. He held three cards to his chest, feeling the hard, rounded edges of mail beneath the hardened leather of his tunic. Two long, thin daggers were concealed in his boots and any member of the city guard shaking him down might quickly find the short sword strapped to his back, beneath his grey woollen cloak. The taverns on the Street of Dogs had not been noted as rough places when he was last in Turnitia, but too many changes had happened in the city during his long absence to take any chances.

The tavern was heaving and, judging by the other establishments he had visited earlier in the evening, business was good in the Street of Dogs. Whether it was the boost in the city's economy by the occupying power or the result of a subjugated populace seeking to forget the realities of the day, he had yet to tell. Certainly some had profited from the occupation, but as he knew too well, others always had to suffer for it. Here, at least, there seemed little evidence of the long war, as the soft tones of flute and harp from somewhere near the back of the common room floated over the raucous cries, laughter and shouts of the patrons.

His eyes snapped open as his opponent, a luckless man in rough clothing and sporting a thick dark beard, grabbed the dice and took a breath. Lucius had taken him for one of the labourers that toiled in the city's warehouse district, perhaps hoping to turn a week's wages into a year's salary in just one fortuitous night. This was not to be his night, Lucius knew, as he focussed his attention on the dice in the man's hand.

"I'll stay," the man said confidently, ignoring Lucius' provocative raised eyebrow. With another glance at his hand, the man shook the dice, blew on them, and then scattered them on the table.

Lucius narrowed his whole world to the tumbling dice. Under the table, the fingers of his free hand twitched as he sought the invisible threads that had become so familiar to him, and he felt the other-worldly power flow under his control. Tiny wisps of air streaked across the table to envelop the tumbling dice. As the dice bounced, Lucius lifted each one by the smallest fraction, buoying them up on a current, while spinning each slightly. When they landed and came to a rest, both cubes of carved bone presented the number four on their top face.

"At last!" the man cried, and his relief was palpable. Lucius had already seen that his belt pouch was getting light, but he had no desire to prolong his opponent's pain. The man took a card from his hand and proudly laid it on the table.

"Eight Princes!" he declared. "Your luck has turned, my friend!"

"Alas, I think not," said Lucius as he produced one of his own cards, also showing the number eight but with a smiling nubile woman seated on a golden throne. "The Queen trumps all but the Fool. I win again."

So saying, Lucius swept the coins lying on the table into his own pouch before snatching another card from the face down deck between them. "Another round? I believe I'm getting the feel for this."

The man, however, was not swayed by Lucius' demeanour. "The ills of Kerberos be on you, no one is that lucky," he spat. "How many times is that now? Eleven, twelve hands in a row? You've played me."

Seeing the man begin to rise from his seat, Lucius swept his legs off the table and stood, reaching into one of his boots for a blade. It was done in one well-practised, fluid motion that caught the man completely off guard. He had no idea of the danger until Lucius was leaning over him, the dagger planted firmly in the wood of the table with a dull thud.

"I'm sorry, *friend*," said Lucius. "But I have the idea that you were about to call me a cheat."

Looking into the man's eyes, Lucius could see what he was thinking. The man was no coward, and he likely had friends here that, in the very least, he would not want to see him backing down. On the other hand, Lucius' weather-beaten face, out-of-town air, and readiness to display a weapon marked him as someone not to casually entangle with. An ear-beating from the wife for losing a week's earnings was infinitely preferable to a knife in the belly.

The man spat again. "Your kind never last long around here, you know that? The guard will have you. Sooner or later, you'll push your luck too hard, and then the guard will have you."

Standing up to face Lucius briefly, the man then turned to grab the long coat thrown across the back of his chair before storming through the crowd of revellers to the door. Lucius glanced around to see if anyone had taken an undue interest in his naked blade – the man had not been wrong about the guard, after all – before sliding it back into his boot and gesturing a maid for an ale.

He slipped the maid a silver tenth with a wink when she returned, then settled down to sip his drink, searching for another mark. He caught men's eyes several times with a pointed look at the dice and cards, but no one was biting. Either they had seen the outburst just now, or their female companions were of greater interest than a game of chance. Cursing his previous opponent for forcing him to draw a weapon, he quickly decided to move on. Downing the last remains of the ale, a Vos-brew he had little love for anyway, he surreptitiously checked his weapons and belt pouch and, finding them to be present and in order, slipped through the throng towards the door.

Outside the tavern, he took a deep breath, glad to have air somewhat cleaner than that inside. Looking up, he saw the huge blue-grey globe of Kerberos hanging above, dominating the sky as it cast its dull twilight glow upon the city while bands of white gossamer clouds played slowly across its surface. The eternal sphere had meant much to his father, his faith rooted in the belief of salvation among those clouds, but Lucius had come to know better.

Glancing to the east, he saw the Street of Dogs sweep downwards towards the cliffs, perhaps a couple of miles away, where they formed a natural defence against the ocean. The waters constantly raged against the land either side of the city, gouging chunks from it every year, and Lucius wondered at the sanity of the original settlers in building a port here. Only maybe one day in ten could a ship brave the barriers shielding the port from the churning waters to dock at the massive stone harbour built at the bottom of those cliffs, and then only with great risk – and that was assuming the harbour could accept another vessel, as one section or another was always under repair. Once a great marvel of engineering, the harbour had fallen into various states of disrepair over the years as the change in the city's leadership began to favour other priorities. It was certainly no coincidence that many of the Vos nobles now running Turnitia had their own existing interests in the mercantile activities of companies that relied on horse and wagon to transport goods, rather than the dangerous and intemperate sea.

Even from the centre of Turnitia, he could hear the roiling surf blasting itself against the barriers, conjuring a constant dim roar that the citizens of the city soon learned to tune out. For someone who had been away for so long, however, it was a reminder of just how precarious the city's position was. One day, the land must succumb to the angry waters and collapse into the sea, taking Turnitia with it. Perhaps that would not be so bad a thing, he thought. It would save many people a great deal of trouble.

"That's the whore's son." The voice brought Lucius back to the present and he turned around to see if it was indeed him being spoken of. It was. The beaten card player had evidently found some friends in a nearby tavern and had either been convinced to take his money back, or was somewhat braver than Lucius had thought.

There were seven of them, though only two had had the presence of mind to bring weapons. One brandished a knife, while the other wielded a crude cudgel. They had come from the high end of the Street of Dogs and were fanning out in a loose semicircle to trap him against the row of buildings behind.

"I really don't need this," Lucius remarked, as much to himself as to the men. His original opponent appeared to take the comment personally.

"Well, I don't need to be cheated out of me money by a charlatan like you. Breezing into the city, hitting up a few of the locals, and then breezing out again with your pouch clinking with our coin. Is that it?"

"Friend, I beat you fair and square, no cheating," said Lucius, raising a hand in an attempt to forestall any violence. It was not true, of course, but there was not much else he could say.

"Hey, no need for us to start trouble," the man said with a crooked smile. "Just hand me the money back – and your other coins, which you no doubt gained from your games – and we'll call it quits."

Lucius sighed, wondering how far he had fallen to have his own marks trying to rob him. He was not worried about his own immediate safety. A half dozen or so labourers, a little worse for drink no doubt, were of small concern. The city guard, however, were another matter and while he spied no patrols nearby, open violence on the street would bring them running in no time. *That* was something worth avoiding.

"I'm sorry, I can't do that," he said, knowing exactly how this was going to turn out. "I warn you now, walk away. Just walk away. There is nothing you can do that will end this well."

"Cocky, ain't he?" said one of the man's companions.

"He'll be less cocksure with this wrapped round his head," the thug with the cudgel growled. He took a step forward and drew the weapon back as if he were aiming to knock Lucius' head clean off his shoulders and send it sailing down the street.

Lucius ran. Behind him, the men whooped and hollered, their blood rising at the sight of prey fleeing. Hearing their footsteps just a few yards behind, Lucius was faintly surprised they had reacted so quickly, as he had bolted without hesitation when it became clear a confrontation was inevitable.

Keen to get away from the main street where any number of well-meaning citizens might raise a call for the guard, he had already spotted a side alley between the tavern and a hardware stall, one of thousands linking the main thoroughfares of the city. He darted for the narrow entrance, feet skipping over the dull cobbles.

Once veiled by the shadows of the tall buildings either side, Lucius smiled. With darkness as his ally and no witnesses, the odds now swung massively in his favour. Skidding to a halt with his back to a greying stone wall, he momentarily closed his eyes and concentrated, feeling the shadows rise up to cloak his body.

The men rushed around the corner, the one in the lead suddenly stopping. Those behind cursed as they ran into one another before the first raised his hand.

"Well... where on Kerberos did he go?" he said.

They all peered into the alley, squinting to penetrate the gloom. Running straight as an arrow, they could clearly see the length of the alley, just as they could clearly see there was no rogue silhouetted against the lights of the establishments in the next street.

"Maybe he climbed to the roof," said one, eyeing up the side of the buildings.

"Idiot," retorted another.

"There's people that can do it!"

"Not in just a few seconds."

"A master criminal, are you?"

"Idiot."

Lucius watched the men, reaching behind his back to clasp the hilt of his short sword. The closest stood no more than two feet away, but they were oblivious to his presence. Wreathed in arcane darkness, Lucius had effectively become invisible. The other things that might give him away, an involuntary movement, a slight sound, those he could suppress from years of practice. It was a fearsome combination and one that was more than a match for an irritated gambler and his friends.

As the squabble spread to the other men, all with theories on what to do next, Lucius moved. Whipping his sword clear of its inverted scabbard in near silence, he reversed the weapon and brought the steel pommel down on the neck of the nearest man. The target sank without a sound, and Lucius was among the rest of them before they realised one of their number had hit the ground.

A foot sank into the stomach of another, while the sword descended once more – pommel first – into the face of a third. The man's shriek bubbled as blood welled up from his shattered nose, but it was enough to alert the remaining thugs.

The mark acted before thinking, and reached for Lucius' throat with both hands. Lucius took a step back and felt threads of energies rush through him as he sought to harness their power. Selecting a strand, he focussed on its structure and form, consciously moulding it into something he could use. He felt its strength swelling inside his body as it always did in battle, somewhere near his heart, and he extended an open palm to the charging man. A crack resounded down the alley, like a miniature bolt of lightning, and a faint, crimson wave of force sprang from his palm, catching the man full in the chest. With no chance of avoiding the blast, the man was picked up off his feet and hurled against the unyielding building opposite. He collapsed to the floor, winded.

"It's a damned wizard!" one of his friends cried out, now panicking.

"Could be the Lord of the Three Towers himself, he still won't bespell us without a head." This came from cudgel-man, and Lucius turned to see him winding up for another swing. The blow, when it came, seemed painfully slow and obvious to Lucius, who raised his sword to block the attack. The sharpened blade dug deep into the club, trapping it briefly.

Two others, seeing an advantage, both rushed Lucius from behind. He felt a hand grab his shoulder and instantly buckled his knees, rolling forward and dragging his weapon free at the same time. Tumbling away, he came up in a crouch, ready for their next move.

While cudgel-man was wondering where his enemy had gone, the other two were not so slow. Both yelled in triumph as they saw what they thought was a beaten man on the ground. As they ran to start raining kicks and blows down upon him, Lucius took another breath, narrowed his eyes in concentration, and then slapped his free hand on the cobbles. A wave of energy spread out before him, pushing up stones as it shifted the ground. All the men still in the fight were thrown off their feet by the pulse, fear registering in their eyes.

Three turned and fled without another word, though a curse from cudgel-man followed them. Another, the first to fall, lay motionless on the ground, though Lucius knew he would wake up in an hour or so with the world's worst hangover.

Cudgel-man faced him once again, seething with anger but unsure of what to do without anyone backing him up. Knife-man helped the mark to his feet, before turning to face Lucius, blade held at arm's length.

"We can still take him," said cudgel-man, sounding as if he needed the encouragement himself.

"I advise you not to try," said Lucius, raising a hand in an attempt to start a parley. "A beating in an alley is a hazard of the city. But if either of you try to use those weapons, I'll start getting serious."

The gambler was suddenly less than sure of himself and started to mumble something, but Lucius caught the flash of the knife's movement from his friend.

"Fool!" Lucius hissed as the knife span through the air. The man's aim was true, but Lucius gritted his teeth as he released the same energy he had used on the dice earlier. This time there was no effort at finesse or style, as he desperately sought to slow and steady the blade. A blast of wind gusted in a narrow line, striking the knife with a low whistle. The weapon stopped suddenly in mid-air, hung motionless for a brief second, then fell to the stones with a clatter.

Knowing a distraction when he saw one, cudgel-man judged the moment right to finally unleash his skull-splitting swing. It was a poor decision.

Ducking under the wild blow, Lucius sprang forward, lunging with his short sword. The blade buried itself in cudgel-man's stomach, and the man gave a curious mewing sound as his brain began to register that the wound was mortal. Knife-man started to back away, but Lucius reached forward with his outstretched hand and grasped him by the throat.

The rage of battle now well and truly upon him, Lucius dug within himself to find the darkest, most vile, and terrible of threads. He felt a chill sweep through his body as he channelled the force from his heart, down his arm, through his hand and into the man. The power mustered was the antithesis of life and it reacted with the living flesh it raced into. The man gasped as he futilely grabbed at the hand holding him, but his strength was already waning. Lucius stared into his eyes, watching them grow dim in seconds. The man's skin greyed and withered, while his cheeks sank into his face and muscles shrivelled, hair falling out in clumps. When Lucius released his grip the corpse looked as if it had been dead for months.

Angry at the men for attacking him, and for forcing him to use such power, Lucius ripped his sword clear of cudgel-man then rounded on the gambler. With blade held menacingly, he turned his free hand palm upwards and conjured wisps of fiery energy, his hand now wreathed in flames of lavender and turquoise.

"You've lost two friends tonight because of your folly," Lucius told the man. "Believe me when I say you got off lightly. Now go!"

Lucius jerked his head to reinforce his command, but it was wholly unnecessary. As far as the man was concerned, death itself stalked that alley, and he wanted no part of it. Spinning on his heel, the man scrabbled for the bright lights of the Street of Dogs, and a life that held no terror.

Briefly regarding the men lying on the ground, Lucius exhaled as the tension left him. Wiping his blade on the tunic of cudgel-man, he sheathed it then cursed. He had not intended to give knife-man so gruesome a death, no matter how much it might have been deserved or forewarned. Lucius knew many different ways to kill a man but, in the heat of battle, there was rarely time to plan and consider. He had reached for the most devastating attack needed at the time, and taken the first that came to his command. That it was the most loathsome of the energies he was able to use and control was almost pure chance, as he had reached blindly, by instinct. The coldness of its touch still caressed him, and he could feel the dark evil lurking just beneath the surface. He would be paying for its help with a couple of sleepless nights at least, as the old dreams flooded back.

Trying to stem images of past haunted nights, he gathered his wits and resolved to put as much distance between himself and the bodies as possible. Heading away from the Street of Dogs, he briefly considered trying to find another tavern friendly to gamblers, but he quickly dismissed the idea. The earnings tonight would keep him for a day or two at worst, and he was in no shape to beguile anyone after the fight. All they would see would be a rogue, a desperado. Or murderer, maybe.

He decided to head away from the lights and aim for the merchant quarter. The inns there were usually sombre affairs, dedicated to traders and other businessmen visiting Turnitia. They catered for higher classes who demanded peace, security and thrills less blatant than those on offer in the Street of Dogs. The peace and security at least were things Lucius could appreciate at this moment.

Stepping cautiously out the other end of the alley, Lucius scanned the wide road it spilled onto. From old memories, he believed this to be Lantern Street, which ran down the hill parallel to the Street of Dogs before jinking north toward the merchant quarter. Houses lined both sides of the street, punctuated with the occasional bookseller, jewellers, or other trader dealing in luxuries. This area marked the boundary between the masses living alongside the cliff-side warehouses and those in the considerably wealthier area higher up the hill. Drawing his cloak about him, he set off with a safe room, warm bath and comfy sheets in mind.

"A display some would find impressive."

The casual remark caused him to whirl round, his hand instinctively reaching up behind his cloak to grasp his sword once more. A woman stepped from the alley he had just left, slipping easily from the darkness as if she had been there all along. Lucius was not so certain that was not the case.

"Who are you?" he said warily, expecting any kind of trouble after events this evening.

"Do you not recognise me?"

Lucius stared at the woman for a moment, racking his mind. Her dark hair was tied up high on her head, in the style common to women used to fighting, and both her poise and manner indicated she was well accomplished in battle. In age, she was beginning to reach her middle years, but he thought she was no less attractive for that, for the leather tunic studded with small metal discs could not conceal the fact her body was extremely well-toned. Lucius had met such women before and he knew they could drive a blade through a man's body as easily as he could. A tell-tale and familiar bulge in one of her boots told him she was armed with at least one blade and he began to wonder what other weapons might be concealed.

Her eyes were the most striking feature though, dark pits that seemed impenetrable and yet likely missed nothing. They assessed him and the potential danger he posed, even as he weighed her in return. Upon seeing that gaze cast upon him once more, he knew exactly who he was talking to.

"Aidy," he said finally. "I hadn't counted on you still being here."

CHAPTER TWO

EYEING AIDY WARILY from across the table as she sipped her wine, Lucius was a little unnerved to realise she was returning his own suspicious stare. It had been eight years since he had last seen her but under the lanterns of the inn, the years had seemed only to brush against her. Those dark brown, almost black, eyes watched him with the same disapproval he began to remember all too well. They were bordered by a few lines he thought had not been there before, but the biggest change was in her demeanour. She seemed... harder. Colder. Half a decade older than he, Adrianna Torres was obviously just as dangerous as she was in the past.

"Damned chance us running into each other," he said, beginning to feel uncomfortable at the easy way in which she carried the silence.

"Fool," she said dismissively. "Have you forgotten already the lessons of Master Roe? There is very little in this world that happens by coincidence."

"Then how... ?"

"Your arrival here was like a beacon. I would be surprised if every Shadowmage remaining in the city did not feel it."

Lucius was perplexed at that but did not feel like pushing the point and risking a lecture. Adrianna had been more advanced in the craft than he had ever been, and she was certainly more committed. He had always seen his control of the magical threads that made up the Shadowmage's art as a tool, a means to an end. For Aidy, it had been something more akin to a religion, with their shared Master the high priest. Still, at least there was some common ground there.

"So, still learning under Master Roe?"

Her eyes suddenly narrowed, and he mentally kicked himself. He should have guessed things had taken a turn for the worse after he had left Turnitia.

"No, I am not."

It was a leading statement, but Lucius found himself hesitating over the obvious question. Not for the first time, he felt as if he were being led by Aidy in the direction she wanted.

"What happened?"

"What do you think happened? The Empire of Vos increased its grip on the city after their occupation, and the Shadowmages were at the top of their list. Some fled." At this she looked pointedly at him. "The rest of us tried to fight. Without support, we were crushed. Master Roe, as one of the most visible among us, was captured by the Vos guard and taken to the Citadel."

"They killed him?"

"Well, they don't pamper you with whores and wine in the Citadel," she said, caustically.

"I'm sorry," he said. She let it pass but continued to stare at him witheringly over the rim of her glass. Her self-righteousness was beginning to grate on him.

"You do remember I had some problems of my own back then?" he said, trying not to sound defensive. "The war affected everyone in this city, not just the Shadowmages. The Final Faith was their vanguard, and they made damned sure the Brotherhood was in no position to raise objections. I lost my whole family, Aidy, and I would have been next. They knew who I was. I had no choice but to leave."

"You always had a choice."

"What, stand and fight?" he asked incredulously.

She leaned across the table, setting down her glass. "Yes," she said fiercely. "We needed every friend we had. Instead, you chose to run. And for what? What are you now? A vagabond, thief for hire, mercenary?"

"What possible difference could I have made? If you were not powerful enough to stop them taking the Master, what could I have done?"

Adrianna did not answer straight away. Finally leaning back in her chair, she broke eye contact with him for the first time since they had sat down. "It might have made all the difference in the world. You have no idea what you..."

She paused and seemed unwilling to continue.

"What?" he prompted, but she did not answer. As the silence between them grew, Lucius began to feel uncomfortable again. He cleared his throat.

"So, what are the Shadowmages doing now?" he asked.

"We are a pale... shadow of our former selves. Hunted by Vos, whose nobles are convinced we are unstoppable assassins, and used by Pontaine nobles who think much the same thing. The guild is directionless with so many members dead and no one training young blood."

Lucius frowned. "Aidy, it was never much of a guild..." he started.

"It was more a guild than many others in this city. We pledged to never attack one another, to re-assign ourselves when contracts clashed, and to take any and all action when one of us was in danger. Some of us still adhere to the old ways." She gave a short, bitter laugh. "Old ways! It has only been eight years, and yet it seems like ancient history."

Draining her glass, she seemed in no hurry to order another, and Lucius presumed their meeting was drawing to a close.

"So, Lucius, just why have you returned? Come to claim your inheritance? Cause more trouble for your former allies? Why have you come back to Turnitia?"

Lucius shrugged. "I've spent the past eight years wandering the Anclas Territories and Pontaine. I wanted to see home again. I've kept out of the strife between the Empire and Pontaine, but I thought there might be someone here who could use my talents."

"Ha!" Adrianna cried, drawing the attention of the few remaining merchants and traders scattered on the tables around them. "I was right – playing the mercenary."

"I have a right to make a living," said Lucius, giving her an injured look. "The guild could help me with that. Just a few jobs, and then I'll be out of here."

"The guild no longer exists, Lucius," Adrianna said firmly. "Not for you. Not for those who ran."

She stood abruptly and threw a few coins on the table to pay for their wine. "You are not welcome in Turnitia, Lucius Kane. Leave. Now. You are not wanted."

Left staring at her back as she departed, Lucius nursed what remaned of his wine, wondering just how he would continue working in the city if Adrianna decided to make life difficult for him.

THE SUN WAS peering past Kerberos as Lucius paced Ring Street, its full daylight strength beginning to warm Turnitia as the citizenry stirred. As the fiery ball moved inexorably clear of Kerberos' shadow, its rays warped and shimmered through the clouds of its giant companion until it coalesced into a solid sphere.

Ring Street was the thoroughfare that bound the Five Markets together, and it was heaving with traffic. Lying east of the merchant quarter and the docks, the Five Markets were the centre of commerce in Turnitia and on any given day they would be thronged with traders and peddlers, all calling and shrieking for custom, be it from the city's own population or foreign merchants looking to secure new goods for their own home markets.

At the centre of the Five Markets lay the Citadel, a giant fortress that leered over the city and its people. As he looked up warily at its ramparts and the guards that lined them, Lucius recalled that it had been merely a single tower used by the watch when he was last in Turnitia. When Vos had fought with Pontaine, the city had been quickly conquered and the Empire, keen not to lose any territory of value, had dedicated its energies to rebuilding the tower, turning it into an unassailable fortress. A double line of high walls had been thrown up around the tower, causing many to speak of terrible crimes being committed within the hidden interior. The tower itself was expanded into an entire keep within just three years, and a law was passed that no other structures in Turnitia were permitted to be built taller than the Citadel. The message was clear; nothing was above the Empire of Vos.

The original tower still stood, but it had been reinforced and rebuilt to match its four companions, each of which loomed over one of the Five Markets. At the pinnacle of each tower, a flagpole rose bearing the fluttering standard of Vos, a black eagle on a red field.

Lucius felt the presence of Vos in the streets too as he wandered this part of the city. Patrols of the guard, now cloaked in the livery of the Empire, were frequent and terribly efficient. Wherever he found himself on Ring Street or within one of the Five Markets, a patrol of five or six red-tabarded guards were always in sight. What he found curious was that the people of Turnitia seemed to readily accept the presence of the guard, even act friendly towards them. Some chatted amiably with one patrol, while others stood dutifully to one side as another hurried past on some errand.

It seemed as if he were the only one to remember the dreadful days after the army of Vos had routed Turnitia's pitifully small guard and entered the city. The persecutions, the dismantling of the existing law and order, and the carefree violence; women violated in the streets and in their homes, men killed casually while trying to defend them, shops looted then burned. The religion of the Brotherhood wiped out and the Shadowmages decimated.

Looking around as he passed through the Five Markets, Lucius began to understand why the people of his city had been so quick to forget those times. Despite the many guards patrolling the streets, despite the constant, foreboding presence of the Citadel in the heart of Turnitia, business was clearly going well.

The Five Markets were packed with crowds, and there were not enough stalls for all the traders, many being forced to set up shop in alleyways and on street corners. Fine Pontaine wines brought in from the captured Anclas Territories were sold alongside clothes of the highest fashion worn in the Vos cities of Malmkrug, Scholten and Vosburg. The people of the city moved easily, dressed in clothing finer than he remembered them wearing eight years before, and the traders themselves seemed to be doing a great deal of business.

He had to admit, it was not the city he had grown up in. The population had forgiven Vos for its crimes in return for an economy that had flourished, the city's coffers swelled by the presence of the invaders. So what if a little freedom had been curtailed and new taxes imposed? Everyone was better off.

Except himself, Lucius thought. Perhaps the old saying was true, and you really could never go back home. Turnitia was no longer the place he had thought it was, and it was unlikely to welcome one of his sort. Adrianna had been right in one thing; he had grown into an adventurer and mercenary.

He was not entirely sure when it had happened, but he thought of his time in Pontaine and the Anclas Territories, working as a sword for hire, trading his skills for gold and silver as the opportunity struck. It had not been a bad life, he decided, and he certainly appreciated the freedom he had experienced more than the people of Turnitia mourned its loss.

As he wandered through a crowd gathering around a stall whose rotund trader cajoled them into buying trinkets all the way from Allantia, or so he claimed, Lucius made the decision to make what money he could in the city, then leave. He needed gold for a horse and supplies. Then he could perhaps lose himself in the Anclas Territories once more, or perhaps journey deep into Pontaine to discover what lay within the Sardenne. Maybe head north to Allantia, he thought as he eyed the trader. Why not? He was free to do as he wished. Money permitting.

Lucius flicked his eyes to each side as he paced the Five Markets, looking for an opportunity, some sign of the old city he would find familiar and could turn to his advantage. An old acquaintance, perhaps, who could push work his way. A rich trader in need of a capable guard. A ship's captain recruiting marines to work the dangerous trade routes. Anything that provided quick and ready gold.

Much of his morning was spent in this way, but Lucius found little that presented itself. He feared he might be reduced to gambling as a means to an end, but even his special skills might not guarantee win after win. There was a reason they called it gambling, of course, and there was always the risk he might meet someone whose luck or skill at cheating might exceed his own abilities; and then he would be back to square one.

Trying to think a little more laterally, he began to eye up the various stores he passed, and his gaze fixed upon a trader whose accent gave him away as Vos born and bred. His stall was bedecked with chains of gold and silver, bracelets and brooches sparkling in the strengthening sunlight as their gems glinted with every colour Lucius could imagine. He stopped in the street and stared, thinking fast. A quick distraction would be easy enough to create, and a faster hand could sweep a cluster of jewels under his cloak before the trader's attention was brought back to his wares. Glancing about, he looked for the tell-tale red of guard patrols and, sure enough, he saw two at opposite ends of this market. However, they were both at least a hundred paces away, and would have to fight their way through the crowd.

The trader was engaged in an animated discussion over a thin gold chain with a young lady wreathed in silks. He was anxiously assuring her that the chain would bring focus to her neck which, he declared, could not remain unadorned another minute. Lucius cast a look at the two patrols, and then began to search for escape routes. He knew he would have to move fast once the goods were in his possession. The alleyways in the area were too crowded for his comfort, with peddlers and customers spilling over the boundaries of the markets. He knew he could make a crowd work for him, but it would be better overall if no cry of alarm went up until he was well on his way. He took a step forward, preparing to draw upon otherworldly energies to create the distraction he would need.

"I wouldn't if I was you," a gravely voice behind him said.

Lucius turned then looked downwards to find the source of the comment. He saw a filthy man sitting on the cobbles, leaning against a rusting horse trough. The man's clothes were a patchwork of cast-offs, each thread entangled with dirt, crusted food and other, less describable stains. A terrible stench of sweat and foulness reached Lucius' nostrils, and he gagged as he tried to form a retort.

"You'd never make it out of the market in time," the man continued as he quite openly scratched at his nether regions. "See, people here don't like thieves too much. Don't like beggars either, as it happens, but we just get moved on from time to time. You'd go straight to the Citadel, make no mistake. And then you really would be in trouble."

Lucius stared at the man for the moment, peering through the dirt and wild greying hair to detect any deceit. He had the feeling he was being played, but could not quite put his finger on how.

"What business is it of yours?" he asked, quickly glancing about to see if the beggar had any accomplices that were about to assault or rob him.

The man shrugged. "Call it some advice from someone who knows. That much I'll give you for free. If you want more, it'll cost." With this, the man produced a tin cup from the folds of his rags and proffered it upwards to Lucius. "Spare a coin for the sick?" he said with a grin that revealed ruined and blackened teeth.

Trying hard not to wrinkle his face in disgust, Lucius shook his head. "You've caught me at a bad time, my friend. I am as desperate for coin as you."

"Oh, I'm not so sure about that," the man said, winking at Lucius. "A man like you is never far from gold."

That checked Lucius and he gave the man a hard look. "And just what do you mean by that?"

The man shook his head noncommittally. "I've seen you about."

"I haven't been in the city long."

"Last evening, for example. Six men was it? Or seven?"

Lucius narrowed his eyes. "How do you know this? I saw no one else."

The ruined teeth grinned at him again. "That's the point. No one sees us beggars. Just part of the scenery. There I was, just minding me own business, trying to get some kip in the door of the local bookseller. But I have a clear view down a certain alley, and what I saw there was... intriguing."

Lucius glanced about nervously, seeing if anyone else was taking an interest in the conversation, but the crowd seemed to be far more intent on securing deals on food, clothing, or luxuries.

"And what, exactly, would a beggar find intriguing about it?" Lucius said dangerously, though he was a little unsure of what he could do to this man while so many people were close by.

"Just going to dismiss me because I am a beggar, is it? Of no use to anyone, a stain on the backside of Turnitia? Well, I'll tell you, my foolish friend. We beggars are the eyes and ears of the city. What we don't see ain't worth knowing. The wise man knows this, and rewards a beggar for the information he has." Again, the tin cup was shaken in front of Lucius.

Pursing his lips, Lucius considered the man and his words. Opportunity had so far eluded him this morning, and the beggar clearly understood the city and its workings. If the man's intention was to call the guard and get a reward for finding a Shadowmage, if indeed he truly understood what had taken place in the alley the evening before, then surely he would already have done so. The greatest danger was, surely, that the beggar was simply fleecing him for a coin. Despite Lucius' own financial circumstances, the beggar certainly looked as if he needed the money more than him. His face full of distrust, he reached into his pouch and flipped a coin into the cup.

The beggar grinned openly as he scooped the coin out. "Ah, blessings of the Faith be on you."

Lucius watched as the coin disappeared in the folds of the man's rags. He coughed to bring attention back to himself. "And you have information for me?"

"Well, it seems to me you're looking for good money."

"How perceptive."

"There's a peddler across the way, near the fountain in the centre of this market. You'll recognise him, has a green awning above his stall. Sells pans and ornaments, foreign junk."

"And?"

"Ask for Ambrose. You'll be thanking me later."

The beggar shifted his position, then stood, brushing himself down as if removing the dirt of the street would have any effect on his hygiene.

"That's it?" Lucius asked, frowning.

"That's it. Can't do everything for you. My thanks for the coin," the beggar said as he waddled away. Then, he stopped and turned back to Lucius. "Oh, and a word of advice while you are in the city. Always pay a beggar. You never know how fortune may smile upon you."

Lucius was left standing as the man disappeared into the crowd. He shook his head in disbelief, for if this had been a scam, it was a lengthy process simply to gain a single coin. Quickly, he reached down for his pouch to make sure that it was still there and was reassured by its bulk, filled with the proceeds of the previous evening's gambling. Giving one more glance at the jewellery on the stall in front of him, he walked past it, heading towards the centre of the market.

Finding a single stall with a green awning was not a simple task, he soon discovered. The market was a riot of colours, with many traders shadowing their goods and potential customers from the sun with gaudy parasols, awnings and wind-breakers. These clashed with the silks, wools and furs, which in turn competed with brightly coloured signs proclaiming that only they had the best deals in the city.

The fountain was likely a new construction, for Lucius remembered no such decoration in this market years before. As he neared its carved grey stone, his thoughts were confirmed as he saw the tall and familiar figure of the Anointed Lord Katherine Makennon. Her statue stood as depicted in the many paintings that were spreading throughout the Empire as signs of piety and faith; plate-armoured, sword held high in readiness to strike down unbelievers and infidels. Long hair flew from beneath an elegant helm, its front plates open to reveal a stern-faced woman. One hand was held low, as if offered for a kiss of fealty, and from this water flowed into a marble basin. People sat around the rim, but all were at an awkward angle, for one did not turn their back on God's own true representative. A squad of guardsmen were never far away to ensure this observance was followed in public.

After circling the fountain, Lucius finally found the stall he was looking for. The awning was indeed green but, unlike many others nearby, it looked as if it had seen better days. A quick inspection of the goods on display revealed that they were indeed best described as foreign junk. A few largely disinterested passers-by were collared by the animated man behind the stall, perhaps looking for a rare, yet cheap, relic or artefact among the detritus spread across the cloth-covered surface of the stall. Another man sat to one side, whittling away at a wood-carved feline creature, either having fashioned it from scratch, or more likely, repairing some sign of damage.

Lucius sidled up to the stall, suddenly unsure of himself. He picked up a model of a ship, one of its masts twisting under the movement to hang by a thin strip of wood across the deck. The trader immediately turned his attention to the newcomer and started a practised spiel that described the model as a rare work of art from Allantia, honed by a fine craftsman whose name would soon spread throughout the peninsula, raising the value of investment in any of his works purchased now.

Lucius quickly looked at the other patrons of the stall then, seeing them take not the slightest notice of him, said quietly, "I am looking for Ambrose."

The trader immediately lost interest in him, quickly jerking his head toward the man whittling wood before turning back to more likely prospects. Lucius took the sign and placed the ship back on the stall.

"You Ambrose?" he asked, standing over the man as he worked. The man did not bother to look up from the carving he drew a knife over, and Lucius saw it was actually some fantastic creature that stood on two legs, with fierce gouging fangs. The man himself was middle-aged, thin, and dressed in a cheap black tunic.

"Depends," the man answered lazily. "You after a commission? Come back next week, I've got enough for now."

"I'm after work."

"Any good with wood?"

Lucius frowned, not certain he had approached this conversation properly. "I don't think that is the kind of work intended."

The man looked up at him curiously. "Who sent you?"

"Some beggar," Lucius said lamely with a shrug.

"You pay him for my name?"

"I did."

"Good. You looking to work inside the law?" Ambrose asked.

Lucius smiled at that. "I have a feeling that if that was what I was after, I wouldn't be talking to you. No, I have no great desire to work purely within the law of Vos."

"Willing to take risks?"

"Of course. So long as the reward matches them."

Ambrose put his wood carving on the ground and stood, looking Lucius up and down as if weighing his worth.

"You look fit. Can you run?"

"Faster than you would think."

"And fight?"

"If I have to. Haven't been beaten yet."

Ambrose shook his head. "Everyone gets a beating once in a while. The sooner you learn that, the better." He paused for a moment, then seemed to make up his mind. "You'll start at the bottom – means you'll be working with the kids, but do well and we'll see what else you are capable of."

"What's the work? And where?"

"Right here," Ambrose said, sweeping a hand across the market. "I'll put you on a team, you'll work the crowd. Earnings get pooled and split, with the guild taking its forty per cent. Listen to the kids in your team, they know more than you do. And stay away from the stalls, we don't rob them – we have too many friends among the traders, and we don't want you pissing them off."

Lucius frowned. "You want me to work as... a pickpocket. That it?"

Ambrose cocked an eyebrow. "Too good for that line of work, are you? Let me tell you, I – and every thief I know, for that matter – started off on one of these teams. And I never regretted a minute of it. Learn the trade, and then we'll see what else you are capable of. If you are as good as you seem to think you are we'll find the right place for you."

"I was hoping for some real money," Lucius said, a little disenchanted as he saw his future boiling away to nothing more than petty crime and humiliating spells in the stocks. If, indeed, the Vos guard bothered with anything as trivial as stocks for captured thieves. He was surprised to see Ambrose smiling at him.

"I tell you what," said Ambrose. "You give me a week on a team. If you don't like it, if you decide it is not for you, if it is not bringing in the sort of money you are after, then we'll call it quits. You can just walk away, no harm done."

Ambrose sat back down and picked up his carving again. "But I have a feeling that once you see what a noble and skilled profession you have joined, you'll be less than ready to give it up."

CHAPTER THREE

THE FIVE MARKETS had changed, at least for Lucius. No longer were they thronged with crowds wandering aimlessly between traders while trying to save a few coins on their latest purchase, nor was a chance opportunity floating elusively away from him. Instead, this place of commerce had become his hunting ground.

Ambrose had assigned him to a pickpocket team that same afternoon, and his new comrades were Markel and Treal, twin brother and sister no more than twelve or thirteen years old. The previous member of their team, a lad named Harker, Lucius learned, had been promoted to work within the guildhouse of the Night Hands, the title given to this band of thieves. Lucius was taking his place, but neither Markel nor Treal made any comment about his advanced years, even though pick-pocketing was a child's game.

Their acceptance of an adult as an equal, if anything, made Lucius even more self-conscious of what he was doing, and more than once he wondered how much further he could possibly fall. Still, Ambrose had promised that he would not regret the money that would soon be flowing through his hands.

The veteran thief kept a close eye on Lucius' team, and several others, directing them to different areas within the Five Markets, rotating each so suspicious guards would inevitably lose track of the children they had started to watch. The proceeds of their work were transferred to Ambrose regularly, and he quickly sorted the guild's percentage and scribbled down what was owed to each team in his own code, to be returned to each member by the end of the day. It was a well-practised system, with more valuable goods, such as jewels and cut stones, quickly fenced through the Night Hands' own network of dealers and traders, to be returned as hard currency at the day's final accounting.

Lucius' first day was humiliating for him, taking instructions from two children barely old enough to piss in a pot, while his own efforts at grabbing purses and pouches without notice were more often than not dismal failures, forcing him to beat a hasty retreat before his mark realised just what he had intended. By the end of the second day, Lucius was about ready to walk away from the deal and take his chances running cards in taverns. What stopped him was partially the realisation that he was getting better in his role, but mostly because Ambrose made good on his promise of real money. Lucius had not been bothering to keep track of the pockets he, Markel and Treal had picked during the day as he descended ever further into depression, and he actually took a step back in surprise when Ambrose read them their total day's takings as the sun fell beneath the rooftops of the city and the Five Markets began to clear of custom.

His share amounted to twelve full silvers, plus a little change, which he gratefully took from Ambrose and swept into his own pouch.

"You see, lad?" Ambrose had said. "I told you there was good money in this."

Treal had told him that skilled teams that had worked together for many months could easily triple or quadruple this on a good day, and he slowly came to believe this was more than just an idle boast. While it was true that he could earn more than this in a single evening's gambling, particularly when he brought his magic to bear, this work carried far less risk of discovery. It was easy, and despite their tender years, Markel and Treal were solid partners with honed tactics that had been passed down to them from thieves with years of experience.

A pick-pocketing team always consisted of three. During his work in the Five Markets, Treal pointed out the 'independents,' as she called them, desperate men who worked alone. Watching them ply the crowd, Lucius saw the flaws in their plan. With no backup or support, they risked their lives and liberty with every mark they robbed. One bad move, one moment of inattention inevitably led to a cry of "thief" being raised, and then it was only a matter of time. The guard would be on the scene in seconds, and there were many in the crowd willing to play hero and delay the thief's escape long enough for him to be collared by a mailed hand. True, the independents shared their ill-gotten gains with no one else, but they would always, *always*, be caught in the end.

In a Night Hands team, every member had their own specific role to play, though they would often switch throughout the day in order to spread experience and practice, as well as throw off any suspicions a mark, or the guard, might have.

Once a mark had been picked out of the crowd, the first member of the team created a distraction. This could be as straightforward as actually approaching the mark and asking for, say, directions to a nearby tavern (something which, being an adult, Lucius found easy, as marks were more likely to pay him attention). The second team member then moved in to grab the belt pouch, purse, sack of valuables, or whatever had been deemed worth the effort. Small and high-value items were the most desirable, and pouches were at the top of the list. It was the role of the third member of the team that impressed Lucius the most. Once the snatch had been made, the second member would disappear into the crowd, where the third would be waiting for them. The goods would then be passed between them and the third would leave the market for a pre-arranged rendezvous. This was done so that if they were made by the mark – that is, the second team member was caught in the act – no incriminating stolen goods would be found upon him when searched. The Vos guard would find it difficult to arrest someone if an accusation appeared blatantly false.

Distract, grab, switch. The secret to making a small fortune from picking pockets.

Of course, even the dullest guard would soon become suspicious if the same group of children were being collared every hour, and this was where Ambrose came in. He monitored the activities of all the pick-pocketing teams working the Five Markets, and he would regularly rotate their patches so the same team would not be stealing from under the noses of the same guardsmen all the time. The guard rotated their patrols as well, but Ambrose kept a close eye on their activities, all noted down in his own code, and was good at keeping his kids one step ahead.

It worked. It worked very well. By the end of the first week, Lucius had earned more than a hundred full silver, less the Night Hands' forty per cent, of course.

He had grown to like Markel and Treal too, though for all the world he could not see why, as he had little in common with them. They had made no judgements as to why an adult had been placed on their team, and they soon spotted that Lucius was a quick learner. By the end of the third day, they had begun to defer to him when selecting marks, and he was able to execute distractions, both subtle and calamitous, with far greater ease.

They had only one brush with the guard during the week and, for that, Lucius was grateful. As had become the norm, he had picked the mark, a lady of good money if not good breeding, escorting her young daughter through the dressmakers of the Five Markets. The girl was perhaps in her late teens, perhaps looking for something suitable to wear in a coming society function in which she hoped to impress. Lucius, however, had first noted her mother's bulging purse, looped around a belt behind her back.

After pointing her out to Markel and Treal, then agreeing a plan, Lucius approached them while they turned from one stall to search for another carrying the fabrics they sought.

"Ladies, I am so sorry to trouble you," Lucius began as he stepped in front of them. He wore a now well-practised smile, feigning a little embarrassment, keyed to set a mark at ease. "I arrived in Turnitia yesterday, and am hopelessly lost."

As Lucius started to ask for directions to the Street of Dogs, where he ostensibly hoped to find an old friend, he kept his attention on his peripheral vision. Markel had sidled up to the woman and, with a short blade, cut the strings of the purse, allowing it to easily drop into his hand. Making no eye contact with Lucius, he turned and walked quickly away.

"Mother! That boy!" The girl's voice was high and shrill, and it caused her mother to immediately reach behind her back to find the purse gone. She looked back at Lucius accusingly, and he felt a rise of panic.

"You've been robbed!" he cried with as much conviction as he could muster. "There, that boy, there! Thief!"

Knowing that the daughter had already made Markel, he could only pray the boy would slip the purse to his sister with all speed. The cry of "Thief!" was picked up quickly by the crowd, who themselves were split between wanting any criminal brought to justice and seeing an exciting pursuit through the market.

Lucius saw some of them make a grab for Markel and he winced as he thought of what Ambrose might say about him giving up one of his own team. His heart fell further when he heard the next cry.

"Make way! Guard! Make way!" Six red-clad and very well armoured men were making their way through the crowd, which readily parted before them.

"I have him!" another voice cried, and a struggling Markel was held aloft as the guard closed in. "Here's the thief!"

"I am no thief!" Markel shouted and Lucius thought he saw tears in the boy's eyes, though whether they were genuine or part of his act, he could not say.

The lady, trailed by her daughter, forgot all about Lucius as she stalked imperiously toward the guard, who had formed a circle around Markel. Her demands for her purse were met by flat denials from Markel, and two guardsmen soon had him hoisted into the air by his arms as another searched his tunic thoroughly. Lucius began to think that they might actually turn him upside down and shake him, but no purse was found.

With no apologies, Markel was released, and he disappeared. Lucius looked about, thinking he might see Treal poking her head from amongst the crowd, a sly wink on her face letting him know the switch had been made and that she now had the purse. She was nowhere to be seen and Lucius reminded himself that, despite her age, she was utterly professional when it came to work. The thought gave him some chagrin, as he was still standing there on the scene when he should have disappeared himself when the daughter had first cried.

With no more excitement seeming to be had, the crowd soon went back to its business and Lucius joined them in filtering away. He took a circuitous route around the market, as much out of habit now as wanting to throw off anyone who might have grown overly suspicious at his presence near the theft, and then headed back to his team's rendezvous. They had picked a sub-alley, which was probably an overly grand term. It was a dark and filthy place, full of discarded food, rags and, Lucius suspected, vermin. The key, however, was that it was quiet, with no peddlers spilling over from the main trading areas, and no pedestrians taking a short cut from one market to another. Lucius' only worry was that they themselves might get robbed here by some desperate footpad, though he trusted in his own abilities to protect the kids.

Markel was already waiting for him when he arrived, perched on top of a stack of wooden boxes. He smiled as Lucius approached.

"Seen Treal yet?" Lucius asked.

"Nah. She'll be here soon. Good mark that one, I'll bet," Markel said by way of compliment.

Lucius shrugged. "Didn't go so well. Sorry about fingering you like that – I thought the woman had made me, couldn't think what else to do."

The fact he was making a heartfelt apology to a twelve year old boy did not strike Lucius as being odd in the least. After having worked alongside the two kids for the past few days, he had begun to treat them as equally as they had treated him from the start.

Markel shrugged the apology away. "Not the first time I've been collared – hazard of the job. Anyway, you did the right thing, throwing suspicion away from yourself. You have to trust in the other guy getting away – that's *his* job."

"And you made the switch?"

"Easy. Treal snuck in and took it just before they grabbed me."

Lucius looked at the boy with a quizzical expression, prompting Markel to ask him what he was thinking.

"I've been wondering," Lucius said. "You earn good money doing this, and have been doing it for a while. What do you spend it on?"

"Oh, you think that kids can't spend money wisely," Markel said, mocking him. "Most of it goes to our parents right now. Doing this beats working at some butchers or tanners, and they don't complain when they see how much we bring in. The rest we mostly give to Caradoc for keeping."

"Caradoc?" Lucius asked.

"He's the lieutenant of the Night Hands. You'll meet him soon, I guess. He takes a special interest in kids who join the Hands, says they are the future. It was him who got Ambrose to start watching the teams in the markets."

"So what does he do with your money?"

"Holds it for us. Says we would just spend it on beer, and he's probably right. When we leave the teams and become proper thieves, we get the money. Spend it on the gear we'll need – lockpicks, a decent blade, silk rope. That stuff's expensive."

"When do you think you'll get accepted?"

Markel pursed his lips in thought. "A year maybe. If we carry on doing well. I'll probably see you in the guildhouse then."

"You think?"

"You won't be with us long. You're too good. They're just testing you, seeing how you work, and whether you can be trusted."

Lucius sighed. "Tell you the truth, wasn't planning to stay around long. Just wanted to earn some money, then leave."

"You mean leave the city?"

Lucius nodded.

"Nah, you'll stay."

"Oh, yes?"

"The money's too good. If you can avoid getting caught, that is, and I don't think you are planning on that any time soon."

Leaning back against the wall, Markel closed his eyes and dozed while he waited, leaving Lucius to his thoughts. Lucius marvelled in the kid's ability to switch off so quickly. He was hard to restrain at times but whenever there was nothing to do, he could fall into a light sleep almost on command.

Stifling a yawn himself, Lucius was surprised to find how weary he could become after a few marks had been worked. He started to chuckle as he considered the idea that thieving for a living could actually be hard work, but was distracted by a flash of movement within the alley beyond. Treal came tearing round the corner, skidding to a halt in front of them.

"Took your time," Markel said without opening an eye.

"Just met up with Ambrose," Treal said breathlessly, and she put a hand on Lucius' shoulder to steady herself as she panted. With her hair cut short and clothes carelessly chosen, she looked much like her brother, though Lucius thought she might become quite attractive in a few years.

"And?" he prompted.

"Just a few silver coins," Treal said, pausing as she savoured the disappointment in Lucius' eyes, before adding, "and a handful of emeralds and sapphires!"

Lucius smiled. Any cut stone that was green or blue was an emerald or sapphire to Treal, for she had yet to develop a thief's keen eye for detail. However, it would be a good haul nonetheless, and he looked forward to their meeting later with Ambrose when they would learn how much the stones had been fenced for.

"We're to move to the northern markets," Treal continued. "Ambrose saw what happened with Markel, and says there is no reason to push our luck. Vern's guys will take over this patch."

"We'd better get going then."

"Yeah – wake my brother up."

THEY SWITCHED ROLES in the afternoon, and it was Lucius' turn to be handed stolen goods, this time by Treal who would make the grab while her brother distracted the mark. The twins looked to Lucius to pick almost all their marks now, buoyed by their success earlier. They all smelled a good day's takings, and were eager to capitalise on their previous trade.

As the day wore on, the crowds thronging the Five Markets peaked, and then started to recede. There was still enough cover for the team to operate, with the ability to lose oneself among people paramount, and Lucius casually leaned against a plinth missing a statue, the original having been torn down during the city's fall. Treal was close by, while Markel sat by the market's edge a little further off, watching for the signal to move in on a mark.

Treal had been outlining a not entirely serious plan on how they could gain fame by being the first team to treat a guard patrol as a mark, perhaps lifting the sergeant's sword, when Lucius hushed for her attention. Nodding into the crowd, he indicated the unmistakable signs, to the trained eye at least, of a team closing in on a mark. They watched as a young lad purposefully tripped in front of an elderly man. Pretending to be in some distress, the boy persuaded the man to bend down to help him back up, even as one of the boy's friends quickly stepped up behind to lift the man's money.

"I thought Vern and his team were moved to our patch," he said.

"They were," said Treal. "That's not Vern. Damn them!"

Her exclamation caught Lucius by surprise, and he was mystified as Treal caught her brother's attention and directed it to the other pickpockets. Markel frowned angrily when he saw what was going on, and he nodded back to his sister.

"Go and get Ambrose," Treal said to Lucius. "We'll keep watch here and make sure they don't get far. Tell him that the Guild has moved into the markets."

Lucius was thoroughly confused. "Guild? I thought we were the guild?"

"Not this one, we're not. Quickly, get Ambrose," she said, shooing him away.

No wiser, Lucius did as instructed, pushing his way through the crowds to Ring Street, which was the quickest route to the knick-knack stall by the fountain. He began to hurry, not knowing what was going on, but driven by Treal's sense of urgency.

It was with some relief that Lucius saw Ambrose in his usual spot, talking to a young boy who he presumed was another pickpocket from a different team. Lucius paused, unsure of whether he should interrupt another team's business, but his seniority in years got the better of him and he marched up to Ambrose.

The veteran thief looked up in surprise, a querying look on his face.

"A message from Treal," Lucius said. "The Guild is in the markets."

"Damn it!" Ambrose cursed, with a virulence that made Lucius wonder just how bad the situation was. Ambrose turned his attention briefly to the boy standing with them. "Move to the east, like I told you. And not a word of the Guild to anyone, understand? If I hear any rumours floating about, I'll know where they came from."

The boy gave a hurried nod, then fled into the market. Ambrose stood and gestured for Lucius to lead the way.

Their pace was quick, with Ambrose driving Lucius on until his legs began to ache. "I am not entirely sure what is going on," Lucius said as they half-walked, half-trotted.

"The Guild is moving in on our territory. No damn respect, that's their problem. Today it's just pick-pocketing, but they'll be watching how we react. Any weakness here and they'll be all over our territory."

"I thought we were the only thieves' guild in Turnitia," Lucius said, beginning to become a little breathless.

"Would that were so," said Ambrose with a grim tone. "Used to be just one, before Vos descended upon us all. They smashed the old Guild, broke it up. Didn't want any rivals in the city, you see. Took a few years for the thieves to get back together again and when they did, they could not agree on who should lead."

"So two guilds arose?"

"That's right. The Night Hands, under our Magnus, while Loredo started his Guild of Coin and Enterprise. Pompous man, pompous title."

"And they've been fighting ever since?"

"No one's died yet, been nothing more than a few brawls. The city got carved up into territories managed by them or us, but no one was completely happy with what they got. When we get to this Guild team, just follow my lead. Remember, they are just kids, whatever the provocation. I am not going to start a war because of pickpockets!"

They reached the northern market quickly and Markel's nod caught Lucius' attention from the people still milling around the stalls. They were quickly joined by Treal, who related what she had seen to Ambrose.

"Just three of them, seen no other teams. Don't recognise them. Could be they've been brought up from the docks. They're good – well practised. Definitely Guild, they've done this before."

"They still working?"

"Moved to the north edge, following the crowd and keeping away from the Citadel. I'll show you."

They followed the twins, threading through the waning crowd. Treal and Markel then stopped and, with a nod of the latter's head, they looked on to see the three young thieves. Lucius saw they were probably younger than his charges, lounging casually around the front of an open forge. To the casual eye they were just a group of kids lazing between chores, but Lucius saw the flickering glances, quiet muttering and sly movements that told him they were carefully combing passers-by, searching for another easy and rich mark.

Without breaking a step, Ambrose took the lead and marched straight up to them, Lucius in his wake and the twins trailing. At sight of the approaching man, the boys looked as if they were about to run but seeing nowhere to flee, one obviously decided to brazen it out, and his friends took his lead.

"Bugger off, the lot of you!" Ambrose's first words were not subtle in the least.

"Says who, old man?" said one of the boys, taking a step forward to meet the challenge. "We got as much right to be here as you."

"You know damn well this ain't your place. Now, clear off, or you'll be in for a beating."

One of the other boys threw a purse at Ambrose. It was empty, having been looted by them earlier, but the sign of defiance made Markel start, and he stepped past Lucius, fists raised. Lucius laid a hand on the back of Markel's neck, and then held it firm when he tried to struggle free.

"Not here," Lucius whispered. "Ambrose's orders."

That was sufficient to restrain Markel, but Lucius could feel his anger.

The lead boy took another step up to Ambrose and, completely unafraid, spat at his feet. "Your time's over, old man. The markets belong to us now."

"Oh, is that so?" said Ambrose and, like a snake, his arm shot forward to grab the boy. The boy struggled until Ambrose cuffed him round the back of the head, and he was not gentle about it. The blow stunned the boy briefly, and he fell to the ground on his backside. When he heard Treal giggling at his misfortune, his eyes blazed with a fury that Lucius had thought only possible in frenzied warriors.

"You'll regret that, old man," he said, as he picked himself up. Despite his conviction, he started to back away, his friends following him. "Loredo will hear of this."

"I'm sure," Ambrose said. "He must take a personal interest in all the kids working for him. Well, you just tell him that the markets are our ground, and we won't stand for any pushing from him. Won't stand for it, you hear?"

The boys left, the last throwing an obscene gesture at the four of them before turning to follow his friends. Markel was still angry, while Treal jabbed Lucius in the ribs, laughing at the memory of the boy being knocked to the floor.

Sighing, Ambrose turned to Lucius.

"There'll be trouble there, mark my words. The Guild has been getting more aggressive over the past few months. Looks like we'll have plenty of work for you yet, and it won't be picking pockets."

Lucius stared past him, watching the boys disappear into a side street leading away from the market, wondering why every time he found an easy living, something always contrived to take it away from him.

CHAPTER FOUR

MARKEL HAD BEEN right, as it turned out. Lucius had not been kept on the team for long. A week later, Ambrose announced he was to be taken to the guildhouse of the Night Hands. Thus would start his true induction into the organisation.

He had not been sure quite what to expect of a thieves' headquarters. Something in the sewers, perhaps, accessible only by secret passageways and coded knocks, backed up by the password of the day. Maybe a rundown and dilapidated structure in the poorest quarter of the city, dismissed by passing guard patrols, and yet readily turned into a defensible fort when assaulted, with assassins and marksmen sniping from windows. Or it could be palatial, hiding behind the guise of some noble's holdings and filled with the proceeds of years of thieving, decked in gold and silver, with rare objects d'art scattered in every room in the most vulgar fashion.

It was none of those things. From the outside, the townhouse looked like every other in the aptly named Rogue's Way. The street had earned its title decades ago from a scandalous merchant who managed to rob several nobles blind before he was discovered and deported back to Pontaine. The house itself was a three storey structure with large bay windows protected from prying eyes by thick curtains and thicker shutters.

The front door appeared solid enough, but it was not until Lucius was permitted entry that he realised its heavy oak exterior was supported inside by metal bands and finely-crafted locks, and he guessed it would take at least a squad of guardsmen armed with a battering ram to break it down.

A short hallway led into a common room, which looked for all the world like that of a tavern. A bar was situated on the far side of the room, while tables were scattered about randomly, their occupants engaged in games of dice and cards, drinking or huddled together while whispering in conspiratorial tones. The furniture had certainly seen better days than that usually found in taverns, as it seemed thieves had better respect for their surroundings, but it was not of unusually high quality. No rare paintings adorned the wall, no golden sculptures graced the bar.

The rest of the ground floor was taken up by the kitchens, a couple of small store rooms (which held essential supplies, and were never used for hiding stolen goods), and several sleeping areas which were shared by guild members. Ambrose informed him that he was free to make use of them, and Lucius accepted, glad to be free of the financial burden his continued stay at an inn in the merchant quarter had imposed. Not that he could not afford it now, but why waste good coin when a perfectly good bed was available here? Rooms were not granted to individuals but instead shared by whoever was in the guildhouse at the time. There was little fear of having one's personal items go missing here, Ambrose informed him, as thieving from another member of the guild was grounds for immediate expulsion. As Lucius would find out, once granted membership, very few chose to voluntarily leave, as the perks were just too good. Access to the guildhouse, which was regarded as a safe bolt-hole for those running from the guard or an angry merchant, was really the least of these. Now he had been granted full membership, Lucius was considered to be on the payroll.

Money was still earned on a commission basis, based upon the success of individual operations, but there was plenty of work to be had in a city the size of Turnitia. Over the course of the next few days, Ambrose introduced Lucius to several thieves, most of whom agreed to take him on their next few missions.

The work was varied and Lucius was surprised to learn that the Night Hands were frighteningly well organised, operating with a professionalism he would not have believed possible among thieves. Though many of the more successful thieves planned their own operations, staking out likely targets, then gathering fellow members to make a hit on a warehouse or rich noble's townhouse, there was also a great deal of regular day-to-day work the guild needed completed in order to run efficiently. The pickpocket teams in the Five Markets were just the tip of this. There were confidence scams down on the docks, protection rackets run on shop owners and innkeepers, a growing prostitution ring that was quickly adapting to serve all tastes while keeping the women (and a not a few men) safe from both their clients and the occasional invasion by the Guild of Coin and Enterprise.

Ambrose arranged for Lucius to attend one of the weekly collections along the Street of Dogs, which was regarded by the thieves he spoke to as a lucrative business. Once you had the muscle, he discovered, protection rackets were among the simplest and yet most profitable ventures the guild invested its time in. It really just boiled down to standing behind the man collecting the money, looking menacing. None of the traders in the Street of Dogs put up any resistance, while some seemed almost grateful. After all, the racket worked both ways; if they experienced any trouble that could not be resolved with the intervention of the guard, they always had the Night Hands to call upon. This could range from tracking down vandals hired by a rival, to 'persuading' a money lender that his rates were too high.

However, Lucius earned less from his time on protection than he did from pick-pocketing and when he raised this with Ambrose, he was told the work was simply a way of him gaining experience in what the guild did each day, and his place had been obtained as a personal favour to Ambrose himself. Such operations, he learned, were treated as a franchise. One thief, a few years ago, had gathered a group of friends together and started the racket. The Night Hands took their usual percentage, and the rest was split between the thieves doing the work. When the first thief died or otherwise left the guild, control of the racket was passed on to one of his colleagues, who then would decide whether to bring more thieves into the enterprise and expand, or simply keep the current profits rolling in. It was very clear that such operations were run only by the most senior thieves, as they were also the most lucrative; the hard work in setting up the operation had already been done and, bar the occasional upset and non-paying shop owner, the money rolled in continually, week after week. Positions in such rackets were therefore highly prized, and to gain entry you either had to buy your way in, or be extremely good friends with a current franchise holder.

This system ran throughout the Night Hands, and Lucius began to realise that Ambrose was one such senior thief, with his franchise being the teams working the Five Markets. He could not help but smile to himself when he realised that despite all the money he had earned during his time there, he had likely been earning Ambrose a good deal more.

Lucius still felt he was being watched and weighed, with the other thieves gauging whether he could truly be trusted, but he was fine with that. Any business that brought in as much money as he suspected the Night Hands had access to was aided by continual suspicion, not hindered by it. So, he spent his time in the guildhouse common room making easy conversation with visiting thieves, taking up any offer of work, and slowly making his presence felt. The work at his low level was fairly easy, the earnings fair, and expenses non-existent. Even food and wine was free here, so long as no thief over-indulged. A quick mission to break into the apartment of a visiting merchant here, a scam to grab a precious cargo as it was unloaded from a wagon train there. And all the time, the money kept flowing in, at a steadily greater rate of coin.

Fundamentally, the Night Hands were no different to any other sort of business. It was just the nature of the work it specialised in that set the guild apart and on the wrong side of the law.

A fortnight passed, and Lucius began to consider setting up his own operation. He had little experience, but Ambrose promised support and, indeed, seemed pleased that his protégé was beginning to bear fruit. After a day spent aiding another thief – an Allantian born man of slight build – in timing guard patrols round a warehouse that was rumoured to hold spices from the Sarcre Islands, Lucius returned to the guildhouse. The common room was almost empty, and the few remaining thieves present informed him that the guildmaster, Magnus, had cajoled many of them to take part in an operation outside the city, though none offered any further details. The atmosphere was easy, and Lucius joined a group throwing dice, though they seemed more intent on discussing women they had recently bedded than the game itself.

A loud crash as the front door of the guildhouse was slammed shut froze their conversation, and angry voices from the hall had them all looking up in curiosity.

"Bastard!"

The man, swearing, blazed into the common room like a comet. He was tall and lithe, cloaked in black, with dark hair and a well-trimmed beard. A leather hauberk clad his chest, but Lucius was drawn to his eyes, which were fired with anger.

Two other men followed him, looking a little uncomfortable with their proximity to such fury. Lucius recognised them as thieves who had been keeping to themselves in the common room over the past few days.

"What's up, Caradoc?" asked one of Lucius' companions, and for the first time he realised that this was Caradoc Grey, the lieutenant of the Night Hands and second in power only to Guildmaster Magnus.

"That bastard Brink, he's only gone and declared for the Guild," Caradoc fumed.

"Eh?"

"Told these two, bold as brass," he said, indicating the men behind him with a sweeping arm. "Said he didn't need our protection when those Coin and Enterprise bastards were gaining so much power in the city. And he's hired mercenaries to back him up."

"What are you going to do?" asked another one of the thieves at Lucius' table.

"Teach him a valuable lesson in manners, that's what. And we're going to do it this evening. Now. You lot, come with us." So saying, Caradoc swept back out the door, leaving the common room stunned until one thief sighed and stood, giving the rest the cue to follow suit.

Lucius saw the others reach for knives and blades, and he put a hand to the small of his back to make sure his own sword was present. As they filed out, he touched another man on the arm who was winding a length of rope around his body.

"Who is this Brink?" he asked.

The man, who Lucius knew only as Hawk, gave him a grim look. "Hieronymus Brink, a money lender on the Street of Dogs. If the Guild is moving in on our territory there, they are stronger than we thought. This is a direct challenge, and they are forcing Caradoc to take action or watch his income drain away into nothing. Today it is just the money lender – if we do nothing, the merchants and shopkeepers will start to go over as well."

As they walked up the hill to the northern edge of Turnitia, Caradoc whispered sharp instructions to his men. In all, they numbered eight, which the lieutenant clearly felt enough to threaten the money lender. He told them that the goal was to scare the living daylights out of the man, to make sure he did not even think of switching allegiance. By striking at him in his own home, they were sending a message that the Night Hands could reach anyone anywhere, that there was no safety within the city's bounds. They were to employ all stealth to gain access to his house, track him down – his family too if he had any – and then leave them to Caradoc.

"And at all costs," Caradoc continued without missing a step, "avoid his mercenaries. They will be well armed and will know how to use a sword. You don't want to get into a running battle with the likes of them, so quiet is the key. With any luck they will be unprepared or even asleep at their posts. They won't be expecting us to do this, so the advantage is ours."

Lucius was less sure of this pronouncement, and he did not relish the thought of locking blades with trained killers.

The northern part of the city was quiet as they marched determinedly to the money lender's home, though the continual bass rumble of the sea breaking against the cliffs mixed with the raucous sounds of revellers in the taverns and inns further down the hill. One thief ranged ahead of them, diverting the group down side streets and alleys whenever he saw a guard patrol, for Caradoc did not want to be distracted by a confrontation with the law, particularly when his men were armed.

As they continued east, the houses grew steadily larger, more opulent, and further apart. The area reminded Lucius much of his old home, and it crossed his mind that he had not visited its grounds since he had come back to Turnitia. He knew the mob had burned the place after killing his father, but he had tried hard to forget the details of that night. He remembered being almost petrified with fear as he heard his parent's cries from his hiding place in the cellar, how his sister had clung to him painfully. The sounds of strangers rampaging through his home, the smell of burning, a hazy memory of bolting through the garden and streets, driven on by nothing but terror. The utter sense of loss when he returned the next morning to find little more than smoking ruins.

The money lender's house was similar to how Lucius remembered his own home, though it seemed smaller. The tall walls adorned with iron spikes looked more formidable though, and Caradoc drew back his men when they saw two mercenaries standing guard outside the main gate.

"We go in pairs," Caradoc whispered as he crouched down with his men around him. "Pick your own partner – Hawk, you take the new guy," he said, indicating Lucius.

"Sure," said Hawk. "What's the plan?"

"Avoid the rear gate, they'll have a guard there too. Probably just inside so as to draw a foolish thief in. We'll take the walls. Surround the place and pick your entry point. Cross the grounds and get into the house by any means you can. Remember, do this *quietly*. Brink is rich enough to have more mercenaries in the gardens, as well as in the house."

"Once inside?"

"If you see a mercenary with his back to you, consider him fair game. But I don't want any family hurt at all. Find Brink and restrain him. Do the same with the wife and any kids he may have. They will be the real problem, as their first reaction will be to scream. If that happens, we'll be drowning in mercenaries. So *don't let it happen.*"

"You'll deliver the message?"

"Aye. Leave the speaking to me. Now, go. Begin your entry on the count of eighty."

They fanned out, each pair of thieves taking one wall surrounding the square grounds of the house. The walls were around ten feet high and built of tightly packed brick. The iron spikes atop looked wickedly sharp, but Lucius saw they were spaced nearly a foot apart, enough to allow a careful thief safe passage. Hawk nudged him in the ribs and pointed up at a cherry tree whose branches stretched over the wall.

"That's our way in and out," he whispered. "Remember where it is once we get inside, case you and I are split up."

Lucius had absolutely no intention of letting Hawk out of his sight but dutifully nodded. Hawk unwound the rope he was carrying and threw it expertly upwards, curling it around a thick branch. He took the other end as it snaked back down to them, and made a loop knot before pulling hard. The knot shot upwards to hold firm against the branch and Hawk tugged to make sure it was secure. He held a hand up and waited. Lucius heard him muttering under his breath.

"Seventy-seven, seventy-eight, seventy-nine... up you go, lad."

A little clumsily, Lucius reached hand-over-hand as he ascended the rope, trying not to gasp out loud with the effort. He ignored the ignominy of Hawk's hand on his rump as the thief tried to speed his partner up, and was soon straining a leg forward to stand on the wall. Letting go of the rope, he crouched, leaning against the cherry tree's branches for support and cover as Hawk followed him. Looking back, he saw Hawk swarm up the rope with practised ease before peering into the grounds of the townhouse.

Lucius could see that the garden was exceptionally well tended, with a paved path running alongside the wall, separating it from a flat lawn that ran to his right, round to the front of the house. A small apple orchard grew to his left, and he imagined the thieves that had gained entry around the back of the grounds were rejoicing in their good fortune, for they would be able to get within spitting distance of the house without any danger of being seen.

The house itself was perhaps a century old, though it had clearly been as well looked after as the gardens. A glasshouse had been built against the side facing him, close to a tall chimney that he guessed served the kitchen. Thick ivy clawed its way up the stonework, and he saw there were no windows on this side of the building.

Lucius took a branch in hand as he prepared to clamber down to ground level, but a quiet hiss from Hawk made him freeze. Movement to his left caught his eye and he watched as a man, thick chainmail glinting dully in the muted light of Kerberos, stepped out of the shadows at the rear of the house, and followed a meandering path that led to the orchard. Peering into the gloom, Lucius noted that the man had a large sword at his belt.

They watched as the man disappeared under the boughs of the trees, and Lucius thought of the thieves taking cover in the orchard, wishing he could warn them. He then considered that they were far more practised at this than he, and that they had no doubt seen the mercenary before he had. Perhaps they had stealthily crept behind the man as he entered the tree line, and even now he was face down in the dirt, a dagger protruding from his back. Another nudge from Hawk interrupted his thoughts, and he reached forward to grab a lower branch of the cherry tree, swinging down to dangle his feet in the air, before letting go and landing on a flower bed in a crouch.

"There's a door to the kitchens just round the side there," Hawk said, indicating where the guard had appeared. "Probably got a friend or two in there, so we'll avoid that. Head to the glasshouse, then go round the front. Stay out of sight. I'll watch your back, then get us in through one of the windows. Go!"

Taking a last glance round the garden to see if any more guards were close by, Lucius drew a deep breath then ran. Keeping low, he brought his cloak around his body, hoping to appear as no more than a shadow. The finely-cut grass of the open lawn provided no hiding places but allowed him to move quickly without a sound. He gingerly stepped over the gravel trail leading to the door of the glasshouse, then flattened himself against the thick ivy at the base of the wide chimney. Creeping round to the front of the house, he quickly spied another mercenary, this one slouching by the front door. A wide path led thirty or forty yards to the wrought iron gates in the front wall, and he saw two more armed men standing there. It was not long before he was aware of Hawk's presence behind him, and he jabbed a finger at the guards.

Hawk nodded to indicate that he saw the danger, then flashed a smile. Lucius looked on in surprise as Hawk crept past him, keeping flat against the front wall of the house, seeming to dare the guard at the front door to look to his right and catch the thief. He was not the only one taking risks, for Lucius looked up and saw another pair of thieves shinning up the ivy on the side of the house.

Having passed the first window at the front of the house, Hawk had positioned himself beneath a second, and gave a gesture for Lucius to follow him. Padding quietly forward, keeping Hawk's body between himself and the guard, he watched the other thief reach into his tunic to produce a curious device, shaped like a small conical cup with a handle at the narrower end. Hawk placed it against the window. Slowly, he began to turn the handle, and it emitted a low whistling sound as he did so. In the still evening air, it seemed impossibly loud to Lucius, and he cast anxious looks at the nearest guard, thinking he must have detected them, but he made no movement at all.

After a few minutes, Hawk carefully cradled the cup in both hands and steadily moved it away from the window. Lucius saw that where the cup had been placed now lay a perfectly round hole in the window, the blades inside Hawk's tool having neatly cut a section out of the glass. With a last look around, Hawk reached inside the hole and unlatched the window, before pulling it open. Lucius could not help but be impressed with this method of entry, and he promised himself that he would get his hands on one of those tools soon.

Hawk was the first in through the window, seeming to flow like a liquid shadow into the darkened room beyond. Lucius gratefully accepted his hand as he crossed the threshold himself, to find they had entered what must be the main sitting room. In the fireplace on the far wall, glowing embers shed a soft orange light across leather-bound furniture as they both crouched next to a carved wooden desk. Pictures hung from all four walls and while Lucius could not discern any details, he guessed they would collectively be worth a small fortune. A shame, it crossed his mind, that they were here on business other than straightforward theft.

"Guard must have been nodding," Hawk whispered, before gesturing to a door on the wall to their right. "That'll lead to the hall, methinks. We need to get upstairs quickly. I doubt there will be mercenaries up there, and I'll feel a lot safer."

Nodding his assent, Lucius padded to the door, winding his way carefully past the settee and tall chairs. The door was ajar, and he opened it a little further, looking into the hall. Nothing stirred on the other side, and he saw a marbled floor leading to a grand staircase that split into two before turning back on itself to climb up to a balcony that overlooked the entire hall.

A low hiss caught his attention, and he looked up to see another thief had beaten them to the balcony. The dark shape motioned him to follow and, with a nod from Hawk, he stepped into the hall and padded up the stairs.

At the top the balcony backed onto a corridor that seemed to run the length of the house. He noticed that Hawk kept looking over the balcony to the marble below, and he realised the man was keeping an eye out for the mercenaries. The action unnerved him a little, for it was a reminder that though this mission had been quiet so far, the penalty for any mistake could be the death of them all.

The thief that had waved him up had continued down one side of the corridor to join his partner, who had started to open one of the many doors that lined the walls. A quick check inside, and then he moved to the next, evidently having not found the sleeping Brink. Hawk gestured to follow him down the other side of the corridor, and Lucius complied, acutely aware of the sound his boots made on the hard wooden floor, as light as his steps were.

Opening the first door they came to proved as fruitless as the other pair, and Lucius caught a glimpse of a study lined with shelves packed with books before Hawk moved on. They both gave a start as the next door opened just as they reached it, and they drew blades instinctively as a man stepped out, before realising it was Caradoc. He smiled back at them as he lowered his own sword, then jerked his head back towards the room he had just left. Inside, Lucius saw another thief binding the hands of a young girl behind her back as she lay flat on her stomach on her bed. No more than six or seven, she had already been gagged and she caught Lucius' eye, her expression one of sheer terror. The window of her bedroom was open, the route by which Caradoc had entered the house.

With Caradoc leading, they proceeded down the corridor, checking each room in turn as they hunted for the money lender. Blade still drawn, he motioned for Lucius to take a door on the left, while he went for its counterpart on the right.

The door opened easily at Lucius' touch and he crept inside as soon as he saw the young boy sleeping peacefully. Perhaps no more than a year or so older than his sister, he was blissfully unaware as Lucius padded across a soft rug, hand outstretched to throw across the boy's mouth in case he should wake.

From somewhere out in the corridor a bell tolled. It sounded almost mournful as it clanged with dutiful repetition, but it filled Lucius with alarm as he looked over his shoulder. He heard a commotion erupt from somewhere on the ground floor, quickly followed by shouts of surprise, then anger. A piercing cry froze him for an instant before he turned back to see the boy, sitting bolt upright in his bed, screaming at the sight of an armed and cloaked intruder in his bedroom, the very vision of a nightmare.

Lucius hesitated for a fraction longer then cursed under his breath. He retreated out of the room, knowing that whatever was happening outside was of far greater threat than a prepubescent boy.

Caradoc and Hawk were already ahead of him, running at full tilt down the corridor, and as Lucius fell in behind them, he saw the lieutenant leap over a motionless form on the floor as they sprinted for the stairs; as Lucius passed over the same spot, he saw it was the body of Caradoc's partner, and he side-stepped the pool of blood in which the man lay.

"There he is!" Caradoc cried as he reached the balcony and pointed downwards with his sword. Lucius skidded to a halt next to him and looked down to see a man being bundled along like a sack of wheat by two armoured mercenaries.

Looking anxiously about, Lucius saw no sign of the other thieves that had also been upstairs and, thinking the money lender had appeared from one of the rooms they had been searching, feared the worst for them. Hawk was already leaping down the stairs, two at a time, but Caradoc climbed onto the railings of the balcony and, with just a second's pause, leapt down to crash among the three escapees.

Tumbling down the stairs in a ragged pile, they came to rest on the marble floor. The mercenaries scrambled for their weapons while Caradoc struggled to his feet, clearly hurt by the fall. The money lender was pushed aside by one of his men as they formed a barrier before Caradoc, their swords drawn as they began to advance. One swiped at Caradoc and he pushed the blow to one side before the other mercenary stabbed forward, forcing him to give ground.

Hawk reached the mercenaries and the area at the foot of the stairs began to turn into a general melee, the sound of metal smashing against metal ringing against the walls.

Having already determined that he would aid Hawk in dispatching the mercenary he faced, Lucius was dismayed as shouts reached his ears just before the main door leading to the front garden was thrown open, and more mercenaries rushed in. Two grabbed the money lender and carried him outside while three others strode into the battle, weapons swinging.

"He's getting away!" Caradoc cried out, and Lucius could not help but marvel at the lieutenant's single-mindedness in the midst of a fight that would very likely prove fatal. He had no idea how an alarm had been tripped – for he knew the thieves would have taken every precaution – but now they faced their worst fears; a fight in which they were outnumbered by skilled and disciplined warriors. It was a fight they could not win.

Hawk was the first to fall, pierced by a sword thrust to his chest as he faced two mercenaries. They had forced him further and further back until he was flat against a wall with no room to move. He collapsed to the ground just as Lucius swung his sword at the head of one enemy, only to have the blow turned by an iron helmet.

The mercenary reeled back under the blow, but his place was quickly taken by Hawk's two killers, and Lucius immediately found himself on the defensive as he fought next to Caradoc.

"This is no good," Caradoc said breathlessly. "You've got to get out of here. Go, I'll cover you."

Though he appreciated Caradoc's willingness to die in his place, Lucius could see there was no way out. The mercenaries pressed against them, forcing them back. When they were finally pushed against the wall, they would die as Hawk had done.

Cursing his luck, Lucius took a breath to steady his nerves, even as his sword arm rose and fell, beating back the blades of the mercenaries. He reached inside himself to find the strands of energy coursing and twisting as they always had done. During his time with the Night Hands, Lucius had resolutely refused to use his magic, partly because he was keen to learn the skills of the trade without taking shortcuts, but mostly because of the fear and suspicion the thieves would have for him if they knew just what he was capable of. Now, left with no choice, he released the magic once more and the familiar surge of arcane energies felt like an invigorating breeze, a cool shower after a voyage across the desert. He mentally pulled upon a particularly destructive strand and pooled its power, waiting for the moment to strike.

One mercenary stepped forward, intending to drive Lucius back another step or two, and his sword swung low. Lucius met the blow with the edge of his blade and pushed it up and to the side, leaving the man wide open. With his other hand he stretched forward, only releasing the power he had held when it was inches from the man's face.

A jet of fire exploded from his palm and smashed into the mercenary's skull, and a bright flash lit the hall for the briefest of moments. The man was dead before he hit the floor, and the remaining mercenaries all took a step back in fear as they turned toward the source of the fire.

Caradoc, no less mystified, nevertheless saw his advantage. He thrust forward, disembowelling one of the men he faced, then raced for the door, crying for Lucius to follow him. The mercenaries did not take long to recover and as one turned to chase after Caradoc, the last two rounded on Lucius.

These men had fought together before, Lucius could see, as they worked in almost perfect unison, standing side by side as they kept their enemy off balance with repeated blows. The winding energies in his mind's eye separated for an instant, and Lucius drew one of them out, imagining its silver coiled force emanating from his heart to travel down his sword arm. He felt new strength coursing through him and, almost imperceptibly, his blade began to hum as it vibrated in tune with the magic.

Shouting a dreadful battle cry, Lucius stepped up to his attackers and stabbed with all the power he could muster, amplified by otherworldly energy. The mercenary tried to parry the blow, but Lucius' sword was irresistible as it sped forward to spear its point through his eye. The man screamed as Lucius yanked his blade free, then pushed him into his friend.

The bulk of the dying man checked the final mercenary's advance, giving Lucius time to release the last of the energies he had prepared. The shadows of the hall flared, spreading darkness in their wake. The mercenary cried out as he realised he was blinded while Lucius, following his memory of where the front door had been, carefully picked his way across the body-strewn marble. When fresh air hit his face, he reached out to find the door frame, then propelled his way outside.

Seeming serene after the chaos of the hall, the front lawn was quiet, and it took Lucius a second to realise what had changed. One of the front gates lay open and, as Lucius dashed towards them, he spotted the body of another armoured mercenary lying still on the grass, the hilt of a dagger protruding from his back.

Grasping the open gate for support as he tried to catch his breath, Lucius saw Caradoc fighting a little further down the street. Evidently he had caught up with the money lender and his remaining guard. Brink was huddled up against a wall, abject terror on his face as he watched the two men fight over him, Caradoc had been wounded, and he clasped his thigh with a bloodied hand as he held his sword out in front of him, trying to keep the mercenary at bay.

Lucius cast an anxious look down both ends of the street, knowing that an open fight here could bring a patrol running with all speed. Violence was simply not tolerated in this part of Turnitia. Trying to control his breathing, Lucius gripped his sword firmly and started to pad up behind the mercenary.

As he closed the distance, he caught the eye of Caradoc, who quickly saw his way out. Holding up a hand and dropping his sword, he smiled at the mercenary sweetly.

"My man, I surrender," he announced.

The mercenary took a step towards him, though whether it was to take Caradoc into custody or murder him in cold blood would remain a mystery, as Lucius' sword entered the back of his neck and drove downwards, killing him instantly.

Such was the force of the blow, pushing the sword half its length down into the man's body, Lucius had some trouble removing it. In the end, he had to position the guard on his side, then use both hands while putting a foot on the man's shoulder to pull it free. As he did so, Caradoc sheathed his sword and drew a knife, holding it at the money lender's throat.

"We're not unreasonable men, Brink," Lucius heard him say with a quiet, dreadful menace. "You pay on time, every time, and you'll see we take care of you."

He patted Brink on the shoulder as he smiled, though his knife never wavered from the man's neck.

"But if we ever hear you have declared for those tosspots in the Guild, we will pay you another visit," he continued. "We'll kill your family, we'll kill more of your very expensive guards and maybe, just maybe, we'll kill you too – after we have seen how many times we can wrap your guts around that grand house of yours. Do you understand me, Brink?"

The money lender was beyond words now, such was his raw fear, but he shakily nodded his head.

"That'll do him?" Lucius asked, anxious that a patrol would turn up at any time.

"That'll do him," Caradoc confirmed, as he pulled a scarf from his tunic and began wrapping it around his injured leg. "Well done lad, we'll have words when we get back to the guildhouse. Now, let's go before we catch the attention of the guard. Split up and make your own way back, usual drill."

Lucius hesitated, eyeing Caradoc's leg. Blood was oozing from what looked like a deep stab wound.

Caradoc waved him on. "Don't you worry about me, I've had worse than this. Now, be off with you!"

Jogging away, Lucius kept the shadows. He cast one last look back at the gates of Brink's place, watching as the money lender dragged himself, sobbing, back to his home. Lights were beginning to flicker on inside the house, and Lucius could hear sounds of activity as more mercenaries scoured the gardens and searched rooms for other intruders.

For a brief moment, he saw a figure silhouetted in one of the first floor windows, arms crossed as it stared down into the gardens. There was something familiar about the figure that tugged at Lucius' mind but, after just a few seconds, it turned and left his view.

CHAPTER FIVE

NEWS OF THE evening's events had already reached the guildhouse by the time Lucius made his way into the common room. As he walked in, a ragged cheer went up from the gathered thieves, and a mug of ale was pressed into his hands. He smiled sheepishly and looked around for the others he had fought alongside. Picking out three, he dared to hope their losses had been much lighter than he had first feared. Each was surrounded by a small gaggle of their comrades, being pounded with questions and asked to recount, yet again, their exploits.

Lucius soon had his own audience, but he elaborated little on what he had seen, unsure of how free he should be with his speech, even here in the guildhouse. When he told them he had seen Hawk fall, and there had been at least one other death, a groan swept over all assembled. He felt the atmosphere of the common room become mixed, elation entwined with mourning for the loss of a respected talent. Mugs and glasses were raised, and he joined in with the toast to fallen comrades. Someone remarked that it was a better death than one might find in the Citadel, a fate all thieves strove to avoid. Ambrose, though, pointed out that no money lender was worth the life of a good thief, and this was greeted with murmurs of agreement.

Louder cheers were raised when Caradoc entered, limping while supporting the weight of another thief. Both smiled at the welcome, collapsed heavily into the two chairs brought to them, then accepted drinks. Caradoc waved a hand at the man he had helped to the guildhouse.

"Sarnol thought the best way out of the house was through the window – seems he forgot we were no longer on the ground floor!"

Sarnol smiled with embarrassment. "Ah, I didn't forget that," he said, before his expression suddenly turned serious. "Twisted my ankle when I hit the lawn. It was the only escape I had. I saw Kernne struck down by one of those damned mercs, and knew I was next."

"Kernne as well?" someone asked sorrowfully.

"It was a tough one," Caradoc said, scanning the crowed as he counted how many of his men had returned. "Hawk also – he died fighting by my side as we held off a veritable army of the bastards. And Lucius was with us too!"

Caradoc raised his glass to Lucius, who nodded in return. One man was inspecting Caradoc's wound, and it was apparent that he had lost a great deal of blood. The scarf was soaked through as the man removed it, and more blood flowed as the pressure was released.

"We best get you seen to," he said.

"Little more than a scratch," Caradoc insisted, though he shifted his weight as he attempted to stand.

"Yes, well, let others be the judge of that. Let's get you upstairs, Magnus wants to see you. Come with us, Sarnol, we'll check you out too."

Several thieves moved to help the two injured men, bearing their weight as they filed out of the common room towards the back of the building.

As he watched them leave, Lucius found himself manoeuvred into a tall leather chair and was instantly surrounded by those who wanted to hear the story all over again, but from his perspective. Lucius gave them a quick rundown, crediting Hawk for keeping him out of trouble early on, much to their approval. He spoke of the desperate fight when the alarm had been triggered, of how he, Hawk and Caradoc had fought side by side, though he carefully neglected any mention of how his magic had swung the battle. Instead, he described how Hawk had sacrificed his life to save both Caradoc and himself, creating a diversion that allowed them to escape and continue pursuit of the money lender.

He lingered on the description of Caradoc's warning to the cringing money lender, and this too met with the approval of his audience. There was clearly nothing they liked better than a happy ending. After his tale, there were more questions, more ale, and as a soft haze began to envelop his brain. Lucius' descriptions of the night grew little by little, until it seemed as though there had been half an army stationed within the house. Not that those listening minded, for it simply made their guild seem all the more daring.

"So, the triumphant heroes return!" The voice that rose above the general hubbub of the common room was clear and confident, needing little raised volume to command attention. All the thieves rose to their feet, causing Lucius to look around in confusion before clumsily scrambling to his own.

A well-dressed man clothed in silk and cotton had entered the room, flanked by two others who strode in his wake. The man was middle-aged and greying, though he possessed an obvious vitality that the years had yet to touch. He smiled and Lucius immediately formed the impression of both confidence and trustworthiness. Of course, having spent time with any number of con artists and tricksters, he had learned to be on his guard when confronted by such people, but this man also had an obvious command of, and respect from, the other thieves present. His face was rounded and nondescript, except for his eyes which seemed to constantly sparkle with amusement.

The two men who flanked him were almost the complete opposite. Dressed in black leather with long knives at their belts, both exuded an aura of menace. Lucius thought, if there were such a thing as natural born killers, these two would be the definition.

It was not until the man was among the thieves and clamping a hand on the shoulder of one who had been on Caradoc's mission that Lucius heard someone thank him by name and understood who he was. So this was Magnus, the guildmaster of the Night Hands. Despite all the time Lucius had spent in the guildhouse recently, he had yet to meet the man, though he had heard plenty of stories about him. He recalled Ambrose once telling him that Magnus had been a lieutenant in the old Thieves' Guild. When the guild had broken apart, it had been Magnus who had tried to centralise the scattered thieves into a new organisation, at great risk to his life from the guard and other, less pleasant forces. If half of what Lucius had heard was true, then he thought this would be a very easy man to admire.

After shaking another thief by the hand, Magnus turned towards Lucius, and smiled.

"And this would be our newest recruit then. Lucius, isn't it?"

"Uh, yes sir," said Lucius, unsure of how to address the guildmaster.

Magnus waved the honorific away, though Lucius was acutely aware of the attention of his two bodyguards, who seemed to be itching for him to make one aggressive move.

"Just Magnus, please," he said. "You've done well tonight. Brink represents a significant account for us, and the return of his business is worthy of congratulations. I believe you are staying here now – eat and drink well tonight, you've earned it."

"Thank you, err, Magnus," Lucius said, as graciously as he could, though ale and discomfort vied to tie his tongue.

"Get some sleep too. Then come upstairs tomorrow, feel free to explore the place. Perhaps we'll speak further." One of his bodyguards whispered something into Magnus' ear that escaped Lucius hearing. Magnus sighed.

"Ah, that's right. I am afraid I must leave you all now." He looked back at Lucius with a smile. "Pressure of the job you know, they never let up. Welcome, Lucius, I have a feeling you will do well for us here."

As Magnus swept out of the room, the others clustered about Lucius, slapping him on the back and shaking his hand. Through their own celebrations, it took them a while to see that Lucius was thoroughly confused as to what was happening. It was Ambrose who took him to one side to explain.

"You've done well, lad," he said. "I knew you would."

"I don't follow."

"Caradoc must have given a glowing report of you while getting his leg mended. Only senior thieves, those who are full members of the Hands, are permitted beyond the ground floor. You, my friend, are now a true thief!"

Lucius smiled nervously as Ambrose thrust another mug into his hand before calling upon the entire common room to toast him. Raising his mug in return, Lucius thanked the thieves and, ignoring a wag calling for a speech, sank back into his chair, happy to listen to his peers talk business for the rest of the evening.

MORNING CAME TOO soon for Lucius, and he awoke to find himself in the same chair he had collapsed in a few hours before. A few other thieves were also in the common room, lying insensible, though most seemed to have had the sense to retire earlier on. As Lucius sat up, the world swam for an instant, and he leaned forward, burying his face in his hands as he waited for the after-effects of the ale to subside.

His mouth feeling dry and pitted, Lucius stayed in that position until he lost all sense of time. No one else stirred in the common room, though he heard someone snoring softly in a far corner. Shakily, he stood, and wandered out to find water, both to drink and to wash. Running into Ambrose as the veteran thief scoured the kitchen for breakfast, he was invited to take Magnus up on the offer of seeing what else the guildhouse had to offer.

He spent the rest of the morning exploring the two higher levels of the building, and it seemed as though his eyes grew wider at each new sight. It was only now, when he could see the guildhouse in its entirety as a functioning, well-oiled machine, that he understood just how sophisticated the Night Hands were as an organisation. And how much work it took to keep the guild running on a day-to day-basis.

Three rooms were dedicated to maps and charts, scattered over tables, pinned onto walls, and rolled up on shelves that reached to the ceiling, ready for inspection when a mission demanded. The patrol routes of the Vos guard were accurately timed and drawn on one map, allowing any thief to see exactly where blind spots would appear and when. Floor plans of many buildings in Turnitia were collected in the stacks, and Lucius watched another thief pore over one as he devised his next robbery. Information was collected on people as well as structures, and he learned that the libraries were considered to be living things constantly added to as the guild learned more and more, for the benefit of all its members. A laboratory was present, allowing thieves to make all manner of concoctions, from smoke and sleeping powders, to deadly poisons that would ensure no enemy of the guild would survive for long. There was even a training room, suitably soundproofed with targets for shooting or knife practice, a ring for blade training and, round the edges of the over-sized chamber, a running course across which could be strewn a variety of different obstacles.

It seemed, too, as though Lucius had not been wholly wrong when he had imagined a guildhouse with links to the sewer system of Turnitia, for that was exactly what this building boasted. Near the underground vaults in which the greatest stolen treasures were kept, as well as the guild's own vast treasury, were several secret passages that took a winding path down into the sewers. These were built to allow members to enter or leave the guildhouse freely, beyond prying eyes.

Lucius was later drawn back to the armoury, which lay next to the training room. Blades, spears, sections of armour and hundreds upon hundreds of various tools of the trade lay on shelves and in racks.

He saw a host of weapons of varying lethality and, having been told senior thieves were free to pick and choose from the armoury, started to inspect an incredibly well-crafted crossbow. Honed from a lamination of light but strong woods, a series of lenses in a wooden tube was mounted over the groove that took the bolt. Standing at a window, Lucius found he could adjust the lenses to bring far objects into focus. Fine wires within the tube marked exactly where a fired bolt would strike, should the target be within range. Other weapons soon revealed similar ingenuity, such as the sword whose pommel could be separated to draw a dagger from the hilt – useful if the main blade was ever broken.

However the weapons were the least of the treasure in this room and Lucius soon found himself exploring the vast cornucopia of tools, such as pots of swordblack used to dull a blade from reflections, dark silk bodysuits that could make even a clumsy thief silent, and the glass-cutting cups Hawk had used to break into Brink's house.

"There is just something about the mind of a thief that makes him fascinated by these toys," said a voice behind him. Lucius turned to see Caradoc leaning against the door frame.

"This was where I came as well, when I was brought into the guild proper," he continued. "Though there were far less toys back then."

"I am not sure I would call that a toy," said Lucius, indicating the crossbow.

Caradoc smiled. "You'll want to practise with it first. It is not as easy to use as you might think – you have to learn how to use the sights, or your shots will never land anywhere near your target. But I think you are quite wrong about these not being toys. All a good thief really needs is a decent blade, soft boots and his wits, the last being the most vital. It seems as if there is always someone trying to get an advantage, however they can. They come up with an idea, and try to build it. Some work. Some need constant revision, with many minds applying themselves to the problem over time. Which, really, is what this place is all about."

Lucius nodded in understanding. "How long have you been with the Hands?"

"Since the beginning. I knew Magnus from the old guild, and he brought me with him when he created the Hands."

"You are close friends, then?"

Caradoc paused and frowned. "We trust each other, certainly."

"You... don't always agree with what he does?" Lucius asked, wondering where the boundaries were in this conversation. For some reason, he knew he would never have been so direct with Magnus, though the guildmaster seemed far more personable than his lieutenant.

"You don't always have to agree with your leader." Caradoc shrugged. "He knows I'm not an automaton. The important thing is that he trusts me to follow his orders, and I trust him to do what is best for the Hands. That is what we have in common – a desire to make the Hands the best guild it can be."

"So what about the other? The Guild of Coin and Enterprise?"

For a moment, Caradoc looked as though he might spit in disgust, before he remembered where he was. "Well, that is where Magnus and I may differ. He believes we can reach an accord, dividing the city between us without bloodshed. He says it is the most profitable route for both organisations, and I guess I can see the sense of that."

"They don't seem very receptive to that idea," Lucius said.

"No. Once, maybe up to a year ago, we might have made an agreement. But something has changed within the Guild. They are too aggressive, pushing too hard." He sighed. "I fear a war is coming. This might not have been the best time for you to join us!"

"I can take care of myself."

"You proved that last night. Look..." Caradoc seemed self-conscious as he mustered his next words. "I wanted to thank you for stepping in yesterday. Those mercs were tough, and I am not sure I could have taken them all. You did well."

Lucius blushed and he felt as uncomfortable as Caradoc looked when confronted with this gratitude. "Anybody else would have done the same."

"Well, you were there and they weren't. Thanks anyway," Caradoc said, looking at the floor. "What was it, flash powder you used to distract them?"

Not trusting his voice to carry the lie, Lucius just nodded.

"Good move. Painful stuff too, when shoved in someone's face. Still, that bastard deserved what he got."

Not having anything more to add, Lucius simply smiled, and the expression was returned by Caradoc. Neither said anything more, and Lucius pretended to look over the crossbow again, doing anything to break the uncomfortable silence. He looked up again when Caradoc coughed.

"Anyway, there's a meeting going on. Magnus asked me to fetch you."

"Me?"

"Just routine business. Magnus thinks that it would be good for you to see how the guild operates."

"Well, if Magnus has asked... Who else will be there?"

"The most senior thieves of the Hands. These meetings are used to track business, spot opportunities, and generally ensure everything continues to run smoothly. Needless to say, your input won't be required. Just watch and learn."

Leading Lucius up to the third and highest level of the guildhouse, Caradoc took him to Magnus' own meeting hall. Lucius had to bite his tongue to stop from gasping at the sight of the room.

The walls were covered with carefully sculpted wooden panels, displaying exquisite craftsmanship in their varnish and carving. No rare paintings hid their natural beauty, and Lucius got the feeling that Magnus was, at heart, a man who enjoyed simpler things.

The room itself, however, was dominated by a long dark wood table, whose polished surface reflected perfectly the light of the oil lanterns standing on pedestals in each corner of the chamber. Around the table were eighteen tall-backed chairs, upon sixteen of which were seated an assortment of men and women. Some Lucius had seen before, passing through the common room, but he did not know any of their names. At the head of the table at the far end of the chamber sat Magnus, and he smiled as they entered.

"Here comes our hero Lucius – welcome to the Council," Magnus said grandly, and Lucius felt acutely uneasy as all eyes turned on him. Caradoc had taken his seat at the opposite end of the table to Magnus, indicating that Lucius should take the last free chair, halfway along the left edge.

Lucius was aware of the short woman seated to his right watching him as he sat, and he nodded in greeting. She was perhaps of a similar age to Magnus, but showed few signs of ageing. Her hair was dark and slicked back along her scalp, while her face was marred by a scar that split her lower lip. Feeling there was something disconcertingly serpentine in the way she looked at him, Lucius turned to glance at the man on his other side, but found he had already returned his attention to Magnus.

Seeing the new arrivals settled, Magnus waved at the group to continue their business. A young man opposite Lucius spoke up.

"We have started to move prostitutes from the docks to the merchant quarter during evening hours, and this has proved a profitable move. Traders far from home still look for home comforts, and our girls are very good at what they do."

Magnus grunted, and then sighed. "There is still something distasteful in this operation, I find myself thinking. To profit so directly from human trade – it seems a little too close to slavery for my liking."

The woman to Lucius' right raised her voice in response. "Better they are in our care than someone else's. Can you imagine how the Guild would treat them? With us, they earn good money, and do so in relative safety."

"Yes, yes," said Magnus, "as you said before, and that is why I have allowed it to continue thus far. Still, it is something I will keep a close eye on."

"It is also a mistake to think that all these girls have been forced into the work," the woman continued. "If you have an efficient organisation like ours behind you, there is good money in it – far better than common labour. I hear they even have their own guild in Allantia."

"You are just too old-fashioned, Magnus," another, younger, woman said, and a few laughs stirred round the table. Even Magnus gave a wry smile.

"Maybe," he said. "Nate, please continue."

The young man across from Lucius spoke again. "The Street of Dogs is quiet after Caradoc's mission last night. Brink hasn't shown up for work yet..."

There were a few more laughs round the table at this.

"... but I think it will be a while before anyone openly challenges us again."

"I disagree, and we must not be complacent," said the man to Lucius' left. "Most of us here profit in some way from the Street of Dogs, and I would not see us risk that. Brink could just be a prelude, and if we were to find that those mercenaries were funded by the Guild and not Brink himself, well... I would advocate more direct action against the Guild."

There were a few murmurs of agreement and Lucius flicked a look at Caradoc, but the lieutenant was staring fixedly at the table in front of him.

Magnus rapped on the table to regain everyone's attention and the murmurs stopped instantly. He opened his mouth to say something, then seemed to think better of it. After a moment's pause, he turned to look at Lucius.

"What do you think, young man?" he asked. "What would you do about the Guild, were you in our place?"

Once again, all eyes turned on Lucius, and he felt himself blush. "I... I wouldn't know, exactly," he stammered.

"Nonsense," Magnus said. "You are clearly an intelligent man, talented enough to be made a senior thief in a matter of weeks. You have your own mind. Speak!"

Lucius thought hard for a moment. It was, he realised, a good opportunity to play politics, to support the guildmaster, to start building up his own phalanx of friends and enemies on the Council. He instantly dismissed the idea as foolish and, frankly, beneath him. He did not know nearly enough about the thieves sitting round this table, and he had a feeling Magnus would see through any disingenuous arse-kissing.

"So long as incidents can be contained, I think we should watch and wait. If we act, we cannot take anything back."

"You're timid, then," said Caradoc, and this burst of shrewishness surprised Lucius until he looked back at Magnus' measuring expression, and guessed this kind of prodding was a play between them, with Caradoc acting as the fall guy.

"Cautious, yes, not timid," Lucius said carefully. "It might be foolish to tip the scales if the possibility of another solution lies round the corner."

Lucius winced inwardly as he realised he had just called the opinions of at least some of the Council members foolish, but he continued onwards. "If my advice were sought, I would say we watch to see what the Guild does next, and do what we can to ensure they do not cross the line."

"Ah ha!" said Magnus. "And where exactly is that line?"

Smiling, Lucius held the guildmaster's eye steadily. "That, I believe, is what this Council will decide."

Magnus returned Lucius' smile, then laughed. "Well said."

The table fell silent for a moment, before the woman seated next to Lucius spoke again. "Are we seeing more pressure round the Five Markets?"

A hairy man next to Caradoc, who for all the world reminded Lucius of a badger, answered her. "We are still getting kids pressuring our teams. Some have taken to wearing blue scarves, round their heads or arms, though Kerberos alone knows why. Dead giveaway to the guard."

"Then they are obviously not worried about the guard. They are likely a warning to intimidate our kids – difficult to concentrate when you know you are being watched, and a collection of blue scarves would tend to stick out in the crowd." He looked up at Magnus. "I recommend we leave it in Ambrose's hands for now. He'll ask for support in the Five Markets if he needs it."

"Agreed," said Magnus. "Though I would be loath to send thieves down there. The pickings will be far less than they are used to, and they'll see it as a step down."

"Perhaps some compensation from the vaults could be made, show we are taking their work seriously," Caradoc said.

"Perhaps," said Magnus. "I'll give that some thought. We can't open the vault every time we want to get something done. The point of a guild is that things work both ways, and sometimes members just have to get on with it. However, the Street of Dogs is the key. If something happens, it will happen there. Nate, you believe our hold there is solid for now?"

"More or less," the young man answered.

"Well, which is it?"

"No one is about to jump, but I am damn sure they'll be courted by the Guild. Maybe they'll spin a story about Brink that will make us look as if we took action against him for no good cause, and *that* was what made him move to the Guild."

"We'll set up watches then," said Magnus. "You pick out a half dozen of the shakiest clients, and we'll station thieves on them. Make sure they are not approached by the Guild and give them the frighteners if they are."

"That will be more revenue deducted from the Street of Dogs," remarked the short woman.

"Money well spent, I am sure," said Magnus. "And I believe we have our first volunteer. Lucius, are you inclined to give us a hand here?"

Lucius was again caught by surprise, and he kicked himself for not being more alert. He certainly should have known that Magnus would take the opportunity to test him, rather than simply allowing him to be a passive observer.

"Of course," he said, after taking a breath. "I was just starting to plan a few things of my own, but I can push them back–"

Magnus held up his hand. "No need! We'll get you working in shifts with someone."

When Lucius looked at him with confusion, Magnus explained. "We always reward personal initiative among the Hands, and if you are planning an operation of your own, I would be most fascinated to see what it is and how you get on with it. However, you must also learn to serve the guild's interests when necessary. So, we'll have you watch some merchant or shopkeeper by day, and give you free reign in the evening to plan and execute your grand larceny, whatever it may be."

Looking round the table, Magnus raised his eyebrows. "Any other business?" he asked.

As one of the senior thieves close to the guildmaster started to propose a tiered percentage of takings for the guild, based on seniority and wealth, Lucius glanced back down the table at Caradoc. The lieutenant gave a brief smile and nodded his compliments.

Lucius had made a good impression, and he knew it.

CHAPTER SIX

ALLOWING THE SHADOWS to envelop him, Lucius held his breath as another patrol of Vos guards marched past his position, their red tabards appearing almost black in the half-light of Kerberos. With a second's concentration, he summoned the shadows of the alley to completely cloak him, but it was an unnecessary precaution, for the attention of the guards was fixed firmly across the Square of True Believers and the grand edifice that was nearing the last stages of completion.

When Vos had swept through Turnitia in its grand war of conquest which was intended to break the back of Pontaine, its arrival had been heralded by a rise in the Final Faith. It had started with preachers appearing on street corners, haranguing the crowds as to the fate of their souls. Soon enough, the Final Faith was using the support of converts who were acting as a network of spies and scouts, marking those in power, officially or not, for the Vos captains to hunt down when their armies moved into the city. The capitulation of the city was therefore accomplished quickly and without many losses among the armies; the people of the city were the ones who suffered.

That the Faith was able to annihilate its rivals, the Brotherhood of the Divine Path, was more than a bonus for the Anointed Lord and her followers. It allowed them to start with a clean slate in the city, making their faith the official religion of Turnitia as much as it was in the rest of the Vos Empire.

In recognition of the efforts the Final Faith had extended during the occupation, the Empire had permitted the creation of the Square of True Believers, the site of a new church dedicated to the dominant religion. Though most of the resources used in the reconstruction of Turnitia were swallowed by the Citadel and its expansion, the followers of the Final Faith had taken what they could from the authorities and then tackled a great deal of the work themselves. They pulled down the houses that stood where their church would rise, excavating the foundations and then piling stone upon stone to create their place of worship.

It was said the square was wide enough to accommodate the entire population of the city, for the conversion of all was the Final Faith's stated aim. The church itself was not yet completed, and scaffolding would surround its southern tower for another year or two at the least. However, the nave was complete and, as far as the priesthood was concerned, that made the church open for business.

Far from alienating itself from the population after the riots it had started before the Empire arrived in force, the Final Faith had worked hard to ingratiate itself within the city. The people of Turnitia had traditionally carried their own beliefs lightly, as befitted a free city, but instead of being a hindrance to conversion it had meant there were no doctrinal barriers for the priests to break down. Once established, the Final Faith had dispensed food and money to the poor, offered shelter to those forced from their homes by the armies and, most of all, created a sense of community centred on the Square of True Believers.

While the people of Turnitia would never become fanatics, in the way those of Scholten were often described, living in the shadow of the Faith's great cathedral, most would now describe themselves as followers, even if they did not observe every holy day on the calendar. As a result, the money started to flow into the coffers of the new church from those seeking to help those less fortunate or those wishing an easy path into the afterlife. This was the reason that Lucius was now staking out the square.

As the patrol moved past his hiding place, Lucius recalled some of the lessons his father had tried to teach him of the Brotherhood and its beliefs. He had never really embraced religion in his youth, and his father had never forced it upon him, believing instead that his son should find his own path in life, and for that Lucius was grateful.

The Brotherhood, Lucius learned, had splintered from the Faith a century earlier, a dispute arising between two factions over the excesses one saw in the other. However, the schism was rooted in just one difference of interpretation of ancient texts. The Faith believed mankind had to be led on a tight and narrow path towards complete unity, in order to achieve salvation of all and ascendance to the next plane of existence. To this end, the priesthood was known to play politics at the highest levels, influencing cities and nations in an attempt to bind the peninsula into one cohesive organism.

Indeed, it was said that the Faith was the prime motivator behind the last war, seeking to make the Empire of Vos dominant over its old rival, Pontaine. That past Anointed Lords had tried to make Pontaine ascendant over Vos did not seem to strike any true believer as contradictory.

The Brotherhood believed mankind was already on this path, and merely had to suffer war, bloodshed and terror as part of the process it was already fated to follow. The rituals and observances differed between the two religions, of course, but this was the centre of their dispute, the one difference responsible for so many deaths over the past hundred years.

Scanning the square, Lucius saw another patrol on the far side, and began to time their approach. Just gaining entry to the church would be problematic, he realised, for the priests clearly had enough friends within the Citadel to ensure the square was watched at all times.

He was confident that a man of his... abilities could do it but he suspected only the most accomplished of thieves would succeed, and they would likely not be interested in the risk/reward ratio of breaking into the church, the ultimate calculation every good thief lived by. Once inside, the pillars, statues and altars, along with the shadows they created, would be his allies, but everything rested upon crossing the open square without catching the attention of the guard. He began to look upwards at the roofs of the nearest buildings, wondering if a more vertical approach would be appropriate, though the closest structure lay over a hundred yards away from the church, which seemed an impossible chasm to cross.

"So, you are running with the Hands now."

The female voice behind him made Lucius start with a fright, and he was ashamed to find that all the excuses he had rehearsed for the event of getting caught by a patrol momentarily fled his thoughts. He caught himself and turned round, his mind working once more as it recognised the voice.

"Aidy, you are forever creeping up on me," he whispered.

Her eyes, dark on the brightest of days and virtually invisible in the shadows, looked at him with what he guessed was utter contempt.

"There is no need to keep your voice low," she said, and he thought something approaching loathing was in her words. "The guards cannot hear us."

Lucius tilted his head to one side as he concentrated on the flow of magic he now realised filled the alley. Adrianna was using her mastery of stealth to ensure a passer-by would neither see nor hear them. He finally nodded in understanding.

"Your training has all but deserted you," she said scornfully.

Not wanting to engage in another verbal duel, Lucius tried to change the subject. "How did you find me?"

His question drew a hiss of frustration. "I told you before, you are like a beacon to me. I can feel your presence from half a city away."

Becoming irritated at her superior manner, Lucius snapped back. "So, what do you want?"

She took a step closer, looking straight into his eyes. Of matching height, he could feel anger radiating from her in waves, and he fought to return her stare without blinking.

"You have caused me no end of problems lately. Do you consider yourself a thief now?"

"I *am* a thief, Aidy."

"So far the mighty fall," she said.

It was his turn to show anger. "I told you before why I had come back to the city. I'm doing alright at the moment, and I'll thank you to stay out of my business. You'll just have to endure my presence a little longer, then I'll be gone."

"Unless, of course, you make yourself too comfortable where you are," she pointed out, then seemed to change tack. "And as it happens, you are not doing me the courtesy of staying out of *my* business."

"What do you mean?"

"I'm working a contract with the Guild of Coin and Enterprise."

Things suddenly clicked for Lucius. "It *was* you there that night. In Brink's house. How can you be working for those bastards, Aidy? Do you have any idea what they are doing?"

"Don't be such a bloody idiot. People like you and I have greater allegiances than the petty concerns of thieves. Or, at least, we should. They are but a means to an end, Lucius."

"They are my friends."

"A man like you has no friends," she said caustically.

Once again, anger flared in him. "You don't know a damn thing about me now, Aidy. Whatever you thought of me before was wrong, and you are no closer to the truth now. People died in that house, and I am willing to bet you were in a position to stop that happening."

"I raised the alarm, nothing more. I had thought the mercenaries we had brought in would be able to handle a bunch of rogues with few problems. They probably would have, had a Shadowmage not been among them."

"Well, you could have done something about that, surely," he said. "You are clearly greater than I, so why not just kill me and let the mercenaries deal with the rest of us?"

She looked at him as though he were being particularly stupid, an expression he was beginning to resent a great deal. "Are you deaf, or just wilfully ignoring what I tell you?"

"Was there something you wanted, Aidy, or did you just come here to torment me?"

Adrianna stopped for a moment, then sighed heavily. When she spoke, it sounded as though she were almost spitting the words.

"If you are going to continue working in the city, there are going to have to be some rules."

"Damned if there will be!"

Her hand shot out of the darkness to close, painfully, around his arm. "Listen to me, idiot! I don't want this conversation any more than you do but, as I have been trying to tell you, there are larger things at work here. Now, shut up and follow me!"

Saying that, she spun on her heel and stalked into the depths of the alley, disappearing from sight almost immediately. Casting a last look back at the church, Lucius groaned inwardly and raced to follow her. The Final Faith would have to wait at least another day.

LUCIUS HAD VISITED the docks earlier, and this time his ears became accustomed to the crashing sea far quicker. The noise was relentless, with immense waves breaking against the grey stone defences that rose from the water like monoliths.

Before men had laid the foundations of Turnitia, the sea had already carved a wide bay from the cliffs, hacking away at the land over aeons. The origins of the architects of the defences that were built across the mouth of the bay were lost in antiquity. Merchants and dockmasters, certainly, couldn't care less about the effort that must have gone into building the immense structures, and scholars had long since moved on to investigating the mysteries of the Sardenne and the World's Ridge Mountains, explaining the construction away as the product of ancient magic and, therefore, unknowable. Some tales suggested the barriers were older than the race of men, though Lucius put little credence in children's tales.

Standing on the edge of the cliffs, he looked down as the water surged against the granite harbour. A complex array of winches, lifts and ropes were fixed to the sheer wall of rock, allowing goods brought in from the sea to be brought up to the city, where they could be traded in the merchants' quarter and, finally, the Five Markets. A dozen ships lay in the bay, heaving constantly as the water surged beneath them. They remained in relative safety, so long as their anchors and the ropes that bound them to the harbour did not break their grip and send the vessels crashing into the barriers or cliffs. After gold had changed hands with one of the dockmasters, Lucius had learned earlier that the captains were waiting for the sea to subside a few degrees before risking an egress that would take them beyond the barriers and into the violent waves. Few risked such voyages, preferring the safety of travel over land. But for those willing to risk the churning waters, rogue waves and, so tales went, immense serpents, the rewards could be great.

Looking out to sea, Lucius wondered what life must be like in that hostile wilderness, trusting chance as much as personal skill. The seamen of Allantia were renowned for their ability to master the waves, as were the barbaric savages of the Sarcre Islands, but there were few truly civilised men who were adept at reading the ebb and flow of the sea, and thus had a chance of making their destinations safely. Even the best captains kept close to shore, and no one knew for certain what lay beyond the horizon.

Adrianna had sped through the city to reach this place, and Lucius had been pushed hard to match her long, determined stride. They had not spoken further, and resentment once again began to flow through him as he realised she was dangling him on the end of a rope, possibly for her own amusement.

She stood, back straight and arms folded, as Lucius had seen her in the window of Brink's house. Not looking at him, she too stared out to sea, though he thought her mind was elsewhere. After a few minutes, his boredom got the better of him.

"Well?" he asked, not without a little sarcasm.

"Wait," she said.

Lucius sighed and turned to walk slowly along the cliff. The immediate area was filled with cranes that leaned over the edge and a wide road that served as a loading area for wagons and carts, separating the cliffs from the row upon row of warehouses. He began to wonder whether his father's warehouses were close by – and who owned them now – when a pungent and heady odour filled his nostrils.

It reminded him of the scent that hung in the air after a storm but, looking back at Adrianna, he saw she had either not sensed it or was ignoring it. A low crackle reached his ears, and it seemed to come from all around. Looking around he tried to locate the source of the sound, but it proved elusive.

A brilliant blue-white flash in front of his eyes made him react, taking a step back. The dull light from Kerberos seemed to dim further for a moment, then another flash followed, this time from the side of one of the nearby warehouses. Lightning crackled around the walls of one of the buildings, shards of light playing across the wood and stone with a sizzling of high energy. With a low rumble of thunder, the electrical discharges coalesced into a tightly packed ball a yard from the ground.

Holding a hand over his eyes to shield himself from the glare, Lucius saw something move within the dancing light, a dark shape stepping through the flashes and sparks. He saw the form of a man walking down to the ground as if on a short flight of stairs. As he placed a foot on the cobbles, the lightning disappeared with the pop of air rushing into a vacant space.

The man was in his later years, and wore a tightly-trimmed beard shot through with grey streaks but was otherwise completely bald. Dressed in the jacket and pantaloons of a wealthy merchant, he walked with a limp, leaning on a cane as he crossed the road to face Lucius. Still looking out to sea, Adrianna introduced the newcomer.

"Lucius, this is the Master of Shadows, Forbeck Torquelle."

Eyeing the man warily, Lucius nodded slowly in greeting, but his suspicion seemed to bounce off the man.

"My dear boy," the man said, extending a hand. "I am so very pleased to meet you. Adrianna has told me a great deal about you."

"I'll bet," Lucius said cautiously as he accepted the man's hand and shook it. The Master's voice had the distinct ring of a Pontaine accent, which Lucius found attractive in women, but slightly effeminate in men. Despite the man's careful politeness, Lucius could sense the underlying power in his demeanour. This was someone who was used to getting what he wanted, smothering his iron-hard will with a veneer of courtesy.

"I hope you will forgive my showy entrance," Forbeck said apologetically. "I normally reserve such things for weak-minded and superstitious fools, but I wanted there to be no doubt in your mind as to who I am and why I asked for this meeting."

"And why is that?"

"We all felt your presence when you came back to the city, Mr Kane. We didn't know what was happening or what portent it held, until Adrianna first tracked you down. But once we discovered the truth, we just had to make contact."

"We?"

Adrianna turned back to face Lucius. "There is a new guild in the city. The Shadowmages are returning, and are slowly regaining both their numbers and their power."

Lucius smiled at this and began to shake his head, raising a hand to forestall any argument. "I'm sorry to have wasted your time—"

Forbeck overrode Lucius, speaking quietly but firmly. "This is a new guild, Mr Kane, with a new attitude. We have been reforged from the disaster of Vos conquering this city and wiping out our old infrastructure. Not to mention many of the original members."

"I already belong to a guild," Lucius said.

"Yes, I know that. But ours is the only one of its type in the entire peninsula. Please, Mr Kane, walk with us for a moment."

Forbeck turned and there was something in his voice that commanded Lucius to obey, despite his better judgement.

As they walked along the cliff top, deviating only to avoid cranes or piles of empty boxes, Lucius heard Adrianna's measured footsteps behind him as he kept pace with Forbeck.

"You see, Mr Kane, Shadowmages are unique individuals, having not only the very aptitude for stealth and secrecy that has led you to find a place within the Night Hands, but also a natural affinity for magic. And I mean natural – it takes many men years and years of study and practice to harness the most basic of spells, if they are even capable of it in the first place. Men like you and I – and, sorry Adrianna, ladies too – can control the magic as easily as we breathe." He laughed. "Well, perhaps with a little more effort than that, but you do take my point."

"I do," said Lucius, wondering where this was going. He knew an offer to join the guild was looming, but he was perplexed as to why. He had already made his case for solitude to Adrianna, and he could not imagine for one moment that she had spoken up for him.

"The combination of stealth and magic is a powerful one, as our predecessors realised, but they never understood its potential. Mr Kane, a Shadowmage, properly trained and in full control of his abilities, makes for an excellent – no, he makes for the very best – scout, infiltrator, thief, spy... assassin. The Empire of Vos fears us precisely because of this. That was why they worked so hard to eradicate our kind."

"Well, I have those abilities now, plus the support of a decent guild."

Forbeck shook his head. "The Hands are decent enough, far easier to deal with than those rogues from the Guild of Coin and Enterprise, as Adrianna has recently discovered. But you are quite wrong in thinking you are anywhere near as good as you can be."

He stopped suddenly, catching Lucius by surprise. His gaze was one of passionate intensity as he spoke. "I see such potential in you, Mr Kane. I can feel the power and possibilities emanating from you as you stand there now. You have no idea of what you are really capable of."

Coughing, Forbeck looked down at the ground briefly before raising his head again to Lucius. "This is the purpose of the guild, you see. We need no guildhouse, membership roll, or shady deals to survive. Our magic and other abilities compensate for all of that, in one way or another. But we can work together for a common cause, and that, Mr Kane, is why you should be with us."

"And just what is the common cause?" Lucius asked.

"That we share information on the practices of stealth and magic both, and through the accumulated wisdom of our members, we become an institution valued and respected. Imagine, Mr Kane, no more disguising the fact that you are more than a mere thief. Think of the lords and nobles who will line up to hire one of our number to engage in the most secret of commissions. Whether it is riches or arcane knowledge that motivates you, you will find it among fellow Shadowmages, not thieves."

"I am not sure I would like serving two masters – remember, I already belong to the Hands."

"Oh, you misunderstand me," Forbeck said, brushing aside the argument with a hand. "Stay with the Hands, you could not do better. I am sure you will learn many techniques in their service that will be of great interest to other Shadowmages. We have no dues to pay, and no chores to fulfil, Mr Kane. Our organisation is one of common accord, nothing more. We only have one ultimate directive."

"Which is?"

"One Shadowmage may never strike at another directly, even if they find themselves on opposing sides of a contract. We have suffered too much in recent years, and to fight among ourselves is folly of the highest order." At this, Lucius noticed Forbeck throw a quick glance at Adrianna. "The consequences of such an attack must, by necessity, be dire. We take an oath to that effect."

Lucius was silent for a moment, thoughts churning through his head. He was fairly sure he did not need another level of complication in his life, particularly one that involved the bitter Adrianna. He had continued to think that his stay in the city would be brief, that he would make his money, and then leave to continue his adventures elsewhere. Yet, he had made himself comfortable among the Night Hands and, if he was utterly truthful with himself, he had made no plans to leave in the near future. There was also that hard edge behind Forbeck's calm exterior that troubled him, and he decided to test his theory.

"You are not going to let me simply walk away, are you?"

Forbeck gave him a grim smile. "You are very perceptive, Mr Kane. We cannot have a rogue Shadowmage at work in this city, risking everything we have worked for so far. Imagine a loose wheel on a wagon – sooner or later, it is going to fall off and bring everything crashing to the ground around it. That's you."

"So my choices are what, join you or die?"

"We are not completely cold-blooded, Mr Kane, and we find it repugnant to be forced to attack one of our own. Think of yourself as a troublesome child who would have to be forced out into the wider world for both your safety and our own."

"Join you or leave, then," Lucius said flatly.

"Please, do not think of it in those terms," Forbeck said. "Think of what we can offer you. Support when you most need it, friendship beyond that of thieves. But most of all, training to bring your full potential to light. I was not merely playing you before, Mr Kane. You do have something within you that could be most magnificent. I do not know quite what it is yet, but it will be a fascinating journey of discovery for both of us, I am sure."

Sighing, Lucius shook his head. "You leave me with little choice. How will this work, then?"

"After taking the Oath of the Shadowmages to never strike directly at another, you will enter my tutelage immediately."

Beside Lucius, Adrianna gasped in shock. "You cannot be serious!"

"Adrianna–" Forbeck began.

"You don't know this man, Master," she said, her voice dark and loaded with menace. "He cannot be trusted – he has already betrayed the guild once!"

"I would remind you that was the former guild," Forbeck said, before turning back to Lucius. "You must forgive Adrianna. By allowing me to restart your training, you will also be ensuring that you two see a great deal more of one another."

Lucius caught Adrianna muttering something about seeing him first, but ignored it. He took a breath, wondering what fate he was sealing for himself, and whether he would soon be fighting someone else's battles.

"Do I have to call you master?" he asked.

Forbeck smiled back wolfishly. "When you feel ready to, Mr Kane. When you feel ready."

CHAPTER SEVEN

THE HANDS WERE present in force during the next round of collections from the Street of Dogs. What would normally have been accomplished over a few lazy afternoons by lower ranking members who had bought their way in to the protection franchise was now being planned and executed with military precision.

Lucius found himself playing watchman, pacing the street as if he had no cares in the world. In reality, he was keeping a sharp eye out for the two thieves who had just entered a tanner's workshop to collect the dues owed to the Hands for another week of relative peace. Three others were also on the street keeping watch and, fifty yards up the hill, the operation was being repeated by another team. The intent, Magnus had explained to them all before they had been dispatched from the guildhouse, was to demonstrate a show of force, both to the shopkeepers and any spies from the Guild of Coin and Enterprise who would no doubt be looking for a sign of weakness in any territory that belonged to the Hands.

Thus the morning had passed without event. It was the same routine every time; the collectors went into a shop, storehouse or tavern, took their money and listened to the proprietor's complaints, then exited, giving those watching a brief nod to announce the visit had gone according to plan. Then they would move on to the next stop. After every dozen collections, the team would leapfrog the one further up the hill and begin the process again. The use of two teams had been suggested by Caradoc, and it served a dual purpose. First, it was a show of force to the Guild, an announcement of the manpower the Hands could field. However, it also would give those under protection less warning that the collection was about to arrive.

As predicted by the Council, the takings for those not directly linked to the franchise, Lucius included, were slim, but most accepted the duty without complaint, realising that this was a time for unity, not argument. It was also an easy role to play, Lucius realised as he stopped briefly outside a wine merchant to casually view the more expensive casks and bottles on display. All part of the act.

For his part, Lucius was grateful for the respite, though not for the early start. He was still considering his meeting earlier in the week with Adrianna and her Master – his now as well, he realised. His relationship with Aidy had clearly soured further when she had learned he was to be taught alongside her, and her venomous looks, split equally between him and Forbeck, made it apparent that she was not going to make life easy for either.

Having taken the oath not to directly harm another Shadowmage, which gave some small comfort in itself considering Adrianna's disposition, Forbeck had talked briefly with him about his past, his time in the old guild, his family, his reasons for leaving Turnitia, and what he had seen on his travels beyond the city.

After that, Forbeck had disappeared, promising that Lucius would be contacted soon to begin his training. He did not reveal how or when the message would be delivered, and Adrianna had been in no hurry to educate him further. So, it was back to the Hands and a thief's work.

The two collectors, junior members of the franchise but, on this operation, very much Lucius' superiors, left the tanners and gave the nod before moving next door to a dressmakers he knew was run by an elderly spinster. From what he had heard in the common room, the collectors would get little real trouble there, but would be forced to endure a lecture that encompassed everything that was wrong with the city, and how the Hands should go about fixing it. He reflected that with such clients on the books, the greater share the collectors were making today would be well earned. Keeping pace with them, Lucius moved his attention to the window of a potter's shop front, looking over the decoratively painted clay mugs, plates and bowls while trying not to look bored.

He was eventually distracted by movement down the hill. One of the other watchmen lifted a finger in signal, but Lucius had already clocked the danger. The collectors had not yet left the spinster and coming towards the team now was a group of perhaps twenty men. It was the tightness of their gathering that first alerted Lucius, for while friends may travel so closely together, no one walked in such a large group unless they had distinct purpose.

Eyeing the men without looking at them directly, he spotted a few cudgels carried openly, while others sported suspicious looking bulges under their tunics that suggested concealed knives and clubs. He glanced at one of the other watchmen, a young man called Swinherd, who returned the look with a shrug, clearly not knowing how to respond.

It was unlikely that the proprietors of the Street of Dogs had banded together to raise a small army in order to dissuade the Hands from collecting their dues, as the tax was mild enough and Magnus had made sure there was always some tangible benefit to paying; burglaries in the Street of Dogs were quite rare. The Vos guard, if they deigned to get involved in a benign protection racket, would send armoured and uniformed men. That just left the Guild of Coin and Enterprise, and that meant trouble.

While Lucius had yet to learn all the intricacies of the unique sign language used by the Hands, he knew enough to get his general meaning across, and a casual crossing of his hands told the other watchmen to stand ready and make no overt moves. He was gratified to see their assent, and they continued watching as the men approached.

As they moved closer, Lucius realised that they were paying him no attention, but one burly man at their centre nudged another and pointed directly at Swinherd, obviously recognising him as a Hand. As one, the men altered their course and steered directly for him.

To his credit, Swinherd stood his ground, raising his head in acknowledgement as they gathered around him in a semicircle. The first words exchanged were quiet and beyond Lucius' range of hearing. One of the other watchmen sent a discreet signal, suggesting they move in to support Swinherd, but Lucius shook his head. He guessed that at least some of his fellow thieves had not been recognised either, and while they remained invisible to the Guild men, they retained an advantage, as badly outnumbered as they were. Lucius found himself anxious to move closer, to hear what was being said, but he steeled himself to remain passive and await an outcome.

It all seemed rather amiable, Lucius thought, as he kept a watch out of the corner of his eye, the potter's wares now completely forgotten. The burly man leading the Guild men kept his hands in plain view as he spoke, and Swinherd was nodding and shrugging as if he were chatting to an old acquaintance. Then things became heated.

The burly man pointed a finger back down the hill, as if ordering Swinherd to leave the street, at which point the young man shook his head in refusal and took a step back. They followed him and men on the flanks began to crowd round, hiding Swinherd from sight as he raised his hands, trying to appease them. Knowing he was about to witness a beating in broad daylight, Lucius gave a quick signal to the other watchers and trotted across the street.

"Swinherd!" he said in greeting as he pushed his way through the tight press of men. Keeping his voice jovial, he also completely ignored the baleful stares that were now being directed his way, and he hoped the other thieves had taken his lead and were just a few paces behind. "We've been looking for you. Come, we've got work to do, no time to stand and chat with old friends."

"We're no friends of that this toe-rag," growled someone in the crowd.

Lucius kept his eyes fixed firmly on Swinherd, whose gratitude at being rescued was palpable. "Well, that's unfortunate."

A bearded man took a step to stand directly before Lucius. He held a club low down one leg. "You spineless dog," he said in a low voice.

"We've got no argument with you," said Lucius, trying hard to put an edge in his voice while ignoring the hostile gazes from the assembled men. "It would be best for all if we went our separate ways."

The burly man jabbed a finger hard into Swinherd's chest, though his words were directed at Lucius. "Your time here is over. This street belongs to the Guild now, and we'll be taking over the collections today."

"You don't want to do this," Lucius said. "This is a fight no one can win."

He was, of course, referring to a wider war between the two thieves, guilds, but he belatedly realised that such grander thoughts of strategy were likely beyond the men who had been sent to scare them off.

"There's more of us," the bearded man piped up again. "I'm thinking we can win this easy."

"Understand this," the burly man cut over him. "The Hands are finished. There can only be one Guild in this city, and that's us. You'll either join us, or spend the rest of your lives as cripples. Those are your only choices."

Lucius and Swinherd quickly exchanged glances, and the young man nodded in understanding of what was about to happen. Lucius stared straight into the eyes of the burly man.

"If you don't leave now, I promise, you won't walk away from this," he said, his voice even.

Someone near the back of the crowd laughed. The burly man smiled and nodded at him in a mock salute. He then grabbed the club from the bearded man and swung it hard at Swinherd.

Lucius had been ready for the first attack. He dove between Swinherd and weapon, catching the man's arms as the club started to descend.

"Run!" Lucius shouted over his shoulder and Swinherd, needing no prompting, turned and fled. Raising his knee Lucius rammed it into the crotch of the burly man, who exhaled noisily before staggering to the ground. Reacting a great deal slower than Lucius, the others began to draw knives and daggers as he turned and ran as well.

The collectors had chosen that moment to leave the spinster, and their faces were almost comical, eyes wide in astonishment as they saw their watchmen running at full tilt down the street, pursued by an angry and cursing mob. They took their cue from their friends and started to sprint away, goaded on by Lucius' shouts.

Casting a look behind him as he ran, Lucius saw the Hands had scattered, diving into alleyways, vaulting over walls, splitting up to ensure at least some would escape unharmed. He decided to continue running directly up the centre of the street in order to provide the most visible target, but the Guild men were not co-operating.

Swinherd had rocketed past the collectors, then dived into an alley that stretched alongside the long wall of a tavern proclaiming itself to be the Grateful Rest. With no real co-ordination on their part, the Guild men had zeroed in on their original target and were pounding just a few steps behind the young man, who was clearly in fear of his life.

Coming to a stop, Lucius turned back and shouted a challenge at the pursuing men, calling out the bearded man in the lead.

"Hey, pig!" he bellowed. "Was your mother wedded to a hog, or was she a sow whore putting it to every merchant in the city?"

He was answered by an angry, inarticulate cry, and the mob surged up towards him. Smiling, Lucius bolted. It never failed.

Hearing the clatter of leather on cobbles gaining ground on him, Lucius tried to measure his breathing as he sought the strands of energy that were never far from his grasp. Control of his magic was difficult while sprinting, but he was only attempting rudimentary control. He caught the needed thread, feeling its power flush through his entire body. Feeling a new wave of strength, he banished all thought of fatigue and ignored his aching legs as he gained in speed, pulling away from the mob.

Within seconds, Lucius was in the territory of the second collection team, and he saw the surprised looks of their watchmen.

"Guild men!" he shouted, jabbing a finger over his shoulder. They reacted instantly, one diving into a shop front to retrieve his collectors while the others melted away into side streets. Lucius grinned, satisfied that the other thieves were retreating to places of safety. It took just one more glance over his shoulder to remind him that he was still in great danger himself. The expressions on the faces of the mob left no doubt as to his fate should he be caught.

Deciding that the chase had gone on long enough, he darted right, vaulting over a fence that ran round a small townhouse. Hitting the ground in a roll, he found himself in an unkempt garden, full of uncut thigh-high grass and weeds. He bolted across the small patch of wilderness and swung his legs over the low wall on the other side. Behind, the Guild's men were cursing as they became entangled in the undergrowth, but enough were making good headway to convince Lucius not to slow down.

Over the wall, Lucius found himself in a smaller street, its buildings a mixture of shabby houses and shops whose owners were unable to afford the prices commanded on the Street of Dogs. He ran a short distance past the nearest buildings, then jerked left into a narrow alley, intending to lose the men in the network of twisting turns and junctions that were common in these districts of Turnitia.

After a few more minutes, Lucius felt safe enough to stop and catch his breath, leaning against the brickwork of an abandoned house. The magic that had propelled him this far and this fast was now ebbing, and a deep fatigue spread through his body. The complaints his bones made at having been pushed so hard finally heard. Crouching down as he drew in painful gasps of air, he rubbed his ankles for some relief, but he stopped when he heard new cries coming from a short distance away. They were just one or two streets over from where he stood.

Fearing one of his fellow thieves had been caught, Lucius forced himself to his feet, shoving the weariness away. He retraced his steps cautiously, heading down a short road that led back toward the Street of Dogs. More calls echoed off the walls of the nearby buildings, and he dove into a doorway as three Guild men ran out of an alleyway a few yards ahead of him, coming to a stop in the middle of the road as they looked about them. Pressing himself against the door, Lucius carefully tilted his head to watch them. They were obviously having a disagreement as to which way they should run next, which was finally resolved by one returning the way they had come, while the other two dashed up towards the Street of Dogs.

Lucius released a breath he'd not realised he had been holding, then caught it again as the door behind him opened, which forced him to grab onto the frame to stop himself stumbling. Turning around, he saw a small girl in a dirty shirt looking up at him expectantly. Winking at her and smiling, he fished out a silver tenth from his pouch and flipped it to her, before running across the road into another alley.

Finding himself between two rows of houses, Lucius saw alleys criss-crossing every thirty yards or so and he skidded to a halt at every junction, checking each intersection. Another shout of anger and the clash of metal on metal from up ahead spurred him on, and he rounded a corner in time to see Swinherd pull a knife from the belly of a Guild man, who collapsed, sobbing, onto the hard ground. Another watcher who had been on Lucius' team stepped out from another alley and, on seeing what had happened, patted Swinherd on the back. Lucius, dismayed, ran towards them.

"What have you done?" he said in a harsh whisper. "What have you done?"

"Bastard tried to jump me," Swinherd said, kicking the man as he groaned and clasped his hands to his stomach in a fruitless attempt to stem the flow of blood.

"Why didn't you just keep on running? You should have just ran!"

Swinherd shrugged. "I was trying to hook up with you guys again. I had to defend myself!"

"Yeah, back off a moment," said the watchman, who seemed to take greater offence at Lucius' interruption that Swinherd had. "So we have a dead Guild man on our hands. So what? One less suits us just fine, I say." The watchman bent down to look the dying man in the face. "You hear that, you worthless bastard? You're going to die soon."

"You fools!" said Lucius, trying to keep both his temper and voice low. He could not see why these two did not understand what was at stake. "Up to now, we have just had a few beatings here and there. This is the first time a Hand has killed someone in the Guild."

When they just looked at him blankly, he sighed and continued, speaking a little slower so his meaning would not be lost. "They are going to be after our blood now."

The watchman looked at Swinherd, then at the dying man, then back at Lucius. "Well... we could hide the body."

Lucius rolled his eyes. "Where? You planning on hoisting it over one of these walls? One way or another, the Guild will find the body, and even if they don't they'll guess what has happened when he doesn't show up at their guildhouse."

"So what do we do?" Swinherd asked, now suddenly less elated at his victory.

Thinking hard, Lucius scratched the back of his head. "We've got to get back to Magnus, tell him what has happened."

"You going to tell him it was me?" Swinherd said in a quiet voice.

"Believe me, he is going to have far greater things to worry about than punishing you."

They split up again, after bearing a lecture from Lucius as to how they would *not* go looking for more Guild men. They were to take their separate paths back to the guildhouse and get there as quickly as possible.

He just hoped Magnus would have the wisdom to see a way through this, and perhaps make some compensation towards the Guild. The alternative was too terrible to contemplate.

CHAPTER EIGHT

LUCIUS CURSED AS the small ball of fire ignited another roll of paper. For the third time in a row. Behind him, he heard Adrianna quietly clack her tongue, though whether it was in amusement or impatience, he could not decide.

Moving quickly for an older man, Forbeck kicked it to one side and stamped out the flames, before replacing it with another roll.

"Try again, Mr Kane."

As the sun descended beyond the western horizon, Lucius had felt a curious itch in the back of his mind. A prickling on the nape of his neck. Unable to shake the sensation, he had left the guildhouse and the turmoil it had fallen into, and quickly realised the feeling grew stronger as he headed north, but weaker when he turned aside from the path.

Arriving at an abandoned warehouse, the itching growing ever more insistent, he discovered this was Forbeck's way of summoning him to their first lesson. Lucius was at first irritated at having been called in this manner, but quickly found himself curious as to the measure of subtle control needed for such magic. Knowing the master had managed to pick him out of the entire population of the city, then plant the urge to follow the signal, was impressive, and it left him wanting to know exactly how it was achieved. Forbeck, however, had other plans for that evening, and Adrianna was her usual implacable self.

Within the empty confines of the dusty and cobweb-strewn warehouse, Forbeck had devised a simple test to measure Lucius' control of his talent. Having quickly divined that Lucius was capable of conjuring fire at will, six rolls of paper had been placed in a row, and Lucius had been asked to summon a small ball of flame, and weave it in and out of the spaces while leaving the papers intact.

It was not an easy test, and Lucius was growing more frustrated with each attempt.

He had thought it a simple challenge when Forbeck had initially spelled it out, ignoring Adrianna's knowing look, but Lucius' first try had blasted the first three rolls into cinders. By the third attempt, he had managed to guide the fireball around the first roll, but had watched helplessly as it wobbled into the second. The trial seemed to be going nowhere fast.

The problem was that Lucius had never, since he had first realised his gift with magic, tried to exercise such precise control for anything more than influencing tumbling dice for a split second. Calling upon the power to blast an enemy with a jet of flame, sending him reeling to the ground with the force of the strike even as the fire consumed him, was relatively easy. Aside from the shaping of the necessary energies, it required very little control whatsoever. Just creating and maintaining a small globe of swirling flames for more than a few seconds was enough to make Lucius break into a sweat. Guiding it with precision was seemingly impossible, though Forbeck had earlier demonstrated a successful attempt at the exercise to prove it was not.

"Remember, all it takes is practice," Forbeck said, as he watched Lucius frown in concentration.

Kneeling, Lucius opened his right hand as a bright spark ignited upon his palm. Growing into a sphere of rolling fire half the size of his fist, he placed his hand on the stone floor and willed the flames to tumble forwards. The fire bounced once and, before he could arrest its momentum, bumped gently into the first roll of paper, lighting it immediately.

"Practice makes perfect," Lucius muttered. "I'm getting worse!"

"Did you really think you would come here, accomplish everything laid before you with so little effort and then leave, smug in the knowledge that there is nothing you cannot do?" Adrianna said.

Lucius bit his tongue to forestall the first retort that came to mind. "That was not my first thought, no," he finally said.

A rap echoed across the rafters and walls of the warehouse as Forbeck struck his cane on the hard stone, silencing the argument brewing between his students.

"I wish I could tell you there was an easy way through this part, Mr Kane," he said, replacing the burnt roll. "I wish there was some secret meditative technique, or command word, that would allow you to control your magic as I have asked. But I am afraid there is not. The only route to success lies in practice, practice, practice. Master your frustration at failure, and direct your energies to trying again."

Narrowing his eyes and laying his palm flat once more, Lucius called upon his magic to bring another fire globe into existence, but this one just fizzled away after the first few sparks.

He sighed. "I am not sure I am in the best frame of mind for this today."

"Have you ever had trouble making your talent do what you want before?" Forbeck asked.

Lucius thought for a moment. "No. Not since the early days anyway."

"I would guess that is because you have only ever used your magic when your life was in peril, or perhaps occasionally for your own amusement. You have never had to influence with such delicate control before."

"Taking the path of least resistance," Adrianna said, but they both ignored her.

"Please, try again," Forbeck said. "Forget the distractions of your ordinary life and fill your mind with the magic. There should be nothing else."

Taking a deep breath, Lucius looked at the line of paper rolls before him. The truth was that distractions *were* intruding on his thoughts. Marching back to the guildhouse earlier that day, Lucius had been filled with dread. He knew they had failed utterly in their mission on the Street of Dogs. The disruption to the collections could be excused – but the death of the Guild man in the skirmish after could not.

They had confronted Magnus, all twelve thieves assigned to the task and, upon hearing what Swinherd had done, the guildmaster had fought visibly to control his anger. The shadow across his face had subsided quickly, but he had told them all how very disappointed he was in them. That seemed worse somehow. Though they all knew that it was Swinherd that bore the brunt of blame, they also all felt in some measure responsible. It had after all, happened on their watch.

Ordering the rest of the Hands to keep a low profile in the city over the next few days, he clearly hoped there would be no direct retaliation, that the Guild would see the senselessness of direct action and chalk the death down to overexuberance on the part of some of its members. It was, after all, what he would be inclined to do in their place. However, Lucius was not so sure. There was a dark feeling in the pit of his stomach that refused to be silenced, and it had been troubling him all day, as if they were now just waiting for the hammer to fall. It was certainly affecting his concentration now.

Lucius aimed the next fireball to the side of the first paper roll, thinking that he could at least bypass the obstacle with little effort on his part. As the globe slowly bounced past the paper, he half-closed his eyes as he tried to imagine an invisible thread between it and himself. Gently, he pulled on the connection, willing it to veer to the left and therefore bounce between the first two rolls.

The fiery globe seemed to hesitate just a few inches above the floor, then, with infinite slowness it seemed to Lucius, curved a lazy arc between the rolls. It was not a neat line, but the globe now bobbed on the other side of the rolls, close to the second. He could feel the connection between himself and the fire grow complicated and tenuous, but he took a breath and willed it forward just a little, then started a new curve to the right, to take it past the second roll and onto the third.

As the fire globe slowly drifted in the new direction, he allowed himself a smile of satisfaction. The break in his thoughts was enough to sever the link he had so far maintained, and the ball suddenly picked up speed, veered left and right randomly, then headed straight for the third roll, blasting it to cinders.

"Damn it!" he shouted, frustration getting the better of him.

"Easy, my boy," Forbeck said, placing the end of his cane on Lucius' shoulder, as if to restrain his anger. It caused him to turn round to face the other two Shadowmages.

"You may not believe me, but you are doing well to get so far so quickly," Forbeck continued. "We have been here little more than an hour, and you are showing the ability to influence your magic beyond the point of egress, to maintain a physical form for several seconds, and to guide it with growing precision. I do not know if I recall seeing someone with so much ready aptitude."

Lucius noticed Adrianna's eyes narrow suspiciously at this, but he said nothing. Scoring cheap points against her was not the way to an easy life, he had long ago realised. Forbeck fell silent with his own thoughts for a moment, then focussed back on Lucius.

"Let's try another tack," he said, pacing a half-circle round Lucius before leaning on his cane with both hands. "Tell me how you see your magic. What do you imagine when you call upon the power?"

"The same as you, I would think," Lucius said.

"Indulge an old man," Forbeck said, smiling. "What do you *see*?"

"Well... It's always there, to one degree or another. You kind of get used to it. It's like I can see many different lines, strands, umm... threads, I suppose. Not see them for real, but they are in my head somewhere. They all wrap around one another as they go off into the distance, spinning round and round, crossing one another's path. I sort of reach in and pick out the one I need, and I feel it right here," he said, putting a hand on his chest. "After that, I can direct and shape the energy into what I need it to do."

"Fascinating," Forbeck muttered. Lucius noticed he glanced briefly at Adrianna, who raised her eyebrows in an expression that seemed to suggest she had won an argument between them.

"And what, exactly, are you able to do with these threads?" Forbeck asked. "How can you manifest your power? What can you *do*?"

Lucius shrugged. "Create fire, as you can see, though normally I only use that to start a camp fire – or catch an enemy off guard. I can increase my strength and speed for a short time, send a stone flying through the air, cloak myself in shadows, bend the branches of a tree, umm... well, whatever I need, really."

He purposefully did not mention the darker aspects of his talent, the powers he knew were at his call but had always seemed black, ruinous... evil. He saw Forbeck was eyeing him with a calculating look, seeming to measure him by the ounce.

"You may be a truly remarkable individual, Mr Kane," Forbeck said quietly.

This puzzled Lucius, for he had expected some ridicule, especially from Adrianna, for how little his abilities had progressed over the years. The test with the rolls of paper was clearly an exercise in humiliation for him.

"What do you mean?" he asked.

Forbeck paused again as he marshalled his thoughts. When he finally spoke, his voice was slow and measured. "Every Shadowmage visualises their power in a different way. However, there are common themes. Most see it as a centralised concentration of power." Seeing Lucius frown at that, Forbeck tried to quantify his remark. "They see something like a large cloud, a lake, or maybe a river. They fuel their magic by metaphorically reaching into that source, scooping out the gas or water, and then forming it into what they need."

"I don't see anything like that," Lucius said.

"No. And that is what makes you at least a little different. Tell me, Mr Kane, what you know about the fundamental properties of magic. What is it, do you think, that guides a practitioner, be they Shadowmage, wizard, witch or priest, and limits what he can ultimately achieve?"

"I am not sure I know," Lucius said doubtfully. "Practice, I suppose, as you said."

He saw immediately from Forbeck's expression that it was the wrong answer.

"Do you think you could move a mountain, Mr Kane?" Forbeck asked.

"Well, no."

"So, there are clearly limits to what can be done. However, there are other boundaries that confine a practitioner to certain tasks that he can accomplish with magic. Do you understand what I mean?"

"Not really," Lucius said.

"Well, we have been watching you create your little balls of fire this evening. Would it surprise you to learn that Adrianna is completely unable to ignite so much as a spark, let alone sustain a fire through its own energy alone?"

Lucius blinked. Yes, he was surprised that Adrianna could not accomplish something he found so easy. She was, after all, far more accomplished as a Shadowmage than he. However, as he cast his mind back, he suddenly realised that, for all the time they had spent together in the past learning under Master Roe, he had never seen her use fire in her magic.

"Why is that?" he asked, completely perplexed.

"There are different types of magic, Mr Kane," Forbeck said. "Or rather, different sources. I am not sure anyone knows them all, but the important thing is that the vast majority of practitioners in this world only ever master one. Just one, Mr Kane. Now, all Shadowmages have an aptitude for magic involving stealth and secrecy; that is one of the aspects of our practice that sets us apart – the other is that we can manipulate magic so easily, almost instinctively, while others require years of study, practice and ritual. However, the very best of us also gain mastery of another source. Do you follow me?"

Looking blank, Lucius just waited for him to continue.

"For example, I can create the same fire you do, but Adrianna cannot. She can greatly influence parts of the natural world –

weather, animals, plants and so forth. But I cannot. We share an affinity for stealth and secrets, for we are Shadowmages, but otherwise we are very different.

"When I see the source of my magic, Mr Kane, I see two clouds. One is still and dark, and is where I reach when I want to clothe myself in shadows or walk silently past an alert watchman. The other is turbulent and frightening, a tempest of power that I often struggle to harness. But reaching for that cloud is what allows me to create fire, animate water, or suck the air from the lungs of an enemy. Most Shadowmages are confined to the magic of stealth, which is where we earned our name. Only the best, those destined to become masters of the guild, can add another weapon to their magical arsenal. And then we have you."

"Me?"

"You are clearly not bound to one, or even two sources of power in your magical endeavours, Mr Kane. Adrianna tried to tell me this earlier, but I did not believe it. And yet when you, just now, described what you can achieve with your magic, you told us of things that would ordinarily take half a dozen Shadowmages to accomplish."

Lucius was quiet for a moment, and the silence of the empty warehouse began to press upon him as he struggled to find something to say.

"So... what does mean?" he asked.

"I am not sure," Forbeck said. "That you have access to formidable powers was obvious to me before we even met. Every Shadowmage in the city felt something when you arrived. But it is also clear you have access to perhaps an unlimited number of arcane sources of power. It will be fascinating to watch what you can ultimately achieve and, because of this, I implore you to continue your training. You can be so much, Mr Kane, and I just hope I can help set you on the right path. There is something about you that sets you apart from not only other Shadowmages, but perhaps every practitioner of magic in this world. It would be a crime to allow that to simply fade away."

"That is a lot to think about," Lucius said.

"I know, and both Adrianna and I will do all we can to guide you through these early stages. I cannot promise you anything, Mr Kane, and I cannot foretell the future. But I very much want to train you, for your own sake, as well as that of our guild."

"Then, in that case," Lucius replied, "I think I will stay around. For at least a little while longer."

"Thank you, Mr Kane," said Forbeck, and Lucius sensed his relief. "I think we have covered enough – more than enough – this evening. Carry on with your practice when you can, try to exercise finer control. That will be key to your later studies. When we meet again, we will see how far you have come. I look forward to that time."

With a slight bow, Forbeck spun on his heels and walked out of the warehouse, the sound of his cane ringing on the stone with each step.

Lucius stared down at the line of paper rolls in front of him, sensing Adrianna's eyes fixed on the back of his head.

"You put a word in for me, then?" he asked.

When she did not answer immediately, he turned back to face her, seeing a dark expression bearing down upon him.

"You are a rogue and a scoundrel," she said accusingly. "But you do have power. That, I have always sensed."

She stalked past him to follow Forbeck, her voice floating back to him as it echoed around the warehouse. "Learn from Master Torquelle, and you will find a home among the Shadowmages, Lucius. Betray us again and, I swear, I will finish you myself."

HIS MIND NOW full of magic, as well as the struggle between thieves, Lucius nevertheless felt as though some burden had been lifted from his shoulders. What passed for an olive branch in Adrianna's mind had been offered to him, and he clearly had an ally, if not yet a friend, in Forbeck. For the first time in many years, he had a sense of purpose, of a greater goal to be achieved, rather than aimless wandering. He had to admit, it felt good. There were troubles to be faced by the Night Hands but he now believed they could eventually be solved and, maybe, he would have a part in that.

When Lucius returned to the guildhouse, after walking the twilight streets of Turnitia for an hour or more, he found that nothing would be solved easily, and that greater dangers now hung above all the thieves.

The sombre mood in the common room was palpable when he entered, for no one spoke above a whisper. Clumped together in their regular groups, the thieves simply nursed their ale or wine, and avoided looking directly at him or one another. Sensing something had gone very wrong, Lucius dashed upstairs, seeking Ambrose or

Caradoc, finally finding the latter in the council chamber with two others that Lucius had seen earlier.

"You can't be here," Caradoc warned him. "The Council is gathering to discuss the attack."

"What attack?" Lucius asked, suddenly anxious.

"Where have you been? One of the pickpocket teams was found in the afternoon, stabbed to death and thrown into Drake's Alley in the Five Markets."

"They were only kids," said one of the Council members, a bitter note in her voice.

Suddenly downcast, Lucius turned to leave, before a thought struck him. "Which team was it?"

"Just been put together," Caradoc said. "Some young lad called Tucker, only joined us this week. He was with two experienced kids; Markel and Treal, brother and sister, I think."

Lucius sagged against the door frame, trying hard not to picture the children, their bodies lying in a deserted alley among the dirt and filth, blood pouring from open wounds in their chests. They must have been so scared, he thought, and cursed himself for not being there to save them.

He barely heard when Caradoc spoke again. "It will be war now, you mark my words. There is no way Magnus can back down from this. It will be war."

CHAPTER NINE

THE GUILDHOUSE WAS alive with activity, rumour and gossip. From the first light of day, thieves had been gathered in small groups, and conversation had stealthily made its way through the common room, armoury, kitchens and corridors; the Guild of Coin and Enterprise were coming.

It had been later in the afternoon when Lucius had been summoned to the council chamber, its polished wooden walls seeming to reflect the mixed emotions of excitement and dread that had permeated the entire guildhouse by now. He had already that heard there had been a noisy dispute among the Council – particularly between Magnus and Caradoc – but the guildmaster had made his wishes clear, vetoing all other proposals. Seeing where violence between the two guilds would inevitably lead, Magnus had called for a summit between them, inviting the leadership of the Guild into his most secret lair as a sign of trust and concession.

That had been the rumour, but as Lucius passed Caradoc in the hall and saw his haunted expression, he came to believe all he had heard. They were waiting for him in the council chamber, the table turned so it stood at right angles to its normal facing, with the most senior thieves hunched together on the far side facing a row of empty seats across an assembly of wine urns and cups. Magnus sat in the centre with Caradoc's empty place to his left, while behind him stood his two bodyguards; Lucius had learned they were brothers, Taene and Narsell, and they had terrible reputations for cruel brutality, but served the guildmaster with complete fidelity.

A smattering of other high-ranking thieves stood against the wall behind the assembled Council, and Lucius was directed to join them. He had no idea why he had been summoned to this meeting, other than it had been at Magnus' direct request, as he knew the others would be present to act not only as witnesses, but also as advisors and counsellors, should information be needed during the discussions. What he had to offer, Lucius could not say, but he was grateful indeed that he would see what happened here first hand, and not have to rely on the guildhouse's own, not always accurate, grapevine.

"Are we certain they will show?" one of the Council members asked, a young man whom Lucius recalled was called Nate.

"The offer caused quite a stir within the Guild," another man answered, "or so our spies have told me. I wouldn't be surprised if they were still arguing about what to do."

"They will show," Magnus said confidently. He noticed a few doubtful looks about the table and continued. "The Guild has as much to gain and lose as we do. Though we have very different ideas about how to run this city, Loredo is not a stupid man."

"He also risks a great deal by coming here, to our home ground," Nate said. "If the situation was reversed, I would be worried about an ambush."

"True," Magnus agreed. "But we risk a similar amount by inviting him here. Look at it this way. If the situation were indeed reversed, would you not be swayed by the chance to see your enemy's stronghold?"

The Council considered that, and Lucius saw a few heads nodding round the table as Magnus' reasoning became apparent.

"More important is what happens after the initial greetings," he said. "I confess, I am not entirely sure what the Guild will be after, nor how aggressively they will negotiate. They must be willing to consider compromises, or we would not have been able to arrange this meeting. However, we must be ready to cede ground if it first gains us territory elsewhere and, second, ensures peace between us. I will not have war among thieves, not while I am guildmaster."

Conversation then turned to the operations and territories the Council wanted to keep and which they might consider for trade. As they spoke, Lucius' head began to swim with information; he had had no idea of the complexity or number of the operations the Hands had an interest in. There was far more than just theft at stake.

The growing prostitute rings were clearly an important element for some of the Council, for while new to the Hands and still small, they showed much promise. They fought against the advocates of smugglers and blackmailers. Lucius learned of a city-wide counterfeit ring that traded in false documents, coin and art. It was confirmed that the Hands did indeed have a burgeoning trade in assassinations, whose franchise owners were considered among the most skilled in all the guild. As well as the pickpockets, protection rackets and general burglaries, the Council spoke of narcotics from the Sarcre Islands, trade of arcane artefacts from ruins in the darkest parts of the Sardenne, and an underground network that could spirit Pontaine agents to and from Turnitia throughout the year.

Lucius began to wonder just how wealthy the Night Hands were, when all their operations were stacked up and accounted for. He thought of the vaults built into the foundations of the guildhouse, and thought of how they must be nearly overflowing with coin and valuables. Not for the first time, he could see the organisation he had chosen to join as a whole, that it was not simply a gathering of those who worked outside the law, but a business, run as tightly and efficiently as that of the richest merchants. Fundamentally, it was all about the money.

A short thief poked his head round the open door of the meeting room. "They're here," he said, before ducking back out of sight.

The mood in the room changed immediately. Council members sat straighter in their seats, while Magnus' bodyguards, Taene and Narsell, shifted their weight ever so slightly, moving their hands a fraction of an inch along their belts to where their blades lay. For his part, Lucius folded his arms and squared his shoulders as he waited for the Guild's delegation to arrive.

They heard quiet voices talking amiably from down the hall, accompanied by footsteps. Everyone in the meeting room seemed to draw in breath at the same time as Caradoc appeared at the door, standing to one side as he politely waved his guests through.

Though Lucius had never seen the leader of the Guild of Coin and Enterprise before, he recognised the man immediately by his bearing and demeanour. He looked exactly like a guildmaster should.

So did Magnus, of course, but Lucius had always seen him as a natural guildmaster because of his authority, leadership and wisdom, all of which became apparent after talking to him for just a few minutes. Loredo Foss was different in just about every way. Lithe and graceful, he was dressed in a black leather jerkin lined with dark red thread. His hair was black and slicked back, while his beard was small and pointed, barely covering his chin. This man was a natural guildmaster, Lucius thought, because he was a master thief, among the very best in his game. That would make him a very dangerous enemy, and Lucius began to appreciate some of the risks Magnus had accepted in opposing himself to the Guild.

Loredo was followed only by one other, which was a statement in itself, considering they had entered the lair of *their* enemy. It was Caradoc's counterpart, Loredo's own lieutenant and trusted confidante, a woman Lucius had heard of but had never seen.

She stalked into the meeting room behind her guildmaster as if she were the leader of all thieves, not he. Her boots, whose hard leather clattered on the floor of the meeting room, ran past her knees, and Lucius could not help but think of all the weapons that might be hidden within them, even though they had been told to divest themselves of any offensive items before entering the guildhouse.

Named Jewel, she had a reputation among the Hands for being utterly lethal, for it was rumoured she was more assassin than thief. Her narrow eyes regarded everyone suspiciously and though she was not at all unattractive, the hardness of her features, which promised quick and silent retribution to anyone who would cross her, seemed to sap any desire.

It was a brave move bringing only one bodyguard to a meeting between thieves of this level, but Lucius thought that, between them, Loredo and Jewel might account for many Hands before they were slain, should the summit take an ill turn.

Magnus stood up to greet his guests, and the action was quickly copied among the rest of the seated Council.

"Loredo, Miss Jewel," he acknowledged as he extended a hand across the table. "I bid you a warm welcome to our humble home, and hope your journey here will prove a fruitful one."

Accepting Magnus' hand with a firm shake and brief nod, Loredo replied. "You show great wisdom in calling this meeting, Magnus. I, too, hope for an outcome beneficial to the both of us."

The Council returned to their seats as Loredo sat down, followed by Jewel. The woman said nothing but eyed each of the Hands methodically, as if judging the threat they might pose to her master. As her eyes swept over Lucius, he drew an involuntary breath, and fought to keep his own gaze even. He had the unlikely notion that Jewel had just given him a number that placed him in the order of people in the room she would like to kill.

As Caradoc joined Magnus' side, the guildmaster remained standing as he took a wine urn and poured four cups. He placed the cups in a row and looked across at Loredo, who smiled. He selected two and passed one to Jewel. Magnus scooped up one of the cups that had been left and drained it, before setting it back on the table with a loud clack. Caradoc followed suit, before reaching for the urn once more and refilling Magnus' cup, then his own.

"I thank you for that show of honesty, Magnus," Loredo said. "But I would think that if you wanted me dead, you would not stoop to poison, nor would you go to the trouble of arranging this meeting."

"Merely demonstrating my willingness to be open here," Magnus said, as he watched Loredo take a sip from his cup. Jewel's cup remained untouched on the table before her.

The two guildmasters regarded one another briefly before Magnus spoke again. "Loredo, you and I have a problem. I run a guild of thieves, and have an interest in making money. You run a guild of thieves and have an interest in making money. Of late, these interests have clashed too many times. If we allow this to escalate, we risk a war that could destroy both of us."

"I have no interest in a thieves' war," Loredo said. "It would prove messy and bring the Vos guard crashing down on us. If you have an easy solution, I would gladly hear it."

"We could perhaps divide the city in two," Magnus said, a hint of sarcasm in his voice. "We could take the west while you have the east, or perhaps we control the north while you take the south."

"Giving you, in the first instance, the docks, and in the second, the Five Markets," Loredo said.

"As we can all see, there is no easy solution," Magnus concluded, and Loredo nodded once in agreement.

"I suggest we make the division based on territory and trade," Magnus said. "If we give something up, you make a concession in return. We will ensure there is parity between us, and that every one of our members understands there are some areas they simply do not work in."

"That, I feel, would be the most equitable solution," Loredo said. "So, where would you begin?"

"Let us start with the disputed territories that have led us here. The Street of Dogs and the Five Markets."

For the first hour, Lucius listened with rapt attention as the two guildmasters spoke, proposing and counter-proposing over and again, as they vied for each advantage. Never once was a voice raised in anger, but each retained a hard edge that served to rein the other in when a demand grew too insistent. After the second and third hours, Lucius' legs began to grow numb, and he noticed others shifting their weight or fidgeting.

Magnus made a point of asking various members of his Council or one of the senior thieves to clarify a point, to list earnings over a given period, or give a rundown on recent activities. By contrast, Loredo never asked Jewel for anything, and he seemed to have the uncanny knack for knowing exactly what Magnus was talking about, citing figures and statistics without fail.

Lucius was startled when Magnus asked him a question, briefly wanting to know the average takings for the pickpocket team that had been slain by the Guild. Lucius answered automatically, but he found his mind drifting back to the brother and sister team he had known, Markel and Treal, and the brutal way in which they had died. It was so very hard not to regard the two thieves on either side of the table as mortal enemies, and yet the meeting was being conducted with both respect and courtesy. He began to wonder if it had been Jewel who had sanctioned the murders, or even had performed the act herself; she seemed just the sort of woman who could cold-bloodedly kill a child.

Throughout the meeting, Jewel only spoke once, while Magnus had been proposing an exchange of trades. The pickpockets in the Five Markets had been placed on the table, and they were considered a valuable operation; while they generated comparatively little money, whoever held the children of the pick-pocketing teams would have a ready source of new blood for recruitment as thieves proper. Loredo was proving intractable over the Hands' control over the Five Markets, and so Magnus raised the possibility of allowing the Guild to take the pickpockets, if in return the Hands could claim complete dominance over all assassinations in the city.

"No." Jewel only said the one word, and when she spoke it was as if ice had been dashed in the faces of the Council. Loredo, ignoring the effects of her input, went on to say that assassinations were a specialised field that had highly specialised agents. The idea of one guild holding them all was simply not feasible.

As hours four and five went by, it seemed as though a little progress was being made, but the guildmasters still proved relentless, neither wishing to show weakness by calling for a break in the meeting first.

Assassinations, it was decided, would be regarded as being outside of the discussion, with a view to perhaps creating a separate assassins' guild in the future. Magnus was able to retain control of the Five Markets, in part because he allowed the Guild free use of his smuggling routes.

An argument brewed between Caradoc and Loredo as the matter of compensation for the deaths of those who had been involved in the earlier 'skirmishes', as they were euphemistically called, between the guilds. Loredo had demanded the princely sum of a thousand gold coin for the death of his Street of Dogs man, which would be an extortionate amount for a rich merchant's ransom. When the subject of the murdered children was raised by Caradoc, Loredo flatly denied any compensation, reminding him that the earning potential of one so young was negligible. Seeing his lieutenant clearly struggling with his temper, Magnus stepped in before voices were raised, announcing that he would not only relinquish any interest in compensation for the pickpockets, but that he would agree to the thousand gold blood price for Loredo's man – but he also made sure the Street of Dogs came down firmly in the Hands' territory because of this.

Scams in the merchant quarter went to the Guild, while the Hands retained the docks. This was an arrangement that suited neither guildmaster well, but both realised something valuable would have to be sacrificed in the meeting. Lucius, for his part, was happy at this decision, for he had been planning his own operation in the docks, and was now favouring it over his plans for the raid on the church of the Final Faith; bothering religious fanatics could prove distinctly unhealthy, he had eventually decided, and he doubted the priests would go anywhere soon, whereas the ship he had been watching was scheduled to depart later in the week.

After seven hours, a weary Council stood as the guildmasters shook hands and toasted one another's success. An accord had been reached. There would be no war among the thieves.

THE FOLLOWING DAYS seemed almost like an anti-climax to Lucius, and he formed the impression that many others among the Hands felt the same. The common room was filled with complaints from those who'd had their franchises pulled, the operations now passing to the Guild of Coin and Enterprise, but there was an equal amount of relief, felt in the quiet conversations of others. Everyone had been expecting the worst, with strangled or stabbed bodies strewn throughout the alleyways of Turnitia. Instead, there had been nothing. If anything, business was picking up.

Those who had been present at the meeting between guildmasters had been forbidden to speak of what they had seen and heard, for

Magnus wanted the changes to the Hands' operations to come from him alone, speaking to each franchise holder in turn and informing them of whether they still had a regular source of income or not. It was not until two days later that Lucius had the chance to discuss the meeting, and that was with Magnus himself.

He had literally run into the guildmaster as he was leaving the training chamber, wiping the sweat from his face with a ragged cloth.

"Ah, Lucius, my boy," Magnus greeted him. Once he realised who was talking to him, Lucius threw the cloth back into the chamber and smiled hesitantly.

"Magnus," he acknowledged with a nod.

"Preparing for your first operation? You are going into action this week, are you not?"

"Tomorrow, all going well," Lucius said. "Still need to find a few more volunteers though."

"You'll get them. Many may not sign on until the last minute, but I think enough trust you now." He gestured up the corridor. "Come, walk with me for a moment."

The request caught Lucius off guard, and he had to stride quickly to catch up with Magnus.

"You opted for the docks in the end, then?" Magnus asked.

"Yes. I had a plan for the church of the Faith, but there were a few impracticalities."

"Indeed. The priesthood would have been straight on to the Vos guard, demanding the entire city be closed down and every thief hung from the cliffs. If you had not scrapped the mission yourself, the Council might have been forced to step in. You demonstrate both ambition and good judgement, two qualities that do not always go hand-in-hand among thieves."

Not knowing quite what to say, Lucius just nodded. He had walked with Magnus past the meeting room, and he glanced into the open door to see if any of the Council were present, but it was empty. Magnus began asking about his training, and Lucius did not realise where they were headed until the guildmaster halted outside a plain wooden door and produced a key. Behind the door was a small flight of stairs, spiralling upwards. With a wave of the hand, Lucius was ushered up, but he hesitated.

Though he had not been in this part of the guildhouse before, it was fairly common knowledge that Magnus kept his own set of chambers on the highest floor. Few were invited into his personal living space, and Lucius wondered why he was being accorded the honour.

"Come along, boy," Magnus prompted. "I have much to do – a guild does not just run itself!"

With Magnus close behind, Lucius ascended the stairs as they rose in a tight spiral.

They emerged into a small study, spartan in appearance with few nods to luxury. A desk lay below a single skylight, strewn with papers, maps and a single oil lantern. A leather-bound chair sat behind it, while in front were three austere wooden seats, of the sort that might be expected in a commoner's kitchen. These were the only items of furniture in the study, and all rested on a tired-looking threadbare rug. Two doors faced one another to Lucius' left and right, and a quick glance told him they were both very thick, with intricate locks holding them fast.

Magnus manoeuvred himself behind the desk and nodded to Lucius to take a chair while he sat. Leaning back casually, Magnus released a sigh, as if happy to have come to the study, and he leaned back in his chair, legs straight out, hands steepled across his stomach.

"As you can see," Magnus said, indicating the piled papers on his desk with a wave, "the business of the Hands is never ending. There is always something!"

Not knowing why he was here or what he was expected to say, Lucius just smiled as if he understood just how much work Magnus was required to handle. In truth, he had little idea.

"It is the *Allantian Voyager* that you are planning to strike, isn't it?"

"Yes," Lucius said. "One of the dockmasters told Elaine that it was taking on silk from Pontaine. When she heard I was scouting out the docks, she suggested I run the operation."

"And her take?"

"Twenty per cent of the gross."

Magnus pursed his lips. "That could be a lot, considering she is taking none of the risks."

"It is my first job, so I thought it fair," Lucius shrugged. "And if I do well on this haul, she will be all the more ready to let me know when the next valuable cargo comes in. I have to pay my dues first, after all."

"You do," Magnus said, smiling. "You seem to be learning the franchise system well, though I would be concerned that there may not be much left for yourself, after you have shared out the profits among everyone you gather to help you – those silks will need a lot of manpower, and any fence is likely to charge a large commission on such a sizeable haul."

"I thought about that. If I am generous on the first job, recruitment for my second will not be so hard."

"But your next volunteers may become greedy."

"I'll always be up front about payment. Everyone will know where they stand."

"That is well. I think you are beginning to understand, Lucius, that when working alongside those who thieve and swindle for a living, the only guarantee one has is mutual self-interest."

Lucius became aware that Magnus was eyeing him closely, and he shifted under this gaze uncomfortably, becoming acutely aware that the hard wooden chair he had taken was beginning to numb his backside.

"I like you," Magnus said at last. "I have been taken in by nobles who promise the earth in the past, and the less said about my romantic attachments to women, the better. But I know thieves, Lucius. I have grown able to spot, very quickly, those who were born to the life, and those who merely pretend. And I see in you the makings of a great thief."

The praise was completely unexpected. "Well... thank you."

"No need for thanks, Lucius, you got here on your own strengths. All learned from your time in the Anclas Territories, were they?"

"Mostly," Lucius said, evasively, but Magnus seemed to either not notice or not care.

"Caradoc recognises your talent too, though he finds it shameful to admit you saved his life."

"Any one of us would have done the same."

"Maybe. You must remember that, despite us all belonging to the Night Hands, some here really are rogues of the highest order. But you will learn that truth soon enough," Magnus said, then suddenly changed the subject. "What did you make of Loredo and his woman during our summit?"

Lucius paused, marshalling his thoughts. "Very capable and very deadly. That woman, Jewel, in particular gave me the shivers."

"A natural killer. Of all the assassins in Turnitia, she probably commands the highest fees. She is very good at what she does."

"But I don't think they can be trusted."

Magnus raised an eyebrow. "You think, perhaps, I was wrong to call the summit and make the deal?"

"Hardly matters what I think, guildmaster," Lucius said, hoping his use of Magnus' title was respectful enough.

"Of course what you think matters. You are one of the Hands, you have a stake in what we do here, that decision affected you directly," Magnus said, then he gave Lucius a sly look. "Of course, your *opinion* may not always count for much, but I would still hear it."

"The summit was important, as it forced both sides to put their cards on the table. And, if nothing else, it has created at least a couple of days of peace."

"True," Magnus nodded. "Anything else?"

When Lucius frowned in thought, Magnus prompted him.

"Why, for example, would I risk inviting them here, into our own guildhouse?"

"A show of trust, as you said," Lucius began, then a flash of inspiration took him. "And to get both Loredo and his woman close – you wanted to watch them, see how they would take the proposals."

"Very good, Lucius," Magnus said. "Loredo I knew before, but the years can change a man. Jewel, I know only by reputation, and most of the tales told of her are likely exaggerated. Or maybe not. I like to know who I am dealing with. And you are right – they cannot be trusted."

"So, what have we gained?"

"Well, time, as you said. Even a moment of peace is infinitely preferable to the immediate onset of war. There are those, of course, who think a good, bloody war would straighten the city out and set things right, but we cannot guarantee we would be on the winning side, can we? At least, not yet."

Thinking Magnus' words over, Lucius looked up at the guildmaster.

"While I appreciate the trust, why are you telling me this?" he asked.

Magnus sat up straight, abandoning his leisurely posture to clasp his hands together as he leaned over the desk.

"Several reasons," he began. "I meant what I said about liking you. It's an instinct. You are going to do well for us here, Lucius, if you work hard and do not cheat us."

"I wouldn't–" Lucius began, but Magnus waved his objection away.

"It occurs to every thief at some time. A few coins here, a few valuables there, before anything reaches our fences. Just... just be warned that we have our own methods for discovering and tracking down those who embezzle from us. However, the one point of real contention between the Hands and the Guild is the docks and outlying merchant quarter. The Five Markets are what attract citizen and visitor both, but the money all flows from the ships and wagons of the merchants. Not having both the docks and the merchant quarter in the possession of either guild makes lasting peace between us impossible."

"You think they will try moving against us so soon?" Lucius asked, thinking of his own operation about to go into action.

"Probably not," Magnus said. "It is probably just me worrying too much about every little thing the Hands get up to. But promise me this, Lucius. If you get the merest hint that the Guild are getting ready to hit us, the slightest suspicion that everything is not quite right when you make your raid, pull out. Don't risk the lives of the men who volunteer to go with you. They may escape only with their skins that evening rather than the goods they hoped for, but that is good enough if danger threatens. Do you understand?"

"Of course."

"I'm serious, Lucius. Whether it is this week, next month or next year, the Guild will be coming for us. I don't want any of us caught in the firing line when they do."

CHAPTER TEN

Lucius cast a wry glance up at Kerberos as the blue-grey giant leered down upon the docks. He had heard the sphere called Thief's Friend, on account of the twilight it cast during the late hours, creating shadows throughout the city in which a rogue could readily hide. Only rarely did it dip completely below the horizon and so shroud the world in the pitch black of night. He ruefully thought he might have liked such a night, with darkness completely clothing both himself and his allies as they surrounded their target.

The *Allantian Voyager* was berthed just a few dozen yards ahead of him, its three masts rising into the faintly star-speckled sky. With its hull heavily reinforced to withstand the battering it would face on its travels across the churning sea, it was a squat and unlovely vessel, but one eminently suited to the journeys it would face. Typical of Allantian designs, the *Voyager* was the largest ship in the harbour, with others from Vosburg and the Sarcre Islands much smaller by comparison, designed to ride the huge waves they would face rather than plough a course through the maelstrom. Such ships would inevitably be smashed to splinters within a year or two, having encountered one natural disaster too many. It was said the best Allantian ships could last for more than a century of continuous travel.

A small flash of light made Lucius look upwards to the cliffs rising behind him. He nodded to himself, knowing the wagon party was now ready. Having commandeered a massive crane, they now awaited the haul of silk to be loaded onto its platform, which they would then raise and transfer onto the wagon they had acquired. From there, the silk would be taken to one of the Hands' affiliated fences to be sold; job done.

The light flashed again as one of the thieves high above lifted his cloak slightly to reveal the hooded lantern he held close to his body, then dropped it, his signal complete. The first part of their task was done. Now they had to wait for the other thieves to board the *Voyager* and make off with its goods before their turn in the heavy lifting began.

In all, Lucius had managed to raise a score of thieves to join him in his expedition, most signing on at the last minute. Quickly briefing them on the plan, and noticing some of the older thieves suppressing smiles as they watched him draw out positions on the many different maps he had prepared, Lucius had led them to the docks and delegated positions. He was, at least, gratified to see Ambrose with them, a familiar face on his first planned mission.

A few members of the party were simply serving as lookouts, though no serious trouble from the Vos guard was expected. The few men of the wagon party were now ready, but the bulk of his strength was in the harbour itself, stalking the *Voyager*, watching for overly curious crew, and getting ready to engage in the toil of heaving bundles of silk from ship to crane.

Crouched behind a large coil of rope, Lucius raised his hand, the signal that started the next part of the process; the approach to the *Voyager* itself.

As the sign was passed from thief to thief, each within eyesight of another in the gloom, Lucius saw dark shapes detach themselves from the shadows, keeping low and taking advantage of any available cover. A single sentry on the deck of the *Voyager* had already been sighted, and the role of silencing him passed to a veteran of such missions.

Lucius broke cover too, a slight manipulation of arcane energies allowing him to bring some of the darkness of his hiding place with him; just enough to give him a little extra protection from prying eyes, and not too much that would alert his fellow thieves to anything unusual.

The ship grew closer and, as he approached, Lucius only just began to realise just how large it really was. There were entire warehouses in Turnitia that were not as long or broad, and he wondered whether they would easily find the silk they were seeking to rob from its hold.

He saw some thieves gaining access to the ship's deck by the ropes that moored it tightly to the dock, clambering hand-over-hand as they swarmed up. Though they had plenty of skill in the use of ropes, he could see even the best of them were having some trouble, as the ship constantly lurched up and down, the ropes binding it creaking with the strain of holding it in place against the constant, surging waves that flooded past the barriers and into the harbour.

Joining a small group of thieves near the bottom of a ramp that led straight up onto the *Voyager's* deck, he crouched and waited with them, ready to charge forwards at the call of the next signal. He did not have to wait long as a low thump and groan issued from the deck, quickly followed by a quiet whistle; the ship's sentry had been dealt with.

Leading the rush, Lucius sprinted up the ramp, still keeping his body low as the thieves behind him followed suit. His first time on the deck of a ship, Lucius quickly looked around to get his bearings. Seeing the wheelhouse, three masts and prow allowed him to picture the deck plans of the ship in his mind, but the reality was entirely more confusing. It seemed as if nowhere was free of stores, debris and rope; lots and lots of rope. Only having the vaguest idea of why a ship needed so much rigging, or why it so often needed replacing, he trotted over to the space between the centre mast and the one ahead of it, knowing the hatch to the forward hold must lie there.

Several thieves, including Ambrose, were quicker and got there ahead of him, already lifting the massive double hatch to reveal a black maw that descended into the bowels of the ship.

"This is it," one whispered. "I'm going down, there'll be a second hatch down there. Someone look about, there'll be a winch round here somewhere."

Another thief was already rigging a winch and pulley to a metal pole jutting from the main mast, lashing it to a square platform, not unlike those used by the cranes on the cliff. Lucius could see each thief attending to his assigned role, and was pleased with how quickly and efficiently they worked together. He was less happy with the noise being generated, and though they had been near silent as they boarded the *Voyager*, the harder work of preparing to lift bales of silk out of the hold inevitably stole their stealth. Casting an anxious eye around the quieter areas of the deck towards the stern, Lucius could not help but think they were being watched.

Clapping Ambrose on the shoulder to let him know he should continue as planned, Lucius padded softly away as the other thieves started descending into the darkness below the deck. Drawing his sword from his back, he kept his body low and stayed to the shadows as he crept away.

Passing the thick masts, Lucius picked his way stealthily along the deck, nodding briefly to another thief who was coming from the opposite direction.

"All clear," the thief whispered, and Lucius gestured for him to proceed helping with the unloading of silk. With the haul the dockmaster had promised lay on board, they would need all the hands they could muster to make their theft before any of the remaining crew on board were wise to their presence. However, Lucius could not shake the ominous feeling he had and, cursing Magnus for putting doubts into his head in the first place, he approached the poop deck.

Raised above the level of the deck, the poop was accessible by two ladders, one on either side of the ship, and flanking a simple wooden door that Lucius knew gave access to the lower decks and the captain's own quarters. Mounting the first two rungs of a ladder, he poked his head over the lip of the poop, and scanned the area.

The wheel lay before him, lashed tightly as part of the precautions to keep the *Voyager* steady while berthed in the dangerous harbour. Two large siege crossbows were mounted to either side behind large purpose-built shields, perhaps intended to keep the ship safe from the pirates and corsairs Lucius had heard roamed the straits between the peninsula and the Sarcre Islands. He could also just make out a slumped form behind one of the crossbows, the bound and gagged sentry, now oblivious to the presence of the intruders.

Seeing nothing out of the ordinary, Lucius hopped back down to the main deck and crept to the door. He had not wanted to risk exploring the rest of the ship but, while his men were busy with their haul, he reasoned that it was better to be safe than very, very sorry. He tried the handle, resolving himself to simply blocking the exit with a barrel or something similar if it were locked, in order to stop any attempt by the crew to storm the main deck, and was faintly surprised to find the door swung easily open. The interior was pitch black and he cast a quick look over his shoulder, suddenly apprehensive. He could see the shadowy shapes of thieves at work at the far end of the ship in the half-light of Kerberos and, seeing nothing more amiss, steeled himself to take a look inside.

Stretching a hand outwards, Lucius summoned a small flame, its purple light flickering crazily. Inside, a small corridor extended ahead. At its end was a stout door lined with metal bands – leading to the captain's quarters, Lucius presumed. To his left was another closed door and to his right, a small set of stairs descended into darkness.

Creeping forward as quietly as he could, Lucius ducked his head down the stairs briefly. He had no desire to pace his way through sleeping crew. Just wanting to ensure no one was awake, he peered into the gloom and was greeted with a rank smell that made him retch until he buried his face into his cloak. He had never smelled anything like it; the stench of a body left in the sun too long, mixed with the pungent aroma of salt and dead fish. It was not pleasant like the scent of a fresh catch being unloaded dockside from a fisherman's boat, but something altogether more sickening. Shaking his head at the hygiene of Allantian sailors, Lucius turned away to approach the door to the captain's quarters.

There was no sound of movement behind the door and for that, he was grateful. Not quite knowing what to do, Lucius eventually settled on snuffing out his flame to call upon a reflection of the same thread of power. Reaching towards the lock, he felt a chill sweep through him as the magic surged in his body. His hand becoming the focus, he concentrated until a stream of cold air blasted forward to envelop the lock's mechanism, softly whistling as ice began to form.

Hoping that would be sufficient to at least delay the captain should he awake to the noise of the thieves working at the far end of the ship, Lucius started to retrace his steps.

He froze as he heard a strangled cry ahead. Though the door to the deck was open before him, he could not see any of the other thieves, and he at first thought they were either hidden by the masts or else working in the hold. That did not make any sense though, for the unloading of silk should have begun by now. A heavy thump seemed to resonate through the ship, as if something very large had been dropped, and this was followed by a shout of warning.

Startled now, and worried by what might have stirred the thieves into breaking their silence, Lucius started to run to the main deck, but was halted by the sound of movement from the stairs leading to the lower deck. The crew of the ship would have been awoken by the thieves on board, and Lucius crouched, sword drawn, ready to skewer whoever came up the stairs first.

Seeing a shadow move, the stench he had smelled before suddenly strengthened and he realised someone was approaching. He felt the comfort of the threads of magic spin in his mind's eye, ready to be unleashed if his sword alone proved insufficient. Stepping forward, blade ready, Lucius prepared to thrust his weapon into the chest of whoever emerged and then sprint out to see what danger the rest of his team faced.

A loud cry of fear and alarm rang out, resounding in the confined space. Dimly, Lucius realised it was he that had screamed. The figure before him climbed up the stairs inexorably, but he was rooted to the spot, unable to move as he watched the horror approach.

Two shiny, black eyes – each the size of his fist – looked back at him unblinking. They were mounted in a bulbous, scaly head, its wide maw filled with rows of razor-sharp teeth. It was naked, but its skin was completely cloaked in the same foul green scales that covered its head. Spines rose from the top of its skull and continued down its back, and they flattened menacingly as it spoke a language he did not recognise, a base slurping and lapping sound that no human could imitate.

Slime covered its hideous body but it was not until it raised a hand, its nails stretching out into wicked inch-long webbed claws, that Lucius was finally galvanised into action, his instinct for survival overriding his conscious mind.

Screaming again, he flailed out with his sword, but it was swatted away with a metallic chink by one of the claws. Reeling backwards from the blow, he knew the creature was immensely strong, and that he was about to die, torn apart by those talons, and then savaged and consumed by those fangs.

Reaching a hand up in defence, his fear and anger mingled, and he was distantly aware of two threads of power smashing together to form one continuous bolt of energy that whipped through his body violently. Crying out in pain now, Lucius sought to unleash the magic building up inside before it burned him to a cinder and he focussed it forward, straight into the creature.

Lightning erupted from his hand and struck the creature in the centre of its chest with a massive impact, sending it flying back down the stairs with an inhuman wail. Standing, Lucius continued to direct the flow of magic, sending bolts of white-hot light down into the lower deck where they smashed into the corpse of the creature, incinerating it, before blasting through the floor into the darkest regions of the ship. The flickering light illuminated the lower deck, and he saw more of the creatures caught in the explosion, shielding their large dark eyes from the glare as they pulled themselves in through open portholes in the ship's hull.

Shouting out obscenities, Lucius directed the pulsing magical energy to wherever he saw movement, striking down one monster after another, their scales sizzling in the blinding heat. Without warning, the magic waned and he felt the two threads separate. The lightning stopped and he staggered back, suddenly weary, before collapsing to the floor.

Breathing heavily from the exertion, Lucius clumsily raised his sword to ward off a sudden rush of the creatures up the stairs, but none came. He had either destroyed them all or at least scared them off, and he sobbed for a moment, overcome by the horror of what he had faced and the sheer exhaustion of focussing so much magic at once.

More cries from the main deck cleared his fogged mind, and he clambered back on his feet. He rushed to the door shakily, and braced himself on its frame as he looked out.

The creatures covered the deck, loping along with a strange gait that seemed unsuited for dry land. Clambering over the sides of the ship, their claws digging into the wood to give purchase, dozens more were rushing away from him – and towards the thieves.

He saw men battling them, but they were completely overwhelmed by the strength and numbers of the horrors. One thief, armed with two knives, circled one of the creatures to find an opening, but – with frightening speed – it whirled round and he screamed as its claws raked his face and tore out his eyes. The creature's mouth closed upon his skull, and Lucius heard the wet crack as his head was torn apart.

Elsewhere arms were torn from sockets and bodies were hurled in great arcs through the twilight air into the sea, where their desperate cries were quickly silenced. One thief had tried to escape the carnage by climbing the mainmast, but he was quickly overtaken by two of the creatures who, using their claws, were able to scramble up the smooth wood with ease. He was cast back down to the deck, his stomach torn open with one vicious swipe.

Panicked, Lucius stalled for a moment, realising the creatures were unaware of his presence as they rejoiced in the slaughter. He saw Ambrose bravely face one creature that had its claws deep in the chest of a younger thief, and was spurred into action.

Trying to summon a wave of fire that would sweep the deck clear of those creatures closest to him, Lucius was alarmed to find the magic stutter and disappear, his concentration too muddied with fear to manipulate the threads. Desperate now, Lucius ran down the length of the ship, closing in on the nearest creature. It was alerted to his presence an instant before he struck, and began to turn just as he thrust his sword forward. The movement was sufficient to turn the blade, its edge skidding across the scales on its back. Keeping his momentum going, Lucius crashed bodily into the creature, knocking it off its feet.

Well aware of the teeth and claws that were eagerly reaching for his flesh, Lucius rolled off the beast then brought the point of his sword down into its chest. Throwing his full weight onto the weapon, he was amazed at the resistance the creature's scales gave before the blade pierced them and slid into its body.

Wailing, the creature slobbered as it died, but as Lucius stared into its large black eyes, he saw no change, no glazing of its stare as its body stopped twitching. Its eyes remained as fixed in death as they had in life.

Jumping back to his feet, he saw his attack had not gone unnoticed. Some embattled thieves cried out for help, while three of the creatures turned to avenge their fallen comrade.

"Lucius, there are too many of them!" It was Ambrose's voice that reached him, from somewhere near the prow.

He knew he could not save them all. Wherever these things had come from, they were strong, fast and deadly, and thieves were no match for them.

"Run!" he shouted. "Save yourselves!"

He saw Ambrose rally a few thieves and they began fighting as a unit, attempting to cut their way to the ramp; after having seen the fate of some of their friends, no man wanted to risk jumping into the sea.

Lucius was closer to the ramp, but his way was blocked by three of the creatures and as they loped towards him he was forced to back away. A bright burst of light illuminated the deck for a brief second, and the nearest creatures to the blast wailed as they turned away from the glare, shaking their heads in pain. Someone had used flash powder, and Lucius cursed himself for not taking some himself from the armoury. The distraction was enough to give the thieves room to manoeuvre, but the creatures were quick to return to the fight, dragging down the thief that had thrown the powder, as well as the man who rushed into the melee in an attempt to save him. Their strangled death cries made Lucius shudder as he reached down to draw a dagger from his boot.

Taking quick aim as the creatures approached, he threw the dagger at the leftmost of the three, and grinned as the blade sank deep into its eye, the size of the black orb making it an east target. It wailed, its inhuman voice cutting into the nerves of every man on board as it dropped to the deck and thrashed in pain, trying to remove the blade.

Seeing the opening, Lucius rushed the two remaining creatures, and they opened their arms wide, claws ready to tear him apart. He feinted to the right, and the creatures followed his movement, crouching as they prepared to leap and drag him down, but as they began to move, he quickly jinked left and leapt onto the railings lining the side of the ship.

He saw more shapes on the dockside moving in the characteristic gait of the creatures, and he inwardly groaned as he realised they would have to fight their way clear of the entire harbour, not just the ship. The railings were smooth but not wet, and Lucius hopped past the creatures on the balls of his feet before lightly dropping down behind them. He raised his sword high above his head before bringing it down on the skull of the nearest creature with all his strength. It staggered under the blow and a deep gash streamed dark blood as it sank to the deck.

The remaining creature hissed and burbled something in its mongrel language as it spun round, a claw whipping through the air. Lucius was forced to take a step back and he felt the creature's talon cut through his tunic as it sliced across his mail beneath. The links in his armour buckled under the attack, but held.

Dropping low Lucius threw out a booted foot, which crashed into its knee. This caused the creature to spit something unintelligible at him, the sound of a jellyfish being thrown against a rock, and he fancied it was a curse of some kind. However, whereas his boot would have shattered the knee of a man, it merely seemed to slow the creature down slightly. Seeing it recover, Lucius jumped to his feet and ran.

Men lay strewn across the deck, a few moaning in pain as they died from hideous wounds, but most were still in death. Ambrose and his cohorts had managed to fight their way clear to the ramp and were starting to run down it at full speed, though they were leaving many of their original number behind.

Lucius ran to join them, the creature behind in hot pursuit, but another reared up before him, just yards away from the ramp. The last thief of Ambrose's group turned as he jumped on to the ramp, and threw something at the creature's feet. Knowing what was coming next, Lucius closed his eyes as he ran and heard the muffled crump of flash powder igniting. Opening his eyes again, he saw the creature clasping its claws over its face, writhing in pain.

The thief grinned at Lucius and held out a hand for him. Lucius smiled back before gasping in horror as another creature sailed through the air, the result of a huge leap. He watched, feeling the creature was moving with agonising slowness, yet he could do nothing to alter its course. It ploughed into the back of the grinning thief, knocking him off the ramp and carrying him down to the hard stone of the dock where they landed heavily.

Lucius screamed in protest and rushed down the ramp, all too aware of the creatures swarming behind him. Something whipped through the air past his head as he ran and he glanced quickly over his shoulder to see an arrow jutting out the chest of the beast nearest him. It had stopped running, and seemed to be looking curiously at the shaft which jutted from its body.

Lucius leapt from the ramp, planting both feet on the back of the skull of one of the monsters, before they both sprawled onto the dock. As he stood, he saw that the creature was groggy from the attack, stumbling on all fours as it tried to pick itself up. Lucius sank his blade into its neck. The creature shuddered for a moment and was still.

Another shout arrested his attention and Lucius saw Ambrose waving to him. Sprinting away from the ship, he saw that the *Voyager* was swarming with the monsters. Others on the docks were closing in on either side, pursuing Ambrose and his remaining men. They caught one, and the man was dragged down, screaming as he thrashed about with his club. The weapon just bounced off the scales of the creature, and his cries turned to a burbled moan as it tore his throat out.

Running, Lucius passed the creatures as they began to feast on the man's body. He launched a kick at one, sending it sprawling, but carried on sprinting, knowing he could do no more for his comrade.

"To the crane!" Lucius shouted to Ambrose and the thieves ahead, and they turned as one, glad to have an order to follow, a direction to head in amongst all the chaos. Lucius looked behind once more and saw that, while the creatures were still following, they seemed to be moving slower than they had earlier. Thanking God for small mercies, he began to hope that the nightmare would soon be over.

As Lucius raced along the docks to the cliff face, he spied the waiting platform. Ambrose waved him over, and he increased his speed, ignoring his complaining muscles. A hand clapped him on the shoulder as he reached the group.

"You made it!" someone said.

Lucius looked around and saw only two other men stood with Ambrose, who was now frantically pulling on the ropes, the signal to tell the thieves working the crane to start raising the platform.

"This is all?" Lucius asked, and was answered only by mute nods.

"Look!" cried one of the thieves, pointing out into the darkness of the docks.

The creatures had massed, and were approaching the platform, fanning out to surround the thieves.

"In the name of all that's holy, come on!" Ambrose screamed, lifting himself off his feet in the effort of jerking the rope, desperately hoping to get the attention of the wagon team above.

The creatures started to move closer, the ring drawing tighter around the men. One of the thieves unlimbered a bow and sent an arrow into the mass, but aside from drawing a hiss out of the creature it struck, it had little effect. He notched another arrow and sent it flying.

"Have they got to the men on top of the cliff too?" someone asked.

Lucius didn't see how but, seeing no movement from the crane, he jumped off the platform, sword drawn. He did not know what he was going to do, only that he hoped he could buy enough time for them to start the ascent.

One creature broke from the pack and swiped at Lucius with its claws. He parried the blow, and took a step back to avoid a second. He heard movement behind him and another creature slobbered at his back. A low whistle punctuated the air and he heard a dull thud as an arrow hit home.

Hearing an angry wail and hoping the creature behind had been taken out of the fight, Lucius stepped to one side, looking to create an opening. The creature in front followed his movements and, as it raised a claw to strike at him again, Lucius swung his sword in a wide arc, catching the creature's arm.

He felt the sword bite deep, and wondered if the creature's scales were not as thick on some parts of its body as others. It shrieked in pain, and scrambled backwards, cradling its injured arm, which was hanging at an odd angle, bone sheared by the impact of Lucius' sword.

Apparently not liking the way the combat was going, the massed creatures hissed, the sound undulating eerily, sending a shiver down Lucius' back. He held his sword out in front of him as they began to advance, their movements a little halted and slow. He made a couple of feints towards the closest creatures, hoping to force them to draw back, wishing he could scare them into at least re-considering their actions. They were relentless, however, and ignored the flashes of his sword. It was not as if he were able to stop them all.

He heard a creaking behind him, and knew the strain had been taken on the ropes of the platform.

"Lucius, come on!" Ambrose cried, but he needed no prompting. The platform was beginning to rise with agonising slowness and Lucius hurled himself up onto its wooden surface. Hands steadied him as he turned round to look down at the creatures.

Seeing their quarry beginning to escape, they hissed in frustration and some shambled forward. Lucius saw their movements were becoming more exaggerated, slow and awkward. Even so, they did not have much ground to cover and they crashed into the platform, causing it to swing alarmingly. Ambrose was thrown to one side and he clutched wildly at the rope to stop himself from toppling into the snarling mass below. Claws whipped over the edges of the platform as it continued to rise above their heads. Lucius carefully grabbed a rope to steady himself before moving to the edge and stamping down hard into a scaly face.

The scrabbling sound of claws gouging chunks from the underside of the platform caused one thief to moan in terror. He screamed as one of the creatures launched itself from below to grab onto the side of the platform, beginning to pull itself on board. Its claws dug deep into the wood, giving it all the leverage it needed. Lucius kicked out again as they all lurched crazily, but the creature ignored the blow, intent on its prey.

It reached out and dug a claw into the boot of one of the thieves. The man cried out in pain as the claw drove through leather and bone, pinning him to the wood. Another thief tried to help him but lost his grip on the rope and fell into the dark, ferocious mass now twenty yards below, the sounds of flesh being ripped apart soon cutting off his cries.

Curling an arm around the rope as he tried to gain his footing on the tilting platform, Lucius hacked down with his sword at the arm of the monster, trying to sever its hand to free the thief, but he could not gain enough purchase to put any real strength into the blow. Blood seeped from the wounds he had caused, but the creature just hissed malevolently.

"Hold on!" Lucius shouted, and the thieves gripped the ropes they were holding more firmly when they saw what he intended to do.

Strapping his sword to his back, he reached into a boot to draw his last dagger. Frantically sawing at the rope he was holding, Lucius steeled himself, closing his other hand around it in a death grip. He knew that if he were to let go, he would fall into the claws and fangs of the creatures below. The threads of the rope sprang open, one by one, until with a final lurch it broke.

Men screamed as one side of the platform gave way completely, leaving them dangling in the air by the ropes they clung to. The creature's grasp was wrenched away by the sudden movement, and the man it had pinned shrieked as the claw was ripped out with brutal force.

Lucius caught a glimpse of the creature as it fell, its shining black eyes reflecting what little light there was, before they disappeared into the churning swarm of the horde below. The crane continued to raise the tattered remains of the platform, leaving the three remaining men to look at one another with the wild eyes of those who have confronted their worst demons.

"What were those things?" Ambrose asked.

No one had an answer for him.

CHAPTER ELEVEN

HUNCHED OVER THE long table in the council chamber, Lucius flicked his gaze over to Ambrose, who sat straight, arms wrapped around himself as he shuddered. The veteran thief looked shaken to his core, and Lucius could not blame him, for the events of the evening weighed heavily on his mind.

It had been his operation, *his* plan. The thieves who had volunteered knew there were risks involved but that did not excuse what had happened. His big ideas had cost thirteen men their lives, unless by some miracle, a few had managed to evade those hideous creatures and were, even now, making their way back to the guildhouse. Lucius now had to explain himself to Magnus and tell him exactly why his operation had gone so tragically wrong. In part, he resented the deaths. Up to now, Lucius had never been responsible for anyone, and this was an excellent illustration as to why he had avoided it so long. He wondered how the Hands had managed to sucker him in, made him feel part of their guild and accept the accountability he now faced. At the same time, he knew it was a childish regret, that the lives of good men – thieves though they might be – was an order of magnitude above his own petty concerns. He had no idea what he would say to Magnus. He still did not understand what had happened.

Of the three who had survived boarding the ship, Lucius was to answer for the tragedy, as would Ambrose, being the only senior thief to emerge unscathed from the *Voyager*. The only other thief to make it out alive, Sandtrist, had been excused on account of his injuries; Lucius had already heard that he was likely to lose his foot, and what use would the Hands have for a one-footed thief? In his own way, Sandtrist had been lost that evening as well.

Footsteps sounded from outside the room, and Lucius braced himself for the confrontation, though he still had little idea of what he would say. Ambrose seemed not to have noticed the sound, and he did not look up when Magnus entered and stood, watching the two thieves.

Since he had known the guildmaster, Lucius had thought him wise, extremely competent and utterly benevolent to those in his charge. But as he looked at the man's face, he could see a terrible hardness in his eyes, an iron will he had always suspected must lie within Magnus, but had never seen. The guildmaster smouldered with barely contained rage, and Lucius swallowed, awaiting the onslaught.

"Would you like to tell me," Magnus said, starting quietly but gradually allowing his anger to take control until he shouted the last words, "just why thirteen of my thieves are *dead*?"

"Ambush–" Lucius began, but his voice was too quiet.

Striding over to the table, Magnus hammered a fist down, the sudden violent sound jerking Lucius back. It even seemed to rouse Ambrose.

"What?" Magnus said in a deafening tone that promised quick punishment to anyone who would chance a wrong answer.

Lucius cleared his throat and started again. "We were ambushed, Magnus, there was no warning, I–"

Magnus' fist crashed down on the table again. "What happened to your plans? Where were the sentries? Why did no one see them approach? Why are my men dead, Lucius?"

"They weren't human, Magnus."

"Who weren't? What are you talking about?"

"They just swarmed all over the ship while we were unloading. I swear to you, we scouted the area, silenced the sentry, and only then started the haul. But they were on us in seconds, too many of them. They started killing..." Lucius broke off at that, seeing again in his mind's eye the terrible carnage on the deck of the ship.

"So who was it?" Magnus demanded.

"I... I think they came from the sea."

Magnus looked utterly confused. "As an excuse, this is a poor one, Lucius," he said dangerously.

"He's telling the truth," Ambrose said, and they both looked at him in surprise. "On my mother's grave, Magnus, he's telling the truth."

Magnus sighed and, drawing out a seat, sat down with them.

"You better tell me what happened, from start to finish. Leave nothing out," he said.

So Lucius explained, with Ambrose adding comments where he could. He told Magnus how he had begun preparations for the operation, using the Hand's resources to learn about the ship and its cargo. He outlined the different teams involved, who was part of each, and what their expected roles were. He told how they had boarded the ship, located the silk, and then started offloading it.

Then he began telling Magnus of the appearance of the first creature, describing how it looked, its strength and deadly, murderous intent. Intentionally leaving out the use of his magical talents, he went on to tell of the slaughter that had followed, of the sheer number of the creatures that had boarded the ship after them, and how men had died. Their desperate escape from the *Voyager* followed, along with the pursuit across the docks and the final, terrifying assault on the platform as they fled the scene. When he finished, Lucius was shaking, the retelling of the events forcing him to relive them once more.

Magnus' anger had subsided, but he shook his head in disbelief.

"I have never heard of such things," he said simply.

"On my *mother's* grave, Magnus," Ambrose said again, and the seriousness of his expression seemed to give Magnus pause.

"You think they came from the sea?" he asked.

Lucius shrugged helplessly. "They seemed... adapted to it," he said, remembering the foul sea stench, the webbed claws and scaled skin. "And they moved slower once they had been out of the water for a few minutes."

"I noticed that," Ambrose said.

"Well, do you have any idea why they were there?" Magnus asked. "Who sent them?"

They both shook their heads.

"I would dearly like to blame the Guild for this," Lucius said. "But I saw nothing to suggest their involvement."

"Then there are three possibilities that come to mind," Magnus said. "First, the Guild has new allies. Second, we have inadvertently wandered into some dispute between the Allantians and these... sea demons."

"And third?" Lucius prompted.

"Third, there is a new power in the city." He raised a hand in a helpless gesture. "But none of those seem very likely to me. What would sea demons want with a city on land? Why have we heard nothing about them before? None of this makes sense."

He prompted Lucius to retell the story again, searching for any information that had been missed the first time, anything that could give him a clue as to what his thieves had faced that night. No matter how many times he quizzed Lucius over particular points, however, they seemed no closer to the truth. Magnus was about to ask Lucius to describe the attack on the *Voyager* again, when shouts and excited cries reached them from the open door. When someone shouted for the guildmaster, panic evident in his voice, they all started.

Leading the way, Magnus rushed from the meeting room and vaulted down the stairs, Lucius and Ambrose in tow, where another thief directed him to one of the rooms used as sleeping quarters. Trotting behind Magnus, Lucius entered the room and gasped.

Tiny though the room was a dozen thieves were gathered in a tightly packed mass that they had to push their way through, some only relinquishing their place when they saw it was Magnus who had entered. Lying on the bed, its sheets already soaked through with his blood, was Caradoc. Helmut, a thief from Vosburg who was versed in some of the arts of healing, was tending to him, fussing over a crossbow bolt that jutted from the lieutenant's shoulder. Writhing in pain, Caradoc looked up at Magnus as he entered.

"Caught me on Ring Street," he gasped. "Tried to kill me."

"Would have done too, but for another three inches to the left," Helmut muttered to no one in particular.

"Who?" Magnus said, leaning over the bed to catch Caradoc's words.

"Didn't see," he said. "Too dark. But... Guild. Has to be... the Guild. They've broken the truce."

Magnus frowned at that, then laid a hand on Helmut's shoulder. "Can you help him?"

The Vos man looked at his patient as he thought. "We need to remove that bolt, and that won't be pleasant. But if he makes it through this evening, I think he will be just fine. So long as no poison was used, of course."

"We'll take care of it," Magnus said quietly to Caradoc. "We'll find who did this."

"Guild..." Caradoc started to say again, but Magnus hushed him.

"We'll find them," he promised again.

As Magnus left the small, overcrowded room, he pulled Lucius to one side.

"You think it was the Guild?" Lucius asked when they were out of earshot of the others.

"What I am thinking is whether there is a connection between the attack on Caradoc and what happened with you down at the docks." Magnus said, rubbing his chin in thought. "The timing is... too much of a coincidence."

"But if we assume that, then we have to also assume the Guild have new allies in these creatures."

"And that, Lucius, is what really worries me. It is just too incredible to believe. Damn it! We need answers, we cannot carry on operating blind like this. We need to reach out to our contacts outside of the Hands. I have a few ideas on who we can talk to, but it will take time to set things up. You are Turnitia born and bred – do you have anyone on the outside who can help us?"

The image of Adrianna and Forbeck flashed through his mind.

"There may be someone," Lucius said. "I'll see what I can find out."

STANDING IN THE centre of the warehouse that had been used for his training, Lucius eyed the scorch marks on the floor ruefully, the evidence of another session that had ended in failure. He had not been able to practice the steering of the flame globes as much as Forbeck had wished for, and he had been chided for it. The Master of Shadows had insisted he try the exercise himself in his own time, but with the events within the Hands of late, that had not been possible.

A tickling at the back of his mind signalled a presence behind him and he whirled round to see Adrianna stalking out of the shadows, her pace measured and confident.

"Well, your training is having at least some effect, I see," she said. "You can now sense the presence of another Shadowmage within, oh, at least twenty yards."

"At least you came."

"It is not often I receive a summons, least of all from you. I was mildly curious."

"I'm glad to see it worked," he said. Lucius had been curious as to Forbeck's ability to sound an alarm in his mind from half-way across the city, and had tried to do the same for Adrianna, concentrating on her disdainful face and willing her to him through the threads of power.

"It was faint, but I sensed it. You need improvement."

Her remark was no surprise to Lucius, for he never expected an easy compliment from her.

"As it happens, I wanted to see you as well," she continued.

"Oh?"

"I have a contract, one that may bring us into conflict. By the terms of the Shadowmage charter, I must inform you of this and find a resolution between us."

He rolled his eyes. "Which, I presume, is Shadowmage language for 'stay out of my way'?"

"As you say." She shrugged.

Sighing, Lucius shook his head, then a thought struck him.

"You've been contracted by the Guild of Coin and Enterprise, haven't you?"

"My employers are making some aggressive moves in the city, and you are within their chief target. I recommend you leave the Night Hands and find a more stable contract. Forbeck can help you out there. I might be able to put a word in with my current employers too, if necessary."

"It's not going to be that easy, Aidy," Lucius said, a smile beginning to flicker on his lips. "Your current employers are scum, and I will do everything I can to bring them down."

"I cannot force you to do one thing or another," Adrianna said. "But I would advise you to remember the oath you took."

"I'm not going to attack you, Aidy."

"It is likely that our current employers will force the issue, one way or another."

Adrianna's inhuman attitude was beginning to grate on his nerves once again, and he marvelled at how little time was needed in her presence before anger flared. He briefly wondered whether he was alone in his constant head-butting with her, or if it was common in everyone she met.

"It was the Guild who drew first blood, Aidy," he said, letting himself ride the wave of anger she had sparked. "There was a truce between us, the city had been carved up – there was an agreement."

She shook her head carelessly. "That is not my concern. The accord has been broken, and my specific role is to ensure my employer is victorious in the struggle ahead."

"And your contract is all you care about? There are good men within the Hands, Aidy, they don't deserve this. The Guild is full of cold-blooded killers."

"While the thieves of the Hands are entirely honourable? Don't kid yourself."

"The Hands are not the ones allying themselves to devils from the sea."

That checked her, Lucius saw, and her scorn was replaced by a puzzled expression.

"What do you mean?"

"You're telling me you weren't there at the docks? Yesterday evening?"

Adrianna frowned, and Lucius was at least gratified to see her stumble when someone was accusing her for a change.

"Lucius, I swear to you, I have not been directly involved in any of the Guild's operations around the docks. I know they want to take that territory away from the Hands, and I know they planned an ambush there last night, but I had nothing to do with it. I am contracted for specific... duties, no more."

"It was my operation they ambushed."

She looked him up and down briefly. "You seem to have survived."

"Oh, I did, but many of the men I took with me didn't. Do you have any idea who the Guild is dealing with these days? I'm telling you, they have an alliance with something truly evil."

"I'm sure you are exaggerating."

"Really?" he said, moving onto the attack. "Scales, bulging eyes, webbed claws. Hordes of them, Aidy, coming from the sea to tear us apart – and I mean, *tear* us apart. They killed most of us within minutes, and damn well nearly got me."

Her next words were slow in coming, as she chose them carefully. "Assuming you are not making this up, I have no idea what you are talking about – truly. That the Guild was planning to disrupt the operations of the Hands on the docks as a prelude to taking them over is all I am aware of. I... I can talk to Master Forbeck, perhaps he knows what you are speaking of."

"Well, that's something," Lucius muttered.

"But if you are right, Lucius, you need to be careful. The Guild is not messing around this time, they want the Hands gone. Smashed, broken, the members either dead, fleeing from the city, or on their side. And they can do it. They have the power and the determination. That is not something you want to be caught in the middle of."

He suppressed a smile. "Well, at least you can spare a thought for me."

Adrianna closed the distance between them in a single long stride and jabbed a finger, painfully, into his chest.

"What I want, Lucius, is for you to go," she said adamantly. "To leave this city, to disappear. What I want to avoid is breaking my oath to the Shadowmages. I will be on the front line in this fight, and woe betide anyone who stands between me and the completion of the contract."

Spinning on a heel, she stalked away, their meeting clearly at an end.

"Well, just ask yourself this, Aidy," Lucius shouted at her retreating back. "If the Guild are capable enough to hire a Shadowmage when most people haven't even heard of us, who or what else have they employed, eh? Do you even know what you are fighting for? Just which one of us is the mercenary here?"

His voice still echoing through the empty warehouse, Lucius cursed the shadows into which Adrianna had disappeared. He had known he would not find a friend in her stern glare, but had hoped to discover at least an ally.

CHAPTER TWELVE

THERE WERE NO smiles among the Council or the senior thieves surrounding the table in the meeting room. Too many deaths had taken place within the Night Hands, and more than a few were thinking about Caradoc. After all, if someone could strike at the lieutenant of the Hands, how safe were the rest of them when they left the guildhouse?

Various theories had been put forward by Council members as to what was happening and who was responsible, but while few doubted the Guild's involvement, Magnus kept demanding proof. With none of the Council able to provide anything more than rumour, he turned to Lucius.

Lucius was acutely aware that all eyes in the room were now focussed on him, and that not all were waiting for his explanation. He was still, officially, a low-ranking thief within the Hands, and though he had not yet been made a senior, many had taken note of Magnus' obvious favouritism toward him. It was breeding jealousy, he knew, and Lucius was distinctly conscious of being part of an organisation whose members, while overtly supporting one another, were just as likely to settle a difference or imagined slight with a knife in the back.

He cleared his throat as he marshalled his thoughts.

"The Council is correct – the truce has been broken," Lucius said to them all. He hoped that by affirming the Council's thoughts, he might find a friend amongst them or, at least, make it look as though he were paying his proper respects and not trying to subvert anyone's position. It was a small gesture, but he knew that when the danger to the Hands was over, differences would be settled one way or another.

"Our operation on the docks was disrupted at the Guild's instigation," he continued. "And they orchestrated the attack on Caradoc, though I have no information on who exactly was responsible."

"So it could just be a few troublemakers in the Guild?" asked Nate.

"It hardly matters," said Elaine, a tall middle-aged woman who controlled the Hands' concerns around the docks. It had been she who had provided Lucius with information on the *Allantian Voyager* from her paid contacts among the dockmasters. "Whether it is just a few or the whole Guild, we are still under attack and we must defend ourselves."

This raised some murmurs of assent from the table.

"Where did you get this information, Lucius?" asked Nate.

Lucius hesitated. "I cannot say," he said and inwardly winced as a collective look of contempt swept the table, but it was halted by Magnus' raised hand.

"He does not need to say. Lucius, for now, has my trust," he said. *That* would create a few enemies, Lucius thought.

"Could he be mistaken?" Elaine asked. "There is always the possibility of another player coming into the city, and starting a war between the existing powers is a good way of getting a foothold. Divide and conquer."

"We use the information we have," Magnus said. "I won't have us jumping at shadows."

"Could it be the work of an insider?" asked a tanned man whose face looked more like that of a weather-beaten sailor than a thief. "After all, it was you, Elaine, who provided the lead for Lucius' disastrous operation at the docks."

"You dare accuse me!" Elaine spat.

A hand slapped the table, bringing all attention to Magnus. "I will not have us fighting each other!" he said, eyes flashing dangerously, challenging anyone to make another charge of treason. For a few seconds, the Council was quiet.

"Then we must hit back," Nate said. "And hit back hard. We cannot just roll over and let them take our operations from us. If they tried to take out Caradoc, Magnus, they are deadly serious. Striking at a lieutenant is unheard of! Who will be next? One of us? You?"

"There will be blood in the streets," someone muttered.

The Council broke down into bickering parties, some wanting to wipe out the Guild in a single night of violence, others supporting the idea of another parley in an attempt to discern the Guild's true intentions.

Clearing his throat, Magnus brought the arguments to a halt. "Reluctant as I am to admit it, Nate has the truth of it. Right now, we are just waiting for another arrow from the dark to strike one of us down, and who knows what our foot soldiers will face on the streets as they go about their work. We *do* need to demonstrate that we will not roll over. More than that, we must show the Guild that we can strike them where it hurts the most."

"We go for Jewel?" Nate asked, a little doubtfully, and Lucius understood his hesitation. He was not sure which of the Hands would be capable of accomplishing that goal.

"We go for the merchants' quarter," Elaine said flatly. "Disrupt their protection rackets, squeeze their main source of revenue. Starve them of gold."

Magnus nodded in appreciation. "Your strategy does you credit, Elaine," he said. "That is how we start. If they are trying to take the docks from us, we will flood the merchants' quarter with our own men, making it impossible for them to operate."

"If I may?" Lucius asked. Feeling a little foolish, he ploughed on. "If we go in mob-handed, someone, perhaps a great many, will die. It will be the start of an all-out war."

"Well, that is what we are discussing here," Nate said, a little contemptuous.

"Let him speak," Magnus said, raising a hand.

"We can be smarter than that," Lucius said. "We rough up their collectors – giving our men strict instructions to spill no blood – we fire a few warehouses, maybe plunder a few. Turn the merchants against the Guild by showing they cannot be protected, and make it impossible for the Guild men to fulfil their obligations. Then we pull out, quickly and quietly, and do the same thing the next day."

The Council was silent as they digested this. It was Nate who spoke first.

"Will it make us look weak, a half-cooked response to the start of a war?"

Magnus rubbed his chin in thought. "It *is* appealing. We have a chance to make the Guild back down, without doing anything irreversible. A chance to avoid all-out war."

"And we can always turn up the heat later, if it does not seem to work," Elaine said, adding her support to the idea.

"Right, we give it a try then," Magnus said, nodding. "We send six teams in, men we can trust not to let their passions get the better of them. Lucius, you will head one of the teams, seeing as this was your idea. You get to share the risks."

Lucius bowed his head once to show his acceptance. He knew this was a chance to shine. He just hoped they did not meet anything unexpected, for a second disaster that cost the lives of thieves might well put him on the hit list of their friends.

SQUEEZING THROUGH THE stacks of large wooden crates marked with a Vos brand proclaiming they were filled with Malmkrug liquor, Lucius nodded at Lihou, who was laying a trail of oil on the warehouse floor. The young thief, like him, had recently been elevated from the ranks of the pickpockets, and he had the unnerving feeling the lad looked up to him.

The warehouse belonged to one Dietrich Schon, a merchant known to have extensive business interests in Turnitia and who was a fully paid up member for protection from the Guild. This evening, Lucius intended to show him that the gold handed over for a quiet life of business and profit was only so much waste.

As they made their way back to the warehouse's loading bay, Lucius and Lihou were joined by other members of their small team – Ashmore, Teton, and Judi – all trailing their own line of oil from other stacks. Looking up at the wooden pillars, supports and rafters of the building, Lucius could not help smiling. Most of the warehouses in the merchant quarter were new constructions, many of the originals having been destroyed by Vos when the army had entered the city as part of its reign of terror. These new buildings were designed to be large, cheap and quick to construct, so the Vos merchants who had all but paid for the invasion could start business as soon as Turnitia was pacified. This meant they had been built entirely of wood – this fire was going to be huge.

The team continued to pour oil from their leather flasks, joining their lines just outside the wide door that led to a street lined with other warehouses. *Phase one of the plan complete*, thought Lucius. Now he just had to wait.

Across the merchant quarter other Night Hands were at work in their teams. At least one other was firing warehouses, though no glow on the skyline had yet made itself visible. Others were paying personal visits to merchants staying in wayhouses or taverns, encouraging them to do business elsewhere or otherwise be forced to pay protection money to the Hands. Another team armed with clubs and saps was actively hunting down collectors from the Guild, intending to convince them they were working in dangerous territory.

Lucius had thought he could kill two birds with one stone, and so he and his team waited until their final member, Banff, appeared, with three Guild collectors in tow. Banff had been brought up from the pickpockets at the same time as Lihou, and Lucius had taken advantage of this, gambling that no one in the Guild would recognise him as a Hand. It had clearly worked.

The Guild collectors were clearly taken aback when they realised they were outnumbered, but bravado carried their leader forward.

"This is private property," he said, eyeing them warily. "Be off with you!"

"This property is under our care now," Lucius said, adopting a polite tone to mock the collectors. "We have a message for you to take back to your masters in the Guild. The first part is this; your time here is over. This quarter now belongs to the Hands."

"Arrogant son of a whore," muttered one of the collectors.

"The second part of the message is this," Lihou said, striking his tinderbox and igniting a rag whose end had been doused in oil.

Lihou glanced back at the collectors, then grinned as he threw the burning rag into the pool that had formed from the joint trails of oil that ran through the warehouse.

"Oops," he said, smiling.

The flame guttered for a moment, then flashed as it greedily consumed the oil. Fire swept out in four lines that shot straight into the warehouse. The look on the faces of the collectors was almost comical as they realised, finally, what was going on.

"You fools!" said the leader. "You have no idea who you have just messed with! They're going to be coming after you for this."

"I wouldn't worry," said Lucius, keeping his voice calm. "We are pretty sure we know what we are doing. However, there is a third part of the message we would like you to deliver."

The leader frowned, puzzled, until Lucius clicked his fingers and the rest of his team moved forward, eager for violence. As one, the collectors turned and ran, but they were brought down within a few yards by Lucius' team, who proceeded to pummel them senseless.

A dull crump from behind told him that the first crate of liquor had been burst open by the flames, which would now be spreading voraciously throughout the furs, spices and other goods of luxury stored in the warehouse. He watched his team go to work on the collectors and, though they were clearly enjoying the job, happy to be able to hand something back to the Guild after having been put on the back foot of late, he was pleased to see their discipline remained. He had warned them to use fists and feet only, unless one of the collectors drew a weapon. The point of the exercise was to frighten them and deliver a clear message. Not kill them in the street.

He had to conclude, though, after watching Judi hiss and spit and curse as she dug her boot into a man's groin – causing him to curl up and start sobbing – that perhaps the use of a dagger might have been more humane.

Seeing the collectors had taken enough punishment or, at least, understood the message, Lucius gave a low whistle. His thieves stood up from their task, all breathing heavily from the exertion. As they hurried down the street, leaving the scene, the open doors of the warehouse began to glow with the orange light of the flames inside as they took hold. It would be a few more minutes before the fire swept through the rafters and became visible to the whole city, but Lucius knew the place was already doomed. Even if a Vos patrol happened by now, it was too late; the only question was whether they would be able to save the warehouses either side.

"What's next, sir?" Lihou asked as he trotted alongside.

Lucius smiled as he drew a rolled parchment from under his tunic. "No need to call me sir, just Lucius will do." Consulting the parchment he nodded. "The Three Springs tavern. That is where our merchant, Mr Schon, is staying for the next week as he tries to sell what remains of his stock."

"There's not much profit in ashes," Judi said.

"True. And less in doing business with the Guild, as we shall prove tonight."

The Three Springs lay just a few streets over from the warehouse and was one of several establishments devoted to visiting merchants who could not bear to be far from their goods. No one else would visit a tavern nestled deep within the warehouses, so such places also formed a natural forum for negotiations and deal making, where traders could talk shop without being disturbed. There were also other pleasures available to those rich enough, even some that could technically be described as illegal in other parts of Turnitia. It was all part of a specialised service.

As they approached the small building, its two floors and narrow frontage looking faintly ridiculous as it nestled between two giant warehouses, Lucius spotted Gunnison and his team coming from the opposite direction. Gunnison waved anxiously at them, and then dove into a narrow alley that lay between two warehouses.

Motioning his team to follow, Lucius trailed the veteran thief. Short, wiry and with a pointed face some might describe as rat-like, he had always thought Gunnison the archetypal rogue. The image most people saw in their mind when thinking of a burglar or pickpocket.

Gunnison gestured him to come closer as he crouched. Joining him, Lucius gave a quizzical look.

"Thought we might find you here," Gunnison said, his eyes constantly darting back to the street they had left.

"What's wrong?"

"The Guild has reacted far quicker than we thought. They've got men on the streets hunting for us."

"Yeah, we saw them," Lihou said cockily. "Gave them a right kicking, we did!"

Ignoring him, Gunnison spoke only to Lucius. "Armed men. We saw Wade's guys get hit. He got away, but left two of his men – killed or captured, I don't know."

Lucius sighed. "We should pull out, abandon this evening's operations."

"That's what I was thinking," Gunnison agreed.

"What? We can handle them, sir," Lihou said. "There's more of us here, I'll bet."

"We are not set up for this," Lucius said, grabbing his arm. "We've already lost two men because we were not prepared for this kind of response. It is too dangerous to continue."

"Besides, if we have running battles in the streets, the guard would be on top of all of us before you could sneeze," Gunnison said. "Keep your team together, Lucius, but we'll make our own way back to the guildhouse. Magnus will know what to do."

Nodding in agreement, he watched Gunnison and his men leave. Before he disappeared into the twilight gloom, Gunnison turned back to Lucius and said, "Looks like the Guild means business after all."

Leading his team down the opposite end of the alley, Lucius poked his head out into the next street, carefully looking up and down the quiet warehouses to make sure the way was clear.

"Come on," he said. "If you see any trouble, run back to the guildhouse. I don't want any heroics tonight."

They padded up the street, moving slower than Lucius would have wished but staying within the shadows of the tall buildings as they went, all but invisible. A patrol of Vos guards marched from an adjoining road, causing them to double back a short distance, and skip between two warehouses to take a parallel street out of the merchant quarter.

Lucius heard shouts in the distance as the burning warehouses dotted around the quarter began to be noted and men rushed to douse the flames. He became more confident then, as he knew the Vos guard would be drawn to the disturbances, likely giving his team a free run all the way back to the guildhouse.

He heard Judi hiss a warning, and looked over his shoulder to see they were being followed. A half dozen men, armed with clubs and short swords, were calmly walking up the centre of the street as if they owned it, not bothering to keep to the shadows.

"Get ready to run," he whispered to his team. "Split up if you must and find your own way back to the guildhouse. Tell Magnus what happened. When I give the word, mind. I'll watch your backs."

"Lucius..." Lihou said in a quiet voice, as they saw a half dozen more men detach themselves from shadowy doorways, alleys and from behind resting wagons ahead of them. They, too, were obviously armed, and Lucius felt a sinking feeling in his stomach.

"Right..." he said. "Go! Now!"

As one, his team scattered, dashing for the narrow passages that lay between the nearest warehouses. As one, the men before and behind them scattered as well, matching their movements as they sought to cut the escaping thieves off.

Only two remained on the street, and Lucius made to draw his sword as they approached then, thinking better, reached down for a dagger with his left hand. Knowing his team would need his support in all haste, he resolved to dispatch the men quickly.

He saw immediately that they were barely trained to use the blades they carried, and he spun to dodge one overhead slash, while catching the other with his dagger. He thrust with his weapon, feeling it enter the belly of his opponent, then kicked out with his boot to push the man back to the ground.

If the second man was aware his friend was already dead, he did not show it as he screamed an inarticulate cry, while swinging his sword at Lucius' midriff. Taking a step back, Lucius avoided the blow, and shook his head in astonishment. The man was using his sword as one would a club. His next swing was easy to counter, and Lucius turned it aside before taking a step forward and driving his dagger into the man's throat. Gargling as blood swept down his chest, the man sank to the ground, a look of incomprehension in his eyes.

More shouts, much closer this time, spurred Lucius into action. Taking a guess, he tore across the street and raced down a narrow alley to follow the sounds. He emerged onto a wide road, one of the main thoroughfares of the merchant quarter, and saw Lihou and Judi running together, their feet barely touching the cobbled surface as four men chased them. Racing after them, he watched as they dived into an alley on the far side, hoping to shake their pursuers off in the network that ran between the warehouses. Panting heavily now, he cursed with painful breaths as he saw they were, out of obvious fear, sticking together and not splitting up.

Shouting a challenge, he gained the attention of one man, who turned aside from the chase to face Lucius with a club. Lucius did not bother to confront him, ducking instead down another alley he hoped would continue to run parallel to the one Lihou and Judi had taken, intending to outpace them to the other side.

Now with his own pursuer, he sheathed his dagger and sought the threads of power, summoning a flame to his left hand. Holding it as one might hold an apple, he stopped and turned, concentrating for a second to bind more energy to his bidding, then threw it at the man. Sizzling through the air, the lavender flames struck the man in the chest with the force of a hammer. He tried to scream, but fire sucked the air out of his lungs as it consumed his flesh. Knowing the man would be dead before he hit the ground, Lucius hurried on.

Racing out into the next street, Lucius looked to his left and saw Judi, standing at the entrance to an alley from which she had just emerged. He tore towards her, seeing the shock and fear on her face.

"They got him," she cried, pointing into the alley where Lucius could see three men kicking at someone curled up on the ground.

"Get out of here now!" he shouted at her. "Back to the guildhouse. I'll look after Lihou!"

He grabbed at her arm and bodily pushed her up the street away from him. Stumbling, Judi found her feet and began to run.

Drawing his dagger, Lucius padded quickly down the dark alley, closing fast on the men who were, so far, unaware of his presence. The first died without knowing what hit him, Lucius' dagger planted firmly between his shoulder blades, and the second had barely started to raise his sword as Lucius' own blade slashed across his face, leaving it a screaming ruin.

The last of the thugs held a hand up as he backed away, and Lucius snarled at him. Casting a last look at his bawling companion who was clasping bloodied hands to his face, he turned and ran.

Lucius silenced the screaming man with a quick thrust, as much to save his ears from the anguished cries as to stop him from bringing the guard down on their heads. He reached down to the huddled mass on the ground, and found Lihou, battered and bruised but alive. The lad's nose was clearly broken, and his whole face was a puffed up mass of injured flesh. As he tried to pick Lihou up, the boy moaned in pain, and Lucius went down on his knees to support him.

"Judi," Lihou muttered. "Tried to save her. Not running fast enough."

"You did fine," Lucius said, checking Lihou's body for other injuries. His hand came away sticky with blood. Running a hand across Lihou's tunic, he was shocked to find a mass of stab wounds.

"She got away," Lucius said, not knowing what else to say. "You showed real courage."

"Knew... I wouldn't amount to much," Lihou mumbled past broken lips.

As Lucius searched for another platitude, he felt Lihou tense suddenly, then relax. A last breath escaped the lad and he was still.

Silent anger boiled within Lucius as he carefully laid Lihou's body on the ground. He had seen plenty of people die in the past, many of them at his own hand, but he felt something different this time. Like the men who had died on the Allantian ship, Lihou had been under his leadership, had been his responsibility. It was not a feeling Lucius welcomed, and he cursed himself for accepting the roles Magnus had placed upon him but, most of all, he felt the need to bring down the men who had caused so much death. The Guild had to be brought to task.

Lucius sprang up and rejoined the main thoroughfare. As he trotted up the street, he kept alert, straining his senses to penetrate the twilight for any sign of Hands in trouble, or the Guild men after them.

More cries, including one prolonged and agonised wail which could only mark a man's death, guided him across a junction and into a side road. Rounding a small lean-to built against a warehouse, he saw a pitched battle in the middle of the street.

Men were clumped in groups, the fight scattered across the entire street. As one combatant sank to the ground, overcome by a deadly sword thrust or clout to the back of the head with a club, those fighting him moved to another victim. Closing in on the melee, Lucius found that he had trouble recognising who was on which side, though he spotted a couple of Hands he had spoken to in the common room on previous days, and rushed to aid them.

Ashmore was there, and Lucius gave him an angry sideways look for having got caught in the fight rather than making his way back to the guildhouse as instructed. To his credit, the thief seemed almost sheepish as he buried his small knife into the kidney of a man attacking another Hand.

"The guard!" someone cried, and Lucius ducked under a club swung at his skull, before rolling away. He glanced down the street in the direction of the cry and saw a patrol of six Vos guard – their eagle-faced tabards menacing in Kerberos' half-light – approaching at a trot, with their swords drawn and mail chinking with each footfall.

The club swung down towards him again and, caught on the ground, Lucius barely had time to raise his sword to catch the blow. The blade dug deep into the wood, locking the two weapons together, and while the man attacking him strained to release them, Lucius hacked down with his dagger, driving it through the man's foot.

Reeling back in agony, the man collapsed to the floor, clutching his injured foot, while Lucius stood on the club and pulled, jerking his sword free. With one thrust, he ended the man's pain.

The guard hit the fray like a bolt of lightning, men starting to go down as soon as they entered the melee. Lucius shouted for the Hands to follow him, to escape, but some were already in a deadly fight with the armoured guard, and others were reluctant to leave them. Hoping it would not be the last decision he made, Lucius charged forward. Catching a guard in the side and bowling him over, he stabbed down, but his sword was turned aside by the guard's thick mail.

Another guardsman, seeing his comrade in distress, rushed into the fight and was about to decapitate one of the thieves when he started shouting "Red diamond! Red diamond!" Lucius was amazed to see the guard turn from the man and march resolutely toward him. Lucius ran.

Shouting again for them to follow, other Hands gradually got the message and they scattered into the alleys, desperately trying to put ground between them and the guard. Instead, they found more guardsmen waiting for them.

Pulling one man out of an alley that another patrol of guard had started to close upon, Lucius ran with him down the street, this being the only clear path he could see. But as he approached the junction, yet another patrol appeared, trotting round the corner, weapons drawn. Seeing an alley to his left, Lucius shoved the man into it ahead of him and together they sprinted down the cobbles, only for Lucius to run into his comrade as the man suddenly stopped.

Blood pumping in fear as much as excitement now, Lucius looked at what had caused the man to halt in his tracks. The two warehouses that formed the alley had been joined together by a new connecting structure that towered above them, blocking their exit. One glance at the smooth planks that formed the soaring wall told Lucius that even Hawk would have found it difficult to scale.

"We've got to get out of here now," he said to the other Hand, and grabbed his shoulder to propel him back up the alley. A Guild man appeared at its entrance, and pointed towards them.

"Red diamond!" Lucius heard him say as the Vos guard appeared next to him. The guard sergeant nodded in understanding, then led his patrol down the alley toward them.

Lucius heard the man standing next to him curse, then throw down his sword. The guard approached two abreast, those marching behind them training crossbows on Lucius' chest.

With an angry cry of frustration, Lucius turned and kicked the wooden wall of the warehouse, having nothing else to take his fury out on. He then hurled his weapons to the ground and stared ruefully at the guardsmen, his hands splayed out to either side in surrender.

CHAPTER THIRTEEN

THE ARMY OF VOS was renowned throughout the peninsula for its efficiency, be it at grinding down the defences of an enemy city or calculating the food and supplies a force would need on a long march and ensuring it would receive them in good order.

That same efficiency was apparent here, in the depths of the Citadel. Lucius cast a rueful eye around his cell, illuminated only by the torchlight flickering through the narrow barred window in the single, stout oaken door. The flagstones were spotless, with any evidence of the previous occupants of the cell removed before he set foot inside himself. The manacles that bound his hands and feet to wall and floor were well-oiled, with secure locks intended to foil the best efforts of any thief who managed to not only get a hand free, but smuggle a pick in with him.

He shared the cell with Luber, the thief arrested alongside him. He was a Vos-born rogue who had sought the freedoms of Turnitia only to find his old empire sweep over his new home with ease. He was well aware of Vos efficiency, and had spent much of his time bemoaning their fate, regaling Lucius with unwelcome tales of torture and mutilation before exhaustion finally overwhelmed him.

Ignoring the man's gentle snores, Lucius cast his eyes around the cell, debating exactly what to do next. The manacles, and even the cell door, posed no problem for him. There were any number of ways he could call the magic to his aid to find freedom, from the freezing of the chains so they would shatter with a sharp strike, to allowing the energy to increase his own strength enough to force the door open. There were few prisons that could hold an accomplished Shadowmage for long.

No, his problem would be with whatever happened next. Lucius was aware of guards passing by his cell door at semi-regular intervals, and he had already begun to count the minutes to the next arrival in order to determine the changing patterns. Assuming he could leave the cell without alerting them, he would then find himself in the heart of an enemy stronghold that had gained a reputation for absolute security. It was the home of every Vos soldier in Turnitia, and he did not relish the idea of providing them all with sword and crossbow practice. They were already too good.

Nor could he await the justice, such as it was, of Vos. Arrested thieves could expect the briefest of trials, followed by a stripping of their possessions (his sword and mail were not much, but they were his and he valued them) and, likely as not, the loss of a hand or foot in order to remind the citizens of the city that while Vos brought many economic benefits, disobedience would not be tolerated.

There was also something larger taking place, Lucius now realised. He thought back to the skirmishes in the merchant quarter, and the arrival of the guard – and the passwords that the Guild men had uttered. If the Guild of Coin and Enterprise had bought the guard... as unthinkable – not to mention unlikely – as it was, it spelt nothing but trouble for the Hands. They may as well try to fight the entire city.

Thoughts buzzing around his head like angry hornets, Lucius jerked himself back into alertness when he heard the now familiar heavy footsteps and chink of mail that signalled the arrival of another pair of guards. He frowned, and gave an angry sigh. The guard, it seemed, were intentionally varying the regularity of their patrols past the cells in order to throw the senses and timing of the inmates. However, there had to be an underlying order to their patrols (they were Vos, after all), and Lucius had begun to think he had discovered it. This patrol threw his calculations right out the non-existent window, however.

A jangle of keys on a chain and the sliding of several locks in the door heralded the arrival of three armed men. The first two stood either side of the cell's entrance, hands on sword hilts but in a casual stance that suggested they expected no real trouble. The third man to enter caught Lucius' attention immediately, for his tight, moustachioed face and narrow, suspicious eyes exuded both menace and authority. His presence seemed to fill the cell, making it seem that much smaller. Wearing a black leather waistcoat studded with metal plates, he might have looked like many of the thieves Lucius knew, were it not for the obvious expense and elegance of his armour. A long red cloak swept behind him, pinned to his waistcoat with elaborate gold brooches, and the hilt of his longsword was similarly well decorated.

"Good evening," he said, and Lucius saw he almost clicked his heels as he bent his head in mock salute. "I am Baron Ernst von Minterheim, Commander of the Citadel, Colonel of the Vos Empire and Master of the Guard."

He smiled briefly at his two prisoners. "I want to know the location of your guildhouse, its defences and a roll of all its members. As Commander of the Citadel, it is within my discretion as to the best methods to obtain this information so, in a way, it is up to you how this will go. We'll start with you."

The commander gestured at Luber, and the two guards sprang into action. One pulled the man to his feet, while the other busied himself with the locks round Luber's ankles and wrists. As he was carried out, Luber flashed a worried look at Lucius, who was paying more attention to the movements of the guards, watching for any opportunity to spring a bid for freedom. For he knew he would be next.

It came quicker than he thought. As the guards dragged Luber out of the cell, another pair stepped around the Commander to haul Lucius to his feet. He felt the manacles release his limbs from their pinching grasp, only to be replaced by an iron-like grip that drew his arms behind his back in a well-practised move. Propelled out of the cell, he was dragged bodily along a corridor and down a set of steps that descended further into the fortress. His mind churned as his feet slid along the flagstones, determined not to aid the guards in their labours in any way.

Any thieves captured by the guard would be in for a hellish evening, Lucius knew, but it would be the morning before anything more permanent would take place. Lucius was betting on this, if the Guild had any say on events in the Citadel, and the Vos guard liked a public display to stamp their authority on the citizens of Turnitia. A good hanging or maiming always drew a decent crowd, regardless of who was suffering.

That gave him some time, at least. He guessed the Vos guard and their commander would be inventive during their questioning, but Lucius had taken a beating before and believed he could face up to another one. His worry was how many other thieves had been caught, and how many of them would be quickly broken.

As they stepped out of the staircase and entered another level, Lucius noted that the environment seemed darker, and it took him a few seconds to realise that the torches down here were spaced further apart, creating more shadows; and a far more foreboding atmosphere. All part of the Vos game he decided, an attempt to convince those brought down here that hope was as far away as the daylit world. The cries and moans from the cells they passed served to add to the atmosphere of impending defeat, a promise of what any prisoner would inevitably face. Lucius guessed that perhaps a dozen men and women were being questioned, though he had no way of knowing whether they were all thieves caught that night.

A painful crack, followed by sustained sobbing caught Lucius' attention as he was dragged past one such cell, and it was followed by a rumble of laughter from within.

Lucius was thrown onto the floor of a nearby cell, this one even smaller than his previous residence. He struck the ground and rolled, but was instantly grabbed again and shoved into the single wooden chair that was bolted to the flagstones. A heavy hand forced him back into the uncomfortable seat while others grabbed at his hands and feet, securing them with iron clasps, holding him immobile. One guard left the cell, while the other stationed himself behind Lucius, out of view but his presence menacingly obvious.

Taking a breath to compose himself, Lucius began to take in his surroundings, inspecting the clasps holding him to his chair, the thickness of the cell door, the space he might have to manoeuvre, should he break free and be forced to fight. His calculations were interrupted by the cell door opening again and another guard entering, followed by Commander Ernst von Minterheim.

"I have little time and less patience," he announced casually, almost seeming bored by this duty. "We already have much of the information we require, and your fellow thieves caught this evening have been most co-operative. I merely require you to confirm some of what they have told us. If your tales support one another, you can all go free come morning. Lie to me, and you will all hang."

Lucius looked up at him with a rueful expression. "I will not co-operate."

The commander gave a nod, and Lucius felt strong hands press down on his shoulders from behind. The guard who had entered the cell with the Commander stepped up and backhanded him with a mailed fist.

His head whipping round with the blow, Lucius gasped with the sudden pain, and he worked his jaw to ensure it was not broken. He glanced back at the Commander, this time with a baleful expression.

"That was just the start of what could be a very long evening for you," von Minterheim said. "Now, what is your name?"

Lucius stared back, saying nothing. Another mailed swipe set his teeth ringing.

"How long have you been with the Hands?"

This time Lucius' silence was met with a blow straight to his face. He felt something in his nose crack under the fist, and his eyes watered.

"Who are the current members of your Council?"

Lucius did not see the next strike coming, and he jerked against the clasps of the chair as the side of his head exploded in pain, causing the whole world to reel, then spin. A hand grasped him under the chin to hold his head upright before another backhanded blow blasted across his face. Hanging his head low, Lucius spat blood down his chest.

"I don't have time for another tight-lipped thief," he heard von Minterheim say, as if from a great distance. "Carry on with him. Let me know if he decides to loosen his tongue."

As LIGHT SLOWLY flooded back into Lucius' world, he felt pain. His face felt like it had swollen to twice its normal size and, as he roused himself awake, the movement sent sharp bolts that lanced through his stomach and chest. Duller was the ache from his wrists and ankles, where they had been bruised from the clasps of the chair. Opening his eyes a fraction, he saw that his limbs were bound once again by chained manacles, and he guessed he was back in his cell.

Low voices made him aware he was not alone and, glancing at his cell mates, he saw he was somewhere else entirely. This cell was much larger, and held more than a dozen other thieves, all bound by hand and foot to the walls and floor as was he. Luber was to his right, and the man looked a wreck, with blackened, puffed up eyes and a dried slick of blood running down his chin. Guessing he looked no better himself, Lucius glanced round the other captives, tuning in to their low, hushed conversations.

"It'll be suicide," said one in a hiss.

"Better that than hang," answered another, a thin, reedy man about the same age as Lucius. "I heard von Minterheim say it himself; anyone not making a deal with them is strung up in the courtyard this morning."

"So, which of us made a deal?" a woman's voice asked, her tone one of guarded suspicion.

"Not me," said the thin man, who Lucius now recognised as a counterfeiter called Aeron. "Can't imagine anyone would."

"Oh, come on. There's, what, fourteen, fifteen..." she said, counting the bodies surrounding her. "Sixteen thieves here. You certain *no one* spoke?"

"Not really a problem for us right now," Lucius heard himself mumble.

"Hey, Lucius is awake," the original voice said. "What was that you said?"

Lucius worked his mouth for a few seconds, trying to find some moisture while ignoring the pain of moving his lips.

"Whether one or more of us answered any of the guard's questions is rather academic," he said. "It does us no good or harm while we are locked up here – and if we hang this morning, it won't matter to us either way."

A mumble of agreement spread round the cell. Aeron spoke up again.

"There are some who think an escape attempt is pointless, that we'll just be caught and killed that much quicker."

Seeing one man lower his head to avoid Aeron's pointed stare, Lucius tried to give a confident smile, but his lips only partially co-operated. "Would anyone here rather they met their end at the end of a noose than while fighting for their lives?"

He was met with silence.

"Thought not."

"So, it just remains for us to get ourselves free," said the woman. Lucius gave her a quick look but while he thought he had seen her in the guildhouse from time to time, he could not remember her name. As battered and bruised as the rest of them, he was impressed that her eyes still shone with the light of defiance.

Rattling her chains, the woman nodded to her manacles. "Anyone manage to get themselves free of these?"

Inwardly, Lucius sighed. He was not ready to unleash his magic with all the thieves as witnesses, however simple it might be for him. Even with the Hands under assault from both the Vos guard and the Guild, it was too dangerous. Looking around the cell for an answer, he was conscious of Luber moaning next to him, and was surprised to realise that the man was chuckling. Others watched the man as he gave a bloodied grin then produced a small hooked bar of metal from his swollen lips. A lockpick.

"Nice going, Luber," the woman said. "But how are you going to reach your chains?"

"Well, Natalia," he said. "There's a little trick I learned growing up in Vosburg. You might want to look away..."

Lucius saw her sneer at that, then followed her gaze as her eyes widened in shock. Next to him, Luber's face had turned into a grimace as he strained his right hand against the manacles that clasped his wrist. He watched as the man flattened his fingers, then brought his thumb down into his palm, before he pulled, shuddering with the effort.

The thieves winced collectively as a dull, wet snap reached their ears, and Luber grunted from the pain. Incredulously, Lucius stared as Luber simply drew his hand back through the manacles. Gingerly, he took the lockpick from his mouth and began prodding at the restraint around his left hand.

Waiting with bated breath, the thieves watched as Luber, with obvious pain and difficulty, probed the locking mechanism of the manacles, the action made harder tenfold with the broken joint of his thumb. He twisted the pick, and they all strained to hear the click of the mechanism unlocking, but instead heard Luber grunt again in pain as his hand spasmed slightly, and the pick fell from the lock, dangling only by a fraction of an inch of its hooked end. Lucius saw the woman jerk against her chains involuntarily, perhaps thinking she could catch the pick from across the cell, but Luber's reactions were up to the task. Giving a pained but wry smile at his audience, he scooped the pick up, and re-seated it back in the lock.

"God's teeth, Luber," someone muttered. "Could do this quicker myself."

"And could you break your own wrist first?" the woman asked caustically, only to be met with silence.

Moving slower and more deliberately this time, Luber continued his probing, then gave another grunt.

"Got it," he whispered, and hushed words of encouragement swept around the cell as they all heard a tiny click. With a shrugging motion, Luber discarded the open manacles and set to work on those chaining his feet.

Eyes began to flicker towards the cell door, as the thieves collectively prayed that the guard would not return before Luber's work was done, but luck remained on their side. He quickly disposed of the restraints tying his feet and then, shakily, stood, grinning in his new-found freedom. A quiet cough brought him back to the job in hand,

and he set to work on another man Lucius recognised as his partner. Once another set of manacles lay useless on the floor, the newly freed thief produced his own lockpick from inside a boot, and together he and Luber shuffled around the cell, releasing their comrades.

Even before the last thief was released, Lucius was by the cell door, inspecting its lock. He was joined by the woman.

"No craftsmanship here," she said. Noting Lucius' quizzical gaze, she gestured at the lock. "Why build a cell whose door gives access to the lock on the inside? Especially one designed to hold thieves. All that money from Vos to build the Citadel, but no finesse in its application."

"Lucky for us," he said. "I'm Lucius."

She took his extended hand. "Grayling. I've seen you around. Rumour has it you can fight." In response, he shrugged. "There'll be plenty of fighting soon," she continued. "Let's hope you are as good as your reputation. Luber, you finished there? We need this door open."

It was Luber's partner who answered her summons and, as he went to work, Grayling ordered the thieves into pairs, and Lucius was faintly surprised at the ease qith which they accepted her leadership.

"When you leave, take your chances to go left or right down the corridor – either is as good as the other, and it will mean we are not all cooped up in one place if the guard see us. Find weapons if you can, but don't take risks. The goal is to get out of this cursed place. Go for the roof or the ground floor, as you like. Find a route out of this tower and then past the walls – that will be the difficult bit. Better to go over than through, but if some of us are found, it may cause enough distraction for the others. Once out..." Here she paused, as the enormity of what they were attempting struck home. "Split up and make your way back to the guildhouse. Standard procedures. Make sure you are not followed, and make wide detours. Understood?"

She was answered by nods and grunts.

"Lucius, you come with me," she said, barely looking him in the eye.

A loud click froze the thieves as the lock of the cell door was forced by Luber's partner. He looked back at Grayling who nodded. Pulling Lucius to one side, she opened the door open a crack and, seeing no movement, swung it open fully. She darted her head outside, looking up and down the open corridor.

"You two," she said, gesturing at a pair of thieves. "Go!"

The two men sprang up and, with just a second's hesitation, darted left. The next pair called by Grayling went right. As the thieves funnelled out, Lucius began to fidget, feeling that the guards could return any moment, trapping him in the cell while the other thieves made their bid for freedom. As the last pair left, Grayling looked up at him.

"Ready?"

Without waiting for a reply, she peered out of the corridor once more, then trotted left, her soft boots making no noise on the flagstones. They passed other cells, and Lucius briefly entertained the idea of releasing all the prisoners held in this tower, but realised that such a mob would as likely get themselves killed as escape, and that the odds were stacked against the thieves as it was.

At the first junction, Grayling cocked her head, then pointed right, and as they made their way down shadowy, torch-lit passages, they caught the occasional snatch of raised voices and the unmistakable clash of metal on metal. Some of the thieves had already been found, and were now fighting for their lives.

An alcove revealed a spiral stone staircase leading both up and down, and Grayling began to vault upwards, aiming for the pinnacle of the tower. However, the stairs stopped at least one level short, forcing them back into twisting corridors. Always one pace behind her, Lucius stopped short when Grayling held up a hand.

"Guard coming," she whispered. "Get him looking at you."

With no other words, she skipped to the left, nestling herself within the shadows of a support buttress that stood proud of the passageway's walls. An instant later, Lucius heard booted feet and the clink of mail from ahead, and realised Grayling's hearing was far more acute than his own. A second later, an armoured guard rounded a corner a few yards down the corridor, coming to a dead halt when he saw Lucius standing in his path.

They stared at one another for a brief instant, the guard surprised at the sight of an intruder, Lucius' mind fumbling for something to say.

He held up both hands. "I surrender."

Frowning now, the guard jogged down the corridor, arm outstretched to seize Lucius, but his motion was arrested by Grayling's foot. Catching the guard off balance, she snaked from the shadows, tripping him with an easy movement, then following his body down with her own. Throwing his helmet aside, one blow to the back of his neck rendered the guard unconscious.

Moving quickly, Grayling tugged at the guard's belt, freeing his weapons. The sword she passed to Lucius, while she grabbed a dagger for herself.

"Sure you don't want the sword?" Lucius asked, surprised she had taken the smaller weapon. She gave him a disparaging look.

"You men are always so worried about size."

Her smile might have been meant purely in jest, but it retained such a look of viciousness that Lucius found himself swallowing involuntarily. Grayling glanced over her shoulder, looking down the corridor.

"Grab that and pull it into the shadows," she said, indicating the motionless guard. "I'll scout ahead."

As quietly as he could, Lucius dragged the guard next to the buttress Grayling had used to ambush him, deeply aware of the grating sound the man's mail made on the stone floor. He tried lifting and shuffling the man as best he could, but it was a dead weight, and he kept flicking glances up and down the passageway, expecting to see half the Vos army bearing down upon him.

By the time he had finished, Grayling had returned, and he noted a triumphant look in her eyes.

"I know how we are getting out of here," she said. "But there is a problem. Come."

Pacing down the corridor behind her, Lucius followed Grayling past two junctions in the mazelike arrangement of the tower. They came to a half-open door, from which he heard the voices of several men. Following her gesture, he looked inside.

Lucius saw the problem immediately. Four more guards were inside, in various states of unreadiness. Two were reclined on cots, propped up against the far wall as they spoke with their colleagues, while the other pair were seated at a table, evidently finishing off their evening meal. Only one was fully armoured, his helmet lying discarded on the table, while another wore only his mail coat. The two on the cots wore only leather under-tunics, their mail hung from crosspieces on one side of the room. Quickly scanning the room for weapons, Lucius saw a wooden rack against the far wall in which rested a variety of swords, maces and daggers.

Grayling nudged him in the side, and he followed her eyes to a corner of the barracks. A ladder rose from the floor to a large trapdoor in the ceiling.

"To the roof," she mouthed.

Lucius frowned at her and jerked his head to the guards. Despite having the advantage of surprise, he was not sure they could defeat all of the men inside before they could launch a highly effective counterattack. If it were just him, with both armour and magic as his allies, he would be confident. However, he had nothing but the sword Grayling had managed to recover for him, and he did not fancy her chances at all, fighting well-trained soldiers with only a dagger.

She grabbed his arm and pulled him back down the corridor. When they were a safe distance away, she whispered her idea to him.

"I go in first. You move as soon as they spot me, got it?"

He nodded, but she took hold of his arm again, squeezing it to underline her point. "As soon as they see me, understand? If I am caught alone in there, I'm dead. I'm relying on you – can I do that?"

Lucius took a breath, still not liking their odds, but he nodded. "You can count on me."

"Good," she said, smiling. "I had heard that."

He frowned at that, but Grayling had already left his side, pacing stealthily back towards the door, dagger held low. Watching as she reached the door, Lucius saw her drop into a crouch and then, slowly, silently, she passed the threshold and entered the room.

Using the half-open door to shield his presence, Lucius watched in amazement as Grayling padded towards the men in the cots. She moved with exceptional grace, each footstep slow and deliberate. He had heard tales in the common room of some thieves with the ability to blend into their environments to such a degree that they practically became invisible, but he had not really believed it up to now. Keeping her back to the wall, Grayling moved with a slow but irresistible motion. Never completely still, yet never drawing attention to herself. One foot was placed in front of the other in total silence. Lucius marvelled at her ability, but felt her luck could not last.

It didn't. A casual glance from one of the men at the table became a double take as he focussed on the creeping woman who, battered and bruised with a naked dagger, must have looked for all the world like some evil spirit come to exact vengeance.

"Assassin!" the man cried out, stunning his comrades into inaction as he whirled around for the weapons rack.

Lucius was already moving, sprinting for the table. Out of the corner of his eye, he saw Grayling uncoil from her crouch, turning her stealthy pose into a killing strike in an instant. The man in the first cot was dead a second later, blood gushing down his tunic.

The last man at the table reeled back from Lucius' charge, falling from his chair and upending the table as he hit the floor. Kicking the table to one side, Lucius hacked the man down before he could cry out. The blade dug easily into the side of the guard's skull, and blood flowed across the floor as he yanked it free.

A hiss from Grayling caused Lucius to look up, and it was by reflex alone that he managed to raise the blade of his sword in time to catch the downward swing of the other guard's mace. The guard snarled at Lucius – spittle flying from his lips – before he reversed the direction of his weapon, and swung the mace again.

Unable to parry such a close blow, Lucius backed away and nearly tangled himself in the body at his feet. Seeing the guard advance and ready another swing, he reached down and grabbed the fallen chair, raising it just as the mace came towards his head.

The chair shattered into a dozen wooden splinters while the force of the attack caused him to stumble. As he went down on one knee, Lucius swung his sword in a backhanded blow intended to disembowel the guard, but the tip of his weapon just skittered off mail. Pressing home the advantage, the guard raised the mace above his head and brought it rushing down, perhaps hoping to blast Lucius straight through the floor and back into the cells.

Caught off balance, Lucius rolled back toward the door, hoping to gain a little ground. The guard followed immediately, seeing a helpless enemy before him. Kicking out, Lucius stalled the advance with a blow to the guard's shin, but his foot just glanced off the metal greaves. Another swing forced him to dive to his left, and his sword clattered on the floor as it fell from his grasp. On his rump and completely defenceless now, Lucius desperately kicked at the floor, trying to drive himself back, away from the guard, whose face was now triumphant with victory.

He felt the wall at his back, and knew there was nowhere else to run. Raising his arms in a futile effort to ward away the guard's finishing blow, he looked up to see the man staring down at him. The guard's fury had disappeared and his expression was almost serene. Lucius frowned in puzzlement, then opened his mouth in shock as the man sank to his knees and collapsed at his feet. Behind the guard stood Grayling, her dagger dripping with blood.

"Can I help you up?" she said.

Grayling was the first to the ladder and after reaching the top, she heaved with her shoulder to force the trapdoor open. Lucius looked past her slight form to see the blue sphere of Kerberos leering down at him, and he felt a rush of relief as he breathed in fresh air.

Vaulting up the ladder, he found himself at the top of the tower beside Grayling, looking down from the parapets. The roof was dominated by a huge trebuchet – its timbers harvested from Vos forests – the massive stones it threw piled next to it, mined from quarries close to the city. A single pole rose higher even than the mighty war machine, but no flag flew from it this evening, that honour having currently been taken by one of the other towers of the Citadel.

The view of Turnitia from this height was spectacular. He could see the entire expanse of the city, from the ocean cliffs guarding it, up the slope to the townhouses on its far side. To the east and north, rows of blank-roofed warehouses held the wealth of the city, while the Five Markets lay empty below.

Closer, the construction of the Citadel was equally impressive. The four other towers stood silent and imposing, acting as sentinels for the entire city, while the main keep – invisible to the rest of the world behind vast stone walls – nestled between them. Those walls ringed the entire complex, high above the level of most buildings in Turnitia, and were lined with troops. More soldiers were scattered in the courtyards directly below, and Lucius saw the frantic movements of an ongoing battle. Some of the thieves had escaped from the tower at ground level, only to find themselves cut off and surrounded.

"We cannot help them," Grayling said, perhaps wanting to forestall any foolish heroics Lucius might be tempted to perform.

"Agreed," he said after a moment, nodding. "So, what now?"

"Still thinking," Grayling said as she looked left and right for a solution to present itself.

"I thought you said you had a plan?"

"Got us this far, haven't I?" she retorted, though there was no venom in her voice. Slowly, Lucius began to realise that she was actually enjoying the moment, their brush with danger and the bid for freedom. He could not decide whether that was a good thing.

"We've got this," Grayling said, scooping up a coil of rope that lay next to the Vos banners that were draped down the sheer sides of the towers on special days marked by the Empire. "But we can't just drop it down into the courtyard."

Staring out at the city, an idea came to Lucius. "If we could stretch it to the walls, they would be the last obstacle."

She looked at him doubtfully, as if he had suddenly turned simple. "Even if we had a hook to tie to the end, could you throw it that far?"

Walking to the edge of the battlements lining the tower, Lucius stared at the wall, trying to gauge the distance. As a horizontal throw, it would be impossible, but from their vantage point, they had height on their side. If they had just a little help.

"Find something," he said. "Anything that can act as a grappling hook. We need something that can dig into stone."

Grayling disappeared back down the trapdoor while Lucius scouted the roof of the tower. He had hoped to find something useful among the tools and supplies surrounding the war machine, but he was unsuccessful. When Grayling reappeared, he could tell from her expression that she had been no luckier.

She looked up at the trebuchet. "You know, there are stories of thieves making their escape by using catapults."

"Any thief telling that story is either a liar or a good deal shorter than he once was."

Grayling sighed. "We might have to go back down into the tower."

Closing his eyes, Lucius cursed. He knew what he had to do, but it would very likely mean an end to his place among the Hands.

"Grayling," he began. "You counted on me before. I need to count on you now."

"Of course," she said without hesitation.

"I mean it."

Something in his voice checked her, and she frowned at him. "What are you planning to do?"

It was his turn to sigh. "Stand back until I say. And you'll need a strip of cloth or short length of rope."

Still clearly puzzled, Grayling nevertheless followed his instructions, and dug around the trebuchet's supplies until she found something suitable.

Lucius took a deep breath as he began coiling the rope in his hands, staring fixedly at a portion of the opposite wall that seemed to have few guards on its ramparts. He turned his attention inward, seeking the threads of magic that constantly turned and twisted, and, like an old friend, they came flooding back under his control.

He began to swing one end of the rope above his head, whipping it around faster and faster as he manipulated the threads to bring those he needed into the real world. An otherworldly strength flooded into his body briefly, hot and fast, and he felt himself shudder as the power whipped about in his chest. Then it was gone, the energy passed to the rope spinning above his head, and suddenly it was moving with its own momentum. Letting go with one hand, he retained a grip on its length with the other. The rope coiled above his head as it span, reaching ever higher speeds.

He heard Grayling gasp in astonishment but his conscious mind was elsewhere, directing the magic that now song along the entire length of the rope. With a command that was part gesture, part vocals the rope arced high in the sky across the face of Kerberos before plunging down towards the wall. A bright flash of light surged along its length, pulling it taut as the tip rocketed downwards, plunging deep into the battlements of the wall. Feeling the magic spent as the conjuration was completed, Lucius pulled hard on the rope to ensure it had taken hold, then ran to the trebuchet to tie the loose end firmly. He cut a short length from it, and then returned to the battlements.

Throughout this, he avoided eye contact with Grayling, but was aware that she was giving him suspicious sidelong looks.

"Come on," he said. "You first."

With the briefest of pauses, Grayling threw her legs over the side of the tower and wrapped the cloth she had gathered around the rope. He saw her shift her weight in preparation to throw herself into clear air but she stopped, and turned to face him.

"I think I know what you are," she said.

He stopped for a moment, then looked directly into her eyes. "The others cannot know."

She nodded in understanding. "I'll make you a deal. We survive this and escape, it will be our secret. If not... well, it won't matter either way."

Cocking a half-smile, Grayling put her dagger in her mouth and pushed off. Grasping the cloth wrapped round the rope in each hand, she quickly gained speed as she flew through the air, down to the wall below.

Lucius sat on the edge of the battlements as he twisted his short cord around the rope then, testing the strain to ensure it could bear him as well as Grayling, he jumped.

He tried to pull the ends of the cord across one another in an attempt to control his speed, but he gathered pace at an alarming rate as he shot down the rope. Feet dangling helplessly in the air, he was aware of shouts rising up from the courtyard, but whether they were directed at him or were the result of the ongoing battle below, he could not tell. Ahead, Grayling had already reached the wall and had dropped from the rope into a graceful roll. Even now, she was throwing her dagger at the chest of a guard but Lucius had greater concerns on his mind.

The wall was approaching at a terrible pace, the thick stone rearing up in front of him, growing ever larger. Belatedly, he tried to find the threads of magic, tried to summon energy that would enable him to avoid the inevitable collision that loomed. With the air whistling past his ears and the feeling of being utterly out of control, he was ashamed to find his concentration completely spent. As the wall approached, he tried to gauge his increasing speed and then let go of the cord.

For a brief second, he seemed to float through the air, and he fancied he might land neatly on his feet, coming to rest lightly on the ramparts of the wall. Instead, he barrelled forward helplessly. Tucking in a shoulder by sheer instinct at the last minute, he smashed into the battlements and the wind was forced from his body.

Lucius was completely dazed, and his head rang as he tried to take in air. He briefly thought he had been run down in the street by a racing wagon, and that well meaning citizens were trying to get him to stand once more. Not caring for their attentions, he tried to tell them that he just needed to sleep, but the words came out wrong. He was not even sure they were audible. Tucking his head under his arms, Lucius was irritated when someone dragged him to sit upright and started shouting in his face.

A sharp sting hit his cheek, and he shook his head. The voices seemed clearer now. He blinked and saw Grayling draw back her hand for another slap. He raised his own palm to show he was back with her, and it was sufficient to forestall the blow.

"Can you walk?" she hissed.

"I think so," he said, feeling the complete opposite. With her help, he stood, and though the world reeled at first, everything quickly settled down as he took a deep breath. The motion was accompanied by a nagging pain in his chest, and he reached down to hold his side.

"A rib, probably," Grayling said. "You were lucky that was the only thing you broke."

"Got to get out of here," he managed to say, and he found no argument from her.

"That's the easy part. Grab that man's sword. I don't know if there are others on this part of the wall, but we can't have gone unnoticed."

"Where are you going?"

Watching Grayling retrieve her dagger from the guard's chest, Lucius leaned heavily against the battlements, aware that the streets of Turnitia – and freedom – were just a few yards below on the other side. No other guards rushed their position and for this, he was grateful, as he did not think he could fight effectively in his current condition. Lucius yearned for a bed and a long rest, but steeled himself for just a little more discomfort before he could claim them.

Grayling had gone back to the rope and, wrapping her legs around it, pulled herself back along its length, hand-over-hand. After she had gone out a little distance, he saw her look back at the wall, as if sizing its dimensions. Then, taking the dagger from her mouth, she began to saw at the rope. Lucius frowned, as it seemed to him to be a remarkably foolish thing to cut a rope one was using for support. And sure enough, it snapped with an audible twang. Grayling dropped from view.

Stumbling to the edge of the rampart, Lucius looked down to see Grayling grinning up at him as she ascended the rope again. He leaned down to give her a hand as she threw a leg over the stone threshold, and instantly regretted it as pain lanced up his side.

As she stood next to him, Lucius looked at Grayling, the rope she held, and the wall.

"Don't get it," he said.

She rolled her eyes. "That fall robbed you of your senses. Watch."

Holding the rope in front of his face, she then threw it over the other side of the wall. It draped itself over the battlements to dangle gently just a few feet from street level.

"You see?" she said. "Simple."

CHAPTER FOURTEEN

HOVERING ON THE border of consciousness and deep sleep, Lucius was only barely aware as his imagination and dreams ruled his mind. He only dimly recalled the flight through the streets of the city, supported by Grayling as he stumbled, taking seemingly random turns as they tried to shake any attempt to follow them. There was no memory of arriving at the guildhouse, but images of mighty Shadowmages commanding vast hordes of creatures from the darkest depths of the sea ran riot, the dreaded demons sweeping through Turnitia, claiming it as their own. He thought his wounds were tended to by the smooth and soft hands of a dozen half-naked virgins, but they were soon replaced by the threads of power twisting around one another, before fusing into a terrible energy that burned his eyes and boiled his blood.

Lucius did not know how long he had lain like this, assaulted by confusing scenes and half-remembered dreams, but a cold, wet touch to his forehead made him groan as his mind slowly travelled through the mental fog, back to the real world. A quiet voice forced him to open his eyes, though he quickly half-closed them again as light flooded his vision.

"You're awake. Finally."

Wetting his lips, which suddenly felt deathly dry, Lucius tried to focus on the woman sitting next to his bed.

"Grayling," he managed to say.

"Indeed."

"We made it then."

She gave a short, humourless laugh. "You nearly didn't. You damaged more than a rib in that outrageous stunt. I had to virtually carry you the last quarter-mile. We had to give you honeyleaf-dram to get you healthy again."

Lucius sighed. That, at least, explained why he had been barely sentient. The dram was known to induce fever, and in sufficient quantities, coma and death. But the Hands had long used it to aid the healing process. With other concoctions from the guild's laboratory, many serious injuries could be countered in a relatively short space of time, as the body's own mechanisms were accelerated. Widely used among the nobility of Pontaine, the dram was eschewed within the Empire of Vos, but the Hands had learnt how to use it with only the merest chance of fatal results.

He coughed and accepted a mug of water from Grayling. Sitting up and taking a sip, he tried opening his eyes fully, and found his senses rapidly coming back to him, though he felt quite nauseous.

"How many got out?" he asked.

"Not enough. We've counted seven in so far, but I do not expect there to be any more. There has been no word of hangings, so we are assuming the others were killed trying to escape."

"Well," Lucius said, then fell silent for a moment. "It beats a noose."

"Yes, it does. But Luber was one of those who did not come back."

"I'm sorry to hear that." Lucius had not known the man very well, but was surprised to discover that he *was* sorry. Sharing a cell with Luber, however briefly, had forged something of a bond. "We might not have escaped at all if it were not for him."

"Maybe," Grayling said, watching Lucius carefully. "Maybe not."

Lucius returned her gaze, becoming increasingly uncomfortable. This was a moment he had been hoping to avoid for some time yet, but it looked as though there was no way out.

"Listen, you and I have to talk. What you saw at the Citadel–"

"You're a Shadowmage, aren't you?" Grayling asked, her voice low and secretive. He also detected a hint of curiosity, and maybe wonder. "I had heard you had all been wiped out when Vos entered the city."

"I left. But others stayed, hiding."

"There are others?" she asked, a little too eagerly, and Lucius winced. This was not a wise conversation to have when his senses were still addled, he realised.

"I can't discuss this. But, Grayling, I beg of you–"

"It's our secret," she said, guessing his next words. "I know why you kept it hidden. Some of the others here are not ready to accept a wizard in the guild."

He shook his head. "I'm no wizard."

"If the stories are true, you are so much more."

"Well... some of those might have been exaggerated. Like thieves that can pass through solid walls, you know?"

Grayling nodded slowly. "Are there others in the Hands too? No, don't answer that. As I said in the Citadel, you can count on me. Mind you, I think the others might be more ready to accept you than you think. Especially now."

"Why, what's happened?" he asked, noting the change in her voice. He suddenly realised that the dram he had been given might well have knocked him insensible for longer than it had seemed. "How long was I out of it?"

"Three days."

"God." He tried to sit up and was pleased to discover that the pain lancing his side had been replaced by a dull ache. His head still swam though, and he took another sip of water to settle his stomach. It was only marginally successful. "Fill me in, then. What's been going on?"

"They're calling it the Thieves War."

He sighed. "It's started."

"In a big way. Killings have spread across the city, and regular operations have all but ceased. Thieves are going round in groups, many with orders to do nothing more than hunt down those in the Guild. They have similar teams, and have been quite successful. We've lost nearly a quarter of our number already, and many are now too afraid to leave the guildhouse. There is a lot of talk about defecting. Of course, all of that just makes this place a bigger target."

He thought briefly of the twins, and the price they had already paid in all of this. "What about the pickpocket teams?"

"Ambrose has completely shut them down. It's just too dangerous. However, some have decided to go freelance, and others have been killed. Magnus sent enforcers to watch over them in the Five Markets, but that turned into a running battle with the Vos guard and more Guild men."

"Is there no good news?"

Her expression was grim. "None to speak of. We've had our victories, but they have been too small and too slow in coming. Caradoc succumbed to his wounds, never responded to the dram. They're talking about poison now. The docks have become a complete no-go area, at least in the dark hours. The thieves we had operating there have just disappeared. Bodies were found the next day, horribly mutilated, but we can only guess as to whether they are ours. The Guild must have hired real savages for that work. I am not sure what manner of man could do something like that."

"I think I know," he said quietly, but ignored her searching look. "What is the Council doing?"

"Panicking, mostly. At least, that is the word among the rest of us. Magnus told me to tell you that he is convening a council of war this afternoon, and your presence is requested if you are fit. I'm not sure though–"

"You can tell him I'll be there."

"I thought you might say that. You do need more rest, though."

"I'll rest until the meeting. But this is more important. We're fighting for survival now."

WHEN HE WALKED into the council chamber, Lucius' first reaction was one of alarm. The large table that dominated the room seemed empty; only four seats were occupied. Magnus took his usual place, and had been joined by Elaine, Nate and the weather-beaten thief he had come to know as Wendric. Magnus' bodyguards, Taene and Narsell, were standing behind the guildmaster, and Lucius had heard they had not left his side since the war began.

With so few members of the Council remaining it would appear that the Guild had been all too successful in its murderous campaign. Lucius found himself desperately hoping that others were engaged in secret missions for Magnus, that some plan was already being enacted that would secure final victory in this dirty war.

Magnus waved him forward, but the motion was slow and weary, and Lucius could see the strain and exhaustion the guildmaster was battling. He guessed Magnus had not seen his bed for the past three days.

"Lucius, good," Magnus said. "I had hoped you would be well enough to join us here. Are you fit enough for action?"

"I'm ready," Lucius said, without hesitation.

"The Hands are in need of every able-bodied thief now. I wanted you to take your place in this council of war, to advise and, if necessary, carry out the plans we make here. While you are not formally part of the Council itself, I believe that may only be a matter of time, to be resolved after this war is done. But that is something we need to set aside for now."

"Of course," Lucius said, surprised at the casual way the promotion had fallen into his lap. He forced himself to focus on the matter at hand.

"We have taken too many losses over the past few days, and it is clear that the Guild of Coin and Enterprise is much stronger than we gave them credit for," Magnus said.

"That may be true," said Wendric. "But it may just be they were better prepared to start a war. While we were concentrating on business, they were planning this from the start, picking targets and building alliances."

If Wendric's remarks were a reproach to Magnus' leadership, no one commented on it.

"We've got to start hitting back in a meaningful way," Nate said. "We've got to pick our own targets. Show the Guild we will not lie down quietly, that we are still to be reckoned with. At worse, we can slow down the assault. At best, we can deliver a killing blow."

"Jewel," Elaine said.

"That's right," Nate said. "They struck at our lieutenant, we must hit at theirs. Tit-for-tat. Loredo clearly prizes her. Removing Jewel will make him less sure, and it must at least damage his own standing within the Guild."

Wendric cleared his throat. "I'm... a little uneasy about that."

"Why?" Magnus asked.

"Well... if we meet Jewel on the street, if she is struck down during a battle, that is one thing. But to plan an assassination on a woman? It seems distasteful, in a way. Beneath us."

"Ha!" Elaine's bark preceded her incredulous gaze. "Best hope she is not assigned to take you down, Wendric. I doubt she will show you the same mercy!"

Lucius discovered that he had been swayed by Wendric's argument. He did not relish the thought of striking a woman down from the shadows. However, he thought of Adrianna and Grayling, women who were clearly at least as skilled as the men around them, and he had seen Jewel was a cold-blooded killer.

"I agree," he said. "Her reputation is well known, Wendric. How many of us is she already responsible for? It might well have been her who attacked Caradoc."

"I concur with Elaine and Lucius," Magnus said softly. "She must be removed. Elaine, with Agar gone, I am making you our Master of Assassins, temporarily at least. See to it."

"With pleasure." Elaine's easy, even grateful, acceptance sent a chill through Lucius, and he was once again reminded of the strength present in some women.

"So, where else is the Guild vulnerable?" Magnus asked.

"What of the Guild's alliance with the Vos guard?" Lucius asked. All eyes turned toward him, and he realised that none of the Council were aware of everything that had taken place during the raids in the merchant quarter.

"What alliance?" Nate asked suspiciously, and Lucius could see a tide of fear and doubt rising in the younger man.

"No one else reported it, then?" Lucius asked, though he already knew the answer. He kicked himself, for he should have known that with so many of the raiding parties killed during the escape from the Citadel, the chances of one surviving who had seen the direct co-operation between guard and Guild were greatly diminished. Luber had seen it, but he had already paid the price.

"When the Guild responded to us in the merchant quarter, fights broke out in the streets," he explained. "It did not take the guard long to respond, and the area was soon full of patrols."

"Well, that would be as dangerous to the Guild as to us," Elaine said.

"No," Lucius said firmly, shaking his head. "They had code words. The Guild, I mean. I heard them. When the guard waded in, code words were being used to identify the Guild from us. When I saw what was happening, I told everyone to scatter. But the Guild started tracking us, and leading patrols onto our trail. It was hopeless."

Nate thumped a hand down onto the table in frustration.

"Well, that's it, then," he said. "We can't fight the Guild *and* the Vos army!"

"Calm yourself, Nate," Magnus said smoothly, but they could all see he was troubled by this new revelation.

"Magnus, the Guild are already stronger than us," Nate said, suddenly very animated. "Maybe, just maybe, with a careful selection of targets and a great deal of planning, we can pull even with them. Maybe win. But there is no way we can send thieves against the Vos army. They know how to fight. It will just be a slaughter."

"So why not just wander over to Loredo and ask if he needs another thief?" Elaine said, caustically.

Nate looked hurt at that. "I'm just saying."

"One way or another, better or worse, I'll stand with you Magnus," Wendric said. "But Nate is not wholly wrong. The combination of a thieves' guild and a city guard – especially one formed from the Vos army – is a dreadful thought. Even in peace time, they could completely shut us down. During a war..."

Lucius considered the sea demons the Guild also evidently had on their side, and he looked up at Magnus to find the guildmaster staring back at him. He thought that Magnus was perhaps thinking the same thing, that the Hands' position in the city was far less tenable than even the surviving Council members believed.

"Then it is obvious," Magnus finally said. They all looked at him with clear relief, clinging to the hope that their guildmaster would still be able to steer them through this difficult time. "If our enemies have built up their strength, then we must do the same. If they increase their reach by building alliances, then we must do the same."

Wendric frowned. "But who can we go to that would be both willing to support us, and provide us with real muscle?"

"We can pull mercenaries in from the Anclas Territories. Battle-hardened soldiers. We'll have to disguise their presence here in the city, but I fancy they will be a match for the Vos guard."

"Expensive though," Nate pointed out. "And we could never afford enough to swing the balance entirely."

"The vault does us no good if the Guild wins this war, no matter how full it remains," Elaine said in reply.

"That is true enough," Magnus said. "We filled the vault before, we can do so again – but only if we survive this war. As for numbers, it will be more important as to how and where we use such men. Our goal is not to launch a coup, remember, just to defeat the Guild or force them to terms. We only need employ mercenaries when we risk running into the Vos guard."

"I'll arrange it," Wendric said. "I have a few contacts I can tap for this."

"It will take time," Lucius said, recalling just how large the Anclas Territories were, and how long the journey to Turnitia could take. That was assuming a company could be persuaded to employment quickly.

"There is something else we can do," Magnus said. "Loredo is acting like a warlord, gathering as much strength in arms to his cause as he can muster. Somewhere along the line, he has forgotten how to be a thief. That will be to our advantage."

"What do you mean?" Nate asked.

"A thief never confronts an enemy head on," Magnus explained. "Instead, he studies his mark, picks the weak points, bypasses the defences and traps. Only if absolutely necessary does he strike, and then only from the shadows."

"We avoid open battle?" Elaine asked. "Seems obvious."

"It is," Magnus said. "But to do so effectively, we need information. We all know this. Information is what drives a thieves' guild, it's what ensures the flow of gold into the vault. We need access to better information – we need to know exactly what the Guild is up to at all times, what their ties to the Vos guard are, and what is happening within the Citadel itself."

"Ah, I see where you are going with this, Magnus," Wendric said. "But you cannot know whether they have not been bought already. They could already be working for the Guild."

Lucius was confused and, from Nate's expression, he was not the only one.

"Who are you talking about?" he asked.

"He wants to bring the Beggars' Guild on side with us," Wendric said.

"The beggars?" Nate said derisively.

"Nate, the beggars are eyes of this city," Magnus said. "They are ignored by everyone, and yet they can be found in every corner of Turnitia. From the docks to the Five Markets, you will find them huddled, lost, abandoned and forgotten. But it is exactly those qualities that allow them to get close to others, to see and hear everything that goes on in the city. How many times have you left a house you have just robbed, and ignored the beggar across the street outside, happily thinking you have escaped notice? I promise you, nearly every one of your operations is known to the Beggars' guild."

"They actually have a guild?" Lucius asked.

"Oh, there is quite some etiquette involved in begging," Magnus said. "And, like any industry, like us, efforts have to be organised if the maximum profit for all is to be realised. You've worked with our pickpocket teams, Lucius. You know how we strategise their efforts. The beggars are no different, with each assigned a rotating territory that ensures no one area is flooded with them, and no purses are drained too heavily or too quickly. And they can actually be quite vicious towards independents who break the system."

"Do they have a guildhouse?" Elaine asked.

"The streets are their guildhouse. However, I think I know where to find their master."

"You're not thinking of going yourself?" Wendric asked, suddenly alarmed.

"You'd be making yourself too easy a target," Elaine joined in. "The Guild will be waiting for something like this, one mistake that would reveal you and allow them to decapitate us."

Magnus held up his hands. "My friends, I will not be swayed in this. We need the beggars with us, and we need them now. If one of you were to go, the negotiations might take too long. If I can locate their guildmaster, and I have a good idea where to start looking, I might be able to make the right promises and forge an alliance on the spot."

"It is far too dangerous," Wendric said.

"Too many of our members have already paid too high a price," Magnus said in reply. "If I do not share the same risks, I am not fit to be guildmaster in the first place. Anyway, I'll have Taene and Narsell with me, and I doubt there are any assassins capable of making their way past these two. If that should prove insufficient, however, I will also have Lucius at my side."

Lucius looked up in surprise. "Of course," he heard himself say. "I would be honoured."

Wendric had the last words of the meeting.

"Be watchful instead."

CHAPTER FIFTEEN

LUCIUS HAD NEVER felt more alive than he did at this moment. Magnus walked within a pace behind him, while Taene and Narsell brought up the rear, flanking the guildmaster. He felt his heart pounding, heard every sound in the crowded street, smelled every scent. Danger lurked in every passer-by, in every alley they passed, within every window that opened as they walked underneath, or so he felt. After the Council had broken up, Elaine had approached him, making him swear to protect Magnus from harm whatever the odds. It was a promise he intended to keep.

Lucius' eyes flicked constantly, sweeping over every member of the crowd that thronged the street. The middle-aged woman manhandling several long Pontaine-style loaves and two children; was she disguised to appear older, her bread concealing a weapon as she moved closer? The kids, were they lookouts, gauging the guildmaster's defences in preparation for an ambush at the next junction? Were those Vos guards intentionally flanking them? Was that a shadow on the roofline, an assassin lining up a shot with a crossbow?

More than once, he had felt Magnus' hand on his shoulder, accompanied with an admonishment to relax or, at least calm down a degree. Magnus had taken precautions, wearing a cloak and wide-brimmed hat to disguise his appearance. To anyone casually walking past the tight, protective group, he might well have been no more than a wealthy trader or official with an exaggerated sense of self-worth. Even so, the mail shirt he wore under his cloak and leather tunic was an added insurance.

They had started their search in the Five Markets which, in Lucius' opinion, was close to madness. The ever-shifting crowds and sheer number of potential threats seemed overwhelming, and he noticed that even Taene and Narsell seemed nervous, their eyes in a permanent suspicious squint, heads turning to face every new sound. Looming over them were the walls of the Citadel, and Lucius could all too easily imagine some guard perched on the ramparts, sighting Magnus and feeling lucky with a crossbow.

Magnus, however, insisted that this was where they start, and he made a rough kind of sense. The Five Markets were among the busiest places in the city, and it was a natural congregation point for beggars. They were, thus, the power centre of the beggars and their presumed guild, though Lucius still had doubts about the homeless being able to organise themselves to any great degree.

Insisting on approaching any beggar directly himself, Magnus was met with suspicion at first, and sometimes a subdued hostility. They all feared the beggars had already been bought by the Guild. However, Magnus was lucky enough to be recognised by one – a foul-smelling woman in the later years of her life – who had a disturbing habit of scratching at her nether regions while holding a hand out for coin. Her directions, which Magnus paid handsomely for, led them to Ring Street and a grain house that lay between the two southern markets.

Crates and empty sacks were piled outside and these had been appropriated by nearly a dozen beggars, all looking dishevelled, miserable, and without purpose. A memory triggered in Lucius' mind, and he recalled seeing beggars gather here before. In the past, he had presumed they were the failures of the city's lowest citizens, those whose begging had been less than successful, and were now just waiting around to die. However, if what the old woman had told Magnus was to be believed, Lucius was in fact looking at the power base of the Beggars' Guild.

"They don't look much," he muttered, and felt Magnus' hand on his shoulder again.

"That is their strength," Magnus said. "Now, remember why we are here, and that we need their help. Beggars are outcasts, spurned by everyone, and so they expect no favours. But we must treat them with the utmost respect. Understand?"

Lucius nodded as he followed Magnus and the bodyguards as they approached the beggars. It was hard to identify some of them as men or women, but Lucius had the feeling they were a mix of both, young and old. Some slouched against piles of sacks made into makeshift beds, while others perched on top of crates. All seemed weary, and yet they regarded the entourage of thieves with guarded suspicion.

"Greetings," Magnus began, holding up a hand.

"You've got no business here, sir, best you move along," said one, a girl Lucius thought, though there was nothing feminine about her appearance.

"On the contrary, I believe there is business that would interest everyone here."

"We're not looking for work, so if you have a ship or wagon train that needs unloading, go find your cheap labour elsewhere."

"You misunderstand me—"

"It's okay, Grennar," said one of the men sitting cross-legged on the crates. He was wreathed in rags, and Lucius had taken him for a leper, or worse. He drew back his hood to reveal a middle-aged face, dirty, unshaven, but otherwise remarkably healthy. "I think we can dispense with the deceptions this time. Magnus here is finding time rather against him at the moment. Is that not right, Magnus?"

"You know me?"

"We know everyone," the man said with a sly smile. "That is why you are here, is it not?"

Magnus tipped his head in acknowledgement. "You have me at a disadvantage."

"I know you are Magnus Wry, leader of the Night Hands and former lieutenant of the Thieves' Guild of Turnitia. You already know my position among the beggars. But you may call me Sebastian."

"I have a proposal for an alliance."

"Of course you have," Sebastian said, his voice warm but his eyes betraying a coldness. "Your little den of thieves stands on the brink of annihilation, and you find many powerful enemies allied against you. You, Magnus, are desperate."

"And you are on the outside, Sebastian," Magnus said. "The lowest of all in the city, ignored by everyone. Only I realise your true value."

"So, we have your respect. Well, that is... nice." The comment drew a small swell of laughter from the beggars, and Lucius saw Magnus turn to him, rolling his eyes at the contrived play between the two guildmasters.

"I can give you a great deal more than respect. Employment. Regular income. Work for all the members of your guild."

"We already have work," said Sebastian. "And many of my beggars are richer than many of your thieves. Show him, Grennar."

The girl smiled up at them, revealing a set of perfect teeth, then reached to her face to pick at a boil. Lucius stomach turned in disgust, then his eyes opened wide as he saw her peel the boil off.

She repeated the action several more times, then spat on a cloth and wiped the dirt away, revealing a not unattractive face. Sebastian noted Lucius' look of surprise.

"It is all about deception," he said. "And yes, we know you too Lucius Kane, once exile of this city, returned a gambler, now rising star among the Night Hands – whatever *that* future is worth. We know your secrets too. We have seen how you fight the men you cheat, and the... methods you employ."

Lucius looked up at the beggar master in alarm, but kept his face neutral.

"You see, Lucius, we are not thieves or blackmailers. We have no interest in power, territory, or fame. So long as the city continues to exist, so will we. Our guild offers protection and a livelihood to the lowest, the most humble. That is why we are here, and that is the only thing we work towards."

"We can help you," Magnus said.

"It seems you are the one in need of help, Magnus," said Sebastian. "Alliances, you see, are built on mutual goals. You are currently engaged in a war, one that you are losing. The bodies of your members are found every night in dark alleys, and your numbers shrink daily. And now the Vos army itself has targeted you for destruction. Why would we want any part of that? I have no wish to see my own people decimated in retaliation."

"The risks to you would be minimal. No active operations. Just information, a regular flow. That is all."

"The role of a spy can be the riskiest of all."

"I suspect you already have much of the information we require," Magnus said. "You need do little more than you do now. As you said, your guild comprises the lowest and most humble. You are all but invisible to our enemies – else they would have approached you already."

"What makes you think they haven't?" Sebastian asked.

"I know Loredo. I know how he thinks."

Sebastian shrugged. "Not completely useless, then."

"In return, I offer you ten per cent of our guild's takings over the next five years. After that, we review the arrangement, see whether it is still beneficial to the two of us."

Lucius stifled a sharp intake of breath. That ten per cent would cut deep into the franchise agreements within the Hands, and he could imagine plenty of thieves loath to share their ill-gotten gains with beggars.

"Plus, we can train any member of yours that wishes to become a thief," Magnus finished.

Sebastian hooted at that, and that encouraged laughter from the rest of his entourage. "I already told you, Magnus, many of the beggars in this city are wealthier than your thieves. And I won't have you sap my guild's strength to bolster your own."

"Then stop playing, Sebastian," Magnus said, allowing impatience to creep into his voice. "What are you after? You already knew I was coming to see you, and if I did not have something you were interested in, we would not have got this far. So, what is it?"

Pursing his lips, Sebastian looked down at Magnus as if considering his options.

"The ten per cent I'll take," he said. "Though only for one year. You will have trouble enough keeping your thieves in line for that arrangement, and you won't get them to agree to it for long when the danger has passed. Maybe we will continue the alliance thereafter, maybe not. It all depends on which guild earns more during that time."

"Agreed."

"Furthermore, you will give us the Five Markets."

Magnus frowned. "I thought you said you weren't interested in territory."

"Oh, we're not," Sebastian said smoothly. "But visitors to the Five Markets all come with a finite amount of coin in their purses. Most they will spend, but some they give to the poor, starving beggars that walk among them. However, a man who has just been robbed has neither the ability nor the inclination for charity, and your pickpockets have become too good at what they do."

"That is too much to ask."

"It makes perfect sense. It is a small price to pay for our support. And what you are doing in the Five Markets is not good for business. People become tighter with their money, the guard move us on that much quicker. It's bad business, Magnus and you only have the greed of your thieves to blame."

Exhaling noisily, Magnus eventually nodded. "I'll withdraw our teams from the Five Markets tomorrow, but they come up for negotiation again when we discuss the continuance of our alliance."

Sebastian, still crouched on his crate, looked down at Magnus imperiously for a moment, then smiled.

"Then we have an understanding. I'll arrange for one of us to report to your guildhouse daily. We'll update you with anything learned, and you can suggest where we concentrate our efforts."

"Good enough," said Magnus. "I presume you already know where our guildhouse is."

He received a look of scorn for his trouble. "Magnus, we already know the knock code to gain entry through your own front door."

"Of course you do," Magnus muttered, and Lucius guessed that the system would be changed wholesale that very night. "Who will be our liaison?"

"Grennar, I think. She is most suited to the task." Magnus looked doubtfully down at the young girl, who stared back defiantly. "Don't let her tender years mislead you, Magnus. She is probably smarter than both of us."

Magnus shrugged. "Fine. Send her to us tonight."

"She'll be there," Sebastian said. "One other thing, a down payment on our side of the bargain. Have a care as you walk about the city, Magnus. Your enemies know you have left the guildhouse, and that disguise is not going to fool anyone"

Lucius looked up at Sebastian in alarm. "How do they know?"

"The Guild's own spy network is not as extensive as ours, but it's still shrewd enough. Loredo is playing his own game at the moment, pulling on the Vos army for muscle and information, while giving as little in return as possible – Grennar will tell you what we have learned there later. But, for now, be careful. Assassins are on the streets looking for you."

"We should go, quickly," Lucius said, turning to Magnus. He glanced at Taene and Narsell, and saw both had their hands on their weapons and were already scanning the nearby crowds for danger.

Magnus agreed, then faced the beggars. "Sebastian, a pleasure."

The beggar master nodded once. "Just make sure you stay in one piece. I don't want to have this conversation with Loredo down the line."

Taene and Narsell hustled them away from Ring Street, choosing quieter side roads and the wider alleys in an effort to avoid crowds. Now their mission was done, there was no need to take unnecessary risks, and the bodyguards placed themselves ahead and behind Magnus and Lucius.

"That was an expensive agreement," Lucius said cautiously.

"It could have been far more costly," Magnus said. "I was expecting him to demand a portion of the vault from the outset, as it will take time for our operations to reach their full potential again, even if this war is won quickly with the minimum of bloodshed. But I think he had already fixed his sights on the Five Markets."

"Ambrose will not be happy with that, nor will the others involved in the pick-pocketing."

"The Five Markets represent a higher cost than that, Lucius," Magnus said. "They are a magnet for everyone in the city, be they resident or visitor. The pickpocket teams are where we have always trained the youngest among us, bringing fresh blood into the guild on a regular basis. Now, those children will become beggars, while we must look elsewhere for recruits. That is the true value of the territory."

Lucius had not considered that, and it began to dawn on him just how complicated the structure of these negotiations could become. Narsell, leading them down a narrow street lined with tanners, ironmongers and other tradesmen, suddenly hissed, and Lucius looked up to see a patrol of Vos guard rounding the junction ahead. They steered right, heading down a short alley behind a carpenters but, as they emerged into the parallel street, they saw another patrol just a few dozen yards away.

"That's no coincidence," Magnus muttered, and Lucius felt the tension rise in both Narsell and Taene. They headed away from the patrols, directly back to Ring Street, with Lucius reaching beneath his cloak to feel the reassuring presence of his sword. They could see the crowds churning along Ring Street just a little distance ahead, but the Vos patrol had already changed its course to follow them, and they were not being discreet about it.

"Get ready to run," Narsell whispered, and Lucius saw him raise a hand in preparation for the signal to take action. Before he could give it, two groups of men stumbled out of opposite alleyways ahead of them, some singing drunkenly, others stumbling as they clutched bottles.

The timing of their appearance set Lucius on edge, and he felt in his stomach that these were no mere revellers in search of another tavern. Magnus and the bodyguards had stopped, and Taene's blade was half-drawn. Lucius looked back at the Vos guards, who had not quickened their pace, but still continued towards them relentlessly. If the drunks proved hostile, they were cut off from any path of escape, but he did not relish trying to smash through the soldiers while fleeing.

"Carry on," Magnus urged. "We'll do better with the drunks than the guard."

They moved to obey, and watched as the two groups of men merged with one another, laughing and slapping one another on the back, seemingly oblivious to the four thieves marching warily toward them. However, Lucius had already noted one or two sidelong gazes directed their way, and knew then they were in for trouble.

A woman strode out from among the press of men and, too late, Lucius recognised her as Jewel. He opened his mouth to cry out, but Narsell and Taene were already reacting, drawing their swords and moving to shield Magnus. She raised a small one-handed crossbow and tightened her grip on the lever. Lucius heard a quiet whistle through the air, then Narsell collapsed to the ground, a short bolt protruding from his throat.

Jewel grinned as she dropped the crossbow and drew a dagger from her belt. The men behind her whooped in excitement, and a range of daggers and short blades appeared in their hands. Led by Jewel, they charged.

Taene showed no fear, and little regard for his own life as he met the attack. Side-stepping one man and kicking out at another, his sword claimed two lives within seconds, and the deaths checked the momentum of the charge. He was soon fighting for his life, but he always manoeuvred to keep himself between Magnus and the bulk of the pack.

For his part, Magnus had already drawn his own weapon, a finely balanced short sword, but Lucius grabbed him and propelled the guildmaster forward, hoping to break through the gang and then disappear into the crowds just a couple of hundred yards ahead on Ring Street. He glanced over his shoulder and saw the patrol had stopped, evidently happy to let the thieves kill one another before moving in.

"Go!" Taene shouted as he fell under a swarm of bodies, his sword reappearing momentarily as it continued to hack down at those around him. Blood was already flowing across the cobbles of the street but Lucius knew the bodyguard's skill and luck would not save him in that tight press.

The rest of the Guild men, frustrated at not being able to reach Taene because of the press of bodies surrounding him, broke off from the fight and ran to cut off Magnus and Lucius from escape. Knowing he could not fight them all, Lucius cursed as he shoved the guildmaster behind him. He felt the threads of power respond to his call and he grabbed one whose energy was deeply familiar. This time, however, he allowed the thread to spiral and grow until he could barely contain the form he moulded it to in his mind. With a loud cry, he brought his arm down in a wide sweep, and felt the energy pass through his body to push the air away from him in an explosive burst.

Hit by an unyielding wall of wind, the men were tossed back, sprawling on the ground as they lay stunned and gasping for breath. Breathing heavily from the exertion, Lucius staggered as he grabbed Magnus again to spur him on, trying desperately to ignore the look of suspicious amazement in the man's face.

They started to run, feet pounding the street, each step taking them further from the murderous crowd behind. Magnus cried out, and Lucius felt the man stumble against him, the weight almost pulling him down to the ground. Catching his balance, Lucius turned to get Magnus back on his feet, and saw a slender knife embedded deep in the back of his thigh. Blood oozed slowly from the wound, but Lucius knew that, as deep as the blade had gone, the flow would quickly speed up if the weapon was removed.

"Lucius!" Magnus shouted the warning and even as he scrambled to one side, Lucius sensed motion beside him. Ducking low and rolling backwards, he grabbed for the sword at his back even as another blade sliced through the air between them.

He jumped to his feet, and saw Jewel standing just a few feet from him, her eyes narrowed to slits as she watched them both, judging which to be the greater threat. Her face remained flat and expressionless, betraying no emotion whatsoever. She apparently decided that, with Magnus already wounded and struggling to get to his feet, Lucius was her priority. Covering the distance between them in two easy strides, she swiped through the air with her sword, as if testing his reactions; she then crouched low and whirled round in a circle, the blade building momentum as it spun towards his shins.

Lucius sprang back, then held his sword forward defensively, as if warding the woman back. Rising to her full height again, Jewel drew a dagger from her belt. Lucius stabbed forward, but a casual flick of her dagger turned his blade, holding it to one side as her own sword was held aloft for an instant, then brought down to slash his skull in two.

Off balance from her parry, but seeing the danger, Lucius reached up and grabbed her wrist, surprised at her sinewy strength as he strained to keep her sword clear.

He tried to muster his strength to drive Jewel down, wanting to pin her to the ground where his weight would give him the advantage, but she yielded only an inch at a time. Straining with the effort, he suddenly felt the air driven out of his lungs as her knee drove hard into his groin. A split second later, his world exploded into stars of pain as her forehead smashed into the bridge of his nose.

Sightless and writhing in agony, Lucius felt the ground rise up to hit him hard. Expecting to feel Jewel's blade pierce his heart at any moment, he shook his head to clear his vision as he tried to get to his knees.

The world blurred in front of him, then suddenly sharpened into stark reality. Jewel's back was toward him as she strode toward Magnus. The guildmaster was limping badly as he tried to circle her, his own weapon held before him. As she slashed her sword at his chest, he met the attack, and a loud ringing of metal echoed off the buildings along the street as their weapons met. Immediately, Jewel drew her sword back and thrust forward again, only to be turned by a desperate parry from Magnus.

Lucius tried to get to his feet but stumbled and he started crawling toward Magnus and Jewel, desperate to aid his friend before the murderess could finish him. He could see Magnus was in a lot of pain, and Jewel was forcing him to keep moving, every step forcing the dagger in the back of his leg to grind against bone. Their swords met again, and Magnus was forced to give more ground, fighting purely defensively, with Jewel giving him no opportunity to attack.

Drawing a ragged breath, Lucius was finally able to force air into his lungs, and he used his sword as a brace to get him back on his feet. He caught Magnus' eye, and a look flicked between them. Magnus hobbled to the left, bringing Jewel round with him, so her back was kept to Lucius. Lifting his sword, Lucius staggered toward her, fixing his gaze between her shoulder blades, where he intended to plant his weapon and so rid the Hands of this dreadful enemy.

Magnus roared as he thrust his sword forward, as much to distract Jewel as score a hit, and the woman easily side-stepped his attack. Lucius was closing on her now and he began to run, painful though the movement was. He raised his sword, its point aimed squarely at her back, and prepared to thrust down with all his remaining strength.

Jewel turned and flung her left arm out, releasing her dagger. It was a hasty attack, but the spinning blade still thumped home into Lucius' right arm. He cried out in pain as his sword fell from suddenly lifeless fingers, his left hand instinctively grasping the wound.

He bent down to fumble for his sword, but looked up as Jewel whirled back to Magnus, her foot lashing out to strike him on his wounded leg. The shock of the impact was enough to make Magnus cry out in pain and he reeled backwards, tripping on the cobbles.

"No!" Lucius cried out as he saw the inevitability of her next action. Jewel calmly thrust her sword through Magnus' chest. The guildmaster coughed blood as he tried to grasp the blade that had ploughed through his breast bone, then he fell limp.

Anger and deadly fury swept through Lucius now, as he saw Jewel casually withdraw her sword and wipe it on Magnus' cloak. Then, she turned back to him.

"Bitch!"

He was not aware of his cry of vengeance, feeling only the threads of power surging forward, each eager to be clasped by his mind and moulded by his rage. Without thinking, he grabbed the brightest and hurled its force, unchecked and barely formed, at the woman.

A burst of argent fire soared from the fist he punched at her, the ball of white-hot energy burning the air itself as it shot forth. He saw Jewel's eyes widen a fraction as the magic surged toward her, and she flinched to one side as the silver flames swept past her face. She shrieked with pain and the smell of burnt flesh rolled over him.

Recoiling backwards and dropping her sword, Jewel clutched at her face, the whole left side having been blackened and scorched by the magical fire. Her hair burned and her ear had been shrivelled by the heat. She took only seconds to recover, and then stared back at Lucius, emotion coming to her ruined face for the first time. He felt her loathing, her fury and terrible desire to inflict pain upon him, and he stood to await the inevitable, having no energy for anything else.

Just as quickly, the hate fled from her eyes, and they flickered down to the corpse at her feet. Seeing no movement, she nodded to herself once, then turned, and walked away. She called out to the men still standing, and they followed her, leaving only bodies lying in the bloody street.

Lucius was alone. Narsell and Taene lay still ahead of him, the latter barely recognisable after having been all but torn apart by the Guild men. He knelt down beside Magnus, hoping beyond hope that he would still feel a pulse in the guildmaster's veins. Magnus, however, had already left.

CHAPTER SIXTEEN

Upon his arrival, the guildhouse erupted into turmoil. Lucius had entered the building, his face betraying no emotion other than a hard, frozen shock. Taking a place in the common room, questions and accusations rolled over him like the gigantic waves pounding at the harbour defences but, like the monolithic breakers that stalled the ocean, he remained immovable.

The absence of Magnus, Taene and Narsell spoke volumes, and every thief present knew something had gone tragically wrong. Without explanation from Lucius, rumour and paranoia ran rampant, with scare stories growing ever more fantastic and yet all the more plausible for it. Within a few minutes, there were a good number of thieves who believed the Vos guard had marched onto the streets with lists detailing all their names, and were seeking to murder every one of them.

Calm was not restored until Elaine entered the common room and, upon seeing Lucius, she ordered everyone to leave. Many seemed ready to protest her authority now the guildmaster was dead, but her withering look broke any resistance.

Sitting opposite Lucius, she stared across the table at him, the silence of the empty common room seeming almost deafening to him. She reached out to touch his hand and asked him what had happened. Haltingly, he told her. The finding of Sebastian and the alliance forged between thief and beggar. The presence of the Vos guard on the streets, and the ambush by Guild men.

Jewel. Terrible, deadly Jewel.

He fell silent when his tale was complete, and Elaine had no words. They sat together, in silence as they brooded and mourned, contemplating the loss of their guildmaster and what the Guild would now do to finish them off.

Lucius found his own melancholy a little puzzling. He had liked Magnus, of course – who hadn't? He had been a good leader, quick to spot talent and loyalty, and ready to reward both. What Lucius had not counted on was how much the Night Hands had become his new home and family, how much Magnus had really meant to him.

Part of the hurt, he knew, was his own failure to stop the assassination, and now anger boiled within him too. He clung on to that feeling, knowing that in the trials ahead, it would prove useful.

Elaine reached across the table to touch him again, this time shaking him firmly out of his darker thoughts.

"Pull yourself together, Lucius," she said. "Magnus trusted you, and so I must too. We are about to fall apart, and we need all the strength we can muster to stop us breaking."

He looked up at her mutely for a moment, then nodded.

"There will be a meeting," she said. "It will be chaotic, so be prepared."

ELAINE HAD NOT been wrong. With the Council decimated and Magnus gone, anarchy began to take hold within the Night Hands. The council chamber barely contained the riot as the voices of dozens of thieves, all packed into the inadequate space, competed with one another to be heard.

The remaining Council took seats around the table; Elaine, Wendric, Nate, and now Lucius. Some of the thieves forced to stand raised objections to Lucius' presence at the table, but a sharp word from Elaine silenced their criticisms.

Grennar was also at the table, at Lucius' side, and her transformation was remarkable. No longer a young beggar girl wreathed in rags, she sat straight and appeared utterly confident. Dressed in a tight-fitting blue gown, she might have been the daughter of a wealthy city official. Most stunning was her face; sharp, lightly freckled, once clean it revealed a girl of perhaps no more than fourteen. Her young age was a great surprise to the Council, some of whom had wondered out loud whether the beggars were taking them seriously. However, Magnus' posthumous endorsement of the alliance proved sufficient for them to invite her to the table.

Before the table, other members of the Hands jostled for position, seeking to get themselves heard. Each with a different idea of how the guild should continue, or not. Of how they could take instant vengeance, or not. One viciously planted a dagger into the table, promising that if the Council were too weak to take the fight to the enemy, others were not.

The overall mood, however, was one of despondent failure, a feeling that the time of the Night Hands was at an end. Most expected the guild to be disbanded in this meeting.

Clearing his throat, Wendric silenced the bickering thieves and all eyes turned toward him.

"As you will have all heard by now, Magnus has been slain by the Guild. The Council has heard Lucius' explanation of what happened, and we are satisfied that he is in no way at fault." At this, Lucius heard someone mutter at the back of the chamber, but he did not catch what was said, and Wendric ignored the interruption. "It was a calculated ambush aided, in part, by the Vos guard. It would have taken a small army to save Magnus. The guildmaster knew the risks when he left this place to forge a new alliance. It is now our duty to continue in his footsteps, to lead the Night Hands to become the kind of organisation for thieves that he always envisioned."

"Well, what's the point?" cried one thief, an old man whose hands shook as he spoke. "We're beaten. With Magnus and God knows how many others gone, the guild is broken!"

"You thinking we should all just roll over and join Loredo, is that it, Hengit?" called out another.

"We split up!" Hengit said, smacking a fist into his palm. "We all go independent. The Guild will never be able to track all of us!"

"Oh, they will," Elaine said, bringing attention back to those around the table. "You can be sure of that. They will track each one of you down and either force you to join their Guild or kill you. If we divide our strength–"

"What's left of it!"

"Yes, Hengit, what is left of it," Elaine said, her anger directed solely at the old thief for a moment. "If we break up the Hands now, we all die. Or, worse, work for a pittance under Loredo. You think he will just welcome you with open arms? He will mistrust all of you, your careers will be broken, doing the worst jobs and taking part in the riskiest operations. No, Hengit, you are far better off among the Night Hands, however long we last."

"And how long will that be, then?" called a voice from the back of the chamber.

"That is what we are here to decide," said Nate. "Elaine, your hit on Jewel clearly did not work as planned."

Elaine sighed audibly. "No. She was spotted on the streets near the merchant quarter but when our agents moved in... well, she either expected their arrival or is far more dangerous than we credited her with."

"What were our losses?" Wendric asked.

"Total." Elaine's simple answer triggered a collective intake of breath throughout the assembled crowd. The assassins employed by the Hands were experts in their field, trained killers capable of evading guards, traps and other defences in order to strike a target down within seconds. For a single woman to not only escape their attentions but strike back so effectively was a stunning achievement.

"After dispatching our agents, she was then able to gather her forces and take down Magnus. We don't know whether it was a chance encounter, or if they knew where Magnus was–"

"They knew," said Grennar. Her voice cut over Elaine's easily and with a measure of grace. In another time, Lucius might have smiled at the ease with which the girl spoke to the thieves but, at this moment, he simply listened as if she were the equal of any in the chamber. In that, he was not alone.

"The Vos army has its own network of spies in the city," Grennar went on to explain. "When Magnus was spotted on the streets, word was quickly passed to the Guild, and the ambush set. Once the guard was used to funnel your guildmaster into a predetermined area, there was nothing anyone could do."

In saying that, she cast a brief look at Lucius.

"So if the Guild has the Vos guard in their pocket, why have they not just finished us off completely?" Nate asked. "It is what I would do. Why not just launch an assault against this guildhouse and wipe us out in one stroke?"

Nate's question had been on everyone's mind and hearing it voiced caused some to start shuffling their feet and looking over their shoulders, as if expecting to see the entire Vos army crash through the door of the council chamber.

"Because Loredo is no fool," Grennar said, and Lucius saw Nate colour slightly as the girl looked at him. "Because the Vos guard have *no idea* where your guildhouse is."

"Well, that doesn't make sense," Wendric said. "The Vos guard won't see themselves as junior members in that partnership. They will want to run the Guild, not the other way around."

"That is exactly what Loredo fears."

"If the Hands fall and only the Guild remains, Loredo wants to retain his independence," Elaine said. "He does not want his thieves to become stooges for the Empire."

"Exactly," Grennar said. "He is playing a dangerous, but – it has to be said – clever game. He has brought the Vos guard onto his side, and that is a powerful ally for any thieves' guild to have, normally only possible in the most corrupt Pontaine cities. He is playing things down the middle, taking what support he can easily get from the guard, while giving them as little information as possible."

"The guard cannot be happy with that," said Nate.

"The captain of the guard, von Minterheim, was seen raging in the Citadel this morning. He has been telling his sergeants to lean on their Guild contacts, to start squeezing them for information. He wants this war over quickly, as it is beginning to make the merchants nervous. If they decide it is safer and more profitable to start trading in another city, Vos' hold on Turnitia is weakened."

Nate gave Grennar a strange look. "And how, exactly, does the Beggars' Guild know what is happening within the Citadel?"

She shrugged. "As we told your guildmaster and Lucius here, we have eyes everywhere."

"In the Citadel?"

"Beggars can go where others cannot. No one sees us, and so if a few beggars remain in the courtyard after a hanging or two, well they will be thrown out eventually, but no one is going to hurry to do it."

"Magnus was right about you," Wendric said quietly, and Lucius could see the man had a new appreciation of their ally, despite her young age.

"So where does that leave us?" another voice in the crowd asked.

"Without much time," Elaine answered. "If von Minterheim is pressuring Loredo, he will be forced to move quickly. He doubtless feels we are crippled and defenceless, so his end game will start soon."

"One thing is certain; he will want this guildhouse," Wendric said. "There are too many treasures and secrets within these walls for him to ignore."

"A direct assault, then?" Nate asked.

"That will come sooner or later," Elaine said. "The streets will become no-go areas for all of us first. And if they discover our relationship with the beggars..."

"Don't worry about us," Grennar said. "We would not enter an agreement with you if it meant suicide. Our presence will be kept hidden, one way or another."

"In that case, we go fully defensive," Elaine said. "We lock down the guildhouse, use only the sewers when moving about the city, and stay away from the areas the Guild controls best – the docks and merchant quarter. This place, we fortify. We'll get our trapsmiths to work and plunder the armoury for weapons."

"Just sit and wait?" Wendric asked.

"We cannot fight them directly," Elaine pointed out. "They are too many. However, if we know they have to come here, and our friends among the beggars can tell us when, then we regain an advantage. Superior numbers will mean nothing when the fight is on our territory."

"There is a sense in that," a thief said in support.

"We can ensure that any enemy trying to breach these walls, be they thieves or guard, will be hip deep in their own blood within minutes."

"That is no way to gain victory," Wendric said.

"The first task is to survive. Once we can prove we can defend ourselves, once we show the Guild that they cannot wipe us out without sustaining untenable losses, their attacks will stall."

"I agree," said Nate. "Once we break the back of their main assault, then we can think about hitting back. If we prolong this long enough, their alliance with the Vos guard may break down. Without that support, it is the Guild that becomes vulnerable."

"It would be ironic if the guard then decided all thieves were its enemy," Elaine said, thinking through the course ahead. "Suddenly, it is the Guild that is the most visible, while we are hidden here. When the guard starts hitting back at thieves, they will be targeting the Guild. How long will it be before the Guild is reduced in strength to our level? Suddenly, things become even!"

A ragged cheer went through the crowd, though only a handful of thieves added to it.

"That is pretty fanciful," Wendric said.

"Yes, of course it is," Elaine said. "What is important is that we realise that there are many other options open to us, so long as we can survive the next few days. We can make this guildhouse near impregnable. We can play the waiting game now – the Guild cannot."

Seeing Nate nod in agreement, Wendric looked down the table. "So, we have a consensus?"

"No."

Lucius had been brooding, following only the gist of the debate at times. He leaned on one elbow as he sat in thought. He was only faintly aware that he had uttered his disagreement, and it was the silence that followed that shook his attention back to the chamber, as the assembled thieves waited for his next words.

Looking down the table, he saw Wendric raise his eyebrows in surprise, while Nate frowned in frustration. He tried hard to ignore the dangerous look Elaine flashed him, there only for a second, but no less threatening for all that.

"Make your preparations," he said. "Build the defences you suggest round the guildhouse. Whether necessary or not, they are certainly prudent. And yes, I agree that no one should leave unless on absolutely essential business. You will need the manpower anyway to defend this place. But I do not suggest that we simply sit here, waiting for the hammer to fall. That, it seems to me, would be a very foolish thing to do."

"So, what do you suggest?" Elaine asked, and he could sense the coldness in voice, the faint warning that now was not the time for the Council to be divided, that they could not risk the Hands disbanding.

Laying his hands flat on the table, Lucius sat straight in his seat, staring at the wood between them. He thought of the attack on Magnus, the guildmaster cut down in the street like an animal. He remembered Markel and Treal, two children who had been butchered by the Guild, just to make a point. The disaster at the docks, and the inhuman allies the Guild had apparently gained, still a secret to those in this chamber. Too much blood, too much killing, and for what? So one group of thieves could run the city the way they saw fit?

It ended here.

"I say we attack."

The suggestion was met with silence, and Lucius continued, his voice even, measured, dangerous. "We have little else to lose, and they will be at their most confident. We hit them. We hit all of them. We start with Loredo, Jewel, von Minterheim, and work down from there. We kill their leaders, their senior thieves, the guard sergeants, and anyone else who gets in the way. We pay them back for the blood they have stolen from us, drop for drop. In one evening, we finish this war."

Silence reigned in the room, until Nate coughed, then laughed.

"I see," he said. "We just kill them all. Why didn't we think of that?"

"Lucius, we have already tried to hit Jewel, and it failed. Badly," said Wendric.

"Then we do it properly this time."

"And von Minterheim as well?" Elaine asked. "You suggest we just walk into the Citadel and assassinate the military leader of the city?"

"Yes," he said. "That is exactly what I propose."

Elaine threw up her hands in disbelief. "And how do you propose we accomplish this great night of murder?"

"It's war, Elaine, not murder," Lucius said. "Never forget that. This is how we avenge Magnus, Caradoc and everyone else taken from us."

He stopped for a moment, then cleared his throat. "I'll make an agreement with you, Elaine. You carry on with your preparations here at the guildhouse. If we fail to end this war, your plan will be the only one open to us anyway. I will take care of von Minterheim. This evening."

"By yourself?" Nate asked incredulously.

"I won't require any of you to come with me," Lucius said. He managed not to sound evasive, but he already had an idea of who he could go to for help. "If I succeed, the guard will be thrown into chaos, at least temporarily, and their ties to the Guild will be weakened."

"This sounds like madness," Nate said.

"I would listen to him, if I were you," said Grennar. "If I were all of you. If anyone here can reach the captain of the Vos guard, I think it is Lucius."

"I agree," said another woman, and Lucius saw Grayling throw a quick wink at him. "Though if he does need any help, I will gladly volunteer for that mission."

He smiled back, but shook his head slowly. *No*, his gesture said, it would be too dangerous for an ordinary thief. Silently, she nodded in understanding.

"If I fail, then you will have lost nothing," Lucius continued, turning his attention back to Elaine. "If I reach him, we go on the attack tomorrow evening. I'll form the team to strike at Loredo and Jewel myself. The other targets we will divide up amongst us. Grennar, the beggars will act as spotters, watching the Guild's movements so we can be ready to strike at Loredo when the guard are at their most distracted."

"They won't be able to sneeze without one of us being nearby to see it," Grennar said. "When the time comes, we'll have your target in our sights."

As arguments between the thieves began to break out, some supporting Lucius' bold plan, others counselling caution, Lucius looked down the table at the other members of the Council.

"Do we have an agreement?"

Wendric looked sideways at Elaine. "We have little to lose. Without being callous about it, we risk only one man."

"I think this is the last time I may see you, Lucius," Elaine said. "But if there is the slightest chance you can succeed... it is an appealing idea. Nate, what say you?"

"I still think it is madness," Nate muttered.

"Then we are agreed," Elaine said, her voice suddenly hard and sure, carrying across the crowded council chamber. "We will start our reprisal this evening."

Lucius stood. "I must prepare."

As he strode out of the council chamber, he ignored the looks the thieves threw him, ranging from outright support to complete mistrust. His mind was fixed firmly on reaching von Minterheim. First, however, he had to enlist the help of someone else. And that would not be easy.

CHAPTER SEVENTEEN

CLOSING HIS EYES, Lucius half-smiled to himself as he felt the threads of power buckle and twist slightly, their natural movements disrupted by the approach of another practitioner. He still lacked the finesse to decipher everything they were telling him, but Adrianna's approach was becoming easier to monitor the closer she came. Whether it was the magnitude of her skill in magic that caused the little fluctuations in the threads, or her emotions at having been summoned once more, Lucius could only guess. He found himself thinking of her anger acting as a bow wave ploughing through their energy, as a ship made its presence felt across the vast ocean.

The analogy seemed to hold true as she strode across the empty warehouse, dust curling up behind her footsteps.

"I am not yours to summon and command, Lucius," she said, contempt evident in her voice. He sighed inwardly, knowing his mission here was not going to be easy.

"You turn your back on us, ignore the calls of Master Forbeck, abandon the training generously offered to you, and then expect... what? Why have you called me here?"

"Good evening, Adrianna," he said, forcing a grim smile.

"Just get to the point."

"Your current employers are finished," he said. "Within the next day, their hold on the city will be shattered, their members scattered and bleeding."

Adrianna's pace had slowed as she approached him, and now she stopped altogether, her expression a mixture of puzzlement and exasperation.

"Perhaps you have not been keeping up with recent events," she said carefully, and he realised she was studying him closely. She had not assumed he was bluffing, instead trying to determine the path he had chosen; she was no longer dismissing him as unimportant. "The Hands are in retreat all over the city, your guildmaster and most of the Council are dead, and you are now just waiting for the end."

"I'm waiting for nothing, Aidy. I told you, this war will be over within the next day."

"This is not your fight, Lucius. Leave them. Leave the Hands. There is no future there, and your allegiance should not be to a den of thieves. You could be so much more than that."

"So you have told me."

"Then why stay with the Hands?"

He smiled wolfishly at her. "I like them."

Snorting at that, Adrianna shook her head. "Are they worth dying for?"

Considering her words, he finally shrugged. "They are certainly worth fighting for, and that is what I intend to do. Without me, they will all die, or otherwise be all but enslaved by the Guild. I can make the difference here, Aidy."

Placing a hand on her hip, she looked at him curiously. "And when did you find something to believe in? Where is the selfish Lucius we have come to know and despise, the one who runs from responsibility? They cannot be paying you that much at the moment, I know. If there is no profit, why are you staying to defend them?"

Lucius opened his mouth to answer, then found precious few words. "That is something of a surprise to me as well," he finally muttered.

"If only you had found a similar loyalty for us."

"I still may." The words amazed him as much as they did Adrianna. Somewhere along the line, he found he had decided to stay in the city, to carve his own niche, and no one would be forcing him out. Not the Guild, not Adrianna and definitely not the Shadowmages. Turnitia was after all, his home. He was done with running.

"What are you saying?" she asked, suspiciously, still expecting a trap somewhere down the line. As it happened, she was not so very wrong.

"I'll tell you what I am going to do," he said. "And I'll ask a simple request. What happens then is up to you. You will have the chance, at the very least, to protect your employer's interests, and perhaps deliver victory in this war to them single-handed. That would do much for the reputation of the Shadowmages and herald their return to the city, would it not?"

"Go on."

"Loredo has been clever, building alliances and ensuring he has some of the best thieves in the city on his side. Even his thugs are well-directed and motivated. He has a Shadowmage in his employ, and can call upon the services of demons from the sea. But central to his plans are his ties to the Vos guard."

"And these are the enemies you are determined to make?" Adrianna asked. "You have a chance to escape all of this, and there are those within the Shadowmages who would protect you from further harm if you walked away now. Remember, we always look after our own."

"In a way, I am counting on that," Lucius said, but evaded her questioning look. "However, it is plain that we cannot fight them all, not in open battle."

He ran a hand through his hair as he debated his next words. If he had misread Adrianna, what he was about to say could finish the Hands before a single attack was launched. Still, he forged ahead, determined to test his own instincts.

"We are going to strike them down from the shadows, hit the power base of the Guild," he said. "The enforcers on the streets, the contacts that form their network of spies, the highest earning merchants in their protection rackets, Loredo and Jewel themselves."

"You have already tried to take down Jewel," Adrianna interjected. "That did not go so well."

"We'll be prepared this time, and she won't have so many allies to call upon when we make the move. I'll do it myself, if I have to."

"Have a care. She is as dangerous as her reputation suggests."

"Your concern is touching," Lucius said, but when he saw Adrianna about to react to that, he waved her fury away. "By the time I reach Jewel, she will have a great many things to occupy her thoughts."

"Such as?"

"This all happens tomorrow evening. The Hands will leave their guildhouse and kill everyone connected with Loredo that can be found." He was acutely conscious that if Adrianna did not do as he expected, he had just doomed every member of the Hands.

"How can you be sure you will be able to find all the targets you seek? You know Loredo has moved the location of his guildhouse, specifically to avoid any reprisal like this?"

He did not know that, and Lucius hesitated before offering up the final part of the plan hatched by the Hands. "We have the beggars on side. They are watching the movements of the Guild, tracking down everyone we have deemed important to Loredo's operations. They'll find their new base of power."

"The beggars? Clever." Her compliment was muted, and he could see her mind was ticking away, gauging the threat he and the Hands posed, and how it affected her position with her employer.

"It was Magnus, not me, that brought the beggars into the fold. And he paid for the alliance with his life."

"And what, exactly, is your part in all of this, Lucius?" Adrianna asked.

"I'll be there every step of the way, Aidy. I'll lead the attack."

"You realise, of course, that this will likely bring you into direct conflict with another Shadowmage."

"I have no quarrel with you, Aidy. I am not looking to fight you."

"If you are leading the assault, it becomes damn well near impossible to avoid, doesn't it?" she said, her anger finally boiling over. "Do you understand what you risk, Lucius? Not the dangers in fighting the Guild, but in taking a stand against us?"

"I'm not taking a stand against you or the other Shadowmages, Aidy."

"My contract with the Guild predates your involvement with the Hands, and so takes precedence!"

"I have no contract, Aidy. I am here because I have to be, because these people need me. Because they will die without me, and that is not something I can walk away from. I fight because I have to fight."

"God damn you, Lucius!" Adrianna spat, and went on cursing him, decrying amateur practitioners and their lack of respect for the Shadowmages' guild. He let her anger ride out, knowing he risked her striking him down on the spot, but also hoping he had understood how her loyalties ran.

When her fury was spent, she whirled back on him. "You don't leave me any damned choice, do you?"

He waited for her next words, though he found it difficult to hold her stare.

Closing her eyes, Adrianna sighed, and with the release of breath, so the fire of her rage seemed to dissipate. "It seems you have a personal stake in this war, Lucius, and it is clear that I don't. I'll release myself from the contract with the Guild. To continue would risk coming into conflict with another Shadowmage and however agreeable that may be on one level, I will not do it."

"Thank you, Aidy," he said.

"Oh, don't thank me, Lucius," she said. "I am well aware I have been played, and there will be a reckoning after this war is done."

He nodded slowly, then played his next card. "After this, I will take up my training in earnest."

That made her look twice at him, and she frowned.

"It is a promise I make to both you and Master Forbeck," he said. "I will dedicate myself to the Shadowmages, learn all I can, and abide by the rules of the guild."

Clearly sceptical, Adrianna cocked her head. "Why?"

"I am going to stay in this city, Aidy," he said. "It is going to become my home again. I'll always have an allegiance to the Hands, but I will also pledge myself to the Shadowmages. I want to learn about our gift. I want to be more than I have been."

"Your record in this matter is hardly sterling."

"True," he had to concede. "But please allow that a man can change. I don't want to be your enemy, Aidy. We should not be enemies."

Taking a step closer, Adrianna dark eyes bored into his own, as if trying to plumb the depths of his mind for the truth. "If you do as you say, Lucius, you will have my support. But my God, if you should prove false..."

"I know," he said simply.

She took a step back, preparing to leave. "We have an understanding, then. I will not interfere with your plans, and will henceforth break off contact with Loredo and his Guild."

"There was... just one more thing," Lucius said.

"Oh, with you there always is," Adrianna said, but waited patiently to hear him out.

He took a breath, preparing himself to see how far his relationship with Adrianna truly stretched. "The Hands' assault on the Guild begins this evening."

She frowned. "I thought you said..."

"Tomorrow is when the Hands move as a whole. In a few hours, however, I will enter the Citadel and strike at the heart of the Vos guard. Their captain, von Minterheim."

Adrianna just looked at him, mouth open, dumbstruck.

"That is the signal for the Hands to begin. With the guard paralysed and leaderless, they will be of little aid to the Guild, for a time at least."

It took a while for Adrianna to find her voice again. "That... is either incredibly stupid and ill-conceived, or..." She trailed off.

"Whatever it is, it won't be easy. However, my request..." He hesitated for a moment before steeling himself to continue. "I wanted to ask you if you would come with me, to fight by my side and ensure the mission's success."

Trying very hard to ignore Adrianna's dark eyes, Lucius began to explain. "I cannot offer you money or anything that would be the equal of the contract you have lost, but this is important to me Aidy, and–"

"Fine."

"What?"

"Fine," she said with a shrug. "I'll come with you. Then we'll see just how good a practitioner you have become."

Lucius had expected argument, threat and disparagement, but not an easy acquiescence. It caught him off guard.

"You better tell me what you have planned," Adrianna said. "Then I can tell you where you are going wrong, and how to fix it."

THE CITADEL LAY silhouetted against the giant sphere of Kerberos that hung imposingly across half the evening sky. Bands of clouds raced across its surface like the wake from a ship moving at speed. The Five Markets were quiet, just a few late traders desperately trying to hawk the last of their day's stock.

Lucius' initial plan had been scotched by Adrianna almost immediately in favour of an easier and less complicated approach. He had envisioned an assault upon the walls, a stealthy dash through the courtyard and then a sweep of the keep in order to locate their prey. Instead, the more experienced Shadowmage had suggested they allow von Minterheim to come to them. The changing of the guard was an event undertaken with typical Vos regularity, and it was always overseen by the captain so long as he was present in the city. That meant not a dangerous and probably futile attempt to gain access to the keep, but instead a hard-hitting strike executed in the main courtyard of the Citadel.

Quickly warming to the idea, Lucius had seen its promise. The point of the attack was not simply to avenge himself and the Hands on von Minterheim, but to shatter the guard. To paralyse their ability to retaliate to the Hands' next move against the Guild, however briefly. The Vos army could not be destroyed in Turnitia, but it could be made to stumble. The aim therefore, was to eliminate von Minterheim and cause as much disruption as possible while inside the Citadel. It was a mission that two Shadowmages, working in concert, could excel at.

They shuffled along the short line of people heading toward the southern gate of the Citadel, cloaked and hooded. The others entering the gate were, for the most part, visitors and tourists who often made it a point to witness the precision display the Vos military enacted while changing the guard. In just a few short years since the invasion, it had become as much a part of city life as the Five Markets or the great barriers at the docks. It was a piece of what made Turnitia what it was.

Lucius had left behind his sword and mail under Adrianna's guidance. Reluctantly at first, but she had pointed out that everyone entering the Citadel legitimately was searched for weapons and contraband, and it would do their mission no good if they were detained at the gate and forced to fight their way through. Besides, Adrianna had said, a real Shadowmage had no need of mundane weapons.

Only partly agreeing, Lucius had refused to relinquish the daggers sheathed inside his boots, and he felt grateful for their hard, metallic presence as they paced, ever so slowly, toward the gate.

The delay was down to the more rigorous than usual searches being performed by the gate guards, halting each person in turn and patting them down before nodding them ahead and turning to the next. The rumour flowing down the line was that the guards had been spooked by a breakout the other night, and their lives depended upon no more trouble erupting in the heart of the Vos military presence. Few believed such an escape attempt was likely, but it made Lucius smile.

He strode up to one of the guards as they approached the gate, its arch soaring high above them while the eight-inch-thick reinforced greywood gates lay invitingly open. Raising his arms, he felt the guard's hands sweep over his chest, back and legs, and was thankful he had not tried to smuggle through his armour or sword, as it would have been found immediately. His hood was jerked back, and the guard, barely more than a lad sporting the first wisps of a beard, stared intently into his face. Lucius smiled back pleasantly, playing the part of a curious visitor, and it seemed to work. The guard jerked a thumb over his shoulder, indicating Lucius should continue, and Adrianna stepped up for inspection. Glancing over his shoulder as he crossed the threshold, Lucius had to suppress a smile as her hood was thrown back and a wilful glare dared the young guardsman to get too familiar during his search. Despite his years, it seemed as though the guard had wisdom enough not to take liberties and Adrianna was quickly directed through.

The courtyard swept before them as they entered, side by side. It was dominated by the keep and the five towers, but was still a vast expanse of open space within a city where real estate was usually at a premium. Around the walls that ringed the courtyard and keep were a myriad of smaller buildings; stables, storehouses, guard quarters, and forges. It was said that the Citadel could be closed for over a year and remain self-sufficient. It was only now that Lucius began to appreciate the grandeur of its design.

Guardsmen were already assembled across the courtyard, lined up in their respective units as they prepared to hand over the watch, long shadows cast from their stationary positions from the lanterns that bedecked the entire courtyard at strategic points, driving back the darkness. The visitors were shown by other guards to a waiting area in front of a wagon house, but Lucius and Adrianna had already split up, taking positions at either side of the crowd. It was not their intention to involve innocents in the attack, and by avoiding the centre of the onlookers, any reprisals from the guard were less likely to inadvertently catch one of them.

Taking a step to one side to put some more distance between himself and a family whose two children had thick Vos accents, obviously from the heartlands, Lucius held his breath as a guardsman approached him, arm held out to one side to guide him back into the crowd. Lucius nodded at the man, who immediately spun on his heels to return to his position a few yards away.

Peering through the crowd, Lucius tried to spy Adrianna, but she had disappeared. She had told him that she would wait for his move, that he would initiate the attack, and he hoped she was merely using subtle magic to conceal her presence, rather than leaving him out to dry. He doubted she lacked sincerity, but he could never quite tell where Adrianna was concerned.

A cheer went up from the crowd, as they all realised the ceremony was about to begin. This drew some frowns from the guard themselves, particularly the older men, but one young guardsman waved until a superior bawled him out, to the amusement of the onlookers.

Movement to his left caught Lucius' eye, and another cheer was raised as the main gates of the keep were opened. From the darkness within strode von Minterheim, flanked by his entourage:

six guardsmen in full dress uniform, only slightly less ostentatious than their captain's breastplate, braids, feathered hat and jewel-encrusted sword. At his appearance, Lucius began to tap into the threads, beckoning them to his reach, but he held his mind steady. It would be too easy for the captain to retreat back into the keep if he struck now.

He watched as the captain and his men paced the courtyard with solemn duty, passing each assembled unit while inspecting each man. At times, von Minterheim would mutter a word to one of his entourage, and the man would stop in front of some poor guardsman singled out for discipline for some slight in his uniform, while the captain continued his march down the line.

This continued for some time, as every active member of the guard in the Citadel was reviewed. Lucius felt some sympathy for the guards who had been on duty for the entire day and were forced to endure this charade in the name of tradition and discipline before they could finally be relieved. Von Minterheim finally rounded the last unit, and strode confidently to the centre of the courtyard, where he nodded to a junior officer. The man gave an order to a unit of trumpeters who rang out a fanfare, the sound piercing the stillness of the evening air. The assembled units began to move, one watch being relieved as another came on duty.

It was a good a time as any to act, Lucius thought.

With so much movement going on in the courtyard, no one saw him slip from the crowd as he crept along the wall past the wagon house, and on past a set of stables. The horses whinnied quietly as he stalked past them, and their agitation gave him an idea.

Stepping inside, he cast about for dry hay, finding it baled near the back of the stables. Looking upwards, he saw more stored in the loft above, and smiled wolfishly.

Checking once more that no one was nearby, he outstretched a finger and felt the familiar surge as a small jet of flame short forth, instantly igniting a bale. It was a small fire, but it grew hungrily. Even as the horses began to stir, he conjured a ball of fire to his palm before launching it into the loft. There, it flashed briefly as it consumed more hay.

He smelt smoke rising to his nostrils, and hastened out, not wanting to be anywhere near the conflagration when it was noticed. Continuing his pace along the wall of the Citadel, he closed the distance to the Keep, wanting to cut off von Minterheim's obvious escape route should the man try to run.

An cry from the crowd told Lucius that the mission had begun in earnest. Within seconds, guardsmen were charging across the courtyard to the stables. Sergeants screamed orders as buckets were grabbed from one of the storehouses and a chain formed to a well.

Von Minterheim had remained calm, though the man was scanning the courtyard, obviously searching for the cause of the fire, trying to decide whether it was an accident or something more sinister. As the man's gaze swept over him, Lucius stopped in his tracks and crouched, tugging on threads to bring the shadows cast by the wall and its outbuildings around him like a second cloak.

It was then that Adrianna weighed in with her assault. Something crackled in the air across the courtyard before, from a cloudless sky, a bolt of lightning shot down from the heavens to strike one of the Vos units square in its centre. The luckiest men flew through the air as the ground exploded beneath them, while those closest to the descending bolt were boiled in their armour. A cry went up, and Lucius saw guardsmen point to the sky. Following their gestures, he looked, then gasped as he saw Adrianna, her powers manifesting themselves for all to see.

Her cloak billowing out behind her as tightly circling winds carried her aloft, Adrianna rose into the evening sky. Gesturing at the ground beneath the guardsmen trying to fight the fire in the stables, he saw their feet become mired as the earth turned to liquid beneath them. Adrianna paid them no more attention as she rose upwards to alight on the wall, now commanding the high ground and able to see the entire courtyard below her. Under the directions of an officer determined to take charge, squads of crossbowmen assembled in front of Adrianna, cranking their weapons back and sliding bolts into place before aiming them upwards.

With a series of clicks audible across the excited courtyard, dozens of bolts shot towards Adrianna, but she stayed her ground, merely holding up a hand to ward them off. As if striking an invisible wall, the bolts sheared off course just a few feet away from her, scattering themselves as they ricocheted back into the courtyard.

A few fell close to the crowd. Fearing they would soon be caught in a crossfire between Vos guard and Shadowmage, Lucius tugged a thread, and sent its energy surging into the fires of the stable. With a low boom, the flames suddenly swelled with intensity, sending the guardsmen fighting them reeling back in shock. The sudden flare and noise was enough to galvanise the crowd and, screaming, they fled as one to the gate. The guards stationed there were trying to close the massive portal, but the frightened people just surged past them into the city streets.

Directing more men towards Adrianna, who even now was racing along the wall for the cover of one of the small towers set along its length, von Minterheim made his move. Whether wanting to bring reinforcements into play or through self-preservation, he began to run for the Keep, his entourage close behind. Lucius was ready for him.

Drawing a dagger from his boot, Lucius forced powerful energies down its blade, feeling them pulse in anticipation of release. Stepping out of the shadows, he placed himself in von Minterheim's path before launching the dagger with a straight throw.

Guided unerringly to its targets, the blade arrowed straight for one of the officers flanking von Minterheim, no spin upsetting the delicate balance of its flight. It ploughed into the breastplate of the man, a shower of blood erupting as the weapon tunnelled through his body without losing any of its momentum. As it blasted out between his shoulders, the dagger continued on its trajectory, and smashed into the chest of the officer behind, sending him flying to the ground with terrible force.

Instinctively, von Minterheim and his remaining officers drew their swords as they warily approached the man who had materialised out of the shadows before them. Lucius waited for them to make the first move, a faint smile on his lips as von Minterheim frowned in recognition.

"You," the captain said, his voice low and dangerous, promising a slow death to any who invaded the Citadel.

"You have cost me the lives of many of my friends, you Vos bastard," Lucius said, feeling both hatred and exaltation at confronting this man. "You are going to die slowly."

Von Minterheim sneered, ignoring the explosions and lightning behind him as his guards tried vainly to bring Adrianna to ground. He nodded to his officers.

"Take him."

The four surviving officers of the captain's entourage spread themselves out, anxious to be the one to slay their superior's enemy. Yet, they were wary of what Lucius could do, the corpses of their comrades a stark reminder that this stranger should not be underestimated.

"You are going to burn in hell's own fire, warlock," said one as he paced to one side.

"What do you know of hellfire?" Lucius cried out, releasing his anger as another ball of flame circled his right hand before being launched forward. The officer tried desperately to lunge out of the way, but the fire curved in flight to match his movements, striking him squarely in the chest. His dying shrieks were cut off as the fire eagerly consumed the air in his lungs, now exposed through the shattered remains of his breastplate and chest.

Sensing motion behind him, Lucius whirled round, collecting the air about him into a solid wall, before flinging it at his assailants in a single smooth movement. Hurled off their feet by the blast, he watched the officers collapse to the ground, then summoned the thread once more to gather the air above them. Going down on one knee to emphasise the action, he raised his arm high over his head, then swiftly dropped it, palm downwards. A sickening squelch echoed through the courtyard as the officers were crushed. In his mind's eye, Lucius saw ribs break and organs burst under the weight before he released the conjuration.

Standing straight, he looked down at the dead men, their still faces contorted in terrible pain as blood seeped from their mouths. Grinning, Lucius looked up at von Minterheim.

"Who are you?" the captain asked, and Lucius was mildly surprised to note von Minterheim was more curious than afraid.

"Consider that a mystery to contemplate in the grave," Lucius snarled, reaching out with a hand as a surge of lightning wreathed his arm. Unleashing the energy, he was stunned as von Minterheim raised his sword to block the attack, bolts of white light crackling around the blade as they were dissipated harmlessly into the air around him.

He had taken the weapon to be purely ceremonial, but cursed himself for not guessing that there was little in the Vos military that was not functional in the extreme, and that von Minterheim was likely rich enough to afford the best equipment in the Empire.

"Nice sword," he managed to say, but was answered only with a derisive sneer as von Minterheim took two steps forward and swung the blade, the rare stones in its elaborate gold crossguard glinting in the fires spreading through the outbuildings of the courtyard. Lucius noted the markings etched into the blade as he pedalled backwards to avoid the blow, a fine script in some foreign tongue. The lettering glowed briefly with the radiance of the lightning he had thrown at von Minterheim, before they finally faded.

Another swipe forced him back, then another. He crouched down to reach for his remaining dagger, but von Minterheim gave him no room for pause.

Behind the captain, Lucius saw that several squads of guards had noticed the fight, and they rushed to join their superior. They fanned out to either side, weapons drawn, cutting off any chance of escape. Conjuring fire to his hand, Lucius held it low, waiting for his time to strike. He took another step back and felt the wall of the keep at his back. Looking left and right at the guardsmen, he saw grim faced men ready to take their revenge for the attack.

"Make it easy on yourself," von Minterheim said. "Maybe we'll give you a quick death. Once you have answered a few questions, of course. Just a gentle chat, then a quick hanging. Believe me, the noose is better than what my men will be wanting to do to you."

The fire at his fingertips began to burn hot, its energies having been kept in check too long. Lucius took a deep breath as he prepared a last assault on the guardsmen as, pace by pace, they closed in for the kill.

"Adrianna, I could use your help now," he muttered, and he was at least gratified to see a few of the guardsmen check their step, fearing he was vocalising some incantation that would bring death to them all.

He saw her then, standing on the wall across the far side of the courtyard. A guardsman lay dead at her feet, and she seemed to be staring straight at him, heedless of the bolts and spears that flew past her. A rush of air swept over him, a gentle breeze that reminded him of calm summer afternoons in the Anclas Territories, and the wind carried Adrianna's voice to him, as clear as if she were standing at his side.

"Unleash the power, Lucius," he heard her say. "Let's find out what you are *really* capable of. Let the magic flow through you. Give yourself up to it."

Von Minterheim had ordered the guardsmen to halt, and they stayed, weapons at the ready, less than a dozen yards away. Their ranks were held tight, at least three men deep, forming a barrier of flesh and iron that trained cavalry would have difficulty breaking. Smiling, von Minterheim took a pace forward and gestured to the ball of flame Lucius still held in his hand.

"Want to try your luck one last time?"

Lucius stared ruefully back at him, before a soothing calm flooded through him. With an instant clarity, he could see the threads spinning and weaving their magic in the hidden part of his mind, begging to be manipulated and used, their only purpose to serve his direction.

Sighing, Lucius held up his hand and let the ball of flame fly high into the sky, where it finally sputtered and flashed out of existence.

"Sensible choice," said von Minterheim, and he lifted a hand to direct his men to take Lucius into custody, but something checked him. His eyes widened as he watched Lucius draw in a deep breath, and a sudden tension filled the air. The shadows around the keep seemed to lengthen and grow, appearing to cluster around Lucius as his eyes shone with a pale, inner light.

"Take him!" von Minterheim shouted at his men, not knowing what his enemy was planning, acting purely on instinct.

Primed and ready to obey, the guardsmen leapt forward, weapons raised, as Lucius closed his eyes and caught the threads. With little conscious thought, he fashioned them crudely, trading finesse for power, raw power. The threads responded, eagerly it seemed, and he opened his mind to their energies, not attempting to hold them in check, acting as a funnel for their escape as if they now controlled him.

His eyes snapped open as the power bubbled violently over the brim and with a wide sweeping motion, he flung fire at the nearest guardsmen. A giant sheet of flame tumbled toward them, its green and purple hues making it look almost tame. As it reached them, it turned white hot and the men were incinerated where they stood, the trailing wake of fire leaving only blackened and shrivelled corpses. Their weapons and armour were melted into slag by the terrible heat.

Only narrowly missed by the fires, von Minterheim leapt forward, the tip of his sword aiming true for Lucius' chest as the surviving guards rallied behind him. Only barely aware of the danger, Lucius continued to let the magic flow unchecked, and he felt himself raise his foot before stamping it down hard. The earth rocked as tremors radiated out from him, throwing captain and guard alike to the ground, their feet kicked from beneath them by the force of magic rippling below.

Scrabbling for weapons, they looked up to see Lucius glaring down upon them, the fury in his eyes replaced by something altogether more primal, smouldering in its release. He sought out von Minterheim from the tangle of weapons and limbs, and his gaze bored into the man's eyes.

"You cannot conceive of the power you have unleashed," he heard himself say, then shuddered as he felt the darkest of threads push itself to the fore, snaking out from his outstretched hands to slither over every man who still drew breath before him.

The strangled shrieks of the guards tortured his ears and drew the attention of everyone left in the courtyard. They grasped their throats as their skin turned deathly pale, the life being sucked out of their bodies. Lucius watched as von Minterheim tried to tear off his breastplate with fingers that rotted as they pulled uselessly at the clasps. Flesh dropped from his hands in blackened chunks, leaving only bone, as the skin drew taut across his face. Hair greyed and fell to the ground, while his eyes lost the sparkle of life, dulled and then hardened. Then the screams fell silent.

Full consciousness returned to Lucius, and he retched as he felt the dark energy pulse through his body. Dropping to his knees, he vomited. He could smell nothing but death, and it seemed like a poison in his veins, charring every part of his being and staining it forever. He spat to remove the foul taste from his mouth, but it felt as though nothing would remove the darkness that gathered in his body and mind.

Standing, he took a shaky step forward, trying hard not to notice the shrivelled corpses that lay all around him. But their sightless eyes seemed to catch his, the dark husks accusing him of a crime humanity had no word for. He felt his stomach heave again, but he continued his march, limping with exhaustion and disgust at himself. Glaring at the remaining guards he passed, Lucius dared them to move against him. After witnessing what he had done to their captain, none did.

The gate was closed as he approached it, and he cast about, looking for a guard to intimidate into opening it, but they had begun to flee back into the keep. He eyed the wooden barrier, knowing he had no strength left to summon the magic, and little desire to give free rein.

The air became agitated around him, and he felt a gale sweep past his body, the current running just inches from his skin, leaving him unmolested. The wind seemed to be formed from a sweeter form of magic, and he felt physically charged as he bathed in its purity, the sickness of his soul slowly receding. Taking a deep breath to savour the feeling, he watched the wind now whistling with shrieking hurricane force, smash into the gate. The timbers exploded in a shower of splinters, leaving the wrecked gates hanging by ruined hinges. Beyond, the streets of Turnitia lay as they always had, a scene of complete normality somehow removed from the devastation of the courtyard behind him.

He felt Adrianna's presence before he heard her footsteps.

"I said you had potential," she told him, placing a hand on his shoulder.

"I swear to you," he said when he found his voice, "I am never doing that again. The magic is... evil. Black. We are not supposed to be using it, not like that."

"Don't you dare blame the magic for that! The power you manifest is a reflection of you, and you alone. That darkness is a part of you, and the sooner you realise that, the more powerful you will become."

"I don't want it," he said plaintively.

"Not your choice. Right now, you need it."

Damn her, Lucius thought. He knew she was right.

CHAPTER EIGHTEEN

MURDER EXPLODED ACROSS the city.

The surviving Hands were astounded at the stories coming from the Citadel: Captain von Minterheim slain in the cruellest fashion, the corpses of guardsmen littering the southern courtyard like so many rag dolls discarded by a precocious rich girl and powerful magic unleashed against their enemies. Many presumed that Lucius had forged an alliance with great wizards, or brought mercenary warlocks into their guild's employ. A few guessed the truth, but their suspicions were over-ridden by a new feeling of optimism among their fellow thieves.

For the first time victory seemed possible. Maybe even likely.

There was little opposition to the next phase of Lucius' plan, and no attempt on his part to curb the enthusiasm of the more bloodthirsty thieves. In the morning after the assault on the Citadel, he unleashed the Hands into the city while the Vos guard were paralysed and the Guild was reeling from the loss of its greatest ally.

Working in concert with the Beggars' Guild, shambling mounds of filth-ridden disease providing accurate descriptions of where targets could be found, the thieves hunted down their enemies and showed no mercy. They killed collectors working extortion rackets, their bodyguards and any client known to sympathise with the Guild. They killed enforcers, lookouts, spies, fences, anyone remotely connected with the Guild and who might raise opposition to the new swing in the balance of power. The assault on the Vos guard continued, with a dagger or crossbow bolt launched from a high rooftop or dark alley to strike down sergeants and corporals. The net closed, with the Hands leaving nowhere for Guild men or their supporters to run to. Everyone in the city knew what was happening, and those with no interest in the outcome – the thousands of ordinary traders, craftsmen and their families – kept clear of the streets, not wanting to inadvertently be caught up in the slaughter. The Vos guard, by now, were powerless to protect them.

Throughout the day, a constant stream of beggars reported to Grennar, now permanently stationed at the Hands' guildhouse. They were bringing back vital information of the Guild's response, allowing the Council to pull their own men away from areas of the city where thugs and mercenaries prowled, looking for the chance to repay the Hands for the blood being spilt. All the time, the beggars tracked the movements of Guild men until, finally, they were ready to reveal the expected location of Loredo's new guildhouse.

As evening approached, a final Council meeting was called, attended by every thief not still wetting his blade with the blood of the Guild. The mood was jubilant, for the day had seen the Guild all but cut down. Now, just the final stroke remained, the last attack that would see their enemy smashed forever.

All eyes were on Grennar as she outlined what her beggars had learned of the Guild's last hiding place.

"They've retreated to the docks," she said. "Their operations have always centred in that territory, ever since it became a no-go area for you."

"I heard they had demons on their side," one voice from the crowd said, and was greeted by a few nervous murmurs. "That's what put paid to Lucius' operation."

"You've been drinking too much, or else listening to old wives' tales," Nate said scornfully. "They employed mercenaries who took Lucius and his men by surprise."

Lucius was aware of Ambrose among the thieves, his eyebrows arched questioningly, and he sighed.

"We will be walking into the heart of our enemy's territory this evening," he said slowly. "They will be at their most dangerous, cornered, afraid and desperate. I would not have you walking into their lair without knowing the truth."

The council chamber was suddenly still, and a few of the older thieves leaned forward to catch every word. Lucius ignored the eyes of the other Council members, especially Elaine, who frowned at him dangerously for withholding any information from her.

"Magnus knew what happened, and he swore myself, Ambrose and Sandtrist – the only other thief to survive that evening – to silence. We knew the Guild had brought new allies into their fold, but we knew nothing of where they came from or what they were."

"They are truly demons, then?" asked the same voice.

"I don't know," Lucius confessed. "I know they are not human, that they came from the sea. That they have brutal strength and are utterly savage. How the Guild contacted them and negotiated an alliance, well, I don't know that either."

"So, what do we do if they are waiting for us?" Nate asked.

"Run," Ambrose said.

Lucius nodded. "That is fair advice. From what we saw, the further they are from the sea, the slower and clumsier they become. Even so, you don't want to be anywhere near them when they attack. They slaughtered almost my entire team within a few minutes."

"Then the Guild might still win?"

"Not if I have anything to do with it," Lucius said. "I have some ideas. If they appear, get out of the way and leave them to me."

"And what makes you so special, Lucius?" Elaine asked. "We have heard strange tales from the Citadel. If the Guild has brought these terrible creatures onto their side, who or what have you brought onto ours?"

He hesitated. "That is a topic for another time," he said, finally.

More mutters floated from the crowded thieves, and they were not charitable ones. Elaine leaned forward in her seat to look Lucius straight in the eye.

"If we are trusting you with our lives, Lucius, we all deserve to know who and what we are fighting for."

He returned her gaze for a moment then, deliberately, turned to the thieves in front of them.

"You are fighting for your lives and continued prosperity," he said evenly. "As for myself... I have brought you all this far. I ask you to continue trusting me for one more evening. After that, I'll tell you what I can."

The thieves were far from happy with that. Once, seemingly a lifetime ago, a word from Magnus would have silenced any dissent, and each thief would be content with knowing what he was supposed to know and no more. Now, with every thief able to take part in the Council's meetings, they all wanted to know every secret. Muttering turned into open growls demanding Lucius reveal what he knew, to answer for the rumours of what happened in the Citadel. Of whether he was in league with Loredo.

"He doesn't have to tell us anything," a clear voice said, riding above the noise of the other thieves, and he saw that Grayling had walked out from the crowd to stand between the thieves and the

Council's table. "Lucius broke us out of the Citadel and, without him, I can truly say I would not be standing here now. I would be dead, either by the neck or with a Vos sword in my stomach."

"Aye," said Ambrose, standing forward to join her. "I brought Lucius into the Hands, and fought alongside him against these sea demons. I tell you all, if he had meant to betray us, he has had plenty of opportunity before now."

"Before Lucius killed the captain of the guard, we were ready to huddle in this place like trapped rats," Grayling said. "Now look at us! We are on the eve of victory, and still you want to quibble!"

"He has the support of the beggars too," Grennar spoke up.

The testimonies to Lucius' character made him feel a little uncomfortable, but they were sufficient to silence the thieves. To his right, Elaine stood up.

"The Council, at this time, agrees," she said, looking pointedly at Wendric and Nate, who both got to their feet to stand alongside her, though Nate hesitated for a second, appearing reluctant to do so.

"We proceed with the plan," Wendric said. "Tonight, we win the Thieves War."

His words gained a few grumbles of grudging assent from the thieves, but if he had been expecting to rouse cheers of support, he was disappointed. Lucius nodded his thanks to Wendric, but his eyes were drawn to Elaine, who had fixed him with a doom-laden stare. He knew that if anything went wrong this evening, he would find one of her daggers planted in his back when he least expected it. Either way, she would be demanding a full explanation from him.

FROM THE GUILDHOUSE, small bands of thieves left through the secret entrances to the sewer system and spread out across the city. Vos guard and the few brave Guild men looking to make reprisals were ignored. For once, they were not the target.

These bands divided themselves and regrouped in new locations, expanding across Turnitia like a dark cancer, taking streets least used and alleys least watched. Slowly, they converged upon the docks, a secret army preparing for its last assault.

Finding Lucius on the roof of a warehouse near the cliffs, Ambrose reported that a dozen sentries had been located and eliminated, leaving the path clear for their own thieves to gather and assemble into an attack force. Nodding his thanks, Lucius gave him instructions to report again when each band of thieves was in position. Watching Ambrose withdraw, he returned his attention to the building he had been scanning.

The beggars had found the new guildhouse by the same manner they discovered everything else. Throughout the city, the ostensibly penniless and dispossessed watched known Guild members, tracked their movements, and informed their spymasters. These senior beggars then worked together to piece disparate nuggets of information together into a meaningful whole. There was little happening within the city that escaped their attention.

Perched on the side of the cliff, at the furthest edge of the sprawl that was gathered around the docks, the warehouse was a two storey affair, designed to accommodate a growing business as well as serve as a repository for goods. The Hands were well aware of the layout of such warehouses, built to a specific design as it was under the direction of the Vos military when they rebuilt the city. Storage area on the ground floor, offices and living quarters above. However, they all expected the Guild to have modified the interior, even in the short time they had been present. No beggar though had managed to approach the building without being turned away.

It was a well positioned site, right at the edge of the city, providing an easy ingress for those wanting to avoid the main entrances. Grennar had told him they suspected that tunnels bored into the cliff led to caves at the base of the cliff face, making it a superb location for anyone wishing to engage in smuggling. A ship need only dock at the harbour and, during the hours of darkness, a small boat could be hauled over the side to deliver high value goods without incurring dock taxes.

Lucius had to admit, it was all very neatly done. Tapping his fingers on the roof of the warehouse on which he had taken position, he mentally urged his thieves to get into place. With the sentries gone they had limited time to launch their attack, as the failure of any sentry to report in would set the Guild on the highest alert. A guildhouse could easily be turned into a fortress, and Lucius had no wish for his thieves to cover dead ground while under fire from secret arrow nests. They had to attack while the Guild was blind to their approach.

There was also the problem of his Shadowmage talents to contend with, and this had occupied his mind greatly since Elaine's silent warning to him. One way or another, he guessed the Hands would know the truth after this evening. Though he knew he had the support of some, there were still too many suspicious of those capable of using magic. Still, he could always look on the bright side – there was a good chance he would be killed tonight, saving him from any explanation.

A low whistle echoed off the walls of the warehouses close by, and Lucius scrambled across the roof to drop a rope off the side of the building. Swinging down, he was greeted by Ambrose and Elaine.

"They're in position," Elaine said quietly. Dressed all in black, she bore two short swords at her hips. She was rumoured to be one of the best blade fighters among the Hands.

"Ambrose, give the nod to the roof-hoppers. Tell everyone else to move on their signal."

Nodding his understanding, Ambrose disappeared into the shadows. Lucius took a place at the corner of another warehouse, allowing him a clear view of the Guild's headquarters. Elaine joined him, drawing a sword and rubbing its blade with a cloth. Gradually, its bright edge lost its lustre, dulled by a lotion concocted to eliminate any chance of light catching the weapon's edge and giving away her position.

"You think this will work?" she whispered.

Lucius considered the question for a moment. "I would give us evens."

"No better?"

He shrugged. "I am pretty sure the Guild has no idea exactly what to expect, but they must know we are coming for them. They will be alert, and traps will be waiting for us."

They were silent for a time, with only the sound of the ocean crashing into the dock's barriers breaking the stillness. Lucius saw thieves move across the skyline, skipping across the roofs of warehouses as they made their way to the guildhouse. When buildings were close together, they would leap across the gap. When the distance was too far to jump, short, stocky crossbows were employed to send a bolt across the chasm, pulling silken rope with it.

"You and I will be having words after this, Lucius," Elaine said.

"I know," he sighed.

"For what it is worth, I have few doubts about your loyalties to the Hands," she said. "You started as an outsider but then, we all did. I know you now have friends among us."

"For what *this* is worth, I count you among them," he said, turning to face her briefly.

"But there are still too many unanswered questions," Elaine said, as though she had not heard him.

He turned away from her, back to face the guildhouse. The thieves on the roofs were about to make their final crossing to the Guild's lair. "You know I wield magic," he said.

"Of course I do. And that is something you are going to have trouble reconciling with some of our members. I am not stupid, Lucius. You left the city soon after the invasion, and now return a spellslinger. I think I know what you are."

"Then you know you have little to fear from what I do."

"I also know that you have obligations to others. But, that aside, we also need to redress the balance of power within the Hands. We are an anarchic mess at the moment."

"We need to rebuild the Council and appoint a new guildmaster," Lucius said, understanding where Elaine was going.

"If we are successful tonight, there will be many who want you as guildmaster, magic or no," she said.

He gave a low laugh. "I don't want it. Truly, I don't. Up until a few days ago, I was not even sure I would be staying here after this."

"You now think you will?"

"These thieves are growing on me," he said. "Look, I'll make a deal with you, here and now. You support me against those who may have trouble accepting what I am. In return, I will do everything to convince the others you should be guildmaster."

She was quiet for a moment. "You really don't want it, do you?"

"That is not where my ambitions lie. You have the experience and knowledge. You also have the assassins in your hand, which should ease the conscience of any doubters to your claim. For my part, I would like a place on the Council – I feel I owe Magnus that much, and some of his more controversial decisions will need a champion. His deal with the beggars, say. That's too important to let slide in any reorganisation."

"I agree. Both to the beggars, and your terms."

"Wendric should be your lieutenant."

"I was thinking you might be more suitable, especially after tonight."

"I told you, I really don't want any of it. Besides, you don't want to split the guild between myself and Wendric, and then let Nate through."

"Then I think we have an understanding," she said.

"We do. We also have the signal."

Gathered on the roof of the guildhouse, a dull glow flashed twice as a thief caught the low radiance of Kerberos on a hand mirror.

From warehouses and alleyways, more thieves detached themselves from the shadows and began the rush to the guildhouse, keeping low. Lucius and Elaine watched them for a moment, then darted forward to follow.

A flash erupted from the windows of the first floor of the guildhouse, quickly followed by a muffled blast. The rooftop thieves had pried open a skylight and thrown bundles of flash powder down into the offices. Cries and screams from inside split the evening air as the thieves followed their flash powder, blades drawn. The killing had begun.

The nimblest thieves had reached a side door and one of them jammed a crowbar into the frame, wrenching it hard. As the door flew open, Lucius saw something dark and heavy inside move with speed, and the thief had no time to scream as a large stone block swung down on chains to catch him square in the chest. The impact sent him sprawling several yards and he landed heavily on the street, completely motionless. More shouts came from the main entrance, where the heavy double doors had been forced open, the thieves there greeted by a hail of arrows and bolts, cutting down any not quick enough to dive out of sight. The assault was stalling before it really began and Lucius knew that if they did not gain entry quickly, those who had entered by the roof would be swiftly killed.

"Come on," he shouted to Elaine. "We've got to get inside."

She ran for the side door with the sprung stone block trap, seeing fighting had erupted at its threshold. The Hands could only enter one at a time, and he imagined several Guild members inside, easily overpowering anyone who made it through. Whenever the Hands backed off, they were chased by thrown blades. Already, four bodies lay in front of the door.

Lucius threw himself against the wall of the warehouse next to the door, and looked about for support as Elaine joined him. Another thief was on the opposite side of the door.

"There's a dozen of the bastards inside," the thief shouted across to him. "Bloody death-trap in there."

Risking his neck, Lucius quickly poked his head round the corner, then hastily drew it back as an arrow thudded into the door frame, its metal head jutting through the wood just inches from his face. He shook his head in despair, having seen the defences inside; three armed men just inside to ward off any attacker, and an overturned table behind them, lined with archers and blade throwers.

"We can rush 'em, but the first of us inside will die," the thief said, clearly not volunteering for the duty.

Lucius cast a quick look back at Elaine, who raised her eyebrows expectantly. He sighed.

"The hell with it," he muttered, then shouted for the other thief's attention. "You, get your men ready. You'll follow me."

Incredulous, the thief grinned, happy not to be the first in.

"Whatever happens, you follow me in, right?" Lucius reiterated.

"We'll be right behind you," Elaine said, and Lucius felt he could trust her at least to threaten and cajole the others into obeying.

"Right," he said to himself, and half-closed his eyes to seek the threads amidst the chaos of the battle. They came to him, ready, almost desperate to be used. "Shut the door!" he said to the thief across from him, and the man swung the heavy wooden door shut.

Stepping out in front of the closed door, Lucius took in a deep breath, and summoned the air around him to his control. A breeze whipped around the clothes of the amazed thieves close by as he raised his fist, the air rolling into a tight twisting wind that followed his movements. Punching forward, he released the magic he had infused into the air, and it blasted forward to crash against the door. The structure had no chance.

The door, smashed by the force of a typhoon, burst from its hinges and was hurled inside, crashing into the table and those taking cover behind it.

Not hesitating, not waiting to see whether Elaine would succeed in forcing the thieves to follow, Lucius dove inside. The upturned table was before him, pinning several Guild thieves to the floor, while others lay on the floor, groaning as they nursed vicious looking wounds caused by the splintering door. He kicked at one who reached for a sword, then rushed forward.

Lucius was in the main storage area of the warehouse, littered with wooden crates, furniture and equipment, all recently transported from the original guildhouse. Much of it had been reformed into defensive posts, and he saw movement everywhere. To his left, stairs hugged the wall, leading up to the floor above, and they were lined with thieves armed with bows and crossbows. Almost immediately, a hail of fire was directed toward him and he rolled for the cover of a crate, missiles impacting on the floor around him.

Behind him, Lucius saw Elaine leading the other thieves in, and they quickly set about ending the lives of any who had survived Lucius' entry until the arrow fire was redirected towards them.

Two fell immediately, long shafts jutting from their bodies as they collapsed to the ground, and he heard Elaine order the others to take cover and prepare to charge their attackers on the stairs. Above the din of the battle, he heard cries and thuds from above, and knew the thieves who had entered by the roof were fighting for their lives.

On the other side of the warehouse, he saw more makeshift barricades in front of the main entrance, the doors now wide open to the evening air. Lanterns and torches had been positioned strategically throughout the building, casting their light around any entry, yet keeping the defenders shrouded in darkness. Every so often, a Hand would dare to peer round a corner to let loose a bolt or arrow, only to be driven back by a hail of return fire.

Seeing a chance to tilt the battle in their favour, Lucius pushed away from the crate and started to creep toward the barricades. He felt a thread come to the fore and eagerly seized it, beginning to mould its energy to his wishes as a familiar ball of fire leapt to his fingertips before he quickly extinguished it. It would be very foolish to set light to the warehouse while they were still in it.

Instead, he pulled upon another thread, and the lanterns near the main entrance seemed to pale and shimmer, as if losing their radiance. Concentrating, he mentally tugged at the shadows cloaking those behind the barricades, lengthening and stretching them towards the open entrance.

Confused for a moment, the defenders ceased their volley of fire, no longer able to see their targets through the unnatural darkness that swept between them and the enemy. The Hands did not question their good fortune, and they swept inside en masse. A few thieves fell to quicker-witted Guild men, the rest leaping over the barricades to engage the defenders with blade and club. The warehouse quickly filled with dozens of individual melees as thief battled thief, swordplay interrupted by an arrow or dagger in the back from a concealed enemy, men howling as poisons burned through their bodies from minor scratches. It was a dirty way to fight, and both sides were very good at it.

Missiles were still coming from the direction of the stairs, picking off anyone too slow to dive for cover once they had dispatched the man or woman they were fighting, and Lucius kept low as he sought to make his way back to Elaine and the men she led. A loud cry made Lucius turn to see a thief running toward him, sword outstretched and eyes wild as bloodlust overcame him.

Suddenly realising he had yet to draw his own weapon, Lucius stumbled backwards as the sword sliced through the air in front of his eyes, and he sprawled over a motionless body. The thief, now screaming incoherently, held his sword in both hands and raised it above his head, ready to cleave Lucius in two. The weapon descended, and Lucius, panicking, held his arms before him, desperately seizing the first thread that spun across his mind's eye. With a loud metallic ringing, the sword stopped suddenly in its downward motion, as if it had struck a thick, invisible shield.

The thief, looked puzzled, jolted out of his bloodletting by what must have appeared as Lucius halting the blow with his own arm. With a grim smile, Lucius rolled out of the way and stood, drawing his own sword. He stabbed forward, and the thief parried wildly, pushing Lucius' blade to one side. Closing the distance between them, Lucius grabbed at the man's throat and felt a warm pulse of energy rocket down his arm. Twisting savagely with his magically enhanced strength, he felt the bones in the neck of the thief grind together, then snap. Releasing his opponent, Lucius discarded the body as it collapsed to the floor.

He found Elaine crouched behind a jumble of hastily piled furniture, surrounded by the bodies of the men she had led into the warehouse. Only a handful now remained alive, the rest having been picked off by increasingly accurate fire.

"We're winning," he said breathlessly.

"We'll win nothing if we don't take those stairs," she said, her frustration evident. "Can you clear the way?"

"Easy."

He closed his eyes, visualising the thieves on the stairs, counting their number and summoning the energy for what he planned to do next.

"Get ready," he whispered, and he was dimly aware of Elaine rallying her remaining men, forcing them to prepare for a charge. They appeared doubtful, then stared, wide-eyed, as the furniture they were hiding behind began to tremble and shift, as if caught in an earthquake.

With a loud shout, Lucius hurled the energy he had been building forward, and the furniture responded to his direction. Heavy chairs, desks and wardrobes flew through the air with deadly speed, crashing into the stairs and the thieves upon them. Most were crushed instantly by the force of the flying furniture, but a few were fortunate enough to merely have limbs smashed into bloody pulp. Their moans and screams were ignored by the cheering thieves below.

"Up there!" hissed Elaine, and Lucius followed her gaze to the ruined stairs, to see Loredo surveying the carnage in the warehouse, his pointed beard quivering in either rage or excitement.

"He's mine!" Elaine said as she leapt forward and began leaping up the tangle of bodies and smashed furniture balanced precariously on what was left of the stairs.

"I want Jewel!" Lucius shouted as he followed her.

Elaine was a few yards in front of him, but where she leapt lithely up the obstacles to Loredo, Lucius found his greater weight was causing the ruined stairs to shift disturbingly, and he was forced to regain his balance time and again. He looked up to see Elaine draw her second sword, intent on duelling with Loredo, but the man smiled down at her as he produced a small hand crossbow.

Screaming a warning, Lucius fumbled with a thread to block the bolt, blast Loredo apart or otherwise alter the course of events, but he saw he was too slow, as the crossbow was aimed at Elaine's chest and fired.

Flattening herself against the wall, Elaine's twisting motion was almost a blur to Lucius, and he was forced to duck as the tiny bolt went skittering through the air past her and shot over his head. Giving no time for Elaine to recover, Loredo dropped his crossbow and drew a sword, a long, thin blade weighted for speed. Leaping down the stairs, he picked his way over the obstacles and broken bodies of his own thieves to confront Elaine. Balanced precariously, they traded blows in a fast display of swordsmanship, he with the advantage of height, she able to bring a second weapon into play to defeat his lightning fast thrusts without losing the momentum of her own attacks.

Within the warehouse, the battle was turning in favour of the Hands, scattering the defenders and overwhelming them through teamwork and foul play. Someone had started a fire near the entrance, whether intentionally or not, and the warehouse was beginning to fill with smoke. Lucius could see there was little danger of the fire spreading out of control before it could be tended to.

Looking back up the stairs, he willed Elaine to make the killing blow, ending Loredo's life and allowing him to vault up the stairs to find Jewel. He was tempted to join Elaine and fight at her side, but he also knew his life would not be worth living if he robbed her of the kill.

A terrible crash reverberated through the warehouse, causing the many fights to cease for a few seconds. Over on the far side, a tall stack of crates had been toppled, and thieves from both sides lay under the debris, calling out piteously for help from their comrades. Leaping across to the remains of a wardrobe for a better look, Lucius saw what had caused the crates to topple.

Within the smoky shadows behind the scattered crates, he saw movement as a heavy trapdoor was swung open in the floor, and he recalled Grennar telling them of smuggler tunnels leading to the foot of the cliff. When he saw the scarred face of Jewel vault from the blackness within the trapdoor, he knew what was going to follow her.

"Hands, to me!" he shouted as he leapt from the wardrobe. "Get behind me!"

A few were quick enough to heed his instruction, while others were either cut off from reaching him, or too shocked by what they saw emerge.

Moving with a terrible grace, Jewel drew her blade and began moving through the thieves, slashing out at anyone she did not recognise from the Guild, leaving a trail of broken and dying men behind her. Clawing their way from the lip of the trapdoor, Lucius saw scaled, black-eyed creatures, their talons black as the deepest night. One look at their fanged maws was enough to send thieves scrambling away, but the creatures moved with inhuman speed, claws snaking out to gouge bloodied chunks from any victim who strayed too close.

The creatures began pouring out of the trapdoor, and Lucius rushed ahead, seeking to gain a vantage point. A score of the monsters had leapt into the warehouse before he clambered onto a table propped up against a pile of sacks, and more were slithering out of the open trapdoor. Bellowing a challenge, Lucius raised his arms to the ceiling and focussed on the energies he felt bubbling above. Some of the creatures looked up at him, their dark alien eyes puzzled as electric tension filled the air, its crackling just barely audible over the screams of the dying and terrified.

The power he sought mastery over erupted, only just within the edge of his control, and the ceiling above burst apart in a shower of splinters and rafters as a bolt of lightning snaked down to explode within the darkness of the trapdoor. The shrieks of the creatures caught in the blast pierced the ears of everyone in the warehouse, galvanising those who kept their wits to flight. A few made it outside, but most were cut down by the creatures moving among them, or by Jewel whose expressionless face seemed all the more terrible in the half-light spilt by the remaining lanterns and growing fire near the main entrance.

Exalted by the energy he commanded, Lucius shouted in a joyous rage as he saw the creatures move away from him, and he sent another bolt of lightning down into their ranks, then another, leaving charred and boiled corpses scattered across the warehouse, strewn throughout the human dead. More holes were punched through the ceiling as he brought lightning down from the sky and he directed the blasts back to the trapdoor as he saw more movement within, the creatures rallying for another attack.

With a loud crack, another bolt descended, and he smiled as he anticipated the terror and pain of the creatures below, only to see the bolt shatter into a thousand shards of light a few feet above the opening. Bolstered by this failure, creatures started flooding from the trapdoor again, and he summoned the threads to his aid, intent on halting them in their tracks.

A sharp pain blasted inside his head, and he reeled, feeling as though his mind was being squeezed by a giant hand. Staggering, he fell to the floor, trying to take in air, but discovering his lungs no longer worked as they should. Suddenly, the gripping agony was gone, and he sucked in precious breath, leaning against the table on which he had been standing for support as he tried to gather his mental energies to launch another attack.

He raised a shaky hand, and fire rolled down his arm. With a flick, he sent the ball of flame flying across the warehouse towards the creatures now scampering toward him but, as he watched, it simply snuffed out of existence before it reached them. Frowning in confusion, he took a step back, raising his sword defensively, and he felt the threads of power twist out of his reach, seeming to fly away from his grasp at speed.

The creatures started to circle round him and, as they parted, he saw one different from the rest. With greying scales, it walked with a stooped gait, and held a coral-encrusted staff upon which it leaned for support. Its eyes were milky and without any life, and yet Lucius knew the creature was watching him.

Raising the staff, the creature pointed its end at him. The pain came once again, forcing him to the ground as he clutched at his head, trying to pull his own skull apart to relieve the pressure. He grabbed, helplessly at an elusive thread, even as his sword slipped from his twitching fingers, but the magic would not come to him. Lucius raised his head to stare up at the grey creature as it approached, shuffling its clawed feet across the stone floor. He raised a hand, hoping – praying – that so much as a tiny ball of fire would come to fingers. But just as the thread started to jerk towards his will, the creature waved its staff in a tight, circular motion. The magic just fled, disappearing into the darkest recesses of his mind. It was quickly replaced by the agony, and he screamed in pain and terror as he grovelled on the floor.

Opening his eyes, Lucius saw a claw just inches from his face, and he looked up to see the grey creature staring soullessly down upon him. Its coral staff pointed down at his forehead. He was paralysed, utterly unable to order any of his limbs to move, and he began to gasp for air as his lungs and heart began, slowly, to shut down. Tears came to his eyes as the pain intensified and he tried to mouth a curse at the creature, but no words came.

His world exploded then, and Lucius thought the end had finally come for him, that the light and sound was part of the journey to Kerberos where he would meet his family and roam among the clouds forever more as a free spirit. It was not until the greying creature collapsed next to him, its milky eyes ruptured and oozing a dark liquid, that he realised he was still alive.

The pain and agony were gone, and with his heart pumping to restore the flow of blood to his body, Lucius managed to claw his way to his knees as he looked about him. It was a scene of complete chaos and carnage.

Panicked, the creatures were moaning in a strange alien tongue as they ran, seeking shelter from something near the main entrance. He struggled to his feet to get a better look, but was forced back down as the warehouse wall behind the trapdoor exploded inwards, nails and shards of wood whipping through the air to shred the fleeing creatures. As debris rained down, Lucius saw four figures standing outside the warehouse, each gesturing at the creatures and each gesture followed by a wave of magical energy. Fire and lightning, stone and ice lashed out at the creatures as they were consumed by the onslaught.

The figures walked steadily into the warehouse, annihilating any creature they saw and any human foolish enough to attack them. Lucius stared, open-mouthed, as he recognised Master Forbeck at their head, his genial face now a mask of hatred and vengeance as he wreathed himself in fire, sending out bolts of multihued flame to engulf every creature that dared to make its way past him.

Near the main entrance, some of the creatures were trying to follow thieves out into the streets, but a solitary figure stood at the threshold, hurling ice and blasts of solid air at any that made the attempt, while planting a sword into any who survived the maelstrom, and Lucius cried out loud in relief when he recognised Adrianna. Stumbling across the warehouse, he ran to greet her.

The battle was over within seconds, and an eerie silence fell across the shattered remains of the warehouse punctuated only by the moans of injured thieves. A few remaining creatures croaked as life fled from their dull eyes, and able-bodied thieves were only too happy to hurry them to their deaths.

Breathing heavily, Lucius stopped as he reached Adrianna, who stared down at him imperiously, and he thought he might be in for another of her jibes or criticisms. Then she smiled, warmly.

"One day, Lucius, you may curb your ability to get yourself into trouble."

"But not today," a voice said behind him, and he turned to face Forbeck. The master was flanked by three young men and even if he had not seen their display just a few minutes earlier, Lucius would have known they were Shadowmages from the magic he sensed emanating from them. He realised he was standing before practitioners of great power.

"What..." Lucius started. "Not that I am ungrateful, but what are you doing here?"

Forbeck nodded to the corpse of one of the creatures, it's back arched as though still in agony. "We heard a Shadowmage was in trouble, had brought more down upon his head than he could handle."

"You knew about these things?"

"We suspected," Forbeck shrugged. "And we had you as a witness to their activities previously. It bore further investigation. When Adrianna released herself from the Guild's contract, it allowed us to take a legitimate interest in what was going on. Though we are still unclear on exactly what that is."

"This may help," Adrianna said. As she stepped to one side, Lucius' gaze was caught by a motionless form on the floor behind her. Jewel.

"She's still alive, though I suspect she may regret that when you take her back to your guildhouse."

"You are handing her to us?" Lucius asked, visions of vengeance suddenly flashing through his mind.

"We are neither thieves nor inquisitors," Forbeck said. "You'll get more out of her than we will. I trust that, as one of us, you will keep us informed of anything we need to know."

Lucius turned back to Adrianna. "Thank you. I mean it. For everything."

She sniffed, avoiding his eyes for a moment. "Just remember your promise to me."

EPILOGUE

THE SHADOWS CAST by the single lantern hanging in the centre of the low ceiling did nothing to hide the baleful malice of Jewel's glare, the hatred she bore for all of them plainly visible. The greater part of her enmity she held for Lucius, the wreck of the left side of her face a twisted mass of burned and ravaged flesh. Her left eye seemed slow to react, but its twin was as fast as ever, seeming to almost glow with smouldering fury whenever Lucius walked in front of her.

He was impressed. With the concoctions she had been plied with, recipes brewed by the expert interrogators of the Night Hands, the woman should have been barely conscious, mumbling truthful replies to every question set before her. Instead, she still spat curses, promising slow death to them all. Elaine was getting impatient.

"Has she been trained to resist?" she demanded as she limped to Lucius' side to stare Jewel full in the face. Her stomach was wreathed in bandages, the legacy of a single thrust from Loredo's sword that had skittered across her lower ribs, smashing one. The guildmaster had fared far less well in their duel, falling to the ground with both of Elaine's swords jutting from his chest. "Has she taken something that nullifies our potions?"

Wendric shrugged. "Either is possible. Or both. For the latter, we may need to just wait for the effects of the counteragent to subside."

"We should increase the dosage," Elaine said flatly.

"No," said Lucius. "She has already taken more than you or I could bear. And I want to know what she knows."

Folding her arms, Elaine regarded the other woman. "She's playing us. We should move to more direct means."

Lucius guessed that Elaine had been itching to say that since they had brought Jewel into the bowels of the guildhouse two days ago. A few yards above them, in the common room and throughout the permitted areas of the guildhouse, thieves still celebrated, getting drunk and retelling stories of their rise to victory. The tales grew with each telling, but no one objected. From daring hits on the Guild's enforcers to the final assault on the guildhouse, every thief had the opportunity to become a hero.

Elaine had granted the Hands a week of celebration, but had made it painfully clear that open Council sessions were a thing of the past and that anyone defying her law as guildmaster would answer for it. She had been accepted smoothly enough, and even Lucius had avoided too many awkward questions, such was the elation throughout the guild. That, he knew, would likely not last.

Picking a knife off the single table in the small, dank room, Elaine crossed back over to Jewel and held the blade in front of the woman's face.

"It will do no good to work on her face," Elaine said, trying to goad her. "You already worked her over well, Lucius. She might have been pretty once, but now she looks like a freak. Like one of those creatures we slaughtered. Remember those? The ones we threw back into the sea."

Silently, Lucius shook his head. He had a fair idea that Jewel had never concerned herself with looking good and that, if anything, those scars aided her line of work. For her part, Jewel just held Elaine's gaze, her face completely neutral and without emotion, except her eyes, which spoke of nothing but promised agony.

"No, we must do something more... permanent, I think," Elaine declared. "Perhaps a few tendons cut, or the loss of a few fingers. That would bother you, wouldn't it, bitch? Not being able to kill any more. Life wouldn't be worth living."

Jewel muttered something then, but it was lost in Wendric's caustic comment: "I think she could learn to kill if you removed all her limbs. And maybe her head too."

Lucius held up a hand to silence him, and leaned over Jewel. Though she was tightly bound to the chair they had placed her in, he still did not get too close. He did not expect her to spit acid or poison into his face, but it would not surprise him if she did.

"What was that? What did you say, Jewel?"

With utter contempt, she stared back up at him and, for a moment, he thought she was going to fall silent again.

"I said, you are all dead and you don't even know it."

"We were the ones that won the war, Jewel," said Elaine. "You might have trouble recognising defeat, I realise, but what you are feeling right now, that is it. Wendric, give her another dose."

"I told you, she is already dangerously high."

"Apparently not," said Lucius. "Go on. Risk it. She's no good to us silent."

Grabbing a small opaque vial from the table, Wendric stood over Jewel, and regarded her as he held the vial aloft.

"We've done this before. You can have it easy, or have it hard." As he reached down, she twisted as far as her straps would allow.

"Hard then," Wendric said, grabbing Jewel's nose and wrenching her head back. For a minute he held her like that, waiting for her to draw breath through her mouth, but she remained resolutely still. Losing his patience, Wendric punched her hard in the stomach and, when this elicited the required response, drove the vial between her teeth, emptying its contents before slamming her mouth shut.

Still Jewel held out, twisting to break his grasp as a trickle of the potion ran from the corner of her mouth. She was finally defeated by the basic need for air, and Wendric finally released her when they heard her swallow.

For a moment, she gasped for breath, then spat at their feet. For a few seconds, her eyes lost focus and her head began to sway.

"It's beginning to work," Lucius said, taking a step forward. Then, as if a torch had been snuffed out, the dullness disappeared from her eyes and she snapped back in her restraints, staring past them as if watching something a great distance away. Both Lucius and Elaine looked at Wendric, but he just shrugged.

Lucius crouched until he was at her eye level, but she just seemed to stare right through him.

"Jewel, how did you contact those creatures?"

"They contacted us."

"What did you offer to get them working for the Guild?"

"Idiot."

Behind Lucius, Wendric smirked. "If the truth drugs are working, I would say that gives you little credit."

Ignoring him, Lucius pressed on. "Jewel, what are they."

"The power of the ancients, the rulers of the past," she said, then added an afterthought. "And the future."

"I don't understand."

Jewel sighed then, long and exaggerated, as if failing to get through to an ignorant child. He decided to try a different tack.

"What do they want?"

"Everything."

"What do you mean, everything? All the gold in the city? The city itself? The Empire?"

"Everything."

"That doesn't make sense, Jewel," he said, wishing the others would join in. "Why would they fight alongside you? What could you offer?"

"Revenge. A tip in the balance."

He stopped, thinking that one through. Turning, he faced Wendric. "Does she have to be this literal?"

"It works differently for everyone," Wendric shrugged. "Some appear drunk, others desperate to please. I always thought it was a reflection of the personality, though I am not sure what that says about her."

Scratching his head, Lucius confronted Jewel again. "You said they wanted to tip the balance. You weren't paying them in gold or goods, were you?"

"Of course not." Again, that exasperated tone.

A thought struck him as he saw her head begin to sag. "Jewel, listen to me. They weren't working for you, right? You were doing their bidding."

"We served them."

"But why?"

"Idiot."

"She presumes the answer is obvious," said Wendric.

"Yes, thank you Wendric, I am beginning to get that," Lucius replied testily. "They served something more powerful than them because they would be rewarded. I withdraw the question – happy?"

In response Wendric shrugged as Elaine pushed past him. As Jewel's eyes began to close, she slapped the woman hard across the face. The sharp sting of pain seemed to revive Jewel and, for a moment, she seemed lucid.

"What are they, Jewel?" Elaine asked. "What do we have to fear from them?"

"They have been here forever," Jewel said slowly. "They commanded us and we obeyed, for that is the only way to survive the war."

"The war is over, Jewel," Lucius said. "You lost."

"No, the war has gone on for centuries, and will continue until every man and woman is dead or lies enslaved at their feet."

Wendric cleared his throat. "I recall hearing stories of the Old Races, those that came before man, and the great empires they built. Is that what you mean?"

"Idiot," Jewel spat. "They were ancient when elf and dwarf walked this world. They fought them too, and won. Now it is our turn."

"But why?" Elaine asked.

"Because they understand hatred. Because they know it is not enough to simply exist."

"What do you mean?" Elaine pressed, but Jewel's head was beginning to hang to one side, as if it were too heavy for her neck. When Elaine shook her, they all saw a slither of froth between her lips.

"She's going," Wendric said. "I warned you."

"Stay with us, Jewel!" Elaine demanded, shaking her harder. "What do you mean by that, why is it not enough for them to just exist?"

Jewel coughed, flecks of bloodied spittle flying across Elaine's face. Her words were barely more than a whisper, forced from her throat by the power of the drugs alone.

"Our presence is an affront to them. War has come, but now they can join the old power with the new. Now, they are unstoppable."

"I don't understand," Elaine said. "What do they want? What *are* they, Jewel?"

She slapped the woman again to bring her back to consciousness, then shook her when she failed to respond, until Lucius laid a hand on her arm. Jewel had stopped breathing.

"It's too late, Elaine."

"Damn her!" Elaine spat, as she pushed away from Jewel's body and stalked across the room in frustration. "She told us nothing!"

"She told us little," Lucius corrected her, but Elaine was in no mood to be placated.

"Riddles and fairy tales! And you, Wendric," she said, turning on her new lieutenant. "You should know better than to spout myths about goblins and elves!"

He seemed ready to respond, but wisely kept silent. Lucius was lost in his own thoughts as he tried to piece together what Jewel had told them. Could her words be trusted? If she had the power to resist the truth drugs, did she also have the power to defy them outright? Still, he had witnessed the power the creatures from the sea wielded and that scared him more than he cared to admit to either of his fellow thieves.

Either way, he had just got this guild back onto its feet, and he was not about to let anything tear it back down. Even if the threat lay at the bottom of the ocean.

THE END

NIGHT'S HAUNTING

Original cover art by Greg Staples

CHAPTER ONE

THE CROSSBOW HAD been specially modified for the purpose, and Grayling could easily appreciate its craftsmanship as she watched Ambrose hefting it into a firing position.

The brass plates along its length strengthened the weapon against the massive pull of its string. Along the top surface, a long tube of variable lenses ensured the weapon would strike whatever it was aimed at. It was these that Ambrose adjusted now, carefully making allowances for range, elevation, even the slight breeze that rolled in from the sea, nearly two miles to the west.

A wicked looking double-hook protruded from the end of the bolt, carefully fashioned to fly through the air with the least disturbance or deviation.

Just ahead of the firing lever, a metal eyepiece stood proud, and through this was threaded a silken rope, fixed to the trailing point of the bolt. The rest of the rope, thin and light but extremely strong, lay coiled at Ambrose's feet as he balanced in the branches of the ash tree that overhung the walled garden. Its other end was tied to the trunk itself, in a slip knot that Grayling stood ready to adjust as soon as the bolt flew.

Grayling glanced over Ambrose's shoulder.

"Guard turning around again, get ready."

"Say when," Ambrose whispered.

The guard strolled past the round pond at the garden's centre, then disappeared into the small cherry orchard.

"Now!" Grayling hissed.

As soon as the bolt left the crossbow, Grayling saw it was flying true. The silk rope trailing behind it, the bolt sailed over the three storey mansion to arc over the roofline and out of sight.

Immediately, Grayling pulled hard on the slip knot while the uncoiling rope hissed through the crossbow's eyepiece. For a few seconds there was play in the rope, then it snapped taut. The hooked bolt had found purchase. Grayling placed a foot on the trunk of the ash tree and pulled, making sure the rope would bear weight. Satisfied, she twisted the knot until it bit deep and the rope thrummed slightly as she brushed her fingers against it.

"Your turn," said Ambrose, as he began to dismantle the crossbow, hiding components in pouches and belts.

Grayling was wreathed in a black silken bodysuit. Hugging every contour of her body precisely, there was no play or loose folds in the material, allowing her to move in absolute silence. Instinctively checking the short sword sheathed between her shoulders, the silk rope coiled around her waist and the small bundle at the small of her back, Grayling wrapped her legs around the rope and began to pull herself along its length towards the mansion's roof.

She was suddenly grateful for the hours of training she had been forced to endure within the guildhouse. She remembered cursing Ambrose at the time, for he had merely been tinkering with his crossbow while she had been climbing up and down ropes for nearly a week in preparation for this job. Now, however, she sailed up the rope, hand-over-hand in easy, practised motions.

Catching sight of movement from the corner of her eye, she stopped suddenly. Grayling was very conscious that she swung just a few yards above ground whose guardians would as soon kill her as catch her. A lone dog had appeared from around the far end of an outbuilding, and it sniffed the air tentatively. A lean creature, she could see it was powerfully built, no doubt bred to hunt and bring down thieves.

As it loped across the lawn toward her, a suspicious growl building in its throat, Grayling reached behind her back and fumbled with her pack, drawing out a small pouch. With a single, swift motion, she flung it over the dog's head, back toward the coach house. For a moment, the dog seemed confused, and it looked up at her quizzically. Then the scent of the pouch reached it and, with a hurried bark, it ran at full flight back to the coach house, head swinging from side to side as it searched for the pouch and its irresistible odours.

The activity caused the guard to emerge from the orchard. He looked across the lawns, hands on his hips, as if trying to gauge whether any investigation into the dog's activities was worth his time. Evidently, he was paid well enough, as he started to march towards the disturbance.

As she continued her climb, Grayling smiled. The guard would likely find the pouch she had thrown, but he would then discover all dogs would take a special interest in him for the next few days, as the mixed oils and powders within the pouch transferred their scent to those that handled it very easily. It was an ingenious design, as it meant that only one dog had to make contact with the pouch for it to affect a whole pack, the scent rubbing off from one animal to another.

Within minutes, Grayling had crossed the lip of the roof and, gently, she lowered herself down from the rope, feet first. Tightly bound canvas pads woven into the feet of her bodysuit permitted her to drop down silently, yet gave enough grip on the sloping tiles to stop her sliding. Quickly glancing around to ensure there were no guards stationed on the roof itself, and that no one in the gardens below had spotted her ingress, Grayling realised she was now virtually invisible against the dark tiles of the roof. She stepped lightly to the top of the roofline, and held up a hand. The signal told Ambrose he could now cross, and that the second team could also proceed in their part of this mission.

Running a hand along the length of the rope as she walked back down the slope of the roof, she felt it twitch as Ambrose started his ascent. He lacked her agility but, at the same time, she was not entirely sure she could have made that shot with the crossbow – this was, after all, why they worked in teams.

Looking out across the gardens, she waited until she saw Ambrose was halfway towards the mansion before looking down at the bay window on the floor directly below. She uncoiled the shorter rope wound about her waist, and knotted one end above her hips. As Ambrose, puffing slightly with the effort of pulling his body up to the roof, dropped down beside her, she handed him the other end of the rope.

"Getting too old for jobs like this," Ambrose muttered, as he sat down on the tiled roof and braced his legs against the guttering.

"Just don't let go." Grayling winked back, and then turned to scrabble down from the roof, head first.

Slowly lowered by Ambrose, she scaled the short distance without sound, inching towards the wide bay window. She looked into the dark interior, taking a few seconds for her eyes to adjust. As expected, the window looked into a wide corridor. She could see a portrait directly opposite her, looking down onto a wood panelled floor. At the foot of the bay itself, a wide upholstered chair was placed, perhaps to provide light to some rich noble looking to get away from the bustle of his household in the company of a good book.

Satisfied that no one prowled the corridor, Grayling crawled down a few feet further so she hung in front of the window's locking mechanism. A cautious probing told her the mechanism was engaged – as she had expected it to be. The owner of the mansion was arrogant, but he was not stupid enough to spend gold on hired mercenaries, then leave a window unlocked.

Reaching for her pack again, she produced an instrument that looked like a small wooden cup, with a butterfly screw inserted into its base. Placing the open mouth of the cup firmly against the glass of the window, Grayling slowly twisted the screw. Inside the cup, gears engaged and diamond-edged blades ground against the glass, scoring a deeper cut with each rotation, the tiny scratching noise barely audible.

After a minute of grinding, Grayling removed the cup and slid it back into her pack. Before her was a perfectly round score mark in the glass. She tapped the bottom of the circle once. The glass tilted free and she swept it clear before it could fall inside.

Pleased with her work thus far, she reached into the hole and grasped the short lever built into the wooden frame. Testing it gently to begin with to ensure it would not grind or squeak, Grayling then pulled the lever to unlock the window.

Lowering herself to the window's level, Grayling spun on her rope so she was upright, then crept inside the mansion, stepping on the chair as she entered. Glancing down the corridor, she saw multiple doors on either side. There was no sign of life. With a confident smile, she untied the rope, then gave it a slight tug to let Ambrose know she was in. Taking an easy breath, Grayling stepped down onto the panelled floor.

And immediately froze.

SHIFTING HIS POSITION on the tiled roof of the old Brotherhood chapel, Lucius Kane moved closer to the chimney stack to avoid being silhouetted against the huge blue sphere of Kerberos. Though it was the dead of night, the gas giant cast an eerie grey light across the city, enough to give thieves cover in the shadows, but not so much that they could be careless.

From his perch, Lucius could see the entire city laid before him like a mosaic of stone and lantern light. Behind him, Meridian Street ran down the hill from the fortified north gate through the heart of Turnitia. There, down the slope, the huge Vos Citadel stood, its five towers imposing themselves over the city, just as the Vos army had done some years before. Beyond, the docks were hidden from view below the cliffs that marked the western boundary of Turnitia. Lucius could hear the savage ocean, constantly pounding at the ancient monolithic defences that protected the harbour. It was a sound every citizen of Turnitia learned to tune out, though visitors often found themselves missing sleep for days on end before they adjusted.

Drawing his cloak tighter about himself, Lucius all but disappeared against the stone chimney stack as he resumed study of the building before him. The mansion and its surrounding gardens were large, but not as ostentatious as many others in the immediate area. The owner preferred to display his wealth and power in other ways.

Henri de Lille, a successful merchant from Pontaine, was well known to the thieves' guild of Turnitia, as he had established an extensive network of business interests in the city while it remained free and neutral from the bickering between Pontaine and the Empire of Vos. When Vos entered the city during the last war, de Lille had had little to fear, for his own empire had been built on servicing the needs of Vos and Pontaine nobles who still wished to trade with one another. He was a broker in the main, and money flowed through his hands like water, maintaining tight control on the flow of goods between Andon and Malmkrug.

Not that any of this mattered to Lucius or any of his fellow thieves, of course. Politics was not their strength, and they shied away from murky entanglements. Their interest was in fleecing de Lille in as efficient a manner as possible.

This meant that, rather than target de Lille's very well protected warehouses and stores of goods he transferred from one nation to another, they ran an extortion racket among the Pontaine man's lieutenants and officers. Insurance, of a type. In return for regular – and not insubstantial – payments, the thieves' guild guaranteed not only that none of their operatives would steal from de Lille's property, but that they would also ensure no independent thieves made the attempt either.

On the whole, a merchant like de Lille was probably better off with an arrangement like this. The guild made sure it operated in a very low key fashion, and the losses paid to them were likely far less than if thieves had free range over his property, without factoring in the reputation a merchant can lose by having his warehouses constantly plundered. However, a man like de Lille never got to be as rich as he was without an over-developed sense of greed, and he had gradually grown tired of paying the thieves for, as he saw it, nothing.

That was when the hired mercenaries were brought in. Well-armed, they protected de Lille's belongings like an iron wall, and were more than capable of seeing off any of the guild's collectors. Revenue from de Lille dried up overnight, and that made certain members of the thieves' guild anxious.

Including Lucius. The entire thieves' guild ran on a franchise system where senior thieves would create missions and ongoing enterprises, and gain a permanent income from them (minus the guild's own take, of course). They would effectively employ lower ranking thieves, and split their share in ever decreasing amounts. The longest serving thieves might have dozens of such operations, all providing a flow of cash, while younger members might only have part shares in one or two. Indeed, with so much of Turnitia sewn up by enterprising members of the guild, it was difficult for a young thief to create a brand new franchise, and as a result many were passed on from one thief to the next in the event of death or retirement.

De Lille had been Lucius' franchise, passed on to him after the war between the original Night Hands thieves and the Guild of Coin and Enterprise. The war had shattered both guilds utterly and the new thieves' guild was an amalgamation of members from both sides. When de Lille had employed his mercenaries and refused to pay the guild its rightful share, he had deprived Lucius, and many other thieves, of a lucrative income. More to the point, if word got out that de Lille was able to poke the thieves' guild in the eye without retribution, then many other merchants might get the same idea.

So, this evening was about retribution, and a lesson to be taught. Maintaining a healthy relationship with the beggars' guild – the spies of the city – Lucius had learned that de Lille had recently brought a large haul into the city from Andon, planning to sell it to Vos nobility. Lucius' interest was in a particular item known as the Torc of Vocator Majoris, an old Pontaine artefact said to protect the wearer from assassination. He doubted its powers were real, but the torc was worth a great deal of money and having it stolen would lose de Lille a great deal of face among his wealthiest customers. That alone would serve as a potent reminder that no one, no matter who they were, ever crossed the thieves' guild.

Lucius had already begun moving from his perch when he saw Grayling shimmy up the rope and distract the merchant's dogs. De Lille's mansion was said to be very well protected, both by guards and traps designed to catch unwary thieves, and so he had decided to take two teams on this mission. More thieves meant a smaller percentage for him at the end of the night, true, but this job was about more than just the money.

Swinging down from a rope he had tied around the chimney stack, Lucius dropped spryly into a shadowy alley between the chapel and a small residence. Taking a quick look out of the alley to ensure the main thoroughfare remained deserted, Lucius sprinted across the road on the balls of his feet, making little noise. In the opposite alley, running straight past the wall of de Lille's grounds, he nodded a silent greeting to Swinherd, his own team mate.

Lucius watched as Swinherd grabbed a pole ladder from the shadows, and laid it against the wall.

Swinherd was on top of the wall in seconds, and he held a hand out as he scanned the surrounding gardens, holding Lucius in check until he was sure the coast was clear.

Had he taken only one team to de Lille's mansion, Lucius might have instead chosen Ambrose to accompany him, the man who had first inducted him into the guild and taught him so much. Or perhaps Grayling, a woman he had fought side-by-side with during an escape from the Vos Citadel. He had not worked with Swinherd a great deal, and the man had a reputation for impetuousness, but Ambrose had suggested Lucius take him on this mission. Swinherd had, of late, started to learn the locksmith's trade and, as useful as that alone might have been inside the mansion, it seemed as though he was also starting to learn patience.

A waved signal from Swinherd saw Lucius scampering up the ladder, and he too perched on the wall, studying the gardens while his partner drew the pole ladder up from the alley, and carefully wedged it between the top of the wall and the side of the mansion. Seconds ticked away as he made sure the metal claws were firmly gripped. While Lucius wished Swinherd would hurry so they could quickly gain entry into the mansion, he also knew that if the pole ladder was positioned incorrectly, it would slip and collapse as soon as either of them put any weight upon it.

Finally satisfied, Swinherd cast a quick glance at Lucius, who nodded in assent, and then carefully climbed the ladder to the roof. As soon as his foot left the last rung of the ladder, Lucius sprang onto it, and proceeded to follow.

"Larken? Where the dogs got to?"

The voice from the other end of the path caught Lucius with alarm, and he instantly went rigid, trying to make himself as invisible as possible. Another voice sounded to Lucius' left, coming from somewhere near a coach house a few dozen yards away.

"They're round here," it said. "Acting crazy."

"For the love of God..." protested the first voice and heavy footsteps, accompanied by the unmistakable chink of mail armour, grew louder as a mercenary came down the path. As he came into view Lucius recalled the old thief adage: if you can see them, they can see you.

Taking a quick breath, Lucius reached within his mind's eye to find the threads of magical energies running through his consciousness. He had been able to tap this sorcerous power for many years now, but his recent training allowed him to gather the threads he needed and wield them almost as a reflex.

Selecting the darkest of the threads, he mentally pulled, breaking it away from the others, and imagined it wrapping itself around his body, the magic twisting and writhing under his direction. To any observer, Lucius' form would seem to shimmer and distort before growing fainter, as if he was being stretched into the nearby shadows. To the mercenary, his mind on the important matter of his employer's dogs, Lucius was no more than an indistinct shadow at the corner of his eye. With the garden full of such shadows, he paid it no more attention than he did the rest, and carried on, oblivious to the thief's presence.

Waiting until the guard had disappeared behind the coach house, Lucius started up the pole ladder again, letting the magical darkness slowly uncoil itself. Once on the roof, he directed Swinherd to the rear of the mansion, where they had agreed they would gain entry. He was about to follow but glanced across at Ambrose, who was still at the edge of the roof, holding the rope that trailed off the edge down to the bay window below. Lucius frowned at that, as he was sure Ambrose would have reached the roof long before he and Swinherd had. He should be inside by now.

Casting a rueful look at Swinherd as the younger man disappeared over the roofline, Lucius padded quietly to Ambrose, a knot starting to grow in his stomach at the thought of his plan unravelling so soon.

Seeing Lucius approach him, Ambrose exhaled in relief.

"Something's wrong," he said, and Lucius had to stifle a groan. "Got the tug from Grayling, but it's gone all quiet now."

Rubbing his forehead in frustration as much as thought, Lucius made a quick decision. He was determined that his plan would stay more or less intact.

"Okay, I'll go down," he said to Ambrose. "Once I'm in, you go over the top with Swinherd. You remember everything about the entry from the back?"

Ambrose nodded. Both teams had been briefed well on one another's roles, in case of any last minute changes.

Following Grayling's descent, Lucius scaled down the rope quickly as Ambrose once again braced himself against the weight. Scanning the bay as he went down, Lucius saw nothing out of the ordinary. As he drew level with the window, he peered inside and saw the black, slender form of the female thief, standing in the corridor, utterly rigid. He put his head through the open window and glanced up and down the corridor, trying to see if perhaps a squad of mercenaries held her at crossbow point. There was nothing.

"Grayling. What's wrong?"

"Thank God it's you. Filcher's floor. Heard it crack as soon as I put a foot down."

"Is the chair secure?" Lucius asked, indicating the furniture in the centre of the bay.

"I think so, yes."

Hooking a foot inside the bay, Lucius entered the mansion, and perched himself on the chair, before tugging on the rope twice to let Ambrose know he was now free to follow Swinherd around the back of the mansion.

He glanced at Grayling, impressed with both her composure and stillness. Other thieves might have panicked at discovering they were standing on a filcher's floor, but Grayling remained stock still. That was when the floor must have shifted, as she put her full weight on to it; the flexible floorboards designed to crush glass and ring chimes mounted underneath. They were carefully built so even a tentative footstep could trigger the trap.

They were lucky, for Grayling had frozen the moment she knew what was happening, and her quick reactions had probably saved all of them.

"Alright, you're safe now – this will probably get a bit cold, so be ready."

Grayling slowly and gently nodded her assent, as Lucius reached down with his right hand, his left holding the back of the chair to support his weight. Again, the threads of magic leapt to the forefront of his mind, and he twisted them around, conjuring their potency as he made their power manifest.

Eyes widening slightly in amazement, Grayling watched as a fine mist grew around her foot and then spread up and down the entire length of the corridor in seconds, forming a carpet an inch thick. Looking over her shoulder at Lucius, she saw him frown in concentration then shiver as he lowered his hand to the floor, his fingers turning pale blue as he allowed the magic to flow through him. She had witnessed his shadowmagic before, but he never used it at the guildhouse and she was awestruck every time.

As he touched the filcher's floor, there was a tiny crackle of energy as the mist around his fingers dissipated, frozen to the wooden boards of the corridor by the extreme magical cold. This effect radiated out from Lucius, spreading down the corridor, causing Grayling to gasp at the cold as it numbed her foot. Within a few heartbeats, the mist had completely disappeared, leaving behind a fine sheen on the floor, freezing it still.

Lucius let go of the breath he had been holding and looked up at Grayling, smiling. Gingerly, he took a foot off the chair and set it down on the floor, gradually adding his full weight. The boards he rested on remained inflexible and no alarms sounded.

"It's okay, you can move now," he said. "Just be careful not to slip on the ice."

Grayling was tentative in her movements at first, but quickly gained confidence in the solidity of the floor. She stooped to massage her thighs, and then straightened to stretch her back, both having suffered cramp from being held immobile for too long.

"We ready?" Grayling asked.

Lucius looked down the corridor to his right, and beckoned Grayling along. The libraries of the guildhouse had borne much fruit for this mission, including detailed plans for the entire house. The thieves' guild had many such plans for buildings across the city, acquired with either great expense or great skill from the architects that had built them, over many years. These plans had formed the basis of many raids in the past, and were a valuable resource.

The members of both teams had memorised the mansion's floor plans, and their methods of entry had been built around them. They could not be sure de Lille or some past resident had not changed the interior, of course, as indeed the filcher's floor indicated, but the main structural design should have remained more or less intact. Both Lucius and Grayling already knew they were on the right floor; now they just needed to head deeper into the mansion, where a small set of windowless interior rooms suggested the prime location for both de Lille's personal quarters and his most treasured belongings.

Counting doors as he padded down the icy corridor, Lucius finally stopped at one, and listened. He felt Grayling tap him gently on the shoulder and, turning around, saw she was indicating that she go first. His first reaction was to refuse, but he quickly reflected on her agility and the bodysuit she wore, designed purely for stealth, then nodded.

Slowly, and with painstaking care, Grayling twisted the door's handle, gauging whether it was locked or not. It wasn't and, with equally measured pace, she quietly opened it, ready to halt her actions immediately if the door should squeal on its hinges or someone should be present on the other side.

She turned back to Lucius, held up two fingers, then one. She then made an "o" with finger and thumb, and finally held up her hand, palm facing him.

Lucius nodded. Two guards, about ten yards away, in front of a door.

Reaching down to his belt, Lucius produced a pouch whose end was sealed but had a wick poking up through the fabric. Not wanting to spend time with a flint and steel, he willed the forces of magic to his bidding, and touched the wick with his finger. Instantly, a flame took to it and it fizzed – an almost trivial spell for Lucius now, though he remembered a time when he had trouble controlling effects so small.

He passed the pouch to Grayling, who took great care not to inhale the smoke streaming from it. Sliding the door open a fraction wider, she flicked the pouch down the corridor.

Inside the short passageway, one of the mercenaries was alert enough to notice the pouch as it slid along the floor. He took a step back, but the pouch suddenly puffed open with a low gasp, coating both him and the other guard in a fine white powder. The powder quickly sank back to the floor, but by then they had both inhaled it. The alert guard suddenly found his senses dulled, as his hearing fled, and the walls of the passageway seemed to bend into one another. He saw a short black form pacing menacingly towards him, but his throat would not co-operate as he tried to shout an alarm. He managed to get his hand around the pommel of his sword as blackness overtook him, and he felt as though he were falling a long way.

Entering the passageway, Lucius and Grayling saw the two guards succumb to the sleeping draught, slumping against the walls as they sank to the ground. Lucius winced as the mail armour of one scored a line in the plastered wall, causing a low grinding noise. Grayling, too, was concerned at the unintended noise, and they both froze on the spot as they listened intently, trying to detect any sign of alarm in the mansion.

There was nothing.

"Guards mean we are on the right track," whispered Grayling.

"So does this door."

Grayling had noted that the door seemed unusually elaborate when she had first seen it from the other end of the passageway, but she had put that down to a merchant's poor taste in interior decoration. As she looked now, she saw that the design was in fact an elaborate mechanism.

The centre of the door was dominated by four short swords, built into large metal dials, each surrounded by strange glyphs and markers. Each dial was linked to the others by shafts of steel and, from there, thicker shafts were driven into the surrounding door frame and, presumably, extended some distance into the wall.

Lucius sighed. He had heard of such doors before, though he had never seen one himself. Built by esteemed Vos craftsmen, such portals were used to secure the most valuable of possessions, and were rumoured to be only in the possession of the richest nobles and best-connected holy men. That de Lille had one made Lucius think he had underestimated the man's wealth by a significant degree.

The swords and dials, Lucius saw, formed an elaborate combination lock, with each sword being turned to face a number of markers. So long as you knew which markers each sword should point to, the door could be opened within seconds. Lucius did not know, as his research for this mission had not even hinted that such a door might be present.

"So, you wish you had stayed with Swinherd now?" whispered Grayling with a smile.

CHAPTER TWO

SQUINTING DOWN THE wooden tube, Ambrose surveyed the doorway from the safety of the adjoining passage. Inside the tube, two mirrors had been precisely positioned so a thief looking at the mirror at the bottom end of the tube would actually see the world from the vantage of the one at the top. As the tube was a foot long, this made it an ideal tool for peering over walls or, in this case, around corners.

Ambrose could not remember exactly what the device was called, so he called it his jerriscope. As impressive as his jerriscope was, however, the doorway that blocked their progress was a great deal more elaborate.

"Passage is clear, but we have a problem," he told Swinherd.

Swinherd peered through the jerriscope, and whistled quietly.

Before him, the width of the passage was blocked by a wall of glass. Set into the panes was a single door, with an exposed locking mechanism. As Swinherd broke from cover to better view the obstacle, he could see that the glass was as thick as his smallest finger.

"Force the lock, you smash the glass," Ambrose said. "Clever. I would guess the glass has been stressed so the whole lot will come down. Very noisy."

Swinherd snorted and reached for his belt, bringing up a small leather pack as he crouched down in front of the lock. He unrolled the pack on the floor, revealing a selection of finely crafted lockpicks, a collection that had cost him four months' income.

"But there is a flaw," he whispered. "By setting the lock in glass, I can see half the mechanism. I'll be through this in less than a minute."

Ambrose had already set his glass cutting cup to the door, just a few inches above the lock.

"No," he said. "You are looking at a false mechanism, designed to lure a thief away from the tumblers. You'll think you have it, force the lock, and then break the glass. Look..."

Frowning, Swinherd reconsidered the lock.

"No, I don't think..."

With a slight crack, Ambrose withdrew the cup, then popped the circle of glass free. Reaching inside, he pulled the latch, and carefully swung the glass door inwards.

"Swinherd, my friend, you may be adapting to the locksmith's trade quickly, but you still have a lot to learn about being a thief."

BEFORE EXPLORING THE junction, Grayling flattened herself against the wall, using the back of her arm to wipe the sweat from her brow. Lucius had finally lost patience with the combination lock, and focussed fiery magics that had, eventually, melted the mechanisms, allowing him to pull the securing bars free, one by one. It had taken time, and Grayling thought the backdraft of heat would boil her alive. Her hair was sodden, sweat ran freely down her face, and her bodysuit was growing more uncomfortable by the minute.

For his part, Lucius seemed less affected by the heat, but the directed concentration of such powerful magic had left him breathless. Their prize was close, however, and the combination door seemed to be the last obstacle barring their way into de Lille's inner sanctum.

On the original architectural plans they had studied before launching this assault, the small complex of three rooms and their adjoining corridors had lit up like a beacon. All interior rooms, with no windows, they were perfectly situated to house valuables – all approaches could be trapped or sealed, unless you could tunnel through walls.

Along the corridor, mounted on wall brackets at regular intervals, were strange orbs, glowing with a yellowish light. Lucius had never seen such artefacts before, but he had heard of them. Crafted by the wizards of the Three Towers in Andon, also known as the League of Prestidigitation and Prestige, the orbs were magical, needing a simple touch by their owner to dull or brighten them. That de Lille could afford to light his entire inner domain with them was further testament to his wealth.

Grayling tapped his arm.

"Two more guards," she whispered, indicating one of the passageways leading from the junction. "The rest are clear."

"We have our target, then."

"You have more sleep powder?"

He shook his head. "No. This one we'll have to do the old-fashioned way."

"I'll go first."

"On your word."

Slowly, Grayling drew her short sword from across her back, the scabbard lined with cloth so the weapon slid free without sound. Behind her, Lucius did the same, but also plucked a dagger from his belt. Grayling padded around the corner at speed, arrowing straight towards the mercenaries and the oaken door they guarded.

Lucius' dagger flew over her shoulder to sink into the throat of one man, causing him to gag while blood flowed between his fingers as he fought to stem the flow. His cry of alarm was little more than a low gurgle.

His partner was taken fully by surprise as Grayling charged him, her canvassed feet making little noise as she quickly closed the distance. He managed to draw his sword and flail blindly, batting aside Grayling's disembowelling thrust by luck more than skill. Grayling winced as the swords met and a metallic clang rang clear, impossibly loud in the tight, quiet passageway.

Changing grip on her weapon, she forced the guard's blade up, over their heads. Seeing the man begin to recover his wits, she jabbed a knee hard into his groin. Air exploded from his lungs, and her face was showered in the man's spittle. He bent low, allowing Grayling to smash her forehead into his nose. She heard the crack over the guard's moan of pain as he tried to draw breath. With one arm, Grayling pushed him back against the wall and rammed her sword into his stomach. He twitched as the weapon entered him, and Grayling clamped a hand over his mouth as she slowly laid him on the floor.

She looked up at Lucius, who was casting anxious glances behind them.

"Did that betray our entry?" she asked.

"I can't hear anything," he said after a moment. "What about within?"

Placing her ear to the door, Grayling concentrated, trying to pick up the slightest noise. There was nothing.

She tried the door handle, and found it was locked.

"You sure this is the right room?" she asked. "Wouldn't put it beyond our man to use a decoy."

Lucius shook his head. "I thought about that. De Lille *is* paranoid, but everything we've seen here tonight suggests he likes his luxury. It's the largest room in this area. I can't see him at ease anywhere else."

Grayling shrugged. It sounded plausible. She inspected the lock, wondering if her own skills in lockpicking would suffice or whether they would have to wait for Swinherd. Hearing Lucius rummage through the guards' mail coats, she glanced behind her.

Finding nothing on the guard Grayling had silenced, Lucius crossed the passageway to check beneath the mail of the other man. Reaching under the guard's chin, Lucius wrinkled his nose as his hand became coated in blood. He then grunted with satisfaction, withdrawing a cord looped around a key.

"Too paranoid," Lucius whispered. "Our merchant feared someone would somehow circumvent the guards altogether, thus he gave them a key so they could come and rescue him at his call. Just makes our job easier, though."

Lucius turned the key in the lock slowly until they heard a quiet click. Looking at Grayling to ensure she was ready, he entered the room beyond.

Inside, the room was illuminated by the lighted orbs, but they had been set to a dim glow, barely casting their light across the soft rugs that littered the floor. The walls to his left and right were lined with overcrowded bookcases, and a single desk covered with stacked sheets and discarded quills stood in the centre of the room. On the far side, behind gossamer thin veils, was a wide bed. Lucius could just make out a motionless form lying beneath the sheets. De Lille.

Waving Grayling in, Lucius padded to the desk, the thick rugs aiding his stealth. Carefully, he began to search for their prize. Grayling, meanwhile, started to work through the bookcases.

Finding nothing of note in the desk, though raising his eyebrows more than once at the figures he glanced at the sheets denoting the value of some of de Lille's recent transactions, Lucius crossed to the bookshelves to aid Grayling.

After a few moments, he started to get nervous. Their entry into the mansion would not remain secret for much longer, as a patrolling guard would inevitably happen across the open window or blasted door, and Lord alone knew what Ambrose and Swinherd were getting up to. Added to that, de Lille could awake at any minute, and if they were caught in his room, they would have to either retreat or kill him; neither of which was the desired objective this evening.

A sniff from Grayling caught his attention and he looked around. The small thief had apparently abandoned her search of the bookcases out of frustration and had started lifting rugs. By the desk, right where Lucius had been standing, she pointed to the floor beneath a large bearskin. Set into the wood was a small metal safe.

Nodding, Lucius prompted her to open it, and she quickly drew a pick from her pack, then began probing. A thought crept into Lucius' mind, a feeling that something was not quite right, and he frowned as he tried to detect what was wrong.

The location of the safe seemed right; hidden, yet easy to access while de Lille worked at his desk. The lock seemed fairly rudimentary but, like that of the door they had just entered, it seemed as though the merchant was confident that no one would get this far into his home.

So what was it? He watched as Grayling flicked tumblers, one by one, working further into the mechanism. Giving up on his search, Lucius instead called the threads of magic to his aid, ready to shape and twist them to face whatever threat was to be unleashed.

In his mind, he saw them, pulsing cords of magical energy, each a different hue, each containing a different potential that could be caught, separated and shaped to his whim, allowing him to conjure fire, give himself inhuman strength, suck the life from another living being, or any one of a multitude of actions.

He noticed then that several threads had started to bend and twist of their own volition, and he frowned. The threads of magic always curled and twisted around one another, making the process of separating and using them difficult without practice and training, but here they appeared to be curving around *something*. He had seen that effect before, but only when in the presence of another mage, such as Adrianna. This did not look quite the same. It was more... subdued, somehow.

Grayling felt the last tumbler click and, with a satisfied smile, placed her hand on the safe's lever, ready to wrench it open.

Lucius hissed, stopping her instantly. She looked at him quizzically.

Waving her back, Lucius crouched down and studied the safe intently. He saw nothing unusual but, closing his eyes and focussing on the magical streams, he saw them split and curve far more acutely.

Opening his eyes, he saw Grayling looking at him with concern.

"Trapped," he mouthed to her, causing her to frown in puzzlement. She shrugged, ready to accept his lead. After all, she was well aware that he could sense things she would never be able to see.

Turning his attention back to the safe, he gently placed a palm flat on its surface and closed his eyes again. This time, the obstacle that forced the threads to split and curve was obvious. He saw a small nest of crackling magical energy resting in his mind's eye, its presence forcing the threads to avoid it. He knew that nest represented the safe or, at least, the magics bound within it.

Mentally grabbing a thread, he pulled it closer to the safe, and saw wisps of coloured gas, the raw essence of magic, begin to siphon off from the safe. After a few seconds, it was done. No more gases were drawn from the safe, and its nest of energy seemed diminished somehow.

For a fraction of a second he relaxed his control of that single thread and energy immediately began to flow back to the safe. Grasping the thread with his mind again, he halted the flow.

Briefly he wondered what to do next, then an idea occurred. Brow creasing with concentration, he tried to reach out to another thread that slipped and bent its way around the safe. He started breathing hard, and felt himself tiring; he had never before tried to utilise two threads at once.

Slowly, wearily, he brought the second thread over to the safe, and felt his confidence grow a little as, once again, gaseous energy began to transfer from the safe to the thread. After a few seconds more, the ball of energy representing the safe was a little smaller still.

Now he knew what to do, but he was dubious about his ability to control multiple threads at a time. Fervently, he hoped the next thread would prove sufficient to disarm whatever protective magic had been placed upon the safe.

As threads were removed from the main flow of magic, the remainder seemed more chaotic in their path around the safe, as if they were becoming less stable, and it occurred to Lucius that he had no real idea of what he was doing. Was he creating a hole in magic itself as he bound more threads to his control? Or was the more violent twisting and curving of the threads a natural result of his low level of training and understanding? He now began to wish he had paid far more attention to Adrianna and Master Forbeck.

The third thread bucked and twisted, and he had the bizarre image of a kicking and screaming child. Screwing his eyes tight with concentration, he forced the thread, inch by inch, toward the safe. It bucked and rolled under his touch, but he managed to move it close enough for the transfer of energy to resume. As the magical essences started to shift away from the safe, he breathed in relief as the energies around the safe shrank by a much greater margin.

That was enough for the rampaging thread to wriggle out of his control. Like a writhing snake, it coiled back upon itself and, for the briefest instant, touched the safe. The safe exploded, blowing Lucius onto his back.

He felt Grayling grab his shoulders and start to haul him up, but his vision was blocked by a thick mist that rolled with unnatural speed from the lighting globes, down the walls, to fill the room. When his hearing returned, he was aware that de Lille's room was ringing to the sound of a large, thunderous bell.

Still shaky on his feet, Lucius shook his head to clear the daze left by the blast, and saw Grayling reach down to the safe, twist it open, and grasp something inside. Grinning, she held a golden chain in front of him, a stone-encrusted, moon-shaped device suspended from its length – the torc.

Nodding his thanks, Lucius gestured that they should leave. The doorway was barely visible through the roiling fog, but as he took a step towards it, he saw Grayling's eyes widen in alarm. He dropped to the floor and rolled as a sword blade hissed through the air behind him. Hearing it thud into the floor, Lucius sprang to his feet, his own weapon in hand.

The fog began to sting his eyes and Lucius blinked to clear his vision. De Lille stood before him. Two quick thrusts from the portly merchant drove Lucius back, and then spun him around as he desperately parried.

He swung for de Lille's head, but his blade was met by the merchant's own before it could strike. Another thrust pierced Lucius' guard and buried itself in the side of his hardened leather tunic. The blow was a glancing one, but he felt a rib give way and wetness start to spread along his side. Lucius began to realise that, for all his bulk and love of riches, de Lille was a most credible swordsman. This was not something he had factored into his plans.

"Go!" Lucius shouted at Grayling.

He saw her hesitate for a second, and then watched her slight form disappear into the fog. He nodded to himself; there was no sense in them both dying here when they were so close to completing the mission. He just hoped the small thief would be able to make her way past the mercenaries that were undoubtedly on their way.

Opting not to play to de Lille's strengths, Lucius backed up a couple of paces, reaching for the threads, but his enemy was quick, closing the distance immediately. De Lille thrust again, a blow aimed straight for the heart, though Lucius was more prepared this time.

Catching the thrust he turned it aside and reached forward with his left hand. Lucius willed. From his palm, a bolt of flame shot forth. Incredulous, Lucius watched it split apart, discharging its energy harmlessly either side of de Lille.

The merchant advanced, chopping and thrusting with easy, almost lazy blows. The fog was starting to dissipate, but that did not help Lucius in the least, as he was beginning to feel himself tire.

Backing off another few paces, he thought hard. The merchant had to be wearing some charm. That made some sense, and if anyone could afford such defence, it was de Lille.

The merchant pushed from his back foot and he lunged with the speed of a viper, delivering a thrust aimed at Lucius' belly.

Lucius twisted away. The blade gouged a line against his leather tunic, which held, though he would carry a bruise for a week. Unbalanced, Lucius crashed to the floor, sprawling on his back, his sword clattering away from his grasp. Upon him in an instant, de Lille levelled his sword at Lucius' face.

Weaponless, Lucius fell back to his magic. He could not disappear into the shadows with de Lille so fully aware of him, and he knew that a direct attack would be instantly nullified by whatever protection the merchant had bought. That just left flight and escape.

Taking a deep breath, Lucius concentrated. It felt as those his veins were burning with the energy being channelled through them. He gestured towards one of the thick rugs lying in the centre of the room.

De Lille saw the rug fly through the air towards him and reacted instantly. He whipped his sword around, but was engulfed by the rug.

Lucius leapt to his feet and pounded out of the room, realising only as he came to the first junction that he had left his sword behind. He had little wish to confront de Lille again in order to retrieve it.

Retracing his steps, he sprinted past the ruined combination door and on through twisting passageways to the corridor with the filcher's floor, all the time hearing the shouts of mercenaries and the stomping of their steel-clad feet. The ice holding the floor of the corridor in place had melted some time ago, leaving a damp sheen, but now the alarm had been sounded there was little need for caution.

With no more pretence at stealth, Lucius ran, feeling the boards shift beneath his weight with each step, every movement eliciting crack, thunder or crash. A mercenary stepped out ahead of him, clad in metal from head to foot. The guard held a spear, ready to gut the thief as he approached.

Lucius closed the distance between them and then dropped, skidding under the mercenary's guard along the wet floor. Once past the mercenary, Lucius scrambled to his feet and vaulted for the chair in front of the open bay window.

Looking down at the courtyard and gardens below, Lucius snorted in frustration. There was no convenient pond or thicket for him to leap into and a drop from this height would leave him with a broken ankle or worse. Glancing upwards, he thought he would have a chance at scaling the bay and getting from there onto the roof, but he was distracted by a roar from back inside the corridor.

He twisted to one side, desperately hanging onto the window frame as a spear was thrust at him. Realising just how precarious his position was, Lucius grabbed the shaft of the spear with his one free hand and pulled. Perhaps thinking Lucius was trying to pull him out of the window, the mercenary relaxed his grip on the spear. That was what Lucius had been waiting for.

Thrusting the spear back into the window, Lucius felt the butt connect with the mercenary's chest, sending him stumbling back. Lucius then leapt upwards to catch the roof of the bay and hauled himself onto the roof.

He saw Swinherd fighting a guard, the thrusts and swings from the mercenary forcing the thief back with every step. Glancing back across to the garden, Lucius saw Grayling sliding down the rope across the wall, followed by Ambrose, mercenaries racing below in a vain attempt to stop them. Gathering what remained of his strength, Lucius pounded up the tiles towards where Swinherd was fighting.

A vicious swipe from the guard caused Swinherd to back up, and the thief lost his footing, slipping down to one knee as he tried to keep balance on the ridge of the roof. However, the guard paid him scant attention, instead hacking down on the escape rope with his sword, the blade passing through it easily. Lucius was sure Grayling had reached safety, but he saw Ambrose fall, disappearing into the hedges. Guards were cleaving their way through the vegetation within seconds.

The mercenary on the roof turned back to Swinherd. Roaring to distract the man, Lucius ploughed into him. The mercenary slid down the incline of the roof, frantically scrabbling to arrest his descent. With a forlorn scream, he disappeared.

Not waiting to hear the crash of the armoured guard hitting the ground, Lucius grabbed Swinherd.

"There will be more of them up here at any moment," he said.

"They've already discovered the ladder and kicked it down," Swinherd said. "I've found something else though. Come on!"

Behind them, the mercenaries had apparently erected their own ladder, for two appeared on the roof at the far end of the mansion. Heading in the opposite direction, Swinherd guided Lucius along the roofline, and then threw himself down its incline, sliding to the rear of de Lille's home. Controlling their descent, they steadied themselves as they reached the edge. Looking down, Lucius saw that an outbuilding butted onto the back of the mansion, its own sloped roof reaching up perhaps half the height of the main building.

"It's a longer drop than I thought," Swinherd admitted.

Lucius looked over his shoulder to see mercenaries rapidly approaching, with more close behind. He groaned in expectation of the coming pain.

"We have little choice," he said.

Grabbing the stone gutters, he swung his legs over and dangled for a few seconds before letting go.

Lucius seemed to fall for an age. Then, with a jarring thud, he slammed into the roof tiles of the outbuilding, shattering dozens of them with the impact. Immediately, he began to slide down, causing a cascade of broken tiles to tumble before him. He was barely aware of rolling off the roof until he hit the grass with a blow that forced all the air out of his body.

Another thud in the ground right next to him marked Swinherd's impact. The thief moaned in pain as Lucius forced himself to stand.

"You alright?" Lucius asked as he reached down to help Swinherd.

"Just twisted me ankle," Swinherd said, though Lucius saw the pain he was in, and wondered if the fall had not broken it.

Quickly looking about him, Lucius searched for an escape route. Swinherd would slow him down, but he couldn't leave him.

More shouts from mercenaries alerted him to hurry, as those on the roof began directing the efforts of those in the gardens. The shortest route out of de Lille's grounds was the tall wall that surrounded them on all sides, but Swinherd was in no shape to scale anything, and he could hardly throw the man over it.

If not over, then through.

Though he was mentally exhausted and in pain, Lucius raised a hand and the threads of magic came to his mind's eye. He reached out for what he knew to be the most destructive of them, a source of magical energy that he had only before used in small measure. Now, he grasped the thread in its entirety.

The magic bending under his control, he gasped at the effort it took to fashion it into shape. It felt like hammering steel with his bare hands, and he cried out with the raw effort as he felt the energy begin to burn into his flesh. Sweat erupted all over his body, and he clenched his fist as he felt the magic begin to build up to its critical point, fingers digging deep into his palm until it began to bleed.

With a roar, Lucius released the magic.

The force of the arcane blast drove Lucius a step back. An invisible fist drove through the air with the speed of a cracking whip and impacted against the wall.

Bricks and mortar flew high into the evening sky as the wall folded under the attack with a thunderous crash, debris raining down to bounce off the roof of de Lille's neighbour.

Swinherd looked up at Lucius, stunned.

"I had no idea..." he began.

"There's no time for that," Lucius said, hauling Swinherd to his feet and ignoring the man's sharp cry of pain as he placed weight on his injured foot. Slinging Swinherd's arm across his shoulders, Lucius half-ran and half-staggered through the gap in the wall. Behind them, he heard mercenaries running for the gap as well, and this drove him to move faster, becoming oblivious to Swinherd's agony and his own exhaustion. Once in the dark of the alleys, he knew they would be safe.

CHAPTER THREE

STRETCHING HIS FULL length, Lucius groaned in contentment as he languished under the soft cotton sheets, and then yelped as the movement twisted the wound in his side, the lance of pain causing him to grab his side, trying to ameliorate the agony.

Elaine laid her head on his bare chest. "That will teach you to move quicker when an angry merchant comes at you with his sword."

He grunted in reply, not rising to the bait. Casting a glance around Elaine's tiny room, he saw how much the guildmistress had changed it since the old master's time. The desk was still there, but it had been shunted to one side along the wall, and papers were neatly stacked along one edge, rather than scattered in loosely organised piles. It was not that Elaine ran a tighter ship than Magnus, Lucius knew, just that she brought only the most sensitive documents into this, the guildmaster's office. The majority of her work was conducted elsewhere in the guildhouse.

The rest of the room was strewn with her belongings. Books – lots and lots of books – sat on shelves or were otherwise stacked in tall towers. Two chests contained Elaine's clothes, another her personal weaponry and tools of the thief's trade. It was amazing that she had managed to fit the wide bed into the room at all, and Lucius had never worked out how she had managed to get it up the narrow stairs.

A cloud shifted, and sunlight streamed through both the skylight and the tiny round window set opposite the door, its rays picking out the motes of dust that floated in the air. Movement from Elaine caught his attention, and Lucius stared in half-amazement as she reached under the sheets and produced the Torc of Vocator Majoris. Holding it up, she stared at it, turning it slowly.

"Shouldn't that have gone into the vault?" he asked.

Elaine shrugged. "Perk of being guildmistress. Do you think it really works?"

"Protection from assassins? I don't see how."

She continued to look at it intently, and Lucius supposed she viewed the Pontaine artefact as some sort of challenge. After all, before adopting the mantle of guildmistress, she had been Magnus' master of assassins, and that was an area of guild business she still took a deep interest in. That had been Lucius' greatest source of unease, reconciling the teasing, reflective and indefatigable woman he slept with, to the stone-cold killer he knew her to be.

"Do you have a buyer lined up?" he asked, after she had remained silent for a few moments.

"We'll keep it for a while," Elaine said as she carelessly tossed the torc onto the floor. "Maybe get some of our men to look at it, determine its true potential. There's no hurry."

"Business is getting back to normal," he said, referring to the reformation of the guild from the ashes of the thieves' war.

She turned back to him, tapping her fingers rhythmically on his chest as she thought.

"There is still a long way to go," she said. "The pickpockets are back in operation in the Five Markets and, gradually, the merchants are being brought back into line with their payments – your work with de Lille will help a great deal there."

"Happy to be of service," he said, running a hand down her back.

"We'll have to start from scratch with the longer term projects. I want to get that prostitution ring going – the kids running the pickpocket franchises do well under our care, and I know we can do the same for these women."

"As well as draw in revenue from them," Lucius said.

Elaine raised her eyebrows. "That *is* the reason we are all here. But I mean what I say – we can provide protection for the girls, set standard rates, invest their shares of the franchise, and give them a chance for a decent future, the same as any of our current members. Overall, they will be better off."

With a fluid motion, Elaine whipped the sheets away from herself, and leapt from the bed. She crossed the small room and went to her desk. Lucius watched her leaf through the pages, taking the opportunity to admire her naked body. Her dark hair fell loose down past her shoulders, and she moved with the easy grace common to all good thieves. Exceptionally well-toned for a woman of her age, her skin was nonetheless criss-crossed with a multitude of scars, a testament to the bloody work she had carried out in the past. Those flaws had never bothered him on a physical level, though they always served as a reminder of what she was capable of; perhaps that was part of the attraction.

They had been sleeping together for several months now, the relationship starting a little after the guild had been put back together. Lucius had still not really worked out why she had chosen him as a partner or, for that matter, why he had accepted.

At least ten years his senior, Elaine was not known for sleeping with other thieves. He might have thought he provided her with mere physical relief, but over the past few weeks they had started talking more in bed after making love, though the conversation tended to revolve around guild activities rather than anything truly personal.

They should have been rivals, of course, for both were aware that Lucius could have easily taken the leadership of the guild after the thieves' war. As it was, Lucius was keen to advance to a position of responsibility, but he had no desire for complete authority. Elaine most certainly did, and what Elaine wanted she tended to get, one way or another.

Still, he had to admit, he liked her. After all, she was an utterly capable warrior, a cold killer, an energetic lover and a superlative guildmistress. He was surprised more thieves had not fallen for her. Then again, perhaps they had and were just intimidated by her manner. There were times when he could well understand that.

"We done?" Lucius asked when he saw Elaine's attention was sinking deeper into her papers.

"We're done," she said, a little distracted, before remembering herself and looking over her shoulder briefly. "Work never stops."

"Too true." Lucius watched Elaine work for several minutes more, rummaging through her paperwork to find the information she sought.

He saw her frown as she looked up from her papers, then cross over to the window. Grasping the latch, she threw it open and looked down at the street below.

"What the hell is going on?" he heard her mutter.

Vaulting from the bed, he joined her, standing behind as his arms encircled her waist. Briefly, he enjoyed the feel of her body up against his, but then he saw what had caught her attention.

The street outside was thronged with a crowd, people streaming past toward the centre of the city. Beggars, merchants, storekeepers, labourers, all pushed past and tripped over one another as they hastened along the street, chatting eagerly with their neighbours.

Turning to glance back at Lucius, Elaine looked at him for answers, but he just shook his head in puzzlement.

THE CROWD THRONGED in the Square of True Believers, people jostling for position even as more filed in from the surrounding streets. Children were held close by their parents, lest they become utterly lost in the sea of bodies, while more adventurous onlookers scaled discarded crates, wagons, and statues for a better viewpoint. At the furthest edges of the crowd, where the press of people was lighter, the pickpockets worked, the occasional cry of "thief!" accompanied by quick footsteps and scattering children.

All eyes were on the wooden dais and pulpit that had been constructed in front of the Cathedral. A sudden influx of funds from Vos had driven the completion of the Cathedral, so that its towers now loomed over the square. Rumours abounded that the Cathedral's quick construction had as much to do with a cut in the height of the two towers flanking the massive wooden doors to the nave as it had with more money being made available. The priests of the Final Faith had originally intended the Cathedral to be the tallest structure in the entire city, presiding over even the five towers of the Citadel. However, the lawmakers within Vos had stood their ground, and the message was clear; even the religion of the Final Faith could not be allowed to overshadow the rule of Vos.

A hush fell over the crowd nearest the Cathedral, and it quickly spread over the entire square as the tall metal-bound doors of the massive edifice opened. Only subdued murmurs rippled through multitude as the first figures strode proudly, in two lines, from the innards of the Cathedral.

Resplendent in white tabards bearing the red crossed circle of their Order, the Swords of Dawn put the garrisoned soldiers stationed to police the population of Turnitia to shame. Their armour was of the latest fashion, sporting plates over the normal mail to protect the shoulders, forearms and thighs. Their helmets remained open-faced but were far more intricately crafted, with state-sanctioned prayers inscribed in gold on their tall, flat surfaces, topped by short red plumes. What arrested the attention of most, however, were their wicked-looking weapons, slab-sided halberds, great pole axes that looked as though they could cleave a full grown man in two with a solid blow. These were new weapons in the Vos arsenal and, though untested in open warfare, they had already garnered a fearsome reputation among the citizens of the Empire.

The Swords filed out of the entrance of the Cathedral and down its steps, marching in perfect harmony, the clanking of their armour echoing across the square. Fanning out, the soldiers assembled themselves in two lines either side of the dais, staring implacably out at the crowd, as if daring anyone to make a foolish move.

No one dared. As one, the Swords raised their halberds a few inches above the paved stones and then brought them down in unison, the sound commanding instant silence from the gathered citizens. None stirred as their attention focussed on the open doors of the Cathedral and its dark interior.

A young priest, flanked by two neophytes, walked solemnly from the Cathedral, swinging a censer in time with his steps. They were all clothed in the white robes favoured by clergy of the Final Faith, though the priest's clothing was draped in a green stole that denoted his rank. With aching slowness, he paced down the steps and, reaching the dais, handed the censer to one of the neophytes before climbing the pulpit.

Sure he had the attention of everyone, the priest raised his arms, and breathed in deeply before speaking.

"Blessed are you, you who attend the consecration of this great city's cathedral, dedicated to the one, true Final Faith. Your devotion is noted by the Anointed Lord herself, for she has sent her humble representative to us today. Pray silence for the Preacher Divine, Alhmanic."

After stepping down from the pulpit, the priest turned to face the Cathedral and waited, his head bowed.

A minute passed with no movement from within the cavernous interior. The people simply stood, almost entranced as they awaited the most powerful member of the Final Faith to ever visit their city.

There was a collective intake of breath as the Preacher Divine seemed to materialise out of the Cathedral. One moment there was nothing, and then there he stood, staring imperiously across the square.

The Preacher Divine was old, with thinning white hair above a majestic beard. However, as he started down the steps, it was clear he moved with the quick and easy grace of a man both young and physically fit. Those closest saw that while his skin was hard and weathered, it was barely touched by age. His eyes were clear and roved constantly over the crowd, as if able to pick out infidels with the merest glance.

He walked with a tall gilded staff that he clearly did not need, its metal butt hammering the ground with each step. A large blue stone was mounted at the staff's tip, grasped by silver claws. Dressed in white robes similar to the clergy on the dais, the Preacher Divine also wore a dark red cloak that trailed behind him as he walked, along with metal bracers on his arms and a thick leather tunic of exquisite craftsmanship. He gave the impression that he had fought a battle every step of the way to Turnitia but had not tired in doing the work of the Final Faith.

Mounting the pulpit, the Preacher Divine gazed down on the people – *his* people now. He nodded approvingly.

"FRIENDS. OH, MY beloved friends. You are welcome here, at the first true house of the Final Faith in the worthy city of Turnitia. You have accepted the inspired leadership of Vos into your lives – now accept the true belief of the Final Faith into your hearts. I am Preacher Divine Alhmanic, and I bring you the blessings of the Anointed Lord and all the benefits that follow."

A few in the crowd cheered, though most merely clapped. He held up a hand again to silence them.

"This city has faced trials and hardships throughout the years. Interference from decadent aristocrats in Pontaine, misguided leaders who told you that safety can only come from that ridiculous idea, independence. Look about yourselves now," Alhmanic said, sweeping an arm over the entire square. "Do you stand alone? Are you not here, now, with your fellow citizens? Does not the merchant rely on the baker to provide the bread on his table? Does not the baker rely on the farmer to provide wheat? And does not the farmer rely on the Vos guard to keep him safe from brigands? We are all bound, one to another. An independent city cannot function any better than a man living on his own in the wilderness."

He paused for a moment to let his words sink in.

"This Cathedral, this magnificent building that will set your city apart from lesser settlements, brings with it a new era for Turnitia, one filled with wealth and prosperity for all decent people. Those of you who toil daily, be it in the docks, warehouses, or your own shops, will gain the full measure of your labours, a just reward for a day's work. For those whom independence and Pontaine ruined, those who are destitute but would willingly work for the betterment of your society, you will have every chance to find the same success as your peers."

The crowd's interest was piqued at the mention of money. It was the same in every city in the world, and Alhmanic had given variations of this speech a hundred times. Identify an enemy or cause for the people's hardships, then promise a better life under the Final Faith. Of course, you had to back up your promises to some extent.

"We have already trained many new stonesmiths, carpenters and other craftsman during the construction of this Cathedral – we did not only pay these men and women a fair wage, but taught them a trade so they can continue to work and to earn for the rest of their lives. And we are doing more; as a part of the Vos Empire, Turnitia is a vital port. This means we need more workers on the docks, more labourers for the warehouses, more taverns and shops for them to spend their hard earned wages, more mentors for their children, more builders for their new homes, and more craftsmen to provide everything they need. Everyone in this city can benefit from our work here."

More cheers rang from the crowd and many reached for him with their hands. Alhmanic nodded magnanimously before continuing.

"New charities are being set up as I speak. Those out of work can draw a stipend, so long as they make themselves available for the new work we are creating. This means no one ever need starve! Physicians are on their way from the Empire, ready to administer their skills to anyone who needs them, for fees anyone can afford – the Final Faith will make up any shortfall! We will also commence building Turnitia's first university within the year. Any hardworking citizen will be able to get an education and better themselves!"

The people before the Preacher Divine were now even more enthusiastic. Offering free money had a way of eliciting such a response, though Alhmanic knew the machinery of the Vos Empire was efficient enough to not only keep the promises he was making, but also claw back the expense through taxes. Not that the people need hear about that now, of course, nor about the nature of work that would be found for them if they wished to avail themselves of the charity of the Empire.

What was important now was the creation of a new enemy. In the end, life probably *would* get better for most of the people in the city, but they would pay through the nose for it and, as always, it would be the Vos Empire and the Final Faith that benefited the most.

"But my friends, my cherished friends, there are those who will work against us. Those who prey on the weak, the innocent, the hardworking. Liars, thieves and murderers, those who would use deception, crime or sorcery to make themselves rich at the expense of decent people like you. They grow fat as your lives become ever harder. Well, no more!

"Magic, in all its forms, has the potential to bring truly wondrous boons to an entire city, yet its practitioners lock themselves away, intent only on their own wealth. The first Imperial Decree of this new, golden era is that all magic within the city of Turnitia will be regulated. Only those with a licence may practice magic, on pain of death. This will weed out the miserable tricksters and charlatans that have plagued you for too long."

Alhmanic doubted whether many of the people here had suffered, directly or otherwise, from rogue wizards, but practitioners were *such* easy targets. By its nature, magic was difficult for most people to understand, and so anyone well versed in its use was always treated with suspicion. After all, what was a simple labourer to make of a man who might be able to read his mind or burn down his house with a mere gesture?

"There is another blight, one that has plagued this city since its formation. Organised crime. From the pickpocket on the street to the thug who extorts decent shop owners for so-called protection, from the con man running crooked games in your favourite tavern to assassins who lurk within the shadows, everyone is affected by these malcontents."

For a moment, Alhmanic lowered his voice, forcing the crowd to keep silence in order to catch his words.

"No longer, my friends, no longer. We will not suffer these criminals to make an easy living at your expense. I vow to you, every resource the Empire has here will be used to smash the centre of organised crime, the so-called thieves' guild. And we will do more, my friends, much more. We will also wipe out that nest of traitors, assassins and infidels – the Shadowmages!"

CHAPTER FOUR

"I REALLY WOULDN'T worry about it."

Lucius glanced at Forbeck Torquelle. His mentor was pacing the perimeter of the empty warehouse they used for infrequent training sessions, the master slowly encouraging his pupil in the refinement of the art of the Shadowmage. Forbeck leaned on a cane as he walked, and was dressed in a fine jacket and pantaloons, for all the world like a Pontaine noble, complete with tight, trimmed beard.

"Vos means it this time," Lucius said. "Have you seen how many troops the Preacher Divine brought with him? Or the money they suddenly found to finish the Cathedral? Mark my words, they will come for you. They'll come for all of us, thieves and mages alike."

Forbeck sighed. "Lucius, my worrisome student, I have survived attacks from the Empire before now, and I will ensure we survive this one. Now, concentrate. You told me before you see the magic as individual threads. I want to focus on that for a while. Close your eyes..."

"He has a point," said another voice. Adrianna rested casually against a wooden pillar. "I've been watching this Alhmanic, and he is top grade material. They say he has the ear of the Anointed Lord herself."

"All preachers like to say that," said Forbeck. "Lucius, lock on to one thread, any one you like..."

"This one has the Swords of Dawn at his beck and call. You don't get that just by preaching to the masses. Alhmanic has clout, and is capable."

"But he has no magic, so how can he stand up to us?" asked Forbeck. "I promise you, he won't even *find* us. It is Lucius here who has more to worry about."

"True, with the promises he made at the Square, he will target the thieves' guild first," said Lucius.

"Vos has the resources to bring wizards into the city," said Adrianna. "They can afford the best."

"Well, not quite the best," Forbeck smiled.

"It *is* a danger," Adrianna said insistently.

"All the more reason for Lucius here to gain greater skill with his arcane manipulations," Forbeck said. "He is your friend. Perhaps *you* can get him to focus."

Adrianna sighed and pushed herself away from the pillar to stalk across the warehouse, her heels cracking on the flagstones with every step. Lucius turned to give her a wry smile as she approached.

While they had certainly had their differences in the past, Lucius had found Adrianna's acceptance of his presence in the city had grown over the past few months. Though the thieves' guild occupied much of his time, his renewed dedication to learning the arts of the Shadowmage, however loosely, had earned her respect.

He still found her cold at times, and wondered just how much emotion she possessed, beyond hatred and anger bent toward any who threatened the Shadowmages. Theirs was a loose guild, devoid of the rules and regulations that the thieves needed just to function as an organised body. In comparison, the Shadowmages received few instructions from superiors, and rank was assumed with experience and skill, rather than structured with rigid promotion. Every Shadowmage pledged to aid others in training, and all swore never to openly oppose another. They worked as spies, infiltrators, sometimes assassins to anyone who could afford their services, and few contracts were turned down on moral grounds. For a true Shadowmage, the principal aim was the betterment of their skills in both magic and stealth, not the accumulation of wealth, knowledge or material power. A Shadowmage would refuse a commission if either another Shadowmage was likely to be found on the side of the target, or if the work simply did not interest him.

This made the Shadowmages' guild incredibly difficult to penetrate or control, and that worried many within the Empire of Vos. After all, any one of them could become a target of a Shadowmage's skill, hired by a rival or enemy from Pontaine, and there was little defence against a skilled Shadowmage. When Vos had first invaded Turnitia, the Shadowmages had been purged and driven underground. Though weakened, enough had survived to continue the traditions and, now they were regaining their past eminence, it seemed as though someone in Vos had decided they needed to be taken down again.

For his part, Lucius considered himself more thief than Shadowmage, but his uncanny natural talent in manipulating magic had caught the attention of both Adrianna and her master, Forbeck. He appreciated their trust in him, but Lucius all too often wished he could be a more regular petty magician, using magic just as an aid to thievery, rather than reaching for something greater.

Standing in front of him, Adrianna wore a pained expression.

"Please, Lucius, he will keep us here all day if you don't do as he says."

"There are worse ways to spend an afternoon," Lucius said, but dutifully closed his eyes and concentrated on the threads of magic.

"Now, take a deep breath, and open your eyes," said Forbeck, "but keep the magic in your vision."

This was an exercise Lucius had been made to practise many time before, and he had become somewhat proficient at it. While using magic in battle or on a thieves' mission, he had grown used to summoning the arcane power in a split second. However, doing it slowly, while training, had always been more difficult. Perhaps it had something to do with the lack of adrenaline, maybe it was simply because his life was not at risk.

Gradually, it had dawned on him why Forbeck continually repeated exercises like this, concentrating on elements of the craft that, in theory, he could already do quite easily. By performing the actions slowly, consciously, he could study the magic more closely. It was like duelling; there were people who were natural talents in the use of a blade, and could be quite formidable fighters. If, however, they were taught to slow down their actions and actually study what they did and *why*, they could be rebuilt as far superior warriors.

In the end, magic was not that different from combat. The source of the power just came from elsewhere.

"Create fire."

Lucius held up a palm and a swirling ball of fire sparked in his hand, then steadied.

"Good," said Forbeck. "Now, pass it to Adrianna."

Adrianna waited patiently as Lucius willed the fire to, slowly, lift from his hand and cross to hers. He felt a mental nudge as her magic briefly brushed against his own. Their eyes met, and she gave him a slight nod. He realised they were both thinking the same thing;

a year ago, this amount of control would have been beyond him. Today, however, Forbeck wanted more.

"Nice. Now, let Adrianna pass into the shadows."

Lucius took a deep breath before starting the new conjuration. He had wreathed himself in darkness many times while working with thieves, and it was something all Shadowmages could do. To pass that ability onto someone else, however, was quite difficult.

In his mind, he saw the threads spinning around the single strand that fed the natural forces sustaining the fire in Adrianna's hand. He could see wisps of energy spiral off that strand as his spell continued to pull energy away. Concentrating, he slowed the other threads down so he could pick the grey, almost colourless strand that governed the magics he used to hide himself from others.

Plucking the thread, he suddenly became mindful of controlling the conjuration he already had manifested. A break in concentration could either snuff out the flame or cause it to swell in intensity, searing Adrianna. He felt his forehead grow wet with perspiration.

"Steady, Lucius," Forbeck said softly.

Lucius visualised draping a cloak of raw arcane power around Adrianna. Before him, her outline turned indistinct and pale.

Lucius could also feel Adrianna's presence in his mind, a vessel that contained a solid core of magic, potent and vivid. He felt the warmth of her arcane power breathe through him. Adjusting his control of the shadow cloak that he had spun around her, he reached out to brush against her presence, feeling the magical energies respond to his touch.

Looking up, he saw Adrianna staring at him, wide-eyed, mouth slightly open in surprise. She then smiled wolfishly, and he reddened in embarrassment. Though he had known Adrianna for years now, he had never had a moment with her that was so intimate.

The cloak of shadows fell from Adrianna and the ball of flame spluttered as Lucius' control was disrupted by a flood of emotion.

"Concentrate," Forbeck said, apparently unaware of what was passing between his two students. "We have a long way to go yet, Lucius."

The next exercises took a while to work through, as Forbeck pushed his levels of concentration further and further. Every time Lucius' mental control failed, Forbeck would start him again from the beginning.

First, Adrianna's cloak of shadows was brought back into existence. Then Lucius was commanded to flood his muscles with power, greatly increasing his strength and physical endurance, before he created an invisible shield that he had to manoeuvre to deflect small stones that Forbeck pelted him with. He was told to cast his mind around the warehouse to locate the nearest vermin – and then suck its life out with the most vile of death magics.

Each new task required a new strand of energy to be pulled, teased and shaped, even as Lucius tried to maintain the other conjurations. He was not always successful, and he received a particularly painful lesson when his shield failed and one of Forbeck's pebbles caught him on the temple. Even then, he was proud that of all the spells that failed from the break in concentration as his world spun around, the flame in Adrianna's hand was not one of them.

Finally, soaked with sweat, Lucius thought he had achieved what Forbeck was searching for. With the ball of fire, stone shield and cloak of shadows, he had three spells running simultaneously, and he felt he could keep them going for at least a minute or two longer. However, Forbeck still wanted more.

"Feel the magic flow through you, Lucius. Reach out with your mind, and search the remaining threads. You have always felt their presence, but I want you to become ever more familiar with them. Imagine a time when you can control any number of them. Don't see them, *feel* them."

Reaching out, Lucius could clearly visualise the spinning threads, three of them static and stable as he continued to draw upon their power.

He brushed against each thread, drawing a murmur of satisfaction from Forbeck as he passed over two of them, triggering a tremor in those forces that Forbeck could feel. While Forbeck was a far more accomplished Shadowmage than he was – would likely ever be – the master was limited to just a few forms of magic, as were all Shadowmages. It was Lucius' ability, perhaps unique, to feel *all* forms of magic that had drawn Forbeck to him.

The threads that he was still taking power from felt taut and straight, while the others seemed to snake around his fingers, ready to be moulded and forged. Slowly, Lucius made his way from strand to strand, sensing each one's energy and potential. He reached out for the next and felt... nothing. An empty place that should be filled. All he could feel was darkness, and a chill cold swept over him, freezing his mind. Lucius stared straight into a void, a region of absolute, utter nothing.

Crying out, Lucius fell, the conjurations forgotten.

Lucius came to and opened his eyes to look up at Adrianna's face, her expression a mixture of curiosity and concern. Her hand was brushing his brow, and his head lay in her lap.

"Are you alright?"

Lucius frowned, trying to recall what had happened. "I think so."

"You gave us quite a scare," Forbeck said. "I've never seen a loss of concentration do that before – not to someone as proficient as you."

"No, it wasn't that," Lucius said. "It was something else. Something cold and dark and... I don't know how to describe it."

Adrianna helped Lucius to his feet.

"Try," Forbeck said.

"I just saw nothing. No, that's not right. It was an empty space. I reached for a new strand, one that, somehow, I knew should be there. But it wasn't."

"Have you used this strand before?"

Lucius thought hard. "No. Never. But I just felt as though it should be there. It's like... someone takes a book from your shelf, but you cannot remember which book they took. And yet you still know it is gone. Does that make any sense?"

"Maybe," Forbeck said. "It is certainly fascinating. Lucius, I have always said you are something of a mystery to me. Most Shadowmages are confined to the study of just one or two forms of magic. But you are different. You have access to all forms of magic, and I don't know why. My interest, of course, is whether this is something that all Shadowmages *should* be able to do, but have just forgotten over the ages."

"So what type of magic is it that is formed of nothing?"

"I really don't know. Maybe some strand of magic is missing..."

He trailed off, prompting Lucius to speak.

"Yes?"

Forbeck smiled. "I can give you a legend, for whatever that is worth. What do you know of the Old Races?"

"They built the harbour outside the city thousands of years ago. Apparently. Every now and again we hear about some artefact of theirs in the guild. That's about it."

"The two Old Races formed two great empires, elves on one side, dwarfs on the other. These two empires were far more advanced than we men have ever been. There are tales of huge towers a mile high, of great magics that could fulfil any desire, of mighty sky ships that, some say, could even voyage to Kerberos itself.

"For millennia, these two empires worked together in peace and mutual prosperity, but something went wrong. Elf began to fight dwarf, and a terrible, terrible war broke out. The land shook and the sea boiled – even the sky itself burned with the magic the two empires unleashed upon one another. The death toll was catastrophic, but still they fought on, each determined to construct bigger and better war machines or destructive spells. In the end, one side went too far. Think on this for a moment. The wizards of Pontaine long ago classified the types of magic: necromancy, natural magic, spells of shadow, elemental forces, and battle magic. Once the wizards had this structure and began classifying individual spells, however, certain issues became readily apparent."

"What issues?" Lucius asked.

"They soon discovered that necromantic castings were naturally more powerful than those rooted in natural forces. In their turn, spells governing natural forces had dominance over shadow."

"That means one wizard will naturally be better than a peer, no matter how hard they both study," Lucius said.

"Well, sort of," Forbeck said. "Effort and raw talent still count for something, I am happy to say. But you have the essence of it. However, think about it in respect to your own abilities."

"If I understand the relationship of magic, then when I face another practitioner, I can gain a natural advantage over him."

"Precisely."

"So why did you not explain this to me before? It might have come in useful!"

"I was interested to see whether this would have been something you discovered for yourself. You may have come across something altogether more fundamental."

"Which is?"

"Well, there are some contradictions with this view of magic. Imagine a circle. We'll call it the Circle of Power. Start with necromancy at the top. It is ascendant over nature, which is next around the circle. Nature, in turn is dominant over shadows. Then follow the elemental forces and battle magic."

"So battle magic trumps necromancy, completing the circle," said Adrianna.

"You would think so, wouldn't you?" said Forbeck. "That is exactly what every master wizard thought for centuries. However, it has never been proved. There has never been one successful experiment or casting that proves that battle magic is ascendant over necromancy, or that necromancy is subservient to battle magic."

"So what is dominant over necromancy?" asked Adrianna.

"Nothing. Or, at least, nothing that we have found."

"So..." Lucius began hesitantly, not sure he had understood where Forbeck was going. "It is like a part of the circle is missing?"

"Precisely!"

"But what can cause magic to go missing?"

"The two empires fought, and one of them went too far. Everything I have ever heard and read has said it was the elves that pushed too hard and brought destruction to both empires. It is said that they had such a mastery of magic that they were able to bring one of your threads, as you call them, into the physical world – permanently. Imagine that, the essence of raw magic, made physical. It would be like... being able to wield the power of the sun. You could control the stars themselves!"

"That didn't happen, though," said Adrianna flatly.

"Of course not. They could not control that much magic. A cataclysm befell them. Huge portions of their empires fell into the sea, which began to churn with endless storms, as it does today. Elf and dwarf were completely wiped out, leaving our race behind. All their knowledge, all the grandeur of their civilisation, wiped out in an instant because of greed and the desire to massacre their enemies. In doing so, they took some part of magic with them."

"Is all that true?" Lucius asked.

"No idea!" Forbeck grinned. "It fits all the known facts, but could still be completely wrong. We may never know the answers! We'll continue your training and see what happens. Still, we have done enough for today. Rest and reflect on the tale. For my part, I must bid you farewell – affairs of other guild members call upon my time."

"I'll come with you," Adrianna said.

"Foolish girl, don't worry for my safety – I am more than capable of taking care of myself."

"She's right," Lucius said, suddenly thinking of Magnus, the previous guildmaster of thieves. "You should not wander the streets alone."

"I thank you both for your concern, truly. But there are some things, I confess, that I must do alone, and I will not suffer interference from those seeking to protect me from an illusory threat."

"Well, just keep an eye open," he finally said.

"My dear Lucius, coming from a thief, that is indeed good advice!"

Lucius became aware of Adrianna standing close behind him as they both watched Forbeck leave the warehouse. She placed a hand on his shoulder.

"He knows more about our craft than you and I are ever likely to know, but I believe he is underestimating the intentions of Vos this time. Keep your ears open, Lucius; see what your thieves can find out about this Preacher Divine. You and I have to work together if we are going to keep Master Forbeck alive."

CHAPTER FIVE

STARING IN DISBELIEF across the Five Markets, Ambrose shook his head, unable to reconcile what he saw with any kind of sense. He had worked the Five Markets for years, managing children the thieves' guild recruited as pickpockets within his own franchise. It was a lucrative business, and served the guild as a tool for bringing young blood into its ranks. He had grown used to working under the shadow of the Vos Empire, personified by the soaring towers of the Citadel that loomed darkly over each of the separate markets.

Now, his worst nightmare had come true. Being so close to the Citadel, small patrols of red-liveried guards were common enough, and it was his role to keep his pickpocket teams on the move, timing patrols so the guards did not see the same familiar faces in the crowd time and again.

As soon as he arrived in the Five Markets that morning, Ambrose saw what had changed. The guard were present in force. Pairs of guards stood at every conceivable entrance to the markets, from the wide Ring Street that linked all the markets, to the smallest alley. Larger squads marched past gaudily coloured stalls, ever vigilant for thievery. Ambrose had also noted that a single guard armed with yellow and black flags stood at the top of each tower, using his vantage point to direct patrols to anything suspicious.

He had already visited the other four market plazas, and the same system was in place in each. Standing beside a statue of the Anointed Lord, Ambrose fumed. Vos had promised to close in on the thieves' guild, and their first target was all too clear. They had shut his franchise down.

Already, several three-child teams had been apprehended before Ambrose could give orders for them to halt their business, and he had seen them led into the Citadel, furious at his inability to help.

"What are we going to do, Mr Ambrose?" asked Jake, a young boy of perhaps nine or ten, already a superior pickpocket who had taken over the leadership of his own team.

Ambrose sighed. "Go home, Jake. Tell everyone to go home. We can't work like this."

SIPPING AT HIS wine to hide a self-satisfied smile, Reinhardt Perner relaxed back in his chair, eyeing the official seated opposite him. He cast a glance past the sacks of wheat, barrels of ale and stacks of bread, over to the Vos guardsman standing outside the front door of his store. A warm feeling spread through him, and he knew it was more than just the wine working through his system. For the first time in a very long time, he felt free. Free to do business and free to earn a decent profit through his labours.

"You have my sincere thanks, Councillor," he said to his companion, a short man dressed in a dark tunic, tidy but not ostentatious. "My business has been terrorised for as long as I can remember by those rogues. Your man there will serve to be an admirable deterrent."

"It is the least we can do, Master Perner. Merchants such as yourself are the backbone of this city, and we consider it our utmost duty to protect your business. As the Preacher Divine himself has said, we are here to ensure decent people do not have to struggle to make a living."

"And you say your man will be relieved every day?"

"Twice a day," the councillor assured him. "And if the thieves are foolish enough to come here in force we can have a full squad here in minutes. Our men are drawn from the core of the Vos army, and many have fought against the finest Pontaine has to offer. A few thieves will be no contest."

"That is all to the good, Councillor. I cannot tell you the fury and frustration I have had to endure over the years. Helpless, I have been, as the thieves and their thugs visited me every week, seeking their 'insurance' money, as they called it. I had to pay them. I saw what they did to Roman's store next door."

The councillor frowned. "There is no store next to yours."

"Exactly. It was burned to the ground overnight."

"Ahhh. Well, you need not worry yourself about such things any longer."

"Again, you have my gratitude."

Reaching into his tunic, the councillor produced a leather scroll case and, unscrewing its lid, withdrew a single sheet of paper.

"There is just one more thing we need to attend to," he said.

"Oh?" Reinhardt set down his wine glass, suddenly feeling uneasy. He took the paper handed to him and started to read. It took him just a few seconds to comprehend what he was looking at.

"This is an increase in taxes – it will be nearly triple what I pay already!"

"In effect from this morning," the councillor said. He took up his own glass and drained it. When the merchant did not respond, the councillor leaned towards him. "Guards cost money, Master Perner. Catching thieves costs money. Charity costs money, and I am sure you wish to contribute your part to help those less well off than yourself."

Reinhardt looked as though he was about to argue, but the councillor spoke first. "You are going to be better off, Master Perner, believe me. You will be able to operate your business in peace, without interference from the lawless elements of the city. You don't need my promise for that, you will see it for yourself over the next few days. You *will* have to pay for law and order, but with peace comes prosperity. Already, immigrants from other Vos cities are arriving, and we will draw more people in from the Anclas Territories. Lord alone knows they will be happy to move out of that hell hole. More people means more customers, Master Perner. I am sure someone with your acumen will find a way to take advantage of that."

Setting the demand down before him, Reinhardt sighed in frustration. Without running precise figures, he already guessed he would be paying the Vos government more than he had ever paid the thieves' guild. On the other hand, he had already seen business start to grow since the Preacher Divine had arrived in Turnitia so maybe, just maybe, there was something in what the councillor was saying. He forced himself to smile.

"Of course, Councillor, you are quite right. We must all pay our share to maintain this fine city. You certainly have my full support."

"That is good to hear, Master Perner. And I am sure we will be seeing you at the service tomorrow morning at the Cathedral. You and your entire family."

"Tomorrow morning? I am afraid that will be quite impossible, Councillor. I have deliveries to take in and customers to–"

"It was not a request," the councillor cut in. "The priesthood of the Final Faith have some important messages to tell you. I am sure you would not want to miss them. *Ever.* I am telling everyone in this quarter the same thing."

Reinhardt frowned, but he took the councillor's meaningful look on board. He cleared his throat.

"Of course, Councillor. Our spiritual health is just as important as the maintenance of the city's economy."

"I am glad you agree. As I said, decent people like yourself are what this city needs. You work for the betterment of Turnitia, and you will find yourself prospering in ways you cannot yet imagine."

The councillor stood and bade him good day before leaving. Reinhardt watched him depart, a worried expression on his face. He always knew the city would pay a price in accepting Vos, but for the first time he began to wonder just who they were all making a deal with.

HARKER REACHED DOWN to feel the mule's leg, pretending to locate a sprain. His eyes, however, were roving up and down the street, searching for any sign of a patrol of Vos guards. He had timed the patrols, of course, and was reasonably sure that his thieves would be undisturbed for at least a half hour, but it always paid to be prepared.

The rest of his team was inside the warehouse and, every few minutes, they trotted out with boxes, sacks and crates. It was a straightforward theft, a relatively easy job here, in the merchants' district. Rows and rows of warehouses supported Turnitia's economy, with goods coming in every day by both sea and road. The city had not lost its reputation for independent trading, even with Vos now in control, and it was still discreetly a hub for merchants of no political affiliation who wished to trade across the divide between Vos and Pontaine.

The thieves' guild monitored the district daily, and Harker specialised in low-cost commodities from warehouse break-ins. Though individual hauls generated smaller profits, they were largely risk free and he could run several in the course of one profitable afternoon, whereas other thieves might spend a week planning one job for a precious prize guarded by mercenaries, soldiers and traps.

A loud rattle arrested his attention, and he saw another cart pull out of a side street, laden with boxes destined for the port, or perhaps just another warehouse. The labourer leading the mules looked tired and bored, but nodded at Harker as he passed.

Harker inclined his own head in greeting; just two low paid labourers sharing the common bond of their work. He returned to his mule's leg, keeping the labourer in his peripheral vision, but the man and his goods kept on plodding wearily down the street. Harker's own cart was about half full, and he tapped his foot impatiently as he waited for his thieves to return with more ill-gotten gains. One more trip after that, and they should be done, he reckoned.

Looking back up the street, he noticed the labourer had stopped opposite one of the many alleyways that ran between the warehouses. He squinted to get a better look, then realised with alarm that the labourer was gesturing towards him. Seconds later, a squad of six Vos guardsmen shot out of the alley, and started running toward him. They did not shout after him or demand his surrender, but their spears were levelled with clear intent.

"Fire!" he shouted into the open door of the warehouse, the pre-arranged warning he had agreed with his team. Bad experiences in the past had taught him that shouting "Guards!" when being pursued was a very, very bad idea.

Trusting his team to make their own escape, he slapped the rump of his mule and dragged it forward into an uneasy trot, hoping it might outrun heavily armoured men. Another squad of guards appeared from an alleyway ahead and he cursed as they spotted him, drawing their weapons.

Hauling his mule around, the animal rumbling its protest at his mistreatment, he headed for the side street the labourer had appeared from.

He skidded to a halt, the mule bucking its head in confusion. In front of him, a third squad waited, spears lowered to receive him, forming a prickly barrier. Behind, the first two squads appeared, the soldiers manhandling Terri, one of his team.

"Excellent work, men," said one of the Vos soldiers – a sergeant, Harker saw from the golden insignia woven into the chest of his red uniform. "Are the secondary squads in place?"

"Yes, sir."

"Good, they'll catch the rest of the scum." He cast a disgusted look at Harker. "Someone arrest that man. I want to get at least one more lot before shift's end."

*   *   *

LEANING AGAINST THE wall of the alley, Sebastian fumed as he watched what was happening in the Square of True Believers. He knew *exactly* what Vos was doing but, as yet, he could not see a way around it.

The square was filled with street traders, entertainers and, of course, believers seeking to make their prayers known to the priesthood of the Final Faith in the new Cathedral. They all stayed away from the western side of the square, however. That had been reserved for the beggars.

Even now, they watched the beggars with a strange mixture of contempt and pity. Massive wagons had been brought into the square, and there was polite applause from onlookers as Vos guardsmen began throwing bundles from the wagons into the outstretched hands of the beggars. More soldiers were on the ground, ready to break up any fights in the desperate crowd clamouring for alms, but there was a strange sense of order in place. The beggars had been promised that there was more than enough for everyone and, looking at the size of the wagons, it was easy to believe, despite the many hundreds of needy people that had gathered.

The bundles were ripped apart, and cries of delight rang across the square, as the poorest citizens of the city discovered that the benevolent Empire of Vos had gifted them not just bread, but fruit, new clothes, a skin of wine, and even a small pouch of silver. These cries fuelled more applause as the richer citizens saw their taxes at work, bathing in their own charity.

Sebastian knew better. Those were his people that had been herded into the square, members of the beggars' guild, all of them.

Someone in the Vos-led government had been very, very clever. He had to give them that. Any other official might have just tried to bribe the beggars with bread, believing them to be poor and hungry. That had been tried before and, predictably, it had not worked. Beggars had still lined the streets after weeks of donations.

What had not been understood before was that the beggars of Turnitia were not necessarily poor and starving – certainly not if they had been part of the beggars' guild for any length of time. The guild turned destitution into a profession, and Sebastian's people were very good at what they did. Beggars feigned diseases and injury, turning their deceptive plight into pity from those who were supposedly better off. It was ironic that many of the beggars that received handouts were actually wealthier than many of the labourers and craftsmen who gave freely. But then again, that was the whole point of begging.

Under Sebastian, the beggars' guild had developed so that every beggar in the city belonged, and all benefited from its membership. Plots were allotted and rotated so that each beggar had a good opportunity for charity and no one region of the city was buried under hordes of begging cripples.

More than that, Sebastian had turned the natural tendency of so-called decent people to ignore beggars into a virtue. The beggars' guild had become the eyes and ears of the city, and their recent alliance with the thieves' guild had borne fruit for both.

Someone within the Vos military had finally caught on, however. For the entire morning, Sebastian had watched helplessly as his people were rounded up by Vos soldiers and piled into wagons. He had first thought they were being taken to the Citadel or perhaps even deported from the city, as part of some Vos scheme to clean up the streets. Their true aim was far more insidious, and Sebastian pounded the wall with an angry fist as he sought, without hope, for a response that would save his guild.

The wagons of beggars had been driven to the Square of True Believers. More soldiers ensured no one was able to leave, much to the chagrin of those who felt they had been picked up like sacks of wheat and then dumped in the square. However, when more wagons arrived, the beggars stopped complaining.

By providing more than just food and drink, the Vos government was buying their loyalty. Better clothes immediately made them look like anything but beggars. Cold, hard silver meant there was little to be gained by begging anyway. After all, why squat in the gutter with hand outstretched to passers-by if Vos was going to give you money for doing nothing? True, some of the more successful beggars would not be taken in, being too wealthy to be turned so easily. However, they were few in number and were certainly not the heart and soul of the guild.

A young girl of no more than fifteen summers came from the depths of the alley to stand next to Sebastian. Wearing an elegant gown, the girl looked more like the daughter of a rich aristocrat than the beggar she was. She had been forced to change from her normal, grubby attire in order to avoid being picked up by the guards with the rest of the beggars. Linking an arm through Sebastian's, she too watched what was happening to the beggars.

"Grennar," Sebastian acknowledged.

"What are we going to do?"

He looked down at the ground. "Go to the thieves. Tell them that, from today, my guild no longer exists."

CHAPTER SIX

THE ELEGANT WOOD-PANELLED walls of the guildhouse's council chamber used to give Lucius a measure of confidence in his chosen career. With the wisest and most experienced thieves seated around the long table that dominated the room, the atmosphere was one of business and considered opportunity, not petty larceny and common crime. Theirs was a true profession, taken every bit as seriously as that of the merchants of the city who planned the continuance of their wealth for years into the future.

The comfort was not there today, and everyone fidgeted around the table as they waited for the guildmistress. The Council had shrunk in size since the thieves' war, and the empty chairs around the long table now felt like an ominous sign.

Opposite Lucius sat Ambrose and Nate. The former had been Lucius' own mentor when he first joined the guild, and Lucius had come to trust the veteran thief completely. Nate, on the other hand, could have been considered a rival. Nate was the youngest thief on the guild's Council and was known to be ambitious, yet Lucius had leapfrogged right over him to adopt a very senior position among the thieves. Some said Nate was merely biding his time to avenge himself, but Lucius had found him to be more or less dependable, though the young man could argue with the best of them during the meetings.

There was an empty seat next to Lucius, as his place was at Elaine's left hand. On her right was Wendric who, officially, at least, was her lieutenant and second in command of the guild. Lucius' presence made that position a little less clear, and many thieves in the lower ranks assumed that he had usurped Wendric as well.

What they did not know was that the void left by the death of the previous guildmaster had been resolved neatly between Lucius and Elaine, one night while on a mission to finish the thieves' war. Lucius did not want the responsibility of ownership of the guild, but he did want a position on the Council. Elaine, on the other hand, very much wanted to become leader of the guild. By allowing Wendric to retain his position as lieutenant, both he and Elaine had worked to dissipate the suspicions that had grown over Lucius' magical talents. Most thieves had been set against allowing wizards into the guild, believing them portents of bad luck, but Elaine and Wendric, helped by Lucius' own actions, had convinced most that having a Shadowmage could only benefit them all.

Lucius' attention was brought back to the meeting by Nate hammering his fist on the table as he stood, leaning forwards.

"Launch a rescue bid or retreat, those are the only choices," he said, his ire aimed squarely at Wendric. "I won't leave our people in the Citadel to rot, but if that is the choice of this Council, then we have no option but to shut down our operations. We no longer have the manpower to operate effectively."

Ambrose laid a hand on Nate's arm, indicating that the younger man should sit down.

"In principle, I agree with you, Nate – we all do," said Ambrose. "In practice, we have to be smart."

"We are in danger of losing control of all operations," Wendric pointed out.

"True," said Ambrose. "But we are not losing them to a rival guild. The merchants and wealthy citizens will still be out there in the days and weeks to come. My point is we need not act hastily."

"Agreed," Lucius said.

"I suspect, if we wait just a little longer, we may have unexpected allies," Ambrose said, and the others looked quizzically at him. "Taxes have been increased fourfold. People are required – *required* – to attend services of the Final Faith in that damned Cathedral of theirs. This is a dictatorship in the making and, if I know the people of Turnitia, they won't stand for it. One day, very soon I'd wager, they'll wake up to realise what cold steel fist they have around their throats."

"That is a lovely idea, Ambrose," said Wendric. "But while the people of this city may grumble about Vos' new regime, they will do little about it."

"That is true," Lucius said. "Vos has been smart, giving people just what they thought they wanted. The streets have been swept clean of crime, trade is increasing and, on the face of it, life is getting better. Maybe they will awake to see what is really happening but by then, it will be too late."

"For that matter, there may not be any real people of Turnitia left," said Nate.

"What do you mean?" Lucius asked.

Nate shrugged. "Have you seen who is arriving in the city, who is responsible for the influx of trade? They are all coming from Vos. And they are buying property here too – they are set to stay. It won't be long before these visitors from Vos outnumber the natives. Then we will be a true Vos city."

That thought floated over the table for a few minutes before anyone else spoke.

"Well," Wendric said finally, "that is something to worry about in the future. Our prime concern right now is that our work as a guild is being severely restricted. Even Elaine's assassins are having a hard time of things, as Vos guardsmen have been assigned to anyone who might remotely be a target for their knives."

The door to the chamber flew open with a bang, Elaine sweeping through it at speed. Behind her trotted a familiar face at their meetings, the beggar girl known as Grennar.

"Gentlemen, forgive my late entrance, but I have just heard something disturbing, and we have much to do," Elaine said as she hurried around the table to take her place. Grennar sat next to Ambrose.

Lucius cast a glance at Elaine, and he immediately saw a haunted look behind her eyes. He could only imagine the pressures she was under as she tried to manage a guild that was falling apart. As she took a deep breath to compose herself, Lucius found he wanted nothing more than to reach under the table and take her hand, but he knew better than to try. They had agreed from the outset of their relationship that any display of affection or over-familiarity between them would only shake confidence in the guild's leadership.

He would hold her close that night but, for now, Elaine would have to stand alone.

Elaine gestured to the young girl opposite her. "Grennar, go ahead."

The beggar girl had been presented to the thieves as a go-between, a liaison, linking thief and beggar in the common causes they shared. At first, many thieves presumed she was a calculated insult aimed at them from beggars who believed themselves superior as an organisation, but Lucius saw she had impressed even the most senior of thieves very quickly.

With a freckled face and the slightest of frames, she had the uncanny knack of getting people to listen when she wanted to talk. She also seemed to know exactly what she was talking about on any given subject that cropped up during the Council meetings she attended, which was not always the most obvious trait of some of the thieves present.

"Sebastian sent me," Grennar said. "You heard the promises the Preacher Divine made. Well, he is carrying them out – right now."

"Giving alms to your people, so they need not beg," said Lucius.

To his surprise, Grennar gave an appreciative smile. "It was very neatly done."

This frank analysis surprised Lucius, and he wondered if she was simply relating what her own guildmaster had told her, or whether she had formed the opinion herself. If the latter, Lucius could see why Sebastian kept such a quick mind close to him, however young the head around it.

"Anyway, it means our guild has effectively been shut down," Grennar said simply.

"You have no loyal members to rely on?" Elaine asked. She was mastering her shock at this turn of events, but Lucius could still hear tones of it in her voice, and he wondered if the other thieves noted it too. Wendric, probably, as he had known her the longest.

"Oh, we have people who have pledged themselves to the guild and Sebastian both," Grennar said. "But not enough. Not enough to function as a guild, and certainly not enough to gather information across the city. The rest... well, they look after themselves before all else. I imagine it is much the same in your guild."

Elaine looked sharply at the young girl, then shrugged. "That is true enough." She looked at each of the men around the table in turn before making her pronouncement. "They will be coming for us next. And quickly."

Round the table, the men shuffled uncomfortably.

"We have to clear the guildhouse," Wendric said.

"We have to do more than that," Elaine said. "As a guild we are almost paralysed in our ability to conduct business. With the beggars taken out of play, we are also blind. We are in a very precarious position."

"What is your plan?" Ambrose asked.

Elaine was clearly reluctant to give her next orders, but she forged ahead.

"Clear the guildhouse. Move the vault too, and get our people to take as much as they can carry from the libraries, laboratory and armoury. Everyone splits into individual groups, each headed by a single senior thief who chooses their own safe location and way of continuing business. No senior thief is to know where any other senior thief and their group operates from."

"You are talking about breaking the guild!" Ambrose protested. Nate was uncharacteristically silent, but looked as though he was going to be sick.

"The senior thieves are divided into groups as well, with each senior thief reporting to one of the Council. Again, each Council member will know which senior thieves work for them, but not who works for anyone else. You are all free to conduct yourselves as you see fit. I will stay in touch with the Council members and no one else to preserve everyone's safety. With luck, we will be able to reform as a guild after these troubles."

"You want us to start clearing the guildhouse right now?" Nate asked, finally finding his voice.

"Nate, understand this. The beggars are finished. The Vos guard could be gathering their forces in the Citadel to march on us right now, and we would not know anything about it."

Nate opened his mouth, and then closed it again.

"Start the evacuation now," Elaine said. "Arrange for sentries to watch every approach, and get them to sprint back here if they so much as smell a Vos patrol. Pick your senior thieves and arrange contact locations. I'll stay here to lead the last of us out."

"No," Wendric said, shaking his head. "As guildmistress it is imperative that you survive any attack. The guild really will fall apart if you are captured or killed."

"Wendric and I will lead the last of us out," Lucius said. "All those in favour?"

"Aye!" said Ambrose and Nate together, as Wendric raised his hand to signal assent.

"Motion is carried by the Council," Lucius said, looking at Elaine.

For a second, he thought she would overrule them, as was her right, then he saw her shoulders sag just a fraction. "As you wish," she said quietly. "In that case, I'll safeguard the transition of the vault."

Breathing a sigh of relief, Lucius nodded in agreement. After the thieves themselves, the vault was the most precious resource the guild had, the store of its most valuable possessions. It would also be the first thing to leave the guildhouse, and Lucius felt better knowing Elaine would be following it.

Elaine looked around the table once again. "Keep the faith, we will prevail. Now, get to work, we have a lot to do, and not much time."

With Grennar the men stood and filed out of the council chamber, but Lucius stayed next to Elaine as they departed.

"Ambrose was right, you know," she said quietly. "We could end up spreading ourselves so thin that Vos just sweeps us up one at a time. Or maybe we do all survive, but the separate groups grow too used to doing things their own way – then we have twelve guilds instead of one, and another thieves' war."

"That might all be true," Lucius said. "If we had a weak leader. You'll hold it together."

Elaine was silent for a moment, then said in an even softer voice, "I am not certain I can. Not this time. Not against this enemy." Giving a short self-deprecating laugh, she ran a hand through her hair. "There is no one else I would have said that to!"

Casting a glance around, to make sure that no one was spying upon them, Lucius reached across and took her hand.

"We won't let you down, I promise. You can rely on us."

GLANCING UP AND down the twilight-darkened street, Lucius rubbed his hands nervously. Vos would make its move against the thieves any time now, he could feel it in his bones, and yet he was standing in the middle of an open street, ready to be taken in by the first patrol that saw him. Still, he had learned not to ignore Adrianna when she sent one of her arcane summons. He doubted the slow chiming inside his head would cease for days if he refused to heed its call.

He waited at a small junction in Lantern Street, barely a quarter-mile from the thieves' guildhouse, the wide roadway lined with small houses and the occasional shop. To his back lay an alley, his location chosen to allow for a quick retreat into its narrow, dark entrance if trouble should arise.

Within minutes, he saw Adrianna stalking confidently towards him, her tied up hair bouncing cheerfully along behind her. Her face did not match its gaiety.

"Aidy," he greeted her. "This is an unusual place for you to want to meet."

"It is close to your guildhouse, and I know you have problems there," she said. "I thought you would resist coming if I tried to drag you halfway across the city."

"Hardly," he muttered, but she pretended not to hear him.

"I see the beggars have gone."

"And with them, our eyes and ears," he said bitterly.

"Then you haven't heard what has been happening up on the hill."

Lucius glanced up Lantern Street, the thoroughfare winding its way up Turnitia's slope. The buildings in that, the far eastern part of the town, were mostly residential, and mostly larger estates with extensive gardens, where the richest of the city lived. It was where de Lille had made his home.

Adrianna grabbed his arm and led him into the alleyway.

"They have started clearing out unregulated wizards – you either sign up, or get taken into the Citadel," she said.

Lucius frowned.

"How can they get away with that? Why start on the richest and most powerful in the city – that has to be causing them problems."

"Ah, that is what I thought at first, but you are not thinking it through." There was just a hint of the old, self-satisfied Adrianna in that comment, the one that had always chided him in the past. "These are the people who think themselves above the common law, and are thus more likely to be caught red-handed. But that is not really the point – after all, what does Vos care if it has to manufacture evidence to carry a conviction in its so-called courts? No, what do these people have that no one else possesses much of?"

"Money."

Suddenly, it became obvious to Lucius what Adrianna was getting at. That rich merchants and titled nobles were prone to dabble in sorcery was no secret. Most saw it as a mere diversion, and were thus no great practitioners. They became bored with their meagre efforts and went on to seek other distractions. However, a few had not only the wealth but the patience to pursue the craft, and these men and women could become quite proficient. They also had the arrogance to think that Vos would ignore their studies, but their wealth was an additional attraction.

"Vos are imposing heavy fines?" he asked.

"No, think larger," Adrianna said. "They take everything. The silver, the jewels, the horses – and the property. Some of the larger families are resisting, but Vos will get what it wants in the end.

Enough grand houses and enough silver to attract nobles from all over Vos."

"And we get a new ruling class."

"There you go," she said. "I knew you would get there."

"Alright, alright," he said. "So, are we in danger?"

Adrianna stopped, and released his arm as she turned to face him. "They have some wizards in the city already. Using them to shut down the magic of those they go after so the guard can make easy arrests."

"Will that work against us?"

"Against proper magic, you mean? No, those fools won't stop a Shadowmage."

"But Vos must have considered that."

"Indeed. Among the other Shadowmages there is talk of a secret cabal, something created by the Anointed Lord herself to be used as a weapon against her most powerful enemies. A group of witches, warlocks and wizards who have trained their whole lives to balance their talent with one another. Some Shadowmages say they can feel them approach, that they are already near the city."

"And what do you say?"

He saw her outline shrug. "My skills do not fall that way. But I can believe this cabal exists. Indeed, I would be surprised if Vos did not have a weapon like that."

Lucius thought for a moment. "So what do we do?"

"We await their arrival, Lucius. And then, you and I will erase them from the face of the city!"

He laughed. "Just you and I?"

"Oh, the others will do their part," she admitted. "But no one can counter a wizard as well as I can, and there is no one here with your raw talent and power.

"You and I are not like the other mages, Lucius. You and I can achieve anything we set our minds to. For years I have watched you waste your talents, despairing that you would ever rejoin the fold. Now you are back, I see that we are a natural fit. Our talent, our... spirits complement one another so well. Let our magic fuse together and there will not be a force in the whole of Vos that can bring us down!"

Lucius had felt the wrath of her tongue many times in the past, but he had never heard her speak with such passion and conviction. She was standing close enough for him to feel her breath, hot and excited. In his mind's eye he shared, just for a moment, her dream, and saw the limitless power two Shadowmages working together could achieve.

He thought of the times Adrianna had scorned him, had insulted him and, ultimately, had pushed him further in the understanding of his own arcane talent. All that dwindled away as he felt the closeness of her presence, the nearness of her body as they stood in that alley. Without thinking, he reached out to pull Adrianna close and kissed her.

For several seconds, he held her until it dawned on him just what he had done.

Their lips parted, and Adrianna stepped out of his hold. Though he could not see them, he could feel her narrow dark eyes on him. At that moment, he would not have been shocked if she had cursed him, struck him, or unleashed the full magical arsenal she held at her command, reducing him to a pile of dust where he stood.

Instead, she just smirked. Then turned and walked away.

Lucius' gaze followed her as she stalked down the alley and into the twilight city. His life had just become a lot more complicated.

CHAPTER SEVEN

WHEN THE EMPIRE of Vos dropped the hammer on the thieves, it came quickly.

As arranged, Lucius and his thieves were among the last to be in the guildhouse, tasked with ensuring documents of tertiary importance were gathered and moved to a safer location; the most critical books and scrolls had already been taken from the vast library.

In command of one cell of thieves was Hengit, a senior man in the guild whom Lucius knew only slightly. However, his reputation was that of an old curmudgeon, what Pontaine soldiers called a *grognard*. Still, he was a senior thief for a reason, and Lucius had been given no reason to suspect his capabilities. The constant grumbling, aimed at the lack of apparent sense in the Council and the decisions it made, were expected.

Elaine had already left. Both Lucius and Wendric had seen to that, watching her spirited away by the most trustworthy thieves they knew. Officially, she escorted the primary contents of the vault, though Lucius was left wondering which was really more important – the money, or the guild's mistress.

He had not been able to properly say goodbye to Elaine, and it surprised him that he felt a cold blade in his chest at the thought. The guildhouse had turned into a site of near anarchy once the evacuation order had been given, and there was no room for privacy, even for the guildmistress. All Lucius could do was fervently hope that no harm would come to her, and that they would be meeting again soon.

Hengit's thieves, those he would be leading under Lucius' direction in the coming weeks, had large backpacks that they stuffed with maps, floor plans, books of record, and anything else that came easily to hand. Their role was to secure as much of the guild's knowledge as possible, knowing that Vos soldiers would likely destroy everything they found. The libraries represented all the information the guild had gathered throughout the years, from detailed architect's plans of important buildings, to records updated regularly of traffic to and from the warehouses of merchants.

A loud crash from the floor below signified the arrival of the guards. Standing at the doorway of one of the chart rooms that served as the guild's libraries, Lucius heard the panicked shout of one of the returning sentries.

"They're coming, everyone clear out!" the man yelled as he ran. "The soldiers are coming!"

Lucius waved impatiently at Hengit. "Okay, that's it," he said. "Get your men out, Hengit, it's time to go."

The veteran thief needed no second telling, and he barked an order at his three younger charges. They immediately filed out of the library, leaving Lucius alone for a moment, looking at the huge multitude of papers and books that remained. In their haste to carry off the most important items, the thieves had left drawers and cabinets open, papers strewn across the floor around them. He wondered how long it would take the guild to recover so much lost knowledge, and whether the thieves could ever truly be the same efficient organisation without it.

Sighing, he turned and jogged out of the door, heading for the stairs.

The ground floor of the guildhouse held barely contained panic. The few remaining thieves darted across the common room in different directions, some heading for the rear door, some the front, others heading upstairs to escape across the roofs of nearby buildings.

They had all spent many hours in the common room, a place set aside for thieves to talk, to plan, to relax after a hard day's – or evening's – larceny. The bar had been stripped of liquor, and Lucius suspected much of it had left the guildhouse before even the contents of the vault. Furniture and various ornaments of questionable value had followed the drink quickly, though Lucius could not find it in his heart to blame those who had taken them – they *were* thieves, after all.

"Forget the doors!" Lucius shouted. "The soldiers will have those covered."

He had been involved in a running battle through the streets of Turnitia in the past, and did not relish the idea of repeating the experience with trained soldiers on his tail.

"Head for the tunnels, we can lose them down there," he said.

Hengit and his three thieves waited impatiently for Lucius, the elder giving him pointed looks. However, Lucius had made a promise to Elaine that he would be the last to leave, ensuring all thieves in her charge got away cleanly. It was not a responsibility he was willing to relinquish.

"Leave that!" he said angrily, grabbing one thief who was burrowing into a niche in the common room wall, likely retrieving something precious stashed there years ago. "There's no time!"

As the last man fled from the common room, Lucius gestured to Hengit that they should move on.

A deafening crash from the front door of the guildhouse hastened them all.

"Capture or kill, it's all the same to me," said a voice from behind them. "There will be bonuses for every live one you get."

Pushing Martelle, one of Hengit's young thieves, through the rear door of the common room, Lucius cast a glance over his shoulder to see a Vos soldier enter behind him, sword drawn. As their eyes met, Lucius drew a dagger from his belt and flung it across the length of the room. At that range, it did no damage, and Lucius hung around just long enough to see it skid off the mail of the soldier's chest, scoring a rip in his tabard.

They raced through the rear passageways and rooms of the guildhouse, coming to the kitchens where a stove had been moved to reveal a deep shaft into which had been set metal rungs. There were several entrances to the tunnels beneath the thieves' headquarters, but this was the largest.

Hengit was helping Martelle down the rungs, almost throwing the young thief down the shaft. Acutely conscious of the sounds of soldiers fanning throughout the building, Lucius considered drawing his sword to defend Hengit and the others, but quickly dismissed the idea. He would likely have need for the weapon later and a naked blade would simply encumber him on the rungs of the shaft. There were plenty of stories of thieves carrying their swords in their teeth, but practical experience had taught Lucius this was a bad idea.

It seemed to take ages for Hengit to swing himself over the lip of the shaft and start descending, while the soldiers moved towards them both with terrible speed. As soon as Hengit had descended a few rungs, Lucius leapt over the edge and began to climb down as fast as he dared.

Cursing the shaft's builder for not installing a ladder they could all simply slide down, Lucius looked up to see the curious faces of two soldiers staring back at him. One of them turned and shouted for more men to join them as the other dangled his legs over the edge and reached for the top rung.

Lucius raised one hand and leaned back as far as he dared. He flooded the top of the shaft with fire, the flames fanning out from his outstretched hand to crawl inexorably up the curving walls, roiling as they engulfed the soldier. The man managed a single, strangled scream before the fire sucked the air out of his lungs. Lucius only just managed to bark a word of warning as the heavily armoured body fell past him into the darkness.

Not waiting to hear the sickening crunch below, Lucius sped down the last few rungs.

At the bottom of the shaft Hengit was waiting for him, a lit torch already in his hands, taken from a rack stood next to him. Lucius nodded at the other torches still in the rack.

"Break them," he said to Hengit. "No sense in making things easier for the soldiers."

Hengit nodded and grabbed another torch for himself, before ripping the others from the rack and snapping them underfoot with the heel of his boot. Lucius, flanked by the other thieves, stared down the two passageways that led from the chamber.

"We could get back onto the streets anywhere along Lantern Street or around the Dogs," one of the thieves said as he gestured to one of the tunnels. Buenwerner, Lucius thought his name was.

"Bad decision, lad," Hengit said.

"He's right," Lucius said. "Vos will have covered every street within a mile with soldiers. They'll be expecting us to come up from beneath the city. No, we should take the sewers."

None relished that thought, but the sewers allowed access to almost every part of the city, and a group of thieves could lose themselves within their labyrinthine twists and turns for days. The drawbacks were, unfortunately, obvious.

Together, they raced through the small network of tunnels that led to the guild's main sewer entrance, a stout stone door designed to look like part of the sewer's brick wall from the other side. The sewer door was cracked open, the mechanism that allowed the heavy bricks and mortar to swing freely groaning quietly as they heaved on it. A terrible, gut-churning stench immediately assailed their nostrils, and Lucius was not the only one who gagged. Martelle raised a ragged cloth to his face to try to mask the noisome smell, but Lucius gritted his teeth and stepped onto the ledge that ran alongside the vile sluggish river.

Hengit did not seem to mind the dark environment. He surprised Lucius further when he closed the sewer door behind them and, leaning against it, placed a palm on its surface.

"She was our home for many years," he whispered.

Looking back at the others, he caught Lucius' stare, and looked down, embarrassed.

"Come on," Lucius said to them all. "We'll head for the docks. It's a long way through this muck, but Vos cannot cover the entire city."

"And don't fall in," Hengit said. "Vos won't need trackers to follow you on the surface if that happens; they'll just follow the stink."

Doing their best to ignore the stench that was beginning to settle into their clothes, hair and skin, the thieves made their way cautiously through the sewers, hopping from ledge to ledge, their passage lit only by Hengit's torch. At one junction that opened into a wider tunnel travelling east to west, Buenwerner cocked his head and stopped.

"Did anyone hear that?" he asked.

"Just rats, keep on moving," Hengit grumbled, anxious to be back on the surface and in the fresh air. Lucius, however, had stopped as well. Straining his ears, he looked down each path, trying to pinpoint the faint noise.

"That is not rats..." he said quietly.

Frozen, they all stood stock still, their senses reaching into the darkness around them. It was Hengit who identified the sounds first, and he cursed vociferously.

"Dogs," he said. "They've brought damned dogs with them."

"That makes no sense. Dogs can't track in the sewers," Martelle said.

Hengit snorted. "Tell that to Vos. They've probably got dogs that are bred in cesspools, just to catch thieves in sewers."

"I can't tell where they are coming from."

"Sounds just bounce around these tunnels," said Hengit. "We won't know until they are on top of us."

"Get moving," Lucius urged.

"But what if we start moving straight towards them?" Martelle protested.

"We'll get as close to the docks as we can before they reach us. Get moving!"

They turned west. The ledges running alongside the effluent here were wide enough for cautious movement, but their speed caused more than a few nervous moments as a foot slipped on slime or a head was cracked against the low ceiling. At every new junction, Lucius paused to listen for signs that their pursuers were closing in.

"I think there is more than one patrol down here," Hengit said.

"I know," said Lucius. "They seem to be moving alongside us, but that doesn't make sense – dogs should follow us directly, right?"

"Right."

"So how can they be matching our movements? If one patrol has our scent, how does it let the others know?"

Shrugging, Hengit turned to follow the others. "No idea. Maybe they have runners on the streets above, going to and from each patrol."

There was a hiss from Martelle up front. "I saw something," he said.

"What?" said another.

"Don't know – flicker of light, or something."

"That's just our torch reflecting off the walls. You're getting jumpy."

"I know what I saw!"

Carefully picking his way along the ledge, Lucius made his way past the other thieves to Martelle. The young thief looked at him, worry evident on his face.

"Just down there, maybe a couple of dozen yards," he said, pointing. "A flash of light."

A howl echoed down the tunnel behind them, chilling them to the bone

"Behind us!" Hengit shouted. "Move! They've found us!"

That was all Martelle needed, and he sprinted off as fast as he dared.

"No, wait!" Lucius cried out, stretching out to grab Martelle, but he was too late. The thief was already out of his reach.

First one soldier, then another, detached themselves from the shadows of a side tunnel, leaping into the effluent. They seemed completely unaffected by its stench and were quickly joined by another pair. All four levelled crossbows at Martelle, who had skidded to a sudden stop before them.

The twangs of the crossbows' mechanisms echoed in Lucius' ears as four bolts shot through the air to skewer Martelle's body. The young man's expression was a mixture of shock and fear as the life went out of his eyes and he toppled into the stream, taking his torch with him.

"Move!" Lucius shouted as he drew his sword and raced forward. Covering the distance in seconds, he was on the soldiers as they were still struggling to reload.

Smashing one man senseless with a hurried blow across the top of his head, Lucius noted curiously that the design of the soldier's helmets was very different from anything he had seen before. Apart from the eye sockets, they seemed to be completely enclosing, and where the men's mouths should be was a complex arrangement of cloth and two wide pipes, jutting out like dark tusks. It occurred to him that Vos might well have been far more prepared to tackle the thieves, even here in the sewers, than any of them had suspected.

Lucius bullrushed the soldiers, toppling them head first into the sewage. Then, raising a hand, he caused a large wave of stinking filth to rear up to the ceiling, before slamming down on the soldiers, smashing the life out of them.

Looking back at his companions, ignoring their wide-eyed astonishment, he quickly made a decision.

"Get moving, to the docks," he said, flattening himself against the curved wall to give them room to pass. "Hengit, you lead."

"What about you?" Hengit asked.

"I'll delay any other soldiers long enough to give you time to escape."

"Don't be a damned hero."

Lucius shrugged. "It's my job, my responsibility. Yours is to your men."

"We only have one torch left."

"You take it," Lucius said. "I'll work better without it. Now go!"

Hengit snorted in frustration, then drove the thieves on. Lucius watched them go as he called upon his magic to wrap him in shadows.

The patrol coming towards him now was stronger than the last, with two dogs leading six men. They wore the same strange helmets as the others, but Lucius had already seen their weakness. While the devices might well make a voyage through the sewers more bearable, they also greatly restricted their eyesight and probably their hearing. That would make achieving surprise far easier.

The dogs bayed as they ran along, occasionally stopping to make sure their masters had not fallen too far behind. Lucius extended his magical concealment, allowing the noisome stench of the sewer to wrap itself around him too, making him invisible to the hounds' heightened sense of smell.

Leaning around the corner of the junction, Lucius took note of the positions of his enemies. The dogs were just a few yards away, the soldiers not far behind. He saw another man move up behind the soldiers. He was tall, and walked with a stoop to avoid scraping his head on the ceiling. He was wearing leather rather than chain and was unarmed. More than that, the stink of the sewer clearly did not affect him at all, as he wore no helmet.

"He's close," the man said, and then closed his eyes. Immediately, Lucius felt a sudden pressure in his head and, searching for the threads of magic, saw them buckle and twist under the strain of a new magical presence.

Lucius knew how the soldiers had found them so quickly. This man had to be one of their highly vaunted wizards.

Maintaining his shadow cloak, Lucius reached forward and mentally grasped a ball of air, no more than a handful, beside the head of each dog. With a quick, savage twist, he shunted the air out of place, creating an instant vacuum.

Two simultaneous bangs echoed around the sewer. The soldiers were startled, but the effect on the dogs was more profound. They bolted, whimpering as they fled back up the sewer and nearly knocking one soldier off his feet.

"He's here," the wizard said.

The soldiers readied their weapons, and Lucius could see how they intended to fight. One soldier would keep him busy with a sword, while another fought past him with a spear, jabbing over the shoulder of his ally.

"Pull back," the wizard instructed. "This is my work."

The wizard stepped coolly past the soldiers.

Lucius dropped the shadows around him, and stepped out to meet him.

"Turn back now, and trouble us no more," Lucius said.

This elicited a chuckle from the wizard.

Lucius felt the strands of magic twist out of synch as the wizard began muttering, his fingers moving in a complex rhythm.

Magic surging from his pointed finger, Lucius hurled a bolt of withering energy, intending to shatter the wizard's concentration and ravage his body with the touch of death.

The wizard continued his incantation but raised one hand, the other still drawing patterns in the air. Lucius' bolt stuttered and dissipated. An instant later, the wizard unleashed his own spell, and Lucius felt his limbs go rigid as an invisible force clasped itself around his body.

Despite himself, Lucius began to feel an appreciation of the wizard's talent. Though it was clumsy and inefficient compared to the grace of the Shadowmage's path, the man had learned enough discipline to block Lucius' magic while continuing to manipulate his own.

He saw the wizard grin in triumph as his spell's hold tightened around him. However, the magic was relatively simple to pick apart.

Not wanting to reveal what he was doing, Lucius picked at two threads of magic, trapping and holding them firm under the presence of the existing spell. Then, feeling the wizard was coming to the end of his ritual, he triggered his own spell.

The magics expanded quickly, blasting the binding spell apart. Lucius swiftly channelled the magic forward, repulsing the force of the spell the wizard was preparing back at him.

The wizard held out a hand to dismiss the attack, but he had not counted on its raw strength. He was thrown backwards against the wall, and buried in an avalanche of bricks and dirt as the roof of the tunnel came down on top of him. Everything suddenly went black.

Gasping for air and gagging against the stink of the sewer, Lucius called a small ball of flame to his palm. He saw that the tunnel had completely caved in ahead of him, the passageway blocked by a wall of brick and earth. Lucius whistled quietly. He had not intended to cause major damage to the sewer itself, but the amount of energy needed to break the wizard's binding spell had been greater than he had first thought. When released, all that power had had to go somewhere.

Resolving to take a little more care in shaping his spells when in confined areas, Lucius started down the sewer again, the ball of fire in his hand lighting the way to the docks.

CHAPTER EIGHT

STRETCHING UNCOMFORTABLY IN the chill morning air, Lucius drew his cloak closer around him. Sounds of people talking animatedly started to penetrate his sleep addled mind, then he snapped open his eyes, suddenly remembering where he was.

Another heap of cloth started to stir within a doorway opposite, and the stink of last night's alcohol washed over him as a vagrant growled irritation and rolled over. Lucius sat up and scratched at his hair, conscious that he still reeked of the sewers himself.

At the far end of the alley, he saw people moving in the main street, and gradually became aware of a low, deep chiming. It took him a further moment to realise he was hearing the newly installed bells at the Cathedral, now used to summon the people of the city to the Square of True Believers. Standing up and shaking the last dregs of sleep from his system, he wandered out to see what was happening.

After leaving the sewers the evening before, Lucius had not found Hengit and the other thieves at the docks, nor had they been present at the pre-arranged meeting point behind the silversmiths near the cliffs. He was not overly worried, as he knew Hengit was an extremely capable thief. Perhaps another Vos patrol had been close on their heels as they left the sewers, or maybe they had run into soldiers above ground and Hengit had decided to lay low for a while. He was sure he would get a chance to rendezvous with Hengit soon.

Rumours were running rampant, it was clear from the excited chattering of the crowd, as friends and strangers alike tried to guess what was going on at the Cathedral. Some were saying that it was to be an open trial of a group of rich wizards, while others opined that a city-wide carnival was in the process of being set up. One old woman told anyone who would listen that the stipend granted to beggars was being extended to all common people, though at a lower rate of course, to demonstrate the generosity of the Empire. Lucius grabbed a young man by the arm to ask him for clearer details, but all he received was a shrug.

He arrived at the square just as the bells stopped tolling, and saw the area was packed with people, the crowd heaving as individuals jostled for the best position. The guard were present in force, their red uniforms and spears or halberds acting as islands in the press of people. However, Lucius doubted any pickpockets or malcontents would dare to make their presence felt today, not after recent events.

The dais at the front of the Cathedral had been reconstructed, but it was much longer now, spanning the whole width of the stairs leading up to the main entrance, with the pulpit offset to one side. As the Swords of Dawn filed down the stairs in two columns, the crowd fell silent, and Lucius waited with them, straining his eyes to pick out the Preacher Divine from the darkness of the Cathedral's interior. He did not have long to wait.

ALHMANIC STRAIGHTENED HIS cloak and pulled his tunic taut before accepting his staff from the acolyte standing dutifully next to him. He waved the man on, indicating he was ready.

"Preacher Divine," the man muttered in acknowledgement before he turned and walked out of the Cathedral, taking the steps with care and solemnity as he approached the dais.

The crowd filled the square outside and he suppressed a satisfied smile, lest one of the nearby clergy see it and think it pride. The people were completely silent, expecting his arrival, and he kept them lingering for a few seconds longer. Alhmanic glanced at the seven sullen looking men, bound and held under the spears of Imperial soldiers just inside the Cathedral's doorway. Today, he would give the crowd something they had never seen before.

Planting his staff firmly on the flagstone floor of the Cathedral, its hammer blow echoing throughout the massive nave, Alhmanic strode forward into the daylight. A few in the crowd dared to cheer his appearance, but they were quickly silenced by a single thump of the guards' halberds on the dais. Straight-backed and majestic, his cloak flowing behind him, Alhmanic descended the stairs of the Cathedral slowly, as much to give the crowd a chance to see him before his words took sway as to continue building the tension of the moment.

Climbing the pulpit, he gazed across the crowd, conveying his absolute authority over the people of Turnitia.

"Beloved friends," he started, raising his hands as a blessing to all. "The past few days have been hard on all of us. Many brave soldiers have been wounded or have died in service to Turnitia. The people of this great city have had their own burdens to bear, which you have undertaken with the same fortitude. We are united in both our pain and determination to make this a better place to live, where freedom and prosperity are not the preserve of a few, but the right of all!"

This time, the guard made no move to stop the crowd from expressing their gratitude. Though many of them were now facing higher taxes, they had also seen their silver being put to work in cleaning up the streets.

"There are many rumours circulating in the city at the moment. As you all well know, loose talk has little value and is rarely the whole truth, or even part of it. However, it is my most humble joy to tell you now that one rumour *is* true. Late in the evening yesterday, noble Vos agents located and wiped out the headquarters of the perfidious thieves' guild. That is right, my friends, the Vos Empire has once again made good on its promises and destroyed crime on all levels in this city."

The ovation Alhmanic received on this pronouncement lasted more than a minute and he let the wave of sound wash over him. When it finally began to subside, he raised a hand to let the crowd know more was to come.

"Of course, you know as well as I that there are those who will always prey on decent, hardworking people, so criminal activity will always be present. However, without an organised guild behind them, these villains will be rudderless, directionless – and easy prey for our town guard!

"This also leaves us free to continue our good work. I promised you the destruction of the thieves' guild, and it has come to pass. I now tell you that we are commencing the next stage in cleaning this city for decent folk. Those terrible practitioners of darkness, the evil merchants of foul sorcery, the Shadowmages, will be next. This I promise to all of you. And to demonstrate our intent, I have another gift for you."

So saying, Alhmanic gestured towards the Cathedral. A line of men, each led by a Vos soldier, were marched down the steps. They looked haggard, and everyone could see that their hands and ankles were bound, allowing just enough movement for them to hobble down the steps. On the dais, other soldiers carried seven heavy wooden blocks, setting them down in a line. There was an audible gasp as a few in the crowd began to understand what was about to happen.

The men, their courage clearly broken, were led onto the dais one by one. None looked out at the crowd. The youngest was weeping, shaking his head as if to clear it of a bad dream.

"These are seven of the worst sinners we found among the thieves," Alhmanic said, turning back to the crowd. "Each one of them is responsible for many murders, rapes, and unspeakable acts. To seal our pledge to you, the decent people of the city, we will carry out their sentence before you, so you can see justice being done."

There were more gasps from the crowd as others began to catch on to what the Preacher Divine intended. Turnitia had never before seen public executions and, indeed, had prided itself in the past on the idea that they were not needed. Some people were clearly revolted by the idea and yet, as Alhmanic had guessed, they could not seem to bring themselves to turn away.

Alhmanic gave a nod to one of the Swords, who then turned to his men and barked an order. As soldiers forced the thieves to their knees, the executioners stepped up to the dais as one. They hoisted their halberds, the silvered axe blades glinting.

With seemingly no signal from Alhmanic, the halberds descended as one.

"WHAT IN THE hell...?"

Lucius' exclamation drew a few stares from those closest to him, but the attention of most was riveted on the events happening up on the dais. He had recognised Hengit the moment the man had been led out of the Cathedral, and saw Martelle following him. The other thieves he recognised, but their names escaped him at that moment.

He listened to the Preacher Divine blathering on about the evils of the city, and knew that any charges levelled at the men were read purely for the benefit of the crowd. They were thieves, true, but not one of them was a murderer. As soon as the wooden blocks were brought out, Lucius knew what was about to happen.

Lucius yelled his defiance and began pushing through the crowd. Some responded angrily and pushed back, but he was oblivious. He took no notice of the shoves and kicks, nor of the soldiers whose attention he gained and were themselves beginning to make their way through the crowd towards him. All he could think of was reaching the dais. He reached out for the threads of magic, trying to decide what manner of sorcery to unleash.

The halberds were raised, yet Lucius had barely managed to push a dozen yards through the crowd.

"No!" he cried, hand outstretched as if he could stop the halberds from descending.

An iron grip seized his arm and spun him around.

"Don't be a fool!" a voice hissed in his ear, and he turned to see Adrianna, her eyes glinting dangerously.

Behind him, Lucius heard the halberds biting into the wooden blocks and dropped his head as the crowd cheered. Adrianna glanced at the soldiers closing in on them, and pulled at Lucius, propelling him away from the Cathedral and now bloody dais.

"Come on!" Seeing the look in Adrianna's eyes, people parted before her.

Lucius stumbled behind her. He vowed that the Empire would pay for what it had done, but first, he wanted to ensure that no other thief would be executed in that manner again. For that, he would have to call the Council together.

HE HAD NEVER seen Adrianna's home before, but it surprised him that she had a very respectable house within the higher end of Turnitia. It was nothing like the mansion of de Lille, but she was well placed among the most respected craftsmen and professionals of the city.

The interior of the house did not seem to match her personality at all, with rich rugs, furniture and ornaments suggesting a lady of means, perhaps a lucky widow. Then again, Lucius considered as he luxuriated in the bath Adrianna had insisted he take after smelling the stink of sewerage on him, anything that could throw people off what she really did for a living was a good thing.

The house must have cost Adrianna a fair sum and he supposed all those years taking Shadowmage commissions while he had been in the Anclas Territories playing mercenary had paid off. The bathroom was tiled, with gilded hooks for clothes and towels lining one wall. A mosaic depicting a forest scene, complete with sunny glade and deer, dominated the opposite wall. The bath was large enough to accommodate three or four.

*   *   *

"ARE YOU COMFORTABLE?" Adrianna asked, and Lucius turned to look over his shoulder. She was carrying his clothes, apparently having just washed them, and was hanging them up on the hooks that ran along the wall. He sank deeper into the water.

"This is divine." He guessed that some soothing herb or mineral had been added to the water.

"It was the first thing I installed when I bought this place." Adrianna stepped out of her long black dress.

As she climbed in to the bath, sighing happily as the water closed over her, Lucius could not help but stare, seeing for the first time her well-toned legs, immaculate pale skin and small but firm breasts.

She slid down, submersing her head under the water, and he felt her legs slide along his. When she surfaced she gave him a quizzical look.

"What's wrong?"

Lucius found that words refused to come, and he ended up shrugging pointlessly.

"There was nothing you could have done for those men, you know," she said

"I know. It was a good thing you were there."

"Where else would I have been? The cabal was there. I could feel them. They were there, in the Cathedral, watching the proceedings."

"For what reason?"

"If I had to hazard a guess, I would say they were looking for us."

He thought about that for a moment. "You think they are as good as Vos believes they are?"

"Yes."

He groaned. "So what do we do now?"

"Oh, I have an idea," Adrianna said, and she moved over so that her face was just inches from his. Lucius was acutely aware of the pressure of her breasts on his chest.

"I have a very good idea," she said, as she pulled herself up to kiss him.

THE SEX HAD been vigorous but brief. Passionate but cold. Adrianna had been skilful, as he had always imagined, in his most candid moments, she would be. But the whole incident had seemed rather abrupt. He sat up in the bed, wondering what to say.

"I want you to join us," Adrianna said. "Properly, I mean. Stop messing around with your little group of thieves, and start fighting."

"What do you have in mind?"

Adrianna's eyes glowed for an instant as the passion took her. "We unite, as an army! With the Shadowmages working together we cannot be defeated! We will smash their soldiers and tear down their precious Cathedral. And then we'll march on the Citadel itself. Their wizards will not be able to stop us, and this cabal will wither under our assault! The city will be released from the yoke of the Empire, and the people will thank us for it. We'll then do as we wish!"

"What does Master Forbeck have to say about this?"

Adrianna's eyes flashed dangerously. "The fool cannot see beyond his own studies," she said, almost spitting the words. "Look at what he is doing with you. Testing and poking and prodding, trying to unearth some great inner secret. What he should be doing is showing you what power you possess and how to use it!"

Lucius began to get the uneasy feeling that seducing him had been Adrianna's way of getting him to agree to her plans. If that were indeed true, it was an unusually clumsy move on her part. He swung his legs over the side of the bed and stood up, gathering the sheets around his waist.

"Forbeck has been very useful, Aidy," he said. "I understand far more now about what we do than I ever did before."

"You still know nothing! There is so much more, Lucius, and I can show it to you. I can be your new teacher. The Master has the talent, yes, but he lacks the vision of what the Shadowmages could be!"

"Are you challenging his leadership?"

She looked at him curiously for a moment. "No. But I do want to show him where he is going wrong. One solid victory from you and me, and the rest will come down on our side. He will have no choice then but to accept what we have done, and then continue the good work. We can do this, you and I."

Lucius looked into her intense, unblinking eyes. "I can't."

He did not see the slap coming, and he staggered under the force of the blow, his cheek stinging hotly.

"Damn you, Lucius! You are deserting us, now of all times?"

Raising a hand, as much to ward off her anger as defend against any further attack, Lucius struggled to keep his voice even.

"In case you had not noticed, Aidy, the thieves have deeper problems right now, and they need me."

For a moment, just a brief moment, Lucius thought Adrianna would strike him down with a powerful blast of magic. She was furious, and he could see her shaking with barely controlled rage. Abruptly, she turned, facing away from him.

"Look," he said, trying to find some way of placating her, yet not daring to reach out and touch her shoulder. "Let me get the thieves together. They are good at what they do. We can use them as spies and find out exactly what the Empire is up to. Then we can hit Vos where it really hurts. You and me. Together."

For a few seconds, Adrianna did not say anything. Then, without a word, she stalked towards the door and flung it open. Her hand still on the handle, she turned back.

"From you, I guess, that will have to do," she said to him. "You can let yourself out."

CHAPTER NINE

LUCIUS HUNCHED OVER his tankard, painfully aware that he looked every inch a ruffian not wanting to be spotted. The common room of the Red Lion was busy with quiet conversation, not yet full of the coming evening's revellers. Known to a few select thieves, the Red Lion and its smooth-talking owner had a long history with the guild. The establishment had provided a safe meeting place for conspiring thieves, a location to store stolen goods and even neutral ground for burglars and their fences. This evening, the inn was serving as the council chamber; or, at least, one of its upper rooms was.

When he entered the tavern, the landlord – Myrklar – had caught his eye, a pre-arranged signal that Lucius should simply sit down at the bar, order a drink and keep a low profile. There was someone in the common room that Myrklar was suspicious of.

More people entered the tavern, demanding drink; a few others left. While pushing three full tankards to a group of tradesmen, Myrklar glanced quickly at Lucius, his blinked signal missed by everyone else in the common room. Standing up, Lucius moved to the back of the tavern and, once out of the lantern light and among the shadows, located the steep wooden stairs and began to climb.

Keeping his footsteps light, knowing that the thin floor could betray him to anyone listening below, he padded to the end of the short hallway. At the far door, he paused, then knocked three times, each with precise pace.

The door opened a few inches, revealing Wendric's suspicious face. Upon seeing Lucius, the man relaxed. As he followed Wendric into the room, Lucius noticed the man sheathing a dagger.

"A little jumpy, Wendric."

"You're late."

It was a far cry from the council chamber of the guildhouse. Small and dirty, it looked as though Myrklar had used it to store things perhaps best left forgotten. There was no table, just a single fragile looking chair occupied by Elaine. Wendric and Ambrose sat on upturned wooden crates.

As he sat on a barrel, Lucius flicked a glance at Elaine. The lines on her face betrayed the strain she was under and, not for the first time, Lucius found himself half-wishing he had accepted responsibility for leadership of the guild himself. Their relationship would certainly be easier under these circumstances and, perhaps, a lot closer. If he were leader, no one would see anything wrong in him betraying affection with a hug or a kiss. It would be a natural thing for a guildmaster to look after his mistress.

"Myrklar delayed me," Lucius said, then looked around, frowning. "Where's Nate?"

Elaine just shrugged, while Ambrose shook his head.

"Like you, he should have been here some time ago," Wendric said flatly, and there was something in his tone that made Lucius look at him curiously.

Wendric looked as though he were about to continue, but Elaine cut him off. "He may turn up later. We'll start without him."

Raising his hands in a helpless gesture, Ambrose said, "Well, where do we start? You have my loyalty as always, Elaine, but what is the Council without a guild?"

"It's a start," Lucius said.

"That's right," Elaine said. "So long as the leadership is intact, the guild has direction – which is what I have called us here to discuss."

Clearing his throat, Wendric took the lead. "It's obvious. The executions in the square were a travesty, one we cannot let go unanswered."

"What do you suggest?" Ambrose asked.

"We hit back," Wendric said. "We go after the Vos officers, those fops in the Order of the Swords of Dawn, their wizards, and then the Preacher Divine himself."

"There are not enough thieves to do that," said Lucius. "And I am not sure we could execute such a large scale attack without some thief turning to Vos and informing them of our plan."

"I'm surprised to hear you being defeatist," Wendric said. "Was this not your plan in the thieves' war, hitting our enemy wherever we could, making them pay for every inch they took from us?"

Lucius looked at him sadly. "This is not the thieves' war. The Empire is far stronger now than it has ever been, and our guild has not just been damaged, it has been smashed."

"Then we go slower," Wendric insisted. "We use only those we trust, we pick our targets carefully. Forget the lower ranks, aim for those who really matter. The commander of the Citadel has been keeping his head low. He's never revealed himself, and with good reason. We find out who he is, where he is skulking, then finish him off! The Preacher Divine too, while we are at it."

"The commander of the Citadel?" Ambrose asked. "You are suggesting a target whose name and face we do not even know?"

"He's right," said Lucius. "We no longer have the resources to gain that information easily–"

"I never said it would be easy," Wendric cut in, exasperated. "However, we can–"

This time, it was Lucius' turn to interrupt. "It's too dangerous, Wendric! It risks the entire leadership of the guild, and for what?"

"For what? For the blood of our fallen comrades, Lucius. As a sign that the guild is still here. As a rallying call for all those thieves that think we are dead and buried, and have started to drift away."

"No." Elaine spoke quietly, but her voice still overrode Wendric's. "Revenge, however much desired, is not the way forward."

Wendric bowed his head to stare at the floor, clearly frustrated.

"Is that becoming a problem?" Lucius asked. "Are they starting to leave the guild?"

"It is quite natural," Ambrose said. "Without the guild around to support them, give them jobs and protection, most will drift off sooner or later and become independents."

Lucius' look of dismay made Ambrose chuckle. "They *are* thieves, Lucius. At the end of the day we deal with people who lie, cheat and steal for a living. You and I may be loyal, but we have a great deal invested in the guild and its members."

"Is that why Nate is not here?" Lucius asked. "Has he gone?"

"Wouldn't surprise me," said Ambrose.

"Bugger Nate," Wendric said. "If he's gone independent we're best rid of him anyway."

"And if he sets up a rival guild?" Lucius asked.

Elaine shook her head. "He doesn't have the pulling power to bring enough thieves in to make a serious challenge. He may try but, trust me, it will be the least of our problems." She changed the subject. "How have your senior thieves done with re-establishing the franchises?"

"They haven't," Wendric said. "Things are just too tight right now, the Empire has made it impossible for us to operate. We can't intimidate a merchant when he knows a shout to the guard will bring an entire squad running, and the streets are so heavily patrolled they might as well be barracks."

"And I won't risk my kids in the markets or the square," Ambrose said. "They have watchers in the towers of both the Citadel and the Cathedral, signalling to guards on the ground as soon as they so much as sniff a thief working the crowd."

No one said anything after that, and an oppressive silence fell upon all four thieves. Lucius could feel the morale sapping out of the others, and he wondered whether this would be the last meeting of the Council. It was Ambrose who finally broke the quiet, with a short laugh that he quickly suppressed with his hand.

"What's so funny, Ambrose?" Elaine asked him.

"It's nothing really. It just occurred to me that this was how the guild first started. A small group of thieves, sitting around, wondering how they could make more money and make it without getting caught."

It took a few seconds, but Wendric finally began to smile at that thought, and then Elaine joined him.

"That's it," she said.

"We operate as if we are starting from scratch. Forget the franchises, at least the larger and more elaborate ones, stay away from the organised stuff. We just offer support for thieves interested in the wider picture."

"Even if it just starts with us and a few we trust," Wendric said.

"Right. Random burglaries, pickpocketing, that kind of thing. We organise the fences, create safe houses for thieves on the run, the basic functions any guild should provide. Keep things compartmentalised with the existing cells, but gradually bring things closer together as we start to gain pace."

Lucius began to smile too. "It could just work. It will be tough, but it could work."

"It needn't be that tough," Elaine said. "After all, we still have at least some of the resources and contacts of the old guild to fall back on, plus the knowledge and experience of the best thieves in the city."

"Well," Ambrose said, "count me in. What do you want from us, Elaine?"

"You were right about the markets and the square. So gather your kids, just a couple of teams made from the best, and start running pockets in the streets – Street of Dogs, Lantern Street, the places where there is healthy commerce and plenty of alleys to lose yourselves in. With practice, the kids will be able to alert you to a patrol before it gets within half a mile."

Lucius found himself enthused with the challenge. Building a new guild from scratch took imagination and experience, and while the grander plans were discounted or at least sidelined, they quickly had a framework of operations that could be enacted by a small number of thieves.

When Elaine finally called an end to the meeting, she caught Lucius' attention and bade him stay in the room with her for a moment longer.

Making sure that the door was firmly closed, Lucius turned to face her and, for a moment, they were both silent.

"I miss you," he said.

She smiled and crossed the few paces between them to embrace him. Resting her head on his shoulder, Elaine held him tight.

"You know I feel the same," she said. "But you also know what I have to do right now. I... I'm not saying the guild is more important..."

"I understand, Elaine, I really do. Whether the guild is more important or not isn't the issue. It is more important *right now*, and I do understand that."

"I do believe we can rebuild the guild," she said, moving away. "But it will be a lot harder than I let on to the others. I think they know that."

"They'll stand with you, whatever happens."

"Which is why they deserve my full attention. If that means I am less attentive elsewhere..."

"Really, Elaine, as I said, I understand. I know how hard this is for you. But we'll do this. We'll succeed. Whatever happens thereafter... we'll deal with it then."

"Thank you," she said. "I need you to do a couple of things for me."

"Name them."

"First, find Grennar or Sebastian. We need to get the beggars up and running again. They can do the same thing we are, start from scratch." She gave a short laugh. "I have a feeling they will find success quicker than we do."

"Consider it done. What else?"

"I never really understood what your other friends were and how they work. You have powers... well, I don't begin to understand them, and I don't know whether your other friends would be willing. But we could use any help they can bring."

Lucius grimaced, thinking immediately of Adrianna. He opened his mouth to speak, but thought better of it. Instead, he said, "It's possible... but unlikely. I'll do my best, but such help... well, it may come with a high price."

"I'll trust your judgement in the matter," Elaine said.

He nodded, aware she was placing no small measure of responsibility on his shoulders. Before he left, he cast one last, long look at her. He admired her, standing tall, though her guild was in pieces, arms defiantly crossed over her chest, a determined look on her face. He felt a longing in his heart, a need to sweep her up in his arms, to reassure her that they would come through this, that he could protect her from any who would dare harm her. He realised then that he cared for Elaine a great deal, and that she would forever have his support.

But he did not truly love her.

FORBECK STOOD JUST inches from the edge of the cliff, the harbour of Turnitia far below him. He could see the cranes and lifts that littered the cliff side, though they rested silent from their labours of hauling goods up from and down to the docks. There were no ships currently in the harbour to service.

Beyond the docks and piers, the water was calmed by the immense monolithic blocks that towered at the harbour's edge, almost as high as the cliffs on which he stood. Their method of construction was a mystery even to the greatest wizards of Vos and Pontaine, though it was generally agreed that the monoliths were ancient Old Race constructions. Together, they formed a complicated pattern that stood as a bulwark against the permanently raging ocean that lay just beyond.

On the cliffs, Forbeck could hear the perpetual storm that broke incessantly against the barrier, expending its energy in a fruitless effort to reach the harbour. For a thousand years, probably more, Forbeck reflected, these monoliths had stood against the sea, and they would likely be around for millennia more.

Forbeck ambled along the cliff's edge, lost in thoughts of old races, deep magics, and the formation of the world and universe. Here, right at the edge of land, where civilisation met the crashing torrent of endless waves, Forbeck loved to think, to plan, to theorise. Quite apart from his vocation as a Shadowmage, it was why he had first settled in Turnitia, a city ostensibly free and independent in deed as well as thought.

That had changed somewhat with the coming of the Vos Empire. This was not the first time Vos had been heavy-handed toward the city, and he doubted it would be the last. The Shadowmages had suffered in the past, but they were wiser now. At some point, Vos would overreach itself, and that would be the time to move.

Forbeck slowed his pace as he approached a group of warehouses and frowned. Vos soldiers stood around the buildings, perhaps seeking to catch another thief.

Not wanting to be stopped and questioned, Forbeck turned and limped towards the city proper, faintly annoyed that his reverie had been disturbed. He picked up the barely cobbled path of Cliffside Way, ignoring the unwholesome odours that emanated from some of the terraced houses.

Another patrol turned a corner ahead of him, and started marching down the street. Thinking their presence and manner a little too coincidental, Forbeck turned abruptly and headed down one of the many alleys that ran between the terraced blocks. Behind him, he heard the unmistakable thuds of armoured men picking up their pace.

Once within the alley, Forbeck stopped and stood with his back flat against the stone wall. Within a single breath he had gathered the shadows about him. As the soldiers turned into the alley, he gave them a scornful look while they searched for him, his magically enhanced stealth rendering him invisible. After a few seconds, their sergeant ordered them forward, guessing their fugitive had run down the alley and was now in another street.

Forbeck allowed himself a quick smirk before he released the shadows about him and continued on his journey.

As soon as he stepped out of the alley, he sensed something was wrong.

Forbeck saw a cowled figure detach itself from the shadows of a rundown block of houses. He saw a flash of fine silks under heavy cloth, as well as a glimpse of a blade. Above all, he felt a surge of arcane power, just hovering at the edge of his attuned senses.

Deciding this was an encounter best avoided, Forbeck turned to head back down the alley, but saw another cloaked figure slowly walking towards him from the other end. This one had the suggestion of a woman in the way it carried itself and, again, he felt a surge of magical energy as it approached. When others arrived, seven in total, all wreathed in the same pale cloaks, Forbeck understood.

"So," he said. "You are here."

There was no reply as the figures closed in. As they approached, each figure raised their hands, and Forbeck felt a wave of power roll towards him. Leaning on his cane, he braced himself, but was still forced to take a step backwards. He felt the power build up within the cabal again, and he realised that they were not casting a spell as such, merely finding links between them that they could use to focus and magnify one another's energy.

"Fascinating," Forbeck said.

He closed his eyes briefly, calling upon his own magical reserves, then brought his cane down with a sharp rap. Fire erupted where he stood and radiated away from him at great speed, incinerating weeds and discarded parchment in its path. The cabal stopped, now standing just a few yards away. He felt a wave of power pulse from them once again, and watched it just roll over his flames, snuffing them out instantly.

Not even slowed down by his magic, the invisible wave of energy continued toward Forbeck and slammed into him with devastating force. He dropped to his knees. The pain, concentrated right into the centre of his mind, was nearly overwhelming.

Gritting his teeth, Forbeck slowly raised himself back to his feet. Looking up at the faceless figures of the cabal, he dimly began to formulate a plan. He doubted any one of them could best him in a duel, but somehow they had developed the ability to fuse their talents together, making them far more powerful than any one mage. However, every chain has a weak link...

Forbeck reached forward to unleash a bolt of arcane fire at the figure in front of him. It was a crude spell, but potent, and Forbeck was counting on its swiftness to beat any defence the cabal would have.

The bolt shot through the air, sizzling as it flew, leaving a smoky trail. Curving slightly as it neared its target, the spell suddenly sputtered and fizzled out. The wave of power that had annihilated the bolt hit Forbeck with a mighty crack that arched his back and dropped him to the floor.

As he struggled to open his eyes, the intense pain blocking all coherent thought, another wave rolled over him, then another, each one coming much quicker than the last, and each building to greater magnitude. Insensible, Forbeck rolled on the ground, only pure instinct driving him to move, to seek refuge.

The cabal resumed their slow, deliberate march towards the Shadowmage. As they built up the last wave of energy, the figures collectively sighed as the power flooded out of their bodies. The last wave smothered Forbeck, holding him in a rigid, pain-filled grip.

Raw arcane energy reduced Forbeck to dust.

As the cabal departed, the sea wind blew down the street, scattering the ashes. Within seconds, only his cane, sundered in two, remained.

CHAPTER TEN

WHILE GRENNAR CUT a beautiful, even faintly aristocratic figure in her long gown, Lucius appeared more as a rogue. He tried hard to ignore the glances he received as the two of them wound their way through the streets of Turnitia.

For her part, Grennar seemed not to notice, and held her head up high as if the streets belonged to her. Lucius had found her lurking near the Square of True Believers, watching the comings and goings of Vos officials around the Cathedral. During their quiet conversation, Grennar had made it clear that while her guildmaster had given up on the beggars, she most certainly had not, and she seemed pleased when Lucius had told her that efforts to rebuild the thieves' guild had begun.

Grennar was only too glad to take him to meet Sebastian, and Lucius was surprised to find himself being led up the hill to the eastern side of the city.

"What, you thought Sebastian made his home in some random alley, or in the sewers?" Grennar had asked. "He is probably richer than any thief."

Lucius doubted that, but didn't argue the issue. Instead, he let the beggar girl lead him to a small but very well-appointed house built within a stone's throw of the city's eastern gate.

As they entered the modest grounds of the estate, Grennar produced a large iron key and opened the front door, revealing a short hall and stairs. She indicated a door set to one side of the stairs, then left, closing the door behind her. Clearly, she had received instructions not to attend this meeting.

Coughing to announce his presence, Lucius entered the door.

A fireplace blazed in the centre of one wall, though the weather was by no means chill. Beside it was a single leather wingbacked chair, placed next to a small table on which Lucius could see an open bottle and glass filled with a deep red wine. Opposite the fireplace, within a wide bay window, was Sebastian, stood over a desk and staring intently at an open book. He wore a tight fitting but exquisitely tailored tunic, and flicked over a page of his book as Lucius entered.

Books lined shelves along each wall and were piled on every available surface. Tables sagged under the weight of many tomes, and further piles on the floor reached Lucius' waist. There must have been several thousand in this place, ranging from small handbooks to massive volumes that would cover Sebastian's desk when opened.

"Do you like my library, Lucius?" Sebastian asked, without looking up.

"It's impressive."

"It's my passion," Sebastian said, turning to face Lucius. "The *Harmonies* of Artitucus, the seventeen surviving plays of Damans, the Kerberos observations of Brach, and Loom's *Histories of the Vos-Speaking Peoples* are all here. Treatises, atlases, encyclopaedias, and satires. I have even started collecting the comedies of Pontaine Treen.

"Finally I have the time to commit to my collection. It really is fascinating. For years, all this knowledge has been stored, uselessly, on these shelves. Now I can begin to enjoy them. I have been planning a trip across Pontaine, and maybe to Allantia, to track down some of the volumes I am missing."

"And what about your beggars?" Lucius asked.

Sebastian shook his head. "They are not mine any more."

"We are reviving the thieves' guild. We would like the beggars to be beside us. For mutual benefit, as always."

"You are on a fool's mission. Vos is too powerful, their stranglehold on the city too firm. One day, maybe, the guilds will rise again. But not in my lifetime. I have been guildmaster of the beggars for many years, Lucius. I have earned my retirement."

"We have adapted! Our guilds cannot function as they once did, true, but there are other ways of doing business. Start small again, like us. There may well be new opportunities that did not exist before. Vos will have its loopholes and blind spots – that is where thieves and beggars thrive. With or without you, the thieves *will* rise again. But it will be easier if the beggars are with us, gathering information in ways no one else can."

"You are not listening to me. There *are* no beggars any more. Even the old hands are drifting away."

"So bring them back to the fold. I know why you are here, reading your books, Sebastian. You are trying to recapture that thrill of discovering something new. When the beggars were reporting to you from across the entire city, you learned new things every day. Some of the information you used, the rest you sold. Remember that feeling, when you learned which Citadel guard could be bribed or blackmailed? And remember how much you could charge me for that little scrap of information? Or which noble's wife was seeing what merchant, or who had bought a new piece of land and what they wanted to use it for?"

Sebastian smiled. "We learned quite a few things about your thieves too.

"But it is all academic. No beggars, no guild, no information. Whether it was the Preacher Divine himself, or one of his administrative lackeys, whoever targeted my guild did it very neatly. The damage has already been done."

"Nothing is irreversible," Lucius said.

"Maybe you are right but, as I said, even my old hands are gone, those I thought might never leave. It really is just Grennar left, and she does not look much like a beggar these days." Sebastian smiled again. "If only that girl were a little older, I would suggest you speak to her about a new guild."

Silence fell over the two men for a few moments.

"I don't know how you would go about it," Sebastian said eventually, "and I would bear no costs, now or later, but... If the thieves were to somehow disrupt the alms-giving, a lot of people would start to go poor and hungry. Under those circumstances, I cannot see how I could do anything *but* reform my guild."

Lucius frowned. "Stop the alms-giving?"

"Either in the city, or hit Vos' silver train as it travels south to Turnitia. That would also disrupt much of what Vos does here, which I guess is a goal for you anyway. Think of what you could do with all those unpaid soldiers..."

The idea of hitting the Empire's silver train was a daunting one, for its defences were near legendary. But that was not Lucius' immediate concern.

"You actually want me to force people into poverty?" he asked.

Sebastian shook his head. "I knew you would have trouble with that. You know, Lucius, for a thief, you have a strange moral code."

"It is one thing to rob a merchant of a few trinkets or take silver for keeping the peace in a busy street."

"Oh, you have done more than that. What about the hardworking labourer whose pocket you pick in the market? I know you have done that yourself in the past. What about the shop that is forced to close its doors because of your extortion rackets? And did you ever stop to think about the girls your people were using in the prostitution rings? Every crime has a victim, Lucius."

Lucius opened his mouth and closed it again, having no real answer for the beggar.

"It is easy to justify, Lucius," Sebastian said. "I've done it myself. Think of it this way. You are not forcing people into poverty – they are already there. They are merely accepting the charity, for want of a better word, of the Empire. You know as well as I do that comes with a heavy price. This is why you are fighting Vos, correct?"

Lucius nodded and Sebastian continued. "Think of those prostitutes. The whole justification for bringing them into your guild, aside from profit of course, was that they would be *safer*. They would have protection, set rates, apothecarial support, and all the rest. In short, they would be better off.

"The same applies to my beggars. They may have to work for their silver, but they are better off working than being completely reliant upon the Empire and its fickle wishes. Young or old, fit or crippled, there is a place for every man, woman and child among the beggars. We support them and train them, and no one *ever* goes hungry. We do not tie them into the guild, and they are free to leave at any time, taking their earnings with them to start a new life – if that is what they want. Can you say the same of Vos?"

"No," Lucius said. "Once Vos decides what to do with them, their fates are sealed."

"Probably in some back-breaking engineering work deep in the Empire."

That caught Lucius' attention. "You know that for a fact?"

Sebastian shrugged. "I heard things in the last days of my guild. But suppose, for a moment, that it is not true, that Vos has only good intentions and, once you and I are cleared out of the city, Vos will leave. What happens then?"

"Well, the guilds will come back. Probably overnight."

"Under whose guidance? You might still be here, Lucius, but I'll be as far from Vos as I can get. The beggars might then be led by a real villain, like the guildmaster in Andon, who uses his people as thugs and whores."

"Alright, you have made your point."

"Will you do it?"

Lucius saw the sense of what Sebastian was telling him, but it was a big leap from making a few robberies to intentionally depriving the weakest and poorest people in the city of food. That was even before he could start thinking about how it might actually be accomplished.

"Let me talk it over with the others. We might find a better way."

"Well, think quickly, Lucius," Sebastian said. "There is not much time."

OUTSIDE, GRENNAR LOOKED at him questioningly. Lucius shrugged and walked past, soon becoming wrapped in his own thoughts. He already knew that he would try to end the alms-giving. He just had to justify the action to himself.

He spent some time meandering the streets of the wealthier end of Turnitia, letting recent events turn over in his mind, thinking about how to resurrect the guilds. Choosing turns at the junctions of the cobbled streets at random, Lucius suddenly stopped, an odd sense of familiarity creeping over him. It took him a few seconds to understand why the area he was in, with its large houses nestled in their wide gardens, had given him pause.

The house before him was notable for being a new construction; while most buildings on this street were at least a century old, this one was younger than he was. Whereas others were built mainly of hewn stone, this used brick throughout its construction, and the materials were not yet weathered. An unfamiliar red carriage was parked in front of the house's main entrance.

Lucius began to pick out features he did recognise: the apple tree on the left, whose branches he had learned years ago; the wooden bridge just beyond the front gates that led over an elongated pond, in which he had sought to catch the fish that lurked in its depths.

It was the place he had been born, and raised for much of his childhood. Standing there, he recalled the events of the night that had altered the course of his life. The rioting mob that had swept over the garden, the deaths of his father, mother and sister, the burning of the house. All because his father had belonged to the Brotherhood of the Divine Path, and not the Final Faith.

One way or another, the Vos Empire had a lot to answer for.

Lucius breathed a silent prayer to the souls of his family, more out of respect to their memory than any belief they would actually hear him. No, he would not make revenge his motive. But that did not mean he was not going to do everything in his power to make Vos' position in his home city as difficult as possible. His own affairs would likely take care of any vengeance his family required in their graves.

Lucius felt a flicker at the edge of his senses, a silent ripple in the fabric of the world about him, and a wall of air slammed into his side, blasting him off his feet.

Hitting the ground hard, he gasped for breath while looking to see what had attacked him. He fixed upon the figure stalking down the street, its long hair tied up behind its head, dark eyes almost black under a frown.

As Adrianna stooped to grab him by the collar and yanked him to his feet, Lucius gaped.

"Aidy, what do you think you're doing? Anyone could see us here."

She threw him against the wall of his old home. The impact knocked the wind out of him again, and he could sense the magic fuelling Adrianna's strength. Looking up at her, he saw she was maddened with rage, magic giving her fury form. He was in trouble.

She seized his collar and drove his head back against the wall.

"Did you feel it?" she hissed at him.

"What, Aidy?" he gasped, the pressure at his throat making breathing difficult. "Feel what?"

"Of course you didn't. You have always been so far removed from us."

Her knee drove into his stomach as she released him. Wheezing, he fell, and lay still as Adrianna ranted.

"He's dead, Lucius!" she screamed, her voice hoarse. "Dead! While you were off playing thief, they *killed* him."

Knowing he might regret it, Lucius climbed to his feet and, leaning on the wall for support, tried to face down her fury.

"Forbeck," he said.

"They tracked him down, like he was no more than vermin. I warned him and I warned *you*..."

As she rounded on him, Lucius could feel the magic surge inside Adrianna, and he braced himself. Then she seemed to droop, her shoulders sagging, and the magic faded. He reached out to touch her, but her head snapped up to face him and he saw that while her magic had been tempered, her anger was still unchecked. The glare she gave him was full of loathing, and he suppressed a shudder.

"How did it happen?" he asked.

She looked down for a moment.

"I'm not sure. Probably the cabal, or maybe it was one of us, trying to make a deal with the Empire."

He frowned. "Surely not."

"This is what I have been trying to tell you, fool. We can't trust anyone! Vos is tearing this city apart, and we must make a stand, or fall!"

"We must be cautious and take our time," Lucius said. "The thieves are making some progress, and we have a few ideas on how to hurt the Empire. We are getting the beggars' guild back on its feet too, and together–"

"Thieves?" she cried. "Beggars? Do you think they are the allies I seek? You are nothing more than a common criminal, Lucius, feckless, lazy, and utterly without spine."

He ignored the insults. "I promise you Aidy, once we are back on our feet, I'll make sure we give you all the support we can."

"And I promise you, Lucius," Adrianna said, her eyes burning, "I will not rest until every Vos-born man, woman and child in this entire city is dead, their corpses lying in the streets. I will drive out the Vos army and destroy this so-called cabal. I will make the slaughter in this city a monument that will burn across the entire world!"

She abruptly turned from him and stormed down the street. He briefly considered chasing after her, trying to reason with her, but he might as well try to placate the ocean. Adrianna was like a force of nature, and one could either stay out of her way or be crushed by her.

He just prayed that, when she struck, he would be in a position to limit the damage. He could not let her carry out her threat against innocent citizens of the city, wherever they were born.

CHAPTER ELEVEN

"RIDERS!"

The cry went up on the thieves' right flank, and they sought shelter in the rough ground, hiding behind boulders and within cracks in the rock.

"Everyone down," Lucius called, though the order was unnecessary; many of the thieves were jittery out in the open countryside.

Along with Ambrose and Wendric, he led a force of nearly two dozen thieves, all that could be gathered from the remaining cells of the guild. They had kept Elaine out of the coming battle to ensure the guild's future, but Lucius was painfully aware that his small army represented the vast majority of the guild's strength, which was a far cry from what it had once been. He just hoped it would be enough for the task at hand.

Wendric crawled across to Lucius, keeping himself hidden as he moved, and joined him behind a large rock.

"Outriders," he said. "Looks like Vos is on time."

"Never thought they would be anything but," Lucius said with a grin. "We can't let the caravan get any warning of our presence. Ambrose's archers ready?"

"Just give the word."

Peering out from behind the rock, Lucius could see thieves littering the broken ground before him, all crouched behind cover. Ahead of his ragtag force, Lucius could see the horsemen, outriders of the silver train they were lying in wait for.

These Vos soldiers were trained to cover long distances around a moving army or convoy of wagons, acting as scouts and sentries. Though they sported wicked looking long spears, they carried food and survival gear in preference to heavy metal armour, relying only on leathers and pot helmets for protection. Perfect prey for snipers.

To one side, he saw Ambrose amidst his archers, looking to Lucius for the signal to attack. Lucius raised a hand in preparation as the outriders advanced.

"If any of them escape, our whole plan is ruined," Wendric said under his breath.

"Ambrose knows what to do," Lucius said.

The veteran thief had already taken action, and Lucius saw several thieves crawling away from the horsemen, flanking them. Picking their way slowly, to avoid twisting a hoof on the rough ground, the Vos soldiers drew closer in a rough line. Lucius dropped his hand.

At Ambrose's sharp order a dozen arrows streaked from the thieves' hiding places. One rider fell from his horse, while three others slumped in their saddles, arrows jutting from their chests and necks. More arrows struck the horses, and their shrieks panicked the others. Within seconds, the discipline of the Vos outriders had vanished as horses reared, slipped on the uneven ground and collapsed, taking their riders with them.

One rider possessed the presence of mind to arrest his frightened mount and, kicking hard as he turned it about, started to race away from the thieves, trusting in his luck and his god to ensure his horse kept its feet. As one, Ambrose's flanking thieves rose from their hiding places and loosed another flight of arrows, the dark shafts tracing a shallow arc across the sky before falling around the fleeing soldier. Two missed and clattered among the stones, while another sank deep into the horse's rump, causing it to stumble. The final arrow struck home in the centre of the soldier's back, and he lurched to one side in his saddle, causing the horse to fall in a cloud of dust and kicking legs.

Lucius could hear men groan above the shriller cries of injured horses, and he waved his group forward to silence both. The men and women drew daggers and short swords, and went about their work with pitiless efficiency; within a few minutes, silence fell across the rocks.

The thieves edged closer to the coastal road and looked down onto the well-used track about eight yards below the escarpment on which they had hidden themselves. Beyond the track was a little vegetation, then a sheer drop as a cliff descended to the crashing ocean far below.

Lucius had remembered this place from a mercenary job he had taken years ago, when he had escorted a merchant's wagon through what had then been bandit territory. With the constant traffic to and from Vos, the bandits had long since gone, but every thief present hoped to teach the Empire that their roads were no longer safe. If what Lucius had told them was true, doing so would prove to be highly profitable.

They did not have long to wait. A low whistle from Ambrose, higher up the escarpment, caught their attention.

"Here we go," Wendric said, checking the tension on his bowstring. Satisfied, he laid his quiver on the ground and drew an arrow. Some other thieves had done the same, while others had removed all of their arrows and driven their tips into the ground. All had their eyes fixed firmly north, waiting for the appearance of more Vos soldiers.

"Here they come," Wendric muttered, sighting his first target.

Lucius looked down the coastal road and smiled.

"This is going to be perfect," he said.

The silver train moved slowly, taking several minutes to come into view. Three more outriders led the column in front of two covered wagons, which Lucius guessed carried more soldiers as well as supplies for the entire convoy. Trailing at the rear was a similar wagon and three more outriders. However, it was the magnificent wagon in the centre of the formation that had all the thieves' attention.

Drawn by six huge draught horses, it towered over the wagons before and behind it. Large metal sheets were hammered onto its sides, each punctuated with a single arrow slit, betraying the crossbow-wielding soldiers inside. On top of the wagon, Lucius could see half a dozen more soldiers sheltering behind crenellated walls, again armed with crossbows.

It was a moving fortress, apparently impregnable.

"That thing is built to wage war," Wendric said.

"It is more for show than practical use," Lucius said. "It would not do much good in a battle. It's too slow. Although it will no doubt cause us some problems."

"Our arrows are just going to bounce off it."

"The horses are still its weakness. Stick to the plan. Once we immobilise it and take care of the rest of the train, it will seem a little less fearsome."

With aching slowness, the convoy began to file past below them. The thieves kept their heads down; only Ambrose kept watch, using his jerriscope to see over the lip of the escarpment.

The minutes dragged by, and Lucius grew impatient, looking to Ambrose for the signal to attack and resisting the urge to crawl forward and look over the escarpment himself.

At last, Ambrose waved a hand, then raised himself to a kneeling position, exchanging his jerriscope for his short bow. The other thieves followed him.

Lucius stood up from behind the escarpment. The lead wagon was right below his position, and the outriders had already moved past, presenting their backs to the thieves. The men closest to Lucius, led by Wendric, all aimed at the target that had been assigned to them – the horses of the lead wagon.

Arrows lanced down on their marks. The horses were soon bristling with shafts, and began to panic. The wagon driver, caught completely unawares, lost the reins as the horses tried to bolt. One fell motionless to the ground, two shafts sprouting from its head and neck.

Another volley of arrows cut the driver down and disabled the other horses. Dead or wounded, they were no longer a concern, and Lucius directed the thieves' fire to the horses of the second wagon.

Further down the caravan, Ambrose's thieves had attacked the trailing wagon, and already two of the horses were immobile. Lucius smiled grimly. So far, the plan was working. The driver of the huge war wagon looked about desperately, caught between his desire to hide and his duty to drive the wagon clear of the ambush. He chose the latter, but the six-horse wagon was not an agile vehicle in the best of conditions, and the thin track ahead of him, winding between the high escarpment and the sheer cliffs, was filled with crippled wagons and screaming horses. There was nowhere for him to go.

An angry shout caught Lucius' attention, and he turned to see the leading outriders gesturing futilely up at him. They were looking for a route up on to the escarpment in order to bring the ambushers to battle, but the closest slope upwards was some way north, and their long spears were designed for charging, not for throwing.

Closing his eyes momentarily, Lucius concentrated, pulling upon one of the threads of magic; he immediately felt the presence of the sparse vegetation around his feet, the rocks behind him, and the ground below. Shaping the thread, he fashioned a huge harpoon in his mind's eye, rippling with arcane energy. Crouching, he hammered both of his fists onto the ground.

Wendric cast him an odd look, seeing only his fellow thief beating at the rocks. In his mind, however, Lucius watched his bolt of energy drive through the ground, through the stone and rock of the escarpment, and under the horses of the outriders. The ground burst open beneath their feet in an explosion of force that threw earth high into the air. One horse and its rider, nearest the centre of the burst, was catapulted over the cliff, to be lost in the churning waves of the sea. The other two horses whinnied pitifully, their legs broken by the spell. One rider was trapped under his mount, the other pulling desperately to free his comrade.

It had taken the thieves just moments to launch their ambush, but the speed at which the Vos soldiers responded was impressive. Crossbow bolts began to fly from the top of the large wagon. A few seconds later, they were joined by shots from inside, the tips of crossbows protruding slightly from the slits in the metal armour.

The shots were hurried, but several thieves yelped as bolts flew too close for comfort, or else found their marks. From their vantage point, the thieves had a clear view down onto the crenellated roof of the wagon, and when the Vos soldiers halted shooting to reload, several arrows fell on the chests and faces of the men stationed there. However, while other thieves targeted the main body of the wagon itself, their shots were not accurate enough to find the narrow slits, and bounced and skidded off its metal hull. When the soldiers inside reloaded, the thieves had no choice but to go to ground.

"This could end up being a stalemate," Wendric said.

"No, we can break the deadlock," Lucius said, and he ran past Wendric to be nearer the armoured wagon and the thieves attacking it.

"On my mark," he called to the thieves. "Stand and fire!"

A few of the thieves looked up at him dubiously, but they dutifully nocked arrows to their strings.

"Wendric," Lucius shouted over his shoulder. "Break out the ropes, and wait for my signal."

He saw Wendric give instructions to his thieves, who buried spikes and hooks into the ground or wedged them between rocks. Crouching at the lip of the escarpment, they held coiled lengths of rope that had been tied to the spikes, waiting for the next order.

"Up!" Lucius said. As one, the thieves stood and loosed, once again watching their arrows bounce uselessly off the armoured wagon.

A second later, crossbows were again pushed through the slits.

"Hold and reload!" Lucius shouted, before the thieves could think about ducking down again. This drew some dubious looks, though all but one held his ground.

Quickly drawing upon the thread of natural magic once more, Lucius reached out with his hand and felt the wind currents flowing in from the raging sea. Binding them to his will, he felt the air itself buckle and reshape itself under his direction, forming a fast moving barrier between the wagon and the thieves.

When the crossbows of the Vos soldiers fired, their bolts travelled just a few yards before being ripped from their courses by the wind, only to fall to the ground half a mile away. Lucius briefly released the air currents from his command, and turned back to the thieves.

"Continue shooting, keep their heads down if nothing else!" So saying, he turned to Wendric and nodded.

Wendric barked an order, and his thieves threw their ropes down the escarpment, throwing themselves over the edge and sliding down to the road. Glancing back up the track, Lucius saw that Ambrose was slightly ahead, with his men already on the road and approaching the rearmost wagon.

The continued volleys from the remaining thieves on the escarpment were sufficient to at least disrupt the return shots from the armoured wagon, and when Lucius saw crossbows begin to appear at the slits, he once more brought down his wind shield to block the flight of the bolts. Satisfied that the morale of the Vos soldiers was at least shaken, he turned to the archers.

"Carry on shooting," he said. "Give us cover down there."

He ran back down the length of the escarpment and swung himself over the edge when he reached the first rope. The ramps at the back of the first two wagons had dropped down, and Vos soldiers were beginning to pour out, brandishing spears and shields. Lucius cursed, praying that the archers had seen them and were already taking aim. The thieves down on the road would be little match against trained and heavily armoured soldiers.

Climbing down the rope, hand-over-hand, he drew his sword as soon as he hit the ground, just as the first volley of arrows from the escarpment started to fall among the soldiers.

The arrows found two of the soldiers, their tips passing shield and armour to bury themselves in their flesh; the rest were caught on shields. Wendric thrust under the guard of one soldier who had raised his shield to defend against the volley, the thief meeting no resistance as he sank his blade into the man's side.

Other thieves were having less luck, and quickly found themselves on the defensive, driven back by the disciplined soldiers. Angling their shields to face both the archers and the thieves on the ground, they paced forward, steadily driving the ambushers toward Lucius' position.

Seeing the attack faltering, Lucius cried out for his men to scatter, clearing a path between him and the soldiers. Taking a deep breath, he summoned his magic forth, holding his hands outstretched, palms upwards. He felt the energy pour down his arms, swelling until he held a large, rolling ball of fire steady, its flames licking just a few inches above his naked skin.

He flung the fireball forwards, feeding ever more power into the spell so the ball accelerated as it flew through the air. It struck the shields in the centre of the soldiers' line with blinding speed, knocking the soldiers back several yards. Seeing his chance, Wendric raised his sword and shouted a rallying cry. His thieves charged.

Once among the disorganised and battered soldiers, the battle became more even. Here a thief was smashed in the face by a soldier's shield and spitted on the end of a spear, while there another parried a soldier's blow with one blade and struck under his guard with the other, finding stomach, thigh or shin.

The soldiers, adhering to their training, tried to reform their shield wall, but were matched by thieves working on instinct and relying on foul play. A soldier confronting one thief would be flanked by another, piercing the chainmail on his back with a well-placed dagger thrust. Within moments, the dead and dying of both sides littered the ground, hindering those still fighting.

Shouts from further up the road checked Lucius' own entry into the fray. Ambrose's thieves had met the soldiers stationed in the rearmost wagon. Their fight was nearly finished, the soldiers outnumbered and already depleted by arrows, but some of the thieves had begun to panic. It took Lucius a few seconds to work out what was happening; he took a step towards them, then stopped as he felt a familiar pressure inside his head.

On top of the armoured wagon, a middle-aged man, looking like a wealthy merchant in his gilded blue tunic, was peering down at the thieves. Lucius saw the magical strands flex and twist at the presence of this man, and knew another spellcaster had joined the battle.

The Vos wizard held his hands out to the sky, then pointed down at the thieves at the far end of the train. Among the thieves, the corpses of the slain Vos soldiers stirred. They grasped the ankles of thieves to bear them down, or dragged themselves to their feet, picking their spears up and advancing on the thieves once again.

Ambrose, unshaken by the obvious sorcery, advanced upon the animated corpses, sword in hand. Following his example, some of the thieves stood to fight the enemies they had only just killed, while others panicked at the sight of the unnatural soldiers, and two broke and fled.

The raised soldiers were uncoordinated and inaccurate, if no slower than they had been in life, and no longer fought as a single unit, but if they could pick themselves up after every death, they would inevitably overwhelm the thieves sooner or later.

Turning to the larger battle at the front of the train, the Vos wizard began to chant his spell once more, and saw Lucius standing before him. Their eyes locked in a grim challenge, and Lucius could not help giving a wicked smile.

He could feel the Vos wizard pluck and twist at the strand of magic that governed death and unlife – necromancy, Forbeck had called it. He could also see that this was the only talent the wizard could manifest. The man, for all his long years of study, might as well have been completely ignorant of all the other radiant shades of magic, and the power that lay within them.

Lucius remained calm as the wizard dropped the corpse-raising spell and prepared an attack that would suck the life out of him. *Alright Forbeck, you old rascal*, Lucius thought. *Let me see if your theory of magic has any weight.*

The strand of death and black hate buckled as the wizard siphoned power from it. No other type of magic held dominance over necromancy, which in turn held dominance over magic of the natural world. However, elemental forces were in direct opposition to necromancy, and it was this thread that Lucius drew from, constructing a cloud of magic and manifesting it in front of him. A thin mist began to form, hanging motionless in the air before him.

A dark bolt of energy leapt from the wizard's outstretched hand. As it collided with the mist, Lucius' magic began to split and break, but he concentrated hard, mending the magical shield. For a few seconds, the two spells vied with one another, and Lucius felt the strength of the wizard's craft. The man was well-versed in his chosen form of magic but, for all his ability, lacked the versatility of a Shadowmage.

The Vos wizard withdrew his spell and prepared another. Lucius went onto the attack immediately, punching the air as he forced his mist cloud forward to envelope his enemy.

The necromancer panicked as he was cloaked by the soft, cool mist, and Lucius smiled as the man fumbled his counterspell. Lucius focussed on the mist wreathing the wizard's body, forcing it to drive inwards, seeping in through the man's clothes and skin. He fed more and more power into the spell as it gained a foothold in the wizard's own flesh, and water flooded the man's lungs and burst through his mouth. Unable to breathe or speak, the wizard could do nothing against Lucius' spell and, held rigid by the magic, slowly drowned where he stood.

Lucius saw the dead soldiers drop motionless to the ground once more and knew the wizard was dead. He released his spell and the wizard fell out of sight behind the crenellations of the armoured wagons.

The corpse soldiers no longer hindering them, Ambrose's men raced down the road, keeping out of shot of the crossbowmen still locked inside the armoured wagon. As soon as they entered the battle alongside Wendric's thieves, the Vos defence folded. Once surrounded, they died.

Wendric staggered towards Lucius, not wounded but clearly exhausted by the short fight. He had ripped a scrap from a fallen soldier's tabard, and was cleaning the blood from his sword.

"That was tight," he said, once his breath had been recovered.

"It's not quite over," Lucius said, nodding to the armoured wagon. He looked back at the thieves behind Wendric, some of whom were noticeably limping or holding blood-sodden makeshift bandages to their sides. "How many did we lose?"

"More than we hoped for, a little less than we feared. A lot of walking wounded too."

"I have a feeling they will feel a lot better about the journey back to Turnitia when they are carrying a sack full of silver each," Lucius said.

"So, what are we going to do about the last wagon?" Wendric asked. "We had not accounted for that."

"Burn it," a young thief said as he walked up to the two of them.

"It's metal, fool," another said, joining them. "Metal doesn't burn."

"It's only metal on the outside."

"He's right," said Lucius, who had been thinking along similar lines. "Stay here."

Walking up to the armoured wagon, aware of the stares of the thieves behind as they wondered what he was going to do, Lucius called out to the soldiers inside.

"Surrender," he said simply. "The rest of your men are dead and you are alone. Surrender."

A single crossbow was thrust through the nearest slit, and Lucius stepped to one side as the bolt was loosed.

"This is your final chance. Surrender, or die where you are."

There was no response. The silver train to Turnitia had to be carrying a vast wealth to fund all of the Empire's activities in the city. Punishment for a soldier deserting such a prize had to be unimaginable. Sighing, Lucius stepped closer to the wagon, taking care to stay out of the line of sight of any of the arrow slits. Standing with his back to the wagon, the nearest slit just inches away, Lucius closed his eyes as he summoned one last spell. Whirling around, he clamped his right hand over the slit, and let the arcane energy pour down his arm and through his hand, erupting as scorching flame that filled the interior of the wagon.

Men shrieked with burning agony, and the stench of burnt flesh blew back into Lucius' face. He kept the fire rolling inside for a few seconds and, when the screams and cries had faded away, snuffed out the flames as quickly as he had created them.

Movement above him caused Lucius to jump back, hand flying to the hilt of his sword. A body, still smouldering, hung over the crenellations above, a single arrow jutting out of its neck. Hearing someone approach behind, Lucius turned to see Ambrose walking towards him, bow in hand.

"He was probably just trying to escape. Didn't want to take the chance though."

Lucius looked up at the corpse and then back at Ambrose.

"That was a fine shot. And it suits our purpose that none of them survive this attack. It will raise more questions in the Empire if the silver train simply disappears."

"Aye, that's true," Ambrose agreed. "So what would you have done if they had surrendered?"

Lucius shrugged. "Given then a cleaner death, perhaps."

"Well, just remember, we did not strike the first blow in this war."

"That's what I keep telling myself."

More thieves started clustering around them, expectant looks on their faces, looking for all the world like children expecting a great gift on their birthday, and Lucius could not help but smile. Within seconds, half a dozen thieves had scaled the sides of the wagon, and called down that they had found a trapdoor leading inside.

"Get inside and see if you can unlock the ramp," Lucius shouted up to them.

They disappeared from view for several minutes, though everyone outside could hear the occasional curse of frustration as they tried to work the locking mechanism. Lucius waited patiently at the rear of the wagon. He was finally rewarded by a cheer from inside and the sound of the heavy latches turning. A slit of darkness appeared at the top of the ramp as it slowly lowered on thick chains.

The thieves stood at the ramp's edge, their expressions a mixture of triumph and revulsion. Lucius waved them out, and sent others in to drag out the bodies. A cursory check was made to see if any still lived, but Lucius' magic had killed them all.

The bodies removed, thieves flooded into the wagon, tearing up the benches that lined the walls in search of the treasure they had been promised. Wendric stormed on board, threatening to make any thief who did not listen to him penniless, and drove them out. He waved Ambrose on, and the veteran thief began a systematic search of the interior, ignoring the suggestions shouted out to him from the thieves clustered outside.

Finally, Ambrose stood, looking critically at the floor of the wagon. He stamped a foot down on the wooden boards, then looked up, grinning. The excitement among the gathered thieves was palpable.

When Ambrose called for crowbars, two thieves rushed to help him, and Lucius followed. The thieves feverishly levered up the boards, snapping the wood in their haste, and Lucius spotted a flash of metal. More boards were removed, revealing six square steel chests. Each chest was nearly two feet to each side, and one of the crowbar thieves whistled as he began to wonder how much silver each chest could contain. The crowbars were employed again to open the chests.

Their contents glinted in the daylight. Lucius stared at them, his mouth open. He had never seen so much wealth. Nearly filled to the brim, every chest was heaving with newly minted silver coins, their pristine edges sharp and unsullied by the hands of merchants and craftsmen.

Wendric boarded the wagon and glanced at the chests, and then smirked to himself. "There's more than a million silver coins there, boys," he said. "Maybe two million."

There was no reaction from the thieves outside the wagon, just a silent awe at being in the presence of so much wealth.

"So, what do we do now?" Ambrose asked after several moments' silence.

Lucius shook himself, remembering that he wanted to be out of the area and back in the city as soon as possible.

"Get your sacks ready," he said to the thieves, unfolding his own. "Form an orderly line – believe me, there is more than enough here for everyone. Take as much as you can carry. It's yours. No guild tithes on this job, you keep everything you can carry."

The thieves had not been expecting that level of generosity, and they whooped with glee and greed, causing Wendric to bark at them to restore order once again. As he left the thieves to stuff as many coins as they could into their sacks, pouches and underclothing, Wendric walked over to Lucius who, having slung his own sack of silver over his shoulder, was near the cliff top, staring out at the sea.

"We had not agreed to that," Wendric said. "You'll spoil them. They'll expect to retain all of their takings in the future."

Lucius shook his head. "There will be plenty of time to restore discipline later, and I daresay few will disobey while Elaine is guildmistress. It's alright this time. Thieves are not usually expected to fight pitched battles against Vos soldiers, and many of them are wounded. It will also do something to stop others leaving the guild altogether. Hopefully, there will be more volunteers next time."

"I suppose," Wendric said.

"But all of that does not really matter," said Lucius. "It is the big picture we must look at. The important thing is that Vos loses its silver, that we begin to starve them out of the city. Without money, we have a much easier time putting the guild back together. I don't mind if a few thieves get rich helping us do that. Besides, if they get to keep all the silver they carry, it will make this next step a bit easier."

So saying, he turned from Wendric and headed back to the wagon. He could not help but smile again at the sight of the grinning thieves, all loaded down with silver.

"One last task, my friends, and then it is back to the city," he said, eliciting a cheer of triumph from them. He pointed to the armoured wagon. "I want you all to push that over the cliffs."

The grins fled from their faces immediately. The wagon was still full of silver and even though not one thief could carry any more about his person, the thought of pitching all that wealth into the endless sea was anathema to any thief.

"You… you're kidding, right?" said one thief among the crowd.

"It has to be done. You know that. If we just leave it here, or bury it, or hide it somewhere, Vos may find it. Our task was not to get rich, but to make the Empire poor. What you are carrying on your backs is… a bonus. Do what I ask."

The thieves moved half-heartedly, some running back on board to cram another coin or two into their boots. When they were assembled around the wagon, ready to push it forward, no one moved.

"Alright boys, it pains me too, but needs must," Ambrose said, and Lucius was not sure whether he was just making a show of solidarity or not. "On the count of three…"

The wagon was weighed down with its metal armour, but the straining thieves gradually got it moving again, and inching towards the cliff edge. The massive structure slowly gained momentum, and soon the thieves were half-running as they pushed it. At a shout from Ambrose, they released the wagon, and watched as it trundled toward the cliffs. For a brief moment, it tottered as the front wheels hit empty air, and then dropped out of sight. Later, Lucius would swear he heard more than one thief sobbing.

Once the haul of silver had been thrown from the cliffs, getting the thieves to clean up the rest of the battleground was easier. Any horse that was still fit was led away, to be taken back to the city, but the dead were dragged to the cliffs and then pushed over. The wounded were killed cleanly and then they too were thrown over. Wagons, dead soldiers and dead thieves quickly followed them, the latter thrown with a degree of reverence and a few words dedicated to their souls.

As the thieves cleared the remainder of the battlefield, collecting stray arrows and covering pools of blood with earth and dust, Wendric approached Lucius.

"So," he said. "We'll call that a success then."

"I think so. It could have been so much worse for us," Lucius said.

"Well, in two weeks, when they send the next silver train, we can do this all over again."

Looking north to the Vos Empire, Lucius grimaced.

"Next time, it will not be this easy."

CHAPTER TWELVE

As MORNING TURNED into afternoon, Elaine wandered slowly through the southernmost of the Five Markets, her arm linked with that of a tall, fair-haired man. Gesturing at the various stalls they passed, his Vos accent was clear as he chided vendors for the prices they tried to charge, or else made disparaging comments about the quality of their merchandise. Dressed in good but affordable clothes, to the casual observer they appeared to be the epitome of middle class Turnitia, hardworking but living comfortably.

Even if such an observer did not miss the man's tone dropping whenever the crowd thinned out, and the couple talking in hushed voices, they might only presume that the conversation had turned to matters only a man and his wife need know. There was certainly nothing in their demeanour to suggest that here was the mistress of the remaining thieves' guild, discussing work with one of her lead assassins.

"I feel we are being shut out," the man was saying, as he steered Elaine away from a meat vendor whose prices had attracted a mob of excited wives and house cooks. "We are poised to act, and yet you are holding us back in favour of operations by footpads and burglars."

Elaine smiled to herself. "There is no disrespect intended, Heinrich. Their talents are useful right now. Yours will come into play soon enough."

"And what of the attack on the silver train? Our skills would have been well suited to that mission."

That question caused Elaine to glance at him and raise an eyebrow, though she quickly reflected that it was difficult to keep any secret from her assassins. After all, she had taught several of them herself and, through her position in the guild, elevated the role of the trained killers.

"The ambush will turn into a battle, and I will not risk our most capable members going toe-to-toe with Vos soldiers. You are better operating from the shadows. You know that."

Heinrich frowned. "I was thinking more of the rewards from the mission. There are a lot of thieves getting rich right now, while the assassins are kept on a chain."

"I thought that might be more to the point. I trust you have informed the others that there will be plenty of opportunities for everyone soon enough?"

"Of course."

"Any talk about splitting and starting an assassins' guild?"

They had entered Ring Street, the thoroughfare that joined the Five Markets and ringed the imposing Citadel. They turned off the busy road and headed for quieter streets.

"No. Not that I have heard of, anyway," Heinrich said. "I wouldn't worry too much about that. Business was always good under your employment, and we all trust that you will steer us back on course."

"There will be some hard work for the assassins before that happens," Elaine said. "Hard, unpaid work."

"I think, after their recent inactivity, your people will happily take it," Heinrich said, smiling. "They will see it as a point of pride, and a chance to refine their skills. What did you have in mind?"

"The chief point of discussion in the next Council meeting. So long as the attack on the silver train is at least a marginal success, we'll see what effect it has on the Vos forces in the city."

"And then?"

A wolfish look crossed Elaine's features. "Let's just say that if the assassins start tracking Vos officials and military leaders, I don't believe their time will be wasted."

"Sounds like war." Heinrich did not seem unhappy with the idea.

"That is what I am trying to avoid, as I am not sure even our assassins could survive a war with Vos. However, a few blades in the dark, a poisoning here or drowning there, might just make the Empire's position here untenable. We avert war and win by default."

"What if that is not enough?"

"Then, so long as we survive, we keep fighting. I'll not be driven from this city."

Heinrich shrugged. "You'll need to find some way to finance our people in the long term. Their loyalty to you is firm at the moment, but it may not last, especially if they start dying."

Nodding grimly, Elaine stopped as they came to a junction where the narrow road joined Lantern Street, a livelier part of the city that was home to many of the permanent traders and craftsmen's workshops. She turned her head to one side slightly as Heinrich leaned over and kissed her cheek.

Turning on her heel, Elaine retraced her steps, thinking hard as she went. The news from Heinrich was encouraging, and she felt she had at least some time with the rest of the assassins. Unlike most of the rogues in the thieves' guild who might engage in the odd murder for silver, her killers were true professionals. They knew when they needed to act, and when they should lie low.

She glanced up to see a woman approaching her from the other end of the street. Elaine found herself unnerved to see the woman walking straight towards her, eyes fixed on hers.

Dropping a hand down to her stomach, Elaine brushed the pommel of the short knife she had concealed under her tunic, and slowed her pace, looking to the alleys she passed and the few passers-by behind her. She suddenly felt very exposed, and wondered if an ambush was about to be sprung.

The woman continued her approach, her pace not slackening in the slightest as she stalked forwards. Elaine saw she was around her own age, with dark hair tied up behind her head. She wore a tunic of black leather, with unusual metal discs woven into the fabric, each dulled so as not to catch the sun. What arrested her attention, though, was the woman's eyes, beautifully wide but almost black as she stared back. Elaine was sure she had seen the woman before.

As they moved to within a few yards of one another, Elaine whipped her knife out from under her tunic, keeping the blade down at her side, but in clear view of the other woman. The only response was a smile as the woman cupped a hand and then thrust it at Elaine, as if she were throwing something.

Elaine had barely started to dodge when she was blasted off her feet by a moving wall of air.

THE THIEVES HAD scattered long before Turnitia had come into sight as they walked back along the coastal road. Wendric and Ambrose had taken the bulk of them in a wide loop around the city, beyond the sight of its walls. There were numerous ways into the city that avoided the two main gates in the east and north walls, from storm drains to overflow pipes leading straight to the sewers. The thieves' guild had long since mapped them all, and they had been a staple of smuggling franchises until Vos had strangled illicit trade in the city.

The journey along the coastal road, in the company of the remaining jubilant thieves, had been an amiable way of passing an afternoon. Though loaded down with heavy coins, even a wounded thief, his left arm strung across his chest with a makeshift sling, was laughing. They were giddy with their success, and while Lucius kept quiet himself, he enjoyed listening to their plans on how they were going to spend their fortunes. Even the hilly terrain through which they travelled did nothing to dampen their spirits, though every few paces one thief or another would stop to shift his sack from one shoulder to the other.

"Going to set me up a dozen new franchises," one said. "Maybe something at the docks, corner all trade coming in by sea."

"Investing in the future, then?"

"Aye, only sensible thing to do."

"Well, in that case I think I'll get myself a new sword. One of those Allantian-forged jobs, perfect balance, they say."

"That's for the future?"

"Sure, I'll need it for when we go for the next silver train!"

"You would be better off investing in a pony and cart, so we don't have to tip so much into the sea. What about you, Alfred, what are you going to do with your money?"

There was a long pause. "I think, on balance," the thief Alfred said, "that I'll take three rooms at the Red Lion, and invite every whore, troubadour and gambler to join me. Oh, and make sure Myrklar never runs out of wine. Think I'll get through this little lot within a month or so, then I'll be ready for more work."

His plans were met with stunned silence, until he turned and winked at the rest of them. They all laughed then, though Lucius was still not sure Alfred was completely joking. He just hoped they would all have the sense to keep their heads down for the next few weeks. Any sudden appearance of huge quantities of cash would lead even the dullest Vos sergeant straight to a guilty thief, once the raid on the silver train became common knowledge.

"Hey, what's going on there?" one thief asked.

The walls of Turnitia had come into view as they mounted the rise, and Lucius' gaze was drawn straight to the thin columns of smoke rising from the centre of the city. He frowned. The smoke was too thick to come from a blacksmith's, and there was too much for it to be an isolated house fire.

"Looks like it's near the Citadel," said one thief.

"A riot, you think?" Alfred asked.

Lucius shook his head. "I can't see the Vos guard tolerating angry crowds long enough for them to light more than one or two fires. It looks like a battle is going on."

That subdued the thieves, though their eyes lit up when Lucius slung his own sack of silver from his back and bade them share the load between them. Telling them to get back into the city through less obvious routes as planned, he jogged ahead, wanting to see what had happened within the city.

It took him nearly an hour to reach the northern city gates. They were wide open, as was usual during the day, but completely untended. Hesitantly, fearing a trap, he approached the gates and peered inside, half-expecting to see ranks of Vos soldiers beyond, spears and crossbows levelled at him as he entered. There was nothing. As he passed under the high stone arch of the gatehouse, Lucius began to pick up speed, looking anxiously for anyone that could tell him what had happened. Every street near the gatehouse was deserted, with the windows of many of the buildings shuttered or barred. He made his way towards the centre of the city, heading for Ring Street and the Citadel.

The northernmost of the Five Markets looked like a battleground, and Lucius wondered if he had missed a sneak attack from some secret army of Pontaine, come to claim the city from the Empire.

On Ring Street, three houses blazed, pouring black smoke into the afternoon sky, the columns streaking across the huge azure sphere of Kerberos. The dead lay everywhere on the cobbles of the marketplace, their bodies looking as if they had been picked up by some giant and then dashed on the ground. Limbs and heads lay at unnatural angles, while some were impaled on the smashed remains of vendors' stalls. He could not see a single wound on any that looked as though it was made by a weapon.

He walked across the marketplace stunned, unable to believe what he was seeing, and he was not alone. Others stumbled over bodies as if in a daze. Every now and again, someone would cry out as they recognised a loved one, falling to their knees beside a body.

It was a massacre, indiscriminate killing on a scale he had only seen performed by the worst mercenary companies operating in the Anclas Territories. The broken bodies of Vos soldiers were scattered all over the cobbles, most near the sealed gates of the Citadel. However, many more of the dead were ordinary men and women, the life blasted out of their corpses. With a shock, Lucius realised that many children were among the dead, covered by the bodies of their mothers or fathers as if they had tried, in vain, to shield them from attack. There were a hundred or more dead in the market.

He walked past the wreckage of one stall, its bright green awning now a tattered sheet flapping in the breeze. The wood used to build the stall was little more than jagged splinters, mixed with the broken crockery the stall had sold. Seated on the ground next to the ruin, Lucius saw an aged woman, her long silver hair shielding her eyes from the devastation surrounding them.

She sat, motionless, staring into nothingness, one hand on the twisted body of a man of similar age. His dead gaze was fixed on the sky, his neck broken.

Crouching down by the woman, Lucius gently took her hand.

"Are you hurt?" he asked, but received no response. He moved so he was crouching directly in her field of vision, and carefully brushed her hair to one side, before repeating the question.

She did not stir for several seconds. When she looked up at him there was fear in her face.

"I will not harm you," he said softly. "Are you injured?"

Slowly, she shook her head. "I'm fine," she said simply. She was silent for a moment more, then added, "Pietre threw me behind the stall. Then he died."

Lucius looked around the market. The scene was being repeated all over, with survivors emerging from the wreckage, aided by those who had ventured to the scene of the battle. The gates of the Citadel opened enough to let a squad of Vos guards through, and they immediately set to work, dragging the bodies of fallen soldiers into the fortress. Only then did Lucius notice that the walls of the Citadel themselves had sustained damage. Great gouges had been torn into the stonework, as if by a powerful siege engine. Mystified, he turned back to the woman.

"What happened here?"

"She said she had come for everyone Vos-born," the woman said after a moment's hesitation. "Then she started attacking the soldiers."

"Who?"

"Some people started cheering at first, seeing the soldiers thrown around like rag dolls. But when she ran out of soldiers, she turned on everyone else. She just… broke them. Threw them into the stalls, the buildings, each other."

"Lady, who did this?"

"Pietre wanted to run, but I was frozen where I stood. Too scared to move. He saw what she was doing, as she killed everyone she could see. He saw her come towards us, and got me out of the way. Then she... she..."

Lucius grasped the woman by her shoulders, shaking her slightly to bring her attention back to him.

"Please, you must tell me," he said. "Who was it?" He knew the answer before the woman spoke.

"Some maddened wizard, some rogue mage. Said she wanted to destroy everything Vos-built and Vos-born. Cloaked in darkness, she was."

Dropping his own gaze to the ground, Lucius sighed uselessly, trying to find some course through the disaster.

"Why did she leave?"

"I don't know," the woman answered bleakly. "I don't think there was anyone left to kill."

Squeezing the woman's hand slightly before he stood, Lucius turned and walked slowly away. He had heard Adrianna's threats, of course, but it staggered him to think she had done this to so many innocent people. She was ferociously dedicated to the Shadowmages and their loose guild, and he could well believe that she would cheerfully slay every Vos soldier and official if it would make them leave the city, but he had never thought she was capable of this level of destruction.

As he left the marketplace, he turned to look at the scene of the massacre. The other troubling thought was that Adrianna was more powerful than he had suspected. Lucius remembered his confrontation with her outside his old home, and how he felt she could easily best him if angered. He had had no idea how true that was. The magnitude of the magics she must have controlled to destroy so much was astounding. He had begun to think he was starting to make progress in the Shadowmage's art, but he was no more than a novice. Adrianna's power and talent were far beyond his own.

Turning into a short dead end of an alley, Lucius leaned against the wall of a small brewing house for support as he gathered his thoughts. He knew exactly what he had to do next, but he feared the confrontation.

Taking a deep, ragged breath, he summoned the threads of magic to his will, shaping them into a quiet clarion call that would find

Adrianna and let her know where he was. He felt the magical chimes radiate away from him, and he turned to leave the alley, wanting to find a more discreet place to meet.

His delicate chimes were suddenly overwhelmed by a massive tolling, a mighty arcane summons that sundered his own spell and caused him to stagger under its force. It felt as if he were inside a huge bell that rang with a deep, bass note, and Lucius clutched at his head.

Breathing heavily under the strain, he built a magical defence that siphoned off a little of the summoning spell's energy. Each peal was still a deafening blast inside his head, but the pain became manageable and, once he was sure his feet were steady, he left the alley. Adrianna was calling him to the harbour, and she had left him with little choice other than to obey.

THE INCESSANT TOLLING had receded by the time he reached the harbour, becoming little more than a constant, dull throbbing in his mind. Tolerable, yet impossible to ignore. It directed him along the cliffs, where labourers toiled with boxed crates and sacks, piling them onto flat platforms that were then hoisted into the open air by sturdy cranes and lowered to the docks. Evidently, a ship was expected, and there were plenty of merchants who wanted to take advantage of another vessel daring to run the gauntlet of the churning seas.

Moving away from the bustling activity, Lucius continued along the cliff top before stopping. He had reached his destination. Looking about, he frowned. The homes of one of the poorer districts of Turnitia were immediately to his left, along with a few scattered warehouses. Gulls circled lazily above him. Beyond them, the calm waters of the harbour belied the crashing storm that raged against the monoliths at its mouth. Adrianna had found a well-concealed lair in which to hide.

Walking to the very edge of the cliffs, he looked down, and fought against the heady sense of vertigo. The docks seemed far below, and their stone foundations, married to wooden piers, stretched out into the harbour like fingers. A single piece of black cloth, perhaps torn from a larger cloak, fluttered in the sea wind, seemingly caught on a jagged outcropping of rock. Lucius smiled.

Calling upon the magical strands, he constructed a spell he had seen performed before, but had never attempted. Shaping the arcane energy to call wind currents to his command, he shaped an invisible, shallow bowl just beyond the cliff's edge. Raising a foot, he stepped tentatively over the lethal drop.

His foot was buoyed up by a solid support of air. It felt like stepping into a bowl of corn and, hesitantly, he brought his other foot on board. Arms instinctively outstretched for balance, he hung motionless in mid-air.

Conscious that a flying man would bring unwanted attention from the labourers working further down the cliffs, he willed the cushion of air into movement, and Lucius gently floated downwards to the black rag.

The cliff side bowed out during his descent, hiding a cleft from casual view. Only someone suicidal enough to try and scale the sheer surface would find it. Shifting the flow of air supporting him, Lucius descended into the cleft and spotted a small cave or tunnel, boring straight into the cliff side. He dropped to its level and stooped as he stepped onto solid ground.

Inside, the cave quickly widened, its ceiling rising so he could stand. He took a few seconds for his eyes to adjust to the gloom, and noticed that, a little further in, the rocky walls seemed to glow with their own dull, green-tinged light. Lucius had heard of luminescent moss in the past, but this seemed different somehow to him, and he suspected the light was being sustained by magic as he felt the threads ripple with the presence of an existing enchantment. The threads began to noticeably buckle and twist as he took a further step inside, causing him to halt quickly.

There was another spell at work here, some sort of ward or trap to discourage unwanted visitors, as unlikely as they might be. Having no wish to inadvertently activate the spell, he created his own shield against it, drawing upon the same shadow magic that created the ward. Wreathing himself in the conjuration, he thus appeared invisible to the spell, and he walked past with trepidation, ready to react if his assumptions about it were wrong.

The tunnel twisted a little before descending on a gentle slope, the route always lit by the softly glowing rocks. He marvelled at the construction of this place, and the effort it must have taken to bore this far into the cliff. Whether it had been done by mundane means or magical, it was something of an achievement.

Lucius felt the presence of Adrianna a moment before he saw her. The tunnel jinked slightly to the left and, as he rounded the corner, widened out into a roughly hewn chamber with two more passages leading off it, deeper into the cliff. Before them stood Adrianna, arms folded across her chest while her dark eyes bored into his.

He did not need to see Adrianna's face to feel her fury, for it punched through the air like a hammer. More disturbing to him were the threads of magic he saw in his mind, pitching and twisting as if reacting to her very presence. Lucius had known that meeting Adrianna was dangerous but, for the first time, he gave himself only even odds for walking out of her lair alive.

"Adrianna..." Lucius began, but immediately faltered. He realised that he really did not know the woman before him at all.

"Useless, feckless, ignorant thief," she hissed. "You have wasted everything you have ever been given. You are no more use than a miserable beggar, scrabbling for whatever scraps Vos leaves on the table for you to steal."

Lucius took a breath before speaking.

"Adrianna, what have you done?" he asked. "All those people..."

"Idiot! If you had accepted our alliance, if you had joined me, this war would be over already! The power of the Empire would be in ruins, and this city would be free again. And where were you instead? Playing bandit in the hills!"

For a second, Lucius was speechless. "And what did you think you were going to achieve? Do you know how many innocent people you have killed?"

She gave him a scornful look. "Together, we could have blasted the Citadel into ruins, then marched on the Cathedral. Vos would have had nowhere to run! We could have blasted every one of them clear out of the city!"

"And how many others would have died? My God, Adrianna, there are dead children in the markets! How does that advance your cause?"

"If it means the Empire withdraws, a few dead, more or less, certainly does not hinder it," she said flatly.

"We don't have to be like this, Adrianna," Lucius said evenly; if there was one thing he was sure of, it was that Adrianna would not look kindly on any display of weakness. "That banditry in the hills you talk about probably did more damage to the Empire in the long run than your own attack. You don't have to become like Vos in order to beat it."

"You fool," she said, as if talking to a particularly slow child. "Becoming like Vos has no relevance whatsoever. What matters is who wins! Who is left standing after this war is done – and it will be done very soon, Lucius, mark my words."

"There is another way."

"No," she said. "Not any more. They have started to strike at us. We *must* hit back, and harder. Show them that we are invincible, that whatever hurt they bring upon us will be revisited upon them a hundredfold."

He tried another tack. "Even if I had been there, two mages cannot defeat the entire Citadel, let alone every soldier Vos has stationed in the city."

Something flashed in Adrianna's eyes, and she looked down at the ground for a few seconds, as if trying to rein in her anger. When she spoke, it was with deliberate slowness, as though each word was difficult for her.

"After all these years, you still do not realise what a Shadowmage is capable of. Forbeck knew, but he kept it chained, muzzled. You do the same thing, but through sheer ignorance. I can show you what power a Shadowmage unleashed has, Lucius. Two of us, working together in concert, would have been unstoppable! I can take over your teaching, shape you into one of the most potent mages this miserable world has ever seen."

"Adrianna..." Lucius began, slowly coming to an unnerving conclusion. "Have you taken over the Shadowmages' guild?"

She waved his question away as if irrelevant. "Two of us could achieve so much, Lucius. The guild as a whole could become all-powerful in this city." She smiled dangerously. "Even almighty."

He stared at her.

"Still, there is time for you to make amends, Lucius," Adrianna said. "I have a task you can aid me with. Follow me."

She spun around to head down one of the other passages, but stopped when Lucius called out to her, keeping her back to him.

"I cannot help you in this," he said.

"You will."

"Adrianna, I don't want to become your enemy."

Looking over her shoulder, Adrianna gave him a dark look.

"No," she said. "You don't."

Lucius watched her disappear down the tunnel. For the moment, at least, he knew he was safe. If Adrianna needed him, she would not kill him unless he forced her hand. Wiping his brow of sweat, he started after her, apprehensive of what favour she would require of him in order to keep the peace between them.

The passage dropped again, a little steeper than before, and opened out into another chamber. Before him was an unfurled bedroll, together with a small store of bread, dried meat, and wine. Adrianna had evidently spent some time in this lair already. As he entered the chamber, his eyes were drawn to one side, and he gasped.

Arms forced either side of her head by manacles of glowing silver energy, Elaine was held fast, Adrianna's prisoner. A similar band of energy blazed across her face, effectively gagging her. When she saw him, Elaine's eyes narrowed with loathing, and he groaned under his breath, dreading whatever Adrianna had been telling her.

"Oh, Adrianna, what have you done?" he said quietly, as much to himself as the two women.

"Your thieving whore has been my guest here," Adrianna said. She stood next to Elaine, arms folded again over her chest.

"As you can imagine, we have had all sorts of things to talk about."

"So what do you want?" he asked, refusing to be baited. He would deal with the fallout with Elaine at a later time, when both of their lives were not in danger.

Adrianna smiled, malice creeping across her face. "There is a ship outside the harbour, waiting for a break in the storms so it can safely negotiate the monoliths and enter Turnitia. I will calm the storms, so it can sail into the harbour–"

"You can do that?" Lucius asked in amazement, interrupting her. The energy that had to be harnessed in order to attempt such a thing was almost beyond his comprehension.

She gave him a contemptuous look before continuing. "The ship is full of Vos soldiers. A lot of them. They are here to lock down the city, and wipe out the last of the Shadowmages."

"You want to destroy the ship."

"Of course."

"So why not just smash them against the harbour defences? It would be a lot easier."

"Because, fool," Adrianna said, spitting at his stupidity, "I want the people of the city to *see* it happen. To understand what is going to happen to anyone who supports the Empire."

His shoulders sagging as he realised he would not be able to reason with Adrianna, Lucius sighed helplessly. While the thieves had certainly killed their fair share of soldiers, the cold-blooded drowning of hundreds of men was not something he could easily stomach. He looked at her bleakly.

"Why are you doing this?"

Eyes narrowing as if she were looking at something deeply repulsive, Adrianna spoke quietly at first, her voice slowly rising.

"Unlike you, I was here when the Empire first came to this city. They promised everything in the world, but brought with them terror and death. You fled. You didn't see them attack the Shadowmages the first time around, wiping us out one by one."

"Adrianna–" he started, but she cut him off.

"You didn't see it. I did. I watched Master Roe die. Now Forbeck is gone, and I won't permit the Empire to kill us off again, not after everything we have achieved since." She took several steps towards Lucius to emphasise her point. "The Vos Empire is evil, Lucius. You know that. They have a twisted bitch in power who sends her lackeys everywhere to act in her cruel name. I will do anything – absolutely anything – to safeguard this city and my guild."

"Even if that turns you into one of them?"

She snorted. "People are going to die in this war, as they die in any war. But I won't subjugate the city. I won't lock people in the Citadel. I won't bleed them dry with taxes. I could not care less how people want to live their lives. I just want to make sure Shadowmages have a place where they can practise their art without persecution."

"And that is worth the deaths of innocents?"

"Defeating Vos is worth the deaths of a few innocents, certainly. It is a means to an end, Lucius, nothing more."

"The end does not justify this means."

He watched as Adrianna walked back to Elaine. "Well," she said. "That is not important right now. You *are* going to help me."

Knowing what was coming, Lucius asked the question anyway. "And if I refuse?"

Adriana looked at him, then crouched down beside Elaine, running her hand through the thief's hair.

"Then your bitch will die."

Elaine turned to look at Adrianna, their faces no more than a few inches apart. Lucius shuddered at the thief's murderous look, realising that, even if he managed to persuade Adrianna to release Elaine, one of them would be dead by the end of the week. He was not wholly sure whose side he would run to, if both asked for his aid.

"You give me no choice," he said softly.

"No," she said, smiling at him. "I haven't."

CHAPTER THIRTEEN

WALKING SEVERAL PACES behind Adrianna, his head bowed, Lucius' mind raced as he tried to find a way out of the horrors he was about to take part in. He would not have liked to take on Adrianna on the best of days, much less when she was prepared for him. How could he match her talent for spellcasting when she held all the cards?

At least Lucius had persuaded her to release Elaine before they embarked on this attack. Adrianna had relented to his demand too quickly for his liking, and he suspected it was all part of a game, a demonstration perhaps that she saw no difficulty in reaching Elaine once more if he reneged on his agreement. For her own part, Elaine had shown no gratitude as Lucius levitated her up the cliff face on his platform of air. Refusing to meet his gaze, she had marched back into the city. He feared what plans *she* was now making, and whether they included him.

Lengthening his stride, Lucius caught up with Adrianna as they approached the cluster of cliffside cranes and lifts that served the docks. He cleared his throat.

"You may be right about working together, Aidy," he started. "Maybe I have been concentrating too much on the thieves. You and I could target the Vos leadership of the city, maybe take out the Citadel's commander, and the Preacher Divine too – he would be a very visible loss for the Empire."

"Now you are starting to think properly, Lucius," Adrianna said. "That is a good idea, and one we will attend to in due course. However, the leadership will be weakened without their soldiers. Trust me, this way is better."

He was silent for a moment.

"So why come to me through Elaine?"

Adrianna shrugged. "Over the past few months, you have reverted back to your old ways. You have become... unreliable. She seemed the simplest route to guarantee your obedience."

"You told her about us, didn't you?"

Adrianna flashed him an amused look.

"I thought she would be interested. It hardly matters, either way," she said with a dismissive wave of her hand. "She might have cared for you quite a lot, I think. But she was not right for you. Don't pretend you were in love with her."

He looked at Adrianna curiously. "Do you think I love you?"

"I think you fear me. For the moment, that is enough."

Lucius sighed in desperation. "I can understand your anger towards Vos – I have lost at least as much myself. But you are courting madness with these attacks, Adrianna."

"Fool!" she spat. "You think me insane? You are not seeing this as I do. There is a wider world, Lucius, one beyond the petty concerns of thieves and their whores. Do you still not understand? There is a chance, a very real chance, for a better future for the Shadowmages. We just have to reach out and take it! We have suffered from leaders who have been too blind to events in the outside world, who have believed that the pure study of magic can fend off the interference of others."

"Isn't that what the Shadowmages' guild is all about?"

She ignored his question. "I will *not* fail. You, you are no different from those doddery old men, the so-called masters. You are no better. You have no gift for leadership – you handed the entire thieves' guild to that bitch because you did not know what else to do."

"Then why invest this time in me?"

"Your training as a Shadowmage is far from complete. It is time you saw exactly what we are capable of."

As they approached the nearest crane, they attracted the attention of the sweating labourers. Two decided that Adrianna would be impressed by cat calls and overly loud comments on her physique, growing lewder when she ignored them.

"I can't work with this noise," she said to Lucius. "Get rid of them."

He looked at the labourers blankly, and then back to her.

"What do you want me to do with them?"

"I really don't care," she said distractedly, and Lucius realised she had already begun to prepare her magic. "Blow them off the cliff for all it matters, though I presume you'll choose to do something less lethal."

Turning to face them, Lucius tried hard to keep an apologetic look from his face.

"Get out of here," he said to them, jerking his head in the direction of the city.

"You what?" said one of the cat callers, standing up straight from the wooden strut he had been slouched over, letting Lucius see his full height.

Looking him directly in the eye, Lucius flooded his hand with raw magical energy and hurled it to the ground just in front of the labourers' feet. With a crashing boom, it exploded, showering them in clumps of earth.

One raised his hands to show he had no argument with Lucius, and ran past him. He was quickly followed by the others, though the cat caller looked surly as he departed.

Adrianna had walked to the very edge of the cliff, where she stood, motionless, the sea wind tugging at her clothing. Eyes half-closed, she seemed serene and calm. Lucius, however, saw something very different.

He saw the threads of magic react to Adrianna's sorcery, bucking and twisting as she drew off vast amounts of energy. Then the strand fuelling the arcane forces of nature that she was attempting to control throbbed and exploded, eclipsing all the others with its radiance. It flashed and strobed as Adrianna took its power and shaped it.

The sound of waves crashing on the harbour defences, a constant noise in the city, disappeared. Mouth gaping, Lucius stared at Adrianna, seeing her eyes alight with the power she controlled. Even at the sea's calmest, when ships dared to negotiate the narrow gaps between the defences, still the waves smashed and thundered. Now, they were utterly still. The magic required to influence something so mighty dwarfed his understanding.

As the sea wind began to blow steady, its usual choppy motion calmed by Adrianna to aid the ship's passage into the harbour, she gave a wolfish smile, and once again Lucius felt the buildup of arcane force as she prepared to unleash her next spell, that would send the vessel to the seabed.

He looked at her curiously now, wondering why she had insisted he join her in this venture. Adrianna's power and ability clearly exceeded his own, by several orders of magnitude, and she certainly did not need him to scare away a handful of dock workers. So why was he there? Did she want to demonstrate to him what

Shadowmages could be capable of? Or was this some lesson in compliance, a warning if he refused her wishes in the future?

Whatever the answer, he resolved to ride her anger out for the moment, and find another way to get through to her later.

As the prow of the ship came into view, appearing from behind the central monolith that dominated the harbour, Lucius frowned.

The ship was a three-mast Vos merchantman, a broad vessel contoured to slice through the largest of rogue waves. He had been expecting to see one of the five-mast frigates the Empire favoured to move soldiers long distances around the coasts of the peninsula, bedecked with weaponry to hurl spears and blazing rocks onto a hostile shoreline.

The merchantman negotiated the harbour defences with deliberate care, sailors crossing the main deck and through the rigging and making adjustments to ensure the large ship did not approach the piers too quickly. As they caught sight of the harbour and cliffs, the sailors cheered, grateful to have survived another voyage across the churning seas. The deck soon filled with more people, streaming from belowdecks. Shielding his eyes from the sun, Lucius squinted to get a better look, as he could not imagine Vos discipline breaking down just because a friendly port had been sighted.

"Something's wrong," he said under his breath. None of those on the main deck were in uniform, and he was puzzled. It then struck him that there were children in the crowd. Some stood atop the railings that ran alongside the main deck, while others were being hoisted onto their parents' shoulders for a better look at their first sight of Turnitia.

"Adrianna, stop," he said. "You've made a mistake, that isn't the ship you think it is."

In return, she shrugged. "It will sink just as well."

Lucius looked at her uncomprehendingly until he realised that this was what she had been planning all along. The tale of more soldiers being brought in to completely flood the city was a fabrication to manipulate him into doing what she desired. Right now, she just wanted to kill.

He took her arm, forcing her to face him. Her attention diverted from the ship, she gave him a mixed look of disgust and irritation.

"Let go of me," Adrianna said.

Suppressing the impulse to swallow, he stared levelly back at her. "I am not going to let you do this."

She narrowed her eyes. "You will. One way or another, Lucius, you will, that I promise."

"More innocents?" he shouted back, losing his patience. "How much more blood are you looking to cover yourself in, Adrianna? All those families, all those children in the market not enough for you?"

"It will never be enough, don't you understand? Whether the Empire chooses to take over this city by force of arms or by colonisation, it makes no difference! Soldiers or civilians, they are both weapons used by Vos, and whichever weapon they choose to employ, I will destroy!"

Lucius could see she was serious in her decision, and cursed himself for seeing a rough sort of logic behind it, but he remained adamant.

"No, Adrianna. Just... no."

For a split second she stared balefully back at him, and he prepared himself for a blast of magic. When she did strike, she caught him completely by surprise. Balling her fist, Adrianna caught him hard on the left side of his chin.

Reeling under the forceful blow, Lucius staggered back until he found his feet. He immediately felt a surge of magic as Adrianna began building up the power to fuel a spell, aimed directly at him. He dragged on a thread, and aimed a bolt of raw energy at the ground before her feet, much as he had done with the labourers.

The crackling energy exploded as soon as it hit the ground, and knocked Adrianna back a step. As Lucius had hoped, the distraction had been enough to stall her spell, but she immediately resumed gathering energy, with far greater speed than he expected. Watching her build up to the spell's peak, he pulled on the power of two threads, more out of instinct than design, crudely fashioning them into large, wide shields that interposed themselves between the two Shadowmages.

Screaming with the intensity of its speed, the sea wind was whipped by Adrianna into a living tornado. The air currents swept past her, barely ruffling her hair, then turned and sped, arrow-straight, toward Lucius. This piston of air smashed into his hastily erected shield, and he struggled to maintain its cohesion as the invisible barrier was flayed by Adrianna's attack. Desperately, he flooded the shields with more energy, opening up a direct conduit from the magical threads.

Lucius was losing. The first shield vanished suddenly, its hold on reality vaporised by Adrianna's attack. He felt a surge of energy as she directed her attention to annihilating the last barrier between them. Gritting his teeth with the effort, he commanded the shield to become tighter and narrower, focussed against her continuous blast. It was whittled away, inch by inch, the energy he was pouring into the arcane defence sapped away quicker than it was filled.

A sharp pain exploded in his head as the last barrier broke apart, and Lucius felt a solid punch on his chest as the column of air blasted into him. He was lifted bodily off his feet and flung from the cliff, spiralling through the sky as Adrianna's magic lifted him higher and higher on a terminal arc. Then, her spell dissipated.

Lucius tumbled from the sky, his vision blurring as the world flashed past him: sky, cliffs, piers, sea, ship. Falling with mounting speed, he desperately sought to regain control of his magic but, for the first time, the threads did not appear in his mind's eye. His attention was rooted firmly on the sea as it rushed up towards him with lethal acceleration.

Lucius was falling so fast that he was struggling to breathe. Closing his eyes, he concentrated hard and dimly made out the threads of magic. They appeared, faint, but calm and serene, as if undaunted by his worldly concerns. Despite their stillness, he had difficulty in reaching out to trap one, as if they receded as he approached. Unconsciously, he opened his eyes a fraction, and saw the surface of the sea was much closer now, and moving swiftly.

Squeezing his eyes shut and clenching his fists in concentration, Lucius groped mentally for the thread he needed. It responded reluctantly to his summons and, as he tried to shape the air beneath him into an invisible platform that would arrest his descent, it fractured then danced away from him.

Panicking now, Lucius screamed in terror, knowing his life would end shortly. The scream echoed in his mind and he desperately clawed after the thread, finally grabbing the strand.

Later, he did not remember actually fashioning a spell; one moment he was fumbling with the thread, then he was in the water and sinking. The force of the impact smashed the air out of his lungs, but whatever magics he had manifested had done enough to slow his fall to a survivable level.

He was carried deep under water and, for a moment, was content to let it be so, mind and body both stunned into inaction. As his lungs began to burn, he kicked out, then reached for the surface, guided only by the dulling light of the sun. Lucius clawed his way upwards, his lungs feeling as though they were about to explode, his world becoming lighter.

As his head burst free of the water, Lucius gasped and choked. He closed his eyes and tried to control his breathing, hardly daring to believe he was still alive. A sharp splintering sound brought him back to the present.

Looking across the harbour, he saw Adrianna's magic destroying the merchantman. He felt the concussion as bolts of compressed water, summoned by Adrianna, punched into the ship's hull. As each one struck, it holed the hull below the waterline, causing splinters to spiral away from the impact. Already, the ship was listing toward the cliffs, the people on board screaming as they grabbed for support.

Feebly, Lucius tried to summon the threads of magic to their aid, though he knew he would never be able to bring enough power to bear to break Adrianna's spells. The threads remained elusive, his control over them shattered by terror and exhaustion.

Water reared up either side of the merchantman, like two huge waves that were held immobile. As one, they came down upon the deck of the ship with shattering force, and with a grinding of wood upon wood the vessel split in two. The masts smashed together in a tangle of rigging and sails as prow and stern both rose to point at the sky, while the crew and passengers on board were crushed inside the wreckage.

Some managed to escape, and Lucius started to swim to a family who had leapt clear of the ship as it broke up, the father gathering his wife and two children closer to him as they began to swim to the piers. More waves of concussion swept over Lucius as bolts of compressed water, smaller than those before but still utterly lethal, started to streak through the remaining wreckage, smashing the life out of anyone who had survived the initial attacks. Lucius stopped, treading water as he gaped at the sheer callousness of what he was witnessing.

Within minutes, all that was left floating on the calm harbour waters before him were jagged pieces of wood and sail cloth – few now recognisable as once having been part of a ship – and bodies. Sailors floated alongside families, all twisted and shattered.

Turning back to see the cliffs, he saw Adrianna, dark and indistinct. She stood motionless for a few seconds, then turned and walked back towards the city, out of sight. Lucius stared after her long after she had gone, knowing that one way or another, she had to be stopped.

He just had no idea how that was now even possible.

CHAPTER FOURTEEN

As he approached the entrance of the Red Lion, Lucius deliberately slowed his step. While this meeting of the Council was critical in planning the guild's next steps, he had no wish to confront Elaine just yet. He had seen the look in her eyes, directed at both him and Adrianna, and he knew there would be no mercy there when the time for settlement came.

It was selfish, he knew, to be more concerned about Adrianna telling Elaine of their brief liaison than about Elaine's abduction. After all, Adrianna was anything but predictable now, and there had been no guarantee that either of them would have walked out of her lair alive. Yet his infidelity, as loose as his relationships with both women had been, seemed the greater betrayal to him. It surprised him to find he actually felt ashamed.

Putting a hand on the latch of the Red Lion's heavy door, Lucius took a deep breath, then entered. The mid-afternoon crowd was light, with just a few scattered patrons nursing their drinks, and Lucius guessed that the Empire's sudden reversal of finances, courtesy of the thieves' raid on their silver train, was beginning to impact the poorer people of the city already. With a sudden tightening of alms, there was less to spend in the Red Lion.

Myrklar glanced up at Lucius as he delivered tankards to two ragged looking men, die-hard drinkers who would spend their last silver on beer even if it meant going without food. He nodded to Lucius, indicating the coast was clear of anyone he deemed suspicious.

Climbing the stairs, Lucius hoped no one would notice the feeling of dread that fell over him. He had deliberately arrived a little later than normal so Wendric and Ambrose would be there, having no wish to be alone in a room with Elaine just yet.

Before opening the door to their ad hoc meeting room, he took another deep breath, then entered. Only Elaine and Wendric were inside, and he cursed Ambrose silently for being even later than he was.

Wendric smiled his greetings, and Lucius nodded in return, but Elaine refused to look him in the eye, taking a deep interest in a stack of parchments she held on her lap. Examining each sheet in turn with great care, she seemed oblivious to Lucius' arrival.

"Well, Lucius, we certainly created a stir with that raid," Wendric said with a smile.

Taking a seat on an upturned crate, Lucius acknowledged the compliment with a wave. "We did well. All of us."

"I have a feeling that Lucius has another similar attack in mind," Wendric said, turning to Elaine. "We should get the word around that Lucius is the brain behind all of this – it could really pick up morale."

Elaine merely responded with a half-nod, not raising her gaze to either of them. Wendric cocked an enquiring look at Lucius, who just shook his head slightly. There was no need to provoke Elaine if she did not want to be brought out into the conversation, and he had no wish to air matters at this time.

"The idea was the beggars', not mine," he said simply.

"Well, true," Wendric said, deflating a little at the obvious tension between the two other thieves. "But it was you who put the plan into motion."

Lucius just shrugged at that, and all three fell into silence, interrupted only by the occasional parchment being ruffled and set aside by Elaine as she worked through the stack. Wendric, clearly unsure of what to do or say, just fidgeted, while Lucius stared into a corner, as if his mind was far away.

Ambrose finally shuffled into the room.

"You're late," Elaine said, and there was a distinctly cold edge to her tone, though Lucius doubted it was actually aimed at Ambrose.

"Ah, yes, sorry," Ambrose said, having heard the undercurrent in Elaine's words. "Small matter of a patrol, wanted to make sure they did not follow."

"Well, you are here now," Wendric said, a little too quickly. He waved Ambrose to another crate. "Let's get started. You want to go first?"

Ambrose shrugged. "I'll give you the bad news first. We are still losing thieves. They are either going independent or leaving the city altogether. Which, it has to be said, is understandable."

"Large numbers?" Wendric asked.

"Large enough. A couple of cells have fallen out of sight completely. The others are reporting thieves missing here or there."

"Any chance they have been taken by Vos rather than just leaving?" Elaine asked.

"That is possible," Ambrose conceded. "However, some of their colleagues have said that there had been talk of leaving, either us or Turnitia as a whole, beforehand. Our people are being cautious, and there is not much opportunity for Vos to act against us at the moment. To all intents and purposes, the guild is barely functioning within the city walls, and the Empire is keen to not draw attention to what little we are doing. I think most have left us voluntarily."

"They'll come back," Wendric said. "Once we start operating as a proper guild again, they'll come back."

"They won't have a choice," Elaine said firmly.

"So the raid on the silver train did nothing to encourage other thieves?" Lucius asked.

Ambrose smiled at him. "Oh, it did a great deal, I think. First, the thieves that came with us, as rich as they are, are now intensely loyal to the guild, and to you."

Lucius noticed that Elaine's eyes flickered over to him for a brief second on hearing that, and a feeling of impending doom fell across him. *My God*, he thought, *now she is thinking that I will challenge her leadership*. As Ambrose continued, he resolved to talk to Elaine sooner rather than later, their personal feelings be damned. The guild, in its current fragile state, could not take any vagaries from the Council, and he certainly wanted to avoid a dagger between the shoulder blades from one of her assassins.

"News of the raid is spreading, and people are liking what they hear. If we were not currently fragmented into cells, we would have everyone right behind us. As it is, the dispersed nature of the guild limits communication."

"That is what it was supposed to do," Elaine said, her voice stern.

"True," Ambrose allowed. "It is just a shame, that is all. Give it another couple of weeks, perhaps another raid, and we'll likely start bringing the independents back into the fold, wanting a piece of the action."

"Getting the franchises up and running will also have a similar effect," Wendric said. "Everyone knows the value of getting in at the start of a new franchise, and we will effectively be wiping the slate clean. Anyone with a bit of nous will be able to set themselves up for life."

"Competition will be fierce, then," Ambrose said.

"That is no bad thing," Elaine replied. "With competition comes better franchises and a healthier guild."

"So, you all set to conduct another raid against Vos' silver train?" Wendric asked Lucius.

"I would like to," Lucius replied slowly, thinking his plan through as he went. "We should have more support from the other thieves this time around, which is just as well, as this battle will be ten times harder. We'll have to pick a new battleground, and Vos will be prepared this time."

"What is the worst they could do?" Ambrose asked. "They had that armoured wagon last time, and a wizard and we – well, you – took care of them both."

"If I were a Vos commander responsible for the safety of the silver train after an attack like ours, I would escort it with an entire legion," Lucius said.

They fell silent again for a few moments, each considering that possibility.

"So... how would we attack a formation like that?" Ambrose asked.

"I am not sure we can," Lucius admitted. "That said, I'll give it some thought. This is what we need in the guild right now, a real bonanza that shows both Vos and the people of the city that we are not dead and buried. It will bring the thieves crawling out of the woodwork, make us a real power to be respected. From there, we can see if we can bring the Empire around to their old way of thinking – tolerate the presence of the thieves, knowing the alternative is worse."

"Sounds like a plan," Wendric said, evidently glad to have some clear direction to the meeting.

"No," Elaine said, causing Lucius to glance up at her. For the first time since she had been taken by Adrianna, their eyes met. Her glare was cold and empty, and determined. There was little left of the woman he had known before.

"We cannot rely on Lucius' plan," she said with some finality, and Lucius wondered if the reference to *his* plan was not a slight intended to let the other Council members know that his position was no longer as privileged as it had been. "We have to, finally, acknowledge that we are once again at war, this time with a far more powerful enemy than a rival thieves' guild. The simple choice before us is whether to surrender and quit or fight on."

"I'm your man, Elaine," Ambrose said. "Where you lead, I'll follow."

"I think you'll be taking on an enemy that can destroy us all," Wendric said. "But I would never let you do that without me at your side.

Lucius opened his mouth to speak, but Elaine spoke first, not bothering to hear what he had to say.

"Then war it is."

Ambrose whistled quietly, and Wendric cleared his throat.

"So, how do we assemble our forces, and what are our targets?" he asked.

"We continue with our current aims, but on a larger scale," Elaine said. "And we aim them directly into the heart of the Vos presence in the city. In running Turnitia, Vos depends on two things; a continuing flow of silver, and order. We cut off the first, and disrupt the second."

"Agreed," Wendric said. "How far do we go?"

Elaine fixed him with a cool and level gaze. "This is war, Wendric. We hit as hard as we can, as often as we can. Mobilise the cells. Rob the soldiers of their pay, raid the Cathedral, and put the word out that any trader, craftsman or merchant who openly supports Vos is our enemy. Steal their tools, drive their customers away, and burn down their shops, warehouses and homes. Conversely, those willing to help us by providing supplies or safe houses will be rewarded. Let them know that we will look favourably on their support after the war is won too – their neighbours will be paying protection money, but they won't. And if they do not agree, lean on them."

"Done right, we could turn whole districts of the city against the Empire," Ambrose reflected.

"And let it be known that anyone wearing the uniform of a Vos officer is an open target. I'll personally pay a bounty of one hundred silver for a sergeant, and five hundred for anyone of higher rank."

Wendric glanced up at her. "Is that just for thieves, or an open offer to anyone?"

Elaine opened her mouth to answer, then hesitated as she reconsidered.

"That is a good idea, Wendric," she finally said with a grim smile. "Open it to anyone. I don't fancy the chances of an untrained thug trying to claim a sergeant's head, but it will cause a great deal of chaos if mobs start attacking patrols."

"And then we keep up the pressure," Wendric said. "Keep hitting these targets, and the whole will begin to fail."

"That is what you need to arrange. However, if this is going to be successful, then the people giving orders to the soldiers will have to fear us too. It is easy enough to send a patrol of soldiers out into the city to protect the holdings of some rich merchant or break down the door of a suspected safe house, but if we can ensure that the men and women giving those orders can expect reprisals as well, then they might start thinking twice about doing it. Which will lead to more chaos as the Vos military becomes paralysed."

"That is where your assassins will come into play, I am guessing," Ambrose said.

"Of course," Elaine said simply. "And, like the thieves on the streets, we will do it in a way that will not be missed. A massacre of those in command, a message that we can reach anyone, anywhere. And that message will be clear to the successors of those we kill too."

"The only way you will do that," Lucius said, speaking at last, "is to enter the Citadel."

"Naturally. We have done it before."

Lucius shook his head. "The Citadel is better defended than it has ever been. They have far more soldiers, and—"

Elaine interrupted him. "And our assassins have become much better at what they do."

He continued, undaunted. "*And* they have much better magical support than before."

"You have beaten their wizards already," Ambrose said, frowning. "They do not seem all that much to me."

"All we have met so far are court practitioners and battle mages," Lucius said. "Whom, incidentally, you should not underestimate, Ambrose. However, there is a new force in the city, a cabal of wizards that are skilled at working together, somehow. They are extremely powerful, and capable of pretty much anything."

"How do you know this?" Ambrose asked.

"Oh, Lucius lies in many beds when it comes to magic," Elaine said, and he gave her a sour look in return. "Though for all his skill, it seems there are some mages he cannot best."

Ambrose and Wendric frowned in confusion, wondering at the animosity between the other two.

"That may be true, Elaine," Lucius said, his patience ebbing, "but I can tell you a bunch of assassins, no matter how well-trained, are going to be annihilated if they try to take on this cabal."

"We don't need *you*."

"He's right," Wendric said. "This is the Citadel we are talking about, not some lonely outpost in the wilds. Even if this cabal is not there, it would be folly to go in without Lucius. I don't pretend to understand what he does or how he does it, but the only time we have ever broken into the Citadel – and out again – was alongside him."

She glared at Wendric. "I would remind you that I am in command of this guild. I decide who does what, and when."

"And I would remind *you* that, as your lieutenant, it is my role to balance those decisions," Wendric said. "I don't give a damn what is going on between you and Lucius, but it seems to me that he is willing to work with you, and I have worked too hard getting this guild back together to squander anything on a disagreement, whatever its cause. If we lose our guildmistress now, that will be the end. The guild will fold, and you do not have the authority to make *that* decision."

"He's right," Ambrose said, adding his support.

Elaine glanced briefly at the floor, fuming.

"Fine," she said.

The meeting developed into a series of discussions covering the technical details of what they had decided, much to the relief of Wendric and Ambrose. Names were drawn up for specific missions, meeting places agreed and targets decided. It was resolved that decoys would be needed for many of the tasks they hoped to accomplish, in order that the thieves would be able to work without interference from Vos patrols. Ambrose's children would once again have gainful employment.

Finally, Elaine called an end to the meeting and, buoyed with the thought of definite action, Wendric and Ambrose left in high spirits to begin their part in the coming war against Vos. Elaine had been content to watch them leave, but when she saw Lucius had hung back, she stood up abruptly and started for the door. Lucius put a firm hand on the door, holding it closed, and she glared at him.

"Elaine, we need to speak," he said.

"I have nothing to say to you," she spat back. "I sent you out to get us new allies, and instead one of them attacks me – me! – directly."

"I had no idea she would do that! I tried to convince her to join us, but she–"

"Oh, I know well how hard you tried to convince her," Elaine interrupted him. "A difficult and exhausting task, I am sure."

Lucius tried another course.

"Alright, Elaine, have it your way. I know I made mistakes, and I doubt you'll ever appreciate how much I regret what has happened. Either way, you and I can't give a damn about it while we are fighting against the Empire. The consequences of us falling out could hurt too many others."

"Why do you think you are still here in the Council?" she asked. "This guild is the most precious thing to me, and I won't let you or anyone else destroy it. So, for now, you stay. And you do as you are told."

She stepped to one side of him and put her hand on the door's handle. Sighing in defeat, he moved away to let her past, but Elaine stayed for a moment longer.

"When this is over, I want you out," she said. "Out of the Council, out of the guild, and out of the city. I never want to so much as hear of you again, and you know I have my own ways to make sure that happens."

Elaine opened the door and turned back to him with an expression of disgust.

"I will never trust you again."

CHAPTER FIFTEEN

THE EVENTS OF the past few days had come as something of a shock to Elouise. Her affiliation to the thieves' guild had been born out of disaffection with the society into which her family had tried to propel her. Endless lessons in etiquette with alternative Vos and Pontaine influences – whichever her family happened to be trying to impress at the time – watching her tongue against unguarded comments, the fashionable balls, ridiculous clothes, the petty politicking that was all the more vicious because there was no real penalty for failure... the list went on.

So she had become a thief, stealing away when her family was not watching, or when she was supposed to be with some man of "quality" that her parents wanted her to court. Thieves did not ask questions, and were interested only in her abilities which, over time, had grown to some measure of competence.

Elouise had no illusions about becoming some criminal master, but the occasional raids and burglaries she attended under the leadership of senior thieves gave her life some substance, and not a little excitement. It had turned out to be quite profitable, too.

That part of her life had turned on its head when Vos had cracked down on the guild, tearing apart its headquarters and beheading those it caught. All of a sudden, being a thief was not as much fun as it used to be, and she had fled into the arms of her family and the society in which they moved. The irony that she had sought sanctuary among the same Vos nobles that had hounded her thievish comrades was not lost on her.

When she heard the thieves' guild was not only still alive but was beginning to fight back, Elouise had been dubious. Being chased by the guard, even caught and fined, might shame her family, but she could shrug it off. She could not dismiss the executioner's axe so easily. However, she had been sympathetic to the plight of her old friends, and stayed in touch. When they returned and said they were planning a massive strike against the Empire, and that there was a role for her, something perhaps closer to her ideals of personal safety, she had accepted the challenge.

So it was she found herself in the Five Markets, clothed in the tight fitting leather tunic and trews that she adopted when engaged in her thievish duties. Trailed at some distance by a group of seven teenage boys, Elouise inspected the vendors and stalls she passed with some care.

Already briefed on which stalls to concentrate on, she carefully gauged each, looking for telltales that would reveal the trader's allegiance. Whenever she came across a trader who spoke with a heavy Vos accent or whose wares were of obvious Imperial origin, Elouise would lean forward and rest a hand on the side of the stall, hunched as if inspecting the goods closely. If her suspicions were confirmed, she would tap her fingers, three times.

Across the other side of the pathway between the lines of stalls, a group of boys gossiped, the breadth of their conversation ranging between girls of their own age, and those perhaps a little older, and who among them would win a free-for-all brawl. They were ignored by traders and passers-by alike, just a typical group of kids wasting time in the markets.

Anyone watching more closely might have noticed that the tallest of the group, a reedy boy called Mattais, spent little time engaged in the debates of his friends, his attention fixed firmly on a young woman as she moved from trader to trader. Every now and then, he would lean across to one of his friends and whisper something, perhaps a simple observation, perhaps an instruction.

Watching all of this, Jake stood with his back to a pile of stacked crates. Arms crossed, he hopped from foot to foot absent-mindedly with impatience, waiting for the fun to start.

Turning away from the older boys for a moment, he sought out Michelle and Emma from amongst the crowd, two girls he had never worked with before. They were easy to spot, as both wore bright tunics, of red and of green, guaranteed to attract attention.

Both were about eight or nine, a little younger than him, but he had been suspicious of them, instead wanting to rejoin his old team. However, when Ambrose had visited with news that the pickpockets were going back into business, the old thief had insisted this was a special team, with each member selected for one primary reason –

all three were exceptionally good runners, and knew the alleys of the Five Markets better than anyone.

This reasoning, the creation of an "elite" team as Jake liked to think of it, had put him in high spirits and he could not wait to get started. He caught Michelle's eye, trying to hurry her on. She shrugged and cast her head about, inspecting those closest to her, and inclined her head, surreptitiously indicating a family that pushed through the crowd past her.

Assessing the mark, Jake smiled. The family was obviously from a humble background, the father probably a craftsman who worked hard for every silver he earned. He also looked fit, and should not drop out of a chase too soon. Jake nodded to Michelle, who grabbed Emma's attention, and then he looked back to see if Elouise was ready.

She was. Jake uncrossed his arms, letting her know that his team was in place and ready to strike. In answer, she reached up and, with great deliberation, tied back her long hair.

The signal was given.

Sidling up to the craftsman, Michelle reached for his belt pouch and, using a tiny blade, sliced the leather straps that held it in place. It dropped neatly into her hand, but instead of turning away with her stolen money, Michelle tripped and brushed against the man.

He looked down at her, frowning, then his hand went instinctively to his belt as he realised that he had been robbed. Giving a cheeky grin, Michelle turned and ran into the crowd, the craftsman just a few feet behind her, giving pursuit.

As the craftsman's family raised the cry of "Thief!" soldiers began to move into the crowd, closing in on Michelle from several angles. Her bright red tunic made it impossible to escape their attention.

Squeezing through the crowd, dodging the grasping hands of citizens quick enough to spot what was happening, Michelle was joined by Emma, and the two girls ran side by side for a few paces as the pouch switched hands. Then, they split, both running as fast as they could in separate directions.

"No, it is that one, the one in green!" the craftsman shouted to the nearest soldiers, pointing at Emma as she sped away.

Confused, the soldiers split up, trying to chase both girls now, but their carefully constructed ring, designed to hem in a pickpocket, had been shattered. People were thrown to the side as the soldiers barrelled past them, sweating hard in their armour as they tried to keep up with the children.

Seeing the soldiers occupied with the pickpockets, Mattais whistled to his friends, and they immediately halted their conversations. As one, they charged the first stall that Elouise had picked out for them, kicking the table over onto the terrified vendor. Goods were crushed underfoot or thrown out into the crowd, where people scrabbled for them, causing more obstacles for the soldiers.

Smiling at the chaos that reigned through the market, Jake trotted over to the drop-off point near a textiles trader. A minute later, Emma came pounding past him, soldiers hot on her heels. She flashed a smile at him as he held out a hand, keeping it low near his waist.

Brushing past him like a feather, Emma kept on running, jinking suddenly as she headed for one of the alleys that ran out of the market. Jake had to jump out of the way of the soldiers who, in their frustration, were beginning to flatten anyone who did not move quickly enough.

Seeing them disappear after Emma, Jake walked away casually, feeling the weight of the stolen pouch within his own tunic.

HIS HEAD HUNCHED over the table, Reinhardt Perner cursed as he read the figures on the sheet before him, over and again. The conclusion was inescapable.

The Vos councillor had been right; more customers were indeed coming to the city. However, the taxes now levied on his business were sucking him dry. The figures did not lie. He was working harder than ever, but earning no more than before.

Sighing, he reached across the table to grasp his beaker of wine but he halted, the drink at his lips. He sniffed at the wine and placed it back on the table. Even the imported vintages lost their taste when his finances were looking so bad.

The sound of a scuffle at his front door caused him to lean to one side to look past the sacks of corn stacked around the central pillar of the main shop floor. With alarm, he realised that the Vos soldier posted outside was brandishing his spear at someone just out of sight on the street. As Reinhardt watched, a scrawny man in ill-fitting clothes sneaked up behind the soldier and with a single, swift motion, stabbed him in the ribs with a broad-bladed dagger. The man withdrew his blade and stabbed the man again and again.

Rendered speechless and immobile with alarm, Reinhardt watched helplessly as more men appeared and the soldier, his struggles growing ever more feeble as blood poured out of his side, was dragged into the shop and dumped on the floor. Stepping over the body, the scrawny man walked over to Reinhardt's table and sat himself opposite. He reached over for the beaker of wine and, after sniffing it suspiciously, downed it a series of gulps.

"Good evening, Mr Perner," the scrawny man said with a leer.

Behind him, other thieves spread out around the shop, selecting sacks of grain, small barrels of ale and cuts of beef. Reinhardt started to stand, his mouth open to protest, but the scrawny man brought his attention back to the table as the large dagger was produced once more, still wreathed in the soldier's blood, and slammed hard, point first, into the table.

"Now, don't you go worrying about my friends there, Mr Perner," the scrawny man said. Reinhardt sat back down, his attention fixed on the dagger embedded in his table, blood running down its blade and pooling on the varnished wood.

"You've been a little bit naughty, haven't you, Mr Perner?"

Reinhardt looked up, blankly.

"What do you mean?" he managed to say.

"Oh, don't be so coy, Mr Perner," the scrawny man said. "You have been just a little bit naughty. Talking to those nasty, rude, Vostypes. And getting them to put a soldier on your doorstep, if you please! It seems you don't remember your old friends, Mr Perner, and that makes us sad."

Realisation began to dawn on Reinhardt, and he closed his eyes as his shoulders slumped. He suddenly knew exactly where this was going.

"What do you want?"

"Well, Mr Perner, we are not greedy men, as you well know, and we really only have your best interests at heart. Even though you have been naughty recently, we are willing to forego all that nastiness. And we won't even be charging interest. Just see to our man when he comes around for the collections every week, and we'll say no more about it. Seems to me that is very fair."

"I can't..."

"What was that, Mr Perner, I could not quite hear you." The scrawny man had stood up, and was now towering over Reinhardt as he leaned over the table.

When Reinhardt finally looked up, the thief could see the worry and fear in the trader's eyes.

"Vos is taxing me through the teeth. I don't *have* anything else!"

The scrawny man took a step back and stood up straight, rubbing a hand across his chin as if in deep thought.

"Well, that *is* a problem, and no mistake," he said. "I could quite easily see how a man might be ruined when he pays two masters, and neither of us want that, do we, Mr Perner?"

Reinhardt shook his head dumbly.

"Seems to me that you can pay us or pay Vos. Hmm... Best you pay us, I think. It would be better for both you and your family. Yes, I am convinced, you are better off paying us. We'll take care of any nasty men Vos sends your way, just like we took care of that poor sad bastard lying on your floor. In the meantime..."

Plucking the dagger from the table in one heave, the scrawny man turned and grabbed the nearest sack of corn, slinging it over his shoulder. He put his other hand to his mouth and whistled. Another thief trotted in, carrying a lighted torch, its flames flickering as it passed through the threshold of the shop. As Reinhardt looked on, the thief began to dip the torch in amongst the dry sacks, then tossed it onto a bale of cloth stacked along a wall.

The scrawny man waved cheerfully as he left with the other thieves, ignoring Reinhardt's plaintive wail as the man rushed across his shop, trying desperately to extinguish the flames with his cloak.

"Think he got the message?" asked the thief who had thrown the torch as they began to walk up Lantern Street.

The scrawny one smiled. "Aye, I believe we did good work there."

"Didn't we just burn down his entire shop?" asked another.

"Nah, he'll put out the flames, if he moves fast enough. And I'll wager he will, men tend to be motivated when their livelihood is at stake. He'll lose a good portion of stock in the process, though."

"Well, that will just make it harder for him to pay us later in the week, surely?"

"It will teach him that, between us and Vos, we are the ones that should be feared. Vos will just arrest him for non-payment of fines. We can finish him off completely." The scrawny man looked over his shoulder as thin trails of smoke began to pour out of the windows and door of Perner's General Stores. "Right now, that is what is important."

LEANING CAUTIOUSLY AROUND the side of the tall wooden warehouse, Grayling watched the red-liveried soldiers of the Vos patrol march stiffly across the street junction a few dozen yards away. As always, they were right on time, their carefully planned misdirection using multiple patrols and rotating routes easily predicted by thieves who had watched them for days on end.

Pulling back, Grayling unslung her short bow and drew a single arrow from the quiver strapped to her back. She took one deep breath, then stepped away from the warehouse, in full view of the soldiers. Aiming for just a second, she let the arrow fly, and watched it thud with a dull smack into the chest of the rearmost soldier along the line.

To their credit, the soldiers reacted quickly, the sergeant shouting commands as his men unshouldered their spears and began to charge towards Grayling. Ice ran in the short thief's veins for a second as she watched the heavily armed and armoured soldiers start pounding for her. Keeping her bow in hand, she turned and ran back around the warehouse, raising her fingers to her mouth to whistle as she went, praying the others heard the signal.

Angry at having already lost one of their own, the soldiers flew around the corner. The sergeant, leading the squad, was run down in a flurry of hooves as another thief, riding a large grey horse, smashed into him. Throwing themselves to either side, the other soldiers managed to escape the horse's impact, but their formation was instantly scattered and, with their sergeant out cold and not giving orders, they split up. A handful continued the chase after Grayling, while the rest tried giving chase to the rogue horse rider, throwing their spears uselessly after him.

Seeing that she was still being followed, Grayling crossed the street and dived into a short dark alley between two more warehouses. A low, terrible growl faced her within the alley, and she kept to one wall, moving quickly but carefully. Lunging from the shadows, a large black mastiff slavered as it barked and strained against its chain to reach her.

Holding a hand out in a futile attempt to calm the creature, Grayling quickly passed it, and hoisted herself over the six-foot fence crossing the alley. She heard the soldiers just steps behind her and unsnared the mastiff's chain from the hook on her side of the fence. The threatening growls changed into a roar from the dog and screams from the soldiers as the mastiff was unleashed.

Trotting out of the opposite end of the alley, Grayling looked up and down the wide road into the merchants' quarter of Turnitia, dominated on all sides by the long warehouses that handled most of the city's trade. A little further along, another thief was being hotly pursued by more Vos soldiers and, seeing the opportunity, Grayling whipped out another arrow and sent it flying. It buried itself in the back of one soldier's leg.

Realising that his squad was in danger, this sergeant barked orders, and one man split off from the rest, running away from the thieves and into the main part of the city. The others continued after their original quarry, leaving their wounded comrade in the middle of the street, writhing in pain as he clutched his wounded leg.

Grayling let the single runner go, knowing full well where the man was headed and how necessary it was to the thieves that he remain untouched, however tempting a target he might present. Instead, Grayling had already settled on her prey – news of the guildmistress' bounty on sergeants had swept through the thieves, and she intended to be the first to claim it.

Running after the fast disappearing squad, she tore past the wounded soldier, breaking her stride only to kick the man hard in the face. The tables had turned, and the forces of Vos were going to feel the wrath of the thieves.

The squad, fixated on the thief they were chasing, pursued him into a warehouse whose doors had been left wide open. As soon as the last soldier ran past the threshold, two thieves jumped from behind a wagon next to the warehouse. Moving swiftly, they flung the doors shut, driving a wooden pole through the handles to seal the entrance.

More thieves appeared from the surrounding area, armed with burning torches, and set light to spots along the walls of the warehouse that had been prepared with lamp oil. The flames took hold fast, and the thieves retreated, dooming the soldiers inside, and eager to move on to the next task. Grayling, however, slowed as she approached the warehouse and waited, pacing outside the building.

The flames clawed their way up the sides of the warehouse, and thick black smoke began to pour into the sky. After a few minutes, Grayling was ready to give up, presuming the men inside had already succumbed to the roiling smoke, if not the flames. Then she heard a crash from the opposite side of the building, and she sprinted around, readying another arrow.

A section of the wall splintered at about head height as she rounded the corner, then the thin wedge of an axe blade appeared as someone started to hack their way clear of the growing inferno. After a few more blows, smoke started pouring out of the gaps growing in the warehouse's wooden walls. The axe blows stopped and the wall thudded once, twice, then three times, as if something heavy was being thrown against it.

In a crash of splintering wood, the sergeant burst through the weakened wall, coughing and spluttering from the smoke as he fell to his knees. Grayling gave a low whistle that made the sergeant look up at her, straight into the point of an arrow. Releasing the string, Grayling smiled as the shaft was buried in the sergeant's throat, its bloody head emerging from the back of his neck. Stooping down, Grayling took the bronze sergeant's crest from the man's chest. The sergeant pawed weakly at Grayling, desperate for aid, but she pocketed the crest and turned, content to let the man die slowly in pain.

Wanting to see how other thieves were faring, Grayling retraced her steps but came to a sudden stop when she reached the main street leading into the district. The runner sent by the sergeant she had just killed had done his work.

Marching down the street, the Vos military had arrived in force. A dozen squads moved toward her in unison, brandishing spears, swords and shields, armed for a real battle. Grayling vowed that the thieves would give them one.

She sent an arrow soaring toward the assembled ranks, but the range was too great and the shot fell short. It was enough to catch the soldiers' attention, though, and two squads detached themselves from the main body to pursue her.

Grayling immediately retreated, diving back among the warehouses and locating a storm drain she had earlier marked as a point of retreat. Lifting the grate, she lowered herself inside quickly, slipping and sliding down the wet, moss-strewn tunnel into the sewers. Too excited to even notice the stench, she quickly got her bearings and headed east to begin the next phase of the plan. With any luck, they would soon have half the soldiers of Turnitia in the merchants' quarter, tied up and useless as they chased fleeting shadows.

DRAWING HIS CLOAK around him, Lucius blew into his cupped hands to ward off the coming evening chill. Balanced on a ledge that wrapped around the spire of a chapel, he had a good vantage point over much of the city and, more importantly, the closest wall of the Citadel.

The chapel was a new construction, one of several that had sprouted up around the city as the Final Faith spread its influence. There were plenty of rich nobles and wealthy merchants who were keen to curry favour with Vos officials by demonstrating their piety in commissioning their own chapels, and these places of worship were quickly filled by less well-off citizens who had their own reasons to attend the regular Mass.

The whole western end of the city, from the Five Markets to the harbour, was in chaos. Fires raged in both shops and warehouses, each carefully targeted by the thieves, and soldiers ran in the streets from disturbance to disturbance with little direction. Columns of smoke rose across the city, the black fog gathering into a great cloud above the streets that smeared across the face of Kerberos' giant sphere; an unintended consequence, but a welcome one.

Their plan was working, that much was clear, Lucius decided as he turned his gaze to the Citadel. Though the fortress was too vast for him to see as a whole from the chapel, he could see the nearest facing wall was undermanned, the few scattered soldiers on its ramparts peering over into the city, wondering when they would be called to rougher duty. Several dead soldiers had already been carried into the gatehouse, nestled in the belly of one of the Citadel's giant towers.

In the shadow of the great wall, Lucius saw other forms moving. The assassins of the thieves' guild had gathered in force for the strike they planned tonight; all the disruption enacted by the other thieves was merely the prelude to unbalance the forces of Vos and give this attack the best chance of success.

The assassins had already begun swarming toward the wall, taking up their final positions before they launched the assault. Some stayed on the ground, using alleys and walls for cover, while others gathered on rooftops. Together, they spanned one great wall, the furthest moving up past the great tower to the next wall.

Shifting his position, Lucius took a couple of steps around the ledge until he was behind the spire, hidden from any spying eyes on the Citadel's wall. His eyes adjusted to the gloom as he looked into the alleys below. He spotted the form he was looking for and gave a short wave. There was a flash of a toothy grin as the young boy below waved back and ran off. Within minutes, the boy would reach Ambrose, and the Pontaine rockets the veteran thief had acquired from a friendly trader the day before.

"So, it begins," Lucius muttered to himself, as he clambered down the side of the chapel, the stepped stone construction of one of its buttresses aiding his descent. He dropped down into the chapel's grassy grounds, and trotted into the empty market that sprawled before the great tower. Moving quietly, he took his place behind a tall wooden stall, its tenant having long since disappeared after the day's trade. Two assassins waited patiently for him.

After glancing to check it was Lucius who approached, Elaine turned from him to look pointedly at the skyline.

"Ambrose is late," she said, gesturing at the empty, smoke-filled sky.

"No," Lucius said coolly, not wanting to start an argument just before the assault began. "There is still time."

The assassins had split into three-man teams, the better to support one another on what would be a very difficult attack. Lucius had seen Elaine's face when she realised that everyone else had simply presumed he would be on her team, and he knew she had not been comfortable with the idea. It frustrated him in turn to think Elaine would not trust him on a mission, regardless of their own personal issues.

He found the third member of their team, Heinrich, harder still to deal with. He was a typical stone-cold killer, the archetypal assassin who killed without thought or conscience for silver. He had taken a dislike to the man instantly, and this was only magnified as he watched Heinrich and Elaine make their final preparations for the assault. Lucius knew Elaine trusted the man and might even call him a friend, but it was not until he saw Heinrich reach over and adjust the scabbards holding Elaine's twin swords on her back that it occurred to him that they could be sleeping together.

That darkened his mood, as he continued to watch them out of the corner of his eye, noting every point of physical contact they made.

He checked himself, then smiled self-consciously. Was that jealously he was feeling? Lucius sighed. The noise pricked the ears of both Elaine and Heinrich, and they threw irritated glares at him which he waved off dismissively.

The hell with it, he thought, *Elaine can sleep with whomever she likes*. He really did not give a damn any more. There were more important things in his life than in whose bed he lay.

With a shrieking whistle that shrilled across the entire city, a column of sparkling fire rose into the sky from close by, then exploded beneath the pall of smoke hanging above. The flash lit up the city for a fraction of a second, then more trails of fire rose into the sky, one after the other, to explode. Ambrose had unleashed both a signal to the assassins and a distraction to the remaining guards within the Citadel who, even now, were running along the walls to get a closer look at the fire trails as they hung for a few seconds in the sky before winking out. Lucius knew Elaine felt the same relief he did that the rockets had worked as intended.

"That's it, go!" Elaine hissed as she rose, running for the wall and keeping her head low, Heinrich close behind.

Along other sections of the wall, the other assassins were moving in. Some, like Heinrich, were swinging grapples up past the crenellations running along the top of the wall; others scaled the walls with climbing spikes or used heavy crossbows to drive bolts trailing rope into the stone wall of the Citadel and swiftly cross the void. Lucius had no idea how the devices had been rescued from the guildhouse before the Vos attack, and began to wonder what else Elaine had managed to save. If nothing else, she was a most capable guildmistress.

Heinrich was already scaling the rope, having ensured the grapple at the top of the wall was secure. Lucius followed, trying not to grunt with the effort, conscious that Heinrich was making it look very easy. As soon as Heinrich swung his boots over the top of the wall, Lucius heard the sounds of a sword fight above him and started to climb faster. While he did not like the man, Lucius knew of his reputation and did not relish the idea of penetrating the Citadel without him.

Peering over the wall before throwing himself over, Lucius saw Heinrich to his right, engaged with two Vos soldiers. One cowered away from the assassin's paired long and short swords behind his shield, his own blade only occasionally flickering out to test an opening. The other stayed behind the first soldier, jabbing at Heinrich with a spear.

Lucius pulled himself over the wall and drew his own weapons, a sword and dagger, before wading in to help Heinrich. There was space on the wide rampart for them to fight side by side, and the soldiers began to give way under their combined assault.

Ducking a thrust of the spear, Lucius slammed his dagger into the top of the shield, forcing the soldier to duck. Lucius hooked his sword under the shield's bottom edge and heaved upwards, and Heinrich stabbed forward with his long sword, a smooth and supple movement that tore through the soldier's mailed shirt to cleave his heart. As the man dropped, Lucius and Heinrich advanced on the remaining soldier, who backed off a few steps to give himself room, the tip of his spear darting forward at head height to slow their step. Lucius could see the soldier assessing the situation, casting a glance at the dead man now behind his attackers and realising his position was desperate.

With a loud cry, the soldier stepped forward and swung his spear sideways, hoping to use the weapon's momentum and his own strength to knock his attackers flat. Heinrich ducked under the blow, but it nearly blind-sided Lucius, who had expected the assassin to block the attack. At the last second, Lucius raised his sword to catch the spear, the blade biting deep into the shaft. Twisting his wrist slightly so the spear could not easily be withdrawn, Lucius tried to pull back, but the soldier had a better grip on his weapon and when he heaved, Lucius followed, stumbling forward.

The soldier took another step back, frantically trying to shake his weapon free, but Lucius and Heinrich were quicker. Even as the spear came free of the sword, Lucius' dagger was plunging into the soldier's neck and Heinrich's own blades were thrust deep into his stomach.

The soldier sank to the floor as Lucius and Heinrich ripped their weapons free. Lucius was about to compliment Heinrich on his style, but a thunder of heavy footsteps and rattling chain caught his ear.

He whirled around to see a third soldier who, having crept up behind them during the fight, now charged at Lucius' back. Lucius spun to face the man, trying to bring his sword into a defensive position against the blow, knowing already that he was too slow. The soldier had raised his sword high above his head for a vicious downward cleave that would split Lucius' skull in two – and then he stopped.

Lucius frowned as the soldier looked at him blankly, sword still held high. With a crash, the man collapsed to his knees, and then fell flat on his face, his sword clattering away before tipping over the edge of the wall to fall into the courtyard below. From his back, a throwing knife protruded.

Beyond the fallen soldier, Lucius saw Elaine clawing her way onto the wall, and he smiled.

"Thanks," he said with genuine relief, and ignored the sour look he received in return.

Elaine glanced at the dead soldiers and then into the compound below. Dominated by the central keep, the bailey was a hive of activity, with the authoritative shouts of officers organising squads of soldiers into platoon and company before dispatching them to various parts of the city. The inner walls were strewn with outbuildings built along their length, a variety of stables, guardhouses, blacksmiths, and stores.

Elsewhere along the wall, more assassins had entered the Citadel, and three teams had already descended into the bailey, engaging the closest soldiers before the Vos forces had time to react. As the officers began to notice the presence of intruders, more and more soldiers peeled away from their formations to take up arms, but the assassins in the courtyard quickly melted away, retreating to the walls or to the towers, where the tighter confines would favour their style of battle, not the soldiers'.

Gesturing for them to follow, Elaine started running along the wall, heading for a stone bridge that ran from the nearest tower to a large gate mounted halfway up the side of the keep itself. As Lucius followed, he eyed the keep, the massive fortified structure that was the centre of all Vos operations and government in the city. He remembered being inside it once before, as a captive.

This time, he vowed, the upper hand would stay with the thieves and their trained killers.

CHAPTER SIXTEEN

THE PASSAGE WAS lit by slow-burning torches that sputtered in wrought-iron brackets as Elaine closed the heavy door, filling the passage with a tangle of wavering shadows until the light steadied. Voices could be heard far off, commanding and authoritative, as the men of the Citadel struggled to keep a rein on the chaos in the city.

Crouching in the shadows, Elaine, Heinrich and Lucius paused with weapons drawn, alert for any reaction to their entrance. The battle within the tower and along the bridge that connected it to the keep had been fierce but brief, and dominated by the assassins. Other teams had briefly joined them and the defenders of the tower, depleted by the need for soldiers to control the city, had been wiped out quickly.

Now they were alone, the other teams having moved off to different areas of the keep. They had all been briefed on a broad range of targets, from the mysterious Commander of the Citadel himself, to various functionaries and officials responsible for the day-to-day running of Turnitia. However, if they were Vos-born and had a measure of authority, anyone could be considered fair game this evening.

While most teams were heading for the higher levels of the keep, where they expected to find most ranking individuals, and a few stayed near ground level where soldiers were still assembling, Elaine led her team underground, into the darkest reaches of the Citadel.

Lucius had guessed why, and who she was hoping to find there. For his part, he was happy with the assignment, for he had been incarcerated within the dungeons of the Citadel in the past, however briefly, and was familiar with the area.

Holding up one hand and pointing forward, Heinrich padded ahead, following distant voices. A few paces behind, Lucius and

Elaine followed, senses straining, determined not to be caught flat-footed should a soldier or official inadvertently happen upon them.

Moving silently, foot by foot, they followed Heinrich, trusting to his keen senses and memorised maps of the Citadel. While the guild had never been able to put together a complete plan of the keep – the Vos military being very careful to guard the identities of its architects – years of bribery, trespass and even incarceration had all led to pages upon pages of maps being compiled and revised. The final picture, while not yet complete, had been invaluable to the assassins while planning the assault.

The light became brighter and voices louder as they ventured into the more populated areas of the Citadel. The corridor widened suddenly and opened onto a long balcony. Hugging the wall as he moved out into the open, Lucius saw they were in one of the keep's large halls, the balcony running along three sides of the immense space to a long, wide staircase that ran to the ground floor.

The hall's floor was a war of order against confusion. Soldiers tried to assemble in tight ranks as their commanding officers gave them instructions for deployment within the city, while officials ran between desks, clutching bundles of parchment. To one side, wine and steaming food were being served to a group of richly dressed men and women – high-ranking members of the city's government, Lucius supposed – while messengers and runners wound their way through the milling crowd, passing in and out of the many doors that lined the hall.

Across the hall, on the other side of the balcony, Lucius saw another two of their assassination teams. He saw their leaders picking targets out from among the crowd and wished them luck striking a few Vos officials down before being discovered and forced to retreat. Beside him, Elaine hissed, and gestured to the wide staircase.

In his full Final Faith regalia, the Preacher Divine had appeared, wreathed in white and trailing his red cloak behind him. Leaning on his staff, Alhmanic mounted the first few steps, then turned to face the churning mob, stretching out his arms to either side.

"Silence!" His voice rang out across the hall, its deep tone cutting across all other conversation. Officers stopped giving orders; officials and servants instantly halted their own discussions mid-sentence.

"This is a time of trial, my friends," Alhmanic said, once he was sure everyone was paying him his due attention. "The criminal elements of the city have turned against us, as we knew they would. But they have made a grave error! For our prey have revealed themselves. Now, instead of sending our brave men into the darkest and dirtiest regions of the city, we can strike them down in a single evening!"

"Would like to see you try," Lucius heard Elaine mutter, and he smiled.

"Remember this, all you of Faith," Alhmanic continued, unaware that a number of assassins had already marked him for a dead man and were even now taking aim. "You do God's work this evening, and your actions are blessed. Together, we will make this city a true child of the Empire, elevating Vos beyond our weak, decadent enemies in Pontaine."

The Preacher Divine went on, but the attentions of Lucius and Elaine were caught by Heinrich, who pointed out a single Vos officer. Wearing the gold epaulets and braid of the military, along with the cropped beard common among the higher ranks, he seemed unremarkable, perhaps no higher than a captain in rank. While that made him a viable target nonetheless, Lucius looked back at Heinrich quizzically.

"That's the Commander of the Citadel, I am sure," Heinrich said.

Elaine frowned. "You certain?"

"The description fits."

"The uniform doesn't," Lucius pointed out, remembering the last commander he had faced, a rich and respected baron. The post of the Citadel's commander was highly sought after, even though Turnitia was still technically outside the Empire's borders. It was generally presumed that it would one day become another Vos city, in name as well as fact, and that meant there were plenty of opportunities here for an ambitious noble. As effective ruler of the city, the commander could do pretty much as he pleased.

"I would say he has learned the lesson of his predecessor," Heinrich said with a rare smile. "He is not drawing attention to himself.

Holding up a hand, Heinrich caught the gaze of a leader in one of the other teams. The two assassins exchanged hand signals for a moment, then the other gave a nod of assent. Heinrich grunted.

"Dressing down will not help the commander now. Come, we should move on."

Creeping along the wall, Heinrich led them to a thin spiral staircase set into the wall and started to descend, sword in hand and ready to spit anyone who should happen to be moving upwards. As Lucius set foot on the first stair, a shriek of pain behind made him look back.

The assassins had started their attack, launching a barrage of knives and arrows at selected targets among the crowd below. Lucius followed an arrow as it lanced through the air and smacked into the Preacher Divine's shoulder with a wet thud. The big man went down with a howl, dropping his staff and clutching at the wound as he rolled down the staircase.

Elsewhere, the agents of Vos were falling with knives in their throats and backs, or else impaled on arrows and bolts. Gradually, they began to recover, officers ducking behind their own men as they assembled rough shield and crossbow lines, while others charged past the wounded Preacher Divine up the staircase to assault the balcony, but after their initial strike the assassins had already retreated. The two teams split and headed deeper into the interior of the keep to continue murdering ranking members of the Vos military and government.

Nodding his satisfaction, Lucius dived into the spiral staircase before anyone thought to look in his direction. As he trotted down the stairs, circling around and again, he started to gain on Elaine, ahead of him. She passed by an entrance leading into the hall, just as a shadow clouded the threshold.

A Vos soldier shoved his head inside the narrow space, having seen movement inside. He spotted Lucius rushing toward him and looked up, alarmed. Fumbling with his scabbarded sword, hindered in the enclosed space, the soldier opened his mouth to shout a warning to his allies in the hall, but was cut off by Lucius' blade burying itself deep in one side of his chest. Lucius caught his fall and lowered him to the floor, glancing through the entrance to the hall.

It had started to empty, with officials running for their lives and soldiers eager to avenge the deaths of their comrades on the assassins. No one was looking his way, and Lucius heaved the soldier's body further into the staircase, lest it be spotted.

There was nowhere else to stash the body, and Lucius knew it would soon be discovered. Trusting to fate, he carried on down the winding stairs into the foundations of the keep. As they opened into a wide, dank corridor, Lucius was greeted by Elaine's withering stare.

"For the love of all that is holy," she whispered. "Keep up!"

He shrugged in reply.

Further along the corridor, Heinrich hissed at them to both be silent and, exchanging looks, Lucius and Elaine moved forward to join him.

Deep beneath the Citadel, the corridors were walled with rougher stone, giving the walls an irregular appearance. The air was cool and damp, with fewer of the slow-burning torches bracketed to the walls. No doubt that helped provide an atmosphere of despair to those incarcerated within, but Lucius was thankful for the shadows they provided.

Advancing cautiously up the corridor, they were soon brought to a halt by a raised palm from Heinrich. He glanced back and held up two fingers, then made a slicing movement across his throat. Two guards ahead.

Straining into the gloom, Lucius picked out a set of alcoves a few yards ahead, though it took him a few more seconds to make out the forms of two soldiers, partly hidden in the recesses on either side of the corridor. Before he could ready his weapons, Heinrich and Elaine were already padding ahead, hugging the walls.

Deciding that this was a task best left to professionals, Lucius hung back, ready to support either should their slaying go awry. He need not have worried.

The two assassins moved slowly but with intent. Swords drawn, they held the blades back behind them, careful not to reveal their presence by an inadvertent flash of torchlight from the naked metal. They froze for a few seconds when the soldiers exchanged a few words, indistinct from where Lucius crouched, but the tone was one of complaint, perhaps a mutter about their shift patterns, locked into the dungeons while their colleagues swept through the city restoring order.

When the assassins moved again, it was as one, and with speed. As Elaine dashed the last few feet to her target, Heinrich copied her motions on his side of the wall. Lucius heard a gasp from the guards as each saw the other's attacker, but the assassins whirled like tightly wound springs, their blades sweeping through the air to embed themselves in the soldiers' stomachs. In the same movement, Elaine and Heinrich grabbed the soldiers' mouths while twisting their swords, holding the men rigid with pain yet silent.

They lowered the dying men to the floor, then slit their throats. The assassins pushed the bodies further into the alcoves, clearing the way. With luck, the bodies would not be found until the shift change.

Pushing on, they were soon in the heart of the dungeon complex, passing cells filled with the misery of the city: traders who refused or were unable to pay their fines, beggars who had not given up their profession, murderers, rapists and drunkards, as well as those that Vos simply found unpleasant or inconvenient. Each cell was secured by a thick wooden door, the only view to the corridor outside through a tiny window set with metal bars. Lucius had spent time in one of these cells, and he did not envy those incarcerated within, oblivious as they were to his passing and that of the two assassins.

The dungeon was quiet, and Lucius presumed most were asleep, or else sunk into the deep depression or half-sleep he had seen in those locked away for months on end without any hope of release. From some cells, they heard quiet snoring, from others gentle moans, though whether they were from pain, loss, or despair, Lucius could not tell. As he passed one cell door, no different from any of the dozens of others in the underground complex, he stopped and cocked his head. Something had caught his attention, and he concentrated to find the errant sound.

"Lucius," someone whispered.

He looked up at the cell's door, and opened his mouth in astonishment.

"Harker, is it?" he said, trying to place the man's face, half-hidden as it was by the bars set into the door.

"Gods be praised," Harker said. "It *is* you! I thought you Council types had forgotten all about us! You freeing everyone?"

Lucius hesitated for a moment, and then considered the options. He had been part of a widespread break from the dungeons before and while many had been recaptured or killed in the attempt, some had made it out of the Citadel. Back then, they had not had the advantage of the Citadel, indeed the entire city, in total chaos.

"Hold on, Harker," he said, as he began to study the door and assess its weak points. He was no locksmith, and any magical method he might employ was sure to attract attention.

"What are you waiting for?" Elaine asked, appearing at Lucius' side. He glanced around, and saw Heinrich a little further ahead, looking back at him with impatience.

"They've got thieves here," he whispered.

She looked at him incredulously. "Well, of course they have. Where do you think they put all the thieves they capture?"

Lucius ignored the sarcasm. "Elaine, we have an army down here, if we release them."

"And we have a mission to perform right now," she shot back.

"But—"

"The answer is no, Lucius," she cut him off, then looked up at Harker. "Sorry, Harker, there are bigger things going on right now. You'll have to wait a little longer."

For a second, Harker was speechless, then he found his voice.

"You've got to be kidding..."

Turning to look at the door, Lucius briefly considered the lock and what it would take to blast it apart, but Elaine saw his look and grabbed his arm.

"I said *no*, Lucius," she hissed, jerking him back up the corridor. "We free them later, when the mission is done, or not at all."

He threw an apologetic glance at Harker, then glowered at Elaine.

"This isn't right," he said. "We can't just leave our people here. They could be dead tomorrow – probably will be after what has happened this evening."

Elaine released his arm, and moved forward, ignoring his protests. He started forward, intending to reiterate his point, but was brought up short by Heinrich's hand on his chest.

"Shut up, right now," the assassin said dangerously. "You give away our presence and I swear I'll kill you right here. And don't think she will give a damn."

Anger suddenly filled Lucius, but he bit his tongue, chafing under both Heinrich's threat and his intimation of knowing Elaine's mind. He had little doubt the two assassins knew what they were doing, but leaving Harker and God knew how many others behind to rot in the cells seemed criminal. The freedom of fellow thieves was a greater priority than the deaths of a few Vos officials, he thought.

Gradually, the corridors of the complex began to appear cleaner and were certainly better lit. They were leaving the cells behind. Elaine still led the way, and Lucius noticed she had become more focussed, as if she were hunting and knew her prey was close.

His suspicions were confirmed when she drew up short at a junction, and peered around the corner quickly. She turned back to glance at Heinrich, smiling.

"He's here," she said quietly. "Three guards with him."

"Officer of the Dungeon?" Lucius asked.

Heinrich gave him a look of annoyance. "Of course," he eventually said.

Lucius nodded. When he had heard that Elaine was intending to go down into the depths of the keep rather than the floors above, he had guessed her intended target. The Officer of the Dungeon, a title currently held by a man known as Jonas Traugott, or simply the Thug to those who had been incarcerated by him, would always be a man much hated by thieves. Jonas had come into the city at about the same time as the Preacher Divine, but had already gained a reputation for brutality and cruelty, treating anyone born in Turnitia as though they were less than human. It was widely believed that his methods of extracting information had been the principal means by which the Empire had found the thieves' guildhouse.

His death might not shake the Vos government of the city to its foundations, but it would be a gesture greatly appreciated by every thief still free, and might shape the attitude of his successor.

"He's mine," Elaine said emphatically, and Heinrich made a sweeping gesture with his hand, indicating the officer was all hers.

Heinrich and Lucius moved up so they were just behind Elaine, as she reached into a pouch and produced a handful of small pellets. They averted their eyes as she threw the pellets down the corridor.

Lucius was aware of a bright flash around the periphery of his vision, like a sheet of lightning, but there was no sound other than startled cries from ahead. Led by Elaine, Lucius and Heinrich charged around the corner, sprinting to the chamber that lay just ahead.

The chamber was small, but well-appointed. Rich rugs covered the floor, and the scattered tables were strewn with clothes, bottles, books, and food. There was a finely crafted lute propped up against one wall; above it, a framed picture of some distant landscape. The chamber was a little palace within the heart of the keep, all of it paid for with the goods and belongings confiscated from those locked up in the cells behind him.

Four men were present in the room, chairs fallen among them. They staggered about the chamber, hands clasped to their eyes, blinded by the explosion of light.

Leading the charge, Elaine and Heinrich hit the men without mercy. Elaine dodged a clumsy blow as a soldier lashed out with his fist, his eyesight beginning to return. She buried one sword in his thigh, and passed him as he fell to the floor howling in pain. She had eyes only for the Officer of the Dungeon, easily recognised by the gaudy gold trim he had added to his plain red Vos livery, and the cluster of rings worn on the fingers of both hands.

Heinrich's short sword finished off the man Elaine had downed, and he moved on to the next soldier, who had recovered his wits enough to scramble for his spear. Heinrich stamped on the weapon, and the soldier jumped backwards to avoid a vicious thrust.

Moving further into the chamber, Lucius ducked a chair thrown by the third soldier and leapt onto the central table, scattering bottles and plates. The soldier was panicked by the sudden assault, but recovered well, reaching for the first thing to come to hand. Advancing on Lucius, he swung the lute, grunting with the weight of the unwieldy instrument.

Jumping down from the table, Lucius blocked the lute with his sword, but it smashed though his defence and slammed into his shoulder, sending him reeling. He ducked another swing, but was forced to step back, knocking into the table. As the soldier swung the lute for the third time, Lucius raised a hand to ward off the blow, but the instrument had too much force behind it.

The tortured strings cried out and were silenced as the neck of the lute shattered against Lucius' skull in a shower of splinters. Staggered by the blow, Lucius reeled, flailing with his sword to keep the soldier back.

The soldier dropped the tattered remains of the lute, grabbed Lucius and threw him against the nearest wall. The impact jarred Lucius' sword from his grip, but he retained hold of the dagger in his left hand. Shaking his head to clear the fog, Lucius saw the soldier advance, fists raised. Lucius held out a hand as if begging for a moment to recover, and the soldier gave him a cruel grin.

As the soldier took another step forward, Lucius pushed off from the wall and sprang for the soldier. He took a punch to the side of the face, but grabbed the man's tabard and plunged the dagger into his neck.

Blood spurted across the chamber and, for a second, they stood face to face, the man looking blankly at him as if not comprehending that he had just been killed. Then, the soldier's eyes glazed and Lucius released his grip, allowing the man to fall to the floor.

He saw Heinrich had already dispatched the soldier he had faced, and had now turned to watch Elaine.

"Stop playing with him, Elaine," the assassin said with a note of reproach.

The Officer of the Dungeon was scared, Lucius could see, and he flailed desperately with a short sword, trying to keep his attacker away. Elaine had scored several hits on him, and blood flowed freely down his arms, legs and chest. Another wound was gouged into his cheek, and Lucius had no doubt Elaine was trying to make a point, prolonging the man's agony in return for all the cruelty he had handed out to his prisoners.

Stepping back, Elaine paused to give Heinrich a look of mock disappointment, turned back to the officer and smiled, before lunging. She buried both her blades into his stomach and released them so they stood proud.

Looking down in horror, the officer dropped his own weapon and grabbed the hilts of her blades as if to pull them out. Gasping for breath, he fell to his knees, looking up at Elaine in a mute plea for help. Still smiling, she grasped the swords, twisting them slightly as he moaned in pain. Then, with a great heave, she ripped them free before planting a boot on his chest and kicking him to the ground.

He lay there, squirming slightly while blood flooded out to stain the deep-green-patterned rug he had fallen onto. Elaine stooped to pick up a corner of the rug and cleaned her blades one at a time.

"You just going to leave him like that?" Heinrich asked.

Elaine shrugged. "No more than he deserves. No less either. The pain will give him something to think about while he dies."

"It's bad tradecraft," Heinrich said, shaking his head slightly.

Sighing, Elaine looked down at the pitiful figure of the officer, who was coughing up blood, crimson trails running down his face. She looked back at Heinrich and nodded, stalked over to the man and ended his life with a blade between the ribs.

"So, job done," Lucius said, looking at the carnage around them. "We release the prisoners now?"

Elaine was looking about herself as well.

"No," she said slowly. "We carry on."

"Carry on?"

"No one has been this deep into the Citadel before. I want to see what else they have here." She saw Lucius frown, as if about to debate her instructions. "We have only presumed the higher ranking officials and officers are on the higher levels of the keep. While we have this chance, we should push on."

Lucius thought he saw a look of concern on Heinrich's face, but it was gone quickly, replaced by a quick nod.

"We push on, then," Heinrich said, "as the guildmistress commands."

CHAPTER SEVENTEEN

Deep beneath the Citadel, beyond the dungeons, they found a vast warehouse.

Lucius whistled softly to himself. The ceiling was not high but, after the low stone arches they had become used to, the double-height chamber seemed to soar above them. Square-carved pillars supported it at regular intervals and, while there were plenty of larger warehouses in Turnitia, Vos had not been idle in using it.

Stretched out over perhaps three acres, mountains of sacks and piles of crates were collected neatly, all ordered by contents, age and usefulness. A cursory investigation of the closest sacks revealed several tons of grain. Clay pots held lantern oil.

"There's enough food and supplies here to last years," Lucius said in some wonder.

"I bet they have a well sunk somewhere inside the Citadel, probably within the keep itself," Elaine said. "They could withstand a siege indefinitely."

"You think they are expecting trouble, perhaps from Pontaine?" Lucius asked.

Heinrich shook his head. "I would expect every major Vos stronghold to have something like this. My people like to be prepared for any eventuality. Given current relations with Pontaine, and the people of this city for that matter, it is a wise precaution."

Lucius looked about him, at all the crates, bottles, sacks and pots, thinking.

"We should destroy it," he said after a moment.

"No," Elaine said flatly.

"It's a legitimate target, if we are waging war!"

"I don't disagree," she said. "But how would you go about it, exactly? Burn it all?"

He was about to agree, then saw the immediate flaw. Billowing smoke underground, especially while they might be stalled by Vos reinforcements on the way out, would be a potentially lethal hindrance, not a victory. Then there were the still trapped prisoners to consider. Another thought occurred to him.

Reaching a hand out to a sack of grain, he closed his eyes briefly, summoning the threads of magic. He felt them begin to work, sucking in moisture from the surrounding air, and concentrating it on the contents of the sack.

As Elaine and Heinrich watched, the sack became sodden before their eyes, the material stained dark as trickles of water began to run down its side.

Lucius looked back at them expectantly, but was greeted by Elaine's sour look.

"That is very good, Lucius," she said with some measure of sarcasm. "Tell me, how long would it take you to do that to all the grain here?"

He looked ruefully at the pile of sacks before him, conscious that it was just one of dozens stacked around him. She had a point.

"We could bury it," he said, eyeing up one of the square columns. Heinrich grabbed his arm.

"Not while we are still down here," he said forcefully. "You can work whatever magic you see fit, after we have left."

Lucius was surprised by his venom.

"Of course," he said, pulling his arm away.

Elaine had wandered off from the two of them, and her voice floated back from behind a row of crates.

"Come and have a look at this."

Glaring at each other, Lucius and Heinrich joined her, and immediately caught sight of what had attracted her attention.

A small oaken door was set into the wall, which Elaine had opened. Inside was another spiral staircase, descending further, and Lucius guessed it must lead to another level. However, he noted that while the rest of the corridors and chambers had shown signs of age, the staircase was new – or else supremely well-preserved. More than that, its walls were completely smooth.

"Either of you heard about a level beneath the dungeons?" Elaine asked, and frowned when she saw them both shaking their heads.

Lucius took a pace forward, and cocked his head as he peered down the stairs into the dark. Something tickled the back of his mind, and he held the mental image of the threads of magic in his mind's eye for a moment, watching them jitter ever so slightly, as if they were troubled by the presence of something that drew upon their energies.

"I don't like this," he muttered.

"What's to like?" Elaine said impatiently. "We've come this far, and if Vos has installed a new level in the Citadel, we need to know about it."

Elaine started for the staircase, but Lucius put a hand on her shoulder. She whipped around, but he held up a hand to stall her.

"I'll go first," he said, then saw her start to protest. "There's magic here, Elaine, I can feel it. I need to go first."

Still, she did not look happy, but after a moment's hesitation, she waved him on.

The stairs wound on, diving much further than those that had brought them to the dungeons. Lucius strained to see into the darkness, and was eventually forced to conjure a small ball of blue fire in his hand just to light the way. The feeling of being in the presence of powerful magics grew as he followed the smooth walls ever downwards.

A light, growing steadily brighter, began to illuminate the stairs beneath him, and Lucius snuffed out his fire. As one, all three slowed, moving stealthily as they cleared the last of the stairs and cautiously examined the corridor at the bottom.

It stretched off into the distance for hundreds of yards. Like the staircase, its walls were utterly smooth, as were the ceiling and floor. There were no flagstones laid here, just the smoothed surface of plain rock; Lucius suspected the whole level had been constructed by magic rather than human labour.

Lucius soon realised that the light, which now allowed him to see for hundreds of yards down the corridor, was emanating from the walls themselves. He recalled seeing something similar in Adrianna's lair and took a breath, marshalling his own magic.

"We should turn back," he whispered.

"Are you mad?" Elaine asked. "There are no guards here, we have the freedom to roam where we wish – and if Vos is planning something down here, we need to know about it."

"I don't wholly disagree, but you said it yourself. If this place is so important, why are there no guards?"

Behind them both, Heinrich sighed. "He may have a point, Elaine. If there are no guards, then whatever is here is either worthless, which I think none of us believes, or else does not require protection."

"Which makes it all the more important for us to discover it," Elaine said stubbornly.

"The magic here is very powerful," Lucius said. "The three of us alone may not be enough."

"You know my feelings for the man, Elaine, but when it comes to magic, I think we should trust him," Heinrich said.

She would not be swayed. "We've handled worse in the past, and what Lucius cannot handle with his own magic, you and I can finish off with our blades. If this is important to Vos, then it is important to us as well."

So saying, Elaine brushed past Lucius and started padding down the corridor, though the bright light from the walls deprived her of any shadows within which to hide. Lucius looked over to Heinrich, and saw him staring after Elaine, a troubled look on his face.

"Come on," Lucius said. "We have to follow her."

Heinrich nodded. "Aye, she'll go by herself just to spite us."

The corridor stretched for an age, and Lucius started to wonder if there was not some deeper enchantment preying upon them, for the passage extended into the distance with no end in sight. They stopped every few seconds, listening for any tell-tale of an ambush: the scrape of a sword drawn from its scabbard, the gentle clink of mail, a stifled breath, anything that would betray an imminent attack.

There was nothing. They were completely alone.

Still Lucius was not at ease. If anything, his nervousness grew, as he saw the threads of magic were still disturbed.

A grinding noise of metal on stone seemed thunderous in the silent confines of the corridor, and they turned to see a heavy portcullis of dark blackened metal slam down from the ceiling behind them. Lucius felt a rising panic, as none of them had spotted any change or mark in the corridor when they crept past. Another portcullis dropped in front, leaving them trapped in an area just a few yards long.

The corridor before them shimmered, as if in a deep haze of heat, and through the distortion, Lucius saw a chamber appear, just beyond the portcullis barrier. Where there had been an endless corridor, there was now a widened area of the same smooth stone, with perhaps half a dozen soldiers led by a tall, fair-headed woman wreathed in green silks.

She pointed a long, aristocratic finger without speaking, and two soldiers ran forward with spears, jabbing at the assassins through the bars of the portcullis. Another two readied heavy crossbows while the rest hefted wicked looking halberds.

Parrying the first spear thrust at her, Elaine side-stepped the blow, then jumped back. Heinrich took the simpler course of shearing the head off the spear nearest him with a powerful overhead hack, then he too paced backwards, eyeing the crossbowmen.

Seeing that they stood trapped, waiting to be spitted with bolts by soldiers who had all the time in the world to aim, Lucius sheathed his sword and dagger, then clenched his fists in front of his chest as he tugged on the invisible threads, drawing power for a new spell. He punched forward with both fists, releasing the energy and roaring in anger, letting his emotion drive the spell as much as his skill.

The pulse of energy slammed into the portcullis with a terrifying crash that caused the soldiers closest to it to yelp and spring back. The metal had yielded a few inches, with the centre of the portcullis buckled and twisted, bars broken and snapped apart. Seeing the barrier resist his spell, Lucius gathered more energy, building it up into a powerful attack that would flatten everything before him.

Sensing the danger, the tall woman reached forward with a casual gesture, and the portcullis erupted into crackling lightning, bright sparks playing up and down its surface. The portcullis surged with energy briefly, then the lightning leapt across to Lucius.

His body jerked in pain as the lightning swept through him and the spell he was forming slipped from his mind to dissipate harmlessly back into the threads. Draining its own power, the lightning relaxed its grip on his body, and Lucius sank to his knees as he tried to catch his breath.

"Cover me," he managed to say to Heinrich and Elaine. They exchanged looks, then leapt forward, using their bodies to shield Lucius.

Elaine had already drawn a throwing knife, and she heaved it at the nearest soldier, but the blade was hastily aimed and clattered off the portcullis. Trying the same thing, Heinrich was more accurate, and sent his spinning knife through the gap in the portcullis that Lucius created. It buried itself in the forearm of one of the crossbowmen, causing him to cry out as he dropped his weapon. His comrade raised his crossbow and aimed straight at Heinrich.

"Lucius, whatever you are doing, do it fast!" Heinrich said, as he jumped onto the balls of his feet, readying for a desperate leap to one side when the bolt was loosed. A strained voice came from behind him.

"Move... now."

Heinrich and Elaine leapt behind the Shadowmage. Lucius had pulled himself to his feet and was holding his palms out as if carrying a great ball. In his mind, he saw the immense energy he had been preparing as a tumultuous, writhing sphere of multi-coloured winds that whipped around at terrible speeds.

With another cry, he threw the energy ball forward, seeing it speed from his hand to the portcullis, though it was invisible to Elaine, Heinrich and the soldiers.

It blasted into the portcullis and detonated. The portcullis collapsed, unable to withstand the assault. Great masses of stone were torn free as it was ripped from its mechanism, and shards of metal and rock were catapulted towards the soldiers with lethal force.

Men shrieked in pain as they were impaled on metal bars or struck by stone. Amidst all the carnage, the tall woman casually, almost contemptuously, raised her hand, palm outwards. The force of the blast, along with its killing shrapnel, seemed to flow around her and the two soldiers standing impassively behind her. They showed no fear as the spell abated and the woman gestured them to move forward over the bodies of their dead and dying allies, halberds raised as they approached Lucius.

Another gesture from the woman froze the air about her into long, thin, needle-sharp ice. The foot-long darts hung in the air for a moment, then arrowed towards Lucius. Lucius raised an invisible shield, deflecting the bolts into the wall where they shattered into fragments of crystal.

Though panting from the exertion, he was now smiling. The tall woman was accomplished enough and, unusually for a Vos-trained wizard, very fast at building spells. Her magic was similar in its discipline to Adrianna's, but he had faced the Shadowmage before, and this woman did not have anything like Adrianna's power or raw talent. His elation at this discovery nearly cost him his life, and Lucius only ducked at the last instant as a halberd hissed through the air above him.

"We'll take this scum," Elaine said. Both she and Heinrich had seen the danger to Lucius, and moved up alongside to protect him. "You take down that witch."

Metal smashed against metal as Elaine raised her sword to parry another halberd swing, and was pushed back by the blow. While the halberd was relatively unwieldy in close combat and easily caught on a blade, the sheer weight behind its attack was enough to send a swordsman flying. Elaine cursed and recovered her balance, ready to face the soldier as he marched upon her.

The Vos wizard smiled at Lucius and beckoned him on. Resolved to tear her arrogance apart, he formed a bolt of black energy that hissed as it fed on the life of everyone present in the corridor. Launching the bolt at the woman, he saw her smile slip as it knifed into her chest. The woman's skin turned ashen, and she looked visibly shaken as she started chanting, preparing another spell.

Heinrich had already dealt with the soldier he faced, moving inside the halberd's reach and driving a sword up through the man's jaw, and the soldier now lay twitching on the floor.

Heinrich advanced on the remaining soldier, who sensed his approach and turned side on to see both assassins. That was all the advantage Elaine needed. Kicking the halberd's shaft to one side, she slashed with one blade, sliding it off his helmet and drawing a deep cut down his cheek. With the other, she stabbed, the blade piercing the mail on the soldier's thigh.

He fell to one knee, bleeding from leg and face, supporting his weight with his halberd. The assassins gave him no time to recover, and savagely hacked and stabbed until he lay still.

Her spell complete, the woman stretched forth her hand and channelled more lightning into Lucius. Lucius had already constructed another invisible barrier and the lightning smashed into it, ripping the strands of energy that bound his defence together, sparks flying to either side as the magics fought one another.

Lucius directed more energy into the shield, repairing it as quickly as she flayed more layers from its surface. He stared grimly at the tall woman, matching and countering her spell as she stepped up its magnitude.

Slowly, tiny flaws started to appear in his shield, and Lucius frowned in concentration as he poured more energy from the threads into the barrier, but still the strength of the wizard's spell increased. When she cried out in pain, Lucius began to wonder if the wizard had not unleashed some terrible spell she could no longer control.

Standing rigid now, the woman was immobile, hand still directed toward him, still funnelling lightning into the shield, though now it was blinding in its intensity. She looked like a puppet, directed by the will of another, and this impression was reinforced as Lucius watched his shield begin to dissolve. He desperately shored up his defences.

From the corner of his eye, he saw the heat haze appear again, this time in the far corners of the chamber on either side of the wizard. An arch appeared in each, with corridors receding away into the distance. Lucius did not know if this was the true layout of this part of the keep, or just another illusion.

He stumbled as a wave of power swept over him, and it took a moment to realise that it had been in his mind alone. It had felt as if someone very powerful and very learned in magics was flexing his muscles before entering the fight.

Screaming now, the endless shriek ripped from her throat, the woman began to shake, though her hand was still rigidly pointing toward him, the lightning pouring out with ever greater intensity. The wizard looked insensible, her eyes rolling in their sockets, glazed over as if she were somewhere else.

The energies channelled by her body had risen tenfold again, and the power was beginning to leak from her tall frame, sparks jumping out through her silk garments, setting them alight. Lucius moaned with the effort of keeping his shield intact, now reduced to the thinnest sliver of a defence.

In the corners of his eyes, he saw a figure appear in each of the corridors now stretching from the chamber. Each was cowled in a pale robe, face hidden within its shadowy recess. They stood, immobile, staring at Lucius and his pathetic efforts to resist the magic of their vassal.

Another pulse of energy swept over Lucius and he staggered under its impact, unaware of Elaine's steadying hand on his shoulder, unable to hear her words. He could feel other centres of power, other crafters of magic, hidden from his view, working together. Perhaps their power was being magnified by the strange construction of this part of the keep, or perhaps they could do it naturally, but he had not felt a force so powerful since confronting Adrianna. Even then, he could not say who was the greater – the Shadowmage, or what must be the Vos cabal.

The tall woman's head now lolled to one side, and Lucius doubted that she was still alive. Still, she was serving as the link to the cabal, their instrument against him. Seeing his shield begin to wither and die, he yelled out loud as he pushed it forward, flooding it with a final burst of energy.

The wave smashed into the tall woman. Unable to offer any resistance, her body folded under the blow, bones breaking as she was thrown off her feet into the wall behind. She fell limply to the ground, unmoving.

The lightning storm ceased with the death of her body, leaving the chamber eerily silent. Lucius became aware of Elaine shaking him. Looking up the twin corridors, he saw the two cowled figures advancing smoothly, as if floating a few inches above the ground.

"I can't fight them," he gasped. "We've got to get out of here."

Heinrich had already hurled a knife at one of the cabal wizards, but the blade had winked out of existence as it spun through the air, not even passing the length of the chamber.

Another pulse, yet stronger than before, hammered Lucius and he reeled, clutching his head as pain lanced through his mind. He looked at Elaine through hazed eyes.

"The portcullis is jammed," Elaine shouted, her voice seeming to come from a far distance. "We can't go back."

"Distract..." he managed to say, but the assassins understood immediately.

Heinrich readied his sword and sprinted towards one of the cabal wizards. Elaine went to follow him, but Lucius grabbed her shoulder. He saw her glance at Heinrich, but he gripped harder, turning her around as he reached out with his other hand, summoning the energy to build his spell. The fog clouding his mind suddenly vanished, and his vision returned with renewed clarity. Lucius knew that Heinrich had succeeded in distracting the cabal wizards for a brief moment. He also knew the assassin was already dead.

With a ragged breath, he drew in air and concentrated, drawing the magical energies he needed to him, conscious that he had but seconds before the wizards behind recovered from whatever Heinrich had done. He formed a blast of energy and sent it streaming toward the portcullis, but collapsed with the effort. He heard Elaine's desperate cries as she threw her weight against the shattered portcullis.

Lucius heard a crash of metal, then Elaine was with him, hauling him to his feet. He stumbled forward, then felt her stop.

"Heinrich..." she said.

"He's dead."

Elaine froze in place, and Lucius saw her look back, though whether it was to seek vengeance or try a desperate rescue, he could not say.

"Don't be a fool," Lucius said. "He's dead."

"Then they die too," she said.

"Elaine, we've got to go now. Too much depends on you. Remember the guild!"

"I don't care about that."

Lucius looked at her, fear and desperation on both their faces.

"Yes you do."

Still she hesitated. He grabbed her around the waist and dragged her through the portcullis.

"For God's sake, Elaine, we leave now!"

For the briefest moment Elaine resisted, then a shadow seemed to fall over her. Her face grew steely; Lucius felt sorry for the next soldier they met.

Behind him, sorcerous energies began to escalate again, poured into a spell of devastating proportions. The thieves fled back up the corridor, and to the spiralled staircase up to the keep's dungeons. Lucius pushed Elaine into the recess and made sure she was climbing before he cast a look over his shoulder.

Pursuing them down the corridor were several cowled figures. No longer floating serenely, he could see them running with desperate speed as they saw their victims escaping. One flicked a hand in an elaborate gesture, and a tiny red spark shot unerringly toward Lucius.

Sensing the power contained within the little spark, Lucius threw himself up the stairs, his legs pumping as he mounted the steps two at a time. He felt the spark build vastly in intensity, and then a thunderous crash blasted behind him just inside the corridor. The dark staircase was lit up in a brilliant orange as flames clawed up the stairs, eager to consume him.

Yelling at Elaine to move faster, he scrambled up the stairs, feeling the heat licking at his boots and cloak. Dust scoured from the walls by the blast was driven up before the flames, and Lucius began to choke as his vision was clouded. Stumbling, he felt his way up the stairs.

The flames receded as the spell subsided. Not wanting to see what the cabal would do as a follow-up, Lucius hurried up the staircase.

Elaine was waiting for him in the underground warehouse. She was bent over, hands on her thighs as she struggled to regain her breath. Looking up as he approached, also gasping for air, Elaine gave him a poisonous look.

"Bastards," she said, and Lucius had the unnerving thought that she blamed him for the loss of Heinrich.

He thought of all the things he could say to her – apologies, sympathies, even an attempt at reconciliation – but dismissed them all.

"We have to go," he said. "They're still following. I can feel them."

"They are too powerful for you to fight?" It could have been a jibe at his skill with magic, or it might have been an honest question. Lucius pushed the thought from his mind.

"I can't face them directly, but I think there is one thing I can do that, if nothing else, will cause them a great deal of frustration."

Elaine gave him a strange look, but followed him as he ran through the lines of stacked crates to the entrance of the warehouse. Stopping at the door, he gestured for Elaine to get behind him.

"Two birds, as they say…"

Feeling the magic surging within him again, Lucius drew the energies together into a jagged bolt of light. With a push of his mind, he sent it lancing toward one of the columns supporting the high ceiling of the warehouse.

The column blew apart under the pressure of the spell, sending chunks of stone spiralling into the furthest recesses of the warehouse. For a brief second, nothing happened, then came a deep, low, vibrating rumble that seemed to emanate from the keep itself. Sacks of grain tumbled from their piles and crates crashed to the floor.

"Now, we really *do* have to go," Lucius said, taking Elaine's arm and pulling her away from the warehouse, retracing their steps into the dungeons.

Behind them, cracks appeared in the ceiling of the warehouse, thin slivers at first, but rapidly growing into wide gashes that streaked across the open spaces between the remaining columns. Rock and earth rained down from the ceiling as the entire warehouse began to shake violently. An ear-splitting crack resounded throughout the lower levels of the keep as the ceiling finally gave way under the pressure of the keep above.

Tons of rock and debris crashed down into the warehouse, instantly flattening everything within.

CHAPTER EIGHTEEN

Thieves and assassins flooded the Citadel, presiding over a reign of terror and death as they took revenge on their oppressors. The assassins remained focussed, locating targets of value and importance and sending them to hell with blade, bolt and arrow. The thieves freed by Lucius and Elaine were less selective. They killed anyone they met, be they official, soldier or servant.

Some, the most experienced and the most terrified, kept their heads enough to follow Lucius and Elaine out. Others rampaged through the keep on a killing spree.

Lucius could do nothing for them. He had given them all a chance for survival and escape; their lives were now in their own hands.

Spilling out onto the bridge between the keep and one of the towers lining the Citadel, Lucius and Elaine found themselves at the head of a mob of the most desperate, those who had seen enough of Vos cruelty and just wanted the freedom of the city. Some had managed to snatch up weapons from defeated soldiers, and a couple had grabbed shields as well, but most were unarmed.

A small group of assassins and thieves had taken up position on one of the walls, holding back squads of soldiers on both sides to protect the ladders and ropes they had deployed down the Citadel wall. Their outlines were barely visible in the soft glow of burning buildings in the city, set against a black sky. No cheers of relief came from the men he led, however; stretched across the bridge, they saw the soldiers of the Order of the Swords of Dawn waiting for them.

The Swords, immaculate in their white tabards, were motionless, and their demeanour radiated discipline, halberds held aloft in perfect ranks.

Lucius cast a glance at Elaine, his eyebrows raised. She shrugged.

"Nothing else for it," she said, turning back to face the rabble of thieves behind her and raising her voice. "We either fight our way through the Faith's so-called elite soldiers, or we retreat, and die in the Citadel. What say you?"

That brought a ragged cheer from the thieves, albeit half-hearted. Not one of them doubted the efficiency of the Swords.

Raising her sword aloft, Elaine marched forward, and Lucius kept pace by her side. After ensuring the thieves were following her, Elaine picked up her pace, first jogging, and then sprinting as they charged the line.

The Swords of Dawn did not so much as twitch their halberds before the baying horde's onslaught. They simply waited for the thieves to hit their line, where their training would ensure short work of the desperate charge.

Lucius cursed, having hoped their line would at least begin to soften and drift apart as they received the charge, allowing some thieves to break through and begin a general brawl. Able to get a soldier on his own, two or more thieves had a chance, but fighting like a disciplined military unit gave all the advantages to the Swords. If they would not break, he would have to force them.

A dozen yards from the Swords' line, Lucius skidded to a stop and dropped to one knee. He thumped a fist to the bridge's stone surface, flooding the area before him with magical energy, pouring it into a wave that rolled inexorably forward.

Few thieves saw the shimmering wave, glinting with a dull sheen as it sped towards the Swords, but they cheered with sudden elation as the centremost guards reeled back, pushed by the hand of a giant. Those who had taken the brunt of the wave flew backwards into the ranks behind them, while those on the periphery staggered, some dropping their weapons as the thieves hit the disrupted line.

Weak after directing such a powerful spell so quickly, Lucius tried to make his way back to Elaine's side, but the mob of thieves swept past him. He saw them crash into the line, and their momentum tore the Swords' formation in two as the centre completely buckled under their charge.

He was aware that those hitting the flanks fared less well, with many being cut down by a sweeping halberd before they had a chance to throw a fist or strike a blow. Most in the centre turned on the guards nearest them with a rare fury, hitting them in the sides and rear, though a few kept on running for the safety of the city. Lucius could not find it in his heart to blame them, though he wished they had stayed to finish the fight.

A stocky knight bawled orders at his men, and the Swords' formation, though broken in two, suddenly became rigid, the soldiers at the front of the fight steeling themselves to face the thieves. Halberds began to swing again, and men and women started to fall beneath their heavy axe-heads.

Lucius pushed his way through the mob of thieves, trying to reach the centre of the fight, hoping to break the line again and reach the knight. With him dead, the Swords' morale might be shaken enough for the thieves to regain an advantage. Elaine had already seen this possibility, and Lucius watched as she railed against the soldiers, ducking their slicing halberds, and thrusting her swords past their clumsy parries. An upswing from a soldier drove the shaft of his halberd into her stomach, and then clipped her across the chin. Elaine reeled back in shock and pain.

Seeing this, Lucius grew frantic, desperately clawing his way through thieves to reach her. He heard another hollered order from the knight, and the soldiers closest to him surged forward as those behind closed in, trying to crush the thieves between them in the shattered centre.

Hefting his dagger, Lucius tried to throw it at the knight, but the thieves were being hemmed in tighter and tighter, and there was not enough room to cast it properly. The blade went wide, disappearing behind the knight to fall into the compound far below.

That gave Lucius an idea.

Side-stepping a halberd thrust at his chest, Lucius stabbed forward with his sword, gouging a deep cut in his attacker's forearm. As the halberd dropped to the floor, Lucius stepped under the soldier's guard and drove his knee into man's stomach. He grasped the soldier's elaborate tabard, then shouted over his shoulder to the thieves.

"Grab them! Push them over the edge!"

Where lack of arms and skill had betrayed them, the thieves now took advantage of their weight of numbers. Halberds flashed, carving holes among the ranks of the thieves, but enough closed in to engage the Swords close up, where large weapons like halberds were useless. Pinned against the bodies of the soldiers, the halberds were held immobile, while small blades in the hands of thieves easily found their way through gaps in mail armour.

"Push!" Lucius yelled, and he felt the thieves behind him surge, pressing him forward into the soldiers. At first, the Swords resisted, but as the thieves grew in confidence, the line began to be driven back. Startled yells from the rearmost soldiers told Lucius they had seen the danger, but it was too late, and he grinned with malicious glee as, over the heads of the Swords, he saw the knight desperately grab at the nearest tabarded figures as he lost his balance. For a second, the knight seemed to hang at an impossible angle over the edge of the bridge. Then, he fell, disappearing from view.

Soldiers quickly followed him, and the pace of the thieves' push increased as the resistance against them waned. With a kick, Lucius pitched the soldier he still held over the metal railings lining the side of the bridge, and watched him fall down into the bailey where scattered corpses of his comrades already lay still. Lucius gave a howl of victory, fairly stunned that his plan had worked, but it was cut short as he realised the thieves behind were still pushing.

"Hold!" he shouted desperately. "Hold!"

Kicking with all his strength, Lucius saw the metal railings approach, saw the yawning emptiness open before him, but his feet slid uselessly across the stone bridge. The air was driven from him as his stomach was pressed into the railings and his body was forced over it, so he was looking directly into the bailey. Beside him, another thief lost his battle against the surge and fell, screaming until he hit the ground with a dreadful impact.

Feeling himself toppling over the edge of the railings, Lucius closed his eyes to await the inevitable. It had been a good idea, and it had saved everyone else, but his quick wits had also killed him.

A hand grabbed the back of his collar and hauled him away from the railings. Lucius remained bent over double as he tried to catch his breath, then he looked up to see the face of Harker, beaming at him.

"Bet you're glad you rescued me now, eh?" Harker said.

"Harker..." Lucius began, then stopped to cough. "Harker, I owe you a drink."

"I'll hold you to that. But for now, I think we'd better get moving."

With no more Swords of Dawn to block their path, the thieves had already started the race to the walls. The few soldiers scattered around the tower proved no match for thieves drunk on their victory over the best the Final Faith had to offer. Elaine led the charge, Lucius saw, while he had to be content bringing up the rear and making sure no thief dallied to torture fallen soldiers.

He was reunited with Elaine at the top of the wall, as she organised the thieves' descent of the wall.

"That was.... inspired," she said to Lucius as he held a ladder steady for thieves clambering to the ground.

"I'm just glad it worked," he said. "If those soldiers had recovered... well, it doesn't bear thinking about. That could have got very nasty, very quickly. Were you hurt?"

She dismissed the question with a wave. "Just a few scratches. I'll be a whole lot better when we leave this place."

Lucius glanced down at the ladder. The thieves had reached the bottom and were already running as fast as they could to their favourite bolt-holes. Waiting until the thieves had found their way out, the assassins were now scaling down their ropes.

"After you," Lucius said, gesturing to the ladder, but Elaine shook her head.

"I'm the leader of the guild, remember? I leave last."

Lucius found himself disagreeing with that sentiment, however noble it might have been, but this was not the place to argue. That could be left to their next Council meeting, preferably voiced by Wendric. Swinging himself over the wall, Lucius gripped the ladder tightly with hands and ankles, and slid down. He hit the ground smiling. They were far from safe, he knew, as the streets would be flooded with Vos soldiers, but just being able to leave the Citadel seemed a huge step.

When Elaine slid down next to him, she beckoned.

"Come on, let's get out of here," she said. "Then we can see just how much damage we have done to the Empire."

"And start planning the next strike?" he asked, still smiling.

"Indeed."

The rest of the thieves had dispersed quickly, spreading throughout the city to brag quietly about their heroic escape, nurse wounds or mourn lost friends. Elaine and Lucius ran through the deserted market, but slowed down once they reached the quieter side streets. The streets were unusually busy for the time of evening, people hurrying past them everywhere they went. Lucius dismissed it as a by-product of the thieves' reign of chaos that evening, but was puzzled as he saw more and more families, parents often carrying children. They all seemed to be heading to the eastern quarter of the city.

It was Lucius who first voiced his doubts. They had turned onto Meridian Street, the wide cobbled thoroughfare that rolled down the gentle slope Turnitia was built on, from the north gate to the harbour. As he looked down to the city westwards, he gasped.

"My God, Elaine, how many buildings did you tell our men to fire?"

"Just..." She trailed off, eyes widening as she took in the devastation.

The entire western quarter of the city was ablaze, a wall of flame that was gradually creeping through the city, consuming one building after another. Rising from the burning ruins, thick smoke poured into the sky, completely blotting out Kerberos and the stars with an impenetrable black pall. A mass of people flooded the lower end of Meridian Street, all of them climbing the slope away from the flames. Those in front were running while others, much slower, struggled with hand carts and wagons full of whatever possessions they had managed to save from the fire.

"No way," Elaine said, still in shock, as the fastest of the fleeing mob began to pass them. "No way did our thieves do this."

"Someone got carried away," Lucius muttered. "Got careless. God, what have we done?"

"One reckless thief did not do all this. What about those who escaped the Citadel? Some were itching for vengeance."

Lucius looked at the rolling inferno, seeing it stretch right across the city, burning through homes and warehouses alike. It was nearing the main commercial hub of Turnitia, the flames beginning to lick around the shops situated on Ring Street, near the westernmost of the Five Markets.

"No, there hasn't been enough time – this happened while we were in the Citadel. Someone planned this, Elaine."

"Not us," Elaine said firmly.

"No, not us," he repeated. He began to feel an icy hand grip his stomach. "Come on. People are going to need our help."

Elaine looked as though she would protest for a moment, then dutifully followed him down Meridian Street. Their progress slowed as they tried to push their way through the crowd, and they were met with dazed, smoke-stained faces. Seeing the crowd get even thicker further on, Lucius grabbed Elaine's arm and steered her off the thoroughfare and into the side streets.

Even these were packed with people, all trying to escape the fires, but squeezing between families and carts, they made better progress. The crowds gradually melted away.

They were near the westernmost market, and though the fires were still at least a quarter-mile away, Lucius could feel the heat from them, swept up through the city by the sea wind which fanned the flames. An orange glow surrounded everything, even when the fires were out of sight.

They heard the crackling of burning wood, and the occasional thundering crash of a burning building, followed by bright cinders spiralling up into the dark sky. Screams and cries for help reached their ears as a steady rain of ash begin to fall, driven before the flames by the sheer heat. The inferno stretched horizon to horizon.

"There is no way this can be stopped," Elaine said. "It's too large."

"Even a fire this big can be made to burn itself out," Lucius said. "Look."

He pointed down a junction of streets where, at the far end, a squad of Vos soldiers were hacking away at a low building with halberds, axes and whatever tools they had managed to find on the streets.

"They're creating a firebreak."

"They're not completely useless then," Elaine said. "Will it work?"

"If there are enough soldiers here, then yes, they have a chance."

"So what can we do?"

Lucius watched the soldiers as they brought one exterior wall crashing down, one of them leaping back as a section of the first floor tumbled down near him.

"I think I can do that," he said. "With magic, I mean."

"You can destroy a building?" Elaine asked, incredulously.

"It will be difficult, but I think I can do enough damage to make a building collapse. After all, they are using nothing more than hand tools," he said, gesturing to the soldiers.

"And if they just happen to be passing by while you are casting your great spell?"

"That's where you come in. Watch my back, and we'll see if we can't help stop this."

Waving a hand to indicate he should lead, Elaine followed Lucius along a side street, away from the soldiers. As they ran, the screams of terrified citizens grew louder, but Lucius guessed they were coming from behind the wall of flame, and were beyond help. Turning back onto a straight road that led to Ring Street, Lucius looked for a suitable building, but his eye was drawn to the bodies strewn across the ground before him.

Many had been burned alive, the blackened, crisp corpses twisted in agonising contortions by the heat, smoke still rising from the motionless forms. He did not need to mention to Elaine that the fire was close but had not yet reached this part of the city, and again, he felt something cold in his stomach. Elaine tugged at his sleeve, and pointed at another set of bodies. These had not been burned but were lying in unnatural positions, their limbs broken, as if they had been thrown against the side of a building or dashed against the ground like a rag doll.

As they stood, dumbfounded, they heard a choking cry. Lucius looked around for the source, finally fixing upon an upended wagon, overturned by the evacuating crowd in their haste. Rushing over, he put his shoulder against the wagon's broad wooden side and heaved, but he might as well have tried to move the Cathedral.

Elaine had dropped to her hands and knees and was looking underneath the wagon, crawling around to get a better look at who was there. She bent lower, so her head was beneath the overturned rim of the wagon, and Lucius heard her speaking softly. Standing up, she walked around to his side of the wagon.

"There's a child there," she said. "Lord alone knows how it survived the wagon flipping over, but I can't reach it. Can we roll it back?"

Lucius shook his head. "It's far too heavy. Stand back though, I think I can move it."

"Careful," Elaine warned him. "If it slides, you'll crush the child. Try to flip it from the front, there may be more room."

"I can do better than that," he said, as he vaulted up onto its chassis.

Feeling the grain of the wooden planks that formed the wagon's floor, Lucius let the flow of magic course through his body, directing it to his right hand. Flattening his palm, he drove it through the wood like a spear, the spell hardening his flesh and lending strength to the thrust.

Wood splintered as his hand broke through a plank and, magic suffusing his arm until it burned, he wrenched his hand back, tearing a hole through the floor of the wagon. The spell dissipated, and he heaved at one of the planks. He studied the hole he had made and waved Elaine over.

"You are smaller than I am – can you get through there?"

Elaine joined him on top of the wagon, but looked doubtfully at the thin gap. She bent over it and whispered down.

"It's alright, don't struggle. I'm going to get you out of there."

For all the time he had known her, Lucius had never heard a single note of tenderness in Elaine's voice, and he felt his heart warm to hear it now. He watched as Elaine lay flat on the underside of the wagon, and wriggled through the hole until her head, shoulder and one arm was buried within it. When she started to shuffle back, Lucius grabbed her waist and helped her. As soon as her head was free, Elaine braced herself with her free arm and pulled a dirty, soot-covered child in a ragged shift free from the wreckage.

The child looked at them with wide eyes, the only part of its body that was not covered with soot or grime. Lucius could not even tell whether it was a boy or girl until Elaine, finally, after gentle coaxing, persuaded the child to talk.

"What happened to you, then?" Elaine asked.

"I was running with everyone," the boy said. Lucius guessed he was in his early teens, but short for his age. "From the fire."

"With your parents?"

The boy shook his head. "No, they're dead."

"Oh, I'm sorry," Elaine said, shocked by the boy's bluntness. He gave her an odd look.

"They died years ago," he said, as if it were the most obvious thing in the world.

Lucius smiled, in spite of himself. "He's one of Sebastian's lot."

"A beggar?" Elaine asked.

The boy looked up defiantly at her. "It's an honest profession."

"You don't need to explain," Lucius said. "Can you tell us what happened here? How did the fire start? Was it the thieves?"

"They started fires, sure. We all saw what they were doing. People started panicking, soldiers started running around. And then death arrived."

"Death?"

The boy shrugged. "That was what people were calling it. It floated, and looked like a woman. It looked like the saints look, in the pictures – but saints are supposed to be nice, aren't they? This one killed. Went from street to street, killing and killing everyone it met. It came along here. Started killing soldiers and when they were all gone, it started killing everyone else. I hid..."

Lucius and Elaine looked at one another meaningfully.

"I've seen bodies like that before, Lucius," Elaine said, venom creeping into her voice.

"Yes," he said quietly. "So have I."

"It's your witch, isn't?" There was accusation in Elaine's voice.

Lucius grasped her shoulders. "Elaine, I want you to leave now. Take the boy with you. Find somewhere safe to hole up."

"The hell I will!"

"Elaine, you cannot fight this woman. She's too powerful."

"No one bests me twice, Lucius," Elaine spat, and she jumped off the wagon to walk away, heading toward the oncoming flames.

She called back to him. "I presume we just follow the screams."

CHAPTER NINETEEN

THE SCREAMS DID indeed lead the way.

As they drew closer to the raging inferno, Lucius and Elaine felt the heat building on their skin. The air was hard to breathe, as though the flames were sucking it from the city, intent on turning Turnitia into a wasted ruin.

Lucius saw that, contrary to what he had seen when further away, the fires were not one perfect straight line consuming all in their path as they advanced, but patches of destruction racing one another through the city. As the fires reached the Square of True Believers, they slowed, perhaps suppressed by the Lord of All Himself as they licked the buildings nearest the Cathedral, which had remained untouched by their terrible heat. As they burnt through the tightly packed houses that spread away from the harbour, the flames increased in pace, surging ahead as they gouged a ragged, blackened wound in the city.

The streets were mostly empty; they saw only a few men and women, usually on their own, stumbling away from the oncoming flames, looking dazed.

Over the crackle of the flames and the crash of broken buildings falling under the onslaught, Lucius and Elaine both heard calls for help. Whether from those trapped in buildings already aflame or watching their loved ones burn, each cry pulled at their consciences, but they pushed on, following the loudest screams, Lucius dreading what he would find.

All around, dogs barked frantically.

As they neared the firestorm, houses burning on either side of the street, the heat became unbearable, and Elaine staggered, gasping for breath. Lucius put an arm around her shoulders and closed his eyes, summoning an arcane, invisible globe about them. Elaine looked up at him in surprise as cool air washed over her, and their breathing became less laboured.

They heard a man cry out in agony, somewhere very close, just beyond the line of low houses on their right. It was a gargled scream, born of pure torture, and it ended abruptly. An instant later, they felt the ground tremble as a tremendous crash resounded about the street, and a column of ash and cinders rose high into the pitch black sky from behind the roofs of the dwellings.

Propelling Elaine forward, keeping her close so she did not leave the protection of his globe, Lucius led them down a narrow alley between the burning houses. Fire arched over them as it leapt from roof to roof, lighting the alley in a deep orange glow, and he began to run as he felt his grip on the shielding globe begin to slip.

Rushing out the other end of the alley, they skidded to a stop, confronted with a scene of horror.

Blackened, burned and twisted bodies littered the street before them. The buildings on either side, two and three storey homes that had once belonged to some of the wealthier trade families of the district, were pouring fire and smoke into the sky, and some had started to collapse. A sheet of flame rose from the far end of the street, crossing its entire width as though the cobbles themselves were burning, and driven against this towering fire were a dozen people, cowering on the ground under the oppressive heat of the flames around them. Already, their clothes and hair were beginning to smoulder, smoke trailing up from each to be quickly lost in the maelstrom of soot and embers.

Before the people was a ragged line of half a dozen Vos soldiers, clearly daunted but resolute in their duty to protect themselves and the people behind them. Most were armed with spears and took cover behind shields, but two were armed with crossbows, and they pointed them upwards, toward one of the burning buildings.

Lucius looked at what they were aiming at, and gasped. The building's entire front wall had already crumbled, opening the rooms inside to the rest of the world. They burned ferociously but, hovering just in front of the second floor, suspended in open space by a column of air summoned to do her bidding, was Adrianna.

Standing motionless in mid-air, she looked down on the small crowd with imperious wrath. She was dressed in her usual black tunic, and wore a dark cloak that billowed out behind her in the air currents that held her aloft.

One of the cowering citizens crawled forward to the line of soldiers. A middle-aged man in clothes that had been half burned away, he started to chant, making obscure gestures with his hands, and Lucius suddenly realised he was a wizard, perhaps one of the Empire's own.

He had no chance to release his spell or even finish its construction, as Adrianna glared down at him and pointed. Lucius felt her magic surge forward, striking the wizard and the soldiers around him. They crumpled before his eyes, as if a great weight had been thrown casually on top of them, flattening them as they fell. Limbs, necks and bodies were twisted at angles that were terrible to behold, and none moved thereafter.

Outside of the spell's effects, the two crossbowmen nodded as they agreed upon a plan, and they broke ranks, each skirting to one side of Adrianna. Aiming high, they loosed their bolts, the dark missiles almost invisible against the glare of fires around them.

Adrianna did not betray any movement or reaction, but the bolts stopped suddenly in mid-air, just a foot away from her heart, as if they had been fired against an invisible wall. Their points blunted, they fell harmlessly to the street below where they clattered uselessly on the bone-dry cobbles.

This seemed to attract Adrianna's attention, and as she raised both her arms high above her head, the two crossbowmen followed suit, kicking and screaming as tightly controlled winds picked up their bodies and hurled them into the sky.

Lucius did not see where they landed, as they were thrown clear over burning roofs. He strode down the street towards Adrianna, Elaine just a few paces behind, neither entirely sure of what they were going to do.

"Aidy!" Lucius called.

Slowly, Adrianna turned to face him, the soldiers and city folk forgotten for the moment.

"Lucius," she said, acknowledging his arrival. Her voice was calm and level, as though spoken in normal conversation, but still he heard it clearly above the howling of the flames and screams of the dying.

"Aidy, what are you doing?" Lucius asked, despairing.

"This is the time, Lucius," she said. "Now. Right now. Help me erase the Vos scum from the city and we will finally be rid of their influence. Finally, we will be free!"

He gestured at the burning buildings around them. "Aidy, there will *be* no city! You haven't declared war on the Empire, you are killing *everyone*."

"They had their chance to leave," she said, nodding towards the frightened people below her. "Instead, they chose to hide behind Vos. They have chosen their path. Their lives and homes are forfeit!"

"What justice is that?" Lucius called up to her, desperate to keep her talking, even as his mind raced to find a way through this.

She looked down with a puzzled expression. "What in hell has justice got to do with anything? Was it justice when Vos soldiers first marched into this city? Was it justice when they started wiping out anyone who opposed them? Or was it justice when they killed Forbeck? No, Lucius, this is not about justice. All that is left is victory for us, and total, crippling defeat for them. It is not enough that we drive them out – they must be too scared to come back for fear of what we will do to them."

"At what cost, Aidy? How many innocent people must die, how much of this city will you destroy in order to save it?"

"As much as it takes, fool!" she spat. "A city can be rebuilt. A city can be repopulated. A Shadowmage cannot be replaced. You, as much as any of us, should understand that."

He shook his head. "I cannot agree."

For a moment, Adrianna just stared at him, and Lucius could not tell whether it was out of pity, disdain or loathing.

"From the day I first met you, I knew you had abilities that could surpass any of us. I also knew you would never reach your true potential. You, Lucius, are the worst kind of traitor to us. You have the talent that could change the entire world for us, but you are too lazy, ignorant and feckless to see that. Go. Take your whore with you, and go. Consider it my last favour to you that I spare your lives."

"I cannot let you carry on with this massacre," he said flatly.

She smiled at him without a trace of humour. "I did not think you would."

With the speed of a coiled serpent striking, Adrianna's hammer bolt of magical energy surged down towards them. Lucius and Elaine dove away from it, rolling on the ground as the bolt smashed into the street, throwing up cobbled stones and earth from the impact.

Rolling back to her feet, Elaine whipped out the last throwing knife at her belt and let it fly at Adrianna. The knife hissed through the air, but was deflected from its path by a gesture from the Shadowmage. In turn, with a contemptuous look, Adrianna punched the air.

Lucius recovered his own footing just in time to see Elaine thrown through the air. He reached out with his own magic, but felt the threads slip from his control as he realised he could not build a spell in time to counter Adrianna's. Elaine soared across the street as if propelled from a catapult, and crashed through the burning front of a small shop. The force of the throw brought down timbers from the floor above, and the flames inside billowed briefly, swallowing the assassin completely.

"By all that is holy, I'll make you pay dearly for that, Adrianna," Lucius said, his voice low.

"This is what I have been trying to get through to you, idiot!" Adrianna shot back. "People like that are barely worth the ground they walk on! You and I, on the other hand, we are precious, Lucius."

He did not wait to hear more. Knowing that Adrianna had access to far greater magic than he, Lucius realised he had to use any advantage he had if he were to survive this encounter, let alone emerge without defeat. Seeing Elaine so casually killed, he finally knew that he had to try to take Adrianna down any way he could.

Quickly tugging on two threads of magic, he sent twin bolts toward Adrianna. They were not powerful spells, and he nodded grimly to himself when he saw them dissipate harmlessly against the shield Adrianna had raised around herself, and was apparently maintaining without effort. In his mind's eye, he saw the bolts completely absorbed. That told him something, at least.

Seeing the distraction, the crowd of people caught near the fire began to move. First one started to crawl away, then another sprang to their feet and started to run. Within seconds, they were all sprinting for their lives, scrabbling to get away from the terror that had nearly claimed them.

Adrianna noticed this and frowned. As they ran past her, she conjured a great ball of air, the currents whipping around inside tighter and tighter. Hurling it down, she threw it into the front of a building just as the people streamed past it. The structural support for the front wall buckled under the strain and started to tumble, even as the flames inside grew with a new intensity as they were fed with the released currents of air.

With a terrible but inevitable slowness, the front of the building collapsed, masonry and burning timbers crashing down into the street on top of the crowd. Only those who had first started to run escaped; the rest were crushed by falling stone or consumed by the flames.

Cursing Adrianna's callousness, Lucius aimed another set of magical bolts at her, this time drawing on different magical threads. One of them, the bolt that took its energy from the darkest of magics, reacted violently with her shield.

His theory, and that of Master Forebeck, was confirmed. Now Lucius had his weapon.

He pulled on the thread of unlife, pouring its energy into a new spell around Adrianna. Almost instantly, she saw what he was doing and began to fuel her own shield, but as he clenched his fist, Lucius felt the pressure of his spell begin to squeeze her shield dry of energy.

The rate at which Adrianna repaired the damage he dealt to the shield was impressive, he could not deny, but the death magic he used simply annihilated the natural energies she was using, draining them as fast as she could funnel magic into her defence. Flooding the air about her with his spell, Lucius felt the crack as her shield buckled and broke.

As his spell reached Adrianna, she screamed aloud, and he saw her skin turn grey as heat, vitality and life were drawn from her. The air currents holding her aloft failed, and she plummeted to the ground, where only a hastily improvised spell saved her from a mortal fall. Hitting the ground hard, she rose shakily to her feet almost immediately.

Her face was a mask of hate, filled with rage that Lucius dared to penetrate her magics and had actually managed to hurt her. Colour flooded back into her skin as arcane energies surged through her, and Lucius quickly reshaped his spell to form a protective wall between them.

The dark bolt of energy that she flung at him ripped through his magical wall as though it were paper and exploded against his chest, throwing him back as it sizzled with a cold fire. Clutching his chest in pain, Lucius cursed himself for not anticipating her move; after all, the shadow bolt she had just sent his way was a branch of magic that Shadowmages were all familiar with. Now he had to find a way to trump the magic of shadows as well as Adrianna's grip on natural sorcery.

He saw Adrianna fuelling another spell, and there was no mercy in her expression. Lucius could feel the thread of shadows twist and lose focus as Adrianna pulled upon it to do her bidding and relinquished all control, knowing he could not compete with her directly. Instead, he plucked the more stable strands of four threads, more or less at random, sweating as he quickly assembled them into a multi-layered shield.

The shield was only just raised in time, and Lucius knew he would have to be quick in its manipulation if he were to survive her next strike. Each layer was painfully thin, having been hastily formed, and the effort of controlling four threads at a time was taking its toll, as his vision blurred and breathing became shallow. He could feel the strength ebbing from his limbs and his thoughts becoming disjointed.

Adrianna's next bolt of shadow was a hammer blow that shattered the first two layers of his shield as though they were no more than air. The next, a gossamer thin construction, formed from the same natural magic that Adrianna was gifted with, held.

Immediately dissolving the rest of the threads, Lucius sank more energy into that single defence. He felt Adrianna narrow her focus as she, too, poured magic into her spell, trying to drive her bolt through the shield and into his body. Lucius' control began to slip as his shield grew in power to match the onslaught, but still Adrianna's spell pressed at him.

For a brief second, Lucius felt the pressure of Adrianna's spell relax, and he wondered whether she had abandoned it. Then she threw a second bolt at him. It sped into the shield, growing in strength as Lucius' own spell began to fuel it. He cried in alarm as he saw his defences falter and felt an icy grip of cold air begin to circle him like a snake. As if a giant had plucked him from the ground, Lucius found himself tossed through the air, flying across the street to land hard on the cobbles.

Choking, Lucius was dimly aware that the throw had stunned him, and struggled to draw breath into his tortured lungs. He knew Adrianna was not far away and would be preparing her next spell, one that would finish him off if he did not get back on his feet.

Shaking his head to clear his vision, Lucius took a deep but painful breath, and then raised himself up on his arms. Slowly, he stood, and faced Adrianna.

She had taken to the air again, and was floating above the ruined shop. Her defences were back up again, and Adrianna was already summoning magic in readiness for their next bout. She looked as healthy and alert as when they had started this fight.

"I never wanted to kill you, Lucius," Adrianna called down to him. "But you are beginning to prove a hindrance. For the good of our future, you cannot be allowed to interfere further."

Lucius felt the energies build up within Adrianna, and knew that he had neither the strength nor the talent to defend himself. He knew he had only a few more seconds of life left to him.

"It doesn't have to be this way, Aidy," he said bleakly. "We could still be allies. You just have to..."

Words failed him.

"You have no idea of what is going on, or what has truly been at stake. You have wasted every opportunity the Shadowmages have offered to you, and now that will prove your downfall. You could have been one of us, Lucius, not a common thief."

"So maybe I am just a common thief, Aidy. You could let me walk away now. I've left this city before, I'll leave it again," he said, trying not to sound as though he were begging. Dignity aside, he guessed how Adrianna would regard any display of weakness.

Instead, she actually smiled.

"You would come back," she said. "You always will. I don't think you could ever stay away for long."

In his mind, Lucius felt Adrianna start to feed energy into her spell. He stared up at her, facing annihilation.

"This would just happen later, if it did not happen now," Adrianna said. "Best we end this now, Lucius."

A flash of movement from behind Adrianna drew Lucius' gaze, and he was astonished to see Elaine. Shakily moving toward Adrianna, sword drawn, Elaine looked ravaged. She was blackened with soot from head to foot, which did not disguise the ugly wound that bled from her scalp or her limp.

Lucius opened his mouth to shout, but he suddenly realised he did not know who to shout to. Despite her injuries, Elaine slithered towards Adrianna with cat-like grace, a look of grim, deathly determination on her face.

Sensing something amiss, Adrianna spun around, and saw Elaine, just feet from her. Before she could reshape the spell, the assassin sprang forward, hacking down with the sword and burying it deep into Adrianna's shoulder. Lucius saw blood spray from the wound, the sword's tip visible through her back.

Adriana screeched, a piercing, inhuman wail. She raised her free arm and let the magic she had gathered flow without control. A firestorm of bright, multi-coloured light sprang from her hand, shards of magic lancing through Elaine's body and spilling out into the shop's crumbling walls where they exploded in a shower of burning debris.

Unable to take this last abuse, the building sagged and collapsed in on itself in a mass of flames, rubble and smoke that billowed up into the sky, carrying burning embers with it.

Lucius stared at the ruin, where Elaine and Adrianna had fought a moment before, now buried deep within the burning rubble.

Lucius fell to his knees and, covering his head with his arms, wept.

CHAPTER TWENTY

WITH THE RISING sun climbing the eastern sky, Turnitia was already a boiling hive of activity. People moved through the streets with purpose, either joining the crowds in the Square of True Believers or near the northern gate, or else hawking their wares to the mob from street corners. A few, no doubt, moved with more nefarious tasks in mind.

Lucius had found one of the few quiet places in the city, on the northern tower of the Citadel, one of the highest points in Turnitia. Since the earliest hours of the morning, the Citadel had been all but deserted, with just a few officials and servants inside. None had even challenged him when he had strode confidently through the gatehouse. From this vantage point, Lucius could watch almost the entire northern half of the city, looking down upon its houses, shops, and squares.

Gazing to the west, enjoying the fresh breeze that washed in over the cliffs, Lucius tried not to look at the great blackened gashes that still marred the city, whole districts still in ruin. In the two months since the great fire, as the citizens had started to call it, the city had rallied and rebuilt a great deal of the destruction, but it would take much longer to erase the last evidence of the attacks. Maybe a lifetime, for those who lost loved ones that evening, and there were many who had lost wives, husbands, and children. Listening to conversations in taverns and inns, it seemed as though everyone at least knew someone who had died, and most had far more personal tales to tell.

Around the cliffs and harbour, many new warehouses and loading stations had sprung up within weeks of the fire, and the merchants' quarter looked much like it always had. Not even a city-wide disaster could interfere with the merchants, it seemed, and Lucius suspected more than a few had made a great deal of money in the rebuilding, and were silently thanking the tragedy.

"You are still an easy man to find," a voice called out behind him.

Turning around, he forced a smile as Adrianna climbed the last few stairs that led up to the tower's roof. Though her hair had begun to grow back, her face would remain a network of burn scars. There was no doubt that it marred her beauty, but Lucius could see something of a change had come about the Shadowmage since the great fire and he suspected she no longer cared for something so trivial as beauty.

Her shoulder would eventually heal, but her left arm was still bound up in a sling, and he had noticed Adrianna still winced whenever she moved too quickly, or brushed her arm against something. There was some comfort to be had in seeing that she was still human.

They had never spoken of the evening of the great fire, nor of the death of Elaine. Neither wanted to pick at old wounds.

Lucius believed Adrianna somewhat unhinged. At first, he had hoped her madness held at its root some measure of shame for the atrocities she had committed, but it seemed there was no room in her heart for mere mortal conscience. She had become drunk on the power she now wielded with such finesse, and was a dangerous person to know.

For his part, Lucius had buried his feelings for Adrianna, both good and bad, deep down. There was simply too much at stake now, and while the sun seemed to be rising on his city, he had vowed not to rock the boat between the guilds. Either way, he had resolved to be very, very wary around her.

He suspected she knew this, and that it amused her.

"I was not trying to hide," he said, gesturing to the battlements, indicating that she should join him.

As she walked over to view the city alongside him, Adrianna smiled, creasing the scars that ran across her cheeks.

"Just as well," she said.

Turning to follow her gaze north, Lucius watched the crowd gathered in the Square of True Believers, spilling out into the North Way towards the city gate. A great column of red marched out of Turnitia, the full weight of the Vos military that had been stationed in Turnitia, along with its assorted officials and hangers-on. The people of the city were respectful in their farewells to the soldiers that had watched over them in recent years, but few were sad at seeing them leave. Some might even have joined the crowd just to make sure the Empire was truly departing.

The day before, the Preacher Divine had made another speech in front of the Cathedral, exalting those in the city who followed the

Final Faith, and urging them to do God's will when he left. He had tried very hard to make the retreat of Vos look positive, as though it was in the natural order of things, but nothing could hide the injury that had been done to the Empire or, for that matter, the Preacher Divine himself. The assassins had crippled his right arm, and the best Vos surgeons had been unable to save it.

For better or worse, the combined efforts of Adrianna and the thieves' guild had made the Empire's position in the city untenable. Within a week of the great fire, when Vos officials and commanders were still foundering from lack of leadership and the demands of a broken city, Baron de Sousse, up to then a relatively minor lord from Pontaine, had decreed that the rule of the Empire in Turnitia was over, and that he would take the city under the protection of his estates.

It was a simple land grab, but it left the Empire with a stark choice: leave the city or go to war over Turnitia.

It was certain that Pontaine could not face war itself, but nor could Vos, and the presence of de Sousse's army so close to the city forced the withdrawal.

"Thought I would find you two up here," a young voice said, and Lucius smiled as Adrianna whirled around.

"Good morning, Grennar," he said. "Won't you join us?"

"I will, thank you."

"How did you know we were here?" Adrianna asked suspiciously. Grennar gave her a pained look.

"You think the mistress of the beggars' guild does not always know where the mistress of the Shadowmages and the thieves' guildmaster are, at all times?"

"Frankly, no," said Adrianna.

"Oh," Grennar said. "In that case, you might want to think about moving from your lair in the cliffs."

Lucius chuckled. When the Shadowmage threw him a dangerous look, he held up a hand.

"Do not trouble yourself with what Grennar does and does not know," he said. "Just be sure to consult her whenever you need to know anything that happens in the city."

Lucius admired Grennar a great deal. She was wise beyond her years, as the saying went, and there was much that she and Adrianna had in common. After Sebastian abdicated leadership of the beggars' guild to go travelling, Lucius had wondered whether Grennar would have the strength of character to govern a guild filled with so many older than herself.

She had risen to the challenge. Just as Adrianna had some very definite ideas about how the Shadowmages' guild should be organised and run, so too was Grennar determined to leave her stamp upon the beggars. With him now running the thieves' guild, the three of them had formed an alliance of sorts and, though Lucius and Grennar did not really trust Adrianna, they could all see the possible benefits and support the alliance could offer. Grennar had nicknamed them the Triumvirate, and proclaimed their ability to run the entire city.

Lucius did not believe their influence would stretch that far, but the possibilities were interesting.

For his own part, Lucius had finally accepted leadership of the thieves. He still maintained that it was not something he wanted but there had been no one else he trusted. A very long conversation with Wendric had left him with the impression that the lieutenant had risen as far in the guild as he ever intended. Wendric liked the authority he carried as the guild's second, but did not want the responsibility that went with overall leadership. He wanted to be the man behind the master, not the master himself. That left Lucius.

Deep down, Lucius had told himself that he would stay just a few years and abdicate when someone better came along. Until then, there was plenty of work to be done and the idea of shaping the guild to his own personality had an appeal.

"Good riddance to them," Grennar said, pronouncing her judgement on the Vos soldiers as they began to wind their way through the north gate.

"What is the word on the streets?" Lucius asked.

Grennar shrugged. "The people seem optimistic. Not sure why. Our new masters may not be that different from our old masters."

"Pontaine has a different way of doing things," he said.

"We will find out soon enough," Grennar said. "Their army will be here before the evening."

"That soon?" Adrianna asked.

"You don't think Vos just picked a random day to leave the city, do you? They wanted to keep their claws in the city for as long as they possibly could."

"Any rumours on this baron?" Lucius asked.

"More than rumours. We have already had an audience."

Lucius and Adrianna turned to face her, brows raised.

"How did you manage that?" Lucius finally asked.

"It's my guild now, thief. We are doing things my way, and I always thought Sebastian limited himself by only having agents within the city walls. I simply… expanded things."

Again, Lucius chuckled.

"Impressive," Adrianna allowed. "How did your contact with the baron go?"

"Well, by all accounts," Grennar said. "The… situation in the city was explained to de Sousse, and he has requested a meeting with the three of us."

Adrianna and Lucius glanced at each other briefly, thinking the same thoughts. It was Grennar that spoke them out loud.

"It seems the Baron de Sousse is an intelligent man. He recognises who has the power in the city and he is willing to do business with us."

Lucius smiled. "That is good work, Grennar."

She gave him a mock curtsey.

They returned to the battlements, each now lost in their own thoughts and plans as they watched the last Vos soldiers leave the city and start the long march back to the Empire.

Lucius knew he would have trouble with some of his thieves, particularly those that had been in the guild the longest. And the assassins, of course. They all knew about his Shadowmage abilities, and not all were comfortable with a wizard among their ranks, especially as they had learned how Elaine had died. The resentment would only get worse when they found out he had also pledged himself to renew his magical training under Adrianna's direction. That, of course, would carry its own dangers, but the recent events had convinced him that he could no longer turn his back on his heritage. For better or worse, he would be both thief and Shadowmage.

So, he thought, there was a new age coming for Turnitia. It might never be the free and independent city it once was, long ago, but if this new Pontaine lord was prepared to deal with guilds on the fringes of society, life was about to improve.

The world was opening up with possibilities.

THE END

LEGACY'S PRICE

Original cover art by Greg Staples

CHAPTER ONE

THE CITADEL LEERED down over Turnitia, its five towers as dark and threatening as they ever had been. Involuntarily, Lucius kept his eyes downcast and wrapped his grey cloak about him all the tighter, as if to avoid scrutiny from the occupants of the fortress.

It was habit. Not three months ago, the Citadel had been the outward symbol of Vos domination and tyranny over a city that had once rejoiced in its own liberty as much as Freiport did now. Dozens, maybe hundreds, of the city's citizens had gone through the huge iron-wrought gates that towered above him, never to be seen again. Many of those had been thieves from his own guild.

What a difference three months made.

Where Vos had once ruled, now Pontaine was dominant, rising in its ascendancy. The ever opportunistic baron, de Sousse, had taken advantage of the weakness with which the Vos Empire had held the city and now his troops garrisoned the Citadel, his court reigning in its keep.

Even Pontaine frippery could not change the outward nature of the Citadel, though.

Lucius passed through the main gates that burrowed through the yards-thick exterior wall, faintly marvelling at the lack of guards. Under the Vos regime, the gates were never opened unless there was good reason, and the familiar red-tabarded guards would be present in force. Now Pontaine held sway, security was far less visible, and the city's people were openly encouraged to enter the courtyard, trade, do business with Pontaine officials, or even just take a look around the place that had dominated their lives.

That was the tradition of Pontaine leadership. To rule without being seen to rule. To interact and build relationships with the populace, not ruthlessly control their lives. As far as the Baron de

Sousse was concerned, Lucius was coming to believe, it mattered less than the fate of a fly what citizens got up to in their own homes or on their own streets. So long as their taxes were paid and the – fairly lax, by Vos standards – rule of law was obeyed, the lords of Pontaine would not even notice you.

That was a good starting position for the leader of a thieves' guild, and Lucius was here this evening to see just how flexible the baron intended to be.

Beyond the gates, the courtyard of the Citadel was mostly empty, with just a few citizens gathering their possessions after a day's trading, watched by a smaller number of off-duty Pontaine guardsmen, their bright blue and orange tunics stretched tight over chainmail. However, despite the spears they kept near to hand, there was little intimidating or frightening about them. They relaxed, joking amongst themselves as they drank deeply from pewter tankards.

Lucius cast a long glance around the courtyard, taking in the various outbuildings scattered along the inside of the main walls, the looming keep that rose even above their height, and the long stone bridge that spanned from the keep to one of the five towers. He had fought for his life on that bridge, infiltrated the depths of the keep, and battled alongside his thieves and assassins against the worst Vos could throw at them. Many had died.

From time to time, Lucius found himself naming the dead. Swinherd, Nate, Helmut, Harker, Hengit.

Elaine.

Many had died here in the Citadel, others had been caught in clashes between the thieves and the tightening grip of the Vos Empire.

If some of their killers had escaped to Vos during the rout, then at least the Citadel itself still bore the scars. The unleashing of powerful magics deep within the keep had shattered part of its foundations, and Lucius could see the metal and wood framework supporting the eastern corner of the giant building as Pontaine engineers laboured to repair the damage. There was talk around the city that the foundations were beyond help and that the Citadel would have to be completely demolished and rebuilt. Lucius would not have minded that.

As he closed the distance to the keep, sounds of music and laughter floated to him across the courtyard. The noise seemed at odds with the sombre surroundings, and even the garish banners hung from the walls of the keep, welcoming various Pontaine lords, did nothing to aid the atmosphere of revelry. Not that this seemed to matter to those inside the keep's main hall.

Two guardsmen dipped their spears in a half-salute as Lucius approached the keep's grand entrance, but they did not so much as ask his name as he mounted the wide stone stairs and passed them. Lucius shook his head silently. Three months.

The keep's entrance took him down a long, wide corridor that arched high above him, the lanterns suspended on iron brackets strategically placed to create shadows across the ceiling. Within the shadows lay murder holes and other defences, but the baron apparently felt that highlighting their presence would perhaps not put people at ease as they entered his court.

Passing through the corridor into the main hall, Lucius was immediately assaulted by the full weight of revelry taking place.

The hall was packed, with long tables arranged in rows down its length. Around each one, people clustered, with lords of Pontaine rubbing shoulders with Turnitia's richest and most ambitious. Everywhere, people were feasting and drinking, taking delight in the bread, wines and cheeses brought into the city from Pontaine. Even the meats supplied by the city had been prepared with a Pontaine flavour, and smells of rich sauces and seasonings wafted around the hall as provocatively-dressed servants scurried to provide the attendees with ever greater courses, a constant flow that emanated from the kitchens.

On the other side of the hall, more food was prepared, this time in full view of everyone. Several large pigs were being roasted whole above fire pits, the smoke only seeming to add to the atmosphere as it wound its way through the enormous hall. Above them, high on the balcony that stretched around three sides of the hall, a large band – perhaps those from Pontaine would call it an orchestra, Lucius did not know – played quietly, its subdued tones of wind and wood draping themselves gently over the banquet below, enhancing the pleasure of the event without dominating it.

Straight across from the main entrance, sat de Sousse himself, flamboyantly dressed even for a Pontaine noble, no doubt enjoying his sudden rise to power and prominence with his victory in Turnitia, albeit won by deceit and good timing rather than force of arms. The baron and his closest allies sat on a raised dais, their table overflowing with the very best the kitchens could amass. A giant roasted elk dominated the table, with some rich golden fruit from

Pontaine's heartlands wedged firmly in its mouth. Cherries had been hung from its antlers and it was these that de Sousse was swiping by the handful as he reached across the table while animatedly describing some battle or tournament to the lords on his left.

Before them stretched a long line of supplicants, people of Turnitia who were looking for some favour, be it leniency for a crime committed, gold for investment or permission to start trading directly with the baron and Pontaine as a whole. For them, this audience was the whole point of the evening, not the rich banquet, and for many their whole lives could rest on the baron's answer.

A young girl caught Lucius' eye as she waved him over to a nearby table. With a freckled face framed by neat, dark hair that sank to her shoulders, she could not have been more than fourteen or fifteen years old. Dressed in a tight gown of pale blue satin, she looked like the innocent daughter of some lord or rich merchant who had finally been allowed to attend her first banquet.

Lucius knew better. As he approached, she grabbed the collar of a drunken man who had passed out on the table beside her and, with a heave, sent him toppling over the back of the bench to make room for Lucius.

Stepping over the sprawled man, who merely groaned and tried to crawl under the bench to escape the noise of the revelry before failing and slumping unconscious once again, Lucius sat down next to the girl and reached across the table to grab a half loaf of long, thin Pontaine bread.

"Grennar," he said with a slight nod.

"You're late."

"Fashionably so, I hope."

She cast a withering look at his cloak and the tough leather tunic underneath.

"Leave the fashion to me, Lucius. I am a much better study."

That, he had to concede.

"How goes life for the beggars?"

Grennar shrugged. "Things change, things stay the same. Business booms ether way."

"You are not finding things easier under Pontaine rule?"

"Oh, it is easier. But that doesn't mean we are earning any more. Despite Vos' best efforts, there were always loopholes and gaps in their policies. That is where the beggars flourish, regardless of who is in charge."

She did not look like a beggar but, again, Lucius knew better.

As young as she was, Grennar had learned from the best and had developed a self-confidence that far outweighed her years. Under her leadership, the beggars' guild of Turnitia had expanded and grown, making life difficult if not outright impossible for those who did not join, and creating wealth for those who did. She was an invaluable ally to Lucius and his own guild, as the beggars were the eyes and ears of the city. What his thieves could not discover, the beggars surely would. Nine times out of ten, they had already obtained the information he sought before he asked. Beggars were all but invisible to cityfolk, and were rarely noticed as people went about their business or confided secrets to one another.

A round of polite applause rose from the other end of the hall as the Baron de Sousse stood to make a pronouncement. He directed his attention to the lead group of petitioners that lined up before his table and pointed at each one individually.

"Yes, yes, no, no, no, and yes," he declared grandly, granting or denying the favours sought before hearing what they were. More than one of the petitioners looked as though they wanted to argue the point, but the baron's attention was already fixed upon a troupe of scantily-clad Allantian dancers that had been ushered into the hall, and the thump of a spear's butt from a nearby guardsmen served to dissuade any further dissent.

"That was quick," Lucius said, frowning. "Erratic to the point of capricious."

"Oh, no," Grennar said with as much of a wolfish smile as a young teenage girl could muster. "I've been studying the good baron all evening."

Lucius gave her a frank look. "Somehow, I think I should have guessed that."

She thought for a moment before frowning herself.

"Yes," she said. "You should. Anyway, our noble baron is a canny mark, and one worthy of some caution. See the servant that attends him now?"

Looking back up to the dais, Lucius saw the baron clapping and howling for more from the dancers, whose combination of thin silks and slow gymnastics had roused the interest of most of the men nearby – and not a few of the Pontaine women.

He almost missed the young man bringing another flagon of wine to the table. It was such a normal, casual act, especially here, in the hall of a Pontaine lord. As the servant leaned over the table, Lucius saw him whisper something, ever so briefly, to the baron, and a swift sleight of hand dropped a small parchment onto the table next to the flagon. Fascinated now, Lucius watched; as the baron continued to harangue the dancers, his eyes flickered to the parchment.

"You see it?" Grennar asked.

Lucius nodded slowly.

"He already knew what those witless fools wanted before they got into line," Grennar said. "There has been a constant flow of information being passed to the baron, always by the servants, never the same one twice in a row."

Even taking into account what he had seen, Lucius was more than prepared to believe Grennar on this point. The girl had a feel for the flow of information and how its transfer worked that made her truly gifted in her profession.

"So, we should be wary," he said.

Grennar considered this. "Yes and no. Don't give anything away that you don't have to when we speak with the baron. He is sharp enough, and you can be sure that whatever he misses will be picked up by one of his own people. Don't be surprised if we are interrupted by something that seems inconsequential – most likely, the baron will be getting a briefing on something we have just said."

"Right," Lucius said, beginning to wish he could delegate such meetings to someone else in his guild. He was skilled at planning, even better at executing a plan, but politics was never his strength. That brought another frown as he considered that, when it came to politicking, they young girl seated next to him was likely his master.

"But do not panic either," Grennar said. "We more or less know what he wants – peace and prosperity, for both himself and the city as a whole. That makes him predictable. If the Triumvirate can guarantee no mess or trouble from our guilds and a continued flow of silver and gold, we will get what we want. Or, at least, what we need."

Lucius had to smile at that. Ever since Vos had left Turnitia, Grennar had started referring to herself, Lucius and Adrianna as the Triumvirate, the true power behind the city. She controlled the beggars, and so controlled information. Lucius was guildmaster of the thieves, and so controlled vast amounts of wealth. For her part, Adrianna ruled the Shadowmages, which was a frightening enough prospect in itself given recent events, but through her guild she wielded power that Lucius and Grennar could not even begin to match.

Little happened in Turnitia's underworld without the say of at least one of the guild leaders. Hence the term Triumvirate. Lucius was less sure that anyone else, de Sousse least of all, thought in quite the same terms, but the three of them were certainly a power bloc of sorts within the city and, thus, people who had to be listened to and, to a measure, respected.

Grennar had determined early on that the baron, who was now smearing warm butter over the naked thigh of one of the dancers he had called to his table, was a man they could do business with. That had never been the case with the Vos management, who had ever been the enemy of all three.

"Speaking of the Triumvirate, has our third member arrived yet?" Lucius asked.

Casting a look over her shoulder, Grennar shook her head. "Perhaps Adrianna is going for unfashionably late?"

"Speak my name and I shall appear," a woman whispered behind them, a mischievous taint to her voice lending her fire-scarred face a dread quality.

Lucius glanced round and nodded a greeting to Adrianna and, with an apologetic look to the man next to him, shuffled along the bench to create room for her to sit. He saw Grennar narrow her eyes briefly, and he guessed why. The girl had looked behind them mere seconds before Adrianna had appeared, and had not seen the Shadowmage. Adrianna had seemed to materialise out of thin air, though whether it had been actual magic or simply a stealthy approach through the crowd, Lucius could not tell. Once, he had been able to sense the use of Adrianna's magic, but those times had passed.

Once, he had called her Aidy, but it was now impossible to think of her in those old, familiar terms. This was now a very different woman sitting next to him, one utterly confident in her abilities which in themselves might well be boundless. She made him nervous and, though Grennar hid it, he knew Adrianna had a similar effect on the girl.

"We were wondering whether you would show up at all," Grennar said, trying to cover her discomfort. Lucius had always felt that Grennar trusted him, as much as anyone could trust a thief, and considered him her equal. However, he also suspected that, around Adrianna, she felt more like the little teenage girl everyone else saw.

Adrianna beckoned and a tankard of wine skidded across the table into her waiting hand. She sipped at it and winced, the curse under her breath decrying all foul Pontaine wines.

"I was *summoned*," she said pointedly, before glaring at Lucius. "Summoned. Me!"

Lucius meant to lay a hand on Adrianna's arm to calm her fury, but stopped before his hand had travelled an inch. He briefly considered it was silly for him to think that she would burn him down with magic just for touching her. He also remembered that, in the past, he had touched far more of her than that, but instantly wiped the memory from his mind's eye.

"I know we don't need this baron," Lucius began, "but we can perhaps make things easier for ourselves."

He did not entirely believe this – many of the things he wanted out of this evening very much required the assent of the baron, but he had learned to talk to Adrianna in her own language, from her own perspective. It saved a great deal of argument and, after events in the recent past, Lucius was still very cautious in his dealings with Adrianna. Her energies seemed to be concentrated solely in gathering power for her guild of Shadowmages these days, but he never knew what might spark another explosion of her wrath. If that happened, the whole city might suffer.

Again.

"If a mere evening's work means we can come to a suitable arrangement with the baron, then Grennar can get back to her beggars, me to the thieves and you can. . ." Lucius hesitated for a second, unsure of how to proceed.

Adrianna cocked an eyebrow at his delay and smiled with all the grace of a viper.

"What, Lucius?" she asked, the mischief coming back into her voice. Lucius wondered whether she had developed a natural cruel streak in recent months, or whether she viewed making him nervous as some sort of sport, or punishment. "I can get back to building the strongest and most powerful guild of mages this poor world has ever seen, perhaps? Start dredging up the oldest of magics and wrestle them under my command alone? Is that what you were going to say?"

"We've all got things we want, and they are things the baron can give to us with very little effort," Lucius said, determined not to be drawn into whatever dark fantasy Adrianna was contemplating.

"He's right," said Grennar from the other side of Adrianna. "The baron is someone we can actually negotiate with."

She stopped her explanation as Adrianna slowly turned to give her a withering glance of contempt. Grennar looked away, under the pretence of studying the baron further, but Lucius could sense how unsure she was around the older woman. Then again, Adrianna had that effect on most people she met.

Adrianna turned back to Lucius. "I will tell this baron what I am after, and he may request certain services of my guild. But this is not a negotiation, you understand that, Lucius? I do not negotiate. The baron wants what only my Shadowmages can provide. My price will be high and I will not be bartered down like some common trader. You remember that."

Lucius nodded dutifully. "I will, Adrianna. I will."

"And I trust you have not forgotten your training tomorrow."

"I'll be there."

"Make sure you are clear headed when you arrive," Adrianna said as she sent her thoughts across the room to redirect a servant who was carrying a silvered plate of cold meats to the baron's table. The boy looked momentarily confused, then trotted over to place the food in front of Adrianna.

Lucius returned the cup of mead he was about to drink to the table. He was not sure if Adrianna had been giving him a pointed direction or whether she was oblivious to his actions, but he decided that getting drunk at the banquet would not be the wisest move. In fact, he would not have put it past the baron for that to be the intention of inviting them to the banquet before meeting them.

The evening continued and the three guildmasters watched, the conversation between Lucius and Grennar somewhat stilted now Adrianna had arrived, as others in the hall steadily became more inebriated with the free-flowing Pontaine wines, spirits, mead and a drink served in a hot bowl they heard described as the Flower of Anclas. Its effect seemed to floor even the heaviest-set drinker quickly.

Many of the men present paired themselves with young female companions and throughout the darker recesses of the hall the couples could be seen in various states of undress, taking advantage of looser Pontaine morals to elevate themselves on the social ladder in a more intimate fashion, or simply to enjoy pleasures of the flesh beyond the copious food and drink. It seemed to Lucius that their visitors from Pontaine took everything to excess without recourse to consequences. He wondered if that would be the case during business negotiations.

An hour or more passed, and Lucius could tell Adrianna was becoming impatient, not from what she said but her growing, cold silence. It was with some relief that he saw the Baron de Sousse finally stand up and declare himself fit to retire, but he gave his blessings to anyone who wanted to continue enjoying his hospitality.

With that, the baron turned and disappeared into one of the many small doorways that lined the main hall, giving a lewd wink to a young man who had cornered one of the female servants against the wall and was trying to clumsily navigate his way through her garments.

"Does he intend to keep us here all night?" Adrianna finally said after another half-hour went by. Lucius was beginning to get worried that she would simply push her way into the keep in an effort to find the baron, and he doubted the lax attitude the Pontaine baron had lent to his security would extend to his personal quarters.

"We'll be sent for," he said. "I imagine you would have much to deal with yourself in your own house."

He received a dismissive snort for his trouble, but a few minutes later a tall man clad in a dark blue tunic bowed low to them and bid them follow. The baron awaited their pleasure.

Once outside the hall, Lucius was surprised at how loud the banquet had been, for the corridors and staircases leading into the more secret parts of the keep were deathly quiet, leaving his ears ringing slightly from the lack of noise.

Leading them on what seemed a circuitous route past many confusing junctions and up six flights of spiralled stairs, the tall man bowed low again as he drew up to a closed door which he rapped upon once with his knuckles, and then swept his hand to indicate they should enter.

Adrianna was first, followed by Lucius and Grennar. The room was large, with an open balcony opposite the door that looked out onto the courtyard. Within, the room was richly appointed, with thick and colourful rugs scattered across the floor, while dozens of framed paintings depicting both landscapes and people fought for space on the walls. In front of the balcony, the baron sat behind a Sardenne oak desk, a finely crafted example with gold-inlaid patterns woven into the legs and rim. The contents of this room alone were worth several of the richer townhouses in Turnitia and served to mark the baron as an extremely wealthy man. The Citadel, after all, was merely an outpost in his wider realm. What must his home castle be like?

The Baron de Sousse was hunched over his desk, taking great care as he wrote into a book with a magnificent feathered quill. He did not look up as he spoke.

"Please, do come in," he said, and Lucius noted immediately that his speech was not slurred in the least. However much the baron had drunk during the banquet, it seemed to affect him little. "I must apologise for my inattention, but I get so little time to work on the important things in life that I am forced to snatch but minutes here and there."

Reaching the end of his current page, he reached across his desk for a pot and scattered powder from it over the wet ink. Holding the book up, he twisted round towards the balcony and blew on it, sending the powder spiralling into the evening air. Turning back to them, he gave a gracious smile.

"My current project," he said, gesturing to the book as he laid it back down on the desk. "A history of expeditions into the Sardenne."

"You have had family engage in such expeditions in the past," Grennar said, and Lucius was not entirely sure it was a question.

The baron graced her with a wide beaming smile. "Indeed, young lady. It was my grandfather who penetrated the northern reaches to bring back the first reliable maps of the interior." His smile slipped a little. "Of course, when he tried the same thing on the western approach, it did not end so well for him."

"Oh, I am sorry to hear that."

De Sousse waved the concern away. "Well, we all have to die, and it was a noble cause he was pursuing. I am just sorry that all his notes and maps disappeared with him. Ah, can't be helped, I suppose."

Leaning back into his chair, the baron gave all three a careful look. "We have common interests, the four of us. I've discussed my ideas with Grennar and she has indicated to me that the three of you are willing to come to agreement on certain issues."

"If... certain accommodations can be made in return," Lucius said.

"Of course," the baron said, raising his hands in a gesture of peace. "That is how these things work. You will find, Mr Kane – or may I call you Lucius?"

Lucius nodded his head once.

"Splendid. And you may call me... well, call me Baron, or Your Excellency, actually. One must observe the forms." The baron closed the book in front of him, and continued. "It seems to me that four groups of people must work in harmony if this city is to remain safe, secure and, just as important, prosperous. That would be the thieves, the beggars, the Shadowmages and those of us from Pontaine."

"What about the merchants?" Lucius asked. "They control the wealth."

"They have wealth, and can guide much of the gold that is on open view to everyone," the baron conceded. "However, the merchants will always follow a strong hand – that is, after all, where the profits are likely to be. They also have little loyalty to one another and no binding organisation or structure – such as a guild. This makes them very easily led and, right now, the one to follow is Pontaine. We hold the balance of power here."

"Until the Empire decides it wants this city back, or Pontaine decides just one city is not enough," Adrianna said, speaking for the first time. "Your move into this city was neatly done, but there will be a reckoning between Vos and Pontaine. You made the first step."

"With all respect, Lady, I disagree," the baron said. "Vos is a spent force in the south at the moment, and they have their own internal problems with the rise of the Final Faith in their midst – contrary to popular rumour, that church and Vos are not one and the same."

"And Pontaine?"

"As you have suggested," the baron said, smiling again, "the Vos withdrawal from Turnitia was a chance we could not ignore. But we have no plans for any continued hostilities with the Empire. Neither nation is in any fit state for it after the last war, and I think it will be beyond the lifetimes of everyone present, even Grennar here, before war blights this land once again. No, Pontaine has no desire for war and Turnitia is, in the overall scheme of things, not important enough for Vos to waste time and money on retribution. We are safe here."

"I am not entirely convinced," Adrianna said. "I have met too many of your type in the past to believe anything you say."

"Of course you don't," the baron said. "But this is how relationships are built. As we continue in our business relationship, you will learn more about me and my people – and I hope you will soon find I am of a type you have not yet met. Until then, we will be cautious. Both of us."

"So where do we start?" Lucius asked.

Sifting through a sheaf of papers on his desk, de Sousse finally produced a single scroll that he handed to Lucius.

"For a start, this is a list of nobles and other notables I would like you to avoid robbing," the baron said. He handed another paper to Grennar. "And these are the areas I would like to keep clear of beggars."

Lucius glanced quickly at his list. There were no names on it he recognised, nor had he expected to. He presumed these men and women were high-borns from Pontaine or wealthy merchant-types that the baron had promised to protect. It was of little consequence, as he would find out who they were from Grennar in due course, and so few names to avoid still left an awful lot of business elsewhere in the city.

Beside him, Grennar was frowning. "The Square of True Believers? We have done some of our best business there in the past."

"Your best business will always be around the outskirts of the Five Markets," the baron answered, "and I would not think of taking those away from you. However, I have plans for the square – changing its name for one, and demolishing that eyesore of a cathedral. We'll be turning it into the finest set of city gardens outside of Pontaine and, I hesitate to say, having your colleagues working the pathways and bridges will not lend to the atmosphere I am looking for."

"The areas outside the gardens?" Grennar asked.

"All yours."

"Done."

The baron slid another paper across his desk.

"Now something altogether more distasteful. This is a list of people I find to be... unpleasant. I want them gone, dead. By the hand of thief, beggar or Shadowmage, I do not care which. Whoever does it, I believe you'll find them either unknown to you or in serious need of meeting a grave. Old Vos officials, Final Faith sympathisers and the like."

"I'll take care of that," Lucius said. His assassins had lacked for decent work since Vos had left the city, and if there was one section of his guild he wanted to keep on his side, it was Elaine's old comrades.

"Finally," said the baron, "I want a bodyguard. A Shadowmage."

Adrianna hissed her disapproval at that suggestion.

"My Lady, I would not think of asking for such a favour without a contract and suitable payment in place. The skills of your guild are much renowned and it would benefit me greatly to have someone at my side who would add so much to my magical repertoire." Seeing she was not convinced, de Sousse quickly continued. "And, I flatter myself, you would have at least some interest in placing someone so close to me, where I could be watched and reported on."

Lucius cocked an eyebrow at that, and the baron favoured him with a frank smile.

"We will all watch each other, Lucius," he said. "That is part of the game we play. We have common interests that can bind us together, but they won't remove our natural suspicions. I see no reason not to be open about that when we all know it."

Lucius noticed how the baron was changing his demeanour and mannerisms depending on who he was talking to. With Adrianna, it was with utter respect, he was deferential to a fault, though that could well have had as much to do with tales of the Shadowmage's attack on the city before he arrived. Grennar he seemed to treat as a girl some years older than she really was, one who had proved her worth. And with himself, the baron was more relaxed, as though they had been friends for some years – though he guessed that was exactly how the baron *wanted* him to feel.

During the banquet, the baron had been the lead rogue among the revellers, but his drunken behaviour had disappeared the moment they had entered his chamber. The baron was clearly a shrewd opponent, very canny, and Lucius resolved not to be drawn in. This was a man he should watch carefully.

"We have some requests ourselves," Grennar said.

"Of course, and I will be happy to accommodate you where I can." The baron picked up a small silver bell from his desk and shook it, the tinny ring barely seeming to escape past them. "But you'll excuse me if I bring in an advisor. My memory is not as sharp as most."

Lucius doubted that.

The door behind them swung open and a heavyset man with a broad moustache entered. He seemed to fill the room as he towered a head taller than Lucius, and his frame was contained within a scarlet cloak that he drew around a bulging dark tunic. There was no hint of fat or lethargy about him though, and Lucius at first suspected he was some kind of warrior, perhaps a knight of Pontaine.

"Allow me to introduce Tellmore," the baron said. "One of my most trusted colleagues."

"His Excellency is too kind," the man murmured. He turned to face the three guildmasters and dipped his head in a short bow. "I am Tellmore, Master of the Three Towers, Graduate with

Honours of the League of Prestidigitation and Prestige, Watcher of the Forbidden Archive, Adept of the Tempest, and Enchanter of Familiars... among other things."

"A most accomplished mage," the baron said, clearly enthused.

Lucius, for his part, found himself impressed by the achievements Tellmore had related, at least those he recognised, and guessed the acquisition of the man as a court wizard was something of a coup for the baron. He did not need to glance over to Adrianna to know she regarded the man as less than nothing.

"My Lord Baron had need of my services?" Tellmore asked.

"Ah, yes. Our friends here have some requests I would like you to document," the baron said, and Tellmore scooped up the quill lying on the desk along with a blank sheet.

Lucius, following a gesture from the baron, was the first to speak.

"There is a ship that comes into Turnitia at the bottom end of every month, the *Sarcre Pioneer*. I would be grateful if no officials board it. Ever."

What followed was an hour of good old-fashioned horse trading that Lucius found himself rather enjoying, and he could see that Grennar was getting into the swing of things too, particularly as they found the baron to be in agreement with much of what they asked, only modifying a few requests slightly to protect Pontaine's interests. Between them, Lucius and Grennar bought the thieves and beggars of Turnitia plenty of blind eyes from the guardsmen of the city, knowledge of their patrol routes, which minor officials were open to bribery, exclusion zones around their guildhouses, pardons for individuals still in the dungeons of the Citadel and even access to the courtyard outside the keep on certain days.

Adrianna requested nothing but complete freedom for her Shadowmages when under contract and a truly extortionate amount of gold for the services of one Shadowmage to act as bodyguard for the baron. He granted both requests without batting an eyelid.

"So, we have an accord?" the baron said at last.

Grennar glanced up at Lucius and Adrianna before answering.

"Your Excellency, I believe we do."

CHAPTER TWO

EVEN AT THIS early hour, Enlightenment Avenue had started to stir, and the broad, cobbled road was beginning to fill with the crowd that would swell and bustle for the rest of the day.

Shopkeepers were busy unlocking their doors and hauling out tables on which to display their expensive – the less pious would say over-priced – wares, each bearing the proud stamp *By Faithful Appointment to the Anointed Lord*. As endorsements went, none was better in Scholten. The shopkeepers paid high taxes for the privilege, were forced to purchase only from similarly endorsed suppliers, and endured regular inspections of their goods to ensure purity.

Few complained, given how much they personally earned under the watch of the Final Faith.

Alhmanic, Preacher Divine of the Final Faith, paid little attention to the shops or the hawkers of scripture that had also joined the commercial procession along the avenue, all getting ready for the day's pilgrims and the silver coin they brought with them. He had far weightier matters on his mind. Like the dull, constant ache in his shoulder that flared whenever he walked more than a few hundred yards. Or whenever it rained.

The wound he had suffered in Turnitia at the hands of a rabble of thieves had come to serve as an ever-present reminder of his failure. That in itself was an unfamiliar emotion for Alhmanic, as blessed as he had been throughout his, to be truthful he thought, great life.

What had been more worrying was the effect that failure to hold on to the city had had upon his career and standing within the Church. Alhmanic, once the trusted advisor and confidant of the Anointed Lord (praise her name) had been denied an audience with his leader since he had returned from the free city, and he had been surprised how callous that dismissive stance had been. It was not just the loss of power and standing among the other clergy and, by extension, the Empire of Vos. The loss of her trust had cut far deeper than he had guessed it would, and he had begun to doubt himself.

That would all change today, he knew. An invitation to the cathedral of Scholten meant his reinstatement, in fact as well as name. No doubt the Anointed Lord (blessed be the ground she walked upon) had encountered some knotty problem the flunky clergymen around her were unable to deal with, and now she required his wise touch once more.

Alhmanic was happy to oblige. Truthfully, the combination of his wisdom and her fiery passion were the most formidable force on the peninsula. There was nothing that could not be achieved, in the name of the Final Faith.

Reverently, his aching shoulder now forgotten, Alhmanic looked up at the cathedral that soared into the sky before him. It was the tallest building in the entire peninsula, he was sure of that, and the broadest too. Its foundations, sunk deep into the earth, supported eleven ornate spires, one for each of the Great Saints. He had always suspected that it was inevitable that a twelfth would be commissioned and built upon his own death.

The stained glass windows that depicted the Trials of Sainthood were shining clear, even at this distance, and the grotesques that leered at pilgrims entering its mighty doors hid a complicated drainage system that provided enough clean water to support the entire clergy within, should it ever be necessary to bar the cathedral's doors. The original architect was a nameless genius and, it was rumoured, had become an intimate part of his design before it was completed, buried within one of its yards-thick outer walls.

The red-tabarded guard that lined the avenue on the final stretch to the cathedral all bent their heads as he passed, and this cheered Alhmanic. He did not consider himself a vain man, but it was right and proper for them to give him his due.

More guards bent their backs to open the massive doors of the cathedral, iron-bound oak that could reputedly withstand a week's attention from a battering ram. The Final Faith was confident in its power over the people, but the Anointed Lords of the past (may history bear them reverence) were not known for skimping on details. The doors swung open, slowly but soundlessly on hinges lubricated with consecrated oil, leading to the yawning interior.

It was not a dark place, the cathedral of Scholten, and everything about its architecture was designed to inspire and encourage piety. There was no need for the building to be oppressive and frightening. Its size alone demonstrated everything about absolute power that the Final Faith needed to convey.

Acolytes worked diligently in the huge entrance hall, careful to remove every speck of dirt and detritus left by visitors the day before. It was as much part of their devotions as prayer, and Alhmanic grimaced slightly as he remembered his own lessons as an acolyte.

One bowed low as he approached and indicated a padded chair with a tall back set alongside one wall, the traditional place of waiting for respected outsiders. Alhmanic frowned at this, wondering what this might portend, but he shrugged it off and sat. No doubt there was to be some ritual of forgiveness led by the Anointed Lord (may her name shine through the ages) that marked his official return, a formal declaration to the rest of the clergy that the Preacher Divine was back and had the full trust of their leader.

As he sat, dwelling on this, Alhmanic considered his assignment in Turnitia and, not for the first time, considered what mistakes he had made. This pondering always returned the same result – he had clearly not been at fault himself, and his imposed exile from the heart of the faith had been a signal, nothing more, to warn others of what might happen should plans go... awry.

It was clear that he had done everything right. No one could have foreseen a motley collection of disparate thieves actually fighting alongside one another. And certainly, no one could have accounted for the witch who burned down half of the city.

Turnitia was a stinking cesspool anyway, a relic from a bygone age without the wit or sophistication of Vos. Its change in leadership to Pontaine was no loss at all.

And had he not demonstrated his own devotion to the cause by taking that terrible wound in defence of the Citadel, while thieves and assassins assaulted its walls?

No, clearly, he was not to blame.

As strains of song from the Eternal Choir, sequestered deep within the cathedral, began to filter through into the hall, Alhmanic began to consider what his new task might entail. Finding out who really was to blame for the issues that had arisen at Turnitia, he supposed, the tracking down of which incompetent strategist among the clergy had been responsible for their irrecoverably weak position there. Then again, perhaps much larger events were afoot, requiring his presence. Maybe the Anointed Lord's plans (may they bear ever-lasting fruit) had accelerated, and the scheme to turn Pontaine into a wasteland was now ready.

Coughing gently to gain his attention, another acolyte bowed low before Alhmanic and gestured to him to follow.

Alhmanic was led, at a pace he found interminably slow. They did not enter the nave with its endless ranks of pews, a new invention that Alhmanic himself had helped to bring to the cathedral many years ago, and instead went down a corridor, past the consultation booths. Later that day, these booths would be turning over a steady procession of pilgrims, each seeking to buy absolution and miracles from a priest for mere silver.

Such was the generosity of the Final Faith. Once the preserve of the wealthy, now anyone could buy their way into a better afterlife. Miracles by volume, that was the key. Another innovation Alhmanic had helped push through the bureaucracy of the clergy.

They turned left into another corridor, and Alhmanic frowned. They were not heading to the Anointed Lord's (may the ground be fertile where she walks) audience chambers, but deeper into the administrative complex of the cathedral, where much of the Final Faith's work across the peninsula was planned and directed. He was tempted to ask the acolyte where they were headed, but decided instead to keep his questions to himself. It would not serve to show his confusion.

They came up short at a solid door set within an alcove of the new corridor, and the acolyte rapped gently on its panelled surface before bowing and retreating, leaving Alhmanic to enter by himself. Taking a breath, and steeling himself to whatever his mistress had planned, Alhmanic grasped the handle and went inside.

"I am glad to see punctuality is not a trait you have abandoned," said a slow, dry voice.

Inwardly, Alhmanic groaned.

The man sat behind the desk, itself piled with papers high enough to nearly obscure him, was older than Alhmanic. Even in the padded chair, he was hunched over, and his thinning grey hair revealed a skin pale from lack of sun, and deeply creased by age.

"Klaus," Alhmanic said.

He saw a thin crease of a smile tug at the corner of the man's lips, and Alhmanic immediately guessed he would not be greeted with the happy news he had been expecting. Klaus was an old rival among the clergy and though officially a mere priest, the man had wormed his way into many aspects of its administration. Alhmanic had always considered that their longstanding and private battle had been fought and won when he had become the Preacher Divine, but now he began to suspect a new front had just been opened.

"I am afraid the Anointed Lord has decided not to join us for this little chat," Klaus said, his voice apologetic, but his eyes almost triumphant in their rheumy mist. "For that, I am sorry."

Alhmanic dismissed the false apology with a wave.

"Blessed be her works, one cannot expect her favours every day."

"Or at all," Klaus said, narrowing his eyes as his voice adopted a slightly harder tone. "We have been most... distressed over the incident that lost us Turnitia. We had built high hopes upon the acquisition of that city."

"The situation was untenable for anyone," Alhmanic said, trying very hard not to sound defensive. "I trust our beloved leader knows that."

"That... remains to be seen."

Alhmanic frowned. "Just what do you mean by that?"

In reply, Klaus shrugged innocently. "That is not for me to say, I am sure. However, I have rather been given the impression that the Anointed Lord is most perplexed at a failure that should have been an early victory. Furthermore there has been talk – not from me, you understand, I know the pressures of high station – that perhaps your time as Preacher Divine has passed. That maybe someone new should adopt the role. Someone younger."

"And I have no doubt you have lent weight yourself to such arguments?"

Again, Klaus gave him a look of pious innocence. "My dear friend, I stand with you in this. I firmly believe that wisdom only comes with age – I have several years on you, how could I say different? Still, young men have their place too, especially in more... energetic pursuits. Besides, it is just possible that placating Turnitia was a poor use of your skills."

Alhmanic did not believe a word that came from Klaus' mouth, but he was not going to give the priest any pleasure in seeing his discomfort. Not from what was being said, nor from the fact that Klaus had seemingly forgotten to ask him to sit down instead of having him stand there like some acolyte-in-training.

That thought set Alhmanic fuming inside.

"I am sure the Anointed Lord, heavens shine upon her, will find the most useful place for me within her designs. She, *above all,*" he made sure to stress those words, "knows the depths of my loyalty."

"Which brings us to why you were called here," Klaus said quickly, straining to reach across his desk to snatch a handful of papers from one of the stacks. "A new mission for you. Very important."

"I stand ready to serve."

"Of course. Now, certain texts retrieved from an ancient site have recently been deemed sacred because of their content."

"Which site?"

"That's not important," Klaus said, showing himself a little irritated at the interruption. Alhmanic could translate that perfectly well – someone had decided he should not know. He had a nasty feeling that the person in question was Klaus himself. A further thought occurred to him.

"And you can assure me that these orders come from the Anointed Lord herself? Blessings upon her," he quickly added.

Klaus pursed his lips and was silent for a few seconds, as if he were choosing his words carefully.

"I can assure you that the Anointed Lord will want success in this mission," he finally said.

Klaus was all but telling him that the mission, whatever it was going to be, had come from Klaus' own desk and quill. Damn him, the man must be laughing inside to have this power!

Keeping his anger bubbling just below what he hoped was the surface, Alhmanic kept his voice low and even.

"What am I to do?"

"Once the texts were declared sacred, proper translations of them could begin. It turns out, we found some rather exciting information. I will spare you the details – here, I have transcribed as much of the texts as was permissible for you to see," Klaus said, handing Alhmanic a handful of papers. "We believe an artefact of most ancient design lies within the southern Anclas Territories. You are to find and fetch it."

"It has not been located yet?"

"We have done as much as we can here," Klaus said. "Now it remains for someone of different skills to actually hunt it down and retrieve it. That would be you."

"I can assume I will be given a contingent of men?"

"Of course! Life in the Anclas Territories can be dangerous, so I am told, and we cannot risk anything happening to the mission."

That was Klaus' not so subtle way of telling him that the mission was being regarded as important, but few people would care what happened to the Preacher Divine. They could have it their way, thought Alhmanic. He would endure these trials, as the Great Saints had endured their own struggles in the past. He would succeed in this test, and the Anointed Lord, praise her, would see what a valuable servant he was. Then he would revisit Klaus and every other lackey within the administration for a little divinely inspired justice. Even now, he saw Klaus in his mind's eye, straining to move a rock-filled cart deep in the mines below the cathedral. The thought almost made him smile.

"Good," he said. "I'll need a full regiment, with attending cavalry."

"Oh, I am afraid that will be entirely impossible," Klaus said, now adopting the posture of some quartermaster who everyone makes too many demands of. "The bulk of our forces are needed... well, elsewhere, I am sure you understand. There will be a half-company waiting for you at the city gates upon your departure. Which will be as soon as we are finished here."

"I see," Alhmanic said. "Anything else I should be aware of?"

"I believe you have everything that you will need. It just remains for me to wish you luck."

Alhmanic gave him a grim smile, before leaning forwards, planting his fists on the desk between stacks of papers as he towered over Klaus.

"I know what is going on here," he said quietly. "Don't think this is over."

Klaus looked up at him, and Alhmanic was a little surprised to see a spark of defiance in the man.

"Let us first see how you perform in this task. If you are successful, I am sure you will be permitted to keep your title of Preacher Divine. If not... well, I would advise you to remember that no Preacher Divine in the past has ever been relieved of his post," Klaus smiled up at him. "They have all, without exception, died in service to the Final Faith. One way or another, I believe you will find the Anointed Lord is a traditionalist in this matter."

Seeing no use for further confrontation, Alhmanic kept his face expressionless as he stood upright and turned for the door. As he placed his hand on the handle, he turned round to face Klaus once more.

"She will get her artefact, Klaus. And you... you will get what is coming to you too."

CHAPTER THREE

As the raging ocean smashed against the huge, towering monoliths that protected Turnitia's harbour, the waves expending their energy in an endless cacophony that could be heard practically anywhere in the city, Lucius glanced at Adrianna out of the corner of his eye. The last time they had both been at the top of the cliffs that looked across the calm waters of the harbour, she had tried to kill him, and had very nearly succeeded.

If Adrianna was thinking the same thing, she showed no sign of it. Lucius had still not figured out whether she felt any shame for the terror she had brought to the city when their master, Forbeck, had been killed by the wizards of Vos, whether she had done her best to forget the incident, or whether she simply saw it as the natural path to her ascension to head of the guild of Shadowmages. He was not sure whether any of those options would make him feel comfortable in her presence.

She was still dangerous, in command of a great deal of magical power, and Adrianna now held sway over every other Shadowmage in the city and, probably, beyond. That was enough to make anyone nervous.

"We no longer have the forces of Vos here to pit you against," she had said as they had walked through the streets of shattered buildings, burnt out wrecks that stood as testament to the power of a Shadowmage unleashed. The baron had started a new public works program to rebuild the areas of the city that Adrianna had destroyed, but human effort alone would not repair the damage for another year at least.

"It would not be politic to set you against the Pontaine occupiers, not that I think they would put up much of a fight anyway. We have to create our own challenges for you, Lucius."

So, they had walked to the cliffs on the edge of the city, bedecked with lifts and cranes that worked to bring cargo from docked ships in the harbour to Turnitia above. Lucius' training under Adrianna continued, as he had promised it would, but there were times he regretted it.

Forbeck had been a demanding master, constantly pushing Lucius to explore the depths of his powers and also reflect upon the nature of the Shadowmage's art. Adrianna was different – she was less interested in the whys and concentrated on honing Lucius' mastery of magic into a finely tuned weapon. Whereas Forbeck's lessons had been tough on both a mental and physical level, Adrianna's were downright dangerous at times.

Using shadow magic to cloak them from the casual gaze of the workers in the harbour and those labouring on the cranes, Adrianna had told Lucius to scale the cliffs, searching for cloth pennants she had placed earlier. At least, that was what she told him. Lucius could not help but suspect the pennants had been placed by another student in an earlier lesson.

This was something that, with the right tools, he could have done without magical aid, but Adrianna soon demanded greater and greater speed from him. Clinging to a rocky outcropping with one hand, trying to ignore the hard surface of the harbour far below, Lucius stretched for a green pennant that lay snagged just below him. It was a tantalising few inches out of his reach.

"Don't strain your muscles," Adrianna's voice floated down to him. "I have few concerns for your physical shape. Use the magic, that is why we are here!"

Not replying, Lucius took a short breath and summoned the forces of magic to himself, seeing them twist and turn in his mind's eye. The cloth twitched as an air current tugged at it and then, with a quick ripping sound, it tore itself free from the rocks and leapt into his outstretched hand.

Quickly tucking it into his belt, where it sat with three other pennants of various colours, Lucius smiled to himself, and then cast about looking for the next target. He saw it immediately, a blue flash of cloth just a few yards across from his current perch. Setting a foot down, he pushed hard, and felt himself buoyed up by a magical force that lifted him clear of the rock to float him across a deep gash that burrowed into the cliffs.

"I told you, I wanted to see speed!" Adrianna said.

Lucius started to draw more magical power within himself to give a boost to his progress but then sensed a build up of energies above him. With barely a second to spare, he refashioned his spell and as he floated to the blue pennant, he swiftly brought his hand above his head, as if to ward off a blow.

The bolt of magical energy was invisible to the naked eye but Lucius could feel its presence, could sense the raw power Adrianna had focussed into it, and he felt it shatter against his hastily improvised shield. He landed back onto the rock, gripping the surface with both hands even as he summoned another current of magic to snatch at the blue pennant. When it floated in front of his face, he quickly snatched it out of the air and tucked it into his belt. Taking another breath, he wiped the sweat that had formed on his brow.

"Better," Adrianna said. "You improvised well enough and spared yourself a painful lesson."

She seemed oblivious to the fact that, had her bolt of energy actually struck him, Lucius would have been dislodged from the cliffs and would have likely fallen to his death without time to recover. He was becoming rapidly convinced that Adrianna now operated on a different level to everyone else, and that the life and death of others was of little moment to her. Even him, who had known her the longest. That, allied to her great mastery of the arts, was what made her so dangerous.

They continued the lesson, with Lucius gradually making his way along the cliffs until his belt was stuffed full of the coloured pennants, all the while fending off the occasional attack from Adrianna. Each was intended to keep him on his toes or force him to use his magic in different ways, and each was potentially life-threatening.

When he returned to the top of the cliffs, glad the lesson was over, he saw Adrianna nod once at him.

"You are somewhat improving. I might even go as far to say you are approaching adequate."

Lucius hid a smile. From Adrianna, that was about as good a compliment as he could expect.

"Tell me," she continued. "What did you make of that... wizard in the baron's keeping?"

He frowned as he thought for a moment. "Tellmore? The baron seemed pleased to have gained his services. The mage seems quite accomplished."

The clicking of Adrianna's tongue alerted Lucius that he had said the wrong thing.

"Don't you dare, Lucius, don't you dare be impressed by *that*. The wizards of Pontaine, and those of Vos for that matter, build great monuments to themselves and their own ingenuity. You have heard of the Three Towers?"

Lucius nodded. "I visited Andon once and saw them."

"The wizard guilds in Pontaine spend their time building themselves pretty palaces, while they hoodwink from the nobility ever greater amounts of silver and gold so they can continue to live a life of luxury. They don't know proper magic, Lucius. Not like us. Not like the Shadowmages. Forbeck always suspected we were the first practitioners of magic, far back in history, and I have begun to learn that he was right."

Again, Lucius nodded, dutifully this time. He did not know where Adrianna was going with this but he wanted to avoid awakening her wrath.

"This play-wizard of the baron," she continued. "He may have some pretty titles awarded to him by fools who know no better. But I'll tell you this, Lucius; he has none of the skills and knowledge I control, and none of the power you can summon in an instant."

Of the baron's wizard's lack of power and magical strength, Lucius was less than sure. He knew that no one got into such a trusted position with an up and coming Pontaine noble without having accomplished at least something. He certainly had no wish to test his own magical powers against the man, if that were what Adrianna was hinting at. Lucius suddenly became uneasy, as he always did when he thought Adrianna was demanding something of him but he did not know exactly what. However, Adrianna's attention was no longer fixated on him, and he felt her grip of his arm weaken.

She was staring up into the sky, her long dark hair tugged by the sea breeze as her face was elevated to the heavens. Lucius noted she was looking away from the huge blue sphere of Kerberos, its great mass half-hidden below the horizon on this day.

"There is something coming, Lucius," she said, but her voice sounded far away, as if she were talking to herself. "I have seen it. The skies are warning us, if we have the wit to see and hear."

Lucius joined her in looking upwards, but saw nothing but the blue sky.

LUCIUS HAD NEVER entered Adrianna's new home, though thieves had kept him abreast of her acquisition. Trading up from her more modest townhouse, Adrianna had used the resources of her guild to buy a sizeable mansion in the city's most eastern, and richest, district, and now used it as the guildhouse of the Shadowmages.

Lucius had not known what to expect when he walked into the mansion's main hall, but what he saw caused all the feelings of dread at what she was becoming to flood back.

The hall was sparsely decorated, with solid carved pillars rising up to support a balcony running either side of its length, and the black and white tiled marble floor shone as though it were new. On the plastered walls were hung an assortment of paintings, a mixture of landscapes and portraits, though none sparked his thief's senses as to any great value.

Others were present in the hall as they entered, and all bowed their heads as Adrianna left his side and marched, confidently, to the far end where a cluster of men and women awaited her. A little more than a dozen people were there, and Lucius knew he was looking upon the core of the Shadowmages' guild for the first time. He recognised none of them, though a couple nodded a greeting to him.

He could almost sense the magical power crackling through the air in the hall, an endless range of possibilities opening up to anyone who could harness the collective energy and direct it to a common cause. Lucius watched as the group at the far end of the hall parted before Adrianna to reveal a gilded chair upon a short dais and observed as, with a flourish he had not expected to see from her, Adrianna sat down and levelled a careful gaze at her guild members.

The moment was not lost on Lucius. Adrianna ruled her guild from a throne.

That realisation made Lucius wish that he had spent more time with this guild in the past, and also that his own guild was in another city, far away from what could easily turn into utter madness.

Raising her head slightly, Adrianna beckoned one Shadowmage forward, a young woman who was dressed in a gown of dark green silk that might have been more appropriate for one of the baron's functions than any guild business. The woman bowed low as she stopped in front of Adrianna, and then went down on one knee.

"My Lady, my petition is for the exclusive right to service a contract with Lord Gilles of Pontaine," she said, the respect in her voice evident.

"He is one of the baron's men," Adrianna said. "That contract is currently held by Torsten."

Another Shadowmage, a man this time of perhaps twice Lucius' age, stepped forward and bowed. He was about to speak but Adrianna held up a hand, silencing him instantly.

"Torsten has squandered the opportunities in working with Pontaine," Adrianna declared. "We will find him work more suited to his abilities. The contract is yours, Miellee."

The young woman bowed her thanks and withdrew as another Shadowmage approached Adrianna.

"My Lady, my petition is for access to the second rank laboratories...'

As the Shadowmages approached Adrianna and had their requests granted or denied, Lucius watched carefully. He had no idea why Arianna had insisted he attend this, well, there was no other word for it, this court that she presided over, but he could see an obvious danger.

The other Shadowmages were either fearful of her – who wouldn't be? – or were willing to be led. It was true, the guild had gained new levels of power and even respectability since Adrianna had taken over its leadership, and they worked openly with the forces of Pontaine, something that could never have happened during the Vos occupation of the city. Business was clearly doing well.

However, he could also see that Adrianna ruled her guild with an absolute iron hand, brooking no argument or dissent. There was no Shadowmage here who had anything like the power or will to oppose her and Lucius doubted whether the combined force of every Shadowmage here, himself included, would be able to do much more than slow Adrianna down if it came to battle. On the other hand, as frightening as she could sometimes be, he did think that Adrianna was holding her emotions in rigid check. Maybe, just maybe, this focus on growing and maintaining her guild was the distraction that Adrianna needed. God knew that his own thieves kept him busy enough most of the time.

Adrianna now had access to more power than she had ever wielded in the past, and a number of sycophants who seemed willing to do whatever she asked without question. That rang alarm bells in Lucius' head. He resolved to attend the Shadowmages' guild more often, to keep an eye on his tutor if nothing else.

As THE LAST Shadowmage departed the hall, Adrianna bent her head and rubbed her eyes, trying to alleviate the growing headache she felt coming on. When she looked up, she saw one still remained, and was looking expectantly at her.

"What is it, Torsten?" she asked in irritation. "Guild business is now over."

"Indeed, my Lady, and I beg your indulgence."

Sighing, Adrianna waved him forward.

"Speak."

"It was good to see young Lucius today," Torsten began. "What made him change his mind to join us?"

"He came because I told him to, and I have no patience for small talk," Adrianna snapped. "What is it you want? I told you, Miellee has the Gilles contract now."

Torsten held up a hand in defence. "Of course, my Lady, and I am sure your decision is final. But I have another matter to raise with you, one I believe should not be conducted openly."

She waved impatiently at him. "Well, out with it."

"I have heard the Preacher Divine is abroad. In the Anclas Territories."

Adrianna stared at him for a second. "Interesting. Vaguely."

"He has the Illkey Prophecies in hand," Torsten said with a slight smile.

"Really?" Adrianna said, her eyes narrowing. "The full translation, or just excerpts?"

"Regretfully, I have not been able to discover that. My information comes from the daughter of Lord Gilles."

"Okay, we'll... review the Gilles contract – at a later date." She thought for a moment. "What do you know of the Illkey Prophecies?"

Torsten shrugged. "Not as much as I might like, my Lady. I know they were supposedly created when man began his rise to power, just before the fall of the Old Races. They are alleged to contain fascinating detail on the magics of the elves and dwarfs, and were supposedly lost when the peninsula suffered some great calamity."

"Oh, there's more," Adrianna said, a smile beginning to creep across her face, her eyes glinting darkly. "There is much that was hidden about those prophecies."

Looking expectantly at her, Torsten waited for Adrianna to speak further, but she held her silence for some minutes as thoughts tumbled through her mind. When she finally spoke, it was with a tightly reined passion.

"I believe I know exactly what the Preacher Divine is looking for in the Anclas Territories. We'll allow him some small success in finding what he searches for, permitting him to do the hard work. Then we'll strike, taking it from him. What is uncovered from the hands of the Old Races, puts us in position to challenge anyone on the peninsula – any circle of Vos wizards, even the Three Towers themselves." Adrianna glanced at the Shadowmage before adding, almost as an afterthought, "And you, loyal Torsten, you will have your share of the new power too."

Torsten abased himself on the floor in front of Adrianna.

"My Lady..."

CHAPTER FOUR

His SCARLET CLOAK fanning out behind him, Tellmore quickened his pace through the corridors of the Citadel's keep, ignoring the curious looks of the few servants and guards that still prowled at this late hour. He kept one arm clasped to his chest, holding his hastily scribbled notes protectively close.

Turning left, he raced up a flight of spiral stairs, coming to an abrupt halt as he ran headlong into an armoured soldier. The soldier briefly smiled an apology, but Tellmore pushed him to one side without a second glance, squeezing himself past the man's bulk in the tight confines of the staircase.

Emerging into another corridor, Tellmore sighed with the exertion as he saw his destination ahead: a closed door with another guardsman standing stiffly outside with a short spear in hand.

The guardsman nodded a greeting and then glanced meaningfully at the door. Tellmore cursed under his breath and then waved his understanding. Drawing up to the door, he rapped hard on its oak surface. For several long seconds, there was no response from within.

"I gave orders not to be disturbed..." The baron's voice floated through the closed door, a hint of exasperation evident. Tellmore knew why.

"My Lord Baron, it's me. You'll want to hear this."

Tellmore could have sworn he heard a growl from within, quickly followed by sounds of movement. After waiting patiently for a few minutes, exchanging a knowing look with the guardsman, Tellmore was rewarded by the sound of the door's heavy lock turning. The door swung open, and a young woman dressed in thin pale blue silks stepped out, smiling shyly as she trotted down the corridor, back to her own quarters.

"Lady Roussin," Tellmore acknowledged, trying hard to avert his eyes from her obvious nakedness beneath her painfully thin clothing.

"Tellmore, you killer of joy," the baron's voice came from within. "Get in here and explain yourself."

Slipping inside, Tellmore saw the baron in his night robes, lighting a lantern and carrying it from his bed chamber to the smaller room he used for private meals. He indicated Tellmore should follow him with a jerk of his head.

Within, a square darkwood table with two matching chairs took up much of the available space, but the baron had managed to squeeze a small buffet along one wall and from this he grabbed a plate of bread and fruit. He gestured to the food, but Tellmore shook his head.

"Please, sit," the baron said, taking a place himself. "And tell me what is so important it could not wait until morning."

"Oh, I think you will want to hear this right now, my Lord Baron," Tellmore said, seating himself and spreading his papers as best he could across the small table.

The baron watched his wizard prepare himself, taking a bite out of a large pear as he waited.

"As you instructed, I started to investigate what Vos was doing in the Anclas Territories, and why they had deemed it necessary to send the Preacher Divine," Tellmore said.

"I still think the duty is a punishment for our taking of Turnitia. It was, after all, his responsibility."

"Maybe," said Tellmore doubtfully. "Maybe. Thing is, if the Anointed Lord wanted to punish him, she has all sorts of permanent ways of doing it. I thought this had the whiff of humiliation, mixed with a chance of redemption, if you see what I mean."

The baron nodded his understanding, prompting Tellmore to continue.

"Your spies in the Territories had already determined that the Preacher Divine was looking for something, and that he was using the Illkey Prophecies to find it."

"Never really trusted those prophecies myself," the baron said. "The source is suspect. I always thought they might have been written far more recently than has been supposed."

"That might well prove to be true," Tellmore said, not wanting to contradict his patron directly. "But regardless of that, they may still hold some useful information – Vos certainly thinks so, and if they are interested...'

"Then we should be too. Yes, I agree. I assume you have gained some knowledge of the prophecies yourself?"

"Far more than Vos has. A benefit of the collected learnings of the Three Towers. More importantly, we hold certain key texts that we know Vos lacks – they are not even aware of the existence of these writings."

Tellmore took a moment to sift through his scattered notes until he seized the sheet he had completed just minutes before in his own chambers.

"Specifically, the Preacher Divine lacks the Illuminated Scrolls of the Thirteenth Elven Dynasty. Luckily, I had the transcribed set in my own collection."

The baron raised an eyebrow. "Really?"

Tellmore looked apologetic. "They are somewhat hard going, and their relevance has always been held in question – as has, indeed, the accuracy of the translations. There have been several made over the centuries, and each has their own proponent as to which is closest to the original text. I won't bore you with the details, but the transcription I possess contains certain references to an Elven outpost – or maybe it's a tomb, perhaps a village, things are not completely clear – that I recalled when I started reading the Illkey Prophecies once again."

Having stopped eating now, the baron leaned forward in his seat. "Tell me you discovered something."

"I must stress, interpretation of anything to do with the Old Races is subject to a wide margin of error at best."

The baron brushed the excuse aside. "You are among the best magical minds on the peninsula, Tellmore. That is why I brought you into my service. I am prepared to act upon your best guess, without thought of recrimination later."

"The Baron is too kind," Tellmore said before taking a breath. He then smiled as he looked back up at his patron. "I believe I have discovered what the Preacher Divine is searching for, where it comes from and, more importantly, where it can be found."

"Well, don't keep me in suspense, man!"

"We have known for some time about an ancient Elven artefact known as the Guardian Starlight. It has been variously described by different sources as a small golden rod, a large crystal staff or a shield the size of a man but light enough to wield as though it were parchment. It was the Illkey Prophecies and the Thirteenth Dynasty that provided the connection I needed. They, with some other, minor texts, have convinced me that the Preacher Divine is searching for the Guardian Starlight, even if he does not know exactly what it is he is looking for."

"So, he is working blind?"

"Not entirely. With the Illkey Prophecies alone, the Preacher Divine *could* find the resting place of the Guardian Starlight. Even if he does not know what he has found, he'll know he has something of value, and if he manages to get it back to the Anointed Lord...'

"Then she will no doubt apply every resource she has to discovering what it is they have found."

"Exactly."

"I have one question for you, Tellmore," the baron said. "Has any of your great research explained what this Guardian Starlight actually *does*?"

"My Lord Baron... umm... no. However, I do not need to impress upon you the potential power invested in artefacts of the Old Races."

"Indeed not. What I want to know is whether, this artefact in hand, you will be able to unlock its mysteries."

"I vow to work ceaselessly until I do. If my Lord Baron will aid me in acquiring this item, I will happily pass all benefits on to him, in exchange for the recognition of being the one who made the discovery."

"My dear Tellmore, you have a deal," the baron smiled. He then brought a fist down hard on the table, causing the wizard to jump. "By God, this could not have happened at a better time. I knew bringing you on board would reap great rewards."

"My Lord Baron?"

The baron waved the question away. "I'll explain when you return from this expedition. You really do know where this thing lies?"

"Well, Vos has a head start on us, but they lack the additional texts that have led me to this discovery. We have the chance to strike first."

"In that case, go now – grab whatever you think you will need. I'll organise a contingent of men to go with you."

"Soldiers?"

"The Preacher Divine would not have ventured into the Territories without military support, and I won't have you facing him without a superior force. Besides, if you are going to be rooting around in elven ruins, you will also need men to dig, move rocks, whatever it is people do in ruins. I'll assign Sir Renauld to lead the men, but I'll make sure he understands you have overall command."

"You are generous in your support, Lord Baron," Tellmore said bowing his head slightly.

"I expect you to succeed. Or, in the very least, to ensure our friend the Preacher Divine fails. This artefact could prove to be a great boon to me, but having it in the hands of Vos would be a far greater failing than neither of us possessing it. Do you understand, Tellmore?"

"As you wish it."

"Good. Now, go, prepare yourself. You leave at dawn."

THE SKY WAS just beginning to lighten, though the sun had yet to break cover from the huge mass of Kerberos. The five towers cast deep shadows across the courtyard of the Citadel, hiding the hundred-odd horsemen that assembled into tight squadrons.

"Lord Tellmore, it is an honour to serve you."

Tellmore rubbed his eyes then shook his head to clear his mind. After preparations for the day's journey, he had managed to snatch but an hour's rest, and his body cried out for more. He was not used to such early hours and he struggled to focus on the armoured knight in front of him.

"Just Tellmore, I am no lord," he said. "You are Sir Renauld?"

"At your service," the knight said. Renauld was a young man, far younger than Tellmore had anticipated, barely into his twenties. The wizard restrained his immediate impulse to ask how many military expeditions he had led before this one.

"You will have a full company of my men-at-arms accompanying you into the Anclas Territories," Renauld continued. "All equally capable on foot as in the saddle."

Renauld, Tellmore saw, wore the heavy half-plate that was currently in vogue among de Sousse's knights, with shining breastplate, half-helm, vambraces and greaves. A green tabard bearing a pair of crossed black axes, presumably Renauld's own family heraldry, hung over the armour, and the colours and design were repeated on the shields and tabards of the assembled horsemen who awaited them in the courtyard. Each was dressed from head to foot in chainmail and carried a long spear in one hand. Large swords were scabbarded at their belts.

Despite himself and his normal disdain for martial prowess, Tellmore found himself impressed.

"What have you been told of our mission, Sir Renauld?"

The knight gave him a rueful smile. "That we are to escort you into the Anclas Territories, to obey your orders to the letter, and to guard your person and possessions with our lives."

"Nothing more?"

"Nothing."

Tellmore considered this for a moment. "Is that the sort of mission you enjoy performing?"

With a sigh, Renauld glanced quickly over his shoulder to ensure none of his men were in earshot.

"Just tell me this. Is this mission important to our baron?"

"I can assure you, it could be absolutely vital to all of Pontaine."

Renauld nodded thoughtfully. "In that case, you may rest assured that we will serve you to the letter, and consider it honourable to do so."

"You have my thanks," Tellmore said. "And Renauld – it is not my intention to keep you in the dark. The more you know, the better you may serve the baron, whatever he might think. I'll tell you what I can as we ride, but please don't think I am being evasive if I don't know everything yet myself."

He noticed that Renauld was giving him an odd look, but Tellmore could not guess whether this was because he was being more truthful than Renauld's superiors had been in the past, or whether he had just breached a major part of knightly etiquette. It was a question that would remain unanswered for now as one of Renauld's men-at-arms trotted up towards them, his every footstep matched with a chinking of the rings in his armour.

"My Lord, the men are ready," he said, saluting with his fist. "We can leave at your command."

Renauld turned to Tellmore. "We have chosen a good horse for you. Just give us the word."

Tellmore glanced once more up at the sky as the first rays of the sun began to streak across the thinning clouds above.

"Sir Renauld, the word is given. Let us go."

CHAPTER FIVE

LOOKING DOWN INTO the shallow valley, Tellmore grew increasingly confident. One by one, the pieces fell together.

On the other side of the valley, a small hump that broke the smooth outline of the rolling hills betrayed the presence of a millennia-old ruin. The untrained eye might have skipped past it altogether, or simply ascribed it to some whim of the Creator when shaping the hills, but Tellmore had seen such markers before and he was sure it was the resting place of a long-forgotten outpost of the Old Races – elf-built, to be exact.

The notes he had compiled over the years used this as a way marker to point towards an even grander settlement of the elves, one that he was now sure had once nestled within the valley below. Ancient stone markers, now worn away by wind and rain, had been followed, the placement of human villages charted on maps copied from fragile texts and compared to the estimated locations of the ir Old Race counterparts. The valley itself had been carved by a river now long since dried up, and a detachment of Renauld's men-at-arms had followed its course north, looking for it to divide in a fork, as the Illuminated Scrolls had promised it would. A day later, the soldiers had returned with the good news. The river bed had indeed forked, confirming that they were in the right placc.

Taking a deep breath, Tellmore allowed himself a smile. Somewhere below him lay the Guardian Starlight. All he had to do was take it.

That would be an effort in itself, Tellmore was under no illusions, but he hungered for the real work that would begin soon after. The work and study that would see him unlock the secrets of the elven artefact and thus elevate himself to become one of the mightiest and most learned wizards in Vos or Pontaine.

It was worth a little effort.

"Is this the place then, Magister?" Renauld asked.

"I believe, Sir Renauld, that we have arrived."

The knight looked around at the surrounding hills.

"I don't like the look of the land," he said. "Far too enclosed to defend properly."

"I imagine this was considered a safe area by the original architects. Perhaps an outpost up there kept watch for invaders, whoever they might have been."

He indicated the hilltop ruin, and then started wondering just what might have challenged the power of the Old Races that they might even need a fort, tower or keep. Did they fight among themselves, the way Vos and Pontaine had done throughout their history? Nothing in the ancient texts suggested that the Old Races were fractured in any way. Even the separate nation states of the dwarfs and elves kept the peace. Well, until their last days, at any rate.

"Unfortunately, elves were not required to take our needs into account when they built their civilisation."

Renauld nodded. True to his word, Tellmore had told the knight what little he could about their expedition, but Renauld had glazed over at the more intricate and technical details of the artefact they were looking for, and did not seem to believe much else about the Old Races and their history. Tellmore could not overly blame him ,for the man, while clearly educated, had not been introduced to the wonders of the Old Races and, like most others, considered them little more than fairy tales. The wizard had seen this reaction before. Even when confronted by direct evidence of the existence of elf and dwarf, many people would simply shrug and go on about their daily lives. Okay, so once, long ago, elves and dwarfs ran the world and they built pretty towers. So what?

"With your permission, I'll want to scatter scouts on long-ranged patrols," Renauld said. "If you are right about a Vos force in the area, I don't want us to be surprised."

"I'll leave military matters to you, Sir Renauld. That is your field of expertise, as this artefact is mine. All I ask is that you do not allow them to interfere with my work."

Renauld coughed, as if a little embarrassed, and that caused Tellmore to look back at him.

"Yes, about that," said the knight. "Once you are sure exactly where we will be digging, I'll be wanting to build a perimeter fence."

Tellmore frowned. "That will take labour away from the digging, and there will be enough of that."

"If it were completely down to me, Magister, I would insist on adding a ditch in front of the fencing," Renauld said, holding up a hand in surrender at Tellmore's look of alarm.

"We don't know what Vos will do if they discover our location, and we have to assume they will. Let me rotate men in scout duty – they will accept the manual labour a lot easier if they can get regular breaks from it – and let me build that fence. I assure you, speaking as a military man, you will be thankful I insisted on that at least if we face an attack."

Sighing, Tellmore relented. There was no sense in finding the location of the Guardian Starlight if he simply had to hand it over to the enemies of the baron soon after.

"I can make things easier, Magister," Renauld said. "I'll get that fence built in no time but I'll assign a few men directly to you, so you can at least make a start on your own work. Then, as the defences near completion, I'll send more and more hands to you. By the end of the week, you'll have all the manpower you need, I am sure."

Tellmore nodded, appreciating the gesture Renauld was trying to make. He had been in the company of knights before, and had usually found them bullish. This Renauld was different, perhaps because of his younger years. Tellmore rather got the impression that the knight was trying hard not only to succeed in the baron's mission but do so without stampeding and riding roughshod over someone another knight might have simply assumed was a courtier. Despite himself, Tellmore found himself beginning to like the young knight.

"In that case, Sir Renauld, I would like to make an immediate start," said Tellmore. "Assign your men to duties as you will, but I would be thankful for a handful to help me set up my tent and tools. Then, I can finally begin work."

"As the Magister wishes."

ALONE IN HIS tent, Tellmore supported his head in his hands as he stared down at the notes that covered the surface of the small desk. More were piled up in discarded stacks behind him, the results of his fruitless labours.

For three weeks he had been stuck in a makeshift fort he was now coming to despise. Three weeks spent in initial elation at getting to grips with the mysteries of the Old Races but quickly giving in to frustration as those same mysteries proved to become more and more impenetrable. After the first week, it had rained near constantly, his tent had flooded twice, and Tellmore was cold, wet, and getting angrier by the day at his inability to find the Guardian Starlight.

He might have consoled himself with what little good news there had been. Renauld had fulfilled his promise to complete the defences around the now exposed elven ruins by the end of the first week and turned most of his men over to Tellmore for the hard labour of shifting earth away from millennia-old foundations. The knight had remained in a good mood, apparently enjoying the change of pace his assignment was allowing him, and that simply grated on Tellmore's nerves all the greater.

The scouts Renauld had deployed had spied an armed force to the north some days ago, but it had continued east without breaking step. Everyone in the camp guessed this was the Vos army sent to recover the artefact they sought, and they took heart not only in the enemy heading in the wrong direction but also that the force was reported to be much smaller than theirs and consisting only of cavalry – not much use against the five-foot-high fence they had erected around the ruins.

Tellmore knew he should be thankful for the small mercies but he had found himself stymied almost as soon as the first pale grey rocks of the elven settlement were exposed to the cold, and wet, light of day.

He still did not know whether they were standing on top of a village, outpost, castle, or some weird elven meeting point. The layout of the foundations they had so far discovered defied easy analysis. The men-at-arms would dig hard at his instruction, at first as eager as Tellmore to discover what lay down some mud and rock filled passageway that had lain dormant for countless centuries.

Then they would hit a dead end.

This happened time and again: a promising passage would simply end in a smooth and unbroken wall that, as subsequent experiments showed, was at least four feet thick. Tellmore could almost taste the whiff of older magics in the air when he descended into the ruins, and had at one point convinced himself that he faced a magical challenge, not one whose solution would be found in mere digging.

And yet, there was no centrepoint to the magic, no obvious ethereal construct that could be moved or manipulated. It just seemed to permeate the area, as if something magical were leaking.

He fervently hoped that the something was not the Guardian Starlight itself, and that they had not arrived a few hundred years too late to take advantage of whatever properties the artefact might bestow upon its wielder.

Tellmore knew his objective might be mere yards away, and he could not reach it. His frustration grew to enormous proportions. Renauld soon learned not to interrupt the wizard's work for any purpose but the most critical.

A few days ago, men had started dying. The first was killed in a rockfall as a ceiling collapsed, and this was put down to inadequate preparation on that part of the excavation, coupled with a weakening of the soil due to the rain. Procedures were revised and work continued. Almost immediately, another man stepped on some sort of pressure plate that triggered a spike as thick as Tellmore's own arm to shoot up from the floor, impaling the poor soldier from underneath.

At least he had died instantaneously but, as Renauld quietly pointed out, any more deaths of this nature were likely to have a negative effect on morale.

The deaths continued and increased in pace. More traps claimed lives. Pits opened up beneath the feet of soldiers, sending them plummeting into a dark void that was too deep for torches or lanterns to illuminate. Scything metal wheels erupted from walls to cut men apart at the waist, or sections of the ruins would spontaneously collapse, burying whoever was walking on top under tonnes of rock. Hidden reservoirs would flood passageways, drowning any who did not start moving at the first ominous rumbles though, it had to be said, the soldiers were certainly more alert now and false alarms were becoming just as common as real dangers. Either would send men spilling out of the ruins, screaming in raw fear.

Not blind to the panic around him and all too aware of stories of bloody mutinies in Pontaine's history, Tellmore started to create protective charms, spells of shielding and absorption that robbed most traps of their lethality. Gradually, Renauld's soldiers began to settle back down into the rhythm of work and progress began to be made.

Tellmore had felt a rush of elation yesterday when they finally broke into a new chamber that seemed to serve as some kind of entrance hall. There were no cobwebs in the darkest recesses of this chamber, nor layers of dust, just the same flat grey stone they had all seen throughout the rest of the ruins. The place might have been deserted only a month ago, and yet Tellmore instantly recognised the unmistakable pull of magic tugging on his senses, ancient though it might be, and he knew they had taken a large step towards their goal.

The flap of his tent was pulled aside and Renauld, his armour dripping with the rain still pouring outside, entered. His face, as it had remained since his men started dying on the expedition, was grim.

"We are ready for you now, Magister."

Tellmore took a deep breath, closed his eyes briefly, and then stood.

"Good. Let's finish this."

Renauld held the tent flap open for the wizard, but could not refrain from the question that burned within.

"Do you think it will work this time, Magister?"

Tellmore gave him a sharp glare, a warning for the knight to keep his questions to himself lest someone in the camp overhear them. Pontaine troops had been known to mutiny before, and he feared the continued deaths would drive the soldiers in this camp to do something very foolish.

Drawing his cloak around him, Tellmore bent his head against the rain as he strode outside, Renauld quickly following. He kept his eyes to the ground, as much to avoid the stares of the soldiers as to shield his face from the rain, though he could feel the cold glare of each one, the blame for lost friends and comrades landing squarely on his shoulders.

Picking their way past the tents that had served as home for the entire camp over the past weeks, Tellmore and Renauld marched through the excavation area. What had once been a picturesque valley with lush grass had been transformed by the industry of the men-at-arms. Within the stockade, great mounds of earth were piled next to long trenches and shallow shafts, the glint of ancient grey stone flashing here and there as it shone in the first rain to touch it for thousands of years. Picking a careful path to avoid slipping on the thickening mud, Tellmore turned past a large pile of excavated earth and stepped gingerly onto a set of narrow stairs that descended underground and into a long passageway. His heart quickened its pace, as it always did when he came to this place. He could feel they were very close to their goal now.

They had broken into the chamber through a passageway that had started to slope downwards, and ended at the top of a wide flight of stairs that continued downwards to the chamber's floor. The floor itself was tiled, though from the same rock as the walls, and spanned perhaps thirty yards from end to end. The ceiling was domed, though torchlight rapidly fell away from its tallest point, leaving it in darkness.

To either side of the chamber were narrow alcoves, two to each wall, and it had been presumed that either statues or guards had once stood there, though they were empty now.

Directly opposite the staircase lay a large stone door, between two pillars set into the wall and decorated with a single line of elven text that Tellmore had been labouring to decipher. No handle or bar was present to open the door, but he believed the text suggested that, under the right conditions, one merely had to push lightly against the portal, and it would swing open. He had theorised the door was at least a couple of yards thick and it had so far resisted any attempt to break through or tunnel round, usually with lethal consequences for the soldiers involved.

Four men-at-arms stood nervously between the alcoves, studiously avoiding a glance at the scorch marks that marred the grey stone floor before them, the results of the last attempt to pass through the door.

Smiling in a way he hoped was both confident and encouraging, Tellmore nodded to the soldiers, and strode past them to confront the door. It remained a grey, monolithic barrier but, as Tellmore reached out, his hand hovering just an inch away from its surface, he could feel the latent magical energies stored within and, just at the far reaches of his senses, the arcane throb of something else that lay beyond the portal, something old, ancient and powerful. He turned back to the men-at-arms.

"I have devised a new spell of shielding and protection," he told them. "However, I won't be using the normal magics taught at the Three Towers, but will instead bind the magic of this place itself into the spell."

The men-at-arms looked at one another, and he cold see the doubt. He decided to use another tack.

"Basically, this means wreathing the protection spell with energies that the elves will have used themselves. It would be like... covering oneself with musk in order to approach a bear you are hunting, without it attacking you."

That seemed to work, for a couple of the men at least, and he saw them steel themselves to the task,

"The spell will take only a moment to fashion – when I give the word, you need only approach the door, push gently, and it will open. You will be the first to see riches that have lain here, undisturbed, since before the nations of Vos and Pontaine even existed!"

Renauld, he noticed, had not come down the stairs and was standing with obvious nervousness at the entrance of the chamber.

Reaching into his tunic, Tellmore produced a small silk bag and, as he paced slowly around the men-at-arms, he reached into the bag and threw pinches of sand. Murmuring a chant as he did so, Tellmore continued his pacing, feeling the magic rush into him as he shaped the spell, infusing the energy into the sand as it drifted through the air to settle on the armour and weapons of the men.

Having paced round them three times, Tellmore stopped and his chant grew louder as he sought to snare the magical energy permeating the chamber, binding it into his own spell to combine the magic of man with that of the elves. It was a strange feeling, like nothing he had felt before; he could liken it to wrapping his naked body in a single expanse of silk, but one that felt at once warm and inviting, as well as utterly alien. There was immense power to be used here, but he saw the dangers inherent in his own lack of knowledge. He just hoped that what little energy he was siphoning from the chamber would not unbalance any other defences that they had not yet discovered.

Abruptly, his chant stopped. Tellmore took a deep breath as he studied the soldiers, reaching out with his mind's eye to test the integrity and coverage of the spell. He could almost see it, a faint haze that enveloped each man-at-arms, subtly twisting and bending, though never yielding, as the passive magic of the chamber brushed against it.

"It is done. Please, gentleman, proceed and bring riches to all of us."

The soldiers drew their weapons. They glanced at one another, obviously debating who should go first, until one, a close-shaven middle-aged man, sighed quietly and took a step forward. A sergeant, Tellmore guessed, leading his men by example.

The others followed him, all taking slow and very short steps towards the grey stone door, as though prolonging the short journey as much as possible. All too soon, they were right in front of the door.

Briefly glancing at his men, the sergeant gritted his teeth and held a hand out, palm open, to the door. Slowly, grimacing as he did so, he stretched out to touch the door and push it open. For a second, his hand hovered just an inch from the smooth grey surface.

From across the chamber, Tellmore's moustache twitched as he chewed on his lower lip, caught between anticipation and fear. He saw the sergeant reach out to the door, hesitate, then push forward.

The effect was instant. A chill wind sprang up from the door itself, whipping through the chamber, tugging at Tellmore's cloak. There was a flash of blue-white light, followed by a terrible crack, and, just for an instant, Tellmore fancied he saw the outline of a tall, thin figure standing imperiously before the men-at-arms, within the door itself.

Then the light disappeared, leaving the chamber in guttering torchlight. All four of the soldiers had disappeared, the only trace of their existence a new set of scorch marks on the cold floor before the impenetrable door.

Bowing his head, Tellmore felt a sudden shudder as the frustration built to a pitch within him. Without a word, he turned and mounted the stairs, striding past Renauld's accusing stare without acknowledgement.

Outside, the rain persisted, but Tellmore no longer felt it. He was instead acutely aware of the murderous looks he received from every soldier he passed. They all knew what had happened. More of their friends had been killed, and at the behest of the wizard in their midst.

Forcing himself not to run back to his tent in fear, Tellmore ignored them all, focussing his attention dead ahead.

He almost dove into his tent when he reached it, and immediately raced across the enclosed space to rummage through one of his cases. After a few seconds of groping, he found what he was looking for: a small pewter mug and a bottle of Pontaine brandy. Pouring himself a judicious amount from the bottle, he drained the mug completely and then stood still, closing his eyes as he felt the warmth of the drink spread through his body.

Replacing the bottle and mug back into the case, Tellmore hunched over his desk, staring at the piles of notes he had written over the past three weeks, as if they were about to give him some new answer, some new inspiration. After a few minutes, he had to admit to himself that no new information was forthcoming.

He closed his eyes and muttered the one thing he had thought he would never hear himself say.

"I don't know what to do."

CHAPTER SIX

IT HAD STARTED raining again. Alhmanic gave the dark clouded sky a baleful look.

The Anclas Territories were notorious for their bad weather. He had once heard a church scholar describe the effects of the Drakengrat Mountains on the area, as the wind swept in over Vos from the ocean but he had neglected to learn the details. However, the effect was that it always rained in the Territories, and not just a few showers here and there, but constant, wet misery interspersed with outbreaks of gales and sleet.

It gave Alhmanic pause to wonder why Pontaine had struggled so hard to fight over these lands, and why the Anointed Lord had ordered their seizure by the Empire. It was a depressing place, with tiny little settlements barely worthy of the title of town, a population who resented whoever ruled over them, precious few minerals and earth that made for poor farming.

Still, the Territories had once been the scene of tremendous glory during the war between Vos and Pontaine, and Alhmanic remembered well his own part in the struggle. He had been younger then, all those years ago, fitter physically and more ambitious, if that were possible. It was funny to think of how much potential that young man had had back then.

Starting the war as a humble but God-fearing militiaman, Alhmanic's devotion to the cause and ability with a sword had caught the eye of the fighting clergy, and thus began his rise. By the time the Pontaine army had been beaten and the Territories claimed by Vos, Alhmanic had been at the head of a force ten thousand strong, every one of them listening intently to the man who would become the Preacher Divine as he gave sermons masquerading as battle speeches, even in the heart of the fighting. They were real fighting men, he recalled, able to march all day and fight a battle at the end of it without so much as a complaint.

He had less faith in his current charges, though they seemed capable enough of following orders. The half-company he led, less than fifty men, had at least been given horses. It seemed as though Klaus had not been as sadistic as he could have been, and had granted that mercy at least.

A pathetic sneeze caught Alhmanic's attention and he threw a contemptuous glance over his shoulder. Traipsing behind him, on a horse that looked as ragged as its rider, was Otto, a mage of the Final Faith that Alhmanic had been able to requisition by calling in a few favours that would remain unknown to Klaus. The intention had been to grant his half-company some magical support. The result was a little more doubtful.

Otto was a young man, in his early twenties but going on sixty, Alhmanic swore. The lad might well have been as competent as Alhmanic had been assured, but he had turned out to be strictly a city mage. His back was permanently bowed as he huddled under his soaking cloak, trying in vain to stay dry.

Now it seemed as though their only mage had caught a cold.

As evening drew in, making the bleak land all the more bleak, the Vos horsemen rode at breakneck pace on Alhmanic's orders, heedless of the wet grassland and patches of sucking mud. One of his scouting outriders had rejoined the force an hour before carrying what he doubtless considered good news. The scout had returned from Soire, a tiny village typical of so many in the Territories, with a report that the site they were looking for was close by, to the west. Unfortunately, a Pontaine force had already ridden through Soire, and had apparently set up its own camp there.

The scout's cheerful face fell as Alhmanic let loose a stream of expletives. They had ridden within a few miles of the Pontaine position and his scouts had failed to spot them. He was furious that Pontaine was ahead of them and already in position, and nervous that he might be too late. Ordering his men to prepare for battle, he rode them hard towards the valley the scout had spoken of, trying to race the fall of night and thus avoid yet another delay.

With the sound of hooves thudding on soft ground all around him, Alhmanic finally allowed himself a grim smile. He had no idea of how advanced the plans of the Pontaine force were, nor even if they were after the same artefact. However, he was no believer in coincidence and an armed Pontaine force travelling through the

Territories was justification for an attack. Whatever the reason for their presence, Alhmanic intended to rid the Territories of every Pontaine soldier he could find.

A cry went up from one of the horsemen ahead of him, and he looked up to see two men standing on top of a small hillock about half a mile away. Barking an order, Alhmanic sent three of his horsemen to ride them down. Perhaps they were just a couple of innocent travellers, shepherds, or traders, but he was not going to take the chance they were not Pontaine scouts. When he attacked their camp, he wanted complete surprise.

The three horsemen veered away from the force and goaded their horses into full gallops, covering the ground between them and the unknown men rapidly. As the distance closed, they lowered their spears as the two men started to run.

They barely made it to the summit of the hill before one was spitted on the spear of a Vos horseman, while the other was ridden down by the other two. Circling around, one of the horsemen plunged his spear into the unmoving body that lay on the ground. Alhmanic appreciated that gesture. It always counted to be thorough.

Ahead, the lead horseman, some sergeant whose name had escaped Alhmanic within minutes of them meeting in Scholten, had raised his hand to call the force to a halt. Impatiently, Alhmanic quickly trotted over to him.

"Scout returns, Preacher," the sergeant said, pointing out a lone horseman slowly becoming visible through the gloom of evening and the ever-present rain.

It was the same man who had returned from Soire to report the presence of the Pontaine force, and Alhmanic noted his demeanour was far more subdued this time.

"What news?"

"Valley up ahead, my Lord. Filled with Pontaine soldiers. They have a camp, seem to have been there some time."

"Have they built fortifications?"

"Aye, just a fence but it completely rings their camp, too high to jump. They seem set in for some duration, pitched up those big tents they use when they mean to stay somewhere for a while."

"Numbers?"

"Against us, at least two to one, possibly more."

Alhmanic was not going to blindly trust the eyes of a scout he had not handpicked himself but felt at least a little encouraged by that. The fence could be a problem though.

"Any notion of what they are doing there?"

The scout shrugged. "They seem to be building something inside the camp. Big piles of dirt everywhere, saw some stone blocks. Couldn't see what though. Maybe some kind of fort, but in the centre of a valley is an odd place for one."

"Think carefully, soldier," Alhmanic said. "Do you think they are really building something... or is it possible they are digging something up?"

Caught between frowning in thought and gulping in nervousness, knowing that the wrong word to the Preacher Divine could have unfortunate consequences on his career, not to mention his life expectancy, the scout seemed almost comical.

"I had not considered that, Lord. It could be they are digging something up, yes."

Alhmanic swore under his breath, an unwieldy diatribe that encompassed Pontaine, the Territories and the demands of the Anointed Lord.

Sighing, he calmed down a little. So, he had to assume that someone in Pontaine knew what he was after and had beaten him to it. Perhaps that was all for the better, especially if they could capture one of the officers. Alhmanic might just be able to save himself a little trouble in rooting out the artefact from whatever dungeon the Pontaine force clearly thought it was buried within.

"Sergeant, take Otto and half your men," Alhmanic commanded. "Circle round that valley and wait for my signal – you'll know it when you see it. Then charge. Otto?"

A sniff at his shoulder indicated the mage had joined the discussion.

"You'll blast the fence apart, letting the horses through, understand?" He did not wait for a response, instead turning back to the sergeant. "Wipe out all resistance, but if you see a decent officer, grab him. I want at least one alive."

The sergeant banged his fist against his chest then extended his arm in salute, then wheeled his troops as he shouted orders for the force to split.

"The rest of you," Alhmanic shouted as he stood in his stirrups, "with me. We'll show these Pontaine dogs that they need a damn sight more than a force twice our size to stake any claim in the Anclas Territories. Let us remind them of what happened to their men during the war!"

The horsemen raised their spears and called out in salute as they goaded their beasts into action. Alhmanic grinned as he unslung his staff, the large blue stone mounted at its tip clasped by silvered claws. Despite everything that had happened, he was going to enjoy what happened next.

With half a dozen Pontaine scouts dispatched by outriders, Alhmanic felt confident enough to dismount as he approached the brow of the hill. Looking down into the valley, he saw the Pontaine soldiers within their camp as they scuttled about, lighting lanterns to ward off the growing darkness. He could make out the perimeter fence, a crude but effective wooden construction reaching perhaps six feet high in some areas, and there were obviously many tents within its circumference. However, he could not pick out any details of the digging his scouts had reported.

Some of his horsemen had voiced concerns about an attack in the dark, but Alhmanic had waved them aside. When the battle started, he assured them, there would be plenty of light for them to slay the Pontaine force by and while the initial approach to the camp would be brisk, there was no reason for them to engage at full tilt.

Directing his men forward with his staff, Alhmanic led them at a walking pace to a point just below the crest of the hill. Looking about him, he took a deep breath. His soldiers gripped their spears and swords firmly, anticipating the coming battle, while a few grinned at one another, perhaps hoping for a rich Pontaine officer who could be captured then ransomed.

Across the other side of the valley, the sergeant would be waiting for Alhmanic's signal.

"Quiet on the way down, and follow my lead," Alhmanic said. "Our comrades will be going in slightly ahead of us, so we will have complete surprise. We charge only at the last moment, when you see a gap in their fencing. Stay close to me until then, and we'll be among them before they know it."

A few quiet murmurs told him they understood.

Raising his staff to the sky, Alhmanic closed his eyes and briefly conjured the image of the Anointed Lord into his mind, feeling the familiar rise of reverence and devotion to the Final Faith.

Fuelled by his passion and belief, the staff shuddered with divine power, and the blue stone at its tip blazed fiercely for a few seconds before releasing its energies. A bolt of blue light shot up into the sky to hang, motionless, directly above the camp. It began to pulse, slowly, growing a little brighter with each flicker.

Cries from the far side of the valley told Alhmanic that the other half of his force had started their charge. With a wave, he directed his own men to make their way carefully down into the valley.

A flash of orange light and a giant crack echoed around the valley as a great ball of fire slammed into the fence on the far side of the camp. Otto had, at least, done his duty in breaking a path through the fence for the sergeant and his men. Through the dying fires of his magic, Alhmanic could see the first horsemen charging for the Pontaine soldiers who scrabbled to their feet to meet the oncoming attack. The quickest of them died at the point of a Vos spear while the others were simply ridden down under the hooves of a score of charging horses.

Alhmanic raised his staff once more and shouted to the men he led.

"In the name of the true and Final Faith, in the name of the most Holy Anointed Lord – attack!"

His men needed no other encouragement, and they kicked their horses into a gallop. The fence loomed before them, a solid barrier impossible to jump with the weight of their weapons and armour, but Alhmanic could feel their faith behind him, and he felt the thrill of pious devotion sweep through his body. He channelled the energy, from his heart to his staff, and he felt the shaft begin to hum as power built up within the relic.

Levelling the staff at the fence they rushed toward, Alhmanic cried out a single word in a language long forgotten outside of the Final Faith, a word that was part prayer, part pure exaltation.

The staff throbbed once in his hand, then bucked as if trying to free itself from his grip. Its stone shone brightly, then winked out as a pulse of divine energy leapt forward to smack against the fence with irresistible force.

The effect was spectacular. Thirty feet of the fence line exploded in a flash of bright blue light, with earth and wooden posts spiralling high into the night sky. A strong gust of wind swept past the horsemen, as if the air itself were trying to escape from the magical explosion. However, the full force of the magic was directed inside the camp, and the wind became a brief but howling gale that knocked men off their feet, threw lanterns through the air and blasted tents apart.

As Alhmanic galloped the last remaining yards to the camp, he vaulted his horse over the wreckage of the fence, now barely more than a shallow crater filled with stone and wooden shards. One Pontaine soldier reacted a little quicker than his friends and stood up to face the charge. A single swing across the temple with Alhmanic's staff, aided by the speed of the horse, caved in the skull of the man before he properly registered what was happening.

Once inside, Alhmanic drew his horse up short, allowing his men to sweep either side of him as they speared and slashed their way through the Pontaine force, knocking over lanterns to start fires and trampling through tents to find more victims for their murderous attack.

The Pontaine force was beginning to rally, remarkably quickly, Alhmanic thought. While the perimeter had crumbled swiftly, there was a strong core nearer the centre of the camp that was already forming into a tightly bound unit, its spears daring any horse to make a charge against them. It would be a hard nut to crack, Alhmanic could already see, and he kicked his horse forward, intending to lend support, hoping they could break the Pontaine soldiers before they became a problem.

Raising his staff high over his head, he allowed its single blue crystal to shine briefly, its light pulling the Vos soldiers nearest to him along for the attack. Alhmanic allowed them to surge forward as they neared the line and the foremost riders drove into the Pontaine defence.

Horses screamed in agony and men yelled in fear as the Pontaine spears sank deep into the flesh of the mounts. Seeing what was happening, Alhmanic jerked the reins of his own horse tight as he pulled up short but several of his soldiers did not see the danger until it was too late. They continued ploughing forward into the Pontaine line which by now had set their spears against the charge, the butts buried deep into the churned mud. The speed of the horses had been turned against them as they were impaled on the waiting spear points.

Cursing under his breath, Alhmanic rode away, determined to find another weak point, as the remaining Vos soldiers drew their swords and attempted to hack their way through the bristling spear line. He knew he had to act quickly, or more of the Pontaine men would rally to this point and their weight of numbers, not to mention their spears, would begin to tell against his smaller mounted force.

Desperately seeking an answer somewhere across the camp, his vision obscured by smoke, burning tents and men pitched in bloody battle against one another, Alhmanic gave a grim smile as he saw Otto cowering behind a line of his cavalry, clinging to his horse as though it would bear him away from this dreadful place.

*   *   *

A FEW SCATTERED shouts roused Tellmore from his studies, as sleep had eluded him once again. Raising his head from another stack of scattered notes, the wizard frowned. Then he heard – and felt – the explosion; a deep bass note, followed by the ground shaking and men screaming. Powerful magics were weaving their way through the air, and that explosion had been no mere alchemist's trickery.

Gathering his cloak about him, Tellmore ran into the camp, the notes behind him scattering in the breeze. All about him was the confusion of men attacked when they least expected it. While some fought and died near the perimeter of the camp, others stumbled bleary-eyed out of their tents, only to find themselves staring at a lance point. Some broke immediately and fled, while others kept enough wits about them to reach for their weapons.

Seeing a familiar face, Tellmore called out.

"Renauld, call your men," he ordered, directing the knight to an open patch of ground between tents they had used to parade the soldiers every morning.

Tellmore was gratified to see that the knight had reacted quickly and had already gathered a handful of men to his side. Seeing what Tellmore was intending, Renauld began shouting at any Pontaine man he saw and, with painful slowness it seemed to Tellmore, the handful of men grew into a reasonable sized unit. Leaving their swords scabbarded, they opted for spears, bracing the long staves against the inevitable charge.

The attackers did not keep them waiting for long, and a near score of horsemen began to charge the line. Having faith in Renauld's ability to defend himself and hold the line, Tellmore trotted away, keeping to the shadows of tents as he sought to bolster the defences elsewhere. He imagined Renauld's defiant stand as the only one in the camp and knew that if that were so, they would soon all be killed as more horsemen flooded in. Two soldiers came across his path, backing down between two tents as more horses thundered past.

"You two," Tellmore said. "Defend me. Let no one come within five yards."

He noticed the soldiers glanced at one another, but their natural instinct was to obey any commander and Tellmore's authority was sufficient to bring them back into the fight.

"As you say, my Lord."

He gestured them to follow as he ran down between the tents to a wider thoroughfare. Looking either side, he saw horsemen had broken into the camp from opposite sides of the stockade. Those to the west were making short work of hacking down some soldiers who had tried to flee through the camp's entrance.

Closing his eyes for the briefest second, Tellmore felt the power of magic flow through him and he fashioned its energy as a craftsman might whittle wood. With a single word of power, Tellmore stamped his foot into the earth, and fire erupted from the ground and streaked towards the horses, leaving a trail of guttering flames as it shot down the thoroughfare.

One of the horsemen saw the incoming attack, its course an unerring bolt that flashed towards them far faster than any steed could gallop. He opened his mouth to cry out in alarm, just as the fire reached him. It flared suddenly, and a wave of flame engulfed both horses and men, their screams utterly silent as the air was sucked from their lungs by the intense heat. As quickly as they had appeared, the flames died away, leaving nothing but charred and smoking flesh scattered across the scorched earth. It was no longer possible to tell horse flesh from man.

"My Lord!" one of his soldiers yelled, and Tellmore felt a hand on his back, shoving him roughly into the thoroughfare. Stumbling, Tellmore heard the dull sound of hooves impacting on wet mud, and he glanced over his shoulder to see a horseman riding through the narrow gap between the tents, bearing down on the three of them with a spear held wickedly at neck height.

One of the soldiers grabbed Tellmore by the arm and spun him to one side, but the horseman adjusted the aim of his spear accordingly and his horse steered towards them. He did not see the second of Tellmore's bodyguards, who had crouched down out of sight behind one of the tents and, as the horse tore past, swung his sword with both hands, slicing deep into the beast's hind leg.

Screaming in agony, the horse collapsed, taking its rider with it as they slid in the mud. Seeing his chance, the soldier that had grabbed Tellmore jumped back up and, raising his sword high, plunged it down into the writhing mass of man and horse. Standing up, Tellmore brushed himself down and looked appreciatively at the two soldiers.

"That was good work," he said, nodding his approval.

"Thank you, my Lord," one said, giving him a half salute. Tellmore was about to ask their names when he saw another small group of horsemen beyond them, riding for the centre of the camp.

"Come on. We still have work to do."

"COME ON, OTTO, you worthless slug!" Alhmanic shouted at the cringing mage.

He had found the wizard cowering behind a row of tents, clinging with fear to his horse as if trying to meld with its flesh and thus become invisible. Alhmanic had snarled as he grabbed the reins of Otto's horse and pulled it bodily back into the fray.

"Ready your spells, wizard," Alhmanic said as they trotted into battle. "Our men have need of you."

He ignored the young wizard's whimpering as the mage gathered his robe about himself and used its corner to wipe his nose.

Hooves churning up the wet mud, they thundered towards the melee at the centre of the encampment that was growing in size and ferocity as both sides began to rally their men and engage in pitched battle. A flash of movement to his right caught Alhmanic's eye and he instinctively pulled hard on the reins of his horse to veer it to one side.

A sword intended to slash his mount's shoulder instead bit deep into one of its hind legs, and the horse shrieked in pain as it collapsed in a torrent of mud, water and flailing limbs. Mindful to keep his staff close to his body, Alhmanic threw himself off the horse as it went down but, even so, the impact knocked the wind out of him.

Using the staff to brace himself, Alhmanic staggered to his feet, ready to face his attacker. Instead, he saw two Pontaine soldiers pacing warily towards Otto who cowered before them on the ground.

On his knees and desperately trying to slide through the mud to get away from his attackers, Otto seemed to be alternating between pleading for mercy and trying to formulate a spell. Arcane words of power, shaken and mis-formed, died on his lips when one of the soldiers plucked up the courage to thrust his sword through the wizard's neck.

Yanking his sword free, the soldier tapped his companion on the arm and pointed towards Alhmanic. The Preacher Divine smiled at the two of them and waved a hand to bid them try their luck. As they took a step forward, Alhmanic thumped the butt of his staff into the wet ground and felt the glorious power of the artefact's divinity begin to spread through his body. The soldiers checked their advance as the crystal in the tip of the staff began to glow.

"Leave this one to me, my friends," a voice said, and Alhmanic noticed a third man had joined them, one dressed in a dark tunic wreathed in a scarlet cloak, and sporting the broad moustache currently favoured by young Pontaine nobles.

The newcomer had the poise of a warrior, thought Alhmanic at first, but he could feel a sense of power emanating from the man that spoke of wizardry.

The two soldiers seemed somewhat relieved to have been recalled, though they did not retreat far, standing behind the wizard with swords still drawn.

"I am Tellmore, advisor to the Baron de Sousse, and you have violated the neutrality of these territories," the man said in a deep, calm voice.

"I am Alhmanic, the Preacher Divine, and I claim everything here in the name of the Final Faith and the Empire of Vos."

That Tellmore sighed at his pronouncement set Alhmanic quivering, and as he made to respond, he almost missed the subtle movement of the wizard's fingers, and the quiet incantation subdued by his moustache.

A bolt of fire streaked out from Tellmore's outstretched hand, building up speed as it crossed the short distance between them. How Alhmanic raised his staff to parry and absorb the spell, he would never know, but the Preacher Divine felt the hot flames blast his face as they smacked against the invisible shield of faith the staff generated.

Scowling, Alhmanic whirled the staff in his hands so rapidly it seemed as though a fluttering fan span in front of him, the glowing crystal creating a pale blue sheen of light at its outermost edge. With a brief prayer, he unleashed the divine energy and a vortex of power shimmered towards the wizard.

Holding up his hand, Tellmore met the attack with magical power of his own, but the strain caused him to take a step back as the force of the Final Faith washed over him in wave after punishing wave. Behind the wizard, the two soldiers and the tent immediately behind them took the full weight of the energy Tellmore failed to block and they were hurled a dozen yards through the air, weapons and tent contents spinning away into the night.

Seeing his attack blocked, Alhmanic quickly switched tactics, and roared as he charged the wizard, the staff held high above his head.

He swung it down hard, intending to split the skull of his opponent, but Tellmore had already recovered from the staff's assault and leapt nimbly to one side as the heavy weapon whistled through the air. Alhmanic cried out again as he swung the staff to his side but, again, Tellmore danced away with remarkable dexterity. Feeling frustration beginning to build, Alhmanic feinted a third blow but then switched his grip on the staff and buried its butt deep into the earth at his feet, uttering a single word of divine power as he did so.

The ground rippled in front of him, the waves spreading rapidly outward as they raced towards Tellmore. The wizard began to cast a quick counterspell but the staff's energy reached him before he could finish, and he was hurled off his feet.

Scrambling to his feet, Tellmore looked up just in time to see the Preacher Divine level the staff at his face.

Then his whole world exploded.

CHAPTER SEVEN

RECOGNISING THE WAX seal of Tellmore holding the folded letter closed, de Sousse leaned back in his chair and hoisted his feet up on to the desk. Shifting his weight in the seat, he settled down to read the latest news from the Anclas Territories but the first few lines told him the wizard was still being stymied by the secrets of the ancient ruins.

With a face that grew steadily grimmer, de Sousse digested the obvious lack of progress, frowning as he came upon the catalogue of troop losses. He had taken a large risk in sending a force into the Anclas Territories where they could easily encounter Vos troops, and he was not ready to start a war. Not just yet, anyway.

Now, it seemed he was suffering a rate of attrition among his soldiers equal to that of a full blown assault on a castle, and yet there was no glory to go with it. They had been dying in a hole in the ground that had, as of yet, yielded no reward.

It crossed the Baron's mind that perhaps Tellmore had not been the right man to send. Perhaps the wizard was not as wise and learned as he imagined.

He shook his head to wipe away the thought. Tellmore was good, de Sousse's gold had ensured he would have one of the best wizards in Pontaine at his disposal. Surely the possession of an artefact like the Guardian Starlight was worth a little time and, yes, even a few lives.

The Baron de Sousse shrugged to himself. Maybe the wizard would be right in saying such things, but that did not mean he could not give the man some aid. What was perhaps needed here, de Sousse thought, was someone who had a more… instinctive grasp of magic, rather than one who had learned it all by rote from dusty tomes.

What might be the result if he sent a Shadowmage into the problem?

* * *

IF THE ANOINTED Lord, bless all ten of her little toes, had created this mission solely to test his faith, she had done a very good job, Alhmanic decided as he stood at the open tent flap, looking out into the continual rain.

The small hours had brought about the defeat of the Pontaine forces, and the dawn had revealed the scale of the carnage. The encampment was now a wreck, with tents and the belongings of the men scattered across the shallow valley. A quagmire of mud, blood and bodies lay at its heart, where the last stand of the Pontaine soldiers had taken place, and where Alhmanic, aided by both his staff's divine power and the speed of his cavalry, had finally overwhelmed the defence.

He had lost nearly half of his men in the attack, but Alhmanic had first thought it a cheap price to pay in order to gain a lead on Pontaine. Now, after his first descent into the ruins, he was not so sure. He also now realised that it had been a mistake to simply blast the wizard he had encountered that night, and perhaps twice as foolish not to ensure the man was dead.

Alhmanic had assumed the wizard had been an advisor, a qualified expert brought along by a Pontaine noble to aid their expedition, but now it became apparent that the man had been the mind behind the excavations, and that his knowledge might have proved useful. As morning broke, they had discovered the wizard's notes, stacks of them, every detail copied down in exhaustive depth – but they had been written in some shorthand or code that Alhmanic was at a loss to understand. When Alhmanic had then searched for the man's body, it had vanished and the wizard was now presumably on his way back to his lord to report what had happened. A handful of scouts had been dispatched to search for him in the wilderness of the Anclas Territories, but Alhmanic held little hope in their abilities and chances of success.

The fact that the wizard had managed to flee did not unduly worry him; after all, it would be some time before Pontaine could mount any sort of response, if they even fancied a larger clash with a Vos army. However, the wizard could have filled in many details of these ruins which would have made Alhmanic's job a great deal easier.

Sighing heavily, Alhmanic turned back into the tent to face the seven Pontaine soldiers kneeling before him, his men holding naked blades at their backs. More had surrendered after their last stand crumbled away but it had taken the Vos horsemen a little while to move beyond their blood lust. At the time, Alhmanic had not overly blamed them for the rampage but now he began to suspect a wiser course of action could have been taken.

"Gentlemen," Alhmanic said. "It has been a long night, and my patience is rapidly disappearing. I want to know what has been happening here and how far you managed to get in your excavations."

A couple of the soldiers glanced sidelong at one another, but the rest kept their stares fixed firmly on the ground in front of them. Again, Alhmanic sighed, then nodded at one of his own men.

The man's sword was thrust sharply down into the shoulder of one of the prisoners, driving past the collarbone and into the heart. The prisoner gasped and died, a fountain of blood erupting from the wound as the soldier withdrew his blade. The others kept their heads down but Alhmanic saw a couple were beginning to shake.

"I can honestly say I do not care what happens to any of you," he continued. "You can all die, right here, right now and I would give it no more thought. Or you can be released and thrown out of this camp to make your own way back to your homes. What *does* matter to me is the completion of my mission, and to accomplish that, I need some information. So, which of you is going to start?"

He saw two of the Pontaine men exchange glances again, and one of them gave the tiniest of nods. In a flash, Alhmanic had stalked over to them and placed the tip of his staff under one of the men's chin to raise his head.

"You have something to say, yes?"

The prisoner, a young man likely not yet in his twenties, cleared his throat then swallowed.

"Sir, I might be able to help you," he said.

"I would hope so. Pray continue."

With his chin still supported by Alhmanic's staff, the prisoner strained his eyes left and right to see what his comrades were doing and, seeing neither support nor condemnation, nodded again and began to speak.

Alhmanic listened intently as he told him of their mission for the Baron de Sousse and his wizard, Tellmore. Though they were not even remotely familiar with arcane terminology, Alhmanic began to put the pieces together and he began to curse allowing the wizard to escape.

It became readily apparent that the Pontaine force had been here for some time, having been stalled in its attempts to descend into the unearthed Older Race outpost. This wizard, this Tellmore, seemed to have worked diligently but that work had cost the lives of many of his men, either through accidents in the excavation or magical defences that had been layered on this place like icing on a Pontaine gateau.

As the prisoners continued to speak, Alhmanic started thinking hard as he picked out the salient points from their confessions. He had inadvertently given the prisoners the impression their information was of little use to him, and they became increasingly agitated, their words more and more jumbled, as they strained to come up with something of value. When he finally turned back to face them and saw what was going on, Alhmanic signalled one of his men again.

"Take them," he said.

The soldier cocked his head. "Release them, sir?"

Alhmanic waved his hand in dismissal. "Yes, yes, they are of no more use to us. Take their weapons and armour, then eject them from the camp. If they survive their crossing of the Territories, they may yet prove of worth to someone. The rest of you are dismissed. Leave me. I need to think."

It was difficult to judge a wizard's abilities in a fight, Alhmanic knew. Some only ever practised battle spells and were useless at everything else. Others could be fine practitioners and yet go completely to pieces when a dagger was drawn. However, he had received the sense that this Tellmore was a mage of some note. While he had not heard of the Baron de Sousse, the lord obviously had enough resources to put together this mission, and such men did not employ fools for wizards. Having faced him personally, Alhmanic had begun to form the impression that while victory had belonged to Vos that night, different circumstances might well see the Pontaine wizard triumphant.

And that put him in a quandary. He might be the Preacher Divine, but what was he going to accomplish in this place that this learned wizard had failed to do in a much longer span of time?

He had little wish to see the magical defences of the ancients in action first hand. If the Pontaine soldiery had taken such heavy losses in their explorations, there was no reason to think his little army would fare differently. And what if the forces of

Pontaine returned; he would look extraordinarily foolish if he had expended the lives of his own soldiers in the ruins when they were later needed to defend the camp.

There were some advantages he could possibly exploit, but still he could not fancy his chances with any honesty. The one tool he had in abundance which the wizard had lacked, of course, was faith. The Anointed Lord had told him that faith alone could move mountains, though he suspected it might have a little trouble with Older Race magics.

He also had his staff which, with its inscribed spellshield, was supposed to be proof against any magic he was alert to. Then again, he did not like the idea of testing its defence against magic that had stopped being used millennia before his staff had been forged and enchanted.

Men could be dispatched to return to Vos and collect the kind of explosives that had recently came into use in the wealthiest mines. He had witnessed their power and had been impressed. However, he suspected even the greatest of the Vos alchemists had little idea of how such destructive force would react to the magical wards and guards laid down for eternity by elves and dwarfs.

Alhmanic fumed. The artefact was here, probably just a few dozen yards from where he stood now. The presence of the Pontaine wizard practically confirmed that. And yet, right at that moment, it might as well have been a thousand miles away, across the World's Ridge Mountains or maybe in the depths of the trackless seas.

On the other hand, there was no way he could return to the Anointed Lord empty-handed. If it cost him every man present and endangered his own life, he *had* to recover the artefact.

CHAPTER EIGHT

THE MAIN HALL of the Citadel lacked the raucous activity present when Lucius had last been there. Gone were the revelling nobles, the musicians, the copious food from around the peninsula and newly introduced couples disappearing into the shadows.

Still, it was anything but peaceful. Servants moved from one doorway to another, some hurrying to errands or carrying messages, others with far weightier burdens, straining to take barrels of wine to the kitchens or bundles of freshly washed tunics to the barracks. A few other townsmen were, like him, seated at one of the long tables that still filled the floor space of the hall, having been left there since the last banquet. They all had appointments for one Pontaine official or another, and they all ignored one another.

Lucius had already seen one change of guard while he had been sat there, and looked up in expectation as he sensed a servant approaching him. However, once again, the servant carried nothing but a flagon of wine that he used to top up Lucius' cup. That was the fourth or fifth time the man had done so, and Lucius decided to set his cup firmly down on the table this time. He could not shake the feeling that the baron was delaying their meeting, one the Pontaine lord had arranged himself, so Lucius could quietly work himself into a drunken stupor and be easier to deal with.

His head already starting to spin slightly, Lucius left his cup alone and instead sat up straight. If someone were watching him from the balcony that ran the length of the hall, or maybe from a spyhole – he would certainly not put that idea past the baron – then maybe they would sense he was done playing games and would get his meeting over with.

It took another visit from the wine-bearing servant, which Lucius pointedly refused, and then, perhaps, someone had taken the hint.

Or maybe the baron had simply concluded whatever business he had been engaged in earlier. A girl, perhaps in her late teenage years, dressed in a tight gown of blue silk, approached Lucius and curtseyed gracefully before him.

"The baron is ready to see you now, my Lord."

Lucius hid a smirk at being called "lord" and studied the girl briefly. She did not dress or speak like a servant, and he sniffed a hint of Pontaine nobility about her. Quite why such a girl would be sent to fetch someone from the hall puzzled him, and he realised he still had a great deal to learn about Pontaine customs.

She did not speak as she led him from the hall on a long journey through passageways and up spiralling stairs that were becoming familiar to him. Through it all, he saw passing servants act in a diffident nature to both of them, confirming his thought that she was not one of them.

Eventually, they arrived at a door Lucius recognised as being that of the baron's own study. The girl reached out with a delicate hand and gently rapped on the door. She barely made a sound to Lucius, but the door opened after a few seconds to reveal the smiling face of the Baron de Sousse.

"Excellent, my dear girl," he said. "You found him. Leave us be, and attend to your embroidery."

The girl curtseyed deeply and turned from them to walk back down the corridor. The baron waved Lucius inside the study.

"Baron," Lucius acknowledged, dipping his head briefly.

"Lovely young girl that one. Blood of my blood, mostly. Her mother died from a chill that settled on her chest, and few other members of our family were prepared to take on her daughter."

"I'm surprised," Lucius said as he walked into the study and took the chair the baron gestured him toward. "I thought Pontaine families relied on marriages to create alliances. An attractive young girl of marriageable age would be something of a prize."

"You are beginning to learn our ways, Lucius," de Sousse said as he walked behind the Sardenne oak desk dominating the room to take his own seat. "I commend you."

Lucius shrugged. "It is obvious Pontaine is not going to be leaving our city anytime soon. It seems prudent to learn the customs."

"Profitable too. Can I get you food or drink? We have some beautiful delicacies recently arrived from Volonne in our kitchens. Shouldn't be missed."

"Thank you, Lord Baron, no."

"To business then. The Lady Adrianna obviously does not accompany you."

"She received an invitation too?"

The baron nodded. "I had hoped to gain the benefits of her expertise as well as your own, but it is of little consequence, I am sure. Do you know what consumes her attention instead of me?"

"I do not. I make it a habit not to enquire too closely into what Adrianna does from day-to-day. If she wants my attention, she normally finds a way to get it."

"Women in general normally get what they want," the baron said, a sardonic smile hovering at his lips before disappearing. "But I do have concerns about Adrianna."

There could be an entire guild of people who feel that way, Lucius thought, but kept it to himself.

"Can she be trusted?"

The bluntness of the baron's question gave Lucius pause, and he stayed silent for a while, thinking how to best answer.

"In general, yes," Lucius said eventually. "If Adrianna says she is going to do something, it will be a rare instance in which she fails. If that is something that you have asked her to do, then maybe you can take advantage of that."

The baron looked at him for a moment as silence hung in the air.

"But..?" the baron finally prompted.

Lucius took a deep breath and wetted his lips. "You can probably trust her. However, never, ever cross her. It does not matter how many soldiers you have, nor how many pet wizards you can call upon. If Adrianna wants you dead, there may be no power in the city that can save you."

"We have heard rumours of her actions during the last days of Vos here. We heard–"

"They are not rumours. Adrianna was responsible for dozens, perhaps hundreds of deaths and single-handedly destroyed a sizeable portion of the city."

"But she was stopped."

Lucius allowed himself a short, bitter laugh at that. The baron looked at him in surprise, and Lucius shook his head.

"My Lord Baron, the only thing that truthfully stopped Adrianna was Adrianna, and a good woman died to ensure that choice." For a moment, he looked past the baron's shoulder, out of the open window behind him and at the greying sky. "Always treat Adrianna with the utmost respect. To do otherwise is to court danger that no one needs."

"But you are loyal to her?"

"I owe her for things that have happened in the past. Then again, she owes me as well, whether she would admit that publicly or not."

"You consider her a friend?"

"I have in the past, certainly. Now... Well, I may be one of the few that actually knows where he stands with her – most of the time, at least – and I am happy to accept that."

"Fair enough."

"Is this why you called me here? To learn about Adrianna?"

"I asked to see both of you. My interest in her, beyond being a Shadowmage and a fascinating woman in her own right, is rooted in Adrianna occupying one of the senior positions in the city, and having gained that position through nothing more than her own efforts and skills. However, I do have something quite different to discuss with you.

"I have several interests in the Anclas Territories, and I believe you have some experience there yourself."

"I worked as a mercenary for a number of years," Lucius said. "Mainly in the north of the Territories. Ugly place after the war."

"Ugly indeed, but also full of opportunity. It is that opportunity that drives me to conflict with other noble families of Pontaine. Resources from crop farms to tin mines often lay abandoned or, better, unprotected after a war. Remember, no one truly rules the Territories, so if a chalk quarry here or a wood rich with timber there is found, who truly owns it?"

"The people of the Territories?"

The baron barked a laugh in response. "Whoever comes along first with enough soldiers to take it and then hold on to it. It is all there, if you can but find it. And serfs, of course. A disenfranchised population like those of the Territories is ripe for use, be it on farms outside their homes or on a man's own property back in Pontaine."

"Sounds a little like slavery."

"I did not ask you here to debate semantics. Nor argue the ways of the world."

"Then, my Lord Baron, may I press you to tell me why I was summoned?"

"I do not intend to be left behind, Lucius. There are many among my peers, nobles of equal or similar rank and title, who already have extensive interests in the Territories. I gained a great deal from seizing Turnitia, of course, but that is only the first step on a much longer road."

"We have discovered an artefact, Lucius. In the Anclas Territories. All indications are that it is a very powerful one, something that was forged in the days of the elves, when their empire was at its very height."

"And you want it."

"Of course. Something like that in my possession would mark me as a cut above all my peers. And once the secrets of the elves are unlocked from it, well, let's just say I have certain ambitions in my own country."

With a sudden shock, Lucius realised what he had been missing throughout the meeting, and he mentally kicked himself for not seeing it earlier.

"You've already sent your wizard to bring it back," Lucius said. "And he has failed."

"He has encountered some difficulties. It seems to me that while Master Tellmore has proved exceptional, not only in his capacity as my arcane advisor but also, let us not forget, as the one who discovered the existence and resting place of the artefact, he may not have the... instinct required here. He is very learned, and there is little he knows absolutely nothing about. But we are dealing with the magics of empires long since turned to dust, Lucius."

"If you are wanting me to take a trip to the Territories, I must decline, my Lord Baron. I have many duties here, in Turnitia and, besides, I have already travelled that way before. Can't say I enjoyed it."

"Ah, of course, of course," the baron said quietly. "Well, it was just an idea. I had hoped that Adrianna might have been fuelled by a desire to prove a learned wizard wrong, but I know that is not your motivation."

"I think that you maybe underestimate Adrianna," Lucius said.

"But you have responsibilities here, naturally. I'm guessing that in what is quite literally a den of thieves, there is no one you can truly trust to run things while you are out of the city. Must be quite restricting. I had hoped the thrill of adventure might be motivation enough for you, Lucius, but I was forgetting myself. A guildmaster retired from active thieving has too many concerns and demands for his attention for a trivial favour for a Pontaine lord."

"Now wait a minute. I never said anything about being retired."

"No of course not," the baron said, a little too hurriedly. He moved forward to lean across his desk. "This task requires a unique combination of skills, Lucius. We have had many men try to retrieve this artefact, but even the most powerful wizard I could recruit cannot get past the first line of defences. What is needed is a deep understanding of magic – not just what can be read in a book, but felt, by *instinct* – allied to a highly developed sense of personal safety and stealth. To my mind, there is only one sort of person who matches that description...'

"Someone who is both thief and wizard," Lucius finished for him. "A Shadowmage."

Sighing, Lucius rubbed his chin thoughtfully as his mind raced. His guild always needed attention, of course. Put a group of thieves together in the same city and their bickering alone would keep you busy. But, this was a quiet time for the guild, with no major operations planned for a while. And the baron was right, in a way. It had been far too long since he had engaged in anything more complex than petty larceny. Here was a chance to put the full repertoire of his skills to use, to achieve something that no one had accomplished before. In spite of himself, Lucius found himself warming to the idea and, in the back of his mind, was already working out who to appoint as lieutenant of the guild while he was absent. Then he caught sight of the glint in the baron's eye.

You unbelievable bastard, Lucius thought.

This was, of course, exactly what the baron wanted him to be thinking. For all his skill and experience, Lucius still found himself being played. It was then the baron landed his final blow.

"I have been giving a lot of thought to the concessions you asked for in our last meeting," he said.

"Oh, I see," Lucius said with an ounce of scorn creeping into his voice. "I perform this task for you or you withdraw your support for my guild."

"Dear me, Lucius, no, what a thing to say. We have already agreed those terms, and I am not a man to go back on his word. Certainly not. No, no, I was thinking that if you were to do me this favour, then it is only right and proper that I perform a similar service for you. After all, we are both ultimately men of business."

"I'm listening."

"It also helps me to have a thieves' guild that is both strong and grateful, of course, but we are all driven by self-interest. Specifically, I was thinking of encouraging the taverns and wine traders to take over the Five Markets by night. You know, liven the place up a bit after the day, as it gets deathly quiet when the sun goes down. I would need you to promise me that the pickpockets will stay away from the place initially – can't have partygoers suddenly losing their purses, after all – but I would be happy to permit, no, encourage your delightful ladies of the night to ply their trade there."

That would open up a whole new market, so to speak, Lucius thought. "That could be doable."

"And of course, with this heightened tension between the Pontaine nobility, things could easily get nasty, very quickly. We have our own way of handling these things in Pontaine, of course, but perhaps it would be of interest if I said I would guarantee all such work within thirty miles of the city to be automatically turned over to your own guild's assassins?"

"It would be of interest, yes..."

"Finally, your guild is beginning to boom but it has still seen better days. I will pass on two parts in every hundred we take from the merchants of this city in tax, straight over to your guild. In exchange for a few more names I want to add to your, umm, theft exemption list."

Two per cent of the merchant taxes, though Lucius. That was an awful lot of money. He began to wonder just how rich a Pontaine lord could become, if de Sousse was throwing his gold about in such a fashion for a mere trinket.

He looked up at the baron and gave a rueful smile.

"Okay, you can stop playing with me, Lord Baron. On behalf of my guild, I gratefully accept your offers."

"And my artefact?"

Lucius narrowed his eyes as he considered the baron. "If this artefact is so powerful and, thus, so valuable, how can you trust me not to run off with it?"

The baron smiled wolfishly. "Two reasons, my dear Lucius. First, I would hunt you down. I would dedicate a great deal of money and resources to do so. Oh, you might evade my efforts for a few years, perhaps forever, but you would never be able to rest easy wherever you fled to."

"In that, I believe you."

"More importantly, I think you are a professional. I don't believe you have any great wish for the kind of power an artefact like this can bring. I *do* think you would be interested in the reputation, the prestige inherent in recovering an item like this, and doing so in the service of, in all modesty, a rising lord of Pontaine. That, I think, is worth a great deal more to you than anything else I am offering."

Lucius sighed. "I think, Lord Baron, that you are probably right. Tell me what you know of his artefact, and it will be yours as quickly as I can move."

CHAPTER NINE

AFTER HAVING SPENT much of the afternoon within the Citadel, with its stagnant corridors, rank soldiery and floating aromas of food and wine, the Five Markets actually hit Lucius with a breath of fresh air. The vendors, standing with their wares under a host of multi-coloured tents and awnings, were at full tilt in their selling, this period of the day being the busiest for many.

"Did you enjoy your meeting with the baron?" Adrianna said, her voice a whisper in his ear.

Lucius turned to face her, but was momentarily surprised to find no one standing next to him. He looked about the market in suspicion, and finally located the Shadowmage, sporting her familiar black tunic, her long black hair tied up behind her head. She was lithely pushing her way through the crowd within the market, still a sling-stone's throw away from him.

Insisting on talking to her normally and without magical assistance, Lucius stood waiting as she walked toward him, his arms crossed in expectation.

"It went well enough," he said when she was finally within earshot. "Though we both noticed your absence."

"I made my peace with de Sousse in our last meeting," Adrianna said in reply. "I have no wish to endure more of his false flattery, nor engage in a debate as to why he still lacks a Shadowmage bodyguard."

"You are going to refuse to provide him with one?"

Adrianna shrugged. "It is not a priority, you might say. But I foresee a time when not sending one of us to babysit him will be more trouble than actually doing it. When that happens, he will find himself served well enough."

"I have business at the guildhouse," Lucius said, then he hesitated. "Will you walk with me?"

"Yes, I believe we should talk," she said, and then surprised him by taking his arm.

They quickly left the Five Markets, with Lucius forced to make small talk about the activities of his guild as Adrianna remained conspicuously silent. It was not until they left the bustle of the markets and Ring Street, and had crossed the main thoroughfare of Meridian Street that she cut him short and began to speak her mind.

"So, tell me, what was our dear baron wanting from you?"

He briefly considered avoiding the question or engaging in some misdirection, but quickly remembered just who it was he was speaking to.

"His pet wizard has let him down in some mission to the Territories," Lucius said.

"Ha! I told you that wizard was not fit to sweep the ground behind you!"

"So it seems. I am to go instead."

"You agreed to it?"

Lucius smiled, as much to himself as anything. "The baron... made a good point."

"Concessions to your guild?"

"Among other things."

Adrianna looked at him curiously for a moment, then snorted. "Oh, Lucius, don't tell me he appealed to your professionalism as a thief."

He glanced back at her in return, his expression serious.

"Please don't think I didn't know how he was trying to play me. I am not stupid. Well, *not* that stupid."

"So... What is the task?"

They turned into Rogue's Way, the quiet street lined with street houses, one of which served as the headquarters for the thieves' guild.

"Apparently his wizard has discovered some ancient artefact in the Territories. Did the research, found an old outpost and has dug it up. It seems the man has failed only in actually getting his hands on the object, something to do with old magics."

"And you think you have the skills to succeed where he failed?"

"You know, Adrianna, I think I do. I may not have his book-learning and I may not have your power, but I think this is one instance where my instincts as a thief may trump you both."

Adrianna smiled at that. "You might well be right, Lucius. Still...'

He closed his eyes. *Here it comes*, he thought.

"I'll come with you. My own guild business is slow right now, and I can more or less trust the others to get on with their appointed tasks."

"I thought you did not trust anyone. Why would you want to come anyway? The Anclas Territories are about the most Godforsaken place I know. Everyone there is poor and desperate, and conditions are hard."

"Well, I am not going as a tourist. But as you know, I have a healthy interest in all things magical where the Old Races are concerned. Like any skilled practitioner. This could be a fascinating trip."

"I have promised the artefact to the baron."

"It is not the artefact that I am after, Lucius. It is the location. An ancient outpost, recently uncovered to reveal the secrets of the Old Races, how they thought, lived, and studied? Revealing their art, medicines and philosophies?" She laughed. "By all that is sacred, man, who *wouldn't* want to go?"

Her words made sense. Indeed, she was saying nothing he had not thought himself during his meeting with the baron, but a quiet alarm was sounding in his head. Lucius knew that where magic was concerned Adrianna could not be trusted.

Then again, he did not get the feeling she was offering him a choice. What would happen if he did try to refuse?

"I was intending to leave tomorrow morning," he finally said.

"Excellent. Get two horses with supplies. I have some errands myself to attend to," she said, before looking back down the street from where they had come. "Until tomorrow then, Lucius."

Lucius watched her walk away, a sick feeling of foreboding begin to cloud his initial excitement. With a heart somewhat heavier than it had been just a short while ago, he headed back towards the guildhouse.

THE MOOD IN the council chamber of the thieves' guild was one of muted excitement. Lucius could well understand it; the boss was going to be going away for a month or so. Now all the senior thieves present at this council had a chance to run their operations the way they saw fit, without interference from him.

Lucius raised a palm and slapped it on the long table to get their attention. Wendric, the lieutenant of the guild and Lucius' second-in-command, raised a palm to emphasise the call to order.

"Just so you understand," he said. "There will be no new franchises created while I am away. You get a good idea, keep it to yourself until I get back. You see a not-to-be-missed opportunity, let it slip past – I promise you, there will be plenty of franchises and wealth for everyone in the near future, and I don't want anyone upsetting the cart with their mad schemes. Is that clear?"

Around the table, the senior thieves nodded and muttered their assent, a somewhat motley collection of men and women who had grown up within the guild and demonstrated the aptitude and trustworthiness to run their own operations. It was a simple system where money trickled up from the ranks, through the senior thieves to the guild itself, where it often became a torrent of gold. It worked, and so long as the money flowed, everyone was happy. Those who chose to buck the system and cream off profits for themselves tended not to stay too long within the guild. The worst offenders could expect a visit from the guild's own assassins.

"Savis, don't look to expand the prostitution rings just yet," Lucius continued. "I'll have some good news for you there soon but, for now, just make sure your girls stay safe and stay clean."

Savis, a light-haired woman starting to push past middle-age, nodded. As the latest leader of the prostitution franchise, she would not want to make any waves.

"Pickpockets, stick to your restricted hours and locations within the Five Markets. Protection, carry on your good work – we have had some complaints from the craftsmen on Meridian Street about a gang hitting their shops and stealing valuables. Probably just some independents, in which case you know what to do, but make sure someone is always nearby. You protect their businesses, and you will find the craftsmen only too glad to pay you their weekly dues. They'll consider it a bargain." Again, mutters and nods.

"The assassins will continue to work their existing contracts, but don't accept new jobs until I return." Lucius received shrugs from the few assassins who had attended the meeting. An enforced period of relaxation was nothing to those men and women as their work, though highly paid, tended to be irregular, even in Turnitia.

"Finally, I want all senior thieves, whether they run their own franchises or not, to stay in touch with the beggars," Lucius said, indicating Grennar seated next to him. "We pay them good money to be our eyes and ears in the city, so I expect you to use them."

Grennar nodded and cleared her throat. "If I may... some of your younger pickpockets have started to stray around Ring Street, probably thinking everyone just keeps an eye on the Five Markets themselves," she said. "That is interfering with our business. I want it to stop."

The current ringleader of pickpockets, an old thief called Callum, shifted in his seat as he leaned across the table in an attempt to intimidate Grennar.

"These are kids you are talking about," he said with a growl. "We can't keep track of them all, not all day. Anyway, there is enough money to go round in Ring Street, don't think you beggars have a sole right to it."

Grennar leaned across the table to confront him, utterly unfazed by his demeanour. Lucius could not help be impressed once again by her nerve and he suppressed a smile.

"Actually, Mr Callum," she said, speaking slowly as if he were the child. "We do have the sole right, as agreed by myself and your guildmaster. Ring Street is ours, but for the few provisions that I know you are already aware of. As for tracking children, if we can manage to watch them, then I am sure any competent thief can do the same. If need be, I can provide you with names...'

There were a few sniggers from the other senior thieves and Callum, seeing himself humiliated by a girl, and one outside of his guild at that, bristled.

"Now look here, girl," he said, beginning to stand.

"Callum!" Wendric said, not raising his voice but putting enough iron in the word to demand attention. When he was sure he had the attention of Callum and the other thieves, he turned and nodded to Lucius, who continued.

"You will be civil to our sister from the Beggars' Guild, Callum. As I said earlier, we pay them a great deal of money for their services, and I consider them vital to our operations in this city. You will rein your kids in or, so help me, I will find someone who can. Is that clear?"

For a second, Callum glared at Grennar who smiled back at him with all the sweet innocence of a young teenager. Then he threw up his hands in surrender and settled back in his seat.

"Do all of you understand?" Wendric said to underscore his guildmaster's words, glancing at each senior thief in turn. Again, mutters and nods of agreement.

"I swear," Lucius said, "if any of you don't know the value of the beggars, you are not fit to be senior thieves. Not in this guild. Remember, Vos is a huge Empire and even they paid the penalty for dismissing the beggars."

A hand went up further down the table. Lucius nodded his acknowledgement to Brynn, a young man barely into his twenties who had been allowed within the ranks of senior thieves due to the creation of a gambling franchise throughout the docks. Lucius had already marked him as someone with potential but with a tendency to leap into situations without thinking too hard about them first.

"What if I see a juicy cargo coming in from the sea? We can't just let it go through, right?"

Lucius sighed and rubbed his temples with a hand, exchanging a look with Wendric.

"What did the guildmaster just say?" Wendric asked the young thief. "No new jobs that aren't already on schedule. No one is going rogue while he is away. Is that understood?"

Brynn nodded, but Lucius could see the reluctance.

"Look at it this way," Lucius said. "Imagine you are a big, fat, greedy merchant. You have a big shipment coming into the city, but you are worried about scurrilous thieves."

That image drew a snigger from Grennar, though she had the sense to stop when she noticed Callum glaring at her again.

"You stock up on guards and informants among the dock workers... but nothing happens. Your cargo goes through, unmolested. So does the next one. Perhaps the thieves are no longer working the docks, eh? Or perhaps they are cowed at how powerful you are and won't dare attack your shipments. So, you decide to maximise your profits and bring a really big cargo in, one brimming with gold."

"And that is when we strike," said Brynn.

"Indeed. My departure, as brief as it will be, is an opportunity we should not miss out on. Run our regular operations, but let any merchant, craftsman, soldier, or citizen live without us for a short while. They could do with the break, and when we come back we will find much richer pickings."

"Clever," said Grennar, nodding her appreciation.

"Thank you," Lucius said. "Now, can I count on you all to watch one another to ensure no one does anything... ambitious?"

"Oh, you can count on us," Savis said, rubbing her hand through Brynn's hair. She ignored his plaintive cry to leave him alone.

"Any other business to raise?" Lucius asked, but no one stirred. "Good. Then I bid you a brief farewell, and entrust the guild to your command while I am gone. For goodness sake, please let there be a guild still here when I return."

* * *

LUCIUS OPENED THE door briskly, his mind full of plans and questions in equal measure as he strode into the small storage room.

"Grennar, I was wondering – oh!"

He stopped short suddenly. Grennar had her back to him as she folded her dark shift. She was completely naked.

"Shut the door, Lucius, I would be happier if I don't have the entire thieves' guild gawking at me while I change."

"Umm, sorry," he manage to stammer. "I'll be back in a moment."

"Don't be simple, man, I am sure you have seen this all before. And we have things to discuss. But do close the door."

Lucius complied with her instruction, but was acutely aware he was confronted by a total lack of modesty. He also could not help but notice that, for a beggar, she was in extremely good shape, with pale skin completely free of blemishes – so far as he could tell at this distance.

She looked over her shoulder at him. "Don't you think I am just a little too young for you anyway?"

He coughed, and dropped his eyes to the floor, wondering just why *he* was the one feeling uncomfortable.

"I was hoping your people knew something about Adrianna that I might not – like why she is so keen to come with me to the Territories."

Grennar pursed her lips as she considered her answer.

"Understand this, Lucius," she said. "Turnitia is doing well right now. It may not be free, it may still have lords and masters from the outside world, but we are doing alright. Business is up for everyone, and no one walks the city scared they might be picked up by Vos soldiers on some trumped-up charge."

"This is true."

"Moreover, this is a very good time for us – not just the beggars, but your thieves and, I daresay, Adrianna's Shadowmages too. It would take an act of monumental stupidity to rock this boat and ruin things for, well, everyone."

"What are you saying, Grennar?"

She sighed. "I am saying, Lucius, that I cannot and will not take sides. Not between you and Adrianna. Placing myself alongside that woman would lose me ties to a guild that has always been traditionally close to us. Placing myself alongside you would just be suicide. No one crosses Adrianna."

"I see."

"Don't get me wrong, I am not unsympathetic to the position I think you will find yourself in, in the weeks and months to come. And while I do not want to upset the cart our Triumvirate is perched upon, I also have no interest in seeing the Shadowmages become all powerful."

She sat down on a stool then grabbed a pair of well-worn boots, the sole of one flapping uselessly as she pulled it on. Then, Grennar looked up at him, giving Lucius her full attention.

"She knows more than you think, Lucius. Much more. Her Shadowmages have been working hard in this city, trying to build their own information network. We are also aware of many scrolls and tomes being intercepted from merchants and wizards alike as they travel to this city."

"Do you know what she is really after?"

Grennar shrugged. "Ultimately, she is after power. I think if she saw a chance to rule this city or, God forbid, an entire Empire, she would take it. However, I also think that is not her goal. Adrianna likes more cerebral pursuits. She wants to become the greatest practitioner of magic the world has ever seen. She wants to surpass the greatest achievements of the Old Races."

"So, she thinks that coming with me might be an opportunity to gather, what, some ancient lore?"

"I'll go further than that, Lucius. I cannot prove it, as she has masked her activities well and, in any case, none of my beggars would have a clue what they were looking at if Adrianna laid down all her arcane plans in a diary. But I *do* think that not only is Adrianna fully conversant in where you are going, she also knows exactly what the two of you will find there."

He thought for a moment. When he spoke, it was with an increasing sense of unease.

"The only logical conclusion to reach from what you have just said is that she knows what this artefact is, what it does, and that she intends to snatch it from me once we find it."

Having finished dressing for the street, Grennar looked nothing like the capable, confident guild leader of just a few moments ago, and could have blended in with any group of homeless children. She stood and crossed the room to face Lucius, putting a flat palm on his chest as a show of support.

"Watch your back, Lucius, and be very careful," she said. "You cannot trust anything Adrianna tells you about this object, and once you leave this city, I won't be around to help you."

CHAPTER TEN

THE FARM WAS a broken, wounded thing, left to bleed in the wilderness. Lucius directed their horses to give the homestead a wide berth, ignoring Adrianna's quizzical glance.

The farmhouse and two outbuildings had seen better days, with gaping holes in the tiled roofs letting the constant drizzle slowly rot them from the inside out. An attempt at using thin wooden boards to repair the worst of the deterioration in the farmhouse had been made, but it seem lacklustre, as if the inhabitants had not really cared whether they continued to live in misery or not, as if it were all they could expect in this world.

Lucius knew the type well, having worked as a mercenary in the Anclas Territories for several years before his return to Turnitia. A broken wall surrounded the buildings, supplemented with a burnt out cart and other detritus. There could not be much more than a dozen family members and farmhands living there, and Lucius could well imagine them living in constant fear.

Even now, he felt eyes upon him, squinting through darkened windows or gaps in the structure of the buildings, wondering whether he and Adrianna were a scouting party for brigands or some other wild, dangerous, adventuring type. When the brigands did come, as they inevitably would in the Territories of today, the farmer was left with a simple choice. He could raise arms – maybe an old family sword, but more likely a rake or hoe fashioned into a makeshift weapon – and fight against the land pirates and die against hopeless odds. Or, he could simply let the marauders take whatever they wanted – food, drink, clothing, perhaps let them borrow his wife and daughters... and then die when the winter came and the food stores were empty.

It was a bleak existence that made Lucius feel sorry for the inhabitants of the farm, but he knew there were thousands more like them across the Territories. This was simply what happened when all vestiges of law and authority disappeared from the land. Even the rule of Vos was preferable to this life.

Entry into the Anclas Territories had been marked, as if they had travelled to a new world. Years of war between Vos and Pontaine had ensured that, and even though the conflict had been resolved long ago, its wounds were still a blight on the contested land.

They might travel for an entire morning over the rolling hills that covered most of the Territories without seeing anything more sinister than a circling crow but then they would clear a rise, and would be struck by a sight that seemed out of place, despite the history of the region.

Mighty spells of destruction had been unleashed here, deep battle magic, the type of incantations requiring several wizards to properly fuel and that could blast half an army apart in one incandescent salvo, leaving nothing but ash. More minor spells left their mark with mere craters, some of them yards across, stones and boulders torn from the earth and hurled into the air lying scattered around them.

One grey morning, they saw a valley filed with the dead, the scene of a vicious struggle between the two empires. Armour rusted where it had fallen decades before, the skeletal owners inside long since picked clean of flesh by animals and of valuables by more human scavengers. Lucius estimated more than a thousand men had met their end in that valley.

At the centre of this open graveyard was the remnants of a massive machine, one that must have towered over the knights and soldiers as they fought. A single, large iron-shod wheel propped up the black structure, canting it at a high angle, while the main hull was rent in two, perhaps from a particularly devastating spell. Lucius did not recognise the device, but he had heard of huge war machines, propelled or pushed in battle by men or horses, large mobile fortresses that were used to crush the enemy and serve as elevated platforms for archers and other missile troops. Heavily armoured, such machines were no longer built by either Empire, each costing as much as a regular fort or small castle. He had little doubt they would appear once more if the peace between Vos and Pontaine ever broke down and war came back to the Territories.

They passed several villages on their route, each as wretched as the farm and little better than a slum. Approaching another, Lucius saw it was little more than a line of tiny hovels lining a worn track, itself blocked by the corpse of a horse that looked as though it had been worked to death.

"Why do these people not move?" Adrianna wondered. "We are little more than a week out of Turnitia, anyone could make the trip and find far better conditions in the city. Even the beggars live better than this!"

"Not everyone can make the journey," Lucius said. "We can protect ourselves if attacked, but what are these people to do? They are just as likely to be killed for their clothing by the people of the next village. Besides, this is all they have known. They saw the products of civilisation when the armies of Vos and Pontaine marched through their villages, trampled their crops and killed their livestock. It is possible they think this is as good as life gets if you are not a knight or some warlord."

He pulled out a map and studied it for a moment, looking up occasionally to gauge his whereabouts. The map was not complete, nor highly detailed, but it had allowed him to count off the number of villages he expected to pass on their journey. Beside him, Adrianna shifted uncomfortably in her saddle. She was no skilled rider, but had so far not complained about her discomfort.

"How much further?" she asked.

Lucius pursed his lips as he tried to judge the esoteric method of scaling the baron's cartographer had used. "We will make Jakus Point... maybe this evening," he said. "Give us a chance for a decent bed, should be cheap enough out here. Then we strike out in the morning. Apparently the Pontaine camp is east of Jakus Point, maybe northeast. About half a day's ride."

"East, maybe northeast," Adrianna stated with some irritation.

He shrugged. "From what I understand, map-making is not as cut and dried as magic. It tends to be less than precise."

"Will anyone in this Jakus Point know about it?"

"That is what I am hoping."

Folding the map away, he gently kicked his horse forward.

"Only one way to find out."

JAKUS POINT MIGHT well have once been a central hub in the Anclas Territories, a common trading area for the surrounding villages and farms, with merchants passing through regularly from Pontaine and perhaps even Vos. If this had been so, it was before Lucius' time.

After the war, the small township could call itself as free and independent as Turnitia had been, or as Freiport was now, with no direct master. However, Lucius could see the entire town was enslaved to something far worse – poverty and neglect. Few outsiders came here and those that did were rarely welcomed by the locals.

As Adrianna and Lucius rode slowly down the main street that was little more than a churned up track interspersed by cobbles, the few inhabitants they saw avoided all eye contact. Children crouched behind dilapidated wagons or ran behind buildings in an effort to hide, while men and women running errands quickened their pace as the horses drew nearer.

"This place is filthy," Adrianna said, wrinkling her scarred face in disgust, and Lucius suspected she referred to the people as much as the town itself.

"This is how people here live. They have no other choice."

Adrianna did not answer, but he could almost feel her contempt, and began to think just how far removed the Shadowmage had become from other people. A large building down the end of the rough street caught his attention and he pointed it out.

"There. I think we'll find what we are looking for there."

Peering through the rain, Adrianna snorted. "Looks like a slop house."

Lucius shrugged. "It probably is, but it is the best accommodation we are likely to find here."

"I would almost prefer sleeping in the rain again."

"You wouldn't," he said, with half a smile. "However, it is not just us I am thinking of. Any outsiders will also be there, likely as not."

"You think people come here intentionally?"

"If the Pontaine camp is as close as the baron's cartographer thinks it is, then I think we might well be in luck."

The inn had no name that Lucius could see as they approached, though the lantern light from the common room spilling onto the street seemed welcoming enough. Whatever Adrianna thought of the place, Lucius was glad to have any bed that included a roof over his head, no matter how many fleas and rats might share it with him. He had certainly spent nights in far worse places.

A young boy hesitantly poked his head out of the low stable next to the tavern, taking a few steps towards them when Lucius smiled and held out a coin. They dismounted and let the stableboy lead their horses into the dry, and then followed suit, pushing open the front door of the inn.

It was little different from Lucius' expectations. The warmth was the first thing he noticed, as a large fire crackled quietly at the far end of the common room, an elderly grey-haired woman using its heat as she stirred the contents of a wide copper pot. The denizens at various crooked tables scattered before him were obviously local, common in appearance with unkempt clothes and sullen expressions as they nursed their drink. Few seemed to have ordered food beyond bread or biscuits and gravy.

Three men carried themselves differently though, and they caught Lucius' thiefes eye immediately. Sitting at a table near the fire, they all had their backs to the wall and were talking in low voices, trying to blend in but not quite managing it. Though none bore weapons or armour, he presumed they were soldiers or mercenaries, warriors of some kind. Two had wide moustaches, as was currently in fashion throughout Pontaine.

He glanced sideways at Adrianna, and she nodded almost imperceptibly. She had noticed them as well.

Nodding in friendly greeting to several of the locals that looked up at their entrance, Lucius fixed a smile on his face and walked straight to the open fire, rubbing his hands as if trying to ward off the cold. The woman stirring away at her pot looked up at him, and a flash of fear passed over her face briefly.

"My husband will be along to see to you in just a minute," she managed to say. "I can take your wet cloaks and hang them by the fire to dry, if that is your wish."

"Lady, nothing could please us more right now," Lucius said, and he meant it. The aroma of the stew she was stirring washed over him and he suddenly felt very hungry.

As the woman hung their cloaks, Lucius saw what he presumed was the owner, an old man with at least ten more years on him than his wife, hunched over by age. He appeared from an open doorway at the opposite end of the common room, carrying two mugs that slopped liquid onto the floor with his unsteady gait.

After laying the mugs down on a table that was taken by locals, he looked up briefly, the movement obviously causing him some pain, to look at Lucius and Adrianna. He started shuffling towards them.

"If that is the pace everything moves round here, this is going to be a very long night," Adrianna said.

Lucius ignored her and smiled in greeting as the man finally reached their table.

"What will you be wanting?" he asked, his voice neither subservient nor hostile. Lucius guessed that, living in this place, the man had seen his fair share of trouble in the past, and had clearly come to deal with it with apathy.

"Beer, milk, mead, whatever you've got. And some of that delicious stew your good lady wife is cooking, if you would."

The man grunted in response and shuffled back to the kitchen. His wife began ladling out bowls of the stew and laid them out before Lucius and Adrianna. The meat was probably from some part of a horse that he had no wish to discover, but the old woman was clearly a cook of some talent. Even Adrianna ate without complaint.

As he ate, Lucius flickered his gaze over to the three outsiders and, finally, caught the eye of one of them.

"Nasty weather out there, eh?" he said.

He received nothing more than a slight incline of the head in response, but Lucius had his way in and he wasn't going to let the gate close on him. Standing up, Lucius took his mug from the innkeeper who had just arrived back at their table, and then walked past the fire to sit himself at the warriors' table.

"I swear, been raining ever since we entered the Territories," he said.

All three looked at him then and one frowned. "What do you want, friend?" he asked.

Lucius shrugged. "We're all travellers here. Always worth seeing where we have all been, let each other know of any trouble we saw on the road. Can I get you lads a drink?"

They wanted to say no, they knew they should say no, but as soon as Lucius saw one of them open his mouth and hesitate, he knew he had them. If there was one common uniting factor among fighting men, be they soldiers of Vos, Pontaine or free company mercenaries, it was their singular inability to refuse a drink when offered freely.

As the drink began to flow, so the looser their lips became. They were duly joined by Adrianna, though her scarred face and stern looks served to keep the men at bay. For his part, Lucius studied the men carefully, though without making it obvious. Two had moustaches, one did not, but he did sport a thin and recent cut to one side of his top lip.

All three from Pontaine? Lucius wondered, and suddenly had an image in his head of all three trying to disguise themselves but two of them being too proud to shave. It was a thought that almost made him smile, but another idea crossed his mind. Why would a man from Pontaine shave other than to hide where he was from? What were they running from?

As the conversation flowed, the men claimed to have been escorting a merchant's wagon from Vos through the Territories but were now out of work, the default position for a sword-for-hire, one joked.

Lucius narrowed in on that. He had heard the joke before, and it was the kind of thing a mercenary would say. But the accent that spoke it... they were trying to hide it, but the trace of Pontaine in the man's voice was too thick to cloak completely, especially from someone who lived in Turnitia and had recently been forced to spot the accent when doing business.

Deserters, then? Lucius thought. If so, he might just have struck rich, as if they had fled from the baron's encampment, then a few more drinks and a flutter of gold might tell him all he needed to know. On the other hand, here in the Anclas Territories, they might well be simple mercenaries.

"I hear there is work for swords at the Pontaine camp nearby," Lucius said, casually enough. The effect on the men seated opposite him was electric, and he saw each had stiffened at the mention of the camp. They looked at one another, almost seeming furtive.

Looking at each in turn, Lucius decided to push his luck.

"If you are from that camp, we are on the same side," he said, lowering his voice.

"How's that?" one of the men asked suspiciously.

"I have been sent by the baron to see what the delay is. And let me make it clear – I am not interested whether you have deserted the camp. Frankly, given where it is, I might have been tempted to do so myself."

His attempt at levity fell flat and he saw all three bristle at the mention of desertion. The man lacking a moustache nearly exploded.

"We are not–" he said, almost shouting before he stopped and checked himself, glancing around to see if any of the locals had taken notice. None seemed to think it wise to trouble themselves with an outsider's problems.

"We are not deserters," the man hissed, still angry.

Lucius held up a hand to ward off his fury.

"I meant nothing by it, only that it would be none of my business." He looked around the common room himself, then leaned forward so his whisper could be heard. Adrianna too leaned in.

"What has been happening there?" he asked.

The men looked at one another again, one of them shrugging.

"You don't look or sound like Vos," he said.

Lucius frowned, puzzled. "What has Vos got to do with anything?"

The man sighed before answering. "We were at the camp. But we didn't desert. The whole place was attacked by a Vos army a week ago. We were captured, but everyone else was slaughtered where they stood."

Rubbing his chin with his hand, Lucius thought fast.

"If you were captured, how did you get free?" he asked, and immediately saw that was the wrong question Though two of the soldiers looked furious, one hung his head in shame, which told Lucius all he needed to know.

"Forget it, not important," he said. "So, the camp is now in Vos hands?"

"Just so," he was answered. "We had set up a fence perimeter and had guards stationed, but they hit us fast and without warning. We rallied for a while, but they were everywhere and half of us were asleep. They also had some powerful wizard on their side, blasting holes in our ranks before we could respond. It was hopeless. Utterly hopeless. As far as I know, we were the only ones to get out. Everyone else is dead."

"Including the wizard Tellmore?" Adrianna asked.

"Didn't see him, and you would think he could have defended us against their magic. Figure he must have been killed early on."

Lucius decided to change tack. "What did you discover there? Before the attack, I mean."

The soldier held his eye for a moment before answering. "Honestly? Not a thing. Some of the soldiers had been drafted in to help with the digging, but all they found was a bunch of sunken corridors and some empty chambers. And the door, of course."

"The door?"

"Big, elaborate thing. We couldn't open it, and any man who tried was burned away in seconds by magic. I don't know anything about that, but it was the thing that consumed Lord Tellmore's attention most. Once we hit that obstacle, I don't think he ever slept. Just stayed in his tent, chanting, casting spells and writing. His tent was overflowing with scraps of parchment."

"But nothing worked," the clean-shaven soldier cut in. "Time and again he would line men up in front of that door, cast some spell or charm of protection, and bid them open it. Every time, they would be... annihilated would be the term, I think. They were just reduced to ash in seconds."

It was Lucius' turn to glance at Adrianna this time, but he found no answer in her eyes. Just a raw hunger that here, at last, was a solid report on ancient magic. He could almost feel her desire to possess it. That would be a problem to face a little later, though.

"I need to know exactly where the camp is," he said.

The soldiers gave him sensible directions, and he was grateful for them as, lying within a shallow valley, he and Adrianna might have ridden straight past it, knowing no better. He stood and gestured for Adrianna to follow him.

Before leaving, Lucius turned to regard all three men.

"I make no judgements on what happened at the camp and, from what I can tell, you are all damn lucky to be alive. Vos soldiers are not known for their temperance," he said, then fished in his pouch to scatter a handful of coins on the table. "Whether you return to Turnitia or have somewhere in Pontaine to go to, you'll find the journey much easier if you have good coin on you. And when I return to the baron, I'll be sure to put in a good word for all of you."

As one, they looked up at him, eyebrows raised in surprise. One recovered sooner than his compatriots.

"Well, bless you, sir," he said, his gratitude obvious. "If you are heading towards the camp, I wish you the best of luck, but... be careful. I see no reason why the Vos army would have moved on."

Lucius nodded his thanks and, taking Adrianna's arm, headed for the inn's front door.

CHAPTER ELEVEN

THE RAIN HAD slackened off with the coming of night, but it gave little comfort to Lucius as he lay on his stomach, peering into the shallow valley where the now Vos-held camp lay. The ground was wet through and it was slowly seeping into his clothing. Adrianna had rolled out her cloak, but he knew she would later regret that when the time came to don it again.

They had both been grateful for the help the Pontaine soldiers had given them, for they might easily have missed the camp among the rolling hills of the Anclas Territories.

Their horses they had released some distance away, which had sparked a brief argument with Adrianna. She had not relished the thought of walking any great distance in what she regarded, not without cause he admitted, as a vast wilderness. However, Lucius had been more concerned with the horses giving away their presence to any wandering sentry or scout and, at the end of the day, he *was* a thief. When the time came to use mounts once more, he was sure the Vos force below them would provide.

The Vos sentries were plainly apparent as they had approached, silhouetted against the darkening sky, and the Shadowmages had wreathed themselves in magical darkness, blurring their outlines and making themselves virtually invisible in the gloom.

Such were the skills of all Shadowmages.

Straining his eyes, Lucius tried to pick out the details of the camp. The Vos force had made sure some areas were well-lit with lanterns and fires, but other parts were shrouded in darkness.

Closest to them, the camp was mainly filled with tents of obvious Pontaine tailoring, which had been taken by the Vos soldiery for their own use. Spaces were cleared in this area for cooking, rest and toiletry purposes. A few lanterns were scattered about here but the larger fires were concentrated towards the far end of the camp, and the earthworks. Even at this distance, Lucius could make out deep trenches, wide pits and, here and there, the exposed grey of long-buried stone.

Around the camp, a perimeter wooden fence provided the main line of defence. Lucius estimated it was at least eight feet high; no real obstacle to any competent thief.

"They've been busy," Lucius said, and turned to look at Adrianna when she did not answer him.

Through the shadowy waves of her concealing magic, he could make out an expression of concentration on her face, and he began to feel the power of her magic radiate out.

"Do you see anything?" he asked.

After a few seconds, Adrianna shuddered and sighed as she relaxed her scrying.

"The Pontaine men said the Vos force had magic on their side," she said. "I sense no wizard down there but... There is something strange. Can you feel it?"

Lucius stared hard down at the camp, trying to visualise the streams of magic that he could see flowing around him wherever he was, but they revealed no disturbance he could see.

"I do not," he said at last. "What do you think it is?"

"We know magic is bound into the ruins to protect them, but this doesn't feel like that. It is not ancient, patient, waiting. If there were active spells used by the Old Races, believe me, I would sense them from miles away. The ruins seem dead, so perhaps their magics are only tripped by certain actions."

"Like trying to open the front door."

"Just so. There is something else down there though, something... different. Maybe some ward, or maybe a weapon, enchanted to give its user power."

"A charm of protection, perhaps?"

"No..." Adrianna said, her voice growing vague for a moment. She cursed under her breath as her spell of detection once again failed to give her a clear answer.

"It is something more powerful," she said at last. "Something powerful enough to make Pontaine soldiers think the Vos army had a wizard with them."

"Perhaps they did, and the wizard was killed," Lucius said.

"Unlikely," Adrianna said. "Wizards trained for battle learn wards as a matter of course and are quite capable of keeping their heads low when swords and arrows start being aimed at them." She shook her head, as much in frustration as anything else. "I can't see clearly enough."

"Well then. The only way we will ever know is to take a closer look."

Whoever was commanding the Vos soldiers had only placed sentries on the rim of the valley. It was a careful enough precaution, as the sentries would likely see anyone approaching and the signals would be seen quickly by those down in the camp, but it meant that, once bypassed, Lucius and Adrianna had a clear passage all the way to the fence line.

Leading the way, Lucius peeled off to the right to follow the fence, searching for the ideal point to gain entry. He pulled suddenly up short as a terrible stench filled his nostrils. Dead, rotting flesh.

"God above," he hissed as Adrianna joined him. They both gathered their cloaks in their hands and held them tight to their faces, trying to block the dreadful stink. Adrianna peered into the darkness, then nudged his arm as she sighted something. Creeping forward, Lucius winced at what he saw.

Earthen mounds lay in strict rows that stretched away to his left but, directly in front, was a wide, open pit. It was filled with the tangled and maimed bodies of Pontaine soldiers, the original occupants of the camp who had not managed to escape the carnage like the men they had met in the inn. The Vos invaders had buried their own dead but left their enemies out for the wolves and birds. It was a sign of the greatest disrespect.

"Animals," Adrianna said, with some venom in her voice, and that surprised Lucius. He had not thought she could be touched by such earthly matters.

There was, however, nothing they could do for the dead. Lucius touched her arm to bring her attention back to their task, and they turned away from the charnel pit.

Returning to the fence line, Lucius continued his search for a point of ingress. He purposefully avoided the bulk of the tents as, while they would provide superb cover for two creeping Shadowmages, he had no wish to be accidentally surprised by a chance Vos soldier walking out of his tent. Instead, he looped round the fence line, stopping when he saw the main, open entrance. That, he knew, would be guarded, so he retraced his steps a short way so they would enter at the edge of the tented area.

Summoning just a little of his magic, Lucius felt his arms and legs swell with power as he leapt upwards to catch the top of the fence. Throwing himself half over, he reached down an arm for Adrianna, who grabbed it. In one fluid motion, he pulled the woman up and over the fence as if she had been no more than an empty cloth sack. Then, he dropped down on the other side of the camp, crouching next to her to see if anyone had detected their entry.

It seemed as though no one was in their immediate vicinity, though they could hear the occasional voice caught on the slight breeze, laughter and a few shouted curses as soldiers did what they always do when not under orders or the watchful eyes of sergeants.

Taking full advantage of the cover provided by tents and the fence line itself, Lucius and Adrianna were little more than dark blurs, fully wreathed in their stealth spells, becoming one with the shadows. Heading towards the excavation site, the tents disappeared and high cover became less frequent. The area was also more brightly lit by larger fires and more numerous lanterns but the flickering shadows provided them with adequate cover as they flitted from earth mound to tool store. After sprinting across a wide open area that had been cleared to allow easy passage to the unearthed ruins, Lucius stopped behind a line of wooden barrels to catch his breath. Wrinkling his nose, he guessed his hiding place was being used to stockpile lantern oil.

Sharp movement to his left caused him to duck down until he realised it was Adrianna joining him, panting slightly from their rapid passage through the camp. She indicated a point beyond the barrels.

"They are working late tonight," she said.

Lucius peered over the barrels, trusting to his magic to hide him but allowing his thievish instincts to make him cautious nonetheless. Adrianna was right, there was a fair bit of activity still taking place in one part of the excavation site when he would have expected any soldier not on sentry duty to be thinking about retiring. Most were involved in heavy labour, carrying baskets of earth dug up by others who manned spades, shovels and picks.

"Looks as though they are starting a whole new dig over there," he said.

"Typical Vos," Adrianna said. "If you can't work something out, give up and try a longer path."

Lucius frowned in puzzlement. "What do you mean?"

She paused for a second, leaving Lucius wondering whether he had said something she considered truly stupid.

"Remember the entrance the Pontaine men told us about? They could not breach the Old Races' magical defences, and I would guess these Vos henchmen have fared no better."

"So... they are trying to bypass it?" Lucius said, hazarding a guess.

"Looks like. They are digging down where they think the outpost extends underground, hoping to break into an unprotected chamber."

"But wouldn't the Old Races have thought of that?"

Adrianna grinned, her blurred face taking on the look of a predator. "Well, you did, so I would guess that the wizards, or whatever they had thousands of years ago, that built this place would as well."

"Might be interesting to stay here and watch the fun and games when they start. But this does give us an opportunity."

"That the main entrance will be relatively unguarded? I agree."

One man moving through the labouring soldiers caught Lucius' eye and he gasped in surprise.

"Wow, Aidy, look at that," he said.

"Well, well," she said. "Our old friend, the Preacher Divine. We could do a lot of people a lot of favours right now."

"By killing him?"

She shrugged. "It is a happy thought, but not a practical one."

"So this is some kind of holy mission for Vos, you think?"

"Oh, Lucius," Adrianna said, a hint of wonder in her voice. "That's it. There is no wizard here, and the Preacher Divine is no mage. Should have seen it before – long before. It's his staff."

"It's a weapon?"

"Weapon, spellshield, focus of his faith. Enchanted, heavily so by the feel of it." She extended an arm towards the Preacher Divine to help focus the silent spell of analysis she was casting. "Very powerful enchantments. If anything goes wrong tonight, don't face him without me being there. Used offensively, that staff could near break you with one word from its wielder."

"I'll bear that in mind. But, really, I just want to get into the ruins, get through the entrance and find what we are looking for."

"Over there," Adrianna said, pointing to an area of the site where the fires had been allowed to die down to crackling embers.

"You sure?"

"I can feel it. Deep, ancient, patient. There are terrifying magics at work in this place, Lucius. Terrifying and wonderful. You must be cautious."

Lucius could not help notice that she had warned *him* to be cautious, not the both of them. Either Adrianna was so confident in her own abilities that she thought even the spells of the Old Races could not touch her – and that was entirely possible – or she was intending to send Lucius down to face them alone. Though the thought rankled, he realised it made no difference. He had first intended to come to this place alone and, frankly, he could count himself lucky if Adrianna withdrew to watch his back for any overly-curious Vos soldier that came their way.

"This way?" he asked, pointing.

Adrianna nodded. Lucius took a deep breath and, letting it go slowly, padded quietly out of cover and headed towards the ruins.

CHAPTER TWELVE

HEAD BOWED LOW, the tired horse clopped dejectedly through the main gates of the Citadel, looking as miserable as Tellmore felt. Behind him, Renauld was no happier on his exhausted mount. They had both failed their baron, and they knew it. At least here in Turnitia it rained less than in the Anclas Territories and, mercifully, the grey sky today withheld its deluge.

The guards at the gate let them both through without a word and Tellmore glanced back at Renauld, feeling as sorry for the knight as he did for himself. Renauld's cloak was gone, lost in the fighting at the camp, and a heavy dent was obvious in his helm where a savage sword swing had nearly taken the man's life. He favoured his left arm, the result of a shallow but painful wound from a spear thrust a Vos soldier had made as Renauld had struggled to get Tellmore on his feet.

Tellmore shuddered to remember that night, the suddenness of the attack, the butchery of Renauld's men, and the irresistible onslaught of the man he had fought a magical duel with. And lost.

By all that was holy, that opponent had been quick. While Tellmore might admit to himself in more candid moments that he might have become a little rusty in the use of battle magics, that Vos leader had been both fast and powerful with his staff. After being thrown through the air by the arcane explosion unleashed by the enchanted weapon, Tellmore had lost consciousness for a few moments. He had been roused by a desperate Renauld who shook him hard. Tellmore had been dimly aware as he came round that the knight was battling Vos soldiers. How many, he did not know, and that was when Renauld had been wounded. One of the soldiers had managed to flank him and a cruel spear thrust nearly took Renauld out of the battle altogether.

Somehow, Renauld had triumphed, and Tellmore had risen unsteadily to his feet, looking desperately about him to regain his sense of how the fight was going.

"We need to regroup at the centre," Renauld shouted above the cacophony of sword on metal and the screams of dying men. "I have men holding there but they need support."

He had started to drag Tellmore with him, but the wizard grasped his arm and spun him round.

"Don't be foolish," Tellmore had said. "We have to get out of here."

"We can still win this fight!"

"The battle is already lost, man!"

A look of anguish came across Renauld's face then, and while Tellmore felt his own guilt at leaving so many men behind to be slaughtered, he realised in that moment he would never know just how close the bonds between fighting men could be.

Tellmore lowered his voice and gripped Renauld by the shoulders so he could speak directly into his face.

"We've lost. We never had a chance. If we leave now, we might escape. If we can do that, we can bring more men back and avenge what has happened here."

For a moment, Renauld hesitated, wracked between the choices of loyalty to his men and loyalty to his baron.

"For God's sake, man," Tellmore shouted again. "We have to go now!"

Muttering a curse, Renauld grabbed Tellmore and hustled him away from the main body of the fighting. From there, it had been something of a blur for Tellmore. He remembered Renauld hacking down a couple of Vos soldiers who had dismounted to start looting fallen Pontaine men before their comrades, still fighting, had a chance. From them, they had taken two horses and ridden out of the camp at the fastest gallop they could persuade the horses to make.

That had been hard, surviving that night. Now came something that Tellmore relished even less. Explaining to the baron just why he had failed.

THE EAST HALL of the Citadel was a much smaller affair than the main hall used for the larger events and celebrations. It was intimate and a great deal more luxurious. This was where the Baron de Sousse entertained those he considered his superiors, or peers that he wanted something from. Today, he wanted something from everyone who sat at the single long table that dominated the hall.

Though the table featured a full spread of wines, cheeses, breads and cold meats, few of the visitors did more than pick at the food. Nor had they paid much more than cursory attention to the finery of the hall itself, to the portraits of notables of the de Sousse family, the shields of its heroes, or even the broken lance that was the sole embellishment above the lone fireplace, the baron's own, splintered on the shield of Francois du Gris at the Grand Tourney in Miramas last year.

No, everyone here took such things for granted, their own families having performed deeds at least equal to those of de Sousse, and often far more impressive. The father of Count Fournier, on de Sousse's left hand, was in the royal court at Volonne. The Baron de Biot, seated at the far end of the table, had lost many family members in the war against Vos and each had covered himself in glory before falling to sword or lance. Baron Fremont, currently sipping at wine while listening to a conversation about the breeding of fine horses between Barons Rousseau and Durand, owned a huge amount of territory near the Sardenne whose riches guaranteed him a place at tables much finer than this one.

They all had two things in common with de Sousse, though. They all found themselves in the mid-strata of Pontaine nobility, rich and owners of large estates, but without strong political power. And they were all deeply ambitious for more.

Up to now, they had all been stymied in their efforts to climb the political ladder of Pontaine but de Sousse had broken the mould when he had seized Turnitia from the retreating Vos forces. Everyone seated at the table knew it had been an opportunistic move, and that de Sousse had merely been in the right place at the right time. However, he had demonstrated both the wit and will to grab the opportunity when it was dangled in front of him and that, at least, they could all respect. De Sousse could turn his chance victory into serious political force, as Turnitia was one of the main cities of the peninsula. If that were to happen, they all wanted to be a part of it.

De Sousse took a knife from the table, and banged its pommel gently on the table to attract attention. As heads turned towards him, he leaned forward in his seat to address them.

"My Lords," he began, respectfully. "I have taken Turnitia and made this city my own – in the name of Pontaine, of course. I would now like to explore how we can share in the further good fortune I now sense is possible, by tipping the balance so Vos becomes weak, and Pontaine becomes strong."

"The Anclas Territories are the obvious target," said Baron Rousseau. His family had lost a lot of land when the Territories had been declared neutral after the last war with Vos, and he was hungry to reclaim them.

"Too obvious?" asked Baron Fremont.

"And in any case," Count Fournier interrupted, "aside from farmland, there is little of true value in the Territories and no good defensive strongholds. We could march in, and be thrown out by an aggressive Vos army within a few months. There is no sense in replaying the last war."

De Sousse nodded. "I agree. I wonder if there is a better candidate for a first strike. If we could hit hard enough and fast enough, then the Vos Empire will recoil, be forced onto the back foot. The Anclas Territories would later fall to us by default."

There was a pause around the table, broken by de Biot. "You are suggesting invasion?"

Sitting back in his seat, de Sousse glanced at the faces before him. "It is an interesting notion, is it not?"

"Alright, de Sousse," said Fournier. "You have called us far from our own lands to discuss this. I believe we can spend at least a little time exploring the idea."

De Sousse smiled to himself. On a political level, the Count was the highest ranking man among them though, in truth, that was measured by degrees. However, his voice carried weight among them and if he said they would talk about war, then war they would talk about. The six pure-bred white stallions de Sousse had sent the Count as a gift a few months ago had clearly not been wasted, but he could only wonder as to how far Fournier's favour would continue.

They talked, argued, and debated, as only the nobility could. For more than three hours, they made plan and counterplan, each trying to ensure he came out just a little ahead of the others, whether the decision was to take action or no. De Sousse found it predictable and just a little boring as, he was sure, did the others.

Options were weighed, and it became clear they all had their own reasons for taking action, just as de Sousse had supposed when he first decided who to invite to this meeting. Some wanted revenge for allies and relatives, either killed in the war or still rotting in some pit of a Vos prison. Others were more interested in the glory and honour of a campaign, and the reputation that went with both. Most were hungry for more practical advantages, such as money and land.

As the debate began to play itself out, de Sousse tapped his knife on the table once more.

"My Lords, it is apparent to me that if we can find a way to take action against Vos, we should. The question remains, do we have that way? There are those among you better skilled in the ways of war, I have no doubt, but it seems to me that we have the perfect base of operations here, in my city of Turnitia. It is well-positioned to Vos' weak southern frontiers and avoids the mess of the Anclas Territories."

He saw Count Fournier smiling at him then, and had to stop himself returning it. *The old rascal has guessed exactly what I am going to say*, he thought. However, if the count had not interrupted him then maybe, just maybe, he could depend on a further favour. Or perhaps the count saw an advantage for himself in the idea – it amounted to the same thing, regardless.

"I have a large military force, twelve companies and still expanding," de Sousse continued. "You all have large complements too. Together, we can form a credible army. As you all know, I have the wizard Tellmore in my keeping, a mage as learned as he is powerful. At this moment, he is in the Anclas Territories, retrieving an artefact of immense power, said to have been forged by the Old Races."

That raised a few eyebrows, but it was Baron Durand that voiced the question they all had.

"And what does this great artefact do?"

De Sousse favoured him with a smile. "The tinkerings of wizards are far beyond a simple knight such as myself. However, this is something Tellmore has been working towards for a very long time, and if he tells me it contains enough power to decimate an army, I tend to believe him. As should all of you."

He stopped for a moment to take a sip of wine, letting the vague implications of magical power settle on all of them.

"However, in truth, I would never bear total reliance on magic," de Sousse said, setting down his cup. "Maybe the artefact is not everything Tellmore hopes, or perhaps he will be unable to unlock its secrets as quickly as we require. The mere fact that we have it will be enough to send shockwaves through both Vos and Pontaine. What will make this venture succeed for us is force of arms, and that we have between us in abundance. My soldiers, Fournier, your knights, de Biot, your archers – just think of the power we would wield on the field of battle if we combine our efforts!"

"So what is your plan?" de Biot asked.

"Speed is the essence. We strike fast, before Vos can mount a viable response. That way, we will face little more than house guards and militia, not a grand army."

"All well and good, de Sousse," said Rousseau, "but sooner or later, we *will* face a grand army. Vos will mobilise quickly."

"Which makes the target so important," de Sousse said smoothly, anticipating the argument. "We already have Turnitia, and that has gained me a lot of attention in Pontaine. Join me, and that attention becomes yours. Whatever we do after that magnifies our achievements – especially if we take something from Vos that is both close and highly visible."

Rousseau stared at him in something approaching horror. "My God, man. You are talking about Scholten!"

Others round the table looked equally aghast. Count Fournier barked a laugh, apparently pleased with the audacity of the plan.

De Biot shook his head. "You are talking about a lot more than a few house guards and militia. Scholten is effectively the capital of the Final Faith. We'll be going up against the Anointed Lord herself."

"Which is what makes the city the perfect target," de Sousse said. "We need to make meticulous plans, of course, but if we can move our armies together and with speed, we can be at that city and in its streets before any response can be made. The main bulk of the Vos army is kept at Vosburg. The fact that the Final Faith is responsible for the defence of Scholten will be its downfall. And the Anointed Lord will be almost as grand a prize as the city itself."

"At which point, Vos mobilises, surrounds Scholten and crushes us," said de Biot.

Again, de Sousse smiled. "That is the beauty of it. Think for a moment. Suppose you were a tired old noble in Andon or Volonne. One day, you hear that a bunch of young upstart nobles of no real political power or name in the south have risen up and snatched one of the greatest Vos cities, overnight. What would you do?"

It was Count Fournier's turn to smile.

"I would order my squire to fetch my armour and summon as many fighting men as I could muster to cross the Anclas Territories and join them." He shook his head, smiling. "Lord above, de Sousse, I had no idea you had the balls for something of this magnitude. If you can convince these other fine gentlemen – all of them, mind – you will have my knights and much more for this adventure."

"Are you serious?" de Biot asked the count.

"If we can take Scholten, and take it quickly, then we will have every armed man in Pontaine at our beck and call in as much time as it takes them to get to the city," de Sousse said. "With that momentum, we can crush the Vos grand army. One battle, that is all it will take."

"That is a bloody great *if*," said de Biot.

"True," said Rousseau. "And I do have my doubts. But we can plan every detail over and over until we are happy, right, de Sousse?"

De Sousse shrugged. "There is no great pressing need on time. I would not want to waste any advantage we get from taking Turnitia, but that will last a while yet. Better to go in prepared, I always say."

"Then, dependent on the actual planning," said Rousseau slowly. "I am in too."

De Biot looked at him as if he were mad.

"Durand, Fremont," de Sousse addressed the two other barons. "These two fine gentlemen are with me. What will it take to get your support?"

Close political allies, the two barons looked at one another before Fremont spoke.

"I suppose, in all of this, you would be, what, the general of this combined force?"

"Given my hold on Turnitia, I believe I would be the logical choice," de Sousse said.

"Well, that is fine, that is fine," Fremont said. "And when every fighting man in Pontaine is under the banner, you will still be the overall commander?"

"I can foresee several older nobles wanting to displace me, but I would naturally look to my closest friends to assist me in retaining the position."

"And there we have the central problem," Fremont said.

"Which is?" de Sousse asked, trying very hard not to look as if he were baiting the baron.

"Let us suppose that, against all sane odds, this enterprise of yours works. There will be no more Vos or, at least, no more Vos

Empire. The peninsula will be united. Under one rule. Yours? The Emperor de Sousse?"

"That is a lovely thought," de Sousse said, chuckling to himself to lend some levity to the notion. "And it would be another logical choice – I would have initiated Pontaine's path back to greatness. But I instead make you this promise. Who sits in the emperor's throne, if we end up calling it that, will be decided on the field of battle. Whosoever distinguishes himself most in the war, who gathers the most honour and glory... he shall be emperor."

"You'll stand by that?" de Biot asked, clearly surprised.

De Sousse shrugged. "Just by attempting this, every one of us round this table will be guaranteed honour and glory for centuries to come – maybe forever! If we succeed, then we will have all the wealth we ever dreamed of. So what is left? Raw power? I have as much interest in that as all of you, but if it is someone else who sits on the throne, we will have their eternal gratitude. And that, as a power behind the throne, is almost as valuable, without making yourself such a visible target. Yes, de Biot, I am tickled by the notion of being emperor, but I do not burn for it. At least, not yet. Thus, I am happy to let a man's sword determine his right to take the throne."

Fremont grinned. "I'll hold you to that, de Sousse. So long as it remains true, though, I am in."

"I also," growled Durand, looking eager to start hacking apart Vos knights that minute.

"And so it comes to you, de Biot," de Sousse said. "What say you?"

De Biot looked at the others, conscious they all now waited for his answer.

"I will say now that this plan is madness, it's foolish, it's... ill-conceived." He sighed, deeply. "But if you think I am going to let one of you become emperor of the entire peninsula without me having a fair shot at it, you have another think coming."

"You are with us?" Count Fournier asked.

De Biot shook his head slightly, as if he could not believe his own words. He opened his mouth to speak, and then closed it. Rubbing his forehead, he sighed again.

"I believe I am," he finally said. "May the good God help us all."

* * *

ONE OF THE Citadel's countless servants had provided a seat for Tellmore as he waited outside the baron's study. He had been patient to begin with, but had steadily grown concerned as first the minutes and then the hours passed. While he did not relish the news he was to deliver, Tellmore could not help but wonder what kept the baron's attention over news from an expedition in the Anclas Territories to uncover the most powerful magical artefact of recent times.

Tellmore sighed. It was the nature of his position that warriors could rarely understand the import of matters magical.

The servant had offered to prepare new clothing for Tellmore, but he had declined. His cloak was ruined, while his tunic was dirty and ripped in several places. He had thought that his appearance might draw some sympathy from the baron, an acknowledgement that, despite his failure to retrieve the Guardian Starlight, best efforts had been made.

Now he was starting to regret that decision and even doubting its efficacy. The thought of a long soak in a rose-scented bath, followed by a good meal and clean clothing, had taken seed and was starting to bear fruit.

The baron was certainly giving him plenty of time for such welcome luxuries.

"My dear Tellmore, my deepest apologies for having you kept waiting," the baron said as he appeared at the end of the corridor. He was positively beaming, which made Tellmore suspect the man had been enjoying the attentions of one of his many women; but the baron had always let such worldly matters fall to the side when Tellmore had something important to discuss.

As the baron approached, his smile slipped a little as Tellmore stood.

"Tellmore, you look an absolute wreck," he said, as he withdrew a key from his belt pouch and unlocked the study door. "Oh, dear, something tells me you have not got the best news for me. Well, don't stand on ceremony, come on in and tell me all about it."

Following the baron in, Tellmore watched as he flopped down into his chair with a satisfied sigh, before pulling off his boots and settling down comfortably.

"My Lord," Tellmore began, then hesitated.

"Sit, sit, sit, man," the baron said, waving his hand in irritation at Tellmore. "And out with it. You tell me your news, then I'll tell you mine."

Tellmore frowned as he did as he was instructed. He had feared his failure would have serious repercussions, possibly being dismissed from the baron's service and a return to the Three Towers. Such a prospect was not wholly bad in Tellmore's eyes, as he would be able to return to pure academic study. He had to admit though, he would miss the baron's patronage. He had a great deal of autonomy here and the pay was very good.

"The expedition is lost, my Baron," Tellmore said. "I was not able to retrieve the Guardian Starlight."

"Ah, well," said de Sousse. "Your information was bad?"

"No, not at all, I am very sure we found the right site. Everything matched – geography, topography, the few ruins we were able to unearth."

"What then?"

Tellmore took a deep breath before continuing. "We were attacked. Looked like a Vos force."

The baron raised his brow at that.

"We lost everyone. I was knocked out during the fighting, and would still be there now, captured or dead, if it were not for Sir Renauld."

"Renauld got out alive too?"

"He did, my Baron."

"Oh, well thank the heavens for that at least," said the baron, and his relief seemed genuine. "I would not have liked to explain to his father just how I got him killed. Add to that, he *is* a good knight. Young, but with potential enough, and I'll have need for him in the near future."

"Pardon, my Baron," Tellmore said. "You do not seem overly concerned about this turn of events."

"Well, you know me, my dear Tellmore," the baron said, rather grandly. "I don't like leaving important matters to chance. I dispatched some additional help for you some time ago."

"Additional help?"

"Our grateful friend, Lucius."

"You did not trust me, my Baron?"

"Oh, Tellmore, don't be so jealous. When it comes to all things arcane, there is none in this world I would listen to more than you. However, delving in ancient ruins? You never know what you might find. I thought a thief would serve you well for anything… beyond your normal experiences."

Tellmore thought for a moment. "What about the other Shadowmage, Adrianna?"

De Sousse chuckled. "Well, I summoned her, but she did not appear. So, I gave the job to Lucius. However, I now hear from my men in the city that our facially challenged Adrianna ... disappeared. Right about the same time Lucius left to join you."

"So she has gone there as well?"

"That is my assumption."

"My Lord Baron. Can you trust these people? I know we have agreements with them, but..."

"It is a finely balanced play," the baron said, conceding the point. "But as far as our thief Lucius is concerned... yes, I actually think I do trust him. In terms of his guild, he is heavily indebted to us, to what extent I don't think he really comprehends yet. However, on a higher level, I really do believe that his reputation *as* a thief matters more to him than the artefact he now chases."

"And the Shadowmage?"

A dark look fluttered briefly across the baron's face. "Now, she *is* a worry. I have no doubt that, between the two of them, she is the senior, magically speaking. And if she avoided me but went anyway, one has to question her motives. I would not like to be Lucius when they find the Starlight."

"You think a thief may outwit a Shadowmage?" Tellmore asked, dubiously.

"No, but remember that Lucius is a Shadowmage too. He may surprise us. And, if not, I have one more insurance over her."

"Which is?"

"You, my dear Tellmore! I presume you can track her through some arcane means?"

Tellmore thought for a moment. "It is not easy, but certainly possible. If she attempts to use the Guardian Starlight, though, I should be able to find her from the other side of the peninsula."

"I thought as much. And use it she will, if she has gone to this much trouble already. When that happens, I'll send you and a full company of men. I suspect there is little that will improve her disposition towards us better than a few swords and spears in her belly."

Nodding, Tellmore found himself begrudgingly impressed with de Sousse. Though he could not help feel slighted at having been displaced by a thief of all people, the baron had made sure the success of the expedition was secure in many different ways, and that kind of foresight had to be appreciated. At the end of the day, recovery of the Guardian Starlight was all that mattered.

"In that case, my Baron, I formally apologise for having let you down on my side of the arrangement."

"Oh, don't be so pompous," the baron said, waving the apology aside. "If it were not for you, we wouldn't even know of this great magical power. What concerns me more is the presence of Vos forces. Did you get the sense they were there specifically for you, and for the artefact?"

"Impossible to say," Tellmore said after a moment's thought. "The attack came quickly and at night."

"Possibly planned then."

"Does that have bearing on this?"

"Not on this, no. I haven't told you my news yet."

"Which is, my Baron?"

"Many things have been put in motion while you have been away, Tellmore," the baron said with a sparkle in his eye that Tellmore found a little disturbing. "Take a look outside."

Tellmore frowned, but stood up and walked to the open window behind the baron. From the high vantage point, he could see across half the city but his attention was drawn to the courtyard of the Citadel, immediately below him.

Within the high walls and in the shadow of one of the Citadel's towers, soldiers, sporting several different liveries, were lining up and making ready for departure. Honour guards for the armoured nobles who sat on powerful horses at the head of their men. While he was not the best authority on Pontaine heraldry, Tellmore recognised the crest of Count Fournier, and knew him to be someone de Sousse had been moving closer to of late. He also thought he could place one of the barons, though the man's name escaped him for the moment.

"My Baron has been busy indeed," Tellmore muttered. Then, louder, he said, "Would my Baron care to share his plans with me?"

"My dear Tellmore," de Sousse said. "I can promise you, you are going to be impressed."

CHAPTER THIRTEEN

Stepping over the body of a Vos soldier, Lucius padded down the first flight of steps, their surface slick from the rain that had fallen, mixed with the mud remaining from their excavation.

The soldier had been one of two guards stationed at the head of the stairs, and Lucius had efficiently dispatched one with a thrust from his short sword into the small of the man's back, while Adrianna had taken care of the other with a focussed thrust of air that had lethally slammed the guard's body into the ground with a dreadful force. Lucius had looked around anxiously after she had cast her spell, as the sound of the guard hitting the earth seemed impossibly loud. However, the sound did not seem to travel more than a few yards. He wondered if that was an embellishment to the spell Adrianna had developed herself.

The stairs were wide and carved from grey stone. Their lack of grip might have caused anyone else to term them "treacherous" but the Shadowmages crept down as sure as mountain goats. Descending into blackness, the stairs led deep into the earth and, lacking torches, Adrianna cast a minor spell, one that caused a pale purple point of weak light to materialise in the palm of her hand. No one casually walking past the top of the stairs would notice its dim glimmer below, but it provided just enough illumination for Lucius to spot his path.

Though there were others in the thieves' guild who had an uncanny knack for always knowing just how far they were beneath the surface when on a subterranean jaunt, Lucius had never developed the skill. Even so, he could count, and he estimated they were the equivalent of three storeys down when the stairs finally came to an end and flattened out into a corridor which extended into the dark, fully four yards wide.

Even in the pale twilight cast by Adrianna, Lucius could immediately see he was in a fantastical place. The paving stones were exquisitely cut, laid so close together that at no point could he have inserted a blade between them. As for the walls and ceiling of the corridor, he had no idea how that had been constructed. A human might have simply left the rock bare or covered it in plaster. Instead, it seemed each wall was sculpted from a single slab of that grey rock, as perfectly fashioned as each pave stone on the floor.

He could not begin to think of the craftsmanship – or magic – required to build such a place.

In the past, Lucius had heard tales of the Old Races, as had every child or thief willing to listen to a wild story. It was only now that he began to appreciate just what the elves had been capable of.

Which begged the question, of course: why did men rule the world now and not the elves?

The steps he took began to falter, not out of a lack of visibility, but a lack of confidence. His thievish instincts were fully alert, but he recognised that they might have no chance of spotting any potential danger. The walls were perfectly smooth, so that suggested no blade or dart traps would be sprung from them. But then again, if the architects of this place could build such walls, what were they capable of hiding within them?

As for the floor, that was even worse. There would be no chance to spot the outline of a swinging pit trap if it followed the perfect contours of the paving stones.

He felt as if he were groping around in the dark like some apprentice thief on his first burglary. The only comfort was that Adrianna was not passing sarcastic comments about his lack of pace, which meant she was either in complete awe of this place, or just as nervous as he was.

Proceeding down the corridor, perpetually crouched and testing each foot before he put his full weight on it, their progress was slow, but Lucius was not in any real rush.

The corridor seemed to go on forever, though Lucius estimated they had perhaps travelled no more than sixty or seventy yards. It came as some relief when, ahead, Lucius saw the corridor widening into a chamber. He gestured at Adrianna behind and she intensified her spell, the purple haze in the palm of her hand brightening to expand his view.

As darkness retreated, the chamber's full expanse came into view. Lucius found himself at the top of another flight of stairs. The ceiling arched out of sight but he could pick out two alcoves in either of the walls, high enough to contain a man standing but currently empty.

Pacing slowly down the steps, eyes darting in all directions to spot traps and other defences, Lucius spied a handful of dark marks lying on the floor at the opposite end of the chamber and, beyond them, a large set of double doors carved from the same stone as the floors and walls.

Halfway down the stairs, he halted and looked back over his shoulder to Adrianna.

"What do you think?" he said, his voice barely more than a whisper.

"I think we are safe for now. If we are to believe the Pontaine soldiers we met, this place has had morons traipsing in and out of it for weeks, with no harm coming to them. I believe that the doors there will be our real problem."

Forcing himself to relax a little, Lucius took a deep breath and continued down the stairs to cross the chamber. As he approached the great doors, he rubbed his eyes, thinking that Adrianna's false light was beginning to play with his vision.

Pale azure lines of arcane light had begun to glow within the doors, forming a tight, geometric pattern that seemed to grow and build in brilliance as he moved closer. Alarmed, thinking an ancient trap was about to be unleashed, he jumped back, sword drawn in a defensive posture.

"You see that?" he said to Adrianna.

She sounded confused. "See what?"

"The door – is it preparing a spell against us?"

There was a pause. The lights in the door had dimmed slightly when Lucius jumped back, but they held a constant radiance now.

"I can feel magics in the background, but nothing active," Adrianna said.

"Nothing active?" Despite expecting to be blasted apart any second, Lucius could not keep a note of incredulity from his voice. "You seen many glowing doors on your travels?"

"Glowing...? Lucius, tell me what you can see."

It began to dawn on him that, whatever was happening on the door's face, it was being concealed from Adrianna. He briefly told her of the strange patterns, sketching them out with his hand, though he did not move any closer.

They seemed to form a linked chain of regular hexagons and pentagons along the edges of both doors, with larger and more complex multi-pointed stars clustered in the centre, at about head height. The shapes caused his eyes to water and blur if he stared too long at them, but he noticed they had started to pulse, ever so faintly, suddenly getting a little brighter before fading, and then pulsing brighter again. He found it disturbingly like a heartbeat.

"Fascinating," Adrianna said.

"You really can't see that?"

It took her a while to answer, and Lucius heard her muttering, perhaps casting some spell of detection or one that sharpened her senses.

"I cannot," she said finally. She did not sound in the least disappointed, which Lucius found a little suspicious.

"Well then," he said. "That begs an obvious question. How can I see it and you can't?"

"I always said you were special, Lucius."

"I never knew what you meant when you said it."

She shook her head, almost absentmindedly. "In truth, neither did I. But I believe we are close to something of an answer, would you not say?"

"Okay," he said. "So, what do we do now?"

"I think it is obvious. You open the door."

He glanced down at the dark patches on the floor, each one about the size of a man.

"You know that this is all that is left of the last guy who tried opening that thing."

"True. But I don't think the door glowed to him and him alone when he made the attempt."

That checked Lucius.

"So..." he started. "So, you are saying the door is, what, inviting me?"

Again, Adrianna shrugged, a habit that, down here among elven ruins and with his life in the balance, Lucius was beginning to find irritating.

"Before I do anything, I want some answers," he said flatly.

"And I am telling you, Lucius, that the only place you will find any of those answers is beyond those doors. Open them, and go through. Or do not, and go back home."

Lucius put a hand to his temple, as if trying to avoid a headache as he thought fast. There was no lock on the door, no handle, no sign of hinging. No features of any kind that his thievish talent could latch on to. As for his magical side, it was completely mystified.

If he were stalled as both thief and Shadowmage, what else did he have left?

"Can you at least create some ward or charm that might protect me if the worst happens?" he asked.

Adrianna smiled, her scarred face adopting a slightly cruel air to it.

"I can mumble a few words over you if you like," she said. "But it didn't do the Pontaine men at your feet any good."

"I thought you didn't rate their wizard."

"I don't. But I also don't think there is any spell from our world that will protect you from what is down here, should it choose to make you its enemy. You can see something others cannot. I would take that as a sign."

He glanced dubiously at the door and then back at Adrianna.

"If it were you in my place, you would open the door?"

"If it were me in your place, I would already have done so, and we would both have been spared a pointless conversation."

The words were condescending enough, but Lucius felt no real malice behind them. If anything, he would have said Adrianna was fuelled with curiosity. More than anything right now, she wanted to know what secrets this place held.

She was right about one thing, though. Without recourse to any great magics, and acknowledging that neither the Pontaine wizard nor Adrianna had any great insight into elven magic, his choices were remarkably limited. Try to open the door, or turn around and go home. Or simply sit here and debate the situation until some Vos soldier discovered them.

Lucius moved closer to the door, feeling his muscles tense as the patterns on the door grew ever brighter, as if they were trying to reach out to him. Their light was intense as he approached to within just a few inches of the doors' surface.

He held a hand up, feeling a warmth flow from it as his palm hovered just an inch from the portal's surface. Beginning to sweat, he glanced back at Adrianna.

"Go on," she whispered. "Do it!"

Closing his eyes, Lucius leaned forward, feeling his hand touch the stone as he put his weight behind it.

With no sound or resistance at all, both doors swung slowly away from him as if they were on well-greased runners. Lucius heard a sharp intake of breath behind from Adrianna, but inside his own chest he felt something... stir.

Before him, another flight of stairs beckoned downwards, descending the height of perhaps another two storeys. At the bottom, they seemed to open up into a new area, from which a soft creamy light glowed.

"I have no idea how I just did that," he said.

"We can debate that later," Adrianna said, stirring herself. "For now, we must see what lies beyond. If we can – *ah!*"

Her sharp cry was joined by a slicing pain in his head that made Lucius wince. Adrianna had been striding confidently towards the open doors but, as she approached, the arcane patterning had flared briefly and Adrianna had been halted in her tracks as though she had walked into an invisible wall.

She looked shocked, and Lucius rubbed the side of his head to alleviate his own pain. He was grateful it receded quickly.

"What happened there?" he asked.

"It won't let me through," Adrianna said, and he could hear the anger beginning to rise in her voice. "Damn it!"

"You don't belong here," Lucius said, with a flash of insight that mystified him as much as it had informed him. "But I do."

That last part made him frown, for while he considered it plainly obvious, he had no idea how he knew that. He just knew it was fact. Looking up at Adrianna, he saw she was glaring at him.

"What does this mean?" he asked, feeling as though he should have been a lot more scared than he felt.

"It means," she said with a hint of ice on her tongue, "that you will be proceeding alone."

"But why can I go through and you cannot?"

"I don't know, Lucius, but you can rest assured we will be having a long conversation after this, during which I *will* find out."

"Okay. Watch for any Vos patrols. If you hear me cry out... well, you won't be able to do anything. Just... just keep an ear out for me, alright?"

Adrianna did not respond so, steeling himself, Lucius turned and passed through the doors to stand at the top of the stairs.

"Lucius," Adrianna called from the chamber.

He turned to look back at her.

"Keep your eyes open. Trust nothing, no matter how inviting it feels."

"I'll be back soon."

As Lucius paced down the last of the stairs, he stepped into a vast vaulted hall. Larger than the nave of the Final Faith cathedral in Turnitia, the place was illuminated with a soft light, though he could not see any lantern or fire that could be its source. It just seemed to radiate out from the walls and ceiling.

Looking up, he saw the hall stretched far overhead into a dome. Smooth pillars were buttressed against the walls and they reached up into the dome, growing thinner until they met at a single point in its centre.

A dais lay some distance before him, and he saw unmoving figures upon it, scores of them standing rigid as statues. Even from this far away, he could see they were clad in silver and golden armour, breastplates and great helms shining in the light.

What this place was and what it had been used for, he could not say, but Lucius stood there for a moment trying to take in its immense scale. He could not even begin to imagine the tremendous engineering skill and effort needed to excavate such a hall far beneath the earth, and he was struck by the utter perfection of the work. It was not gaudy or intricate, with finely detailed friezes or mosaics, as the stories of elven buildings would have their credulous listeners believe. Everything was very simple, very smooth, with a softness to the architecture that would never be found in anything built by men. It was just... perfect.

Nothing moved in the hall, and his beating heart was the loudest thing present. The air was clean, fresh even, and he thought he could smell the soft scent of tulips.

As he walked into the hall, his boots made no echo upon the paving stones that covered the floor. Looking around, Lucis could see no other entrances but he began to feel this was a central hub of sorts, with pathways radiating out from it, invisible to him though they might be right now.

How he knew this, he could not say but, once again, the thought just felt *right*.

His attention rested on the dais and the armoured statues standing upon it. As he closed the distance to them, he began to pick out details. Each statue seemed to be carved from some sort of marble. Each set of armour decorating the statues was unique, yet each was crafted in a fashion Lucius had not seen before. Contrary to the architecture around him, the armoursmithing of the elves was apparently very intricate, with minute designs and geometric patterns chiselled and hammered into every surface. Each plate was gold, silver or bronze, but most were inlaid with other metals and the occasional gem. Between them, chainmail of the finest mesh he had ever seen provided further protection.

It was a thief's delight. A fortune great enough to buy a city stood before him.

As he reached the foot of the dais, Lucius took note for the first time of the size of the statues. He had thought the dais had given them height but he now saw each stood half as tall again as he. The thought of these titans going into battle, both strong and lightning fast, chilled his blood. They could be unstoppable.

Looking up, he saw the face of an elf for the first time. At first, he found it distinctly alien, with the sharpened features and hawk-like nose of the legends being very apparent. However, as he continued to stare, he began to see the magnificent perfection inherent within these beings. Perfectly proportioned, they had wide eyes that seemed capable of communicating both deep compassion and great fury at the same time. The broad foreheads were smooth and unsullied by emotion, while the prominent cheekbones lent a fundamental beauty to every figure before him.

Lucius mounted the dais to look closer at the creatures. He tried to imagine what it must have been like to see the elves walking, talking, trading and fighting. It was no wonder man did not rise to prominence until this race had passed on. They were superior in every way.

The statue before him had a tall, conical helm of gold sporting silver decoration. Wide shoulder guards the shape of delicate pine leaves extended outwards, their silver filigreed edges catching the surrounding light as Lucius moved for a better look. The breastplate was of a gold so pure it almost hurt to gaze upon it, and the intricate detailing of lines and regular shapes, each so tiny they could be barely seen from more than a few inches away, must have taken some craftsman years to complete. The statue held a tall shield of gold and silver in its left hand, something close to the towered design popular among Pontaine armies, but with elegant curves that provided its user with both visibility and protection when held tight to their body.

In the statue's right hand was an elegant rod or sceptre. It had a grey marble shaft, shot through with red veins, leading to a golden cap that splayed out like the wings of a great eagle. Set in-between the two wings was a large red crystal, carved to form the likeness of a heart.

Again, without quite knowing how, Lucius knew what he was about to say was true.

"You are mine," he said softly, looking at the rod.

Reaching forward with an outstretched hand he touched one of the golden wings, hesitantly. Nothing stirred in the hall, and no spell struck him down.

Controlling his nerves, Lucius grasped the rod by its shaft and pulled it to him. It had not been affixed to the statue in any way, and slide from the stone grasp.

The rod was heavy, but Lucius could already begin to feel its power, as arcane warmth spread through his hands, up his arms and into his body, his whole being electrified by contact with the artefact.

"What are you?" he whispered as he gazed at the rod in awe, turning it over in his hands, noting every detail.

Light flooded the hall, dazzling Lucius. His first instinct was to run, but he found his legs were not functioning properly. They seemed sluggish and, as he moved away from the statues, he lost balance and fell from the dais.

The light grew ever brighter until it blocked any sight of the hall, and the statues became mere silhouettes against a backdrop of brilliance. Squinting in pain, Lucius held up an arm to try to block the light. He cried out in alarm as he saw something move; something very large and yet very graceful.

Moving in-between the statues, a tall figure appeared. It towered above Lucius as he cowered on the floor, kicking his feet uselessly as he tried to crawl away from the apparition. He could see no detail in the figure, but it seemed as though the bright light blinding him emanated from it alone.

Then it spoke, a voice that seemed to come from the entire hall – deep, resonant, a sound that spoke of ages long since turned to dust.

"Why were we lost?" the voice said, booming around Lucius, forcing him to clasp his hands to his ears as they burned with the strain of the words. "Why was the magic lost?"

Lucius felt these were not questions but demands, and they seemed to pound into his body with each syllable. He knew an answer was required, but he could not think of how to even begin to respond.

"Why were we lost?" the figure challenged him once again, much louder this time, and Lucius felt blood begin to trickle from his ears. Unable to rise to his feet and run for safety, Lucius curled up, bringing his knees to his chest as he desperately tried to cover his ears.

He screamed in pain as the figure spoke once more, demanding an answer to its question whose words now seared into the very core of Lucius' mind. Then, mercifully, he lost all sense of self and was surrounded by darkness.

CHAPTER FOURTEEN

LUCIUS AWOKE TO find himself standing on a balcony. Before him was an utterly alien vista; a city of dreams, breathtaking in scope.

The buildings were constructed of a smooth, golden stone that, like the corridors of the ruins, betrayed no sign of join or individual brick. Many had balconies like the one he stood upon, or wide archways halfway up their heights large enough to swallow a small ship. Many had domes of filigreed silver while others had tall, thin towers reaching up to the clouds high above.

Though he towered above the streets far, far below, he was by no means on the tallest structure in the city. At least a dozen buildings before him climbed much higher, as if they had been built to reach the sun itself.

As Lucius looked up at the furthest reaches of those buildings, he gasped to see, moving majestically around their silver spires, several ships.

They had curved hulls made of wood, just like the vessels Lucius had seen in Turnitia's harbour, but they were *flying* through the air as though it were water. Their decks bore sails, though Lucius saw they also had masts and canvas stretching horizontally from the sides of their hulls.

He watched one as it flew in front of the great sphere of Kerberos and, again, gasped as it suddenly struck him that the great blue giant of the sky was much smaller. Had it shrunk? Or had it somehow moved further away?

Steadying himself on the polished wooden railing of the balcony, Lucius again focused on the buildings before him.

Some of the towers, he noticed, had great carved crystals the size of his guildhouse, suspended above them with no visible means of support. The crystals were all of different hues, glowing with an inner light he could only ascribe to magic. Every so often, a tiny bolt of energy would shoot out from one crystal to be quickly absorbed by another.

To his right, the structure of the city changed slightly, as towers became less common and gave way to impossibly large buildings, each perhaps the size of the entire Citadel. Next to these colossal buildings, large chimney stacks, themselves nearly reaching the heights of some of the smaller towers, poured long columns of smoke into the air, constantly changing colour, moving from red to purple to a rich blue, and then back again.

There was a terrible scream and a shadow passed over him as a massive form whipped past above. He had a sense of gossamer wings and a long wooden hull but it quickly disappeared out of view behind the building he was standing within.

With a rush of air, the object appeared again, its long hull slicing through the air as cleanly as any blade. Its hull was almost needle-thin, while lace wings fluttered effortlessly to keep the flying boat aloft.

Ahead of its wings, a man in brilliant silver and gold armour, much like those he had seen in the ruins, sat astride the hull and, as he flew past, raised his long lance in salute to Lucius. Then, he was gone, carried higher into the sky by his strange craft.

As he watched the boat, entranced by its flight, Lucius began to focus on what lay beyond it, and suddenly felt weak at the knees.

Beyond the city lay the ocean – but it was calm, with only gentle waves rolling across its surface. However, three immense blocks of stone were being slowly guided through the air, shepherded by flying ships. Though the stone blocks were a brilliant white, Lucius recognised them immediately.

He realised he was watching the construction of the harbour of Turnitia, with its great monoliths protecting it from a raging ocean.

Just what in the name of all that was holy was going on?

It did not – could not – make sense. Was this how Turnitia had once looked? Slowly, it began to dawn on him that he must have triggered some sort of trap in the ruins, some elven magic that had, somehow, transported him out of his own time and back to theirs.

He did not even want to think about the implications of that.

"Magus, your pardon."

The voice behind him made Lucius whirl round, its deep tones instantly setting his nerves on edge.

He found himself looking at an elf.

"Soluun, it was good of you to come," Lucius said, but in a voice that was not his own. It was deeper, with far more bass and power. The words had come bidden to his lips but not by his will. Moreover, he knew he was speaking some alien tongue, and yet the words and their intent were known to him.

Lucius, quite without willing it, stepped away from the balcony and into the room beyond. A very large and wide desk lay before him. Shelves contained neat rows of books and there was none of the clutter he had associated with such places before.

The elf before him had appeared from a narrow archway and was dressed in a regal grey gown encrusted with vertical lines of blue gems that changed to sparkle a more golden colour when they caught the light. Such stones were beyond Lucius' experience as a thief and he marvelled at what their value could possibly be.

"If one of the Magi has concerns, it is only natural we should consult him," Soluun said.

Studying the elf, Lucius marvelled at the physique of the wonderful creature. It moved with a certainty of purpose that he would not have quite described as graceful – perhaps natural was the correct term, as if every movement and gesture the elf made was in perfect accord with the world and everything in it. Indeed, that every move was necessary for the world to remain as it was.

Extremely tall, the elf seemed quite fragile but Lucius could see, even through the elaborate gown, that powerful muscles lurked below. It took him a moment more to realise that, somehow, he was looking at the elf at eye level.

"I fear my concerns are too little, and too late," Lucius said. "We are on a course that could destroy us all."

"It will not come to that," Soluun said. "The dwarfs may provoke us, that may even be the likely course, but we will remain triumphant."

"We do not always attain victory. The battle on the Plains of Seazzor saw even a phalanx led by a windlord routed."

"A loss that was countered the next week by the breaking of the siege at Antrium."

Lucius sighed. "And so it goes on, they beat us, we beat them, on and on it will go until one of us is foolish enough to do something unthinkable."

"Would you rather we capitulate and lose everything?"

"I would rather we never started this idiotic feud in the first place. What started as a diplomatic slight has been allowed to grow into outright war–"

"A few minor skirmishes," Soluun said.

"Into outright war," Lucius repeated. "This should never have been permitted, and damn the Council for allowing things to progress so far."

"You forget the dwarfs have denied us further diplomatic contact. The only way forward now is to beat them, and beat them hard, so they are forced to renegotiate for peace."

"I am sure, somewhere in the darkest reaches of the minds of the Council, that makes sense. However, it also means things will escalate, and the arcane power both we and the dwarfs now have access to is fundamentally without limit."

"Ours maybe," said Soluun. "But not the dwarfs. They very much have limits. I have not seen them preparing skyships to sail to another world above us."

"And that project is almost as foolish as war with the dwarf nation state." Lucius said, taking a step back to the balcony so he could point to the sphere of Kerberos, hanging in the sky. "We have no idea what that place is or what landing there will do. We have no idea what we might awaken."

"That is why we go, to explore and discover."

"There are better ways of doing it," Lucius hissed. "For millennia our society has grown, at a steady and measured pace, precisely because we were not foolish enough to just rush in. What changed, Soluun?"

For a moment, the other elf was silent. When he spoke, it was in a thoughtful tone.

"I think, perhaps, it was inevitable. The rate of progress increases as we learn more and more."

"You may be right, Soluun. But it does then beg the question; at what point does our reach exceed our grasp? And if we find that answer it may be worth thinking about the consequences of reaching that point."

"Surely a question for the future, Magus. What is important right now is that we protect ourselves from the dwarfs. If they cannot hurt us, then our victory is assured."

"No, Soluun," Lucius said. "It is no longer a choice between us winning this war or the dwarfs doing so. There is now a third possibility that becomes steadily more inevitable with each passing day."

"Which is?"

"Total annihilation for both. That one of us unleashes something so powerful, so terrible, it consumes every living thing in this world."

"We have heard these arguments before, Magus, and the dwarfs just do not have that kind of knowledge. Right now, in our harbour, we are countering the dwarfs' new mighty weapon. And even if they can create a magical vortex at sea, even if it works, even if it succeeds in creating a massive wave, it will be defeated by the new barriers."

"You underestimate the dwarfs, just as the Council has always done," Lucius said. "One day, they will surprise you and launch an attack for which there is no counter. But that is not what truly scares me."

"And what could possibly frighten a Magus of the elves?"

"What we do, Soluun," Lucius said. "What we, the elves, might become capable of. If we had ultimate power in our hands, just what would we do with it."

"Well, that is not for me to say and, with all respect, it is not for you either. That is the very definition of the role the Council plays in our civilisation."

"I know, Soluun. I know."

"It troubles us that you have these doubts. You should be proud of your accomplishments, not thinking about retiring."

"I have played my part, and have no wish to bring closer the end I am beginning to foresee. A quiet life in the Great Forest is what I crave now."

"Cataloguing wildlife and training the growth of trees?" Soluun said, not without a measure of scorn.

"Well, there will be rather more to it than that."

"Either way, we will be looking to you to finish your current work before you can depart."

Lucius took a deep breath and then walked to one of the cabinets that sat between his books. Opening its two doors, he became aware that Soluun had moved up next to him, and was now gazing inside the cabinet.

"Guardian Starlight," Soluun said under his breath, almost reverently.

Inside, nestled on a tray carved from a single block of ivory, were a dozen marble and gold rods, identical to the one Lucius had found in the ruins.

"The power you have invested in these weapons is almost a holy thing," Soluun said.

"We abandoned religion aeons ago, and with good reason," Lucius said sharply. "Would you have us go back to the pagan beliefs practised by the primitive human tribes?"

"I stand corrected, Magus. But your work here has unmatched beauty."

"I find them repulsive. They are, however, yours, whenever you need them."

"You have the gratitude of the Council, Magus," Soluun said. "And our final victory will be ascribed to you. Of course, if Guardian Starlight fails...'

Lucius looked at the elf, an expression of utter dismay crossing his face, completely unbidden.

"Don't tell me the Council went ahead with the contingency."

"We have the utmost faith in you, Magus," Soluun said.

"That is madness," Lucius said after a pause in which he rattled the dread possibilities through his mind. "Utter madness!"

NOT WANTING TO inadvertently set off some mundane trap a clever elf might have left behind, Adrianna had confined her movements only to the sections of the chamber she and Lucius had already walked. After the first half-hour, she had retreated to the stairs leading out of the chamber and sat on the top flight. From there she would be able to see both Lucius' return, and the coming of any inquisitive guards. God help them.

More than an hour had passed, she was sure, and she drummed the fingers of her right hand upon her knee as she waited. She had always thought that if great harm befell Lucius, she would somehow feel it. After all, they had spent enough time together and she had learned how his presence shifted the flow of magic around her. Here, in elven ruins surrounded by Old Race magic, however, she could not be so sure that any break in their connection would make itself known to her.'

She was not worried for Lucius' safety – she would not allow herself to feel that emotion – but his death and failure in this place would cause her some problems. First, the Guardian Starlight might remain forever beyond her reach, and that was an artefact she desperately wanted to get her hands on.

Just the thought of holding the artefact and plumbing the depths of its mysteries caused a rare feeling of joy to surge through her. She likened it to first learning what a Shadowmage was capable of and seeing her first attempts, clumsy as they were, at casting simple spells.

She expected the arrival of the Guardian Starlight, and the awesome magical power it contained, to mark another great shift in her. Everything that had transpired before would be as nothing compared to what she would attain thereafter.

If Lucius returned with the artefact, of course.

It had also occurred to her that life in Turnitia might get more difficult without Lucius as well. The Shadowmages formed a trinity with the thieves and beggars, but Adrianna was under no illusion that it was the thieves and, specifically, Lucius that held them all together. There was no way that she could work with that idiot child Grennar and as powerful as the Shadowmages had become, there was much the guild could not do if unsupported by the thieves and beggars.

That would be the first thing to change when she unlocked the power of the Guardian Starlight, she promised herself.

Movement from down in the chamber startled her, and Adrianna leapt up to a half-crouch, a spell already winding its way to her fingertips. She snuffed the arcane energies out when she saw Lucius stagger through the large doors on the far side of the chamber.

Running down the stairs, eager to see what he had found, Adrianna saw that he appeared uninjured but, more importantly, he clasped a rod of marble and gold in his hand. She suddenly felt the waves of magic flowing from the artefact and gasped at how deep and strong they ran. It was if the rod was the centre of the entire world and its presence could change anything it touched.

Wiping the shock off her face, Adrianna gave a smile of welcome as Lucius looked up at her.

"Safe and whole then," she said. "And you found it."

Lucius sank to his knees, breathing heavily. Wearily, he raised his hand to brandish the rod.

And then Adrianna winced as the strength left Lucius' arm and the rod fell, striking the chamber floor hard.

"Careful," she said as she grabbed him under the shoulder and helped him stand, though even she could not tell whether she was speaking of Lucius or the artefact.

Adrianna led Lucius to the foot of the stairs and helped him sit down.

"There is something wrong, Aidy," he said, beginning to recover his breath.

"What do you mean?"

Hand on his chest to steady his breathing, Lucius began to tell her what he had seen, first in the great hall below them, and then the strange dream – he could think of no other way to describe it.

When he had finished, Adrianna sat back from him, contemplating his words and studying the Guardian Starlight.

"Well, there is obviously some connection between you and the artefact," she said.

"How can that be?"

"I always said you were special!"

He looked up at her, a dour expression on his face. "Is that really the best explanation you can give me?"

"It is the best I can give you right now," she said. "However, we will have time on the way back to deliver that thing to the baron. Time enough for us to do a little testing and perhaps get you some answers. You do... still intend giving it to the baron?"

"I said I would deliver it, Adrianna, and I will."

"This is your commission, Lucius," she said, trying to placate him. "I only wanted to come here to see how elven ruins might appear, to get a sense of the magic within. You want to fulfil your obligations, that is no business of mine."

He continued to look at her, balefully. She felt obliged to continue speaking.

"If it turns out that thing has some value, I'll make a deal with the baron. I am sure I possess things he wants for himself."

"Right," Lucius said after holding her eyes for a while longer.

"So," Adrianna said as she stood, "we best get out of here. We have what you came for, and I have no wish to battle half the Vos army in trying to leave. Let's get back to the city."

As they retraced their steps down the long corridor leading out of the ruins, Adrianna's mind whirled with possibilities. Just what was the connection between Lucius and the elves? It went far deeper than just the Guardian Starlight, that had been made clear when he had been able to pass the barrier below but she had not.

That was troubling, for whatever that connection was, it would likely prove necessary in unlocking the power of the Guardian Starlight, and she was not altogether sure Lucius would be a willing participant.

One thing was clear though. She had never, in her life, seen something she wanted to possess more than that artefact.

Whatever transpired, she vowed, it would be hers.

CHAPTER FIFTEEN

THE SERGEANT STOMPED up the mud bank to Alhmanic, and the Preacher Divine did not need to see the expression on his face to sense dissent in the air.

"My Lord," the sergeant said, and Alhmanic could hear the struggle in his voice to keep his words neutral. "My men have not been trained to perform this sort of labour."

This mission had been a frustration. Even now, when they were within spitting distance of their goal, his efforts had been stymied by elven magic and a few tons of mud. Mud!

The interrogation of the Pontaine soldiers had pointed them in the right direction but Alhmanic had arrogantly assumed his divinely enchanted staff was superior to any protection a Pontaine wizard could give, and so he had marched a squad of his own men to the underground entrance of the elven outpost and ordered them to open the doors.

As it turned out, elven magic saw his arcane defences as no obstacle at all, and the sudden vaporisation of the soldiers had robbed the rest of his force of their high morale after the defeat of the Pontaine army.

He had even thought himself clever by trying to dig around the entrance, to break into some chamber beyond that point, deeper within the ruins, but despite having sunk two holes into the ground, both of which had rapidly filled with water to hamper the efforts of his men, Alhmanic had no luck. They had dug deep and had found nothing.

Alhmanic had considered it might be some cosmic joke, whereby nothing but rock lay behind those infernal doors, and the artefact he sought was nothing but a myth. More likely accursed elf magic was somehow interfering with his efforts...

Suddenly feeling old, Alhmanic leaned on his staff before he opened his eyes and looked at the sergeant.

"Sergeant," he said, "your men will do as they are instructed or they can return to Scholten and explain to the Anointed Lord herself, blessed be her wisdom, just why we failed to succeed in our mission. Especially when we are but a few yards away from the artefact we seek!

"I realise this is not what they are trained to do, but we need men to dig, and they are the only men present. They fought admirably against Pontaine earlier, but the time for fighting is now over."

"Yes, my Lord. I'll instruct the men to continue."

"Instruct them to work faster, or we'll be here come winter."

Alhmanic felt a peculiar vibration in his staff. He looked curiously at his weapon. The blue crystal mounted in its silver-clawed tip was flickering gently, like a faint candle flame caught in a breeze.

The sergeant looked quizzically at him, but Alhmanic ignored the man as he tried to recall his staff acting this way before. He could only think of it reacting to the presence of some of the relics kept in the deepest vaults of Scholten cathedral, those most precious possessions of saints long gone. Frowning, Alhmanic played a hunch and lifted his staff up high before slamming its butt down hard into the soft earth. Immediately, it almost leapt out of his hand as it strained to pull away from him, and it took a firm grip to hold it in place.

"Gather your men – quickly!" Alhmanic shouted at his sergeant.

So saying, Alhmanic stormed away from the fresh excavations, heading towards the ruins the Pontaine force had uncovered – where the staff had been pulling him. Behind him, he could hear the sergeant shouting to rouse his men but only those closest reacted fast enough to keep up with the Preacher Divine.

As he reached the top of the stairs that descended into the elven ruins, Alhmanic noted that only half a dozen of his soldiers had kept up with him.

"You two, get down there," he ordered.

They hesitated and looked at one another.

"My Lord?" one asked, as if he might have misheard.

"For God's sake, man, just go to the bottom of the stairs, you needn't go anywhere near those blasted doors!" Alhmanic roared, and his anger was enough to make them lose their inhibitions and brave the darkness.

Impatiently, Alhmanic waited, resisting the impulse to start pacing. Moments passed, and the group of soldiers around the top of the stairs began to swell as more joined them. Finally, the sergeant brought up the rear with the rest of his men. Still, there had been no sign of the two Alhmanic had dispatched down the stairs.

The sergeant walked over to Alhmanic and, in a low voice, said, "What is it, Lord? What did you sense?"

Alhmanic just shook his head as he wondered whether he should send more men down or if he should go himself.

A bright flare of green light that lit up the lower reaches of the staircase, followed quickly by a loud crack, made them all jump. Alhmanic took a few steps back and brought his staff up in front of him in a defensive stance.

The blurred, shadowy form of a man leapt from the darkness of the staircase and sprinted toward the nearest group of soldiers. There was a ringing of steel and a soldier screamed, clutching his neck as blood spurted over one of his comrades. Chaos exploded among the Vos soldiers as they drew weapons and desperately sought to find a target in the darkness. Alhmanic tried to keep his eye on the shadowy form that was wading through his soldiers, flashing blades sneaking out to bury themselves in a chest or cut through an arm, but the illusion seemed to throw his sight to one side so he could only sense the presence of something very fast and very deadly from the corner of his eye.

All around, men were screaming and dying. Alhmanic pointed his staff, quite prepared to blast chunks out of his own men if it meant silencing their attacker, when a solid blast of air erupted from the staircase and bowled him over as if he were no more than a leaf. More movement caught his eye as he fell on his back, and he immediately scrambled to all fours. The figure before him had made no effort to conceal herself.

Rising out of the staircase and into the sky, as if borne by the wind itself, a fierce looking woman gazed vengefully down on Alhmanic and his prostrate soldiers. Her dark hair, tied into a pony tail, whipped behind her head but her face was baleful, dreadfully scarred and with black eyes that seemed hungry to consume them all.

She gestured to a group of soldiers who had struggled to their feet and casually flicked her hand. The men screamed in sheer terror as they were lifted and hurled over the fence, far into the night.

Alhmanic braced himself with his staff and the movement caught the eye of the woman. She hissed at him, and punched forward with both hands.

Alhmanic did not need to be a wizard to sense the bolt of energy she had sent his way and he desperately raised his staff, crying out as the woman's spell smacked into it, the magic splintering against the spellshield.

Not waiting to see what she would do next, Alhmanic barked a single word of holy power as he pointed the staff at the woman. A bolt of energy hit her with a sound like stone splitting, and the spell flared a brilliant orange as it surrounded her. The woman fell out of sight.

With a grim smile, Alhmanic turned to search for the other attacker. He saw that a ring of soldiers had surrounded the shadowy form. Within the circle the sergeant madly parried each blade that sailed out from his blurred attacker, the clash of sword on sword ringing out clearly with every strike. He lunged once or twice, but never connected, his target just seeming to skip out of the way leaving only formless shadow behind.

Pushing through the ring of soldiers, Alhmanic resolved to end the combat quickly. He stamped his staff into the ground with another word of power and the earth rippled outwards, sending the sergeant reeling.

The sergeant looked up at him accusingly, but Alhmanic ignored him, his attention instead on the attacker. As had he hoped, the staff's earthshaking power had broken the shadowy spell of concealment, and the man sprawled on the floor.

Dressed in dark leathers with a grey cloak, the man was close to middle age and bore a sword in his right hand and a long, wickedly sharp dagger in his left. His expression was one of almost comical surprise, but Alhmanic's gaze was drawn to the object tucked into the man's belt, a short rod capped with golden wings.

Not bothering to think about how this man had succeeded where he had – so far – failed, Alhmanic did not hesitate. He strode purposefully forward, raised his staff and drove the butt down into the man's face. However, the man's reactions proved equal to Alhmanic's, and he threw himself to one side before kicking out with a boot.

The heel connected with Alhmanic's knee, and he grunted in pain as he sank down to the ground. His attacker was already up and circling him, looking for an opening through which to drive a blade and end Alhmanic's life.

Growling, as much in rage as pain, Alhmanic swung wildly with his staff, forcing the man to keep his distance.

"Get him, you bloody fools!" Alhmanic shouted to the soldiers who still ringed them.

That seemed to jerk them back to awareness and, as one, they levelled their spears and swords and took a pace inwards, drawing the ring tighter.

The man flicked a hand towards Alhmanic. A jet of flame erupted from his open palm, forcing Alhmanic to dive to the ground again to avoid having his face burned off. He looked up in time to see the man crouch briefly before leaping up with incredible agility, somersaulting through the air, over the heads of the soldiers.

One proved quicker than the rest, and a spear was thrust upwards, catching the flying man in the torso. Alhmanic grinned as he saw the escape curtailed, and the man fell to the ground a short distance away. Several soldiers started to move towards the fallen man, but Alhmanic got back on to his feet and pushed past them all, wanting to deliver the final blow and claim his prize at long last.

Groaning and spitting blood, the man was clearly hurt, and Alhmanic summoned his will, focussing the power of the staff.

Before the spell could be unleashed, there was another rush of air and the earth exploded around him, great clods of mud and rock thrown into the air as something very heavy and very dense smacked into it. Alhmanic stumbled under the assault, and he turned to see, floating high in the air behind him, the dark woman, her face a perfect picture of hate and vengeance.

She snarled as she reached up and seemed to grasp the air above her head with her right hand. Then she cast forward, as though throwing a stone. She repeated the gesture with her left hand, then back to her right, over and over.

The effect was devastating. With each gesture, a bolt of invisible energy struck the earth, felling soldiers and raising small craters. One soldier fell next to Alhmanic and, as he tried to regain his footing, another blast caught him squarely in the chest, shattering his ribs and hammering him to a bloody pulp. He did not even have time to scream.

Alhmanic crawled away, desperate to escape, knowing he could not repel spells of that magnitude – not forever. One would finally get past his defences, and that would be the end of him.

As quickly as it had started, the magical assault ceased, and Alhmanic looked back to see the woman floating gently to the ground, her eyes fixed firmly on him. For the first time in a very, very long time, Alhmanic felt true fear grip his stomach in an icy clasp.

He stood, bracing himself with his staff and taking assurance from its solid construction, as the woman walked towards him.

"The Preacher Divine," she said softly. "This will be a distinct pleasure."

"Who are you, lady?"

"Your death!"

She raised her hands to summon another spell, and Alhmanic matched the movement with his own staff, hoping to deflect whatever arcane energies were thrown at him.

A sudden cry and rush of movement diverted the attention of them both, and Alhmanic felt his mouth open in surprise as he saw his sergeant rushing the woman, sword drawn and with three men behind him. He also saw the contempt on the woman's face as she prepared to redirect her spell to wipe the sergeant and his men off the face of the earth. Seeing his opportunity, Alhmanic shouted a word of prayer as he extended his staff and unleashed an explosive bolt of magical power.

The spell was a powerful one, and Alhmanic felt his staff grow cold and weak in his hands as it expended its reserve of energy. The rolling ball of fire that struck the woman exploded to engulf both her and the sergeant.

Alhmanic did not wait to see more. He turned, and ran.

THERE WAS NO sun at dawn, just a lightening of the usual grey, cloud-bearing skies. They revealed a sight of devastation. Bodies were strewn everywhere, and had already begun to attract carrion birds who circled under the grey clouds. Craters of all sizes had been cast in vast swathes across the area. It was carnage. But Alhmanic alone had survived, no doubt another sign of the divine providence that guided his life.

Alhmanic had retreated into the darkness outside the camp, and he lay still as he heard his men dying, sliced apart by the man of shadows or blasted by the spells of the dark woman.

He felt no shame in this. His mission was of importance to the Anointed Lord, may her valour shine across the world, and, as he was obviously the only one who could fulfil it, his survival was paramount.

The deaths of his men did present certain problems, however. There was little chance he could retrieve the artefact from those... thieves without an army at his back. As they already had the artefact in their possession and were gaining a lead that was extending even now, due to the horses they had stolen after the battle, he could not return to Scholten to pick up more soldiers.

Especially as Klaus would be there to witness his lack of success.

No, this would take a great deal of thought and cunning.

At least he still had his staff and, after its extended use that night, it had just begun to regain its energies. Even now, it quietly hummed in his hands, reacting to the presence of the elven artefact in the surface world. That meant he could track it, pursue the thieves and visit vengeance upon them for their intervention in his affairs.

Just who were they, though? Agents of Pontaine? That seemed possible, as the staff felt as though it wanted to pull him south, and Turnitia – curse that city – was the only settlement of any real note in that direction.

Were they Shadowmages, he wondered. If so, that raised a lot more questions than it answered.

Sighing, he got back to his feet and started looking for a horse, hoping to find one that had not stampeded right across the Anclas Territories in terror during the battle.

He could not fail, Alhmanic told himself. That could not be permitted. The Anointed Lord, praise be to the light she brings, had put her trust in him and he desperately needed to prove he was not to be found wanting.

The consequences for failing in that duty were likely to be dire in the extreme.

CHAPTER SIXTEEN

GRIPPING HIS SIDE as another ache of pain washed over him, Lucius found himself coming to truly hate the Anclas Territories. Their route back to Turnitia saw them pass the same miserable hamlets, the same derelict farms and face the same relentless rain.

It had not been helped by the wound he had taken at the elven ruins, a savage spear thrust that had torn open the side of his leather jerkin and grazed a couple of ribs. The cut had been shallow enough but had bled profusely until Adrianna had helped him bind it. She had not been gentle, and he still winced when he remembered her pulling the dressing across his chest.

She had now taken to riding to one side and a little behind him, out of sight unless he turned round, and this had begun to prey on his mind in the days since they had fought the Vos soldiers. Lucius had to admit that she had probably saved his life after he had been surrounded and faced the Preacher Divine, but he had seen the look on her face as she tore apart their force, the hatred and pure exaltation as the magic flowed through her. That was the old Adrianna he had seen for a moment there, the one who had killed so many people and destroyed a sizeable portion of Turnitia.

He could only hope such fury was reserved for those born in the Vos Empire.

Time had been wasted at the site of the ruins while Adrianna scoured the area for the Preacher Divine as dawn threatened to break. Neither of them had seen him since their last confrontation and both were convinced he still lived. Which meant he could still cause trouble for them.

"We should detour," Adrianna said. "I know some places where we can stay, completely undisturbed."

Lucius knew where this was going. Every evening during their journey home to Turnitia, Adrianna had quizzed him on the Guardian Starlight and had cast various spells in an attempt to crack its secrets. Though she had tried to hide it, he guessed she had learned nothing more about the artefact, and that had frustrated her hugely.

A frustrated Adrianna was not his ideal travelling companion, so he tried a little levity.

"Our guilds won't last long without us," Lucius said. "We should get back and see if either of us still have a guildhouse standing."

"The Anointed Lord take the guilds. You know we have more important things to do."

"We've already agreed. This rod goes back to the baron, to fulfil my commission. What happens to it after that is up to you two. As you said, he is likely to negotiate."

Lucius did not think that was true, not for an elven artefact the baron had gone to a lot of trouble to secure, but anything that kept Adrianna's attention on the future rather than on him right now had to be a good thing.

"We still have a few evenings before we get back to the city," he said when she did not respond. "Plenty of time for you to examine it."

It then occurred to him that Adrianna had not actually touched the Guardian Starlight yet, seeming to have been content to leave it in Lucius' possession. Why, he could not say.

Throughout the long afternoon, they travelled across the wet landscape in silence, and the worries Lucius had began to multiply. He had always intended to hand over the artefact to the baron as he had promised. The favours to the thieves' guild were substantial and, more than that, he wanted the prestige, the reputation that came from having unearthed such a treasure.

Now he began to wonder whether he should not just hand it over to Adrianna. In the short term, certainly, it would be the safe thing to do in terms of his own personal safety. He might even make some sort of ally out of her, and he thought back to the times when he could work alongside the Shadowmage without being in constant fear for his own life. That seemed so long ago.

There were two problems with that course of action, three if you counted the fact that Lucius would never feel safe around Adrianna, no matter what favours he did for her. She had always treated him as a witless fool, and he saw no reason that would change any time soon.

First, he had precious few ideas what the Guardian Starlight was capable of, only that it obviously contained some very deep magics. If Adrianna, already the most powerful Shadowmage in Turnitia, managed to unlock those secrets, she might literally be capable of anything. That was a deeply troubling thought.

The second was getting to be a greater issue. As soon as he had seen the Guardian Starlight, Lucius had faced the deep-rooted feeling that it was his – as in, it actually belonged to him, personally.

As they had ridden away from the ruins, that feeling had grown ever stronger, day by day, hour by hour.

Lucius no longer knew whether he could give it up, even if he wanted to.

EYES CLOSED, ADRIANNA lay on her side, her head leaning on a balled fist. Ignoring the grunts of pain from Lucius as he redressed his wound and the sound of faint raindrops pattering on their simple canvas shelter, her mind was wide open as she felt the raw power of the Guardian Starlight.

It was a puzzle, a true conundrum, and she found herself revelling in it. So far it had resisted all her attempts to break into its mysteries but once she got it back to her guild, the combined might of all her Shadowmages would surely pry it open. For now, she found herself content to simply float upon the arcane power that washed over her like gentle waves lapping at the shore of a quiet lake.

The Guardian Starlight was also having an effect on Lucius, she could see. Up to now, he had been decisive in his intentions to hand it over to the baron as he had promised, but she could now tell he was beginning to see this might be a waste. That would play into her hands, for there was no way he could hope to learn more about the artefact without her help. In time, he would *have* to come to her.

That opened more questions about Lucius himself, of course. The Guardian Starlight was inert in her magical caress, but it positively overflowed with energy whenever Lucius reached down to his belt and touched it. Just what was the connection there? Neither she nor that fool of a Pontaine wizard, or the Preacher Divine for that matter, had been able to enter the elven ruins to retrieve the artefact, but Lucius had walked into them as if he had been all but invited.

Her old tutor, Forbeck, had seen something special in Lucius and as time went by, despite her initial contempt, she had begun to see it in him too. There was something in the way that magic reacted to Lucius that was beyond her understanding. No one could master all fields of magic, but Lucius seemed able, the only practitioner she had ever *heard* of to do so, let alone actually seen. He lacked her dedication, ambition and sheer mastery of sorcery, but she had come to believe he could be truly great, if only he applied himself.

That he wasted this gift by concentrating on his feckless thieves rather than the pure pursuit of magic made it all the more infuriating.

Was that an answer though? Was Lucius some new breed of mage, maybe an evolution of the Shadowmage? Was he the future all mages should aspire to?

No, it was more subtle than that. Assuming there was a connection between Lucius' use of magic and the Guardian Starlight, of course.

But what?

Little was known of elven wizards and how they practised magic, but few of their relics surviving to this age spoke of divisions in magic or of the need to specialise in spells that affected nature, fire, battle, or death. It had always been presumed that elven magic was so mighty that its practitioners had no need to split it up – they could naturally fashion any part of magic to any use they demanded.

Suppose there had been a change in magic though. It might be a flight of fancy, but suppose that elven mages could cast any spell they wished, just like Lucius could. Lucius was also able to enter the elven ruins, he had a dream about elves, and now he seemed to be able to unlock an elven artefact that closed itself off to her.

Was that an answer? Was this link Lucius had directed toward the elves, and not a certain type of magic?

If so, what did that mean?

"I know you are not asleep," Adrianna said as she heard Lucius stir.

For a moment, he did not answer.

"I was getting very close to it until then," he said at last.

"Let me see the artefact again. I've had some more ideas."

"Please, Adrianna, I hurt all over and I am very tired."

"I think I am on to something," she said, a little testily.

Sighing, Lucius rolled over to face her.

"I've been doing some thinking of my own," he said.

"Oh?"

"I can see that you have not had a great deal of luck in your poking and prodding of this thing," he said, as he placed a hand on the Guardian Starlight. In her mind's eye, she saw its power flare briefly at his touch.

"And what would you know about it?"

"I know a lot more than you give me credit for, Adrianna. I can feel what you are trying to do with it, and I can feel it retreating away from you. It doesn't do that with me. Do you know why?"

"Do *you?*"

He shrugged. "I'm... feeling it grow with me. It is difficult to explain. Somehow, I am feeling more and more in tune with this thing – it is almost as if I was meant to have it."

"What, you think God has miracled that artefact to you?"

"No, it isn't God," he said, and Adrianna did not like the way he was so certain of that. Did he know more about his connection to all things elven than he was letting on? "But there is something there, and I am beginning to think that I might do better if I tried to... understand this thing without any help."

"You think you can do this without me? You think you can do anything without me? You would be dead now, lying in a pool of your own blood while Vos soldiers pissed on your corpse, if it weren't for me.

"Everything you have achieved is a direct result of what you have learned from me, and you damn well better start remembering that," she said, beginning to feel the old fury building up. "And now you want to cut me out, when what I have been after for so long is so close? Damn you, Lucius, I won't permit it, you hear me? Never!"

"And I thought you were just coming along to experience the great elven ruins," he said. "You knew exactly what we would find in there, didn't you? What, you thought I would be too slow-witted to figure that out?"

Adrianna's fist smashed into Lucius' jaw with enough power to send him reeling backwards.

"You idiot!" she shouted as he staggered away, rubbing his face. "You think there is anything that enters your mind that has not crossed mine first? You wanted to keep things civil between us, and I was happy enough to enter that fiction if it meant getting my hands on the Guardian Starlight. If you want to dispense with that, I am more than happy to comply."

So saying, she wreathed herself in magic and the air began to whip round her, circulating ever faster. Adrianna floated a few feet above the ground. She flexed her arms, opening and closing her fists, feeling the surge of arcane energy.

Lucius looked up at her, eyes wide in terror.

"God, Adrianna, I don't want to fight you!" he shouted above the sound of the wind.

Adrianna gradually let the magic ebb out of her control and, slowly, came down to earth.

"Look, we can work together," Lucius said, almost tripping over his own words as he spoke fast. "Maybe I cannot get this thing working without you. I just think that you won't get far without me either."

"You may not be entirely wrong in that assertion," she said, all trace of rage and malice gone from her voice.

"But look, I really am in some considerable pain at the moment," he said, holding his side. "Let's sleep on it, eh? We can start work on the artefact tomorrow."

"You no longer wish to take it back to the baron?" she asked.

He took a breath as he considered this, then firmly nodded his head.

"I think that might be a foolish move. We will do more good with it than he ever would."

"Alright then. It is agreed."

As Adrianna lay on her back, eyes closed, she could not help smiling to herself. That Lucius was a key to unlocking the Guardian Starlight was very likely. However, she had seen his face during that brief confrontation. He truly was frightened of her.

A frightened Lucius would prove to be exceptionally pliable in the days to come. She was now so close to ultimate arcane power, she could feel it. Her dreams that night were going to be good ones.

LYING PERFECTLY STILL, Lucius concentrated on his breathing, keeping it slow and steady. His senses were alert as he strained to hear every rustle of Adrianna's movements. When her breathing started to slow, still he waited. He waited until the embers of their fire had been completely drowned by the drizzle of rain, and then he waited some more.

Not until he was absolutely sure Adrianna was asleep did he begin to move.

Rolling over slowly onto his stomach, Lucius took a deep breath as he thought back to his argument with Adrianna, and remembered the look in her eyes as she had called upon her magic. At that moment, he had seen the old Adrianna, the one that had destroyed so much of his city. He had never been so scared as he was right then.

This had sealed his decision to escape. He did not know how far he would get or how long he could evade her grasp, but he knew beyond all doubt he had to get away. The Guardian Starlight had driven Adrianna's lust for magical power beyond all reason, and he saw nothing but madness or death – probably both – if he stayed with her.

Lucius crawled out of the tent, inch by inch, in perfect silence. He could have used shadow magic to cloak his movements but he dared not. Any use of magic on his part might be felt by Adrianna and be enough to rouse her from sleep.

Lucius had decided the very best place for the Guardian Starlight was in the baron's possession. Let the baron and Adrianna fight one another for mastery of it. So long as they kept far away from him, he could live with the results.

Getting to his feet, Lucius risked a glance at Adrianna. She had rolled over so her back was to him, oblivious to his presence as she dreamed whatever a mad guildmaster of Shadowmages dreamed of.

Placing one foot gently in front of the other, Lucius made his way out of the camp, feeling as though any moment he would hear Adrianna's voice behind him, shortly before feeling one of her spells smash him apart.

He made his way gingerly to where they had staked their horses. Placing his hand on the side of his mount's head, he whispered, so very quietly, to keep the creature calm. Bending down, he untied its reins from the stake and, after glancing at Adrianna's horse for a moment, untied it too.

Leading the horses away from the camp, Lucius prayed to the heavens that their heavy feet would be muffled by the soft ground. It was not until the camp had been swallowed by the darkness behind them that Lucius finally mounted his horse and, leading the second, started trotting away into the wilderness. It was not long before he was at full gallop, putting as many miles as he could between Adrianna and himself

Adrianna's horse constantly pulled at its reins, wanting to be given the freedom to run without his direction, but he kept firm control of it. And, closing his eyes for a second, Lucius manipulated the threads of magic he saw in his mind's eye to fuel the muscles of the horses. They both started slobbering foam as the energy surged into them, allowing them to gallop ever faster.

Holding on tightly, knowing his life depended on the speed of the horses, Lucius knew it was likely that the magic, combined with his own weight, would explode the hearts of both mounts.

He could only hope that he reached the city before that happened.

DAWN AWOKE ADRIANNA and she flexed her muscles before reaching out with her mind to feel the familiar pull of magic about her. Opening her eyes, she rolled out of the tent and stood to stretch, eager, as she had been for the past few days to get out of the Anclas Territories and back to civilisation.

She looked down and saw Lucius' sleeping mat was empty. Her brief puzzlement was punctured a second later by deep suspicion. Looking round at the surrounding grasslands, she saw no sign of Lucius. She then realised there was also no sign of the horses.

She delayed the onset of anger and frustration long enough to close her eyes and reach out to feel the passing of magic in the area. Tilting her head to one side in concentration, she reached further and further out until she eventually found what she was looking for.

The unmistakable aura of the Guardian Starlight was many miles south of her and moving quickly.

Raw fury erupted then. Adrianna howled in rage at the sky. Maddened, she quickly fashioned hard bolts of dark power and flung them downwards, tearing the camp apart in a cataclysm of naked arcane power.

Closing her eyes against the oncoming wind, her hair streaming out behind her, Adrianna soared above the earth, a dark shape in the sky that moved like a diving falcon with terrible purpose. After a few minutes, she cursed as she felt her grip on the spell begin to weaken as the energies dissipated. She ordered them to carry her safely to the ground before they vanished altogether.

Standing on a low hill, Adrianna panted as she tried to regain her strength.

Lucius had the horses, and she had her magic. She was much, much faster than he, but Lucius did not need to constantly stop and rest, not if he was willing to ride his horses into the ground.

It was obvious that he would go to Turnitia – where else could the fool run to? Whether she caught him in the Territories or within the city made little difference to Adrianna. All she could think about was the price she would exact from the trumped-up little thief for his betrayal.

CHAPTER SEVENTEEN

REACHING OUT ACROSS the table, Tellmore adjusted one of his prisms, altering the pattern of light that dispersed though it. Concentrating for a moment, he subtly turned the flow of magic through his spell and the coruscating ball of green light sparked yellow flares briefly.

His mind was focussed solely on the spell of scrying, utterly ignorant of the baron standing, watching intently, behind him, of the cold, wet dungeon cell they were performing this rite within. The baron had thought it amusing that Tellmore insisted on casting such spells within the foundations of the Citadel, as if the magic required a dank and gloomy place; it suited his sense of theatrics.

In truth, Tellmore had selected the place purely because it was quiet. Few ever ventured down here, not since Turnitia had fallen to Pontaine.

Before Tellmore, the table was strewn with a complicated arrangement of finely cut glass prisms, each reflecting and refracting the fierce green light generated by the physical manifestation of his spell. Immediately before him, a map of the peninsula provided him with a reference point.

Stretching out with his mind, Tellmore focused the magic upon his target, riding the arcane flow as it twisted across the land. Few wizards had the concentration, willpower or stamina for such a long-ranged scrying and both he and the baron knew the latter was getting his money's worth.

A small ripple in the fabric of magic caught Tellmore's attention, and his mind descended to a point that shone as bright as the sun.

"It has been uncovered," he said.

"Lucius succeeded?"

"Yes, it is Lucius who bears the Guardian Starlight. He is coming back to us now – he is travelling fast. Very fast."

"Eager to claim his rewards, no doubt."

"No… he is being pursued."

"Who by?"

"A terrible force. Angry. Powerful."

"Some elven demon he woke?"

"Another Shadowmage."

"Adrianna. I knew I could not trust her. Will he make it?"

"Yes… Yes, I think he will get here before she catches him."

The baron started pacing. "We better prepare a welcome – for both of them. We can keep Lucius in the Citadel, even a Shadowmage like her cannot breach these walls.

"It is time to put my plans into action, my good Tellmore. You have done well, indeed, and soon this Guardian Starlight will be in our possession. Everything is coming together as I had hoped."

Tellmore stood up from his chair and coughed.

"My Baron, I must caution you. An artefact like the Guardian Starlight is powerful, to be sure, but its mysteries may not be cracked easily, or quickly. It may be weeks, possibly months, before I am able to utilise it."

"You worry too much, Tellmore. It will take time to amass my army, and we cannot waste a single day. Now we know the artefact is on its way to us, we can start taking steps."

"My Baron–"

"Leave the strategy to me, good Tellmore. I'll leave the magic to you."

His smile was gracious as he turned to leave, but Tellmore had heard a note of steel in his tone. As the baron disappeared down the dark corridors of the dungeon, Tellmore heard him call out for messengers.

There was still much preparation to accomplish to receive the Guardian Starlight. Tellmore was mystified. When the baron said they had to start moving now, surely he did not mean right now? A little dazed, Tellmore left his scrying equipment and the dungeon cell to follow the baron.

THANKS TO SERVANTS who had sprinted through the corridors of the Citadel, the messengers of Fournier, de Biot, Fremont and the others, stationed here since their masters had left for their own fortresses, were waiting in the main hall. As the baron entered at a brisk pace, they stopped lounging behind the long tables and stood in line, bowing low.

Nodding once to acknowledge them, the baron climbed the grand staircase a few steps, and looked down upon them. He glanced across the hall as Tellmore entered, and waved impatiently for the wizard to join him.

"My compliments to your lords," the baron began, his voice echoing across the hall. "You are to depart immediately. Tell your masters our time is finally here. The artefact is with us.

"I humbly request their presence, and that of their armies and allies, to fulfil the next, glorious stage of our design. I bid you Godspeed on your journeys home."

Bowing, the messengers turned and trotted out of the hall. De Sousse smiled. Within minutes, they would be on their horses and riding hard to rejoin Count Fournier and the rest of his little cabal. A few short days thereafter, Pontaine knights, men-at-arms and militia would be heading towards Turnitia, a force so large as to be unstoppable. Turning to leave the hall, de Sousse noticed the worried look on Tellmore's face.

"Okay, Tellmore, out with it. What's wrong?"

"My Lord Baron, as you please."

"Oh, get on with it, man!"

"I feel you are moving prematurely. I am not sure I have impressed upon you just how difficult – and thus time-consuming – activating the Guardian Starlight may be. And even then, we still don't know the real effects of the artefact. You may have to adjust your plans to fit in with what it can actually do."

"Tellmore, Tellmore, Tellmore," the baron said, putting his arm around the wizard. "My respect for your magical knowledge and abilities is boundless, it really is. But strategy is my skill, remember? You think just any baron of Pontaine could choose the perfect time to march into this city and take it from under the noses of the Vos Empire? I know what I am doing!"

"Granted, my Baron, but your plan hinges on using the Guardian Starlight, does it not?"

"One plan does, certainly."

"One plan?"

"Did you learn nothing about me in the Anclas Territories? I do try so very, very hard not to rely on just one shot of the bow."

Tellmore looked a little crestfallen. "Is my Baron beginning to lose confidence in my work? After all, you sent Lucius after me."

"I swear I am talking to myself at times. Were you not listening earlier? I have the utmost confidence in your work. Believe me, I would not pay the gold I do if I did not!"

"Then...'

"I also know how difficult magic can be, Tellmore. I may not know all the ins and outs, I may not be any sort of practitioner myself, but I have eyes, and I have seen magic is a complicated thing that does not always obey the wishes of its masters. That is just the nature of the beast."

"So you always had another plan in case there was a problem with the Guardian Starlight?"

"Now you are catching on! Yes, Tellmore, I have another plan working in the background.

"And this plan has come to fruition?"

"Political bridges, Tellmore, alliances – that's the key."

Tellmore frowned. "I don't follow, my Baron."

"Court Fournier was always the core of my design. If I could bring him over to my way of thinking, I figured it would be much easier to get the visiting barons to come with him. However, the noble families of Pontaine create a vast network, Tellmore. Vast. If you start tugging on one string, others will move as well."

"And with the strings of the count and barons, you could tug several at once?"

De Sousse smiled. "You follow the metaphor, that's a good sign! Yes, with the right word in the right ear, it became inevitable that more families would throw their lot in with us, especially with the prize on offer – the fall of the Vos Empire. The Knights of Angue have pledged their allegiance to our cause, along with the Verte Rangers. Count Fournier has persuaded Baron du Fillimont to levy a new militia from the towns along the Sardenne, bringing another two thousand spears to the army."

"That's... clever, my Baron."

"Not yet it isn't – but it will be! You see, the tugging does not stop there. Our invasion of Vos territory will be another tug on the web of Pontaine noble families, and a few more will join us. Give them a victory, and yet more will follow. We keep tugging, and gradually we will pull the whole weight of Pontaine behind us. Vos will not be able to stand!"

"So the Guardian Starlight is, what, no longer needed?"

"Of course it is! It is another tug on that web, Tellmore, and a bloody big one too."

"How so?"

"It becomes like a banner. An outward sign that the path we are on is irresistible destiny. We will persuade any dissenters that our way is the only way for Pontaine. Even if the artefact does not work, even if we cannot figure out how to use it, it still has great value. We have a powerful elven artefact in our possession! Few are going to argue against that."

"And no doubt the Guardian Starlight will be of use in the later stages of the war you are planning, or perhaps when the war is done and you need its magic to rule."

"Just so."

"It just seems you are moving too far, too soon and too quickly, my Baron. Things threaten to spin out of control."

"For heaven's sake, Tellmore," the baron said. "Please remind me, are you growing into an old man or an old woman?"

Lowering his head, Tellmore did not answer. The baron looked at him for a while, then sighed.

"I know your concerns, and I have taken note. However, a bit of chaos, a bit of disruption to the old order is exactly what is needed right now.

"It is our time at last, Tellmore. Do try to find it within yourself to enjoy it."

CHAPTER EIGHTEEN

LUCIUS ARRIVED BACK in the city in late afternoon, and Turnitia bustled as it always did at this time, with merchants and craftsmen pursuing their trades, even as beggars and thieves chased theirs. Resolved to hand over the Guardian Starlight to the baron as agreed, he nonetheless wanted to see what had been happening in the city since his departure. The baron had waited this long for the artefact, a few hours more would not hurt him.

Presuming his guildhouse would be watched by the baron's men, he stuck to the alleyways of the city, only venturing out when he could hide in a large crowd, outside a general store that had just received a new shipment of goods from the far side of Pontaine, or surrounding a troupe of street performers. It was on the outskirts of one of these crowds he found what he was looking for.

An aged woman, crippled by long years on the streets, tightened her ragged beige shawl as he approached. Looking up at him with an age-creased face, she revealed large gaps in her teeth as she smiled and raised a ceramic bowl.

"Copper for an old lady, good sir?"

"You know who I am?" he asked.

"A generous soul is what I am hoping, good sir."

"I need to speak to Grennar, immediately."

"Oh, I am not sure I know any Grennar, not round these parts," the woman said, and pointedly slid her bowl along the ground towards him.

Lucius fished in his belt pouch and threw two coins into the bowl.

"So, where can I find her?"

"Find who, dearee?" the woman said, cupping a hand to an ear. "You'll have to forgive me, quite deaf you know."

Lucius sighed in exasperation, and reached into his pouch to deposit another two coins into her bowl.

"Ah, you mean young Grennar. Ring Street, near the second market. Look for a path next to the cobblers. You'll find her there."

Nodding his gratitude, Lucius stood and made his way to Ring Street, using the crowds and alleyways to veil his journey.

Nearing Ring Street, he sighted the cobblers the beggar woman had described, and headed down a narrow alley next to it. There, among a dozen discarded wooden crates stacked against the wall of the cobblers' place, he found Grennar.

Wearing a thin smock that had seen better days, her exposed skin was covered in muck and filth. Surrounding her were more beggars, of all ages, equally filthy.

"We need to talk," Grennar said, pre-empting Lucius. "Leave us, all of you." And with that, her street comrades scattered. "You have been away a little longer than I expected," she said, turning to Lucius.

"Complications."

"Isn't that always the way?" She swept dirt off an upturned crate next to her and gestured for Lucius to sit. "If such things were easy, of course, everyone would be doing them."

"So I keep telling myself."

"Were you successful?"

Lucius drew back his cloak so that Grennar could see the Guardian Starlight. She gave a low whistle.

"Looks pretty. I hope it is worth the trouble it will bring you."

"What have you heard?"

"I am not certain the baron has been entirely straight with you."

"You mean he intends to renege on our deal?"

"Oh, I am sure he will fulfil whatever concessions you asked of him."

"Then what?"

"Our glorious baron has been receiving visitors of high rank for quite some time now. At first, we thought it had little to do with us, presuming it was merely an extension of Pontaine politics.

"But when you consider the large orders that have been placed and paid for with the city's weapons and armoursmiths, the tanners and bowyers, it becomes clear what is happening. More men-at-arms are arriving from his estate in Pontaine – large numbers of them. We estimate his military force here in Turnitia has doubled and is still growing."

"An army? You think this is leading to a new war with Vos?"

Grennar nodded. "And your artefact there is a central part of their plan."

"Great, so I deliver my commission, and it sets off a war between Pontaine and Vos!"

"I don't believe it is quite as easy as that. Vos and Pontaine have been spoiling for war ever since the day the last one ended."

"It will still aid their course, though."

"Possession of an artefact of great and ancient magical power likely tipped the baron towards this course of action, yes."

For a long moment, Lucius just sat on the battered crate within the dirty alley. Finally he stood and turned to face her.

"Grennar... I must go."

"What are you going to do?"

"I don't know yet. I... don't know."

"Lucius... Where is Adrianna?"

"I left her in the Territories."

"You mean you ran from her?"

"Yes. This thing, so close to her," he said, touching his belt, "it was driving her mad. She was becoming dangerous again."

"Like before?"

"Just like before."

"By the heavens, Lucius. She will tear this city apart trying to find you."

"I can feel her approaching, even now."

"For what it is worth, I am sorry, Grennar. Thank you, though. Thank you for everything you have done for me."

With that, he turned and walked away, not even seeing the beggars at the end of the alley as he pushed past them. He thought furiously as he walked through the back streets of the city.

Above all else, he wanted things to be simple again. Why did everything these days have to get complicated?

He cursed. He was feeling sorry for himself, and that was not going to help anyone. Even if it did feel like the weight of the whole city was now on his shoulders. He had a nasty thought that the decision he was about to make had been decided before he had even returned to the city.

His own professional pride aside, it felt like Pontaine was about to open a door it would find very hard to close again. The last war had almost broken both nations, and it had not just been the people of the Anclas Territories that had paid the price. Turnitia had always been pivotal between Vos and Pontaine. The latter was now ascendant, though the city had prospered under its fairer rule. But what would be the cost when war arrived? Any response from Vos could easily devastate the city and break everything that had been achieved in the past few months. That included the work he had done, building the thieves' guild into something he was surprised to find he was quite proud of.

That was odd. He had never really wanted the power or responsibility of guildmastery, and he had certainly not actively sought it. As Lucius looked back at his time in Turnitia, it seemed remarkable that the choices he had made just seemed to follow a natural conclusion to him being a master of thieves.

What was even stranger was that he might enjoy the position. For all its irritations, the guild posed him not only suitable challenges but also great compensations. Though he rarely gave the matter much thought, he had become a very wealthy man.

Then there was Adrianna. Grennar had been right when she said the Shadowmage would tear the city apart to find him and the Guardian Starlight.

He did briefly consider handing the Guardian Starlight over to the baron as he had planned, and letting him fight Adrianna for it. It was almost a very neat ploy, getting both sides to destroy one another. The end result would be a shattered Pontaine force that had its energy spent before it could even consider starting another war, and a Shadowmage that might be... what? Killed?

As much as he hated the thought of Adrianna dead, if it were a choice between that and everyone else in the city, then what kind of choice was it anyway?

However, this was all foolish thinking. Even if Adrianna attacked the baron, one of them would survive, and they would have the Guardian Starlight in their possession. At that point, either the war would start or Adrianna, if she were the survivor, would begin whatever reign of terror she was planning.

And so it came back to this. The decision that had already been made, and Lucius felt his heart grow heavy as he finally accepted what had to be done.

Even as he had entered Turnitia, Lucius had felt somewhere in the back of his mind that it was for the last time. With Pontaine on one side and Adrianna on the other, he had no choice but to keep on running. It was likely they would catch up with him, in some other city or in the wilderness, catch him and kill him to take the Guardian Starlight. Maybe, though, he would discover how to wield the artefact, unlock its secrets and make it work for him. Perhaps it would allow him to hide safely away from Adrianna and anyone in Pontaine with thoughts of war.

When he had first returned to Turnitia, long before he became guildmaster of thieves, Adrianna had accused him of always running from his problems. Now, he was running again. This time, however, he was sure it was the right thing to do.

There was just one thing to attend to before he left.

Veering his path towards the heavier crowds in the commercial areas of the city, Lucius studied the people intently. It did not take him long to find what he was looking for.

Three children of perhaps ten or eleven years old were working a crowd that had been stirred together by the presence of a street pedlar offering bottles of miracle cures that she guaranteed would heal any ailment. The woman bravely endured the jeers and heckles of disbelief, and continued her patter, slowly bringing some of those listening to her way of thinking. She was good, Lucius could tell, but it was the children he was after.

They were in the classic three-pronged position he had learned when he first joined the guild, winding their way from different directions among the crowd. The tallest boy among them was the distraction, while a freckled lad would grab a purse. Then, a red-haired boy hanging at the entrance of a side street was the runner, who would spirit away their ill-gotten gains. That was the one he could use now.

The youth gave him a disparaging look that said "go away" as Lucius approached, until recognition dawned.

"Guildmaster," the boy said, attempting something of a bow crossed with a curtsey.

"Go back to the guildhouse, boy, and find Wendric. You understand?"

Though confused at the sudden appearance of his boss, the boy nodded.

"Tell him to meet me at the eastern gate with all speed. Tell him 'gold over blood', use those exact words, clear?"

"Gold over blood." The boy nodded as he repeated the words.

"Go now," Lucius urged. "Run!"

The boy disappeared into the side street with an impressive turn of speed.

Waiting among the wealthier townhouses that lined the

thoroughfare leading to the eastern gate of the city, Lucius saw Wendric approach and intercepted him before he walked into line of sight with the men-at-arms manning the gatehouse. He did not expect them to give him any trouble in this part of the city, but caution was over-riding everything now.

"Gold over blood?" Wendric asked. He looked rattled that Lucius had used the pre-arranged phrase. "What the hell is going on, Lucius?"

"I can't explain fully – and believe me that is for your own safety as much as mine – but you have to listen carefully and do what I tell you."

"You are in trouble."

Lucius nodded. "The worst possible kind."

"Alright, we can work through this. What do you need from me?"

"You are not going to like it. I want you to take over the running of the guild."

Wendric shrugged. "That is never a problem, you know that. Believe it or not, the guildhouse *is* still standing since your last departure."

"No. I mean I want you to take over the guild. Permanently."

"That is not funny, Lucius."

"I am really not joking, Wendric. I know you are content with the position of lieutenant, and I can sympathise with that. I never really wanted to be guildmaster either, but there is no one else I can trust to look after the thieves. It has to be you."

"God's teeth, Lucius, this is a hell of a thing to just land on me."

"For that, I apologise, but I have no other choice. I'm leaving the city, and I don't ever expect to come back."

"Hold on there. Just what kind of trouble are you in?"

"I told you, the worst kind." Lucius sighed. "I can't tell you what is going on, only that it has nothing to do with guild activities and any trouble it brings you will be minor and easily handled. The guild is not the target. It will just be me."

"Can you tell me where you are going?"

"Absolutely not. As I said, I do not expect to be able to return here. Ever. This will be the last time you see me, Wendric."

"Well… at least let me help you in some way. You have provisions? Travelling gear?"

"I have everything I need. I'll steal a horse from the gatehouse stables. I really need nothing more – except the knowledge that my thieves will be looked after."

"I'll keep them safe, Lucius. You've trained them well, the guild almost runs itself these days."

They stared at one another for a moment, both having run out of words. It was Wendric that broke the silence.

"You really cannot tell me anything?"

"Not about what is happening right now. I can tell you that war is coming between Vos and Pontaine, and that it will probably be bad for the city. But Grennar can fill you in on that."

Wendric paled at that news, and looked as though he was going to be sick.

"I am very sorry to see you go, Lucius," Wendric said when he found his voice. "We've had... good times since you were in charge."

"You know what they say – all good things come to an end."

"Never thought I would see the day. You look after yourself, Lucius, and try to get out of this hole you are in. If you ever need anything, no matter how difficult, you be sure to send us a message. You promise me now."

Lucius smiled. "Thank you, Wendric, I promise. But I can also tell you, this really is the last time we will speak."

He looked up and down the path, then pulled the hood of his cloak over his head.

"Take care of my thieves, Wendric. That is all I ask."

CHAPTER NINETEEN

GALLOPING ALONG AT speed across the open grassland, Lucius might have enjoyed himself if he were not fleeing his home city. The horse, a fine pure-bred he had relieved from a wealthy merchant near the eastern gatehouse, seemed to be escaping its own kind of hell, such was its vigour.

Together, they had left Turnitia at some pace and soon the walls, tall townhouses and even the mighty towers of the Citadel had disappeared behind the horizon. They encountered a steady stream of travellers: a merchant train here, a Pontaine knightly delegation there, and farmers, craftsmen and their families, streaming in from the farms and hamlets that surrounded Turnitia, all hoping to seek greater fortune.

At an opportune time, Lucius pulled on the reins and they swung south, off the road that led to Andon, riding cross-country. As evening started to descend, the small settlements and farms grew less frequent, and he started to feel a little more comfortable with each mile he put between him and real civilisation.

Though the horse was strong and well looked after, Lucius fuelled it with a minor enchantment.

He had not given a great deal of thought to where he would flee before he had crossed through the gates of the city, his mind more focussed on evading Adrianna and the baron, and ensuring his guild would be in safe hands. As it happened, he discovered he had little choice in the matter anyway.

Northwards was out. That would be heading straight into the clutches of Adrianna, which meant instant death after what she would regard as his deepest betrayal of her. If he avoided her, there was always the possibility the Preacher Divine still lived and, if he had perished in the Territories, then his successor would likely have an interest in the Guardian Starlight. The thought of that artefact in the hands of Vos and the Anointed Lord made Lucius shiver.

Eastwards would be just as foolish, for that meant Pontaine.

He had not even considered west and the ocean. Lucius was no sailor and he firmly believed the extent of man's voyages across open bodies of water should be restricted to calm lakes, at least as far as he was concerned. He had taken a short voyage on the open ocean just once, an aborted attempt to reach the Sarcre Islands, something both he and the inexperienced captain quickly regretted.

That only left south, and the trackless wilderness beckoned to Lucius, promising anonymity and safe hiding within its empty expanse. Having no real plan for where he was headed or what he would do when he got there, he simply pointed his horse south and trusted to fate.

The World's Ridge Mountains, still many, many miles away, began to rear up in front of him, and he imagined that perhaps he could find some small village in their foothills, a place cut off from the schemes and politicking of city people, inhabited by those who bore no allegiance to Vos or Pontaine. He could turn his hand to anything, and such a place would surely welcome such a multi-talented individual once he had proved himself. Or maybe he would carry on travelling, and explore the furthest recesses of the world, seeing things no one had set their eyes on before. Perhaps he would find a secret pass through the impenetrable World's Ridge Mountains and be the first to stagger though their rocky trails to discover what lay beyond. Maybe it would be a strange but wonderful new world where there were no separate nations, and all men lived in peace.

Well, he could dream, surely?

His good mood remained throughout the evening and night.

Making camp, he felt wonderfully alone as he chewed his way through the dried meats he had packed. Sleep came quickly that night and, for the first time in a long time, it was peaceful and unbroken. Lucius woke as the sun started to rise over the mountains and immediately felt wide awake and alert. Putting it down to having escaped his problems or possibly just the fresh breeze that blew down from the mountains, he discovered he was hungry. After walking the horse a short distance to give it a new patch of vegetation on which to graze, Lucius jogged away from his camp, eyes scanning the middle distance as he watched like a hawk for movement. There!

In the lee of a small rise, a colony of brown-furred rabbits had already spotted him and were all staring in his direction suspiciously, trying to gauge what threat he might represent. Lucius purposefully turned side on to them and then walked slowly, appearing to keep his distance but actually spiralling inwards, closing the range by an inch with each step.

The rabbits went back to their own grazing, but soon became alarmed at Lucius' behaviour as he began to circle them. He saw one sit up on its haunches and sniff the air, while another hopped a few feet away from him. Then another started hopping.

Seeing his chance slip away, Lucius turned towards them and broke into a run, mentally gathering the flow of magic around him as he fashioned a spell.

His quarry ran as soon as he started running, white tails flapping as they crossed the uneven ground at a pace he thought amazing for creatures so small. Barely breaking his stride, Lucius squinted his eyes as he aimed, and then threw a hand forward. A small ball of green fire leapt from his palm and sailed unerringly towards one of the rabbits. As it struck the target on the back of the neck, it flared briefly, causing Lucius to shield his eyes.

When he looked again, the rabbit lay still on the ground, smoke rising from its singed fur.

Lucius regarded the dead creature for a moment before he stooped to pick it up. No, hunting with magic was never fair, but he was hungry and no huntsman, and a man used what tools he had. After the dried meat of the night before, he very much liked the idea of roasted rabbit.

The sun continued its climb into the crisp morning sky, and Lucius found himself rather enjoying the skinning and gutting of his meal, as unskilful as he was.

He laid with his back on the grass, staring up at the sky while listening to the sound of his horse snatching at clumps of grass and his rabbit beginning to sizzle over a fire. Inhaling deep the fresh morning air, Lucius smiled to himself, but the breath stuck in his throat. Frowning, he sat up and looked around, trying to work out what was wrong. His eyes floated over the camp fire, grass, horse, mountains, and then settled on the Guardian Starlight, as ever tucked into his belt.

Lucius held the artefact up in front of his face. He began to feel its magical aura pulsing, sweeping over him as he stared, trying to work out what it was doing, or what it was trying to tell him.

Suddenly, his vision went blank, the grasslands and mountains disappeared to be replaced with the threads of magic running through the world as he perceived the arcane power he drew upon. Streaming around him, the threads spun round the Guardian Starlight like tightly wound cords, drawn into it and through it, gaining a vivid vibrancy as they streamed out of the artefact. Then his perception twitched and he was aware of other forces pulling on the magic of the world, strong, powerful forces that were loaded with deadly intent.

One shone like the sun, repelling several threads of magical energy as it pulsed. Adrianna, Lucius thought. She is looking for me still. It was clear she was getting closer to him all the time.

His attention was drawn to two other entities, and he knew they were looking for him also. One was studious, disciplined, and measured, throwing off pulses of magic that rippled down the threads towards him, rebounding upon his touch and flying back to their point of origin. Was that the baron's wizard, he thought, using some spell of seeing?

The third had a wild, desperate edge to it, a feeling Lucius was coming to know well. There was nothing subtle about this point of power as it too pulsed. He could feel the raw ambition and blind faith behind it, and knew he was looking at the Preacher Divine.

Lucius came back to the physical world with a jolt, gasping for breath, a trickle of cold sweat running down his temple.

The baron's wizard, the Preacher Divine and, worst of all, Adrianna. All three were not just vainly searching for him, they knew exactly where he was, right there and then.

With a start, he bolted up straight, and kicked earth onto the fire, smothering it quickly. The horse looked up from its grazing in surprise as Lucius flew around his small camp, gathering up what few belongings he had managed to steal in the city. Without breaking his pace, he threw himself up onto the horse's back and gave it a kick.

Once again, he was on the run.

IT TOOK ANOTHER two days of mad flight to reach the rocky foothills that lay beneath the World's Ridge Mountains. Neither the baron's wizard, the Preacher Divine, nor Adrianna made an appearance, but from time to time, he would feel the urge to reach down and grasp the Guardian Starlight.

The artefact would give him a brief flash, as though a warning, of the effect all three had on the threads of magic. They were obviously getting closer.

It seemed to Lucius that these flashes were beginning to get more frequent, and he wondered if the Guardian Starlight was somehow trying to communicate with him. Was it intelligent? Sentient?

Dreams of a quiet mountain village nestled between the peaks soon gave way to a reality of broken and craggy land, strewn with boulders and with only the meanest and hardiest vegetation finding sustenance enough to grow.

During his moments of communion with the Guardian Starlight Lucius began to feel it was not just warning him of nearby threats, but also drawing him onwards, encouraging him to take the path he was travelling. He took some encouragement from that, but could not help wondering whether the artefact had been subtly guiding him since he had left the city.

The horse stopped abruptly, almost shaking Lucius from its back as its head jerked up, ears flattening against its skull. He leaned forward to stroke its neck.

"What's up, boy?" he whispered to it. "You smell something bad?"

He looked about, trying to see if a mountain lion or some other predator was lurking among the rocky terrain, but saw nothing. Dismounting, he staked the reins to the ground, and padded ahead, one hand on the hilt of his sword.

A faint grunting, like swine, came to his ears, and he frowned. A herd of boars, perhaps?

Keeping his footsteps silent, Lucius inched slowly towards the summit of the rise, edging closer to the source of the noise.

As he looked down into a small valley, he saw a large camp, comprising what must have been more than a hundred... beings. There was no other way he could describe them. They were not human, of that he was sure.

The creatures were brutes, heavy in build, stocky, and muscular. They moved with a strange gait, as if stooped or crippled, but, despite their posture, each stood at least as high as him. Their skin was a light brown, leathery, as if beaten into a hard surface by the rugged environment. Few clothed their nakedness with anything more than a fur wrapped around the waist or torso, and many were armed with heavy clubs. Just a few carried battered swords and shields that looked man-made but had obviously seen better days.

There was a grunt louder than the others and of a slightly higher pitch. Too late, Lucius realised how exposed he was, silhouetted against the sky atop the rise, and cursed himself for poor judgement. One of the creatures had spotted him, and one by one, the entire camp was turning to look up at him.

For a moment, there was complete silence as man and beasts stared at one another. Lucius saw their faces were just as malformed as their bodies, some sporting terrible growths sprouting from their chins or cheeks, while others had lop-sided tusks jutting from their jaws. All had the same beady black eyes that contained no emotion at all.

Then one screamed, a bestial roar that galvanised the others. A rock flew past Lucius' head with stunning speed, and it was quickly followed by more.

Backing away, Lucius fled, racing for his horse. Already, some of the creatures were beginning to scale the rise behind him and he could only marvel at their agility and raw, physical power.

Yanking the reins from the stake, he flung himself on to the horse's back in one fluid movement. The horse needed no further instructions, and he gripped tightly to its mane as it bolted. A small group of the creatures ran to one side to try to head him off. One, a particularly ugly brute with a face pock-marked from some plague, leapt through the air to seize the horse's neck.

Lucius lashed out with his leg, his boot catching the creature under the chin. It grunted and fell, but as he flashed past, he saw it already beginning to rise and give chase.

One threw a spear, a crude weapon with a bent shaft and stone tip, but hurled with enough force to fly straight. Ducking at the last moment, he felt the force of air whip past the back of his neck as the spear sailed over him.

More creatures appeared ahead, running from behind a pile of boulders. They spread out along his path, bracing themselves as if they were strong enough to halt his horse in its tracks.

Not willing to find out if they could, Lucius conjured a short but powerful spell that sent a ball of fire spinning past the horse's ears. Crackling as it flew, the fire landed in the centre of the line of creatures, immolating them immediately.

Near crazed with fear, the horse almost veered away, but Lucius drew hard on the reins, forcing the animal to keep running straight. Its hooves churned up blackened dirt as it galloped over the smoking earth where the creatures had stood just seconds before.

Seeing his way clear, Lucius kicked the horse to run ever faster, looking over his shoulder to see if they were being pursued.

It was quite some time before he felt relaxed enough to allow the horse to slow its mad rush.

CHAPTER TWENTY

FLANKED BY SQUARE buttresses, each the width of a typical townhouse, the archway had been concealed by the folds of the mountainscape, and Lucius had not been aware in the slightest of its presence until he rounded an ancient pathway and gasped as it appeared before him.

Now deep within the World's Ridge Mountains, Lucius had, with some regret, abandoned his horse days ago and proceeded on foot, drawn on by a growing conviction he felt emanating from the Guardian Starlight. He had seen more of the brutish creatures he encountered before, and they seemed to congregate in immense tribes. The chances of his horse surviving with those savages marauding were low.

Once, he had seen a creature very similar to those misshapen beings, but this one had been a real monster. Standing at least ten feet tall, so far as Lucius could tell while trying to avoid its notice, it had the same hard, leathery skin as the other creatures, the same stooped gait, but was far more muscular. Its arms, thighs and chest bulged with power, and Lucius had no problems imagining the monster uprooting a tree or tearing his arms from his body with brute force. Fortunately, it had not seemed very attentive to its surroundings, and he had been able to sneak past without provoking it.

As he walked cautiously under the arch, Lucius noticed that strange writing was carved into its stone frame, some script he could not decipher. Looking up, he saw it continued far above his head, perhaps up to the very tip of the arch. This simple entrance could have swallowed one of the towers of the Citadel, and still have plenty of room to spare.

Lucius had already guessed the Guardian Starlight had led him to an ancient dwarf stronghold, and he felt the architecture confirmed this, having the same form and function as the structures he had seen in his dreams. Everything the dwarfs had built seemed to have an air of indestructibility about it, a sense of permanence.

The darkness inside the archway was soon broken by a spell of illumination as he held up an open hand upon which danced a pale blue flame. It revealed a wide hall bored into the mountain. He could feel the emptiness around him, the sense of being in a wide open space, and he fed more magic into the spell until the blue flame shone with a brilliant radiance.

It did not help greatly.

Peering into the gloom, Lucius could make out the shadowy form of one wall to his left, but its opposite was still shrouded in darkness and he could only guess at how far above him the ceiling lay. It was as if the dwarfs had built everything for people a hundred feet tall.

Not even the sounds of his footsteps echoed within the hall, any such noise hopelessly swallowed by the immense interior.

A slight tug pulled at his magical senses, a familiar nudge he had long ago associated with the Guardian Starlight. It had led him to this place, that much was clear, and he had at first thought it was leading him to safety. Now, as the feelings dancing at the edge of his arcane vision grew stronger and more persistent, he was not so sure. It was as if there were a great weight threatening to press down upon him, hidden yet obviously there, much like the ceiling of this great hall, millions of tons of rock supported by a barrier invisible to him in the darkness. Quite what that weight was, he did not know, but its presence had a sense of destiny to it, a final end.

Whether it was for him or the Guardian Starlight though, he could not answer. Lucius was content to follow its directions for the moment as it had not led him astray yet and he was all too aware of the magical wrath incarnate that was Adrianna not far behind him.

As he walked further into the mountain, Lucius began to realise that, while covered by the dust of ages, the hall was otherwise remarkably clean. The archway had borne no door or barrier, and he had expected to be fighting his way through more of the savage tribal creatures, but there was no evidence they had ever ventured inside. There was no nests, bones or bodily waste scattered about. It was possible they had never found this place. Possible, but unlikely. He guessed they knew every inch of their environment. Which begged the question, why had they not used this place as shelter?

One hand on his sword's pommel, the other never straying far from the Guardian Starlight, Lucius continued down the hall until he reached its end. There he saw a sight more incredible than any he had witnessed before.

HANDS SPLAYED ACROSS the rock, Alhmanic pulled himself forward to get a better look at the figure walking cautiously into the immense archway. His staff had led him this far, and he was sure the man he now followed was the same Shadowmage that had attacked his camp. He could not see the other, far more dangerous one, but that was fine as far as he was concerned. It would make the next step all the easier.

The Preacher Divine was dishevelled, filthy. He was exhausted and hungry, but all thoughts of discomfort fled the moment he saw his quarry.

After the Shadowmages had left the site of the elven ruins, Alhmanic had scoured the surrounding area for a horse, then had ridden, hard, southwards, led by the rumbling vibrations his staff emitted as it tracked the elven artefact, as a hound fixates on a fox. He had ridden his horse harshly, cruelly, and with all speed until its heart simply gave out.

A nearby farm had supplied another mount, requisitioned in the name of the Anointed Lord, blessed be those who give her succour. Throughout the Territories and into southern Pontaine, Alhmanic had requisitioned, bargained, and bullied common folk for their horses and whenever that had not worked, he flat out stole them.

It was all for the greater good, he reminded himself. Those farmers and craftsmen eking out an existence away from the cities were doing God's own work by providing him with a horse. Even if they did not realise it until after the fact.

All the time, he chased the elusive Shadowmage who had disappeared into the darkness of the huge archway, a brief blue light flaring up from within as he cast a spell to help him see. Alhmanic needed no such tricks, having learned long ago that faith alone could make a blind man see. Well, faith and an enchanted staff.

Alhmanic unlimbered his weapon and felt its power course through his hands. He felt that it knew he was close to journey's end, that the artefact was within his grasp.

No more almost this time. He would enter that archway and claim his prize, or die in the doing.

* * *

HITTING THE GROUND hard, Adrianna tried to roll with the impact but her limbs would not obey her commands. The impact forced the breath from her body and, for a moment, she lay still on the stony ground, chest rising and falling as she drew in air. Eyes closed, she rested both body and mind. It would be a battle, she was sure. Lucius *had* to know that she would not take his betrayal lightly. He *had* to know there would be a terrible price to pay.

She had not yet thought exactly what course her retribution would take. Maybe, just maybe, if Lucius surrendered and handed over the Guardian Starlight, she would spare him. The wretched thief had had his uses in the past, after all.

Adrianna opened her eyes and took another deep breath. Just a little longer, she told herself. Rest just a little longer and get some of your strength back.

She had been so close to cornering Lucius in Turnitia, his presence still lingering within its walls as she walked its streets. She had arrived perhaps just an hour or two, no more than that, after he had departed.

The race across the Anclas Territories had taken its toll, draining her body and leaving her weak. And so, Adrianna had continued her pursuit of Lucius on horse, sparing her magic and allowing her to regain her sapped energy. There were, after all, few places he could run to, and none that would shield him from her. She was already close to him, and now it was only a matter of time before he was caught and the Guardian Starlight became hers.

Then the real work would start.

Lucius' course did not surprise her, making a crow's line to the southern mountains. After all, where else could he try to hide but in the trackless wilderness?

Her problems began as she entered the foothills. Ambushed by a large ogre, Adrianna had lost her horse to a blow from a wickedly heavy club before she had blasted the creature into the earth. From that point, she had been forced to use her magic to travel again.

After the encounter with the ogre, a tribe of orcs had dared cross her path. None would make that mistake again, though more time had been wasted as she tracked the last fleeing creatures to properly demonstrate the folly of attacking a Shadowmage.

That had fired her emotions and the old anger came back. Adrianna embraced it, used it to counter fatigue and fuel her spells, feeding it directly into the magic. The effect was almost explosive, and she shot into the sky once more, the air rushing past her at eye-watering speed. The Guardian Starlight was close, she felt as though she could almost reach out and touch it. The foothills sped past below, a blur of browns and greys interrupted only by patches of sparse vegetation clinging to life among the rocks.

As Adrianna lost altitude, the spell of transportation beginning to wane in power, she spied a remarkable structure coming into view. The rugged mountains gave up their secret, a huge archway built into the rock face, obviously dwarven in construction. A single pulse of magic, released with a single word from her lips, confirmed that Lucius had gone inside.

She had no idea why Lucius had come to this place nor how he knew of its existence. Indeed, Adrianna had been half-expecting the Guardian Starlight to lead him to some abandoned elven outpost like the one it had been recovered from, perhaps directing him to what it perceived as safety.

Whatever his reasons, he was now within the dwarven fortress. Trapped, and alone. It was now only a matter of time.

The Guardian Starlight was as good as hers.

CATCHING THE SUN briefly, the prism in Tellmore's hand flashed with blinding white light, causing him to wince as he continued to stare into its depths. He tuned the discomfort out, along with the clattering of armoured soldiers behind him and the growing cold of the wind. Through the prism, his mind soared, seeing a ghostly representation of the terrain around him, as well as the tell-tale glowing blood-red spots that marked the positions of the three other practitioners who were close by.

Tellmore sighed, seeing the trouble ahead that had become inevitable, and this caused a worried Renauld to hover at his shoulder.

"Is something awry, Magister?" Renauld asked.

Frowning, Tellmore considered this before answering.

"Perhaps..." he said, then hesitated. "Maybe an opportunity, it is difficult to say at the moment. There are other wielders of magic here."

"Other wizards?" Renauld said, a degree of apprehension in his voice.

"Stand firm, Renauld," he said. "And remember, the lowliest man-at-arms can strike down the greatest wizard if he is close enough. We just need to close the range."

Renauld looked doubtful at this, but said no more.

"I can at least see them all through this," Tellmore said, holding up the prism once again. "They will not be in a position to surprise us."

Tellmore and Renauld had headed a column of twelve mounted men-at-arms, but had been forced to abandon their horses as the terrain turned against them. Dispatched by the Baron de Sousse, Tellmore had been left under no illusions that he was now expected to complete his mission to retrieve the Guardian Starlight, and return to Turnitia in time to join the first invasion force. Even now, the first of the baron's allies were arriving in the city, leading their troops which were being garrisoned within the Citadel.

To this end, Tellmore had cast a spell of enchantment within his finest glass prism, one he had ground into shape himself over many months. It was as near perfect as any in Vos or Pontaine and he was using the spell to track the Guardian Starlight and the "interested parties", as the baron had described them, who were pursuing it.

Sir Renauld and the men-at-arms would give Tellmore an advantage in any confrontation with the other practitioners of magic, but Tellmore knew he could not rely upon them for victory. Shadowmages were crafty opponents, and Adrianna was as powerful as any wizard Tellmore had seen in his life. He regarded her as a formidable opponent. Lucius, less so, but the man was still a thief and in Tellmore's mind that made him damn near an assassin – the thought of a knife in the back in some dark corner of this wilderness was not an appealing one.

And then there was the third participant in this little drama. Tellmore had not been able to divine who this was but both he and the baron had assumed it was some agent of Vos, perhaps connected to the force that had destroyed their camp in the Anclas Territories. Through the prism, the shifts and twists in the forces of magic marked the agent as no wizard but the bearer of a powerful artefact – perhaps some relic if they were truly from Vos. Tellmore had little experience of such things, though he had studied them in the Three Towers and knew not to underestimate the power of the Final Faith in creating offensive magic from the belongings of their saints.

He turned to face Renauld.

"If we are attacked by magic, I want you and your men to stay close to me," he said. "I will do everything I can to protect you and keep our enemies off balance. When the opportunity arises, follow my lead and strike. I would be quite as happy to see them fall to a sword in the throat as from one of my spells."

Renauld nodded. "Understood and agreed, Magister. I know you are no glory hound."

Smiling, Tellmore put a hand on the knight's armoured shoulder.

"And I know your reluctance to face wizards, but I promise you this, Sir Renauld. I trust you to keep me safe from harm of the mundane variety. I will do my best for you and your men to defend you against enemies magical."

"The baron has given us a task, and I would see it done."

"Indeed. Now, gather your men and let us proceed," Tellmore said, pocketing the prism as its inner light faded and died. "I believe a confrontation is due very soon. It seems we are close to our final destination and the others are already waiting for us."

CHAPTER TWENTY-ONE

WHAT LUCIUS HAD thought was a hall had turned out to be a mere passageway. Perhaps that great archway was only a minor entrance to this dwarven mountain stronghold, though he found it difficult to imagine anything grander in scale or design.

The place that confronted him now was a real hall, by the standards of the ancient dwarven architects.

Lucius found himself staring across a chamber that was more than half a mile across, and he marvelled at the carved buttresses that rose from six points to climb the walls and meet at a single point high above him. Together, they held back the weight of the mountain from this cavernous place, and had done so for millennia.

The high walls were lined with stairways and balconies, seeming to be guardpoints or perhaps dwellings burrowed into the bare rock. However, it was the sight below that took his breath away.

He snuffed out his spell of illumination, as it was no longer needed. All the light needed to illuminate the huge hall was provided by swift-flowing rivers of lava far below, funnelled into channels by canals of thick bronzed metal that seemed impervious to their heat. Suspended above them were stone bridges, elaborately carved yet immune to the decay of time, wide thoroughfares that sported small buildings along their length. Seven of these bridges led to a central plaza, at least as large as any of the Five Markets in Turnitia, a broad platform suspended by nothing more than the bridges themselves. The plaza was a wide-open paved space, perhaps used as a gathering point or trading area in ages gone, though it was filled with nothing but dust now. Like the bridges, small stone buildings lined its perimeter.

The end was close, he could feel it. Murmuring to him through its magical connection, the Guardian Starlight felt as though it was almost crooning, lightly encouraging him toward their final destination. The centre of the plaza, Lucius felt. Was that where everything would finally be revealed to him, the mystery of the Old Races and their tragedy, his link to them and the Guardian Starlight?

Gingerly, Lucius descended the staircase immediately before him which wound down to a platform that jutted out from the rock face and was connected to the nearest bridge. The descent was not as easy as it had first looked, as the dwarfs must have had some posture, size or gait that made taller steps easier for them; they proved hard work for Lucius.

Hands, shins and knees cloaked with the grey dust that had been lying on the steps, Lucius finally reached the bottom and brushed himself down. Looking across the hall to the plaza, he saw the buildings lining the bridges, some with single entrances and glass windows, others with wide open lower floors – a mixture of homes, shops and tradesmen's workshops, he presumed.

"Infidel!" The shout ricocheted round Lucius, bouncing off the walls. He just had time to look round before he was struck full in the chest and knocked off his feet.

Writhing in pain, Lucius staggered to his feet to see the Preacher Divine, clothes ragged and face haggard, clambering down the steps, brandishing his staff as he did so.

Cursing under his breath, Lucius ran for the bridge, wondering just what it would take to kill the damned Preacher Divine.

STANDING MIDWAY DOWN the staircase, Alhmanic felt the full power of the Final Faith flow through his staff as its crystal tip gleamed with energy. Holding the shaft down three-quarters of its length, he pointed the weapon downwards to the platform and unleashed another magical bolt.

Incredibly, the Shadowmage dove to one side and avoided it, the bolt kicking up a cloud of dust and leaving a blackened stain on the stone. Continuing his roll, the Shadowmage bounced back to his feet and raced for the bridge, his image flickering and blurring as he cast a spell of concealment.

Alhmanic smiled as he whirled his staff in a high arc, calling upon the power of past saints to create a gust of wind that flowed down the steps, rolled over the platform and drove over the bridge, causing a roiling tide of dust. Having witnessed the trickery of

Shadowmages before, he had given some time to thinking how to defeat them.

As the wind swept past the Shadowmage, the dust swirled about his form, making him easy to pick out. Laughing at his own ingenuity, Alhmanic jumped down the last few steps and chased after the fleeing Shadowmage.

UPON ENTERING THE great hall, Adrianna quickly surveyed the arena and spied Lucius and Alhmanic already engaged in battle. Her eyes lit up at that, for the death of the Preacher Divine was collateral damage she could well accept.

Adrianna stepped off the staircase and levitated across the hall to hang high above the plaza. She saw Lucius try to evade the Preacher Divine's attacks as the two crossed the bridge, and she swooped to deliver an early end to the fight.

Screaming like a harpy as she plummeted, she unleashed rocketing balls of compressed air, each as hard as a rock. The salvo impacted around both men below, and she heard Lucius cry out in surprise as he was thrown off his feet.

The Preacher Divine reacted faster, and she saw him brace for the assault, his staff spinning in his hands as it deflected her magic away from him to expend its energy harmlessly against the buildings lining the bridge. Small shards of stone were splintered from the buildings but they otherwise resisted the attack. In return, the Preacher Divine altered the rhythm of his staff, keeping it spinning in front of him but adding a flourish to every rotation that cracked off a bolt of energy from its tip, sailing at speed back up to her.

Twisting in mid-air, Adrianna looped and spun to avoid the Preacher Divine's attacks, all the while continuing her own rain of destruction down upon him. Together, they traded magical blows and counterpunches in a fearsome display of arcane skill and power.

TELLMORE HELD UP a hand to halt his small column of soldiers. Cocking his head to one side as he drew the prism from a concealed pocket, he tried to work out who was fighting and how they were faring.

"Two – no, three wizards ahead," Tellmore said quietly to Renauld. "It would appear we are the last to arrive."

"So long as we are the only ones to leave. I'll be a great deal happier when they are dead," Renauld said.

"One using natural magic, the other… something else. I can guess that would be the Vos agent, though."

"You said there was a third?"

"Yes. Faint, but it is there. Trying to avoid battle, not face it head on. Our Shadowmage, I fancy. If he is not waging full-blooded war, we may be lucky."

"Especially if the other two take each other out."

Tellmore nodded. "Well, it has been known, Sir Renauld, it has been known. However, I won't count on it. Come, let us see what confronts us."

As they reached the great hall, Tellmore heard the gasps of astonishment from the men-at-arms as they saw the huge interior but he immediately focussed on the pitched battle between Adrianna and the Vos agent.

The Shadowmage was using her magic to stay airborne and mobile, proving a difficult target to hit as she dove, unleashed an attack and then twisted out of the way of the inevitable reprisal. Below her, the Vos man was using his staff to block her attacks while delivering his own. That at least answered the question of the fourth practitioner of magic and the strange divinations Tellmore had gained from his prism.

Tellmore could plainly see the folly of the man's position – he might be well matched against the Shadowmage while his staff remained at full power, but such items had a habit of fading during prolonged use and he would not bet a bucket of horse dung on the man's future after that. Frankly, the odds would not be good as they stood right now, if Adrianna's reputation was anything to go by. One slip, and the Vos man would be dead.

He could not see Lucius from his vantage point, but that did not surprise him. No doubt the Shadowmage was hiding, seeking to gain an advantage over his opponents or, perhaps, simply escape.

"Spread your men out," Tellmore said to Renauld, and the order brought a frown to the knight's face.

"Your pardon, Magister, but will you be able to protect us if we are strung so far out?"

"It is a risk, but one worth taking, I think. They are too focussed on their own battle at the moment, giving us the upper hand. You stick with me, and we'll go down to pick our time to attack. Your men will be safely out of the way until we are ready to act. Make sure they keep their heads down, and we can catch everyone off guard. Think of it as an ambush – with a bit of magical support from me, of course."

Renauld smiled as he considered the plan.

"I like that, Magister. We'll see it done."

"Good, good," Tellmore muttered, as much to himself as the knight, who busied himself giving orders and directing his men to their hiding places.

Tellmore then directed his full attention to Adrianna and the Vos man, watching their battle, studying their methods and abilities. The potential within Adrianna was readily apparent, and Tellmore did not look forward to confronting her. If possible, he would evade her completely; that was not cowardice, just common sense.

The Vos man he was more comfortable with. With any luck, the man would be killed by Adrianna or otherwise have his staff, his only source of magical power, completely drained in his duel. If Tellmore picked his time correctly, there would be no danger there.

Casting his eyes across the other bridges and plaza, Tellmore could see no sign of Lucius.

The presence of Adrianna and the Vos man complicated things, certainly, but Tellmore clung to the hope that, somehow, his course of action would suddenly appear clear and simple.

SKIDDING TO A halt inside one of the stone buildings ringing the plaza, Lucius fought to control his breathing lest it give him away. There was little chance of that, given the cacophony of Adrianna's duel with the Preacher Divine.

Entering one of the houses, Lucius inched forward to take position beneath a window. Through its perfect transparency, he could see the centre of the empty plaza and, while he could still feel the tug of the Guardian Starlight suggesting he make his way there, it was depressingly far away. Simply sauntering across the open ground would be suicidal.

Outside, the magical duel came to a sudden end. Briefly, Lucius felt guilty as he found himself hoping it was Adrianna who had fallen; he might have a chance in open confrontation if it were the Preacher Divine who had survived.

Any such wishes were quickly dashed as a breeze fluttered through the building, quickly building up to a gale. Dust began to drift down from the ceiling as the entire building began to shake violently. A giant crack caused Lucius to peer up through the descending dust as light penetrated the ceiling through cracks that quickly spread across its surface. With a wild wrenching movement, the ceiling gave way, breaking apart as it tumbled onto the concourse.

Adrianna rose into view above him. Her fire-scarred face held a baleful look.

"You will not escape me again, Lucius," she cried out above the howling of the gale. "The Guardian Starlight is mine!"

"You have become twisted, Aidy. You are the *last* person who should have it!"

"It has corrupted you, don't you see, Lucius?" Adrianna said as the gale died down and she drifted towards him. "You do not have the knowledge or the will to control an artefact of the elves. It would be better if you simply gave it to me."

"It doesn't want you. I know that much. Whatever this thing is, it chose me. It is in my blood, Aidy, that is why it wanted me. I have some connection to the elves, however diluted by the years since their passing. No amount of study can replace that."

"You are wrong in that assumption, Lucius, very wrong. Unfortunately, I have neither the time nor the inclination to school you further. Hand it over to me now or, I promise, I *will* kill you."

So saying, Adrianna's eyes blazed with an unholy light. Lucius raced for the door only to find it blocked by the Preacher Divine.

"Harridan!" the Preacher Divine screamed as he ignored Lucius and gestured with his staff towards the airborne Shadowmage. A jagged bolt of brilliant white light erupted from his staff and struck Adrianna full in the chest, sending her spinning through the air to fall out of sight in the plaza beyond.

The Preacher Divine seemed to notice Lucius then and, as his gaze travelled to the Guardian Starlight, his eyes gleamed with desire.

With a flick of his wrist, Lucius sent his dagger tumbling pommel over point in an arrow-straight throw that ended with the weapon embedded in the Preacher Divine's shoulder.

Grunting with pain, the Preacher Divine staggered back. Lucius threw himself through window and tumbled to the ground outside. Rolling with the momentum, he bounded back onto his feet and raced for the next building.

Nearby, Adrianna was getting to her feet.

Anger flooded into her heart, and Adrianna embraced it, feeling its energy. It boiled and erupted, raw fury flowing through her veins, binding itself with the rush of magic she summoned. And she rose into the air again, her hair forming a wild halo around her head, fizzing with sparks of arcane energy.

TELLMORE AND RENAULD had managed to advance nearly the full length of the bridge without having attracted any attention, and the wizard found himself daring to hope that he might just accomplish his mission by picking the Guardian Starlight from the dead body of one of the combatants. He had seen Renauld throw more than one unnerved glance at him as they witnessed the titanic magical furies unleashed close by. Adrianna had pulled the roof off one house, shortly after to disappear from sight as the Preacher Divine blasted her with magic, and Lucius had dived out of the small house to sprint to another building, no doubt to lay another ambush.

Tellmore then saw the agent of Vos stagger out of the roofless building, clutching at a dagger buried in his shoulder. They both saw one another at the same time, but pain slowed the Vos agent's reactions and Tellmore released his spell first, a hastily cast enchantment designed to coat the man in a web of magical strands that could bind or crush him as desired.

The Vos man waved wildly with his staff, just catching the edge of the incoming spell with enough force to turn it aside. Before either could call upon another magical attack, Renauld charged, shouting out to their men-at-arms as he raised his sword to strike.

"Renauld, no!"

Tellmore reached out a hand to stop him, but it was too late.

THE WAR CRIES of several men caused Lucius to frown and he cautiously peer over the top of a stone. Racing down two of the bridges leading to the plaza were armoured men sporting the colours of the Baron de Sousse.

More sounds of spells discharging came to his ears and he decided to move away from the source, figuring the longer he spent in hiding, the more chance that everyone else in the hall might wipe one another out.

He crept out of the shop and his attention was immediately drawn upwards. Floating about thirty feet in the air, in complete silence, Adrianna looked the very vision of his worst nightmare.

Her skin was a deathly pale, while her hair streamed behind, twisting and sizzling with raw, untempered magic. It was her face that scared him the most, though. For once, there was no anger in it at all. She was completely devoid of any emotion and he knew in that moment that she was more dangerous than she had ever been.

Adrianna's head whipped round and her cold gaze nearly froze him in place. Instinctively, Lucius grasped the Guardian Starlight and plucked it from his belt, brandishing it as he called upon his magic.

He felt the threads of power running inside his mind's eye and called upon the power of the blackest of them, the one that felt chill to his mental touch. It throbbed and grew as he hastily sculpted it into shape. The arcane presence of the Guardian Starlight was a beacon in his hand and the spell flowed through it, magnified and focussed as it soared towards Adrianna.

Caught within the spell's binding power, Adrianna stopped in mid-air and Lucius channelled every ounce of energy he could summon into it, feeling his skin grow cold as ice crystals formed in his hair and his breath steamed from his mouth.

Adrianna shrieked as the threads of magic wrapped around her, sapping her vitality and ageing her before Lucius' eyes.

"It did not have to be this way," he managed to say through gritted teeth.

That was enough for Adrianna to find the briefest gap in his spell. She broke free in a dazzling pulse of magic, sending waves of dust spiralling away from her and causing Lucius to stagger.

Raising her hands, she let loose a long, keening wail of anguish, the rising crescendo building into a spell of terrible potency.

Lucius hastily erected layers of invisible magical barriers between himself and Adrianna, hoping that the Guardian Starlight would aid him in maintaining their integrity when she unleashed her onslaught.

He did not have to wait long. Head snapping down, Adrianna uttered a single word of power and the air above Lucius groaned. Glancing up, he saw roiling black smoke gathering above him, spreading outwards like clouds driven by a storm. It rained fire.

The breath was sucked from Lucius' lungs as the fire flayed his clothes and skin, and set his hair alight. Feeling his skin begin to peel, Lucius reeled blindly. Every inch of his body seemed to boil and there was no relief.

Then, it was gone.

Lucius did not move for a long time. The fingers of his left hand showed signs of life first, twitching as he slowly extended his arm out, searching.

The Guardian Starlight was gone.

*   *   *

HOPING THE PREACHER Divine's staff had all but spent its power, Tellmore left Renauld to bury his sword in the man's chest in order to search out the two Shadowmages. He stopped short when he saw Adrianna floating towards him, her deadly intent clear, but she was then distracted by something she saw behind a row of buildings beyond his line of sight.

The power he saw Adrianna release then all but took his breath away. He had never seen the like.

Tellmore's mind flicked through dozens of incantations as he approached the area Adrianna had devastated. She had disappeared from view, but he had no illusions that she wouldn't rematerialise soon. He tried to think fast for a spell to use against her.

THE CRYSTAL AT the tip of Alhmanic's staff had begun to fade, and he had been reduced to parrying blows from the Pontaine knight's sword with its shaft, an undignified treatment for a relic. Every movement brought pain as the Shadowmage's dagger, still buried in his shoulder, began to grind against bone.

Alhmanic knew he needed to withdraw, to allow the staff to regenerate. Without it, he was utterly outclassed by the mages present here.

But he was not willing to return to the Anointed Lord, may he be graced with serving her forever, empty-handed.

Alhmanic limped backwards a couple of steps, and held up a hand as if pleading for mercy. The knight backed off slightly, his sword held at arm's length in the traditional Pontaine signal for surrender.

"Your staff, sir, drop it," the knight said.

Alhmanic managed a nod. He made to cast the staff aside, but whipped it up suddenly, smashing it against the knight's sword to throw the blade to one side. Then he thrust the staff forward with all his remaining strength, so the butt thudded right between the knight's eyes.

The knight fell to the ground, out cold.

"Bloody Pontaine idiot," Alhmanic muttered. "No wonder you lot lost the damned war."

Turning away from the knight, he paused to grasp the dagger with one hand. Closing his eyes, he tore the weapon from his flesh.

Gasping with the effort, he cast a baleful look down at the unconscious knight. It did not sit well with him to leave an enemy at his back, but Alhmanic knew he was weak and getting weaker. If he was going to claim the blasted artefact in the name of the Anointed Lord, may her farts part the clouds, he had to act now.

LUCIUS COULD NOT see. Pain screamed at him from every joint, with every movement, and his skin burned. His greatest dread though was that he was blind. Had his eyelids been melted and sealed by Adrianna's flames?

The Guardian Starlight still called to him and he tried to reach out with his magical senses to find it. The artefact was close, but the constant waves of pain shook his concentration with every tremor.

He felt he had been so close to a final understanding of the device and, perhaps, of his own origins. It burned to think he could give up so easily.

Crawling forward on his knees, Lucius swept the ground before him, hoping to feel the familiar cool touch of the Guardian Starlight.

THEY MET IN the plaza.

Tellmore instantly let loose with a salvo of raw magical energy that chattered his teeth as its power swept through him. He had hoped the rapid but powerful bolts would throw Adrianna off balance, perhaps even send her tumbling down into the rivers of lava far below, but the Shadowmage waved a hand and the spell diverted its energy into the plaza below her, blasting a crater into the stone.

She responded by sending shockwaves through the stone at Tellmore's feet and he had to leap backwards to avoid plummeting to his death. He retaliated by creating the ghostly apparition of a sword above Adrianna's head and with a chopping motion, brought it down.

The blade cracked on an invisible shield Adrianna created, shattering into a thousand ethereal fragments.

Tellmore tried again, this time clapping his hands together and allowing the magic to amplify the sound so it would burst the ears and crush the heart of anyone in front of him, but the Shadowmage seemed impervious to it.

Not wanting to wait around for her reprisal, Tellmore wrapped a spell about himself, and disappeared, only to find that Adrianna had created a vivid pink mist that silhouetted him perfectly. He managed to raise an arcane shield just a fraction of a second before a bolt of black energy burnt itself out against its surface.

She was too powerful, he knew. A graduate of the Three Towers, his spells were insignificant against hers, while his own defences would eventually be breached. However, Tellmore had not gained stature in Pontaine society by charging at problems head on, and he resolved to try a different tack.

Seeing Adrianna floating towards him and preparing to throw another attack, he bolstered his shield and drew upon his power to create a very different spell.

The air before him seemed to thicken and twist, before a dark blue fog spiralled out of nothingness to quickly envelop first him, then the whole plaza. Though it blinded him, Tellmore was thankful it also concealed his position.

Already, he could hear the savage discharge of powerful spells as Adrianna threw spells randomly before her, hoping to strike him by chance. He turned and ran before she summoned a wind to blow his fog away and leave him naked before her fury.

The plaza shook as spells impacted again and again on its surface, and the stone itself began to groan under the punishment it had sustained. It would not be long before the plaza could no longer support itself and the whole structure, bridges and all, would plummet hundreds of feet down to smash upon bare rock or sink into molten lava.

Amidst the clouds of dust and wisps of blue fog, a hand reached out, straining for the marble shaft of the Guardian Starlight.

CHAPTER TWENTY-TWO

THE WOODEN HATCH opened and then banged against brick as it fell. Poking her head out, Grennar peered about, then hoisted herself up the last few rungs of the ladder into a small chamber. A single door led out, and it was already open. Breathless from the long, long climb, she held her side as she walked out into the open air.

Outside, she found herself on a balcony that circled the spire just a few yards down from its spiked peak. The view this high up was amazing, with only the central keep of the Citadel rising above her.

Before her was the ocean.

Waves that would easily swallow the spire on which she perched raged high, cresting in a deluge of white foam. Further out, they seemed calmer, though she knew that was deceptive. What looked like gentle rolling hills of water were in fact a nightmare to navigate and could easily swamp a ship.

Grennar had never been to sea but hoped to one day. Perhaps when things had calmed down in the city and the Beggars' Guild did not teeter on a precipice of failure and destitution.

Getting her breath back she followed the balcony as it rounded the spire. On the opposite side stood Wendric, now guildmaster of the thieves. She had not quite sussed him out as yet, and so remained wary in his presence. Lucius had trusted him enough to run the guild in his absence, and she supposed that should be recommendation enough. Trust was not an easy thing for her to bequeath, though.

"Good morning, young miss," Wendric said without turning, and Grennar grimaced.

He had insisted on calling her "young miss" since their first meeting as guildmasters. Nothing was meant by it, she knew, it was just Wendric's way to address her as such; in his mind, he was showing the deepest respect. For her part, it merely reminded everyone who heard how young she really was.

Lucius had always treated her as an equal, not some child off the street.

"Wendric," she said and joined him leaning against the balcony, staring down at the city going about it business below. Today, that business was unusually loud and colourful, and it filled her with nothing but dread.

Grennar decided to avoid the uncomfortable truths happening below them for at least a little while longer.

"Have you heard anything from Lucius?" she asked.

Wendric shook his head.

"No. I thought you would have heard something before we did."

"Well, that's what we do," she said.

Wendric looked down at her and, after a moment, put an arm gently across her shoulders.

"I miss him too," he said. "I'll never be the guildmaster he was."

"You'll do alright. So long as you listen to the beggars."

He smiled at that. "The one lesson he continued to pound into me, day after day. Beggars are the eyes and ears of the city. You'll get far better return of information from them than you will on all the bribes you pay to guards, merchants and nobles."

"Well, it's true."

"Aye."

For a few moments, they stood in an awkward silence. Wendric finally dropped his arm.

"Can't say I miss those crazy Shadowmages though."

"Oh, they are still about," Grennar said. "Just nothing like what they were under Adrianna."

"She was the craziest of the lot of them."

"You'll get no argument from me there. I just hope she never found Lucius."

He looked down at her, hearing the forlorn tone in her voice.

"Don't you be worrying overly on Lucius," he said, trying to put a hint of mock reproach in his voice. "You are talking about the man who joined the thieves as a pickpocket and became guildmaster in a matter of minutes."

Grennar smiled. "And brought down the Vos rule in the city, single-handed."

"Indeed, bringing freedom and prosperity to all in his wake. What is one mad Shadowmage compared to all that?"

"Wendric," Grennar said. "I am scared for him, you know."

"I know, young miss. I know."

Grennar shuddered and wrapped her arms about her body. "She's different now. It is as if she doesn't see people as, well, people any more. We are all just here to be used by her, and crushed when we get in the way."

"Then I daresay it is a good thing that Adrianna is far away from here. And I don't think she'll catch Lucius. They may both be Shadowmages, but he is a thief as well. He can stay one step ahead of anyone."

"I hope so," Grennar whispered, then suddenly felt the need to change the subject. She stopped staring at the horizon and forced herself to watch the procession in the streets far below.

The forces of Pontaine had been roused from their slumber and were now marching through Turnitia in all their glory. Winding through the Five Markets, which had been closed by the Baron de Sousse to mark this special day, a long trail of troops meandered through Turnitia. Unlike the uniform Vos troops, however, the army of Pontaine was a brightly coloured array of nobles, men-at-arms, knights and assorted hangers-on. Each noble had his own livery and this was transposed onto the men following him in a variety of ways. It almost seemed more like a carnival than an army marching.

Though she knew it was just as likely she would never see any of the fighting men again, Grennar had taken the trouble to learn the different units that comprised the army. After all, you never knew what piece of information would prove useful in the future.

Immediately below them, crossing the Square of True Believers, were the Sardenne Militia, drafted from a hundred different towns and villages scattered across the great forest's borders. They were a ragged looking lot, wearing their own clothes for the most part, and many bore only farming tools as weapons. They were all identified by the small red and golden shield that had been granted to them by the Baron du Fillimont, their leader. There was a lot of them in the militia but talk around the city had already suggested they would not be of much account in battle. Most would turn tail and run at the first sight of an aggressive enemy, while the rest would be cut down where they stood.

Du Fillimont brought up their rear, leading his own household guards, magnificent looking knights in full plate armour that gleamed silver and gold in the morning sun, while from their red lances flew long blue pennants that fluttered in the breeze. As they rode past the crowds lining the square, children scampered forward to cast handfuls of petals under the hooves of their horses.

They looked impressive enough, but talk said they would be of little more use than the militia they followed. Still, no one would say that to their baron's face, not if they wanted his continued patronage and friendship within the realms of Pontaine politics. That was a skill he very much possessed, by all reasonable accounts.

A crowd looking even worse off than the militia followed, but there was something in their gait that suggested a rare potency. They wore unclean clothing of greens and browns, but it was the dirt of the country that covered them, not the filth of the city. A mercenary band, they roamed the Pontaine countryside, offering their services to whichever feuding landowner paid the most or, as rumour had it, could serve the best wine.

Still more troops came, and with every salute, every blow of a horn, Grennar became more depressed. There was a damning inevitability to it all, as far as she could see.

Vos hits Pontaine, Pontaine hits Vos back. Pontaine gets stronger, begins to push Vos around. Sooner or later, a knockout blow would be delivered by one or the other that would consume them all. And for what? The lives of the common folk, who far outnumbered the nobles and soldiers, would not be improved. Quite the reverse.

She did not pray often, but Grennar hoped to God that Turnitia would not become like some hellish urban version of the Anclas Territories.

It was her home.

From her lofty vantage point, the army looked almost pretty, and she wished it really were a carnival.

The reality was altogether different. Pontaine was finally making its move against Vos.

A new war had begun.

THE END

ABOUT THE AUTHOR

With a solid history in roleplaying and miniatures game design, Matthew Sprange has written over three dozen gaming books, including the *Babylon 5* and *Judge Dredd* roleplaying games, and has won two Origins Awards. He has four novels to his name, including his Twilight of Kerberos trilogy.